Christian Reid

Morton House

A Novel

Christian Reid

Morton House
A Novel

ISBN/EAN: 9783337026332

Printed in Europe, USA, Canada, Australia, Japan

Cover: Foto ©Andreas Hilbeck / pixelio.de

More available books at **www.hansebooks.com**

Frontispiece — MR. ANNESLEY FOUND IT WAS TIME TO GO. — Chap. VIII.

BY

THE AUTHOR OF "VALERIE AYLMER."

WITH ILLUSTRATIONS.

NEW YORK:
D. APPLETON AND COMPANY,
72 FIFTH AVENUE.
1895.

CONTENTS.

CHAP.	PAGE
I.—OUT OF THE DUSK	1
II.—MR. WARWICK'S GHOST	7
III.—PAULINE MORTON	11
IV.—WHAT MRS. ANNESLEY DID	14
V.—AFTER TWENTY YEARS	19
VI.—WHAT MORTON SAID	26
VII.—HOW A PALADIN STORMED A CASTLE	30
VIII.—THE ADELAIDE	37
IX.—MR. WARWICK MAKES AN OFFER	42
X.—THE GORDON PLAID	49
XI.—AT MORTON HOUSE	53
XII.—THE TUG OF WAR	58
XIII.—MISS TRESHAM ASKS ADVICE	62
XIV.—R. G.	69
XV.—MERRY CHRISTMAS	74
XVI.—ST. CECILIA	80
XVII.—THE APPLE OF DISCORD	85
XVIII.—ST. JOHN	91
XIX.—YOU CANNOT LET ME HELP YOU	97
XX.—MR. WARWICK'S NEW CLIENT	103
XXI.—MISS TRESHAM KEEPS HER WORD	110
XXII.—SPITFIRE PLAYS AT HIDE-AND-SEEK	115
XXIII.—A MORNING-CALL	122
XXIV.—OLD FOES	126
XXV.—MORTON'S CHOICE	133
XXVI.—MR. MARKS ASSERTS HIMSELF	138
XXVII.—MRS. GORDON'S SUGGESTION	142
XXVIII.—ON GUARD	149
XXIX.—THE SICK LADY	153
XXX.—AN OLD FRIEND	161
XXXI.—FATHER MARTIN	168
XXXII.—LIFE AND DEATH	173
XXXIII.—MRS. GORDON'S SUSPICION	180
XXXIV.—MR. WARWICK'S INVESTIGATION	184
XXXV.—TWO AND TWO MAKE FOUR	191
XXXVI.—CHECKMATED	200
XXXVII.—TO WIN OR LOSE IT ALL	206
XXXVIII.—MEA CULPA	213
XXXIX.—MISS TRESHAM'S REPLY	221
XL.—GOOD SAMARITANS	227
XLI.—THE LAST DEFIANCE	234
XLII.—ON THE THRESHOLD OF MORTON HOUSE	241
XLIII.—THE VALLEY OF THE SHADOW OF DEATH	247
XLIV.—IN THE DAWN	252
XLV.—A TURN OF FORTUNE'S WHEEL	259

MORTON HOUSE.

CHAPTER I.

OUT OF THE DUSK.

It was drawing toward the close of a soft November day, some thirty years ago, when the sound of children's merry laughter burst suddenly into the quiet garden of a quiet house, situated on the outskirts of the moderately-sized village of Tallahoma, in the populous and wealthy county of Lagrange. The sun had gone down, leaving behind him broken masses of gorgeously-tinted clouds, which were forming themselves into fanciful shapes of mountains and castles, while over the distant landscape the brooding haze of the Indian summer began to melt into the deeper purple of the gloaming; and the peculiar coolness that betokens coming frost, to make itself perceptibly felt in the pearly atmosphere. It was only the first of the month, and as yet but few of the trees had shed their leaves. The russet of the oaks, the pale yellow of the elms, the burning scarlet of the maples, and the vivid gold of the chestnuts, were all in their glory, and formed a bright autumnal background for the sober house which overshadowed the blooming garden, and the noisy groups that were scampering up and down its paths.

Very noisy groups they were; and yet their noise did not seem at all disturbing to a young girl who had followed them out, and stood leaning over the low garden-gate, while they played hide-and-seek among the rose-bushes. Perhaps this noise had grown an accustomed thing to her ears, as a great deal of it was her daily portion; or, perhaps, she liked children well enough to like even this their most disagreeable attribute—a conclusion devoutly to be wished by all interested in her welfare, since Fate had made of her that much-tried being, a governess. At all events she did not heed it in the least. The worse than Mohawk yells of uproarious Dick, the squabbling of Jack and Katy, the indignant remonstrances of elder Sara, and even the lifting up of baby Nelly's voice in injured weeping, were all unnoticed by their young teacher, who kept her eyes steadily fastened on the distant horizon, where the line of dark woods melted into the hazy atmosphere, and the pale-blue smoke curled upward from several unseen chimneys. Not that Miss Tresham did not hear the various disturbances. But, even in the school-room, she ignored a great deal, for peace' sake, and, once out of that durance vile, she left the children much to themselves—giving them, in unimportant matters, that blessed freedom of conduct and speech which no human creature is too young or too ignorant to appreciate.

She was a stately creature, this Katharine Tresham; and one of the women who possess a power of attraction quite apart from personal gifts. Her face was not a beautiful one, by any means; yet few beautiful faces pleased either so well or so long as this, notwithstanding its faults. The gray eyes were very clear and honest in their glance, but there was none of the sunny gleam of violet orbs, or the dusky splendor which dwells in dark ones; the complexion was very fair and pure, but rather pale, unless some quick emotion or pleasurable excitement, sent a clear carmine glow to the cheeks; the nose was straight and delicate, but not in the least classical; and, if the mouth was all that a mouth could or should be, the unusual squareness of the chin gave a finish to the face that was far from adding to its symmetry. Still, no one could deny that Miss Tresham was handsome—handsome in a very striking and aristocratic style—that her hands and feet were irreproachable in size and shape, that her lithe, slender figure was so well developed that not even an artist could have wished for it a pound of flesh either more or less; and that she carried herself with a very distinguished manner. Most women, looking in their mirror at a face so fair and a form so noble, would have been tempted to murmur at the fate which had dealt with them so hardly; but this was the one point wherein Katharine Tresham proved herself something more than mediocre. She did not indulge any vain regrets, or still more vain aspirations; she did not mourn any withered hopes, or bewail any blighted existence: but she took life as she found it, and bore its burden with a courage as cheerful as it was patient. Her employers were always kind and considerate, the children were warmly attached to her, she was beyond the reach of storms that had once beat very roughly on her head; and as her disposition—a disposition more to be prized than gold or precious stones—was eminently one of content, she furled her sails, and rested quietly in the pleasant haven into which she had drifted, where the sea was smooth beneath, and the sky was bright above her. No genius, the reader will perceive; no unsatisfied yearning being, full of repressed passion and morbid longings; only a brave, bright young gentlewoman, who was Christian enough to be satisfied that God knew what was best for her; who took the good He gave, with grateful heart, and rarely murmured at the ill.

She was leaning over the gate now, softly singing to herself a verse of song, and gazing over the scene before her, with eyes that took in and enjoyed all its beauty. But, after a while, the children began a game very near, and sent their shouts ringing through the clear autumn air, with such hearty good-will, that the young governess was fain to put wider space between herself and their merriment. So she turned away, and began pacing up and down a sheltered walk—a walk bounded on one side by the garden-fence and a hedge of Cherokee rose, on the other by tall gooseberry-bushes. A bright-red glow of the flaming western sky fell over her as she moved to and fro, lighting up her rich brown hair, her clear, bright eyes, and her tall, slender figure, and making a very attractive picture of youth and grace, in the midst of the lovely autumn scene. At length, she drew a small volume from her pocket and began to read. Thirty years ago. Tennyson's fame was yet young—not so young, however, but that, even in the backwoods of America, men had heard his name; and the girl who paced up and down the garden on that soft Indian summer evening, was steeping her soul in the beauty and music of those early poems which no after-efforts can ever supplant in our hearts. Enthralled in the sweeping rhythm, it was rather hard to be suddenly recalled to commonplace reality by a child's eager, uplifted voice.

"Miss Tresham, Miss Tresham!" sounded the cry, "Look, oh, look, what a pretty horse Mr. Annesley's on! May I—please—may I ask him to give me a ride?"

"Certainly not," answered Miss Tresham, speaking with great decision, but without looking up from her book. "Katy, you know your mother forbade your ever again asking Mr. Annesley for a ride."

"But she did not forbid her taking a ride if Mr. Annesley asked *her*, did she?" said a gay voice; and the next moment there appeared at the end of Katharine's walk, between the Cherokee hedge and the gooseberry-bushes, a slender, handsome young cavalier, in riding-boots and spurs, who stood with Katy mounted triumphantly on his shoulder, one tiny hand clutching nervously at his coat-collar, and her blond ringlets falling in a golden shower upon his crisp dark curls.

"No, I don't think she forbade that," Katharine replied, looking up with a smile, whether merely of recognition, or of welcome also, it was hard to say. "But indeed you are spoiling that child dreadfully, Mr. Annesley! She never sees you that she does not expect some marked attention, and almost breaks her heart when you do not notice her."

"And do I ever fail to notice her—when I see her?" asked he, swinging Katy to the ground, and coming nearer to Katharine—seeming, at the same time, to bring sunshine with him in his hazel eyes and brilliant smile. "I am sure I am always very attentive—am I not, my little coquette?"

The little coquette said "Yes," very promptly; but Miss Tresham shook her head.

"It seems I must refresh Katy's memory," she said. "You would scarcely believe that the other afternoon—last week some time, I believe it was—she cried all the way home because you passed her without notice, when you were accompanying two ladies down the village street. It was vain to reason with her—both her mother and myself tried argument unavailingly—and she sobbed herself to sleep that night in profound disdain of bread and milk, or even bread and jam, for supper."

"I remember the afternoon," said the young cavalier, a little confusedly. "I was riding with my sister and a friend of hers. But Katy cannot say that I did not speak to her."

"Ah, but you didn't!" said Katy, eagerly, forgetting her contrary assertion of the moment before. "You spoke to Miss Tresham, but not like you always do—and you didn't notice me at all."

"You shall have a ride this evening to pay for it, then," said he; "and I will be more careful in future. Miss Vernon's horse was rather unmanageable, and occupied all my attention. She does not know how to ride as well as you will when you are grown."

"Is she 'fraid?" asked Katy, with great interest.

"Very much afraid," he answered.

Then he turned to Miss Tresham, and asked if she would not come and look at his new horse.

"So you have another new horse?" she said, smiling. "Of course, I will come and look at him. You know horses are my weakness, and —oh! he *is* a beauty!"

"Is he not?" responded her companion, pleased with her burst of enthusiasm. "I was sure you would admire him.—Soh! Donald!—Steady, boy!"

They had approached the gate, and were leaning over it together, while the horse, which was fastened outside, began to move a little restlessly at sight of his master.

"Look at him!" said that master, eagerly. "Did you ever see a more symmetrical form? And his head—is it not superbly set on the shoulders?"

"He is a paragon," said Katharine, playfully. "And—he is not dangerous, is he, Mr. Annesley?—I must go and speak to him."

"He is as gentle as a greyhound," said Annesley, opening the gate for her to pass out. "I only wish—"

But what he wished was left in doubt; for he paused abruptly, while Katharine went up to the paragon, and patted his straight nose and his glossy, satin neck, calling him many pet-names in her clear, young voice.

"What an intelligent eye he has!" she cried, suddenly. "I really believe he understands all I am saying to him. Mr. Annesley, what is his name?"

"Donald is his name; but I do not like it."

"Donald? No; it is not good at all; it is not suggestive in the least; and it is not pretty either. He deserves a beautiful name."

"Give him one, then," said Annesley, quickly. "He will be only too proud to own you as a sponsor. I have no aptitude whatever for such things, and my horses are usually 'the bay' and 'the sorrel' to their dying-day."

"I thought you were more imaginative," said Katharine, absently. "Is he fleet?" she went on, still looking at the horse.

"He is like the wind, or the lightning."

"Is he? Then I will give you a name for him at once. Call him Ilderim."

"Ilderim? You mean—"

"The sobriquet of Bajazet, of course. It signifies 'The Lightning,' you know. Will it do?"

"It is excellent," he answered, as, indeed, he would have answered to any thing whatever of her suggestion. "From this moment, Donald dies, and Ilderim rises like a phœnix from his ashes.—Soh! Steady, sir!"

For, arching his handsome neck like a bow, the new-made Ilderim began pawing the earth so energetically with his fore-foot that he made Katharine beat a hasty retreat.

"What a racer he would make!" she cried, suddenly. "Is that what you intend him for?"

"Why, no; I had not thought of it," he replied. "I was merely attracted by his beauty, and thought myself lucky to get him."

"Lucky!" she repeated, looking up at him with a smile. "Most people are lucky when Fortune has never said them nay in any one desire of their hearts. I suppose you never wished for any thing in your life without obtaining it."

Standing there in the soft, purple dusk, with one arm thrown over his horse's arched neck, with an unconscious grace in the careless attitude, a suppressed eagerness in the handsome face, and a chivalric deference in the uncovered head, it was not hard to believe this—not hard, indeed, to tell that here was one of those to whom had fallen the purple and fine linen of a world which gives to others only serge; one of those to whom its wealth and fame, its love and pleasure, came, as it were, by right divine, and who now and then flash across the path of our work-day lives, and make our twilight seem more dun by contrast with their own radiant sunshine.

"Yes, I have been very fortunate all my life,'

he answered, more gravely than Katharine's gay tone seemed to warrant; "but the future may overbalance the past, and you may give me my first lesson in denial this very afternoon. I mean to ask a favor of you after a while."

"I hope it is one that I may be able to grant," she said, quietly. "But you know my opinion on that subject."

"That friendship is best kept free from favors?—yes. But I should like to convince you how wrong that is. I should like to make you believe that *real friendship* never hesitates either to give or accept a favor."

"Don't try," she said, lightly; "you might fail, and that would not be pleasant to one who has never known failure. I will grant you this much, however—that, where friendship exists between two people of equal position, they may afford to meet each other half-way in the matter of favors; but, where one occupies the worldly vantage-ground, it is not well for the other to accept benefits which may assume the weight of obligations."

She spoke very calmly; but a hot, red flush mounted swiftly to the brow of her listener. He made one hasty step forward, and then fell back again, irritating Ilderim very much by the unintentional jerk of his rein.

"Why do you say such things? why do you take such a tone about yourself?" he cried, with a sharp accent of reproach in his voice. "You of all women! It is grievously wrong to yourself! It is even more grievously wrong to me!"

"And why should I not look truth in the face?" she asked, gravely. "To say that I am not your social equal means nothing that either you or I need blush to acknowledge. It is merely a conventional accident, and does not even touch the other ground, the personal ground on which we meet—meet, I am glad to think, as friends. That you are Mr. Annesley of Annesdale, of gentle blood and almost princely estate, is a mere chance of fortune; and that I am Katharine Tresham, governess, who teaches Mr. Marks's children for six hundred dollars a year, is equally a chance. I am of the Old World, you know. Perhaps that is the reason why these things seem to me at once a matter of course and a matter of small moment."

The young republican by name, the young aristocrat by race and nature, looked at her in wistful silence for a moment.

"Yet you think of them far more than we do," he said, at length.

"Because I have been trained to do so," she answered, moving toward the half-open gate, "and, perhaps I ought also to add, because I am unfortunately very proud—much 'too proud to care whence I came.' You see I have not forgotten that apprenticeship to the conventionalities which I served when I spent a year as governess in England—a year I would not live over again for untold wealth."

"But that was in England. You are in America now, thank God!"

"Yes," she answered, with an arch gleam in her eyes, "I am in America now—America, where I am theoretically supposed to be the equal in all points of any among your county gentry—we will say, for instance, that lovely Miss Vernon. What would she think, do you suppose, if you suggested that she should call on Mrs. Marks's governess?—But poor little Katy! See how downcast she is looking! She evidently thinks you have forgotten all about her ride."

"I have not, though," said Annesley, half absently; and, looking up, he beckoned Katy to come to him.

The little girl gladly obeyed. She had left her companions to their play, and had been leaning wistfully against the gate, pushing back her bright curls, so as to see what was going on outside, and longing for the signal that was so slow in coming. When, at last, it did come, she bounded forward, and stood impatiently beside the horse, while Annesley gathered up the reins and sprang into the saddle. He bent down and lifted her from the ground to a seat before him, made her kiss her hand to the governess, and they were off, the child's short dress fluttering in the evening breeze as they cantered down the road and out of sight.

Katharine watched them, with a strange sort of yearning in her eyes. Perhaps she was thinking how pleasant it would be to ride down that road, under its crimson and golden woods, in the lovely autumn dusk, with a crescent moon faintly gleaming above the still tinted west, and such a stately and gallant escort by her side as he who had just passed from her sight. Perhaps she thought of those to whom such pleasure was common, and—even the best-disciplined of us will sometimes do such things—contrasted her own life with theirs. Perhaps she remembered that scene of last week, to which she had alluded—the two elegant ladies in their sweeping habits and waving plumes, the curvetting horses, the flashing bits and jewelled whips, the young cavalier, and the golden sunshine streaming over all, while she plodded by in the dust and shadow. Perhaps she wondered if this dust and shadow were henceforth to be her portion; or perhaps she thought of a time when the sunshine had slept on her path too, when kind eyes and loving tones had followed her, when life had seemed for a short while the fair and pleasant thing which it never seems to any long, when a young girl who bore her name had smiled and talked and jested beneath the waving palms of a distant tropic island, and when—but her thoughts went no further than this. It was only Mrs. Marks's governess who turned abruptly from the gate, and, with a resolute compression of the lips, that brought lines too hard for so young a face, began the same pacing up and down the walk that had been interrupted half an hour before. It was not long before she was interrupted again, for Mr. Annesley did not give Katy a very extended ride. Ilderim was brought up before the garden-gate once more, and Katy, flushed, smiling, yet regretful, lowered to the ground. Then Mr. Annesley sprang off also; but this time he did not fasten his horse to the iron staple so conveniently placed in a large elm-tree near by. Probably something in Katharine's face warned him not to do so—he was very quickly sensitive to any change in that face. At all events, he kept the rein over his arm, and, uncovering as he advanced, spoke, half apologetically:

"I am going in a moment, Miss Tresham, but—you know I told you I had a favor to ask of you. The evening is so lovely, I am sure you will not mind a few minutes longer in the open air."

"Yes, the evening is very lovely, but rather cool," answered Katharine, in a tone which was cool also; "and I cannot promise to make it more than a few minutes, Mr. Annesley, for Mrs. Marks expects me to see that the children come in before nightfall."

"I did not know that you were the children's nurse as well as their governess," he said, somewhat hastily.

"There you are right," she answered, quietly. "But they don't obey their nurse very well, and they do obey me. So this duty has devolved upon me—and it is not a very irksome one. I wish I had none that pressed more heavily."

The young man leaned forward over the closed gate which divided them.

"And I wish to Heaven," he said, passionately, "that I could make your life what it should be!"

She shrugged her shoulders slightly.

"Now, that is very kind, but not very wise. There is One who knows what is best for us; and you might spoil the whole aim and intention of my life, if you went to work to improve it after your own device. Really, I am very well content with it as it is. You must not let that foolish speech make you think otherwise"

"Content! How can you possibly be content with such occupation, such surroundings, such compan—"

"Hush!" she said, quickly; for several small listeners had grown tired of their game, and drawn near. "It is all very pleasant—sometimes I think too pleasant, to last long. But you said you had something you wished to ask me."

"Yes," he answered. "I wish to ask you—well, for one thing, why you will never let me do any thing to make your life more endurable?"

"You do a great deal," she replied, a sudden cordial light springing into her eyes and making them beautiful. "You do more than any one has ever done before in—oh, such a long time! Do you think I am ungrateful for the books and papers, the flowers and music that brighten my life so much? Can you imagine I do not see how much more generous you would be if I could allow it? Surely, Mr. Annesley, you do not think that I have so many friends, or receive so much kindness, but that I feel this in my heart of hearts."

"Then grant me one favor," he said, impulsively. "Promise to give me one pleasure, which will be the greatest I have ever known."

"I cannot promise in the dark. What is it?"

"It is not much—to you, that is. Only that you honor Ilderim by riding him."

Katharine drew back a step in her surprise.

"Mr. Annesley, you are surely jesting! Ride Ilderim!"

"Yes," he answered, with a desperate attempt at *nonchalance;* "ride Ilderim—why not? You cannot say you would not like it; and I only bought him because I thought how well he would suit you. And—Miss Tresham, pray do not refuse me this my first request!"

Katharine was silent for a moment. Not that she had a thought of yielding to any thing so inadmissible as what he asked; but simply because she was touched by the desire to give her pleasure, which was so delicately veiled

"How kind he is!" she thought, "and yet, poor fellow, how foolish!" Annesley, who had begun to feel uncomfortable at her long silence, was certainly relieved, but yet more surprised, when she suddenly held out her hand to him.

"Thank you so much," she said. "You are so good—so kind! But, then, you know it is impossible."

The action was only one of frank gratitude; but the next instant she was sorry for having given way to it. Very sorry indeed, when, glancing up, she saw that a carriage had approached unperceived by them, and was passing by, while several pairs of eyes looked curiously from the windows at this way-side scene. Katharine drew back her hand hastily, and a shying movement of Ilderim made Annesley turn at the same moment. Thus they both looked full at the equipage, which, truth to tell, was rather a strange one for that road, at that hour.

Not that the equipage in itself was at all remarkable—only a dusty travelling-carriage, with two worn-out horses, a cross-looking driver, a large trunk behind, and numerous boxes on the driver's seat and under his legs. But the fact that it was leaving the village at such an hour, that the road was a retired one, ouly leading to several country-houses, and to a town distant some forty miles, and that the faces which looked forth from it were totally unknown, conspired to make its unexpected advent surprising. Strangers did not often come to Tallahoma; and when they did, it was generally in the stage-coach, and they ordered supper at the "Tallahoma Hotel," and went to bed like orderly and ordinary mortals. These travellers plainly intended to do neither; and they certainly did not seem very ordinary. The only outside passengers were the driver, who, as before mentioned, looked very cross, and a small spaniel, who looked very tired and patient. But three faces were gazing from the inside, when Katharine with haste drew back her hand, and Annesley turned round. The first that attracted their notice was one which would have claimed attention anywhere, or from anybody. A hollow, attenuated face, with features so finely marked that they stood out like pure Greek chiselling, and eyes so large and dark that they seemed shedding a flood of light over every thing on which they rested, was partially revealed under a black bonnet and heavy crape veil, and showed itself for a minute only—sinking back out of sight immediately. The two others kept their positions, and were hardly less remarkable—hardly less remarkable, that is, to Tallahoma sight; for one was a beautiful bold-eyed boy who was staring with all his might, and hugging closely a small monkey; the other a woman whom Katharine at once recognized as a French *bonne*, in the usual dress of her class. It was a very brief gaze that the two parties interchanged as the carriage moved by, and rumbled away in the dusk. As it disappeared, the eager little voices of the children standing around Katharine found utterance.

"O Miss Tresham, did you see the monkey?"

"Miss Tresham, did you see the little boy?"

"Miss Tresham, wasn't that a pretty lady?"

"Miss Tresham, how funny the little dog looked!"

"Dog! you're crazy! It was a monkey!"

"It wasn't no such thing! It was a dog! Didn't I see it?"

"And didn't I see the monkey? Silly!"

"You're a silly yourself, sir! Miss Tresham, wasn't it a dog?"

"Hush, children," said Miss Tresham, in her governess tone. "There were a dog and monkey both." Then she turned to Annesley. "Who can they possibly be?"

He shook his head. "I have no idea. Strangers, evidently; but where they can be coming from, or where going, at this hour, I can't tell."

"And such strangers! They would not be extraordinary objects on a French or Italian highway; but in this remote corner of the world, they are rather astonishing. Don't you think so?"

"Yes," he answered, "rather astonishing." But it was obvious that they had made but a momentary impression on him, for he turned at once to the subject that had been interrupted by their appearance. "Miss Tresham, seriously, is there any reason why you should not give me this great pleasure?"

"There are many reasons, Mr. Annesley," answered Miss Tresham, gravely. "But I have only time to give you one at present, and with that you must be content—by doing as you wish, I should make myself the object of countless remarks; and I might probably in the end lose my situation. That would be paying rather dearly for a ride, even on Ilderim. Thank you again, though; and now, good-by."

The young man looked at her in the waning light with a passion of resolve in his eyes. "You will not think of this?" he asked. "You will not even give me time to try and change your resolution?"

"I am sorry to say that I can do neither," she answered, a little coldly. "It is late, and I must really go—and so ought you, for that matter, since Annesdale is five miles off. Here! let me return your 'Tennyson.' I have enjoyed it so much."

He received the volume, and thrust it carelessly into his pocket; then, while drawing on his gloves, he said:

"I have received a packet of new books to-day; may I bring you some, when I come again? There are one or two I am sure you will like."

"Then bring me one or two—not more," she said, laughing. "Poor Mrs. Marks must not be frightened by another such imposing sight as those dozen volumes you sent the other day. Bring some poetry, please. Formerly I did not care much for poetry; now I like it—I suppose because my life is so very prosaic. Once more, good-by."

"Good-by," he echoed.

He vaulted on Ilderim, rode away a few steps wheeled suddenly, came back, and leaned out of his saddle toward the gate where Katharine was still standing.

"Perhaps I ought to tell you," he said, "that I am not at all discouraged. You may yet ride Ilderim, and I may yet thank you for my first denial."

With this, and before she could answer, he was gone.

CHAPTER II.

MR. WARWICK'S GHOST.

Miss Tresham remained standing in the place where Mr. Annesley had left her, for a minute or two, gazing with slightly-knitted brows after his vanishing figure; then she turned, and told the children that it was time to go in.

"It is cold," she said, with a little shiver; "and I don't think there is any use in looking for your father. Since he has not come already, he is not likely to be here for an hour yet."

"We'll have to wait a long time for supper, then," remarked one small murmurer; but that was all.

The legion knew better than to offer any open signs of disobedience to their chief; and, although discontent was rife among them, they followed her to the house.

A flight of steps led from a side-piazza down to the garden, and across this piazza a flood of cheerful light was already streaming from two windows and a glass door which opened upon it.

"Why, papa's here already!" cried Katy, who had bounded up the steps before any one else and taken an observation through the window. "Papa's here already! Where did he come from?"

Then the door flew open with a sudden burst and the merry little crowd rushed pell-mell into the room.

A very pleasant room it was, with a sparkling, light-wood fire on the hearth, and a well-set table in the middle of the floor—a room abounding in comfort but lacking in luxury, and with little or no evidence of what are called refined tastes. That is, there were few books visible, and they were chiefly of an unused kind. No pictures excepting some ugly daubs supposed to be family portraits, and not even a vase to hold the royal flowers blooming by in such prodigal profusion. The aspect of the place proclaimed substantial ease, nothing more. There were comfortable chairs, and one or two chintz-cushioned couches; there were various tables, with carved legs and bright-red covers; there was a glowering mahogany sideboard, there was a pretty little work-stand that stood in a niche near the fireplace, and there was a clock on the mantel that told the quarters with remorseless exactitude. But the proprietors of the apartment were plain people, of no fashionable pretension, and still less fashionable ambition—people who were "in business," and were not ashamed of the fact; who were well-to-do in the world now, but who had known a hard struggle before becoming so; who were of the best morals, but of moderate culture; and who, while they were always glad of social advancement and social recognition, never went out of their way to seek either—people, in short, who were types of the best portion of the middle class—the portion that is neither hopelessly vulgar nor absurdly aspiring—and who, in consequence of sturdily respecting their own dignity, were universally respected by those above as by those below them on Fortune's ladder.

The head of the household, Richard Marks, had begun life as a very small tradesman, and it may readily be conceived that the man who sold coffee by the pound, and calico by the yard, across a village counter, was scarcely able to command, or even hope for, any very exalted social elevation. Yet social elevation of a certain sort came with time—as it comes to all men who trust less to fortune than to their own endeavor. To his diligence and energy, and to the scrupulous honesty which made all men recognize his word to be as good as his bond, Richard Marks owed at last an assured competency and an honorable, even an enviable, position among his fellow-townsmen. To these things he owed it that the most aristocratic gentlemen of his native county were proud to hold out the hand of friendship, not patronage, to him; and that, after many years of hard labor, he was now resting on his oars as cashier and virtual controller of the one bank which did all the monetary business of Lagrange County.

His wife, although the daughter of a gentleman—if a spendthrift insolvent deserves the name—had sunk so easily to the social level of her husband that those among her friends and acquaintances who still spoke of her as "Bessie Warwick," were forced to explain the obvious fact as best they could.

"She never had much sense," they would say, "and certainly no great amount of refinement—though she was so pretty—pretty in a certain style, that is; and then she inherited low tastes, no doubt. Her mother was shockingly common, if you remember. It was his marriage that ruined Arnold Warwick—at least his friends always said so."

But, notwithstanding this unflattering opinion, Mrs. Marks certainly proved that she had found her right place in the world as helper of a good man's upward career. The best of wives and mothers—yet, like most best of wives and mothers, apt at times to become a little tiresome, especially if she once began the circumstantial history of Dick's dreadful accident when he fell and broke his collar-bone, or how little Katy whooped through an entire summer with whooping-cough. But a sensible and kind-hearted woman with all that; one of the large class of women of whom the world knows little, and hears nothing; who are not remarkable either for beauty or mental capacity; but who fill their own position in the world better than a Lady Blessington or a Madame de Staël could do it for them; who live a life all pure and blameless in the domestic relations, and who at last go down to the grave leaving in the hearts of their children a good example and a fragrant memory.

In her own way, too, Mrs. Marks was a good business-woman; and the only time in her life that she had acted without due foresight and deliberation was in the matter of engaging a governess for her children. She had accompanied her husband on a short business-visit to Charleston some two years previous to this autumn evening, and while there met Katharine Tresham.

The young foreigner, who had but lately landed, was entirely alone in the strange city; and something in her refined, ladylike appearance, together with her deep-mourning dress, touched the kind heart of the elder woman. They were boarders in the same house, and, when she heard that Katharine was anxious to procure a situation as teacher; that she could give good English and West-Indian references, and that she would much prefer the country to any city as a residence, Mrs. Marks's mind was at once made up. She did not even wait to consult her husband; she made her an offer on the spot, and it was gratefully accepted.

"Indeed, my dear, I could not help it!" she afterward humbly confided to her lord. "It seemed so pitiful to see such a pretty young thing entirely alone; and then, you know, the children learn nothing at all at school. You said yourself that Mr. Watson was good for nothing but to drink whiskey and pay attention to Lucy Smith."

"I did say so," Mr. Marks replied, "but are you sure, Bessie, that your new friend will be worth much more? I don't mean, of course, that she will drink whiskey or pay attention to Lucy Smith; but, after all, there may be worse things than that. What does she engage to teach the children, and what are her terms?"

"She engages to teach the children—well, every thing that is usually taught, I suppose," answered Mrs. Marks, a little vaguely; "and, as to her terms, she does not seem to know very much about them herself. She taught one year in England, and received forty pounds—that is all she knows."

"Why, that is a little less than two hundred dollars," said Mr. Marks, opening his honest eyes. "Teachers must be plenty over there at that rate. Poor thing! I'll tell you what we'll do, Bessie. She *is* a nice-looking girl, and there'll be no harm in trying her. We will offer her four hundred dollars, and take her for one year."

So it was settled; and so Katharine Tresham came to Lagrange.

At the end of the year her employers requested her to remain, and Mr. Marks voluntarily raised her salary. The children had improved so rapidly that Mr. Watson would not have recognized his quondam pupils; and the bright even temper of the young governess made her presence in the house a kind of moral sunshine. Altogether, as Mrs. Marks was accustomed to declare, she could not have been so exactly suited by anybody else in the world; and she would have had no possible fault to find with Miss Tresham if—there is an *if* to every thing earthly—she had been an orthodox member of that religious denomination to which Mrs. Marks herself belonged. But, dreadful to relate, Miss Tresham was that strange off-shoot of iniquity, in the eyes of Tallahoma, a blind and bigoted Papist. She had given Mrs. Marks fair warning of that fact before their engagement was concluded.

"There is one thing I must mention," she said. "I am a Catholic. I know that most Protestants are very much prejudiced against the faith, and don't care to admit Catholics into their households. If this is the case with yourself, we will not say any thing more about the proposed engagement."

But Mrs. Marks, although very much staggered by the information, replied:

"My dear, I don't see that it makes any difference. You will be uncomfortable, I am afraid, for there is no Romish church in Tallahoma; but, as far as I am concerned, I—I suppose we are all Christians."

When the young governess followed her noisy charges into the sitting-room, a pleasant-looking woman glanced up and smiled from her seat by the work-table, while a much older man, with gray hair and frank blue eyes, gave her a hearty greeting.

"Good-evening, Miss Tresham. How do you and the little ones come on?—Well, Nelly, can you spell 'ab,' yet?"

"Spell it, Nelly, for your father," said Miss Tresham, smiling. "She knew it to-day, sir; but I am afraid that hanging head doesn't say much for her recollection of it now."

"Speak up, little woman," said her father, lifting the shame-faced scholar to a place on his knee. "Speak up—and I'll give you a sixpence."

But bashfulness or ignorance continuing to hold the little woman's tongue, Jack and Katy, tempted by the promise of the sixpence, burst out with the spelling of the word desired, and were rewarded by being informed that the offer was not intended for irregular claimants.

"I tell you what I will do, though," said the indulgent father, seeing the disappointment legible on their faces. "Nelly must have her sixpence—but another shall be found for the first one who brings me the mail from your Uncle John's coat-pocket."

"Is this mail-day?" asked Katharine, looking up. "Then why did you not bring it yourself, sir?"

"Because I have been in the country on business, and didn't come through town on my way home," answered Mr. Marks, good-humoredly. "I wish Warwick would come along! I want my papers—and I expect you want your letters, Miss Kate."

"Letters!" the governess repeated. "I thought you knew that I never receive any letters. There is nobody that I care to hear from. Indeed, the worst luck that could befall me would be a letter—unless it came from Father Martin."

Father Martin was the priest of Saxford, a somewhat larger town than Tallahoma, boasting a small Catholic chapel, to which she went occasionally for ghostly shriving—and it was certainly true that his rare letters were the only ones that had ever come to Katharine Tresham, since she first set foot on the soil of America. Nor did she ever write any that were not addressed to him. She seemed to have severed every link that bound her to her former life, and, save in a few general particulars, her present friends knew no more of that life than if she had not broken their bread for the period of two years.

"John is very late to-night," said Mrs. Marks, glancing up at the clock, as if it was its fault that the waffles were burning in the kitchen. "I really think we need not wait for him any longer. Some troublesome man has kept him, and he always begs me not to wait.—Sara, go to the door and tell Judy to send in supper."

Sara obeyed; and, the next minute, two mulatto boys began bringing in plates of biscuit and waffles. Then came some broiled partridges, the tempting odor of which caused Mr. Marks to look round with interest.

"By George! that is delightful to a hungry man! Where did you get such fine birds, Bessie?"

"They were brought this morning, with Mr. Annesley's compliments," answered Mrs. Marks, rising and going to the head of the table. "Sent to me, the boy said—you have forgotten the cream, Tom—but I expect Miss Katharine knows more about them than I do."

Miss Katharine smiled slightly, but without the least tincture of embarrassment. "How could I possibly know about them?" she asked. "I saw Mr. Annesley this afternoon—did I tell you that he gave Katy a ride?—but I assure you he did not hint that even one of the partridges was intended for me. You will spare me one, though—won't you, Mr. Marks?"

In the clatter of plates and knives which followed, a step crossing the piazza outside was unheard; and when the door suddenly opened, Katy was the first one to observe it. She sprang forward with a cry of "Uncle John!"—a cry the eagerness of which was more for the letters in Uncle John's pocket, and the promised sixpence from her father, than for the every-day presence of Uncle John himself.

The new-comer surrendered the letters to the quick little fingers that dived at once into his pocket, watched the payment of the sixpence, with a smile, and then walked to the fireplace and sat down, while Mrs. Marks sent out a requisition for hot coffee.

"Never mind about that, Bessie," he said, in rather a tired tone. "What is on the table will do well enough. I only want to get a little warm before moving again—it is quite cool to-night."

"What on earth made you so late?" asked his sister.

"Business," answered Mr. Warwick, briefly. Then he sank back into his chair, and into silence.

It was not an ordinary face, by any means, across which the fire-light played so fitfully—no more an ordinary face than John Warwick was an ordinary man. There was little beauty in it; and that little was more the beauty of expression than of feature; not much grace of outline or delicacy of coloring. But there was force of will and power of thought; there was a keen habit of observation, and sometimes there was an almost womanly gentleness—the latter not habitual nor often to be seen, but coming occasionally to melt the eyes and soften the mouth, around which some hard lines lay dormant. Take it all in all, a face so full of moral and intellectual strength that the wonder grew how this man could possibly be brother to the pretty commonplace woman who sat at the head of Richard Marks's table. Yet her brother he undoubtedly was; and, if Mrs. Marks loved her husband with all her heart, she certainly reverenced her brother with all her soul—for in him all the gentlemanhood of the father stood confessed, without the father's weakness or the father's vice. He it was who had raised their name from the mire where it had fallen, and given it once more an honorable rank. He it was who had claimed his birthright of social position, and placed his foot, when that foot was yet young, upon the place his father had forfeited. Men already forgot the poor drunkard who had ruined others as well as himself, and only remembered that "Mr. Warwick is decidedly our most rising lawyer." Indeed, they had long since begun to be very proud of him in Lagrange, to put him forward on all public occasions, and prophesy great future advancement for him.

The hot coffee came, and Mrs. Marks announced its arrival to her brother; but he did not move. He seemed, indeed, so deeply sunk in thought as not to hear her; and it was Mr. Marks's brisk tones that roused him at last.

"What's the matter, Warwick, that you sit there staring in the fire, instead of coming to supper? I hope you haven't heard bad news of any kind?"

"Bad news!" repeated Mr. Warwick, looking up with a start. "Why, of course not.—Did you say the coffee was ready, Bessie? I beg your pardon, but I did not hear you."

He rose as he spoke and came to the table. The light thus falling for the first time upon his face, some change there attracted the attention even of the children.

"Unky, you've got a bad headache, haven't you?" inquired womanly little Sara, by whom he sat down.

"Unky, Jack says you've seen a ghost!" cried Katy, with her mouth full, despite an angry "You hush!" and a push under the table from Jack.

And Mrs. Marks herself said, "What is the matter, John? You look pale."

"Nothing is the matter, excepting that I have had a hard day's work, and am tired," he answered. Then, catching the gaze of a pair of eyes opposite him, he added, "Do I look so shockingly, Miss Tresham, as to merit all this?"

"You look as if your day's work had been a very hard one," said Miss Tresham. "That is all, I think."

"I don't know," said his sister, doubtfully. "John, are you certain that is all?"

"Not quite," he answered, with a flitting smile. "Jack was right in his conjecture—I have seen a ghost."

"A ghost!"

"A ghost, Bessie. As veritable a ghost as ever came out of a church-yard."

"My dear John, please recollect that I don't like such things talked of before the children."

"Oh, there is no rawhead and bloody bones in this," said Mr. Warwick, glancing round at the various pairs of eyes that stared at him from over various mugs of bread and milk. "The ghost was not even dressed in white, Katy—what do you think of that?"

"Oh, it wasn't a real ghost, then," said Katy, breathlessly.

"Yes it was, though.—Come, Marks, put down your paper, and guess whose ghost I saw this afternoon."

Mr. Marks laid down his paper as requested; but confessed himself unable to imagine, unless (with a sly glance at the children) it was that of old Mrs. Packham, who was buried about a fortnight before.

But Mr. Warwick shook his head. It was not old Mrs. Packham, he said; but somebody who had gone away at least twenty years before; somebody whom they all had known. And then he told his sister to guess. Whereupon, after much consideration, Mrs. Marks inquired if it could possibly have been that wild son of old Joe Williams, who ran away ever so many years ago, and had never been heard of since. At which Mr. Warwick shook his head yet more impatiently.

"Then tell us who it was," said she.

And Katharine was struck by a husky tone in the lawyer's voice, as he answered—

"I have seen Pauline Morton!"

CHAPTER III.

PAULINE MORTON.

If Mr. Warwick had announced the entire destruction of Tallahoma and all its inhabitants by an earthquake, there scarcely could have ensued a more astonished pause than followed the utterance of that name. For the full space of a minute, an entire silence reigned around the table—a silence which Mrs. Marks was, of course, the first to break.

"You have seen Pauline Morton, John?"

"Yes," answered he, laconically.

"Is she in town?"

"She was in town, or else I could not have seen her."

"But, bless my soul!" cried Mr. Marks, "where did she come from, Warwick?—when did you see her?"

"Of course she came from Europe. I saw her as she passed through Tallahoma, this afternoon, late."

"Well, tell us all about it," cried his sister, a little impatient at these brief replies. "What is the use of doling out news like this? Tell us how she looked, and what she said, and where she is going, and what she means by coming back here?"

"Did you happen to see a travelling-carriage pass here about dusk, laden with trunks, dogs, and monkeys?"

At this question there rose a shout from the children—the eager little pitchers, whose eyes and ears were open to all that was going on.

"We did! Uncle John, we did! And a pretty lady, and a little boy in it, too."

"Yes," said Uncle John, quietly. "That was Pauline Morton, on her way to Morton House."

"To Morton House?" repeated Mr. Marks. "Then Shields, at least, must have known that she was coming."

Again Mr. Warwick shook his head. "No. Shields was in my office this morning about that business of a trespass on the land; and I will answer for it that he had as little idea of seeing the owner of the land as you or I might have had. Besides, she told me that she had not announced her coming to any one."

"And yet you say she went to Morton House?"

"Straight to Morton House.—Heaven help poor Shields's brain this night!"

"Surely you must have mistaken," urged Mr. Marks. "Surely she went to Annesdale—her own first cousin's, you know."

Mr. Warwick shrugged his shoulders. "I should think you would remember how little love there was between her and her first cousin, of old."

"I remember," cried Mrs. Marks, "and I am sure that Pauline Morton would never go uninvited to Mrs. Annesley's house. But oh, John, she could not have gone to Morton House to stay to-night!—why, think of those beds that nobody has slept in for twenty years!"

"Twenty years or not, she meant to do it; and I don't think there's a doubt but that she has done it. Twenty years! Can it be really twenty years since she went away, Bessie?"

"Twenty years this past summer," said Mrs. Marks, decidedly. "I remember the very day. Did her brother come back, John?—and surely her husband is with her?"

"Her brother, she tells me, is dead. She did not mention her husband; but I judge that she is a widow."

"And she came alone?"

"With the exception of a child and a servant, quite alone."

"Her brother dead!" repeated Mr. Marks, whose somewhat slow ears this last item had just reached. "There must be some mistake about that, John—you must have misunderstood her, or his death has happened very lately. It is not more than a few weeks since Shields showed me a letter he had just received from him."

"I only know that she is in deep mourning," Mr. Warwick answered; "and that, when I glanced at her dress, she said—or, if she didn't say, she intimated—that it was for her brother she was wearing it."

"It is very strange," said Mr. Marks, reflectively. "He must have dropped off like his Uncle Paul; for all the rest of the Mortons that ever I heard of were very long-lived people. She did not mention his complaint, did she?"

"No. She said very little—in fact, I saw her for a few minutes only."

"But her looks, John!" cried Mrs. Marks, with a woman's curiosity on this important subject. "Is she as handsome as ever?"

"How do most women look, Bessie, when a gap of twenty years separates them from youth?"

"Why, rather the worse for wear," answered Mrs. Marks, with a glance toward her own face, as reflected in the burnished coffee-pot. "But I cannot imagine Pauline Morton any less beautiful than when I saw her last."

"You had better not see her again, then."

"Has she changed so dreadfully?"

"She is the wreck—the ghost, as I told the children—of her former self."

"Dear, dear! to think of it! But she *has* been married, has she not?"

"Certainly. I told you she had a child with her."

"And whom did she marry? You know there were all sorts of reports at the time—people said she had married a count, or some such person."

"Which was as true as reports generally are. Pauline Morton has come back as Mrs. Gordon."

"Mrs. *what?*"

"Gordon. Did you ever hear the name before—in connection with her, I mean?"

"Never!" cried Mrs. Marks, with a decision which rather surprised the governess, sitting by in profound ignorance of the subject under discussion. "I heard that she had married some nobleman, and that she lived in Europe in grand style; and—and—for her to come back like this, to a place she always hated! Oh, John, I don't believe it!"

"That's just as you please," Mr. Warwick answered, rising and walking to the fire. "I assure you, I have the name on her own authority; and, as for those ridiculous stories of counts and the like, of course no sensible person ever credited them. I remember hearing that she had married an officer in the English army; and, no doubt, this is, or was, the man.—Miss Tresham, did you see the carriage this afternoon?"

"Yes; and the lady also," Katharine answered. "I had only a glimpse of her face, but it struck me very much. Does she belong to the Morton House where the children and I go to walk almost every evening?"

"Morton House belongs to her," Mr. Marks answered, dryly. "I am afraid, if she has come back for good, your walks are at an end, Miss Kate."

"Oh!" cried the children, in chorus. "Can't we go to Morton House any more, and make Ponto chase rabbits in the garden? Oh, papa, why not?"

"Don't you hear why not?" asked Mrs. Marks, a little sharply—"don't you hear that the person who owns Morton House has come back to live in it? Now hush—or I will call Letty and send you straight to bed!—John, dear, you haven't told us yet where you met—Mrs. Gordon."

"Haven't I?" said Mr. Warwick, a little wearily—he was evidently tired of the subject that was still so absorbing to his sister. "Well, it is not much to tell, Bessie. I left my office at dusk, this evening, and was on my way to the post-office to get the mail, when the carriage of which I spoke came down the street. I glanced at it a little curiously, wondering where it was going at that time of day, when a face, that I should have recognized among a thousand, looked out, and made a sign to the driver to stop. Before I knew what I was about, I was shaking hands with Pauline Morton."

He paused, with a half smile at the expression of eager interest on his sister's face; but, notwithstanding the smile, more than one of his hearers noticed that it cost him an effort to resume.

"The first thing I remember was her saying, 'How changed you are! And I looked at her, and answered, 'I am sure I cannot be more changed than you are.'"

"Why, John!" cried Mrs. Marks, reproachfully.

"You think that was rather plain speaking? I thought so myself when it was too late to recall the words. But she did not seem offended by my candor. She only smiled a little, and said, 'Yes, I am very much changed—you will believe that when I tell you that I have come back to Morton to live.' I don't know what I said—something about my surprise, probably; for I was surprised, as you may well imagine—but she repeated the statement, and then, noticing that I looked at her black dress, she added: 'My poor brother!—you see I am all alone in the world.' 'Excepting,' said I, glancing at the child opposite. 'Yes,' she answered, quietly, 'excepting him.' Then she told him to shake hands with one of his mother's old friends; and the boy, who is a splendid-looking little fellow, held out his hand at once, and spoke to me—no hanging of the head, and putting the finger in the mouth, Dick. After a few more words, his mother said they must go on, as she wished to reach Morton House before night. So she held out her hand, saying she would be glad to see me; and you will be shocked to hear, Bessie, that, in responding to the invitation, I called her Miss Morton."

"Good gracious!"

"It was very thoughtless, and, of course, I began a hasty apology, being more annoyed at my awkward mistake from perceiving the effect which it produced upon her. First she flushed, and then she turned so pale that for a minute I thought she was going to faint. But she only gasped for breath a little, and cut short my apology by saying: 'There is nothing to excuse. I am very foolish; but it has been a long time since I heard that name, and it brought back so many recollections—just here. I am Mrs. Gordon now.' Then she drove off. And now that you have heard all that I know myself, Bessie, I hope you have no objection to my going out on the piazza to smoke a cigar."

Mrs. Marks would willingly have detained him for the purpose of further questioning; but she had an instinct that it would be useless. So she only watched him as he left the room, and then turned to her husband.

"You laughed at me several years ago, Richard, when I said that I did not believe John would ever forget Pauline Morton. Pray what do you say now?"

"Why, exactly what I said then," answered Mr. Marks, looking up from the paper which he thought he should never be left to read in peace. "I say that Warwick is much too sensible a man to be hankering after a woman he was in love with more than twenty years ago; and that—"

"Oh, my dear, hush a moment!—Miss Tresham, will you touch the bell for Letty?—Now, children, say good-night to your father, and go to bed; it is after eight o'clock."

The children were evidently well drilled. They were dying to hear what was next to be said; but they went through the good-night ceremony, and filed off obediently, when a tall negro-woman, in a bright red-and-yellow turban, appeared at the door. It is true, there was a riot in the nursery that night; but no sound of it reached the precincts from which the young insurgents had been banished, for Letty was quite equal to the emergency herself, without invoking aid from the higher powers.

Meanwhile Mr. Marks obstinately declined to canvass any further either the arrival of Pauline Morton or the state of Mr. Warwick's affections—at least until he had finished that article from which he had several times been so ruthlessly torn.

"Those subjects will keep for some night when I haven't got any papers, Bessie," he said, to his wife's infinite indignation—an indignation which she forthwith manifested by taking herself and her sewing over to Miss Tresham's side.

"You never heard much about the Mortons, did you, my dear?" she asked, after admiring the pretty braiding that Katharine was putting on an apron for Nelly.

"I never heard any thing," the young governess answered, "excepting that they owned Morton House and lived abroad."

"Ah!" said Mrs. Marks, with something of a sigh; "people don't talk much about things that happened twenty years ago. But oh, my dear, if you could only have seen Morton House when the Mortons lived there, and when Pauline was in her prime! Such troops of servants as they had! such splendid horses! such furniture and such grounds! Why, you can see for yourself, even now, how magnificent the grounds were!"

"They must have been very beautiful when they were kept up," said Katharine, "and they are certainly very extensive."

"I should think so, indeed! Why, there used to be fifteen acres in gardens alone! I remember, when I was a girl, going to a camp-meeting once, where one of the preachers said that the best idea of heaven he could give was that it would be even more beautiful than the grounds of Morton House."

"Why did its owners leave it?"

"Ah, you may well ask! But it was all Pauline's fault. She was so beautiful and so proud that she scorned everybody and every thing here. She was never satisfied unless the house was full of strange company from the cities, and at last she told her parents that she would rather die than live in the backwoods. So her parents, who would have tried to get the stars for her if she had wanted them, left their beautiful home and went to Europe—never to come back, as it turned out."

"Did none of them ever come back?" asked Katharine, becoming rather interested.

"None of them ever came back—until to-day. There was a young brother—only one—who grew up in Europe; and I have heard that he laughed at the idea of returning to America to live. He must have spent money at a dreadful rate after his father's death; for Mr. Shields told John that the crops were always mortgaged before they went into market, and we heard, not long ago, that the house itself was to be sold. If that had been the case, I expect Mr. Annesley would have bought it."

"Why? Is he—"

"A relation? Oh, yes. His mother was a Morton, and as handsome and proud as all the rest of them. She was poor, though, for her father squandered every cent he had. But her uncle always treated her exactly as his own daughter, and people say he settled a very good sum on her when she married. She and Pauline were raised together like sisters; but they never liked each other. I don't know which was in fault; but they made no secret of the matter. For my part, I rather took Pauline's side, though most people were on Eliuor's; but Pauline was very generous, with all her pride, and I don't think she ever made her cousin feel her dependence. They even say that Mr. Annesley was Pauline's admirer, and only went over to Elinor after he was rejected. Then there's—O John, how you startled me!"

"I am very sorry," said Mr. Warwick, who had come in upon them unawares; "but I have been waiting some time for a chance to speak, and, as you seemed determined not to give me one, I was obliged to take it.—Miss Tresham, I wonder if you will excuse me when I tell you that I have just found a letter of yours in my pocket, which was left there through the joint carelessness of Katy and myself, and might have been lost?"

The girl looked up at him wonderingly.

"A letter for me, Mr. Warwick? You must be mistaken."

"How often am I to hear that to-night?" he asked, smiling. "I think, if you will look at this address, you will acknowledge that, with all my stupidity, I have hardly made a mistake."

He laid a letter down on the table before Katharine, who either would not or could not hold out her hand to receive it—a letter written on thin foreign paper, stamped with a foreign post-mark, and bearing her own name in clear, legible address.

Not so clear and legible, however, but that it swam before her eyes as she bent over it; and John Warwick was startled by the pallor of the face that raised itself, and by the anguish-stricken tone of the voice that cried out, as if unconsciously:

"Oh, if you had but lost it! if you had but lost it!"

CHAPTER IV.

WHAT MRS. ANNESLEY DID.

It would be difficult to exaggerate the excitement prevailing in Tallahoma—Tallahoma, which was very stagnant just at that time, for want of something to talk about, and which was blessed beyond its most sanguine expectations in the arrival of Mrs. Gordon. The news of that arrival spread rapidly through the village; and, while Mr. Warwick was telling his story at the Marks's tea-table, it would be hard to say how many other tea-tables were entertained by different renditions of the same facts. True, there was a very general and unsatisfactory haziness concerning the why and wherefore that had brought back the wanderer's steps, concerning her intentions, or even her appearance. But, then, these things promised an abundant harvest of gossip for the future; and all-absorbing for to-night was the simple fact that Pauline Morton had returned.

But on the morrow, after there was time for reflection, after the news had spread through the county, after the first shock of surprise was over, and people looked each other gravely in the face, they began to ask, How had she returned?

The answer was not long in coming. She had gone away in the flush of her youth and beauty, guarded by her parents, and with all the pomp of style and attendance which wealth could secure. She returned alone and unattended, with no husband to guard, no brother to protect, no friend to vouch for her—no word of warning, no single order of preparation! She came to her childhood's home and her childhood's friends with no pleasant stir and bustle of happy arrival, but silently and unexpectedly, more like an outcast seeking shelter than a daughter claiming her rightful heritage. Other people besides Mrs. Marks remembered when the Mortons had gone away, and, contrasting that departure with this return, almost involuntarily shook their heads. The first impulse of the world is always to distrust mystery. "Something is wrong," they said; and many of them said it the more readily because Pauline Morton had been one of those shining marks which envy loves, and because in her proud youth she had rather provoked than conciliated such a feeling.

It is exceedingly doubtful whether any state of society has ever existed since "Adam delved and Eve span," when those who were subordinate in the scale of worldly advantage have not felt a sort of carping dislike, and at times a bitter enmity, toward the few whom chance or fortune has elevated above them. We can imagine how the rabble of Athens spoke of Pericles and Alcibiades; we can conceive that hatred which from first to last the Roman plebeians bore their patrician masters; we can guess how bitterly the serfs and retainers, the scorned burghers, and oppressed Jews, spoke in bated whispers of the great feudal lords; we can read how often and how fiercely the great unknown have lashed themselves into fury against some class, some order, or some individual that birth, merit, or circumstance, rendered illustrious; and we can well believe that the same envy which we see manifested in a dozen petty instances every day, the same envy which was tired of hearing Aristides called the Just—has been the great moving spring of many of earth's revolutions, and is equally the moving spring of half the ill-nature and more than half the ill-speaking of the world. To make a small application of a wide truism, it was certainly the moving spring of most of the ebullitions of spiteful spleen in which for many years Lagrange had permitted itself to indulge regarding the Mortons. People more generous, more frank, or more hospitable, than these Mortons, it would be hard to find; but they were of good blood, and very proud of their descent; they were immensely wealthy, and spent their wealth liberally. These two facts were amply sufficient to excite that alloy of popular dislike which otherwise their many good qualities—qualities that even envy could not deny—might have disarmed. Not that they were unpopular in the general sense of the term; not that men denied their genial uprightness of character, or failed to respect them as only the honorable are respected. But they were too prosperous! The world and the things of the world went well with them; Fortune favored them in all their undertakings, while those who were less lucky could only look on and wonder why and how it was. They kept great state, and, although some of the best blood of the country was to be found in Lagrange, still there was no family that quite ranked with the Mortons, to whose wealth and enterprise Lagrange was indebted for much of its prosperity. The oldest and by far the most stately residence of the county was the house which had been built by the representative man of the line—one Hugh Morton of three generations back. The village of Tallahoma had begun its existence merely as the post-office of this house; and the same house had been for many years the centre of such a lavish and refined hospitality that its reputation spread far and wide throughout the entire State.

Considering their social importance, then, it was no wonder that all Lagrange was thrown into a commotion when it was announced that Mr. and Mrs. Morton were going to Europe, ostensibly for their son's education, but really to gratify their daughter's whim—the daughter who was accustomed to say that life in America was worse than death, who panted for the rush and fever of the Old World as ambitious men pant for fame, and to whom it was solely due that her indulgent parents went abroad, leaving their noble home to pass into decay while they dwelt in Parisian hotels and Neapolitan villas. She had the more easily compassed her point because there was no one of sufficient moral force to resist her. Some men—most men, in fact—would have been utterly lost in the *dilettante* existence thus forced upon them; but her father was just the exceptional man who enjoyed it. If he had been born among the lower classes in Spain or Italy, he would have spent his life on a door-step basking in the sun; and, as it was, he spent it in morally doing the same thing. He was frank and generous to a fault; but he was intensely indolent, pleasure-loving when the pursuit of pleasure did not involve too much trouble, and fond of ease and luxury to an almost womanly degree. Mrs. Morton, for her part, was bound up in her daughter's wishes and her daughter's triumphs, with a great sympathy for both, and a great liking herself for the things that were so attractive to Pauline. The only son was a mere child. So, with none to put an obstacle in her path, Pauline's impetuous will carried the day. The desire of her heart was granted her, as the desires of our hearts are rarely granted to us here on earth; and, when she took her life in her own hands and went her way, it was as some gallant ship sails away from a familiar harbor to cruise in unknown seas, where happiness and fortune may be attainable, but where shipwreck and disaster are much more likely to be encountered.

For some time after the departure of the voluntary exiles, fragmentary news came back of their wanderings; of their cordial recognition by the English relatives they had partly gone to seek; of Pauline's fresh triumphs; and of their glittering life in foreign cities. But all this was very vaguely told, and soon ceased altogether—fifty years ago the country-districts of America were farther removed from such scenes than is the interior of China to-day. Soon all tidings of the Mortons ceased, and before long the Mortons themselves might have been forgotten, had not the house which bore their name and seemed gloomily mourning them, stood as a perpetual reminder of their existence. Only at long intervals certain items of intelligence still gratified the gossips of Lagrange. First came the tidings of Mr. Morton's death; then news of Pauline's marriage to some one, who was variously represented of every imaginable nationality and rank; and, lastly, the announcement of her mother's death. Then silence fell, silence complete and unbroken, although the county leader of fashion, handsome Mrs. Annesley, was first cousin to the surviving brother and sister, had been reared in their father's house, and married from it. But everybody knew that Pauline had never liked her cousin, and that it was a happy day for both when Edgar Annesley (who was killed in a duel a few years later) took his bride from the door of Morton House.

Remembering all these things, a thrill of intense interest and surprise ran through the county when Lagrange heard of Pauline Morton's return. There was not a family of good rank within its borders that did not own some connection of blood or ancient friendship with Morton; and not a family, therefore, which was not personally interested in this unexpected arrival. Still even these people paused and looked at each other full of doubt. If Pauline Morton had come back among them with the state which, to their imagination, was always associated with the name; if she had thrown open the old hospitable doors, and lighted up once more the old hospitable rooms; if she had bidden her friends around her, and asked their welcome with the matchless grace they still remembered—they would have been the last people in the world to question whence she came, or why she chose to shroud her past life in mystery. But the singularity of her course awakened in them the first chill of suspicion. Why come back in this way to her own house? Why write no letters? Why give no warning to the friends who had a right to know of her intention? Why ask no aid from their support, she coming back so strangely alone to claim her old position? Why offer no explanation of her marriage and widowhood? Why think that her old acquaintances would take for granted the twenty years passed away from them—the twenty years in which she might have climbed any height, or plunged into any depth, unknown to them? Truly it was no wonder that the elders among them shook their heads; and truly it did not look as if Pauline Morton had come back to win any very warm welcome from her kinsfolk and friends.

Yet among the former class was one person at least to whom no neutral position was possible, one person on whom the burden of positive action was incumbent, and from whom every obligation of gratitude that the world counts binding commanded a speedy and cordial welcome to the returned wanderer. This person was Mrs. Annesley; and yet her worst enemy —if, indeed, the handsome, charming lady owned any enemies—could not have contrived for her a more disagreeable surprise than the news of her cousin's arrival proved. When she heard the particulars of this arrival, she turned very pale; and then—went to bed with one of those bad nervous attacks which always stood her in such good stead when an unpleasant exertion was demanded, or an unpleasant duty was to be performed. She deplored this necessity very pathetically; and assured the friends who came to see her that she was especially sorry because she could not go at once to meet and welcome "dear Pauline." But these friends were by no means obtuse; they understood the matter perfectly,

MOTHER AND DAUGHTER. Chap. IV

and told each other when they went out that it was evident Mrs. Annesley felt very awkwardly about meeting her cousin, and that they did not wonder at it.

"It is unfortunate that I should be ill just at this time," Mrs. Annesley said to her daughter, Mrs. French—a pretty, fashionable-looking girl two or three years younger than her brother Morton, and lately married—on the evening of the day when these visits had been paid. "I certainly ought to see Pauline at once, and it is quite impossible for me to do so. Yet people will be sure to think it very strange."

"Mrs. Raynor told me to-day that everybody is waiting to see what you mean to do," Mrs. French answered. "If I were you, mamma, I would let them wait. A woman who comes back like this does not deserve any consideration."

"I am not thinking of her," said Mrs. Annesley, truthfully enough.

It was a little before dark, and the mother and daughter were quite alone in the chamber of the former. With the outside world it was still daylight, but here the shades of twilight had already gathered, deepening in all the nooks and corners of the room, and only dissipated by the ruddy glow which a bright wood-fire cast over the polished furniture and the softly-tinted walls. On one side of the hearth sat Mrs. Annesley in a deep arm-chair. Her cashmere dressing-gown, her dainty lace cap, and her velvet slippers, were all perfect; for she had made a tasteful invalid toilet in expectation of those compassionate visitors who had just departed. Opposite, and if possible in a still more luxurious attitude, Mrs. French was sitting—the firelight flickering over her silk dress, and glancing back from her gold *châtelaine*. She had been busy with some netting; but the rose-colored web had dropped in her lap, her hands were loosely folded over it, and her eyes were roving absently from the fire to her mother, and from her mother to the heavily-draped windows that commanded a view of the lawn before the house, and the belt of dark shrubbery beyond. Finally, she said, languidly:

"It is a good thing that Morton is away."

"It is a most fortunate thing," answered Mrs. Annesley, with energy. "Morton is so Quixotic in his ideas that there really is no counting on him, and he is so unfortunately straightforward that he cannot understand the delicate management which some things require. I am sure he would give me trouble if he were here; so I agree with you, Adela—it is a good thing that Mr. French wrote for him just now."

"It will be at least a fortnight before he can get back," said Adela, who had been making some calculation of time and distance while her mother spoke. "Perhaps it may be longer, if Frank decides to come with him, as I hope he will. Then I shall keep him here until I am ready to go back to Mobile."

"It is very provoking that you should need to go back," said Mrs. Annesley, pettishly. "I shall never be satisfied until you are settled in Lagrange. If I could only carry out my plans! If you could only live here—"

"Frank would never consent to it, mamma," interrupted Adela, placidly. "He says, very truly, that Morton will be marrying some day, and, of course, bringing his wife here; and, then, the arrangement would never do."

"Of course, there could be no question of it under those circumstances—that is, if Morton decided to make this place his home," said Mrs. Annesley. "But that was not my plan, Adela, as you very well know."

"I know you thought of Morton House for him, and Annesdale for us. That would certainly be very nice. But I suppose we must give up all hope of it now."

"That remains to be seen," answered Mrs. Annesley, quickly. "It is almost beyond patience," she went on, "that this woman should come back now to defeat all my plans. Every thing was so well arranged. Alfred Morton was perfectly willing to sell the house, and Morton could well afford to give even the exorbitant price he asked. It is true that for the same amount he could have bought the finest plantation in the State; but then no other place could be to him like that—his great-grandfather's house. Nobody knows how my heart has always been set on this. Ever since Morton was a child, I have counted on seeing him owner of Morton House. It seemed to me it would even make amends for all I once endured in that house, to know that *my* son was master there. And now this kind cousin, who always hated me, has come back—simply to disappoint my wishes."

"It would be very nice," said Adela, whose mind was still bent on the arrangement, as it affected her own comfort. "Frank and I could settle here, and I need not trouble myself any more about his disagreeable relations in Mobile Morton could marry Irene Vernon, and live in that tumble-down old barn that you have such a fancy for· and you could have your rooms at both places, and visit between us, just as you liked. It is a pity that one of your cousins took it into his head to die, and the other one to come back just now."

"Gordon!" said Mrs. Annesley, slowly; "Gordon! I am confident that I once heard the name of the man Pauline Morton married; and, if I could recall it now, it might be worth remembering. I am almost sure—as sure as I can be of any thing which did not dwell positively on my mind—that it was *not* Gordon."

"Goodness, mamma! Has she come back under a false name?"

"I am not certain, of course; but my own impression is that she has. Don't mention it, though, Adela. People are talking enough about her already, and we need not circulate a fact which undoubtedly looks very badly."

"You may be sure, mamma, that nobody ever acts as she is acting without some reason for it."

"There is no doubt of that," answered Mrs. Annesley, with a sudden flash of something like triumph in her eyes. "But it does not surprise me in the least—nothing that I could hear of her would surprise me. Her pride and insolence were so great that they paved a fall for themselves. Times have changed, Adela; you don't know how strangely it makes me feel to realize that twenty-five years ago Pauline Morton was the queen of Lagrange, and to-day it is doubtful whether there is a single person of good position in the county who will move an inch to welcome her."

"It all depends on you," said Adela, in her languid way. "Mrs. Raynor told me that. She says that everybody is in doubt what to do, and they mean to wait and see how you will act."

"There, again, times have changed," said Mrs. Annesley, gazing into the fire "Twenty-five years ago I was the dependent cousin whom Pauline Morton barely tolerated; and to-day it seems that here, in her own home, the question of her social recognition depends on me."

"It depends on you how people will receive her," said the matter-of-fact Adela. "If I were you, mamma, I would let her see this, and then—you might perhaps make your own terms, and get Morton House after all."

Mrs. Annesley gave her daughter a glance, and laughed a little.

"You are tolerably quick-witted, Adela, and would make a pretty good diplomatist. Certainly, I don't owe Pauline much, in the way of a good turn; and certainly, also, the advantages of the situation are on my side now. If Morton is not the owner of Morton House yet, you may be sure that it will not be my fault. By-the-by, did Mrs. Raynor tell you any thing of those reports we heard about Pauline several years ago?"

"Nothing at all, mamma, for she did not seem to know any thing. She said there had been reports, but that they were very vague, and she had never been able to make much out of them. She said, also, that you would not speak of them; but she was sure you knew more about the matter than anybody else."

"She is mistaken," said Mrs. Annesley; "I know nothing about it. How or with whom the reports originated, I cannot tell; and, simply because I did not choose to contradict them, people took it for granted that I believed them and was well acquainted with all the particulars."

"I expect you looked as if you believed them. That is a way you have, mamma."

"I certainly could not look as if I did *not* believe them, when they were so entirely in keeping with Pauline Morton's character," answered Mrs. Annesley, a little coldly. "She was always imprudent and reckless to the last degree. If she has learned wisdom, it has been since she left Lagrange.—Will you ring the bell there, Adela? I must order some chocolate for my supper; coffee keeps me awake, and is bad for my nerves."

The bell was rung; the chocolate was ordered; the servant who received the order delivered a message to Mrs. French about some household matter which demanded her presence downstairs; and, with the regretful sigh of an indolent person, the lady tore herself from her comfortable lounging-place, and departed. The door had scarcely closed on her, when Mrs. Annesley rose and walked to the window. The dusk had fallen by this time, and she could not do more than distinguish the outlines of the familiar objects before her—the piazzas and wings of the house, the graceful trees and well-trimmed shrubs that were scattered over the gently-sloping lawn. Every thing at Annesdale was in the most perfect taste; but every thing was undisguisedly new, and just now Mrs. Annesley's heart was longing for something which was old. Her husband had begun, and she herself had completed, the house in which she stood; yet, charming as it was in every appliance of luxury and comfort, her perverse fancy went back to the stately rooms, dark and mellow with age, where her youth had been passed. She looked steadfastly out of the window, over the trees and shrubbery which her own hand had planted, beyond the dark woods and broad fields, until she saw—in imagination—the noble oaks of Morton House, and the tall chimneys, from which, for the first time in twenty years, the smoke of household fires was curling upward. Then her brows contracted in a slight frown—a frown not sufficiently marked to darken the handsome face, or give a severe aspect to its smooth lines. "Times are changed," she said, once more, but this time only half aloud. "Will she recognize that as plainly as I do, I wonder? Will she see that, indeed, the advantage is with me now, and that it is for me to decide whether Pauline Morton—the beauty, the heiress, the belle of Lagrange, twenty-five years ago—shall not be a social outlaw in Lagrange to-day? whether, six months hence, Morton House shall not be in my Morton's hands?"

Before long, Mrs. French came back, and found her mother sitting as quietly as ever beside the hearth, in the dim, fire-lighted apartment. The two ladies spent the evening together, and, when they separated for the night, the last thing Mrs. Annesley told her daughter was that her inconvenient illness would at least serve one good purpose, in enabling her to see what other people meant to do in the case of her cousin.

Several days elapsed. Then she found that Mrs. Raynor was right, and that other people had made up their minds to the same masterly policy of inaction which she herself had been practising. So, urged partly by this fact, and partly by a growing fear of her son's return, she became suddenly convalescent, thought a drive might benefit her, and ordered the carriage.

"I won't ask you to accompany me, Adela," she said to Mrs. French. "If I should go to Morton House, the meeting would, of course, be very painful on both sides, and had better be as private as possible. Besides, I don't care to draw you into a connection that may prove a very awkward one. Frank might object to it."

"Frank is not of any importance," said Frank's wife, carelessly. "But I wouldn't think of such a thing as going—not for the world! I hate disagreeable people, and this Pauline Morton must be very disagreeable. Don't tell her I am here, mamma—I beg you, don't do that!"

"I am not sure that I shall go to Morton House," said Mrs. Annesley. "It depends on how I feel," she added, gravely, as she went down the piazza-steps and entered the carriage which was drawn up before them. "Mrs. Taylor's, John," she said to the coachman, who stood waiting his orders. And, as the carriage drove off, Adela, who was still on the piazza, saw her lean back and put her *vinaigrette* to her nostrils.

Her point of destination was not more than two or three miles from Annesdale; so she had not time to feel her nerves in any unpleasant degree before the mettled horses swept up to a red-brick house, set in the midst of a bright-green lawn, with a brilliant hedge on either side, and an ornate fence in front. Here the languid invalid was warmly welcomed by Mrs. Taylor and some half-dozen daughters, whose ages ranged from fifteen to thirty, and whose ugliness was from comparative to superlative degree. Mrs. Taylor was a widow; her daughters were all unmarried; and, since country-life is stagnant at best, and a large household composed exclusively of women must certainly bestow its energies upon some employment, the Taylors, mother and daughters, were widely famed for devoting themselves, like the Athenians of old, to "telling and hearing something new." Their house was the headquarters of all news (reliable or otherwise) which was afloat in Lagrange, and the mint where all reports were stamped for current circulation. If Mrs. Annesley had wished to put her finger on the public pulse, and feel how strong or how feeble were its beats on the Morton question, she could not have chosen a better place for the purpose.

Perhaps this had been her intention. At all events, when she left the red-brick mansion behind, and was on the high-road, she gave the order, "Morton House."

CHAPTER V.

AFTER TWENTY YEARS.

Half an hour later, Mrs. Annesley's footman was unfastening a large, rusty iron-gate, and holding it open while the flashing carriage rolled majestically through. Then he let the wings fall together with a loud clang, and Mrs. Annesley felt that she was within the domain of Morton House.

It was rather a dreary-looking place into which she had entered; and none the less dreary because showing evident signs of much by-gone beauty and care—dreary with a forsaken air of neglect under the soft November sky, and with the mellow glory of the November sunshine streaming upon it. In all Indian-summer weather, there is a pathos of intangible sadness —even on the bright road, and under its glorious golden woods this was sensibly to be felt; but here it deepened into something almost approaching pain, something which even a nature as wholly prosaic as Mrs. Annesley's could not but feel. "One might believe it was a graveyard," she thought to herself, as her eye swept over the broad, park-like extent around her. A sudden break in the closely-planted trees of the avenue spread a fair picture before her eyes—a picture fair in its decay. True, the noble lawn was thickly strewed with the fallen and mouldering leaves of many autumns, and the once magnificent shrubbery, which on the south side stretched away into far-reaching gardens, was now little more than an overgrown wilderness. But there was an almost regal air of space spread over all; and even neglect could not entirely destroy the matchless landscape gardening that had once been displayed here—the artistic grouping of trees and shrubs, the forest vistas, and the enchanting vicissitudes of light and shadow so skilfully blent and arranged. The avenue was at least a mile in length, and led almost directly to a broad, green terrace, which extended around the house, and from which stone steps descended to the drive below. The house itself was now in sight—old, large, brown, and weather-beaten. Yet, notwithstanding all the dreariness of falling shutters and rotting roof, there was something about it which made it not difficult to believe that it had once been the gayest and most hospitable dwelling in the county—a something which had survived all the long twenty years when no feet had crossed its threshold save those of the servants, who once every six months opened the windows and let God's sunshine stream for a brief space into the darkened chambers!—the twenty years when no household-fires had blazed on the cold hearths, when no master's voice or mistress's laughter, or children's merry tones, had sounded along its galleries, or broken the silence of its deserted rooms.

"There only need a few repairs to make it again the most beautiful place in all the county," Mrs. Annesley said to herself, as she leaned forward for a better view of the house, which she was now rapidly approaching—the house that had sheltered her childhood and youth, and from which her husband had taken her a bride. And, as she bent forward in the bright sunshine, and looked at the dark old front, with its lofty stone portico, a sudden vision seemed to rise before her—a vision of a royal-looking girl, with a face that was brilliant as an oleander blossom, with hair that seemed to have caught the sunshine on every thread, with eyes of matchless splendor, with the profile of a Greek cameo, and the bearing of a Greek goddess. She saw this lovely vision standing where Pauline Morton so often had stood, just within the shadow of the arched door-way, wearing the fresh-flowing muslin that Pauline Morton so often had worn, and turning as if to greet her with the winning smile she had seen so often on Pauline Morton's lip. It was only a moment that this picture of the past stood framed there; but so vivid was it that Mrs. Annesley almost seemed to look through the open doors behind, and see the sunshine of long ago falling on the tessellated floor of the wide, cool hall—almost seemed to see the servants passing up and down the broad staircase, the gay faces at the drawing-room windows, and all the life, the stir, the bustle, so long since fled forever. It was only for one moment; the next, the yellow sunshine slept as peacefully as before on the closed door and vacant step.

But the past had not come back in vain even to this woman's selfish heart, and, for a few minutes, she wavered in the purpose which had brought her there. For a few minutes, she remembered how long that roof had sheltered her, how constant had been the kindness, how lavish the generosity she had received there; she remembered the dead who had befriended her, and, for once, the ingratitude she was meditating rose up to reproach her. Then her son's handsome face and gallant presence seemed also to appear on that threshold where she had so long hoped to see him master; and the mother's heart steeled itself again. "It is for him," she murmured; "and I should not hesitate at any thing, however painful, to serve his interest. Besides, it will depend upon herself—that is the only light in which to look at it. It will depend upon herself; and any one else in my place would act as I must do."

As if to give emphasis to her concluding words, the carriage at that moment drew up before the terrace-steps, and the footman was on the ground lowering the steps, and ready to guard his mistress's dress from any contact with the dusty wheels. It was too late to retreat, even if Mrs. Annesley had felt inclined for any thing so recreant. But she alighted at once ascended the steps and crossed the terrace, her ample skirts sweeping grandly over the neglected walks; entered the portico, and, finding the door-bell gone, gave a summons with her parasol on the panel. She was forced to repeat it more than once before the door opened, creaking a sullen protest on its rusty hinges, and a gray-haired servant appeared. He looked a little doubtfully at the lady standing before him, shading his eyes with one hand, for the sunlight streamed full in his face; but she smiled at once in cordial recognition.

"Why, Harrison, is it you?" she said. "And so you are back in the old place. How are you?"

"Oh, it's Miss Elinor! I beg your pardon, ma'am, but I didn't know you at first," the old man answered, as he took the delicately-gloved hand she extended, in the momentary clasp of his horny black one. "Yes'm, I'm back. Miss Pauline said as how she would rather see the old faces about her than any new ones, Miss Elinor."

Miss Elinor! Yes, she was "Miss Elinor" yet, to these old servants of her uncle's household; and, although she often met them, and heard the name, it had never brought back the memory of her youth as it did now, when she was standing at the door of Morton House, and heard it from the lips that had repeated to her the messages of friends and admirers in the days gone by.

"And Pauline?" she said, eagerly. "I have been sick, Harrison, or I should have been to see her before this. How is she?"

Harrison shook his head.

"You'll see for yourself, Miss Elinor," he answered; "and I'm afraid you'll be shocked, ma'am. But I'm glad you've come—mebbe you'll cheer her up a little."

"Does she need cheering? Is she sick?"

"Oh, no, ma'am, not sick, but so changed like. It was an awful shock to me, ma'am. I'd never a-known Miss Pauline."

"I am changed too, Harrison. We all change in twenty years."

Harrison shook his head again. "Not like her," he said—"not like her."

Then he led the way across the hall, threw open the drawing-room door, with something of his old formality; said, "Walk in, ma'am," quite grandly, and, after Mrs. Annesley had walked in, shut the door, and left her alone with the chill and the darkness—for it was both chill and dark after the glowing softness of the outer air.

Standing where she had been left, the lady looked round and shivered, as if with a sudden ague. This was one of the suite of reception-rooms, which she well remembered—the first one looking to the front—but the curtains were looped back from the arch that divided it from the adjoining apartment; and, when her eyes grew accustomed to the dim light, she gazed straight into the room where she had been married—straight at the very table near which she had stood, and at the very pattern of the carpet which she had traced with her downcast eyes while the ceremony proceeded. Nay, not more than a few steps from her, was the sofa upon which she sat when Edgar Annesley asked her to be his wife, and told her, in his frank, honorable way, that, although he could never love her as he had once loved her cousin, yet he would be to her a true and tender husband. There was the piano on which she had so often played duets with Pauline—there was her aunt's favorite chair; and there her uncle's whist-table. Turn where she would, some memory of the past assailed her; and exclaiming impatiently, "It is worse than meeting a procession of ghosts!" she suddenly crossed the room, and threw open an end window. The sunshine streamed in as if glad of an entrance; and then she perceived the ravages of time—the mildewed walls, the moth-eaten furniture, the faded curtains. "Repairs are needed worse than I thought," she said, half aloud; and, as she said it, she fell to thinking how well these lofty rooms would look newly fitted; how admirably a rich deep green would do for the one in which she stood; and how well green became the blond beauty of Irene Vernon—the girl of all others whom she most wished to see her son's wife. She was so engrossed by these fancies, that the opening of the door did not rouse her, standing as she was with her back to it; neither did a quiet step which crossed the apartment; and it was not until a light touch fell on her arm, that she started, turned, and stood face to face with the cousin from whom she had parted twenty years before.

They stood and looked at each other—neither speaking for a moment. They had lived together in the past as intimately as sisters; but neither of them had ever entertained a sister's regard for the other. Therefore, they felt no affectionate impulse to rush into each other's arms; and, honest in the present as in the past, they did not feign it. They did not break into any noisy greetings, or take refuge in the commonplaces of ordinary welcome; they did not even shake hands—they only stood and looked at the faces over which twenty years had passed.

A greater contrast than these two faces presented it would be hard to imagine—one so handsome and well preserved, so smooth of skin, so clear of outline, so suave and smiling of aspect, with not a silver thread in the shining black hair, or even an incipient crow's-foot around the cold black eyes; the other so worn and haggard, so deeply lined and darkened over, so bereft of all beauty save the mould of feature and the magic of glance, so stamped with the dreary stamp of suffering, so marked with the bitter signet of anguish, so utterly lost to all the bright bravery of the world, that, save for a proud nobility which still dwelt in, and redeemed it—save for the lovely pathos of the eyes, and the haughty curve of the lips—there was no depth of tragedy in which it was not possible to fancy that this woman might have played a part.

This, at least, was the first tangible idea which came to Mrs. Annesley's mind, as she saw that not even Harrison's dismal prophecy had prepared her for the extent of the change, and as she recognized how far below the surface that change had struck. *This* her cousin! *This* Pauline Morton! *This* the girl who had gone away in the spring-tide splendor of her youth and beauty! "Good God! I can believe any thing of her now!" she thought, as she gazed in mute dismay on that world-worn face.

It was Mrs. Gordon who first broke the silence.

"How little changed you are, Elinor!" she said, in a rich, sweet voice; "and how it brings back the old time to see you again—here!"

"But you!" cried Mrs. Annesley, thrown for once entirely beyond the range of her usual conventionalities—"you! Pauline, for Heaven's sake, what have you been doing to yourself that you look like this?"

"Am I so very much changed, then?" asked her cousin, with a smile—oh, so different from the smile that shadowy beauty had worn who stood in the door-way and greeted Mrs. Annesley half an hour before!

"Changed!" She stopped, abruptly; but the tone that said that much had said enough.

There was a moment's silence. Then the other, taking her hand, leaned forward, and lightly kissed her cheek.

"Yours is the first kindred face I have seen," she said, gently, yet with a certain dignity. "Let me bid you welcome to Morton House."

And in the tone, the action, there was that which took the ground from beneath Mrs. Annesley's feet. She had come, meaning to patronize with all the grandiloquent patronage of her changed position; and one second seemed to place her back on the old level, to which Pauline Morton had once bent with this same stately grace, but never succeeded in making her cousin forget that she did bend. For an instant, Mrs. Annesley caught her breath; for an instant, she almost forgot that she was not again the penniless relation who was bidden welcome to a home she might share, but never inherit. Then she recovered herself, and returned her cousin's caress with more effusion than that cousin's manner seemed to warrant.

"My dear Pauline, those words are more mine than yours. Welcome, indeed—welcome to your old home and your old friends!"

"Thank you, Elinor," her cousin replied, quietly. "Pray sit down."

"Of course, I should have come to you at once, if I had not been ill—really ill. I am here to-day in defiance of the doctor."

"Indeed! I should not think you looking badly. But it was one of your old nervous attacks, I suppose?"

"Yes, one of my old nervous attacks," replied Mrs. Annesley, unblushingly. "They seem to grow worse as I grow older."

"I am sorry to hear that.—You must be tired by your drive. I will order some refreshment."

She moved away a few steps to ring a bell, and Mrs. Annesley had a good opportunity for observing how straight and rigid was the dress she wore, how hideous the cap that covered all save a little of the hair so thickly sown with gray, and how every harmless beautifier of the toilet seemed sternly banished from the costume. When she returned, the latter said, wonderingly:

"Have you turned Romanist, Pauline, and are you going to establish a nunnery, that you dress in such a style as this? You look like a nun, I assure you."

"If you had ever seen a nun, Elinor, you would not think so," the other answered, with a faint smile. "A nun's face is always sweet and serene—not world-battered and world-worn, like mine."

"Then, what do you mean by this?" and the gloved hand touched the black fabric near it.

"I only mean that I have renounced the world as much as if I had gone into a cloister."

"My dear Pauline!"

"Does that surprise you, Elinor? Ah! you have not drunk the dregs of life, as I have."

"Surprise me? Of course, it surprises me. But I don't understand."

"No, I don't suppose you do. I hope there are not many people who would fully understand. —Do you know what I have come back here for?"

"How should I?"

"True, how should you! Well, I will tell you; for I want to make my intention clear to all whom it may concern, and you are one of those whom it does concern. I have come back to bury myself."

"Pauline!"

"Is there any thing strange in that?" said Mrs. Gordon, with another faint, flitting smile. "Women have done such things before—the nuns of whom we spoke, for instance."

Mrs. Annesley did not answer. She gazed at her cousin with blank amazement, and yet more blank apprehension, which might in time have found expression, if the door had not been suddenly burst open, and a boy of eight or nine years old—a magnificent incarnation of blooming health and beauty—rushed into the room, exclaiming, "Mamma!" and did not pause until he stood by his mother's side, staring with unabashed eyes at the elegant stranger.

"Oh, what a handsome child!" cried Mrs. Annesley, surprised for once into an enthusiastic truth. "Pauline, is this your boy? How like you he is! and yet, how unlike!"

"He is not like me at all," Mrs. Gordon answered, in a hard voice. Then it softened suddenly, as she turned to the child. "Felix, go and speak to that lady; she is your cousin."

Felix did as he was told—extending a hand by no means very clean, but given with the grace of a young prince.

"I am glad to see you, my cousin," he said, quite loftily.

And, while Mrs. Annesley surreptitiously wiped her fingers on her handkerchief, she turned again to her companion:

"What charming manners he has! If he does not resemble yourself—and I can see now that he does not—I suppose he looks like his father."

"Yes," was the brief reply.

"Poor child! How young to be fatherless! I presume he cannot even remember—Mr. Gordon?"

"Yes, he remembers him," said Mrs. Gordon, quietly.—"Felix, go and ask Harrison if he did not hear the bell."

"He heard it, mamma," said Felix, promptly. "He's cutting the cake; and I came to ask you if I mayn't have some wine—*he* won't give me any."

"Certainly not. You can have cake—not wine."

"I don't care about cake, mamma."

"There is no necessity for you to eat it, then, my dear. But we shall see if your resolution lasts when it comes—and here it is."

As she spoke, Harrison made his appearance, bearing a salver on which were set forth the orthodox cake and wine of country hospitality—the former in rich silver baskets, and the latter in slender, old-fashioned wine-glasses. While Mrs. Annesley refreshed herself with a glass of the golden sherry that had been mellowing in the cellars of Morton House for forty years, exchanging with her cousin a few matter-of-course remarks about the weather, expatiating on the beauty of the child, who was still present, and even upon the becoming costume he wore, she was revolving in her mind the altered aspect which the last few minutes had given to the hopes she had so long and so sanguinely entertained.

How easy it is to arrange mentally a suppositious scene and conversation! But when was such scene or conversation ever enacted *as* arranged? From the moment in which she heard of her cousin's return, Mrs. Annesley's busy fancy had been going over and over again a rehearsal of the present interview; and each time she had acquitted herself to her own entire satisfaction. She had spoken—suavely patronizing, but uncompromising in her demands; her cousin had answered—gratefully submissive. Not a shade of doubt or distrust of her own powers had crossed her mind; she had believed herself to be absolute mistress of the situation. And, alas! the very first tone of her cousin's voice, and glance at her cousin's face—changed so inconceivably though that face was—showed her the mistake she had made, the self-delusion with which she had been pleasing herself. Memory had played her false—memory, and the vanity that had been fostered by years of uncheckered prosperity. At the first glance, she recognized the fact that the Pauline with whom she had been holding her imaginary conversations was but a lay-figure, an automaton of her own creation, which had moved, breathed, trembled, yielded, as her own inclination pulled the wires upon which she had suspended it. The Pauline before her—ah! how could she have forgotten that haughty nature so strangely as to dream of gaining a moment's ascendency over it? She felt that she was defeated even before she had struck one blow in furtherance of her "plan.' This resolution of retirement from the world—why, it destroyed every vestige, even to the very foundations, of the fabric she had so remorselessly reared! The old, bitter hate and envy—the old, still more rankling sense of impotence to harm, even to move, this woman, who had always seemed so unconscious, if not contemptuous, of her enmity—rushed over her soul in a tide of almost suffocating passion. Baffled—defeated—now, as ever before! She could have gnashed her teeth in fury! Baffled—just when she thought success certain! And must she submit unresistingly? Might she not sting, wound, if she could not subdue, this proud nature? She would see.

"Felix, my dear, you make too much noise. Go to Babette, now," said Mrs. Gordon, as the boy began a romp with the little spaniel which had followed him into the room. "Go!"

"Yes, mamma." And he obediently departed.

Mrs. Annesley cleared her throat nervously, rose, and set down the wine-glass from which she had been sipping, and, returning to her chair, drew it a little nearer to her cousin's before she again seated herself. Then, laying her hand on the sleeve of the close black dress, she said, confidentially:

"My dear Pauline, you quite took away my breath by what you said just now. I am glad you sent the child out, so that we can talk freely. Surely, you do not mean that you intend renouncing society altogether?"

"That is what I mean."

"Impossible! impossible!" cried Mrs. Annesley, assuming an expression of grave remonstrance. "Why, what would the world say?"

"The world of Lagrange, do you mean?"

"Yes. Your own old friends, and those of your parents."

"If the subject interests them sufficiently for them to say any thing, I suppose it will be some of the good-natured things which they used to say of me in the old times. But what does it matter?"

"It matters every thing!—if you do not wish to lose your reputation."

Mrs. Gordon regarded her cousin's face for an instant in astonishment. Then her brows contracted slightly, and a haughty light came into her eyes. "My reputation!" she repeated. "And pray, Elinor, will you tell me what possible connection there is, or can be made, between my voluntary seclusion and the loss of my reputation?"

Mrs. Annesley paused a moment, partly because she was a little doubtful as to what her next words should be—partly with an affectation of reluctance to speak. She looked down at the carpet, thoughtfully—then lifted her eyes to her cousin's countenance, hoping to find there signs of alarm and perturbation. She was disappointed. Mrs. Gordon was waiting quietly for her to proceed.

"Your question places me in a very embarrassing, a very painful position, Pauline," she began, with well-acted hesitation. "But—I think you will agree with me that plain speaking is always best; particularly in a case of this kind, and between friends and relatives."

"Undoubtedly. Plain speaking is always best between people who have a right to speak plainly to each other; and friends and relatives do possess this right," answered Mrs. Gordon, with the dignified simplicity of manner which, to her cousin's elaborate mannerism of dignity, seemed, as it always had seemed, like virgin gold to pinchbeck.

Mrs. Annesley cleared her throat again, and, lifting the top of her *vinaigrette*, bent her head and inhaled the salts before she replied, slowly:

"My dear Pauline, I do not know whether you are aware that, to the eyes of the world, your life is veiled in profound mystery; that, until your return, your friends were ignorant of the very name of the man you married; that, even now, the name itself is all that is known. Under these circumstances, is it much to be wondered at that some very unpleasant reports have crept into circulation?—reports which you would be shocked to hear, my dear, I assure you! And, if you take this strange step of secluding yourself from the world, I cannot answer for the consequences."

Mrs. Gordon had listened unmoved to her cousin's words, until Mrs. Annesley came to the last sentence. She smiled then—not scornfully, but with a sort of half-sad amusement.

"Human nature is the same all the world over!" she said. "In the little stagnant pool, as in the great ocean of life, impertinent curiosity and gratuitous ill-nature are the most marked features of 'society.' But, my dear Elinor, I am surprised that you should have forgotten all about my character so entirely as to imagine that the 'opinion of the world' could move me.

or give me a moment's uneasiness. Don't you remember how I used to shock you with my disregard for the ideas and dicta of this narrow world around us? And do you think it likely that a cosmopolitan life of twenty years has taught me to rate its importance more highly?"

"Good Heavens, Pauline! You do not know, you do not realize what you are disregarding!—what the reports *are*—" began Mrs. Annesley, with a consternation which was perfectly genuine—for more and more did *she* realize that her anticipated power over her cousin had been a chimera of self-flattery. But Mrs. Gordon interposed, quietly:

"I have no more curiosity now than formerly about Lagrange gossip. If it amuses people to talk about me, I have no objection to their enjoying that gratification."

"But, surely, you object to setting a stain on your good name!—on the Morton honor!" cried Mrs. Annesley, driven beyond all self-control by the careless indifference with which the other spoke.

Mrs. Gordon's lip curled in a disdain so contemptuous that her cousin shrank abashed with that consciousness of utter discomfiture in all endeavor to annoy, which had been so familiar and so galling to her in the old days, while the former said, sternly:

"I have returned to my old home, soul-weary and grief-stricken—to seek the shelter of my father's roof, as people sometimes quit the world for a cloister. You tell me that the 'old friends' of my parents and myself are bandying about 'reports' concerning me; that they 'know nothing of my life,' and yet are slandering it! Well, I answer that their gossip and slander are less to me than the hum of the insects around him to the anchorite of the desert; that, for the people who disseminate or believe slanders so false, so malicious, so unprovoked—who dare to suspect my father's daughter of any act unworthy of his name and honor—I entertain a contempt too profound for it to be any thing but passive."

Mrs. Annesley was effectually silenced; but her countenance showed so plainly the dismay, mortification, and chagrin, by which she was literally overwhelmed, that Mrs. Gordon, reading the expression (though not, of course, its cause), and attributing it to a fear of being personally compromised, said gravely, but kindly:

"I know, my dear Elinor, that your ideas and mine do not agree as to the value of the world's opinion. And, if you fear that, you may yourself incur the censure of this opinion—"

"Pauline, how can you wrong me by imagining that I am thinking of myself in the matter! It was alarm for you which, ill as I felt this morning, urged me to the exertion of showing the world at once *my* position toward you—*my* estimate of the reports that are in circulation—by coming to offer you the support and advice of a kinswoman."

A smile of irrepressible amusement swept over Mrs. Gordon's face, brightening it into a stronger likeness to its former self than Mrs. Annesley could have believed it possible it would ever again wear. "And have these good people of Lagrange really proceeded so far in their amiable canvassing of my affairs, that you thought it necessary to extend a hand to save me?" she said, with almost a laugh. "I am afraid they would be disappointed, if they knew how much unnecessary trouble they have given themselves. My first order to Harrison, on my arrival, was, that no one but yourself, your children, and one or two of my oldest and dearest friends, were to be admitted. To all others he was to say that, being in deep mourning, and in deep grief—" her lip quivered with anguish as she spoke the last words—"I must decline society. You see, therefore, that it was premature, to say the least, in the social authorities of Lagrange, to decree ostracism to one who, for reasons entirely apart from any consideration of their existence, had no intention of accepting, far less of asking, their suffrage. It was kind of you, Elinor," she added, with a perfect good faith that made Mrs. Annesley wince, "to wish to throw yourself into the breach in my defence."

"It was useless, I perceive," answered Mrs. Annesley, endeavoring to regain her usual manner, "if you persist in this strange resolution you have expressed. Nothing, which I could say or do would have any effect in righting the public sentiment, so long as you maintain the mystery which was the cause of these dreadful reports If you would only authorize me to contradict them—to—"

"Excuse me," interposed Mrs. Gordon, quietly. "It is a matter of perfect indifference to me."

"But for *my* sake!" urged Mrs. Annesley, who remembered well that she had many a time gained concessions from Pauline's generosity, which Pauline's pride would never have made—"for *my* sake, Pauline! Think what an embarrassing position I am placed in. Pray, reconsider your resolution!"

"My dear Elinor, I cannot do that," answered

her cousin. "I came here, as I told you, to seek rest. I married very unhappily, and have suffered much—have suffered so terribly that, but for the sake of my child, I think I could not have lived through all I have endured. This explanation I make to yourself—not for the benefit of the gossips who, it seems, are busying themselves with my name. Yourself, and the few old friends who, I think, have a right to that consideration from me, shall be always welcome here, if—" she smiled—"you and they are not afraid to brave public opinion by coming."

"You do me injustice by the doubt you imply," said Mrs. Annesley, quickly. "But, for that matter, you always did me injustice."

"Did I?" said her cousin, with a softer light coming into her eyes, and a softer tone into her voice. "Perhaps I did; for I was very prone to rash judgment in those wilful early days. I sometimes think that all I have endured since has only been a just punishment for the faults I cherished then. I am glad to believe I did you injustice, and to beg your pardon for it. Forgive me, Elinor—and let us be friends."

She held out her hand, and Mrs. Annesley could not decline to take it. But she hesitated a moment before doing so, and paled slightly, as she said:

"We won't talk of the past, Pauline, for I dare say the fault of our misunderstandings was as much mine as yours. Tell me about poor, dear Alfred. I was so shocked to hear of his—"

"Death," she would have said, had not the sudden ghastly change that came over her cousin's face stopped the word. It was not the acute grief which cannot bear any mention of its bereavement from careless lips, but the presence of an unutterable horror, which blanched the cheek, and gave so deep an agony to the eye, that Mrs. Annesley saw she had made a great mistake, and stammered hastily:

"Pardon me; I did not mean—"

Then Mrs. Gordon seemed to rally with an almost convulsive effort; and, after a minute, spoke hoarsely:

"It does not matter. I—I only have not learned to bear the mention of his name. Yes, he is dead. Be kind, Elinor—do not ask me any more."

Mrs. Annesley could not disregard such a request. She was silent for some time; half from astonishment, half from offended pride at her cousin's reserve. Then she gathered her wrappings round her, and rose with that motion which indicates departure.

"I am sorry I cannot stay longer," she said, "but I dare not risk over-fatiguing myself. I will come soon again, however."

"Pray do," said Mrs. Gordon, cordially. "Give my love to Morton and Adela. Are they not with you now?"

"Morton lives with me, but he is not at home just now. He has been absent for a week or two. Adela is married, and lives in Mobile," replied Mrs. Annesley, telling the truth—but not the whole truth. "Do you remember your old admirer, Colonel French? Well, one of his sons died, and Adela married the other—a very good match indeed."

"Colonel French—the wealthy widower, as you used to call him? How strangely such news makes me feel. To think that Adela should be married—and to one of those little boys!"

"I ought to feel old, ought I not? And yet—"

"And yet you feel young, looking at me. Is it not so?"

"I did not mean to say that, I assure you; but you do look shockingly. I hope you will seem more like yourself when I see you again. Good-by. I cannot tempt you even to Annesdale?"

"Not even to Annesdale."

They shook hands, parted—if any thing more coldly than they had met—and, ten minutes afterward, the Annesley carriage was rolling out of the Morton gates.

CHAPTER VI.

WHAT MORTON SAID.

"It is a good thing that Morton is not at home," Mrs. Annesley had again remarked to her daughter, when she finally made up her mind to action in the case of her cousin; and the event well justified that self-congratulation. A fortnight after the visit in which she had been so signally worsted, Morton returned, and, for the first time in his life, asserted his right of interference as head of the house.

"Mother," he said, when they were at breakfast on the morning after his arrival, and the servants had left the room—"Mother, is it true, as I hear, that our cousin, Pauline Morton, has returned among us?"

There was something unusually grave and formal in the tone of this inquiry, something which made Adela French look up and open her eyes; but Mrs. Annesley answered with admirable nonchalance·

"Yes, my dear boy, she has really returned. I forgot that we heard the news the very day you left. How it must have astonished you! It was quite a shock to me; but my nerves are so easily affected I can stand very little. I suppose you heard it in Tallahoma, as you came through?"

"Yes, I heard it in Tallahoma," the young man answered, "and, mother, I also heard something else, which cannot be true."

"It is a very sad affair altogether, my dear Morton," said Mrs. Annesley, quietly; "but there is nothing more likely than that you heard some exaggeration of the matter. What was it?"

She asked the question with honest indifference, for, since her visit to Mrs. Gordon, she had felt, so far as herself was concerned, upon safe ground. She knew that she had always been to Morton a sort of enthroned divinity, who could do no wrong; and it was evident that he hesitated now before saying any thing which might seem even the mildest censure on her conduct. At last, however, he spoke.

"I heard in Tallahoma that our cousin"—he uttered the last two words with emphasis—"has come back to her old home, without having received any welcome from her old friends; and that even you, mother, have failed to give her one."

"I should think you would know by this time how much reliance is to be placed in Tallahoma gossip," said Mrs. Annesley. "As usual they have told you something entirely without foundation; and"—with gentle reproach—"I cannot help thinking it strange that you should credit such a thing of me."

"I did not credit it!" said the young man, eagerly. "I was only afraid that it might be so, because public opinion seems dealing so hardly with this poor woman. And you *have* been to see her, then?"

"Of course I have," answered she, promptly. "How could I possibly neglect such a duty? We were raised together as sisters, you remember."

"And has she been here? Mother, she ought to be here now."

"Morton!—what do you mean?"

"I mean," answered Morton, quickly, "that when a woman is slandered is the time, of all others, for her kindred to close around her; and that Pauline Morton's proper place now is under this roof."

"But, good Heavens! why?"

"Why?" he repeated in surprise. "Dear mother, don't you know why? Don't you know that she is doubted, suspected, slandered, if you will have a plain word; and that it is only thus we can pay the debt of gratitude we owe to those whose roof once sheltered you?"

He looked like a young paladin, with the kindling fire on his handsome face, and the shining light in his dark eyes; and even his mother's heart was touched as he lowered his voice over the last words.

"My son, you do not understand," she said, in a grave, troubled voice—for it was never her policy to come to an issue with Morton, "you do not understand—and you should trust to me in this matter."

"You know how much I trust to you," he answered. "But in this matter—"

"Why do you think it necessary to take up your cousin's cause with so much zeal?" said Mrs. Annesley, as he hesitated in his sentence.

"I thought I had already explained what really does not seem to require any explanation. Seeing any woman in a position of social difficulty, I should not feel myself a gentleman if, believing her injured, I did not make at least an effort in her defence. And when I see my own kinswoman, one to whom I am bound both by ties of blood and obligations of gratitude—mother, can you ask me why I should take up her cause with all the zeal of which I am capable?"

"One word, Morton," said Mrs. Annesley, who had been watching him during the last speech, and knew to a nicety how far it was prudent to carry open opposition—"one word, if you please. Has it never occurred to you that Pauline Morton may not be the injured victim you seem to consider her?"

If she had sent a rifle-shot into her son's plate, she could not have taken him more completely by surprise. He looked for one moment in mute amazement at her face, then a crimson flood shot over his brow, and was visible even beneath the black curls that rested on it.

"Mother!"

"Don't misunderstand me," said Mrs. Annesley, quietly. "Don't think that I mean any thing more than I say. I only repeat my question—has it never occurred to you that Pauline Morton may not be that injured victim which you seem to consider her?"

"No," answered he. "Is she not a Morton?"

"She is, indeed. But, in short, as I told you before, you had better trust to me in this matter."

"And, as I told you before, that is impossible," he replied. "Tell me what you meant by such a question."

But, what Mrs. Annesley meant, it was very hard—indeed, impossible—for her to explain in Morton's straightforward fashion; for her only real meaning had been to impress him with a belief that the matter was too delicate for his management. She hesitated before answering; and then said more than she had perhaps intended to say.

"I only meant, Morton, that I am sure you would not like to force me into giving countenance to a woman who may not deserve it."

"God forbid!" said Morton, hastily. "But, mother, surely you consider what you are saying?"

"Is it likely I would not consider?" asked Mrs. Annesley, dreadfully conscious that the exigence of the occasion was forcing her into doing just the opposite. But then it was so necessary to quiet Morton by saying something.—"Is it likely I would not consider? Ah, you don't know how I have suffered about this, or you would never reproach me for not doing more."

"Reproach you! My dear mother, I must have expressed myself very badly if you think I meant to reproach you. Pray forgive me, if I have been hasty or disrespectful—but I feel this matter so deeply."

"You cannot feel it more deeply than I do," said Mrs. Annesley, putting her handkerchief to her eyes. "My poor aunt, and my dear uncle, what a blessed thing it is that they did not live to see this day! You may think me unfeeling, Morton, but Adela there could tell you that I have been really ill, and about nothing else but this affair."

"I could as soon suspect a saint of being unfeeling," said Morton, much concerned, but smiling a little.

"Selfish, then, when I had only your welfare at heart."

"You could not be selfish if you tried. But I really don't see what my welfare had to do with the matter."

No, he did not see in the least, and, what was more, Mrs. Annesley dared not enlighten him. She knew how much he desired to own Morton House, but she also knew that Morton House would be worse than valueless to him if he once suspected that it had been won by such means as those she had not scrupled to propose to herself.

"I only mean," she hastily corrected, "that neither you nor I can help a woman who is so utterly reckless that she will not help herself."

"And Pauline Morton?"

"Pauline Morton refuses absolutely to accept any aid that we can give her."

"Refuses! How? Pray be more explicit, if only in consideration of my stupidity."

"I don't see how I can be more explicit, Morton. She distinctly declines to give any explanation of her singular appearance among us, of the death of her brother, or of the absence of her husband—indeed, whether he is alive or dead, nobody knows. She looks as if she might have walked through a furnace of fire, or been buried alive and dug up again, or lived in garrets on crusts of bread, or—or done any thing! And she will neither receive her friends nor accept any hospitality they offer."

Morton, who had risen from the table, was now standing with one hand on the back of his chair, and he did not speak for several minutes. Then he said, slowly:

"Well, all this only proves that she has suffered, nothing more. Surely we may respect this suffering sufficiently to refrain from prying into it. Can the gossips say nothing more of her than this?"

"You can best answer that question," said Mrs. Annesley, stiffly. "I am not likely to hear what gossips say of my own cousin. But I think it is more than ought to be said of any woman."

"Mother, that does not sound like you," said her son, gently. "Remember how often you have agreed with me that misfortune should never be confounded with fault. We have no right to suspect more than misfortune here."

"Not if Pauline had come back as her position demanded she should come—with some guarantee for her past, and some regard for appearances in the present. Not if she—"

"In one word, if she had not needed your friendship. Oh, mother, that I should hear such social cant from your lips! Her old associates, then, would have been willing to extend their hands to her, if she had not needed them; as she does need them, they consider that a sufficient reason for holding aloof. What a pitiful world it is!" said the young man, with a sudden scorn flashing into his face; "and how much it is alike in every place and condition of life!

Mother, one more question, and I have done. I am sure I need not beg you to answer me frankly. Do you, or do you not, believe that Pauline Morton deserves the suspicion that seems to have fallen upon her?"

Was ever diplomacy placed in a more trying position than this? Reply in the affirmative Mrs. Annesley could not, without a more daring violation of truth than even *her* conscience would allow; and, to answer in the negative, would be to undo all her previous work. Clearly, then, the only resource left was that of evasion, and this she employed with commendable quickness.

"Good Heavens, Morton! How can you ask me to decide such a question, and about my own cousin, too? You should be more considerate of my—my feelings!"

"I am asking you to be considerate of the honor of your name, mother," said Morton, half-sternly. "Do you know what people will say if you do not face that question and answer it boldly?"

"I must consult my own conscience, and not what people will say," answered she, with dignity.

Morton took his hand from the chair, and made a quick turn up and down the room before he spoke again. He stopped abruptly then, and fastened his eyes on her face:

"Then, mother, you, too, doubt this poor woman?"

"Doubt her?" She hesitated a moment, but saw her way to no other answer than the truth. "No, Morton, I do not."

"In that case, you consider her unjustly suspected—do you, mother?"

There was something truth-compelling in the direct question, in the earnest eyes, and still more earnest voice. Before Mrs. Annesley knew what she was about, she had uttered a reluctant "Yes."

But, even after this, she was not prepared for what followed. She was astonished when Morton crossed the floor, rang the bell, and said to the servant who answered it:

"The carriage."

The door had hardly closed before Mrs. Annesley cried:

"Morton, what does this mean?"

"It means," said Morton, "that I am going to see our cousin, and that I hope you will accompany me to urge her return with us to Annesdale."

His mother looked at him in silent exasperation. If she had given way to her first impulse, it would certainly have been one of fierce reproach, since anger was burning hotly enough in her heart against this ungrateful return for all her exertion. But one thing which she had learned in life was the folly of passion. So she curbed herself with the steady curb which long habit had rendered easy, and answered quietly:

"I am afraid you must excuse me. Dr. Reynolds expressly forbade my leaving the house until he saw me again. Besides, Morton, since you absolutely refuse to be guided by me in this matter, I cannot think that I am called upon to expose myself to another repulse for your sake."

"Another repulse?"

"Yes, another repulse. I thought I told you that Pauline has already declined the visit which you wish me to urge on her a second time."

"Did you really *urge* it the first time, mother?"

"Did you ever know me lacking in hospitality? But, since you distrust me, go your own way, and find who is right."

She spoke gravely, but without any touch of pettishness; and Morton hesitated. Perhaps, after all, she was right—perhaps, after all, he was wrong. Who was so likely to be wrong as himself, thought the young man, with the humility which was his most prominent characteristic. Surely his mother was better able to judge of her cousin than he who had never seen that cousin. In trying to act up to the standard of his chivalric creed, he began to fear that he had not only been very obstinate, but also very foolish. So, after a pause, he spoke quite humbly:

"I have never done such a thing as distrust you in all my life, mother; and I am sure I have no desire to go my own way simply because it *is* my own way. If you think the invitation had better not be given just at present, I am perfectly willing to defer it. But that is no reason for deferring my visit. Since you cannot accompany me, I am sure Adela will."

He looked at his sister as he spoke; and Mrs. French shrugged her shoulders, as she answered carelessly:

"Indeed, I would not advise you to be too sure, Morton, for I have not an idea of doing any thing of the kind."

"Why not?"

"Simply because I don't choose to."

"Adela!" This was Mrs. Annesley who broke in with a tone half-warning, half-reproachful.

"Well, mamma," was the saucy reply, "you

surely don't think I am going to let Morton tyrannize over me as he does over you? When one doesn't mind one's husband, one isn't likely to mind one's brother—do you think so? He must get him a wife, if he wants somebody to go with him whenever he takes a fancy to visit superannuated beauties."

"I did not ask you to go as a favor to myself, Adela," said her brother, a little haughtily.

"So much the better," answered she. And, at that moment, a servant opened the door and announced the carriage.

"I was wrong," said Morton, turning to her. "I do ask it as a favor to myself. Will you go?"

"Not on any account," said the young lady, with emphasis. "Nothing would induce me to go. I hate disagreeable people—besides, the Raynors and Irene Vernon will be here to dinner to-day, and I would not tire myself out for the world. If you will go, that is no reason why I should be so silly."

"Have the carriage taken back, and my horse brought out," said Mr. Annesley to the servant.

After this, there was ten minutes' rather uncomfortable silence in the room. It was broken at last by Adela, who had sauntered to the window, and, with admirable nonchalance, announced the appearance of the horse—adding the gratuitous information that he did not look quite as well groomed as usual.

"Probably not; those scamps grow careless if I am away from home a week," said her brother. He turned to leave the room, saying to his mother, "I shall not be back until dinner."

"But you must be back in time for dinner—don't forget that, Morton," she said, anxiously.

"I shall not forget it," he answered.

When the door closed on him, Mrs. Annesley drew a deep breath of relief, and looked at her daughter, who was still standing by the window. Their eyes met, and Mrs. French laughed.

"Poor Morton, how simple he is!" she said. "I wondered you had patience to fence with him so long, mamma. Do you think he means to spend the morning at Morton House?"

Mrs. Annesley shook her head. "I wish he did," she answered. "He means to spend it in Tallahoma.

"Mamma," said Mrs. French, setting her teeth sharply, "I would make an end of that business, if I were you."

"Suppose you could not, Adela?"

"As if you could not always do any thing you want to."

"Morton is terribly obstinate."

"Morton is like wax in your hands."

There was a moment's silence. Then, not very relevantly, as it seemed, Mrs. Annesley said, "When does Irene Vernon leave?"

"Not before New Year. You know she is engaged to spend Christmas here."

"Yes, I know."

They said nothing further—but, after another minute or two, Mrs. French kissed her hand, and gayly waved it to some one outside the window.

"It is only Morton," she said, as her mother came forward and looked over her shoulder. "I am wishing him good luck."

They both watched the graceful rider out of sight; and Mrs. Annesley, as she turned away from the window, said, with a low and somewhat bitter laugh, "Let him go. He will not be admitted farther than the door of Morton House."

CHAPTER VII.

HOW A PALADIN STORMED A CASTLE.

In all the sweet South there never was a softer or more beautiful morning—robed in gorgeous autumnal dress, and glorying in a lavish affluence of balmy air, and golden sunshine, and draping haze—than that on which the young owner of Annesdale rode forth to try his fortune at Morton House.

Shortly after leaving his own gates, he overtook an open carriage full of ladies, who were chattering gayly, and who burst into a chorus of welcome when Ilderim's handsome head appeared beside them.

"Mr. Annesley! What a surprise!"

"Why, Mr. Annesley, where did you come from?"

"When did you come back, and how are you?"

Only one of the fair bevy—the fairest among them—said nothing; but she smiled and held out her hand; and neither the smile nor the action left any thing to be desired.

Mr. Annesley answered all the inquiries, and exchanged all the civilities of the occasion; and then rode along by the side of the carriage, resting one hand lightly on the door, while with the other he restrained Ilderim's eager impatience; and the stream of conversation flowed on in easy and lively current.

"You have been to Mobile, Mr. Annesley?" asked the gay young chaperon of the party—

pretty Mrs. George Raynor, who had been a Miss Vernon and a Mobile belle before she married, and came to dazzle Lagrange with her beauty and her fashion. "Oh, do tell us something about it, for we are almost dying—Irene and I—for news of all our friends."

"With all my heart," said Morton, smiling; "but where shall I begin? I was only in Mobile for a few days, and I scarcely saw any thing of the people you would care to hear about."

"Ah, I care to hear about anybody," cried she, with fervor. "And, if you did not see anybody, just tell me what they are talking about in the city. I wish I had known you were going, I would have asked you to take a package to Aunt Lucy—and, perhaps—to bring me a bonnet back."

"You are glad she did *not* know, are you not, Mr. Annesley?" said Miss Vernon, laughing.

Morton smiled only, in reply to the last question, preferring, it seemed, to answer Mrs. Raynor's remark. "If I had not left home so hurriedly, you should have known," he said. "But I did manage to see your aunt, and she charged me with a great many messages to yourself and Miss Vernon—the chief of which," he added, turning to the latter, "I feel tempted not to deliver."

"Is it so very disagreeable, then?" asked she.

"It will not be at all disagreeable to you, I am afraid; but she urges your speedy return to Mobile, and that will be very disagreeable to Lagrange."

"Lagrange will have to support the desolation as best it can, and I have no doubt will be able to endure it," said Miss Vernon, a little coolly—thinking, no doubt, that the compliment would have gained point and strength by a more personal application.

Then a cry broke from the other two young ladies, who were both Misses Raynor, plain in looks, plain in manners, and therefore blindly admiring the Vernon beauty, and emulous of the Vernon style.

"Oh, Irene, you surely will not think of leaving us!"

"Irene, that is *very* mean of your aunt, for she knows you promised to stay until after Christmas."

"Nonsense!" said Mrs. Raynor. "Irene knows she is not going until I am ready to go with her; and only George can say when that will be—he is *so* provoking! Mr. Annesley, I do hope that when you are married, you will treat your wife with some consideration."

"I shall endeavor to do so, Mrs. Raynor," answered Morton, with mock-gravity—for all Lagrange knew that George Raynor was the most thoroughly hen-pecked husband in the county—"I shall come to you for instructions how to act. But you have not told me what has been going on here since I left."

"Nothing has been going on in any way," said Mrs. Raynor.—"Irene, what have we been doing?—any thing at all?"

"Vegetating and yawning, I believe," answered Miss Vernon. "But these principal occupations have been varied by much gossip, and a little scandal, lately."

"Oh, yes!" burst in Mrs. Raynor, with the greatest animation. "Lagrange has been in a perfect ferment of gossip for the last three weeks, Mr. Annesley, about that curious Miss Morton, or Mrs. Gordon, or whatever her name may be, who has come back like a ghost, and set everybody talking themselves hoarse. Of course you have heard of her?" (She did not give him time to reply.) "For my part, I believe that she murdered both her husband and her brother, and that she has come here to bury her remorse, and give Lagrange a standing topic of conversation. I am sure— Good gracious, Louisa, what is the matter? Is there a caterpillar on my bonnet?"

The inquiry was not entirely without reason, for the elder Miss Raynor had been making signals of silence and distress for the last five seconds, without being able to attract her heedless sister-in-law's attention.

"No, indeed, Flora," she said, blushing with that ever-ready and not always becoming blush of eighteen. "But you surely forget—Mr. Annesley is related to—"

"To my murderess?" cried Mrs. Raynor, extricating herself from the difficulty with the merriest laugh in the world. "A thousand pardons, Mr. Annesley! But you know how heedless I am! I am sure I need not apologize for mere jesting."

Mr. Annesley's face had taken an expression which few people had ever seen upon it before. A stern coldness transformed it so entirely that the ladies exchanged glances of surprise and dismay. He bowed quite haughtily, as he said, with gravity:

"Personally, I could not of course be offended by what was not meant to touch myself. But I must confess that my ideas of 'jesting' do not agree with those of Mrs. Raynor."

"I am very, very sorry," cried that lady, eagerly, coloring a little, and slightly disconcerted by his manner and words. "You must really forgive me, Mr. Annesley! I did not remember at the moment your connection with Mrs. Gordon. Indeed, it never occurred to me that you would care. Adela talks just as everybody else does."

"I am sorry to hear it," said Mr. Annesley, in the same tone as before.

"And, really," continued Mrs. Raynor, rallying from her momentary embarrassment, and recovering her usual nonchalant gayety—"really, Mr. Annesley, you are very unreasonable. I only repeated what everybody is saying. Pray don't hold me accountable for the reports!"

Mr. Annesley's face relaxed into a smile—rather grave, it is true—as he answered: "You are right, Mrs. Raynor. It was unreasonable, nay, it was folly in me to resent what is in itself so trifling a matter as these reports. Gossips must have something to talk about, of course. It is I who must beg your pardon for having forgotten this."

"Why, Mr. Annesley, I don't know you!" exclaimed Mrs. Raynor, astonished, annoyed, and amused, all at once. "I always thought you a model of amiability; but you are not amiable at present, I assure you. I did not know that you had laid lance in rest, in Mrs. Gordon's defence, or I should not have said a word. And, by-the-way, don't flatter yourself that you are her only champion. Irene has been doing battle in her defence from the first."

"Have you?" said Morton, turning quickly to Miss Vernon. "I hope you will let me admire and thank you for it."

"Pray don't," answered she. "I only heard a woman assailed, and felt for her—that was all."

Before the gentleman could reply, Mrs. Raynor's light tones broke in again:

"I positively victimized myself by going to church last Sunday in order to catch a glimpse of this ghostly lady; and would you believe it, Mr. Annesley, she did not come! I wonder if she never means to come? But somebody said that a splendid-looking child, who sat in a pew next the pulpit, was hers."

"Oh, yes," chorussed the Misses Raynor, "and *such* a woman with him! If you *could* have seen her bonnet! And, what do you think, Mr Annesley?—she actually sat up and said her beads all the time Mr. Norwood was preaching—and that under his very eyes!"

"She is evidently a Frenchwoman," said Miss Vernon, "and of course a Catholic. No doubt she took that means to avoid joining in what she considered heretical worship.—Are you going, Mr. Annesley?"

"I am reluctantly compelled to do so," said Mr. Annesley, who had drawn Ilderim from the carriage-door, and himself from that soft contact of silk and lace; that near neighborhood of a slender, well-gloved hand; that faint, dainty fragrance of fresh millinery; that capricious parasol fringe which was never still, and which would persist in sweeping his face, and that subtile, intangible charm which, like an aroma, seems constantly exhaling from a lovely and well-dressed woman—"I am compelled to do so—for here is Morton House, and to it I am bound. You dine at Annesdale to-day? Then you may expect a full account of the wonders and mysteries within these gates. Good-morning."

He lifted his hat—the ladies bent their heads with a general flutter of plumes and ribbons—the carriage swept on in a yellow cloud of dust, and the young man found himself alone before the gates of Morton House.

Like his mother, he too felt, when those gates closed behind him, as if he had entered an enchanted domain—a domain over the neglected beauty of which there rested a mournful stillness, deeper and more pathetic than mere solitude; where brooded a solemn air of repose, and a subtile power of awaking thought and association which we have most of us observed in those places where life once ran riot, and from which it has long since departed forever.

The young man involuntarily bared his head as he rode slowly along beneath the drooping trees; and patches of golden sunshine, flickering softly down, fell on the rich black curls and the face that was subdued almost to mournfulness. There was to him an indescribable pathos in the stately quiet around him. He thought of the by-gone voices that had once sounded along this avenue, of the gay hearts that had gone their way brimful of life and joy, and the sad hearts that had found even the beauty of Nature a weariness and a mockery—well, they were all equally at rest now. He thought of the bright children who had played beneath those trees; and of the fair ladies who had dreamed sweet fancies under their shade, or—who knows?—dropped bitter tears upon their mossy roots. The sod lay heavily enough over those lovely faces now; and it mattered little whether they had known most of the smiles or of the tears. Then he thought how often his father had passed here, with all manhood's brightest hopes stirring at his heart, and all manhood's proudest resolve in his breast—yet how little either the hope or the resolve had availed to change his fate. Morton felt a bitter pang at the recollection of that father who had gone so early out of his life, but whose memory had ever remained with him as a vision of all that was most noble in simple chivalry—a lesson which had done more to mould the boy's character than all the precepts of living teachers. And he was going now to see the woman whose fatal beauty had wrecked the happiness of that father's life! He knew—everybody knew—that Edgar Annesley had poured out his love like water at Pauline Morton's feet, and that she had scorned him as she scorned all others in that proud heyday of her youth and power. And now there seemed a retribution in the fact that Edgar Annesley's son came forward as her sole defender against the fickle world that had once fawned at her feet. "It is the only revenge he would have wished," thought the son, placing, as he always did, the father in his position. "But he would never, for one moment, have considered it revenge. He would have regarded it as a duty, and thought himself happy in performing it. Ah, I shall never master the whole essence of his knightly creed and practice —he who was a very Bayard, and yet thought that he only fulfilled the common duties of a gentleman." And here, after all, had been the great secret of that resolution which so much surprised Mrs. Annesley. The young man had set out in life feeling himself his father's representative, and he had never felt this more than when slander set its mark on the woman his father had loved. He had spoken to his mother as a Morton; but his warmest interest in Mrs. Gordon's cause rose from the fact that he was an Annesley. There, indeed, rose his true animating impulse; and there was an anchor to hold him steadfast through any opposition.

Suddenly, when he was about half-way to the house, a sound broke on the stillness—a shrill, childish voice that caused Ilderim to start and prick up his satin ears with ominous haste. When he had been brought to order, Annesley was able to comprehend that words of alternate entreaty and command were apparently being addressed to himself by some unseen person.

"Holà! Monsieur! monsieur, come here!" cried the voice, in a strange mixture of French and English. "Pardonnez-moi, but that nasty Babette—"

The rest was lost in consequence of a sudden movement on Ilderim's part, which demanded all his rider's attention. When this exigence was passed, Morton stared about him in utter bewilderment, for "the silence was unbroken, and the stillness gave no token" of any human presence beside his own.

"Who is there?" he demanded at last—sending his own voice in the direction from which the other had proceeded. "Holloa!—who is there?"

Then the same childish tones replied, impatiently:

"It is me—Felix Gordon. I wish you would make haste, monsieur, for my arm is very tired."

Guided by the voice, Annesley now saw in the grove on his right a small figure clinging half to the trunk and half to the lower limb of a large tree, and thus suspended fully fifteen feet above the ground.

"Good Heavens!" he cried. Then, springing from his horse, one or two quick bounds carried him at once to the foot of the tree, where he perceived the peril of the child's position more clearly. The limb had evidently broken under him, and left him clinging with one hand to a fragment of it while he braced his feet against a gnarled knot of the tree, and thus partially relieved himself of his own weight. But it was only partially; and relief from the precarious position was impossible without the aid which had so opportunely and so accidentally arrived.

Morton did not waste any time in words. He saw that the face which looked down upon him was very self-possessed; but he also saw that it was very pale, and marked the painful rigidity of the attitude. He threw his gloves near a small velvet cap that lay on the grass, and the next moment was climbing the tree with the agility of a school-boy.

But when he began to approach the child, he saw that caution was necessary, or he would dislodge the boy's foot and send him crashing to the ground, for he could do little more than steady himself by his hand. Therefore, the rescuer crept carefully on the opposite side of the trunk, hardly allowing himself more than the merest clasp of it, and, when he was once safe among the boughs, ascended to a considerable height before he paused. Then, with extreme care, he descended from limb to limb until he reached the one immediately above the boy. There he seated himself, and finding it secure spoke for the first time.

"Now I am going to draw you up to me. When I take hold of your collar, you must let go the clasp both of your feet and your hand. Don't be afraid; for I shall not let you fall."

"Ma foi! I am not likely to be afraid," said the boy, half-scornfully. "But, if you are going to do it, you had better make haste."

Bending over, Annesley took a firm grasp of the clothing that encircled the soft young neck, and with one vigorous lift placed the child before him.

His eyes were closed, and he was white to the lips, so that at first Annesley thought he had fainted. But the next instant the fringed lids lifted, and a smile of triumph came over the pale face.

"Babette said I could not do it; but I *have* done it," he cried. "It was not my fault that the limb broke."

"It was not your fault," said Morton, kindly; "but it was an accident which is likely to happen at any time, and you must not risk your neck in this way again. I may not be within call next time."

"No," said the boy. He glanced rapidly and somewhat wonderingly over the face and form of his deliverer. "I am very much obliged to you, monsieur," he added, with the grand manner which had impressed even Mrs. Annesley. "But, je ne vous connais pas—that is, I do not know you."

"I am your cousin," answered Morton, smiling; "and my name is Annesley."

"Ah!" said the boy; and as he strove to steady himself by altering his position, he gave a faint cry of pain. "It is nothing," he said, quickly, in answer to his companion's look of inquiry, "only my arm—I hurt it."

"How?"

"When the limb broke. Ah, I should have got down if I could have used it—but I couldn't, you know."

"Let me see if it is much hurt," said Annesley; and, after the child had unflinchingly borne an examination, he pronounced it only sprained. "The bone is all right," he said; "but you were a brave fellow to hold on with one arm when the other was in this condition."

"I'd have hurt both, if I had fallen," said his new acquaintance, with a half-comic grimace—adding quickly, "but, monsieur, let us go down."

"I have been thinking how we shall manage that, and I don't see very clearly yet. This is the first thing to be done." He drew a small flask from his pocket, and held it to his companion's lips. "Drink, my boy—it will burn your throat, but never mind that—you need it."

The boy drank eagerly—far too eagerly, Annesley thought; for he soon drew the flask away.

"That is enough—I don't want to unsteady your head for the descent."

"Bah!" said the child, in the scornful tone which came so strangely from his childish lips. "Bah, monsieur! Do you think I could not drink twice that much, and be steady yet?"

"I should be sorry if you could," said Annesley, gravely.

The dark eyes flashed upon him suddenly "Pourquoi, monsieur?"

"Because it would show that you must have had very bad training," said Morton, quietly. "No child of your age ought to know the taste of brandy—much less, drink it as you did just now. Who gives it to you?"

"Alas! no one now," answered the boy, with candid regret. "Papa gave it to me sometimes—but that was only to worry mamma—and St. John gave it to me very often."

"But surely your mother does not like it to be given to you?"

The small shoulders achieved a Gallic shrug which was simply perfect. "I should think not, indeed, monsieur! Mamma will not even let me drink a glass of wine—and Babette, nasty thing! always tells her if I do."

"Then, if I had been in your place," said Morton, impressively, "I would not have taken that brandy, unless your mother had given it to you herself."

The boy gazed at him wonderingly "Monsieur, why not?"

"Because I should have felt bound by her wishes, especially as she was absent," said Morton, as gravely as befitted the character of Mentor, with which the occasion had invested him. "A trust, my boy, is a thing which cannot be held too sacred. Come, I see you are very sensible, and I need not talk to you as I would to most children—I can speak to you almost as if you were a man. You mean to be a gentleman, do you not?"

"I am a gentleman," was the quick reply.

"I am glad to hear you say so. But do you know what is the chief thing that makes a gentleman? Not blood, not birth—they are good in their way, but they won't do by themselves—

not any one thing so much as the capability of being trusted."

"Mamma says so—but she is a woman."

"Well, I am a man, and I tell you the same thing. What is more, I tell you that nobody who bore the Morton name was ever lacking in this capability. Look round! do you see all this, which will be yours some day—these noble trees, and those broad fields yonder? Well, the men who owned all this before you were men who, if a trust had been given them, would have held it till they died—held it as you held that limb a little while ago. You are a Morton in courage, why not be a Morton in honor as well?"

The sudden question took his listener entirely by surprise. He looked up—still with wonder—into the earnest face which bent over him, as he said, slowly, "I am a Gordon, monsieur."

"I know. But you are a Morton also; and, whatever the Gordons were, the Mortons, at least, have always been brave and loyal gentlemen. I could tell you many a story about the men of your name—and then, perhaps, you would think that such a name was worth bearing."

"Tell me," said the boy, eagerly. "St. John used to tell me about the Gordons; and I liked to hear how they killed men and ran away with women, and drank wine and brandy."

"Then I am afraid you would not like my stories," said Morton, "for I have nothing of the sort to tell you. The men of whom I speak never did any of those things. They were simple, honorable gentlemen, who lived quiet lives, but who knew how to be true to their friends, to honor their God, and to serve their country; but not one of them would have put that flask of brandy to his lips!"

Felix's large eyes opened widely. "Monsieur! Did none of them drink brandy?"

"Oh, yes," said Morton, "I suppose all of them drank brandy, and sometimes more than was good for them. But none of them would have done so if they had been put on their honor not to do it by somebody who had a right to exact such a promise."

Felix looked thoughtful. It was evident that a new light had dawned on his mind—a light very different, when presented by this handsome young cavalier, to that which had been urged by his mother. At last, as he did not speak, Annesley broke the silence.

"Now, we must get down, or your mother will be uneasy about you. Were you alone when you climbed up here?"

"No; Babette was with me. She said I should not do it, and I said I would—and I did! She tried to hold me; but she isn't strong, though her arms are so big; and, when I kicked her, she had to let me go."

"Who is Babette?"

"My bonne," answered the boy, with a grimace. "St. John says I am too old—I shouldn't have a bonne."

"But, as you have got one, you ought to treat her properly. I am sorry to hear of your having acted as you did. Horses kick—not gentlemen."

"St. John says I ought to torment the life out of her, and then she will go away."

"And then your mother would get another, perhaps a worse one. Who is this St. John? He seems to have given you very bad advice."

"He was papa's secretary, and I liked him; but mamma hated him."

"Then you certainly ought not to obey him so well. Now let us move forward. How does your arm feel?—well enough to bear a weight?"

"N—o," said Felix, regretfully. "What do you want me to do?"

"I wanted you to clasp your arms round my neck, while I go down the tree. But we must compromise with your feet. Do you think you can hold on with them?"

The boy laughed. "It will be funny," he said, "but I think I can."

"This way—let me lift you to my shoulder. Are you firmly seated? Now, hold tight—take a grasp of my collar."

"I'll do it."

And he did do it, with a vigor which threatened strangulation unless their descent was very speedy.

"Here we go!" said Morton, gayly. "Pity we haven't got an audience for this feat in gymnastics." And, lightly swinging loose from the bough on which they had been perched, he clambered down the trunk, without in the least seeming to feel his burdened condition.

In less than a minute they were standing on the ground laughing together in friendly good-fellowship. Ilderim had taken his departure some time before, so the sylvan solitude was all their own.

"Now for this arm of yours," said Morton. "It must be attended to at once; and your clothes are considerably the worse for your mishap. What will your mother say?"

The boy shrugged his shoulders. "She will think of *this*," he said, touching his arm. "Babette will scold about the clothes."

"Oh, I dare say you can hold your own against Babette. Is the avenue the shortest way to the house?"

"No; I'll take you a shorter one."

They set forward amicably, talking as they went. And, as they talked, it would be hard to say which of them conceived the most cordial liking for the other. On Morton's side it was more than half pity, for he perceived the moral perversion of the child's nature, and read plainly his reckless rebellion against the curb held over him by feminine hands. But he saw the elements of much nobility, together with the proofs of much bravery, and the latter in itself delighted him. The boy's face kindled when he spoke of heroism, and, if it did not kindle when he spoke of chivalry, it was because the principles of chivalry were foreign teachings to his mind—not because the nature was incapable of holding them. Some sinister influence had plainly been at work with him—some influence like that which has marred many another gallant nature—and had indissolubly associated valor with evil, and weakness with good, in the boy's apprehension. Pride of a certain sort had been duly instilled, but it was very far from being pride of a right sort—if, indeed, there be a right sort. Annesley was puzzled by the strange contradictions that unfolded themselves before him. But he was more interested than repelled, and he could not help thinking how pleasant it would be to draw these warped conceptions straight. Perhaps he was something of a Quixote in those early days—too prone to amateur philanthropy. But there was that about him which caused most people to forgive the failing; and, considering how soon such impulsive generosity is cooled and cured by later years, they could well afford to do so. His heart yearned now over this fatherless boy—this boy who was his own kinsman—and even while he talked to him of sports, and dogs, and horses, and on all the topics most dear to a boy's fancy, he was mentally considering how he could gain a sort of right of tutelage over him. It all depended on that unknown woman whom he was going to eet—that woman whose sworn defender he had already constituted himself; and he began to feel more anxiety about her reception of him, than he had suffered himself to entertain before.

This anxiety was soon set at rest; for, as they came in sight of the house, Felix uttered an exclamation.

"There is mamma now, and Babette, too—the horrid thing! They are coming after me."

"Go and speak to them, then," said Morton, quickly. "They do not see you yet. Go at once."

The boy hesitated a minute; but, at the second bidding, he went—speeding like an arrow straight to the terrace-steps, which his mother was hastily descending, accompanied by Babette—the latter talking eagerly, with many gesticulations—while a group of servants followed behind.

Annesley advanced deliberately, an amused spectator of the scene which ensued of Babette's stormy outcries and reproaches, of the mother's passionate caresses, of the half-defiant, half-triumphant story of Felix, of the interested servants who brought their dusky faces near and nearer—and of the final moment when all eyes turned toward himself.

Then he came forward more quickly, very gallant and handsome in presence, very easy and graceful in bearing, yet with a slight tincture of embarrassment at the semi-heroism of his position.

Mrs. Gordon met him with outstretched hand, and so warm a light in her eyes that he marked none of the ravages of time, but only saw that they had spoken truly who called Pauline Morton's beauty without peer. "Oh, thank you, thank you!" she cried in that soft and melodious voice which had never yet failed to fascinate any one who listened to it. "I owe my darling's safety to you! How can I thank you enough!"

"You must not thank me at all," said Annesley, bending to kiss the fragile-looking hands that had grasped his own—and there was something very courtly in the action, though it was one of unstudied impulse—"or you will make me fear that you forget I have a kinsman's right to serve you and yours."

She read his face all over with one glance of her eyes, then spoke impulsively: "Ah, my kinsman, indeed—for I see you are Edgar Annesley's son."

There was something in the tone which pronounced his father's name that touched Morton's heart to the quick—won it, indeed, for this woman who had wrecked that father's happiness. It seemed to him that in her voice there was an echo of the admiring reverence, the regretful tenderness, which always thrilled his own soul when he thought of that brief life and premature death—an echo he had never before heard on any lip—not even his mother's. He felt that one other beside himself appreciated the spirit which had passed from earth without its due meed of lasting honor; and an emotion of almost passionate gratitude sprung up within him. Perhaps Mrs. Gordon read the meaning of the swift change that came over the frank young face; for she smiled kindly, and, laying her hand on his arm, said

"Come. Let me welcome my kinsman to Morton House."

And then Annesley found himself led forward into the castle which had been declared impregnable—a paladin, invested for the time being with a sort of chivalric triumph, and quite the master of the situation.

CHAPTER VIII.

THE ADELAIDE.

"Now, Katy," said Miss Tresham, in a tone of authority, "you must say this lesson, my dear—and you must not mumble the words so that I cannot hear them, either. Take your finger out of your mouth, and hold up your head. Now begin—'A verb'—"

"'A verb,'" drawled Katy, "'is a word which signifies to be, to do, or'—to do—or—or—is that all a verb signifies, Miss Tresham?"

"'To suffer,'" prompted Jack, in a loud whisper, with his eyes fastened on the pages of his arithmetic.

"Jack," said the governess, severely, "take your book and go and stand up in the corner, at the other end of the room. In a few minutes I shall see if you know your own lesson well enough to be prompting Katy with hers. You will have to learn a French verb after school, for breaking rules.—Now, Katy, I will give you one more trial. 'A verb is a word which signifies to be, to do, or to suffer.' What next?"

"'As, *I am, he runs, she loves.*'"

"Very well. Go on." For Katy, having delivered this much in a very loud voice, came to a sudden, dead stop.

"'Verbs are—are of two kinds'—ain't they of two kinds, Miss Tresham?"

"Go on, my dear," said Miss Tresham, with severe patience.

"'Verbs are of two kinds,'" repeated Katy, dubiously, as if the statement was, in her own opinion, a very doubtful one; and there she paused, and fell to twisting the corner of her apron.

"Hold your hands still, and go on, Katy," said the much-tried governess.

"'Verbs are of two kinds,'" repeated Katy, once more, and apparently in a state of despair. "'Verbs are of two kinds—positive, comparative, and super—'"

Here an audible titter from the other scholars was silenced by a look from the teacher, and a well-thumbed grammar was held out to its owner. "Take your book, my dear, and put it aside. After school, you will have to learn this lesson. Now, children, get your slates and let me see your sums."

A slamming of desks and shuffling of books ensued, followed by the appearance of various slates, more or less covered with cipherings, all of which were submitted to Miss Tresham. She took the one nearest her, and began casting up the column of figures.

There was a temporary silence in the school-room, for all eyes were anxiously following the movements of the governess's pencil, and the only sounds were her strokes on the slate, as she made her firm, round numerals, and the swaying to and fro of some boughs before the open window—boughs that were faintly stirred by a soft, southern breeze, and between which the golden sunshine streamed across the school-room floor, across Katharine's dark-blue dress and bright brown head, across Jack's darned jacket, and Sara's neat check apron, and smooth little tails of plaited hair. Unfortunately, however, this window was directly over the front-door; and when a quick tread was heard advancing up the walk, and into the piazza, followed by a knock which echoed through the house, there was an instantaneous end both of silence and attention.

"Hallo! who can that be?" cried Jack. "I bet it's Tom Ford, come after his gun, Dick! I told you you'd no business—"

"Hush, Jack!" said Miss Tresham.—"Here, Sara—here is the mistake in your sum. When you added up this line of figures, you forgot to carry there—"

"Miss Tresham, if it's Tom, mayn't I go and give him his gun?" asked Dick, anxiously. He had been listening with all his ears to the muffled sounds below, but had failed to distinguish any thing to set his mind at rest.

"I'll go and look over the banisters, and see who it is," said Jack, briskly, and he made a dart toward the door, but was promptly arrested by the governess.

"Come back this instant to your seat, Jack! It does not concern you to know who is downstairs.—Dick, if it is Tom Ford, your mother car have the gun given to him. Now, be quiet and attend to me. Five into thirty-eight goes how often? I am asking you, Dick."

"Five into thirty-eight," repeated Dick, removing his eyes hastily from the door, upon which they were fixed. "Five into thirty-eight goes—"

"It's Mr. Annesley," announced Katy, in a loud voice.

"How do you know?" demanded Jack, eagerly.

"I heard him," she answered joyfully; and she jumped down from her seat, and ran to the window. "Yes, it's Mr. Annesley—I see his horse!—Oh, Miss Tresham, please let me go down!"

"Take your seat," said Miss Tresham, briefly, "and don't let me hear another word."

"But he will go!" cried the child, turning first red and then pale, "and I won't get to see him at all. Miss Tresham, please let me—"

"Katy, did you hear me tell you to take your seat?"

"But he will go!" repeated she, half-passionately, half-entreatingly.

"Ba—a! Now, cry like a baby about it," said Jack.

"I'll cry if I want to!" was the angry retort.

"I don't think you will," said Miss Tresham, quietly. "If you don't come this instant to your seat, I will lock you up in the closet."

Katy gave a great gulp; but she knew the battle was an unequal one. She remembered how often she had got the worst of similar encounters, and she moved slowly and sullenly toward her chair. When she was fairly seated, Miss Tresham turned again to the arithmetic.

"Dick, you have not yet told me how often five goes into thirty-eight."

"Seven times, and three over," responded Dick, who had, meanwhile, been ascertaining the fact by the aid of his fingers.

"And how often does—"

"Tap, tap, tap," at the door—which was promptly thrown open by Jack, before Miss Tresham could utter a word. A servant stood outside. "Mr. Annesley's down-stairs, ma'am," he said, addressing Katharine.

She looked up and frowned a little.

"Whom did he ask for?"

"For you and mistis both, ma'am."

"Tell him he must excuse me. I never see any one in the morning. You know this, Tom. Why didn't you tell him so at once?"

"I did 'm. But mistis come out, and asked him to walk in, and told me to come up and tell you he was here anyhow."

"He must excuse me. I never see any one in the morning," Katharine said again, and returned to the lesson she was engaged with.

"Yes'm."

The servant disappeared, and blank dismay, seasoned with discontent, settled over the children. They had been unusually trying during the whole morning, and this interruption left them almost unmanageable. They felt that Miss Tresham's refusal to see Mr. Annesley was an outrage on themselves; and the perversity and stupidity with which they revenged themselves would have exhausted any patience less long-suffering than hers. Perhaps it exhausted even hers; but, if so, she did not afford them the gratification of seeing it. On the contrary, she sat, a model of quiet authority, and held them unflinchingly to the task in hand; but it was of so little effect that, when at last the welcome stroke of twelve told their release from the school-room, only Sara was able to close her books and take her departure.

"The rest of you are kept in," said Miss Tresham, looking at her watch, "and it will depend on yourselves whether you get through in time for dinner. If not, I shall leave you here, and send some bread-and-water up to you. —Jack, take Levizac there, and study 'moudre' for recitation; Katy, go to your grammar; now, Dick, let me see if you are still unable to cipher out this sum."

The threat of bread-and-water was not without effect on Dick's hitherto obtuse brain, giving to it a sudden insight into multiplication and division which it had lacked before. With little further trouble the sum was worked out to Miss Tresham's satisfaction; and, when he had seized his cap and scampered off, she was able to turn her attention to the other delinquents, who still sulked in different corners over their respective grammars.

They found the struggle which they had provoked a very hard one; for the young governess stood steadfastly at her post, and never flagged in word or sign all through the weary hour which followed. A very weary hour it was, and, when the dinner-bell pealed through the house, she was looking pale and exhausted, though the battle was fought and won. The two valiant champions had just finished their recitations, and were looking quite crestfallen as they put away their books and closed their desks. Katharine did not even have time to smooth her hair, or add a single adorning touch to her plain morning-costume. Mrs. Marks was very punctual herself, and liked punctuality in other people, especially with regard to meals; so, with one deprecating glance at the little school-room mirror, Miss Tresham ran down-stairs.

As she saw Ilderim still standing beside the front gate, she did not need the sound of a certain ringing laugh, which came through the open door, to tell her that Ilderim's master was in the dining-room. The next minute she was shaking hands with him.

"See how forgiving I am," he said, with a smile. "You refused to see me, and I not only wait your pleasure, but I encroach on Mrs. Marks's hospitality without the least remorse. Have you been victimizing those poor children for the last hour on my account?"

"The matter lies just the other way," she answered. "It is they who have been victimizing me on your account, until I wished that you had timed your visit better. I make no apologies for not seeing you. I believe you know my school-hours."

"I do know them; but I thought you might relax your rule for once, since I have been away so long. However, Mrs. Marks was kind enough to see me, and has entertained me so well that I did not find the time long."

"Indeed, then, Mr. Annesley, you must be fond of hearing about children and chickens," said Mrs. Marks, with a good-humored laugh; "for I don't remember talking about any thing else. I felt sorry for you, but I knew there was no use in going after Miss Katharine. She never will come down in her school-hours."

"And you're quite right, Miss Kate," said Mr. Marks. "Work is work, and play is play, and, in my opinion, the two should never be mixed up together.—Mr. Annesley, let me help you to a piece of this duck.—Bessie, what is that you have before you?"

"Some beef of my own corning," answered Mrs. Marks, with all a housekeeper's pride.—"Mr. Annesley, you must take some, and tell me what you think of it."

Mr. Annesley accepted a mammoth slice, and, with commendable industry, ate a considerable portion of it, praising it the while highly; it is to be hoped, sincerely.

Then the conversation turned upon the different methods of corning beef, and a grave discussion ensued, in which Morton acquitted himself with credit, and much pleased his host and hostess.

These good people, though even to their own hearts they would not have acknowledged such a thing, were not a little flattered by the attention which it had lately pleased the young owner of Annesdale to show them—attentions the source of which they were shrewd enough to suspect, but which in themselves were no slight tokens of distinction, as distinction was reckoned by the Tallahoma world. Already more than one envious friend had said to Mrs. Marks:

"How often Mr. Annesley comes to see you!"

To which Mrs. Marks replied, quite indifferently:

"Yes, he is so fond of the children, and Richard likes him very much."

Therefore, although she sometimes had serious doubts concerning what was to be the end of his evident fancy for Miss Tresham, she could not find it in her heart to discourage his visits.

"He is such a gentleman—there *can* be no harm in it," she once said to her husband, when she felt an unusual qualm on the subject; whereupon honest Mr. Marks answered in his way:

"Harm, indeed! What harm could there be? I'll warrant him for a gentleman—Edgar Annesley's son couldn't well be any thing else—but, even if he wasn't, I should think Miss Tresham was old enough, and had sense enough, to take care of herself."

On the understanding, therefore, that Miss Tresham was old enough, and had sense enough, to take care of herself, Mr. Annesley's visits had not been discouraged. Indeed, he was so bright a visitor that it would have been hard for any, either gentle or simple, to close their doors to him.

As he sat at the table now, it was wonderful how he managed to adapt himself to the tone of his entertainers. Often gay, always pleasant, and invariably courteous, he talked household economy to Mrs. Marks, politics to her husband, and nonsense to the children, with an ease that amused Katharine. There was none of that offensive air of "You see I put myself on your level," which some people assume when they attempt this kind of thing; but, on the contrary, such a frank charm, such an art, or rather such a gift of throwing, not a pretence, but a reality of interest into every thing he touched, and such a happy power of enlivening the dullest subjects, that the most sensitive person could not have found a shade of patronage to resent. He proved so entertaining that even Mr. Marks lingered over the meal, which was usually a very business-like ceremony; and, when at last he rose to go, apologized for his departure.

"I am sorry to say that I must be going," he remarked, with genuine regret. "But I leave you to the ladies, Mr. Annesley, and I don't expect you'll miss me much."

He knew perfectly well that his young guest had not come to see him; but he could not rid himself of an idea that it was "impolite" to leave him in this way.

But Morton replied that, though he was sorry to lose Mr. Marks's company, he had no doubt the ladies would manage to take care of him. And, as the bank was in need of its cashier, Mr. Marks said good-day, and departed.

Immediately thereupon Annesley turned and looked at Katharine, who was still seated at table, showing Nelly how to eat rice-pudding without sharing it between her dress and the table-cloth:

"What do you say?" he asked, with a smile. "Will you accept the responsibility?"

"Is it a very heavy one?" she inquired. "I expect—ah, Nelly, see how you have spilled that spoonful!—I expect to be equal to it, Mr. Annesley, if you won't ask too much in the way of entertainment."

"I will only ask one thing," said he—for they and Nelly had all that end of the table to themselves, as Mrs. Marks was at the moment giving some order to one of the servants at the other, while Jack and Dick squabbled over a custard in the middle.

"Well, and what is it?"

"That you will let this child alone, and come and sing something for me. I have not heard any good music in such a long time. Not since—"

"Since when?" she asked, as he paused.

"Since I heard you last," he answered, with grave sincerity.

Katharine laughed, and made him a little bow.

"After such a compliment, I should be very ungrateful if I could refuse.—Mrs. Marks, will you come with us to the parlor?"

"After a while, my dear," said Mrs. Marks. "But don't wait for me.—You, Jack!—you, Dick!—Tom, take that custard from both of them."

A stormy scene ensued, in the midst of which Annesley and Katharine made an escape, shrugging their shoulders in sympathy as they crossed the passage and entered that gloomy solitude known in the Marks household as "the parlor."

A very gloomy solitude it was, for the children were strictly forbidden to enter it, and, being used only on state occasions, it had none of that air of comfort which pervaded the rest of the house. The stiff horse-hair chairs were ranged with regular uniformity against the walls, while a long sofa, with hard back and harder seat, occupied a position on one side of the fireplace, where a brass fender, polished to the extreme of brightness, enshrined two equally bright andirons and a paper screen of wonderful device. Over the mantel there was a bouquet of flowers, which bloomed all the year round (under a glass shade), a pair of silver candlesticks, a pair of empty vases, and various similar articles, arranged with due attention to mathematical precision. A round table occupied the centre of the floor; and on this reposed various books in gorgeous bindings—chiefly standard devotional works. In a corner stood the piano, and near it a stand on which lay a music portfolio bearing Katharine's name.

The owner of this name gave a slight shiver as she entered the sacred apartment, and, instead of proceeding directly to the piano, she walked across the floor, and opened one of the closed windows. "No, no; not that one," she said, as Annesley moved toward another, with the manifest intention of following her example. "If you open that, it will let in the sunshine; and Mrs. Marks will not allow such a thing, for fear of fading the carpet. Though, I am sure," added she, with a comical glance at the vivid hues spread under her feet, "I think the carpet would be much improved by a little fading. However, that is all a matter of taste. Now, what shall I sing?"

"My old favorite," said Morton, lifting the lid of the piano. "You know what that is."

She smiled, sat down to the instrument, and, softly touching the keys, began to sing the "Adelaide" of Beethoven—that most pure, most tender, most spirit-like strain that ever breathed in immortal tones the common story of our common human love! And as she sang it—as the glorious notes of the great master soared aloft in her rich young voice, as all the sordid things of life seemed to fade away, and all earth to grow more lovely in the divine glory of that tide of sound—it was not strange that the passion which is ever fed by such strains as these deepened on the mobile face beside her until one glance would have told her the story of his heart, without any need of words.

But she did not give that glance. When the song ceased, when her voice fell into silence, and the last vibration of those mournfully passionate cadences had died away, she made an effort to speak lightly; and, without taking her eyes from the keyboard, said, "Will you please look in that portfolio and find me the *Ave verum?* I will sing it for you to-day, though I could not do so the last time you asked me."

Half-mechanically, he obeyed—glad of a moment's time in which to collect himself before the words were uttered that he now felt impelled to speak. Temptation had gone so far, that he could resist no longer. Whatever might be the result, he must lay his heart at this woman's feet, and tell her that it was hers to accept or reject. That magic song had stolen away all his most steadfast resolves; for he had never intended to declare himself thus prematurely. He always had meant to make a formal demand for his mother's consent, and then to woo the girl he loved as if *she* had been the one whom Fortune placed so far above the other. It was always the way of the gallant gentlemen who had borne his name—if poor and humble the maiden whom they loved, they sought her with more state than if she had been the highest in the land. So, Morton had meant to come, when he offered his hand to Mr. Marks's governess; but the sudden force of passion was too strong for him. Words suddenly rushed to his lips, and in another moment Annesdale and all its belongings would have lain at Katharine Tresham's feet, if Fate had not intervened.

But, turning over, with absent mind and careless hand, the sheets of music, he came to a copy of the song he had just heard, the song which had stirred every fibre of his heart—the sad, passionate, beautiful "Adelaide." As he took it up, there fell from between the leaves an open letter. He caught it, as it was fluttering to the floor, and almost unconsciously his eyes fell on the first lines. They were written in a man's hand, and stood out black and clear on the white paper.

"MY DEAREST KATHARINE: I am terribly uncertain whether this letter will reach you, but at least—"

This much Morton could not avoid seeing—more than this, he did not read. Indeed, the hot, sharp pang which shot through his heart sent a mist to his eyes which would have prevented his doing so, if he had felt such a thing possible. Then he strove to steady himself. Might not Katharine, for aught he knew, have brothers, uncles, cousins, a dozen relations, from whom such an address might naturally be permitted? What a jealous fool he was! He would speak to her immediately, and her first look would show him his folly. So he did speak—with just a slight quiver in his voice to betray his anxiety.

"Miss Tresham."

Katharine turned quickly, and, as her glance fell from his face to the open letter in his hand, Morton's heart gave a great bound—then suddenly stood still.

For she did not smile in recognition of a friend's epistle, nor blush that rosy red which greets a lover's missive; she did not hold out her hand or utter one word—she only turned ashen pale, and shivered from head to foot as if with a sudden chill. There was an instant's pause: then Morton spoke hastily, as if eager to relieve a possible fear.

"I found this a moment ago, Miss Tresham. Do you leave your letters where any one might find and read them?"

She did not answer—only held out her hand toward him.

"It may not be of importance," he went on; "but still—"

"It is of importance," she broke in, passionately. "To think that I should have left it here! I must have been mad!"

She took the letter, and, walking to the fire-place, struck a match, set it on fire, and watched it burn until the last fragment was ashes. Then she shivered once more from head to foot. "I must have been mad!" she repeated.

And there was something in the tone and action which settled like ice upon the man who loved her—the man who, a moment before, had wellnigh asked her to be his wife. He could sooner have put his hand into the fire she had kindled than ask that question now. Not that any suspicion of any kind had entered his mind against her, but simply that he felt chilled to the very heart. The women who had always made his ideals of the sex were women into whose stainless lives there entered no pages that all the world might not read; and not a worldling of the world held more firmly than this chivalric but most fastidious gentleman the great maxim of the world, "Distrust secrecy."

So, when Mrs. Marks bustled in a few minutes later, her advent was a relief to him as well as to Katharine, and, for the half-hour which ensued, that good woman had all the burden of conversation on her own shoulders.

Then Mr. Annesley found it was time to go; so he made his adieux and took his departure—riding very slowly from the gate where Ilderim had stood so long, and unmindful of the wistful glances sent after him by poor little Katy, whose heart had been set upon a ride.

When Katharine was left alone in the parlor, her first act was to go and toss over the little feathery heap of ashes on the hearth, to see that no end of paper remained. Then she raised her face with a weary sigh, half of relief, half of pain.

"All gone!" she said, aloud. "But God only knows when that may come to me which I can never, never cast from me, as I now cast these ashes!"

CHAPTER IX.

MR. WARWICK MAKES AN OFFER.

After that day, the Marks household saw no more of Mr. Annesley for some time. Even in the walks which Katharine regularly took with the children, they ceased to meet him, as often before; and they might have thought him absent from home, if they had not seen him occasionally ride past on his way to and from the village. Katy mourned this sudden desertion faithfully; but even for Katy's heart there proved at last to be a balm in Gilead, and it came in this way.

Between the well-cultivated fields which Mr. Marks called his own, and the stately Morton woods that stretched to meet them, and bore the Morton name for many a long mile, there lay a strip of land belonging to the latter, which, having been "thrown out" for years, had made that place dear to every child's heart—an old field where broom-straw and young pines disputed possession with blackberry-bushes and wild fruit-trees; where strawberries by bushels were to be found in spring, and sweet, delicate wild-flowers bloomed in profusion; where the boys of Tallahoma came when they wanted to arrange strictly private racing or shooting matches; where there was always a ring ready for amateur circus performers; where there was a "branch" in which minnows and crawfish abounded (not to speak of the best possible mud for mud-pies), and where the Marks children spent as much time, the whole year round, as was left at their own disposal.

One day they came home from this favorite resort full of momentous intelligence—they had made a new acquaintance. When the name of this new acquaintance was heard, the interest of the elders was scarcely inferior to that of the children; for it was Felix Gordon—the little prince, as people began to call him, on account of his proud young beauty and grand young manners.

"And he's downright jolly, mamma," cried Jack, in his vociferous way. "I thought he was a baby, you know—having a great big nurse following him about all the time; but he isn't a bit of a one. And he says he hates her; and he says she ain't going to mind him any more."

"But he's got a boy that follows him now," said Dick; "and he orders him about just as if he was a man."

"But I thought his mother kept him so close, he was never allowed to see anybody?" said Mrs. Marks. "He must have been there without her knowledge."

"He says he can go anywhere he pleases now, provided this boy goes along with him," answered Jack, whose volubility made him spokesman for the party, whether the others would or no. "He says Mr. Annesley talked his mother into 'lowing it; and he says he's going to have a pony soon as ever Mr. Annesley can find one for his mother to buy."

"And he says I may ride it!" broke in Katy, determined to have an utterance on this point at least.

"My daughter!" said her mother, reprovingly. "I hope you were not such a forward little girl as to ask him."

"Oh, no, mamma; he promised me his own self."

"Oh, did he?" cried Jack, sarcastically. "Well, I reckon he did—after you'd been hinting like forty! She told him she liked riding, mamma, and she kep' a-telling him so, till he was '*bliged* to ask her. Yes, missy, you know that's so!"

"I don't," retorted the little lady, angrily.—"'Tain't so, either, mamma; he asked me his own self."

"Why didn't he ask Sara, too, then?" inquired provoking Jack. "She's a great deal prettier than you are—you stuck-up, forward thing!"

"He did ask me," said Sara's quiet little voice.—"He turned round and asked me just after he asked Katy, mamma; and just like he was a grown-up gentleman. But I told him no, I was much obliged to him, but I was afraid of horses."

"And that was what Katy ought to have told him," said Jack, looking severe reproof at Katy.

"But I ain't afraid of horses," cried she, indignantly; "and I oughtn't to have told a story.—Mamma, he is so nice. Mayn't we please go to see him?—he asked us."

"Yes, mamma, he asked us—mayn't we?" chorussed all the rest.

But of this, Mrs. Marks would not hear. "You may go to see him, if he comes to see you," she said; "but otherwise—certainly not."

With this condition, the children were obliged to be content—trusting to their new acquaintance for its fulfilment. But their new acquaintance either would not or could not fulfil it. He met the little Markses every day in their favorite place of resort; and every day they brought home more wonderful accounts of Felix's sayings and doings; but Felix himself never appeared.

And so the Indian summer came gradually to an end; the soft, blue haze faded from the landscape; a few fierce storms tore all the bright leaves from the trees; and Winter—at least as much of winter as the fair South ever knows—was seated on his throne. His first act of power was a nipping frost, accompanied by such a "freeze" as had not been known in that region of country for a fabulous number of years —a freeze which, to the amazement of everybody, spread a sheet of ice over a small mill-pond near the town, and put all the boys of Tallahoma figuratively on their heads, and literally on their backs.

In the new field of amusement thus opened, neither Jack nor Dick were behindhand; and one day they joined in begging Miss Tresham to come and witness their prowess. "Sara and Katy want to see some skating," said the boys, who were not bad brothers as boys go; "and mamma says they can't come out to the pond, 'less you'll come too, Miss Tresham. Please, do; it's such good fun."

"Is it?" said Miss Tresham. "But it is cold fun, too, for people who don't skate. Have you got a fire out there?"

"Oh, the biggest sort," cried both boys, in a breath. "And we'll make it up splendid, if you'll come, Miss Tresham."

Miss Tresham looked doubtfully out of the window. It was certainly cold; but the boys were anxious; Katy and Sara looked unutterable things; she herself felt that she needed exercise; and, then—the wind was not blowing! That is such a great point in a climate where still cold can never be very dreadful.

"Do you want to go very badly?" she asked, with a smile, of the two little girls.

And they—who knew by that smile how their cause was won—answered, eagerly: "Oh, yes'm; oh, Miss Tresham, indeed we do!"

"Very well, then; we will walk out after dinner. And as for you"—she shook her finger at the two young skaters—"if you deceive me about the fire, I will never trust either of you again."

They made the most effusive promises, the two young scamps, who were secretly burning to be off. "Never mind, Miss Tresham, *I'll* see about it," said Jack, grandly. "I'll make them bring heaps of pine-knots, and they shall all be put on when you come.—But, I say, Dick, look sharp—it's time we were off."

"Off!" echoed the governess. "Are you not going to wait for dinner?"

"We can't," said both in a breath. "But Mom Judy promised to have us a basket ready and we'll eat it on the road." (They did not mean the basket, but its contents.) "Don't change your mind, Miss Tresham—we'll look for you."

"You shall see me," answered she. "I hope you will enjoy yourselves."

They had the grace to thank her; and then were off, running down the passage, leaping down the staircase, as if the fate of a nation depended on their speed; and filling the house with that stir and clatter, that healthful noise and pervading sense of vitality, which only the presence of boys can diffuse.

After they were gone, Miss Tresham and her two young charges drew near the school-room fire, and waited for the sound of the dinner-bell. It came at last, breaking in upon the oft-told story of the "Fair One with the Golden Locks;" and they went down together, the children claiming each a hand of their young teacher, and making quite a pretty picture when they entered the dining-room.

At least, so a gentleman thought who was standing before the fire with a paper in his hand and at sight of whom Katy burst into an exclamation.

"Why, unky! I thought you never came to dinner."

"I have come to-day, at any rate," said he. "Do you mean to say you are not glad to see me?"

"Oh, yes, so glad—ain't we, Sara? But, unky—" Here a sudden pause, and a tiptoe peeping into "unky's" coat-pocket.

"Well?" said he, apparently unconscious of this fact.

But Katy was too busy for speech. She had detected a brown-paper parcel in that receptacle, and she was now intent on an abstraction of the same—a design very well favored by Mr. Warwick's deep interest in politics. Then came a shout.

"Oh, Sara, look! Mamma—Miss Tresham—look!"

"French candy, I declare!" said Mrs. Marks. "John, you really ought not to be so extravagant. You ruin these children."

"Oh, mamma, it's so nice!" said Katy, with a crystallized fig in one hand, and a rose-flavored triumph of confectionery in the other.

"So nice, is it?" said her mother, severely. "And pray, where are your manners? Have you offered Miss Tresham any?—or even your uncle? No; you need not do it now" (as Katy penitently gathered up the paper in her two little hands), "I hear your father's step on the piazza, and dinner is ready.—Tom, put that candy on the mantel-piece."

"May I have it as soon as dinner's over, mamma?" asked Katy, watching, with regretful eyes, the elevation of the candy.

"Yes, you may have it; and I hope you will offer the rest of us some," said Mrs. Marks, taking her seat at the head of the table. "I am fond of candy myself.—Well, my dear, it is cold out—is it not?"

This was addressed to Mr. Marks, who, coming in from the outer world with the state of the thermometer written legibly on his nose, made straight for the fireplace.

"Cold! I should think so, indeed," he answered. "Almost cold enough to nip a man's ears. I never saw such a spell of weather but once before in my life."

"And that was not in December, I am sure," said Mr. Warwick, surrendering possession of the hearth-rug.

"No; I never saw any thing like it in December before," answered Mr. Marks, standing with his back to the fire, and critically scanning the table over his wife's head. "Our mild weather always lasts until after New-Year."

"Last Christmas we had garden roses on the dinner-table," said Katharine; "but the poor bushes are melancholy sights now. Did you notice them as you came through the garden, Mr. Warwick?"

"Yes," answered Mr. Warwick. "Your cloth-of-gold buds, especially. The frost did not spare you even one."

"Mr. Annesley'll send her some prettier flowers," remarked Katy. "He always does; and I like them better than ours."

"No doubt of that, you true daughter of Eve!" said Mr. Warwick, who had sufficient discretion to remove his eyes from Katharine's face. and transfer them to the saucy little speaker "It would be all the same, too, if we had the japonicas, and Mr. Annesley sent the roses.—What is it, Bessie?"

"Do come to dinner," said Mrs. Marks, who had finished piling the ham before her with well-cut slices, and was at leisure to observe that the leg of mutton, at the other end of the table, had ceased to steam. "Richard, you are surely warm by this time?"

"Moderately," said Mr. Marks, as he left the fire with a regretful sigh and went round to his seat, which had two comfortable sluices of air blowing upon it from two ill-fitting windows. After his short grace was finished, and he began to carve the leg of mutton, he observed the absence of Jack and Dick.

"So those young scamps are off to the pond again!" he said. "I wonder they don't kill themselves. Everybody seems pond-crazy! All Tallahoma has gone out on a general jollification."

"We are going, too, papa," cried Katy, eagerly. "Miss Tresham is going to take us this evening."

"Is she? Well, I'm sorry for Miss Tresham, then. I know you little ones have tormented her into it."

"No," said Miss Tresham, speaking for herself, "I shall really enjoy the walk. How far is it to the pond?"

"A good two miles," said Mr. Warwick "Rough miles, too; so I would advise thick shoes and warm wrappings."

Dinner went off in short order; and, when it was over, the children ran for their cloaks and hoods without demanding the candy, which Mrs. Marks suggested should be taken along and feasted on beside the pond.

"Wrap up your best," said Mr. Warwick, with a smile, as the young governess rose to follow. "I shall stay here to see—and admire."

be added, when the door had closed on her.—"What a pretty creature she is, Bessie!"

"And as good as she is pretty," said Mrs. Marks, enthusiastically. "The children love the very ground she walks on; and, if ever I had a lucky day in my life, it was the day I met Katharine Tresham."

The table was cleared off, draped with its bright-crimson cover, and wheeled into its accustomed corner; the last plate and goblet whisked away to the pantry, the fire replenished, the hearth swept, the cheery dining-room looking the cheeriest, when Katharine came in again.

She found Mr. Warwick the only occupant of the room—Mr. Marks having gone into town, and Mrs. Marks into the kitchen. It was that important era in housekeeping known as "hog-killing time," and the lard and the sausages absorbed Mrs. Marks almost as much as the pig-tails and the roasting thereof distracted the children. Katharine was not surprised to find her gone, but she was surprised to see Mr. Warwick, who looked up from his newspaper as she entered.

"Ready?" said he. "I gave you thirty minutes, and you have only taken fifteen. Well—" with an amused glance from her bonnet to her shoes—"I think you can safely defy the weather."

"I think I am ridiculously wrapped up," answered she; "but panics are infectious. You have all been talking about the cold till I deluded myself into a belief that it must be Siberia; while the truth is, that I opened my window just before I came down, and it is absolutely pleasant."

"So much the better for your walk, then. But I think you'll change your mind when you are once out-of-doors."

Just here there was a rush in the passage outside, and the two little girls flashed into the room in their warm cloaks and bright-crimson hoods. Then came an outcry.

"Why, Miss Tresham's all ready, and we don't have to wait—how nice!"

"Katy, don't forget about the candy."

"Unky, please hand me down the candy."

"Do it up tight."

"Miss Tresham, please tie this knot. I can't get my gloves off."

"You little torment!" said Miss Tresham. "How can I do it when I have my own gloves on? Ask Mr. Warwick."

"Unky, please."

"I suspect Miss Tresham could do it better with gloves than I can without," said "unky."

But he tied the knot very deftly, nevertheless; and then slipped the package into his pocket, much to the astonishment of Katy and Sara, who raised a frightened cry of expostulation.

"Unky!"

"Oh, that's Indian-gift!"

But the Indian-giver turned quietly to the governess.

"May I go along, if I promise to show you the best road, and not to promote any disturbances?"

Katharine looked surprised.

"Are you in earnest, Mr. Warwick?"

"To be sure I am in earnest," said Mr. Warwick. "I came home for the purpose of taking these little ones out; but they will enjoy your company more than mine. Only, as I don't like to break up my day for nothing, may I go too?"

"Of course, you may.—Children, do you hear? Your uncle is going with us."

The afternoon was dazzlingly bright when they went out into it; and Mr. Warwick was soon forced to acknowledge that Katharine's judgment of the temperature was better than his own. Being bright and still, the atmosphere had softened very much, and seemed to them almost mild as they walked in the full glow of the winter sun.

"This will be the last day of skating," said Mr. Warwick. "Indeed, I doubt if the ice is safe now. I think I shall stop Jack and Dick as soon as we get there."

"Even if the ice broke, is the water deep enough to drown anybody?" asked Katharine, to whom a mill-pond did not suggest any thing much to be feared.

"It is not less than twelve or fifteen feet in depth," said her companion. "I used to swim in it when I was a boy, and I know it well—besides, the waters are very full just now. On the whole, I think those young gentlemen had better rest on their laurels."

"If there is any danger, yes, indeed. But we can't stop them now; so please don't let us talk about it and make ourselves uncomfortable."

They did not. On the contrary, they talked of other things much more agreeable. Mr. Warwick could not help feeling that many a man might have envied him his position, and that there had seldom been a lighter form or a brighter face than the one now walking beside and smiling upon him; while Katharine, for her part, had never been one of the girls who can find little or nothing to say to a man who is not young enough or foolish enough to be converted into an admirer. Indeed, these two had been friends in a certain reserved but sincere fashion ever since the young governess entered the Marks household. She was often more nearly approaching the confidential with him than with any one else; and they fell into something of a personal strain now as they walked along the rough footpath, and troubled themselves no more about the children than just to keep their crimson hoods in sight.

"Yes, I pity you," Mr. Warwick was saying, "and all the more because you don't seem to pity yourself. If you were discontented, probably I should not trouble myself to sympathize with you. But, as it is, I think very often that you have a hard lot for such a young person."

"Many people younger than I am have a much harder one," said Katharine, quietly. "Does that never occur to you? It always does to me."

"But not people who seem so essentially born and fitted for other things."

"What sort of things do you mean?"

"I think you know. Wealth, luxury, the appliances of refinement, the power of being generous—for I think you would be generous if you had the power—and of putting your talents to some better use than their present one."

A flush came over the girl's face as he spoke, but died away before he finished.

"That is the way my own vanity speaks to me sometimes," she said; "but I never listen to such suggestions. I go and get Dick's sum, or Sara's exercise, and drum away the phantom with the rule of three or the vocative case."

"But it comes back?"

"Yes, sometimes. Then there is nothing to be done but to face it boldly, and ask myself if I am really so weak and vain as to think myself better than the millions who have toiled to their lives' ends, more humble and more unknown than I am; if better talents than any of mine have not gone down into the dust soundless; and if"—her voice sank slightly here—"I am wiser than He who orders our lives for us from their beginning even to their end."

"And then?"

"And then I think that I cannot be sufficiently grateful for all the blessings my life has known; and I try to crush down the vanity and self-love which—let us disguise it as we may, is, after all, the root of most of our discontent. We think too highly of ourselves and our own deserts. If we would only try to recognize ourselves as we really are, we should feel so ashamed of our repining that I think we would be content ever afterward to take whatever God is good enough to give us, and leave the choice of good or bad fortune to Him."

"Do you speak from experience?"

She smiled a little.

"Can't you tell that? One reads such things in books, but one only learns them in one's own heart. It seems to me it is always easy to tell whether it has been read or learned."

Mr. Warwick did not reply; and they walked on silently for some time, no sound breaking the stillness save the echo of their own tread and the children's merry tones floating back through the clear air. Just here their road was through a pine-forest; the tall, straight trunks rose on every side; the deep, sombre green stretched away far as the eye could view; the golden sunshine streamed with a mellow brightness through the stately arcades; and, although there was only a slight breeze stirring the tree-tops, the sound above their heads was like the distant murmur of the sea. It put Katharine strangely in mind of the ocean; and, together with the soft carpet of pine-straw under their feet, and the aromatic fragrance of the forest around, came back to her afterward—recalling that afternoon, and giving its events a picture-like distinctness in her memory. At last Mr. Warwick said, thoughtfully:

"It is not even as if you had been born to this sort of thing."

"But I was born to it," she answered, quickly. "All my life I knew that some day I must earn my own bread. That was the reason why my aunt—my dear, kind aunt—was so careful to educate me thoroughly. She could give me nothing besides an education."

Almost before he had time to consider the incivility of the question, Mr. Warwick had asked "Why?"

"Because she was an officer's widow, and her pension ended with her life," Katharine answered. "But, while she lived, I had a very happy time—and, after that, it did not matter."

Her voice choked, as she uttered the last words; and her companion did not need to glance at her, to know why she drew down her veil so hastily. He gave her time to recover herself, and then said, kindly:

"Courage. Remember how young you are. Happiness may come to you yet, in the form you like best."

"And what is that form?"

He shrugged his shoulders slightly, as he had a habit of doing over any knotty point of legal evidence.

"I may be mistaken, but it seems to me you would like best the happiness that could give you all those things of which you have so keen an appreciation — pictures, music, amusement, and the admiration which all women value so highly."

"I certainly like all those things," said Katharine, with a little sigh; "but I assure you, I can live without them and be happy too. No, Mr. Warwick, you have not hit upon the one great gift which Happiness must bring in her hand when she comes to me—or else not be happiness at all."

Mr. Warwick looked at her intently. Did she mean Morton Annesley's love, he wondered. If so, why did she speak of it thus frankly to him? It was not like Katharine Tresham to do so. "Tell me what it is?" he asked.

The clear, gray eyes—pure and truthful as God's noonday—met his own, as she answered, quietly: "It is the gift of peace."

After that, nothing was said for several minutes. Katy came dancing back with a spray of holly which was duly admired, and which, at her request, Katharine fastened in her brooch. Then, after she ran forward again, Mr. Warwick spoke:

"Miss Tresham, I am going to say something which may seem impertinent, but which, I trust, you will take as it is meant—in simple kindness. I have noticed, for some time past, that you have not been quite yourself, that you have grown thin, that your spirits are less even than heretofore, and that some trouble is evidently preying upon you. Is not this so?"

Katharine caught her breath, paling perceptibly. "I hoped no one had noticed it," she said.

"I am sure I may safely say that no one but myself has done so," he answered. "I am a very close observer—Nature gave me the habit, and my profession has taught me its importance —but you are a very good dissembler. The trifles in which you have betrayed yourself were light as air; but the driftwood shows the direction of the current, you know. I did not need to hear what you said a moment ago, to convince me that something is wrong with you. If it is any thing ideal, I can do nothing for you; but if it is any practical trouble, such as comes to us all sooner or later, why, I trust you believe me to be your friend."

"Yes," she said, simply; "I am glad to believe it."

"And I am glad to hear you say so; for I have watched you closely, ever since you entered my sister's house, and I have never yet known you to trifle with truth. That, first, made me like you, I think—for, of all virtues, it is at once the greatest and the rarest. If you believe me to be your friend, there is not much more to add. A woman—even a woman as brave as you are—is such a helpless creature in the world, that she is often made to suffer acutely through her weakness and her ignorance. In any emergency, therefore, I hope you will remember that my services are at your command."

"Thank you," said Katharine, lifting her face toward him, with a grateful light shining over it. "You are very kind, and there is no one to whom I would as soon go. But—" she paused a moment, and added, slowly—"I must bear my burden alone."

He turned and looked at her. The light had faded, and the young face seemed to have hardened into a self-contained power of endurance. The mouth was set, the eyes were resolute, and, as she met his glance, she repeated her words in the same tone:

"I must bear my burden alone."

"I cannot help you?"

"No. You are very good; but only He who laid it on me can take it away."

Again they walked on silently; and the lawyer felt half inclined to indulge in his quiet, cynical shrug. "It is Annesley, after all," he thought. "What a fool I was to suppose it could be any thing else—and a still greater fool to make such an offer! The very pine-trees might afford to laugh at the idea of my playing *confidant* and consoler in a love-affair!"

Then he glanced at the face beside him, and felt again a sudden conviction that it was *not* Annesley—not any cross in love, or ordinary heart-disaster—which brought such a look of suffering and resolve to those earnest eyes. An impulse hardly to be accounted for, and not at all to be analyzed, made him suddenly extend his hand, and place it on Katharine's arm.

"One word more," he said. "You are entirely unprotected by any friend or relative; this fact must excuse the request I am about to make. Will you promise to come to me if you ever stand in greater need than you do at present of service or advice?"

Katharine paused and looked at him wistfully. "Mr. Warwick," she said at last, "I cannot promise what I am never likely to perform."

"You mean—?"

"I mean what I said before—that I can only carry my burden to God, and He only can release me from it."

The keen lawyer-glance regarded her earnestly—searching, perhaps, for some shadow of shame or fear—but it only found a steady dignity on the pale face, and an open candor in the eyes that looked brave enough to face death itself unflinchingly.

"You are strong—for a woman," he said, after a while; "but your hour of weakness may come. I hope you will remember, then, that my offer still holds good."

"Yes," she answered, quietly, "I will remember it with gratitude."

There was nothing more to be said. They resumed their walk, and, after a minute, fell into other topics—talking until they caught a glimpse of frozen water shining through the trees, and Katy called out, joyfully:

"Here we are! here's the pond!"

"Here is the pond, certainly; but here are not the skaters," said Mr. Warwick, glancing over the sheet of water which lay all silent and glittering before them. "They must be lower down—ah! yes, I see them now. This way, Miss Tresham."

He led the way around a small headland, for the outline of the pond was very irregular, and a picturesque scene burst suddenly upon them—a scene vivid with color, and bright with animated motion, set in the midst of the winter landscape. This portion of the pond was alive with skaters in every stage of proficiency and non-proficiency. One or two seemed at home on their skates, a few managed to keep their feet and move with a tolerable degree of ease; but the vast majority were hopelessly sliding about, and ignominiously falling down every other minute, to their own discomfiture and the immense amusement of the spectators on the shore. These spectators were not by any means contemptible in point of numbers, for three large fires were blazing as only lightwood can blaze, and grouped around and about each were knots of young people, children, and servants. In the background stood several empty carriages, and quite a goodly array of horses. Camp-stools and baskets abounded, bright shawls were laid over the roots of trees to form impromptu easy-chairs, gay scarfs and hoods dangled from the boughs, the golden sunshine streamed over all with a glory and beauty entirely its own, and the majestic forest stretched around in its solemn grandeur.

Katy and Sara darted forward, while Miss Tresham and Mr. Warwick followed more slowly toward the nearest fire. As they approached, two ladies and two gentlemen, who were standing directly in front of it, drew back, and Katharine found herself facing Mrs. French, Miss Vernon, Mr. Annesley, and a stranger whom she had never seen. Neither of the ladies noticed her, excepting by a stare—well-bred on Miss Vernon's part, ill-bred on Mrs. French's—but Morton bowed as if to a *grande dame*, and the other gentleman gave a glance of the most undisguised admiration.

"What a pretty woman, Annesley!" Katharine heard him say, after she had passed. "It can't possibly be one of the Tallahoma belles."

Annesley's reply was inaudible; but its tenor was easily to be surmised, from the long "Whew!" which was his companion's comment, and which, evidently, would not have been the only one if Mrs. French had not broken in.

"Quite a nice person, too, I have heard—that is, for her position. She has something of good style about her, don't you think so, Irene? I wonder where she got that pelisse—the cut of it is excellent. But look at the fur on it—real sable, my dear, as sure as you live. What very bad taste—for her!"

"Why for her, Adela?" asked the bluff, frank tones that were certainly not Morton's. "Why shouldn't she wear a pretty thing as well as other women? I suspect she needs all the consolation that pelisses and furs can give her."

"Don't talk so loud, Frank, and don't be so silly," was the unceremonious reply. "People ought to dress according to their rank in life, or else what's the good of there being ranks in life? For my part, when I see anybody dressed so absurdly, I feel as if I never wanted to put on a handsome thing again."

"I wish you would stay of that mind," laughed the gentleman. And Katharine felt certain that he was the legal possessor of all Mrs. French's pretty toilets, and all Mrs. French's long bills!

"Shall we go over to the next fire?" asked Mr. Warwick, whose face looked amused and contemptuous both at once. "I think it is better than this."

Katharine assented, and they moved away, just as Miss Vernon's clear tones sounded with quite a bell-like distinctness.

"I think a pretty woman has a right to adorn her beauty to the utmost of her power, wherever she may be placed. That is one right of the sex for which I shall always be an advocate, Adela."

"But the working-classes, Irene—"

"We are not speaking of the working-classes," interrupted the other, with a very cool disdain in her voice. "We are speaking of a member of a liberal profession, I thought. I hear that Miss Tresham is very charming, and for a long time I have had a fancy to know her.—Mr. Annesley, you are a friend of hers; will you introduce me?"

"With pleasure, Miss Vernon," said Morton, coloring quickly. "I shall be very glad to do so, if you are in earnest."

"Of course I am in earnest.—Adela, won't you come also?"

"I?" Mrs. French drew back in astonishment. "Irene, you are surely jesting—you are surely not going to be introduced to Mrs. Marks's governess?"

"You will see," said Irene, with a slight nod and a merry laugh. "Carry her to the carriage if she faints, Frank.—Mr. Annesley, may I take your arm?"

CHAPTER X.

THE GORDON PLAID.

The latter part of this conversation Katharine had not heard. She had moved away to the other fire, and was talking to Mr. Warwick about Jack's skating. So her surprise was entirely unaffected when Annesley's voice spoke her name, and, turning, she saw him standing close beside her, with a beautiful, golden-haired vision leaning on his arm.

"Miss Tresham," he said, hurriedly, "allow me to present Miss Vernon. She is anxious to make your acquaintance, and—"

"Hopes you do not object to having it taken by storm," interrupted Miss Vernon, offering her hand. "You must excuse me, if this is an unceremonious proceeding, Miss Tresham; but I am very anxious to know you, and I hope you do not object to knowing me."

It would have been hard to do so under the influence of that gracious smile—for Irene Vernon could be very gracious when she chose—and Katharine answered, with her usual simplicity of word and tone:

"You do me too much honor, Miss Vernon. I am very glad to know you."

"Are you?" asked Miss Vernon. "Is not that speech a mere effort of courtesy?"

"It may be an effort of courtesy," answered Katharine, smiling; "but it is true, also."

"Then I may congratulate myself upon making a favorable impression for once in my life," said the young lady. "People don't usually like me when they first know me; in fact, some of them don't ever like me at all."

"Don't they?" said Katharine, amused at this frank confession. "That is strange; for I should think you would always be liked."

"Are you always liked?"

"Well—really, I don't know. But I think I am rather popular—at least with these." And she laid her hand on Katy's curly head.

"Their good-will is not worth much," said Miss Vernon, carelessly. "It is so cheap—a few sugar-plums will buy it."

"And won't different sugar-plums buy the good-will of older people just as easily?" asked Morton, abruptly.

"So you have turned cynic!" said Miss Vernon, glancing round at him. "I thought you left that to me."

"Don't slander my favorite objects of trust, then," answered he, laughing. "I must believe in children, or in nobody.—Katy, don't you mean to come and kiss me?"

While Katy, nowise loath, went to bestow this favor, Miss Vernon turned with a shrug to her new acquaintance.

"I wonder if he thinks that child would like him if he were poor and ugly?"

"She likes me," said Katharine, smiling, "and I am neither rich nor beautiful."

"You are lovable, though, and that is better than either," said Miss Vernon, with a slight sigh.

Katharine looked up in surprise; but, before she could answer this unexpected compliment, the young lady had turned to Mr. Warwick, and was asking him if he meant to skate.

"I?" he said, laughing. "What have I done, Miss Vernon, that you should suspect me of such an indiscretion?"

"You have worn a pair of skates, Mr. Warwick; for I heard Mrs. Raynor say this morning that John Warwick—isn't your name John?—was the only person she ever saw who seemed at home on the ice."

"Twenty-five years ago, the compliment may have been merited; but I hardly think I need blush for it now."

"Have you forgotten how to skate?"

"I don't know. I have not attempted it since I was a boy."

"Ah, pray try!" said the young lady, with the air of one who was not accustomed to ask favors in vain. "I never saw skating before, and I am so anxious to see at least one good skater!"

"You would see a very poor one, if I were so foolish as to expose my awkwardness," said Mr. Warwick, smiling.

"Who can skate, then? None of those people out yonder can, unless skating is a very ugly thing."

"Annesley ought to," said Mr. Warwick, glancing at that gentleman, who had drawn near and was talking to Katharine. "He spent four years at a German university, and they learn skating as well as metaphysics there."

Miss Vernon turned to Morton, as if intending to speak, and then as hastily turned back again.

"He would not thank us for disturbing him now," she said. "Look at those people out yonder, and tell me who you think gives most promise of learning to skate."

Her companion looked as she directed, and at once singled out a child with floating, blond curls and a plaid scarf, the fringed ends of which fluttered in the wind as he skimmed along the ice.

"I cannot tell from here who it is, but there is no one else to compare with him," answered Mr. Warwick. "He skates as if he had been born in Russia."

"And don't you know who he is?" cried his companion, eagerly. "Why, I thought everybody knew him! That is the little Gordon—don't you see? He looks as if he might have been born in the purple."

Mr. Warwick said, "Indeed!" And then they both watched the elfin skater, who only a few minutes before had made his appearance on the ice. He was, indeed, without peer; the very spirit of grace seemed to animate his motions, and his skating was such as is never seen out of a northern latitude, and of which the inhabitants of southern latitudes can form, at best, but a faint conception. The lithe young figure was so slenderly fashioned, and every movement of every limb was so harmonious with the spirit of the whole, that, aided by the floating curls and waving scarf, it almost looked as if the wind wafted him over the ice. He soon became fully aware of his own skill, and began to indulge in vagaries quite impossible to the novice in this slippery amusement. He made wide circles, then swooped suddenly upon some knot of inexperienced amateurs, scattering them to the right and left out of his path, and generally leaving two or three prostrate behind him; he seized the hand of some unlucky trembler, and carried him forward at a rate which soon left him breathless in a waste of ice, with no hope of return, his malicious guide having taken flight to another quarter; he snatched some half-dozen hats, and made for the centre of the pond, scattering them broadcast on his way; he indulged in solitary waltzes and ballet-like *pirouettes;* he played a thousand antics for his own amusement and that of the many eyes watching him; and then he suddenly darted away down the pond.

"Oh, I hope he is not going out of sight!" said Miss Vernon, with a very genuine tone of regret. "I never saw any thing more beautiful. Do, somebody, make him come back. Mr. Annesley, I believe he is under your charge—please speak to him."

"Speak—to whom?" asked Mr. Annesley, turning. "I beg your pardon. Miss Vernon, but I did not hear—has Felix been doing any thing?"

Miss Vernon replied by pointing to the slender figure and floating scarf which were already vanishing round the headland. "You are the only person whom he has not been entertaining," she said.

"Good Heavens!" cried Annesley, "and I promised his mother that he should not venture on the ice! How could I have been so careless; —Felix, come back! Felix!—don't you hear?"

Felix paused a moment, as the clear voice came ringing over the ice; showed that he heard, by waving his hand with a gesture of gay defiance, and then showed that he did not mean to heed, by coolly continuing his onward course. In another moment he had vanished from sight around the jutting point of land.

Miss Vernon laughed—she evidently sympathized with the bravery of this open rebellion—while Mrs. French, who was standing by, shrugged her shoulders significantly.

"People can't manage to conduct a flirtation and take care of a child at the same time," she said to her husband, in a tone sufficiently audible for Morton to hear.

But Morton took no notice of the remark. He only turned round to the by-standers, and asked if anybody could lend him a pair of skates.

Unfortunately, nobody was able to do so. Skates were very scarce articles, and whoever was so fortunate as to own a pair, lent them to his friends by turns—an arrangement which resulted in the temporary possessor being worried out of all his enjoyment by two or three impatient candidates who wanted to know "if he meant to keep agoing all day, or if he didn't mean to give anybody else a chance to do some skating?" Therefore, all shook their heads when Morton made his request, and several voices replied that Tom Jones had a pair of skates, but that Frank Smith was using them.

"What do you want to do, Mr. Annesley?" Katharine asked.

"I want to go after the little scamp," Annesley replied. "I ought to have paid more attention to him; but how could I think of his playing me such a trick, when he knew, too, that only my persuasion induced his mother to let him come?"

"This is very ungrateful conduct, then."

"Is it not?—Katy, run yonder to that knoll, and see if he is coming back."

Katy obeyed, bounding up on the rising ground at the headland, where a stately group of young pines stood like sentinels; and, in a few minutes, returned with the intelligence that he was coming back.

"You will not need to go, after all," said Miss Vernon to Annesley.

"That remains to be seen," he answered. "I don't much think he will come to shore of his own accord.—Thank you, Price." This to a young man who handed him a pair of skates over two or three intervening shoulders. Then, while he sat down to buckle them on, Felix came bearing back into sight—a more beautiful picture than ever, all alone in his childish grace on the glittering expanse of ice.

"Oh, the little darling!" cried several enthusiastic young ladies; while the boys of all ages stared in open-mouthed, admiring wonder of his skill.

"Is he coming to shore?" asked Morton, who could not see, partly because he was sitting on the ground, and partly because several people were standing before him. Two or three voices answered the question—not very satisfactorily.

"I think so."

"No, he isn't."

"There he goes—he's off again."

"That's splendid! That is skating!"

"He's bound up the pond this time."

"Yes," said Katharine, to whom Morton looked inquiringly. "He certainly has no intention of coming to the shore. He is going up the pond at a rapid rate."

"It's a pity somebody can't make him come back," said a man's voice near. "All skating is something of a risk to-day; but the ice is very unsafe in that direction."

"Are you sure of that, Mr. Mills?" asked Morton, starting to his feet.

"Very sure, sir," answered Mr. Mills, gravely. "My wagon was hauling ice from there this morning, and I don't think it would have borne the weight of a man then."

Morton made no answer, but Katharine saw that he changed color, and immediately swung himself down the bank, which happened to be quite high just there. The next minute he was gliding over the ice with a swift, steady ease of movement which proved his own proficiency quite equal to that of Felix. A chorus of admiration followed him; but the young man evidently heard none of it. He was bending every nerve in pursuit of the gay little will-o'-the-wisp who fleeted forward all the faster when he perceived that a chase had been instituted. Away went the two figures up the pond, the pursuer steadily gaining on the pursued, and both nearing fast the dangerous ice of which Mr. Mills had spoken. Once Annesley paused and uttered something half-warning, half-command; but the young insurgent paid no attention to it, and the only result was that it lost Morton several yards of distance. When he started again, however, he seemed scarcely to touch the ice, and the interest of the spectators had reached a very exciting point when a cry of mingled dismay and triumph rose from a knot of boys on the water's edge.

"He's got him!"

"No, he hasn't!"

"Hurrah! He's slipped away!"

"Well done, little one!"

And Katharine looked in time to see Felix dart out of the grasp Morton laid on him, and, shooting under the outstretched arm, skate away faster than ever, leaving only his scarf as trophy in the disappointed captor's hands.

"Well done, indeed!" cried Miss Vernon, with a ringing laugh of enjoyment. "I am so glad he got away. I should be so sorry if it ended. It is better than horse-racing, and I adore that! Who will make a bet?—Adela, will you?"

"Certainly not," replied Mrs. French, severely. "I think it is disgusting. Morton ought to have more dignity than to make such an exhibition of himself. I really think—"

But Miss Vernon was already speaking to Katharine.

"Miss Tresham, will you? As many pairs of gloves as you please on the Gordon plaid."

"Do you mean Mr. Annesley?" asked Katharine, laughing. "He has the Gordon plaid at present."

"No, indeed; I mean on the rightful owner of the Gordon plaid. Bless his brave little heart! Where is he now?"

"Yonder he is," said Mr. Warwick, who was standing by, a quiet and much-interested spectator. "But Annesley is gaining very fast upon him; so perhaps you had better not register your bet just at present. See! he almost laid hold of him. There, now he has doubled again. After all, you may—my God!"

A sudden wild cry from Mrs. French—a murmur of horror from the crowd—and out on the ice, where there had been two figures a moment before, only one.

This was a terror-stricken child, while, where the ice had broken through, there still floated one fringed end of the Gordon plaid. On the shore, a rush, a commotion, a sound of many voices, and a lady in violent hysterics.

Katharine never knew much of what ensued. She heard Mr. Warwick's tones take the lead, and bring some quiet out of the uproar; she saw a confused mass of men and boys dash across the ice with a reckless disregard of danger, and she sat down sick and shuddering to await the result.

Miss Vernon sat down by her. Neither said any thing, yet there is no doubt that each was conscious of the presence of the other. Mr. French, meanwhile, had left his wife to get out of her hysterics as best she could, and had gone to the rescue with the rest; so, finding nobody to take any notice of her, she somewhat subsided, and stood sobbing and asking questions which it was impossible for any one to answer yet.

To those watchers on the shore it seemed hours, but it was in reality only a short time before the many strong arms which broke up the ice and buffeted the water so bravely, gained their reward—before they raised to the surface and bore shoreward, with a rush of triumph, that which seemed so awfully still and white when they laid it down at Katharine Tresham's feet.

They said it was not Death, but she could scarcely believe it was Life, when she looked at the pale face with the wet hair clinging round it, and at those rigid hands which still grasped the silken scarf.

But, even while she looked, there came a long, gurgling sigh through the half-parted lips—the lids slowly lifted—the dark eyes gazed up at her pitying countenance as if in a bewildered dream—and her name was spoken with that tender, yearning accent which would make any name of earth beautiful.

"Katharine!"

Then, before she could utter one word, they closed again, and Mr. Warwick said:

"He has fainted!"

A little while later, after Mr. Annesley was sufficiently recovered to thank his rescuers, to answer all the inquiries of his friends, to enter his carriage, and be driven home, Mr. Warwick came up to Katharine, and asked her if she felt inclined to perform a deed of charity.

"It depends a good deal upon the amount of exertion required," she answered, with a smile. "I am a little tired. But let me hear what it is."

He pointed to Felix, who stood at a little distance the centre of an admiring group, and quite as nonchalant as ever.

"I promised Morton to take that young gentleman home, and to give as mild a rendering of his exploit as is at all consistent with truth. But I begin to doubt my diplomatic ability. I think you could do him more service than I; and, in short, I want you to take the matter off my hands. Will you?"

Katharine looked slightly aghast.

"Mr. Warwick, I would be glad to oblige you, but—but I am a mere stranger—and *Morton House!*"

"That is the very reason why I ask you," said Mr. Warwick, coolly. "Considering all things, I think a mere stranger might be more welcome in Morton House than an old acquaintance like myself. Will you go?"

She hesitated a minute longer. Then, remembering what might be his reason for wishing to avoid Mrs. Gordon, answered quickly:

"Yes, if you think I can do any good, I will go."

"If you cannot, I am sure it will be for the first time," he answered, smiling. "Yonder comes the carriage which Annesley promised to send back, so you see you have no time to change your mind. Let me put you in, and see you off. Then I will take the children home."

He put her in, called Felix and presented him, closed the door, watched them drive away, and never thought, until long afterward, that he was the direct means of first bringing Katharine Tresham under the roof of Morton House.

CHAPTER XI.

AT MORTON HOUSE.

The whole of that afternoon, which looked so bright to the gay loiterers beside the pond, Mrs. Gordon had spent in the silence and shadow of the Morton-House library, deep in dusty and tedious accounts which had been submitted to her inspection by Mr. Shields, the agent of the Morton estate. It was not a pleasant occupation, but it was one to which she had courageously set herself immediately on her arrival, and in which she had not flagged even when the terribly-involved condition of affairs had been brought plainly to her perception. Debt, difficulty, mortgage, ruinous sacrifice! That was the sum-total of the heritage to which she had returned; and, what the old agent unhesitatingly called "the most tangled business in the country," was what she took in her woman's hands to attempt to make straight again. She succeeded better than might have been expected—succeeded sufficiently to rouse Mr. Shields's honest admiration, and make him tell Lawyer Worruck that he had never seen such business capacity in any woman before. But it was weary work at all times, and never more weary than on this afternoon. So weary that, when she came to the end of a long column of figures, she dropped her pen with a tired sigh, and, leaning her head against the back of her chair, sat motionless for some time.

On this repose, however, Babette broke in suddenly and unceremoniously, just as the last rays of the setting sun flashed a gleam of vivid light across the pale, tired face.

"Madame, pardonnez-moi," she began, hurriedly, as her mistress's eyes opened wide in somewhat haughty astonishment. "But madame always said that if any thing happened to M'sieur Felix, she must be disturbed, and I dared not—"

"Felix!" cried the mother, with a sudden start of alarm. "Felix! Is any thing the matter with him?"

"Indeed, madame, it was not my fault; but that stupid—"

"Babette! *Is* any thing the matter?"

"Non, madame, non," cried the maid, startled by the tone of her mistress's voice. "M'sieur Felix is all safe—but that stupid Harrison has let in a lady."

Mrs. Gordon gave a deep sigh of relief.

"You frightened me very much," she said, rebukingly. "You should not talk so much at random. What has Felix to do with a lady? He is at the pond with Mr. Annesley."

"But, madame, the lady has brought him home."

"The lady! You must be mistaken."

"Indeed, no, madame. I saw them; and that stupid—"

"Then it is Mrs. Annesley?"

Babette shook her head. "*C'est une demoiselle*," she said decidedly. "I saw her myself, madame; and M'sieur Felix—"

"Hold your tongue!" cried a shrill, indignant voice at the door. And the next moment, "M'sieur Felix" himself had rushed into the room, and thrown his arms round his mother.

"Mamma, don't listen to her! *I'll* tell you all about it—but promise first you won't be angry."

"That depends on whether there is good cause for being angry," said his mother, pushing back the bright curls from the glowing face, and looking anxiously into it. "But I can promise not to be very much displeased if you will tell me the exact truth."

"That's what I mean to do, mamma. But kiss me first, and—go away!" he added, with a sudden stamp at Babette.

The Frenchwoman looked unutterable things at him, tossed her head, and held her ground firmly, until Mrs. Gordon herself bade her go.

"But the lady, madame?"

"I will see her in a minute—you need not wait."

Babette gave another glance at Felix, and then retired, with offended dignity rustling in every garment. Her only solace was to go and rate Harrison, and this she immediately proceeded to do.

Katharine, meanwhile, left alone in the large empty drawing-room, began to revolve the awkwardness of her position. She was sorry now that she had acceded to Mr. Warwick's request. It seemed so much like forcing an entrance into Morton House. As for mediation or explanation —Felix's impetuosity had spared her all question of that. Was nobody ever coming? Would it be very wrong to go away without having seen the lady of the house? Perhaps, after all, that might be best. She would wait ten minutes longer, and, if by that time Mrs. Gordon had not made her appearance, why—she would go. She had hardly arrived at this determination, when the door opened, and a pale, stately woman stood on the threshold.

Katharine rose, but before she could utter one of the words of apology trembling on her tongue, Mrs. Gordon crossed the floor, and extended her hand with a warm and cordial gesture.

"Miss Tresham, I owe you many thanks. It was kind of you to take charge of my wilful boy. Pray forgive me that I have kept you waiting; but he has been giving me an account of his adventure."

This, or something like it, was what she said; but no words can embody the gracious and exquisite charm of manner which at once set Katharine at ease—at once made her feel that, instead of being an intruder, she was a welcome guest. A few words told why the duty had devolved upon herself—a few more gave the leading facts of the matter; after which, she rose to take her departure. But this Mrs. Gordon would not permit.

"You are cold, and you must be tired," she said. "It is a point of honor with Morton House that no guest has ever left its door in either of those conditions. This room is my aversion, it is so cheerless. Let me take you to my sitting-room."

"You are very kind," said Katharine, overcome with wonder; "but the carriage is waiting for me, and—"

"If you will allow me, I will have it dismissed, and take the responsibility of sending you home."

"I am afraid Mrs. Marks will be uneasy."

"I am sure she will be able to spare you," said the lady, with a slight smile. "Come, Miss Tresham, I am not accustomed to pressing hospitality; but in this instance I really cannot consent to let you go. Shall I put my request on another ground? Shall I tell you that I am lonely this evening, and that a strange face is a great relief to me? I have not felt this desire for companionship before in many a long day Will you have the heart to disappoint it now?"

"No," said Katharine, with her frank, bright smile. "If my society can gratify your desire, I shall be very glad to stay. But—"

"But I regard the matter as settled," said Mrs. Gordon. Then, after ringing the bell, and sending an order of dismissal to the waiting carriage, she led the way across a large, cold hall, into one of the most thoroughly-charming rooms, Katharine thought, she had ever seen.

A first glance only gave the impression of rich color and luxurious comfort. It was some time before the eye recognized the different elements that went to make up such an attractive whole —the heavy curtains, the velvet carpet, the deep, inviting chairs and couches, the many appointments where taste of the most rare and judicious kind had presided. When Katharine entered, it was empty, but a faint fragrance of flowers came over her as the door opened, and a soft moonlight seemed to fill the room—the glow of two large lamps being toned by tinted shades. Dusk had fallen by this time; and the lamp-light and ruddy firelight made a pleasant contrast to the cold, frosty night gathering outside the open hall-door, and melting into indistinctness the outlines of the rolling hills.

"Oh, what a beautiful room!" cried Katharine, so involuntarily that Mrs. Gordon smiled.

"I am glad you like it," she said. "It is the only room I have refurnished; but I cannot endure the stiff old-fashioned furniture which reigns paramount in the rest of the house. Excepting my cousin, Mr. Annesley, you are the only person who has been admitted here."

"It is beautiful!" Katharine repeated, as she sat down by the glowing fire, sunning herself like a tropical flower in its heat. "I have never seen any thing more luxurious—and I love luxury."

Mrs. Gordon smiled again, perhaps at this candid confession, perhaps at the undisguised enjoyment which prompted it. Then she drew forward a large chair, and seating herself leaned back in its soft depths. The firelight played quiveringly over her face, and Katharine had time to mark every furrow which marred its beauty before Mrs. Gordon spoke again. At last she turned to look at the young girl, and said, rather abruptly:

"Miss Tresham, my desire to keep you was not entirely without reason. I have heard Morton Annesley speak of you very often, and I was sure of one thing—either that I must like you, or that he exaggerated as even a lover has no right to exaggerate."

Katharine started. This was plain speaking, indeed. She started, and, if she also blushed, it might have been surprise as much as any thing else that caused the emotion.

"Excuse me," said Mrs. Gordon, who noticed both the start and the blush. "Perhaps I have not paid sufficient regard to the proprieties of expression; but when one grows a little old, they seem so useless. Why should we hesitate to call a thing by its right name?"

"Why, indeed," answered Katharine, quickly, "if it be a right name?"

"We won't argue that point," said Mrs. Gordon, with a slight laugh. "I don't think a lover's tale is worth telling, excepting by himself. And here comes tea."

The door opened as she spoke, and Harrison brought in a tray. No other servant appeared; but in a few minutes—without even so much noise as the rattling of a plate—a small round table stood between the two ladies, bearing a glittering equipage.

"Are you still English enough to prefer tea, Miss Tresham, or will you let Harrison give you a cup of coffee?" asked Mrs. Gordon, as she poured out a cup of the first, which was strong enough and black enough to have satisfied even De Quincey. "For my part, I always take this. Will you join me?"

"Not since you have given me my choice," said Katharine, with a smile. "I have never yet learned to endure tea—though I have tried heroically, in compliment to other people's taste."

"Not people here, surely?"

"Oh, no. Everybody here drinks coffee. I meant the people in England."

"And yet you are an Englishwoman?"

"No; I am a West-Indian—and very proud of it. I love my dear island, with its brilliant skies and tropical palms, as much as I hate the mists and fogs of England."

"You have been in England, then?"

Katharine shrugged her shoulders ruefully.

"To my cost, yes."

"In what part? I ask because I am very familiar with it, and perhaps you saw the country to disadvantage."

"I was in the north, near the Scottish border. I saw the Scottish shore from my window every time the fog lifted, and did not enjoy it nearly as much as I should have done if I could have stopped shivering even for one day."

"But was there no summer while you were there?"

"There was a time they called summer—a time when the trees had leaves, and the sun shone with tolerable brightness. But our winter-days in Porto Rico are much more balmy."

"Porto Rico! But I thought—that is—"

"You thought I was a British West-Indian. Well, so I am. I was born in Jamaica; but I scarcely remember it at all. When I was very young, my aunt moved to Porto Rico, and took me with her. We lived there entirely, and I never was in England until I went to an old friend of hers, who obtained a situation as governess at Donthorne Place for me. It was a very—"

She stopped—uncontrollable surprise forcing her to do so. Mrs. Gordon had suddenly turned so pale that even the dim light failed to conceal it, and her hand shook until she was obliged to put down untasted a cup of tea which she had been in the act of raising to her lips. There was a moment's silence; then she looked up, white as a sheet, but forcing herself into a sort of rigid calm.

"Pardon me, Miss Tresham; and pray don't look so much alarmed. It is only an old pain that came back to me just then. My nerves are shattered, and I show it—that is all.—Harrison, you will find my case on the side-table there. Give me two spoonfuls of the bottle on the right as you open it."

Harrison obeyed. Mrs. Gordon drank eagerly the dark liquid which he brought her in a slender wineglass; and a faint, subtile odor rushed over Katharine, which told her at once what the draught had been. After that she needed one explanation the less for the lines on her hostess's face.

It was the latter who, after a short silence, spoke first—quietly, but with a certain suppressed anxiety which Katharine's ear was quick to detect.

"You surprised me very much by the mention of Donthorne Place, Miss Tresham. I was once in the neighborhood, and I remember it quite well. How long were you there?"

"A year," answered Katharine, concisely, having her own reasons for reticence on the subject; "a year—one of the most disagreeable of my life, and one that I would not live over again to win a crown. I cannot bear to talk of it, and, of course, it does not interest you."

"On the contrary, if you will pardon me, it interests me very much. Do you"—she leaned forward with an eagerness which startled Katharine—"do you ever hear from them—the Donthornes?"

"Never. To judge by their unconsciousness of my existence when I lived in their house, I should say that they would not even remember my name now."

"From no friends—no one that you left in the neighborhood?"

Katharine drew back. She was not only surprised; but she looked—even her preoccupied questioner noticed that—as if awakened to some sudden fear.

"No," she said, slowly; "I have no friends—there or elsewhere. I had not even an acquaintance in the neighborhood. No one ever writes to me. Why do you ask?"

"I might truly answer, because I am very uncivil," replied Mrs. Gordon. "Solitude fosters many bad habits, and I must beg you to excuse me on that score. I will not offend in the same way again. Indeed, there is nothing I so much detest as curiosity.—Harrison, you may take the tray; we have finished."

Harrison and the tray made an exit as noiseless as their entrance, and, after the door had closed, Mrs. Gordon was again the first to speak—very pleasantly and graciously.

"Miss Tresham, I see that coincidences have left us no option but to think that we are meant to be friends; and one must never gainsay Fate, you know. Do you think you have Christian charity enough to come to see me sometimes, without exacting the ceremony of visits in return? I am such a recluse that I cannot think of leaving my cell to encounter daylight."

Katharine looked up with an astonishment which showed itself in every line of her face. She could scarcely believe that these cordial words of invitation were addressed to herself by the same lips that had declined the visits of all the old hereditary friends who had a right to enter Morton House. The cordiality was in Mrs. Gordon's eyes as well as in Mrs. Gordon's tones, however. So, after a short pause, she answered, with the frank grace that all her life had won for her so much liking:

"Indeed, you are very kind, and I shall be very glad to come. I have few acquaintances—none who consider my society of any importance; so it would be strange if I were not flattered by your invitation. It will be a great pleasure to me to see you again when I can. But my time is not my own, you know."

"I cannot help forgetting that," said Mrs. Gordon, smiling—"you seem so little like a governess. What a disagreeable life you must find it, especially in your present situation!"

"No; very much the reverse," said Katharine, quickly. "Mr. and Mrs. Marks are both kind to me; and I shall never forget how generously they took me into their service when I was an entire stranger to them."

"It was like Bessie Warwick," said Mrs. Gordon, quietly. "I remember her in the old time as very warm-hearted and very impulsive, but rather silly. She was pretty, but so decidedly underbred that nobody wondered when she married much beneath her."

"She seems to have found her right place in the world, however."

"Most women do, or else have sufficient sense to seem as if they do. It is seldom you find one weak enough, or strong enough, to beat against the bars. Then, what are we most inclined to do—pity or scorn her? Either, God knows, is hard enough to bear." She paused a moment, then changed the subject abruptly. "Do you see much of John Warwick? Is he often at his sister's house?"

"He lives there," Katharine answered; "and yet I cannot say that I see much of him. He is absorbed in his profession, and seems to take very little pleasure in society."

"But you like him—do you not?"

"I like him extremely. He is very quiet; but no one could live under the same roof with him and fail to see that he is one of the most thorough gentlemen, as well as one of the kindest of men. I have heard that he can be very hard sometimes; but I can scarcely believe it, when I remember how gentle he is to his sister and the children."

Mrs. Gordon looked at her with a smile. "You are his friend, I perceive," she said.

"I ought to be," the girl answered, quickly, with the remembrance of what he had said to her that afternoon stirring warmly at her heart. "Ingratitude has never been one of my many faults."

"I hoped he would have married long before this," said the other, with a wistful light in her eyes, that Katharine was not slow to interpret. "I do not know any one whom I should better like to see happy—any one whom I would sooner exert myself to help along the road to happiness."

"Mr. Warwick is not unhappy, I am sure," said Katharine, almost resentfully. "He is not one of the men who have no life if they have no fireside. I think a wife would decidedly bore him. He has his clients and his law-books—that is all he wants. No one need pity him for imaginary loneliness."

Mrs. Gordon unclosed her lips, as if to reply; but, before she could do so, the door opened, and Harrison startled them by the announcement that Mr. Warwick had come for Miss Tresham.

Katharine started up at once, full of self-reproach.

"How very inconsiderate of me to have stayed!" she cried, eagerly. "I might have known they would be uneasy; and it is such a long walk to have given Mr. Warwick! How very, very inconsiderate of me!"

She repeated the last expression several times, for her vexation was not least in the thought that she had forced upon Mr. Warwick the very thing he wished to avoid, and brought him to the very house he least desired to enter.

"Don't look so distressed and penitent," said Mrs. Gordon. "It was my fault, not yours; and I am sure he will not mind the walk, especially as he need not repeat it.—Harrison, order the carriage, and show Mr. Warwick in here."

"No! no!" cried Katharine, hastily. "He has had so much trouble about me, pray let me go to him at once, and—and not keep him waiting. I shall not mind the walk at all."

She was drawing her wrappings around her as she spoke, and evidently meant to go at once, if Mrs. Gordon had not interfered very decidedly.

"I will not hear of such a thing," she said. "You must wait for the carriage, and I must send for Mr. Warwick.—Harrison, show him in at once."

Evidently, Mrs. Gordon had been accustomed to the habit of command. Her quiet tones had so much authority in them that Katharine found herself yielding without a word. She sank into her seat, and the next minute Mr. Warwick entered the room.

Whatever he felt, he certainly showed nothing beyond gentlemanly self-possession, as he came forward, meeting Mrs. Gordon's cordially-extended hand with his own, and answering her words of welcome so easily that Katharine felt relieved. What she expected, she could not have told; but certainly something unlike this. Not any faltering, or trembling, or turning pale—she knew the grave, reserved lawyer too well to fear that—but at least some token that his pulses were beating as fast as they surely must beat in presence of the woman who, for twenty-five years (if his sister spoke truth), had stood between him and all thought of other women—some token different from the quiet presence of every day, from the cool glance that saw so much, and the terse speech that said so little—yet they were all there, and as much unchanged as if Pauline Morton's eyes were not looking into his face from the grave of the past.

Presently he crossed over to Katharine and stopped at once the words of penitence with which she was prepared to greet him.

"No," he said, "you must not think any thing of the kind. I came because I wanted to—and a little because Bessie has been uneasy. You know how highly developed her nervous system is. Well, she has been arranging the programme of a very tragic entertainment—Mr. Annesley's horses running away, and leaving you senseless and bleeding in some wayside ditch."

"I am very sorry," said Katharine, too much disturbed to laugh. "It is very kind of Mrs. Marks to take the trouble to be uneasy about me—I am very sorry. I ought to have thought, Mr. Warwick; and then you need not have had all this trouble."

"I told you a minute ago that it was no trouble," he said, a little shortly. And, as Mrs. Gordon advanced, he turned and began speaking about Felix.

"He is quite the hero of the hour," he said. "In fact, he has taken Tallahoma so entirely by storm, that I hope, for the sake of example, you will not let him enter the town to-morrow—he would certainly receive a popular ovation."

"He is not likely to leave the grounds of the House for some time to come," answered his mother, gravely. "I have had a lesson by which I shall profit. Felix's management has been a point at issue between Morton and myself, and the occurrence of this afternoon has showed me that I am right and he is wrong."

"May I not intercede on the side of mercy?" said Mr. Warwick, half jestingly, half in earnest. "You will not think me presumptuous, I am sure, when I tell you that nothing so much shames, or so soon cures untrustworthiness—even the slight, childish form of it which Felix showed this afternoon—as the sense of being trusted."

She looked up at him, with a deep flush on her pale cheeks, and a sudden light in her eyes, that startled both Katharine and himself.

"You speak of what you know," she said, in a low voice. "You speak of those in whom the sense of honor, and the power of being shamed, is born. But you don't speak of, you don't know, the blood that child has in his veins. I know—and, believe me, I can best deal with it."

"Excuse me," he said, hastily. "I did not mean—"

She interrupted him. "Any thing but kindness, I know—only you don't understand. Now tell me if you have heard from Morton. I sent to inquire, and the answer was very satisfactory—but I fear he may have sent it merely to quiet my uneasiness."

"Hardly. No doubt he is well by this time, and probably will make his appearance to answer for himself to-morrow.—Miss Tresham, I am at your service whenever you feel inclined for the walk before us."

"The carriage—" began Mrs. Gordon.

But, at that moment, Harrison once more opened the door, and announced that the carriage was waiting.

"You will come to see me, will you not?" asked the lady, as Katharine bade her good-night. "I don't like to see you go, without an assurance that you will return."

"I will certainly come," said Katharine, with a smile even more bright than usual.

After a few words they took leave, and Miss Tresham found herself rolling rapidly along the road to Tallahoma, and assuring Mr. Warwick that she felt much less tired than excited by her unusual adventures.

CHAPTER XII.

THE TUG OF WAR.

The morning after his escape from drowning, Morton Annesley woke with that uncomfortable weight on his mind—that sense of something disagreeable, either past or impending—with which every one is familiar who has ever sought sleep rather as a refuge from tormenting thought, than as that "sweet restorer" which Nature intended it should be.

For the space of several minutes he could not think what had occurred; then suddenly a throng of recollections rushed over him; he recalled every thing that had happened. He remembered the adventure at the pond, and the scene that followed his rescue; he remembered the looks and tones of the people who had addressed him; and, above all, he remembered the expression of Katharine Tresham's eyes, when, for one brief second, he glanced up into them! With a sharp, impatient exclamation, he sprang up and began to dress. Some reminiscences prick worse than needles, and to him there could scarcely have been a more disagreeable reminiscence than this. Not even Katharine's eyes could take the sting out of it! There was such a mock heroism about the whole affair, that he fairly ground his teeth over it. Some people would have enjoyed the *éclat* thus conferred upon them, while others, recognizing the ludicrous aspect of the adventure, would have laughed it off with that genial good-nature which it is the best policy in the world to affect, if it be not really possessed. But Morton, poor fellow, did not possess, and could not affect it. Which aspect of the matter—the heroic or the ridiculous—was most distasteful to him, it would be hard to say, or against which he chafed most impatiently. It provoked him to think how Lagrange had gossipped and would yet gossip over the occurrence; and it is to be feared that, in his irritation, he was not so lenient in his feelings toward Felix, as Felix's quixotic protector ought to have been. But there was a good deal of disappointment mingled with this irritation. He had taken so much interest in the boy, he had striven so hard to make him comprehend the moral obligation of a trust, and the chivalric standard of honor, that he was chilled and disappointed by his failure; and felt, if the truth must be told, not a little out of patience with the ungrateful wilfulness which had placed him in his present position. What this position was with regard to Miss Tresham, he had only a faint idea. He knew that he had said something—that he had committed himself in some way—out there beside the pond, before all those people (in his own mind, he was ungrateful enough to call them those confounded people); but what it was he did not know, and certainly had no intention of inquiring. Only it made one thing certain—he could not hesitate any longer. The tug of war—did any misgiving of his heart tell him what a tug it would be?—must come with his mother, and, one way or another, his fate must be decided as only Katharine could decide it.

With his mind full of these thoughts he went down-stairs, across the hall, and out of the open front-door. The morning was very bright, for the atmosphere had capriciously changed; the thermometer had risen from its unwonted depression of the few preceding days, and the air that greeted him was soft, as if the dead Indian summer had returned, or the spring was about to burst. The sunshine was pouring in a dazzling flood over the lawn and piazzas; the gravelled sweep before the house sparkled as if its stones had all been precious gems; the evergreens, dotted about in every direction, seemed to have put on a brighter emerald hue; and a bird that was perched on a magnolia near by, was pouring forth its whole heart in glad rejoicing that the cold was over and gone; that the blue skies, and the soft air, and the golden sunshine, had returned. We are all more or less susceptible to such influences as these; and Annesley, as it chanced, was keenly alive to them. At the first sight of the bright outer world, and the first note of that trilling lay, his depression suddenly vanished, and his spirits rose like mercury. Almost unconsciously he caught up the notes of the little feathered songster, and, as he went down the steps and turned toward the stables, he was whistling to himself almost gayly.

He found Mr. French talking to the head groom, while one or two subordinate stablemen were rubbing down a large, black horse, that stood patiently undergoing the operation.

"Good-morning, Frank," said Annesley, coming up. "What brings you out so early? Nothing the matter with the Captain, I hope?"

"I am sorry to say there is something the matter with his shoulder," said Mr. French, looking round. "He fell lame while I was riding home, yesterday afternoon. By-the-way, how do you feel after your ducking?"

"I am well, of course," said Morton, a little ungraciously, resuming his usual manner as he went on: "I am concerned about the Captain.—Lead him out there, Jim, and let me see how he walks."

The Captain was led out, and the Captain walked very badly. Some accident had plainly befallen his right shoulder; and the two gentlemen were soon in deep discussion and examination, aided by Isaac the groom, and John the coachman. Various remedies were suggested, and one or two were tried. It was some time before the poor Captain was remanded to his stall, and the two gentlemen bethought themselves of breakfast. "You can take him to the stable, Isaac," said Mr. French, at last. "I'll be out again after breakfast and look at him.—Morton, are you coming?"

Morton said "Yes," rather carelessly; and they turned into a broad walk which led to the house. With the Captain dismissed from his mind, Mr. French remembered something he wished—or, rather, had promised—to say to his brother-in-law. "A man's opinion always has so much weight with a man," his wife had remarked to him. "You must be sure and tell Morton what you think of this nonsense." Mr. French had promised that he would; but now he began to wish that he had not been so rash. Suppose Morton were to be offended? "Hang it!" thought the other, candidly, "I should be offended myself if anybody were to meddle in my private affairs. I wish I had not promised Adela. It is none of my business if he chooses to make a fool of himself." Then he cleared his throat and looked at the abstracted face beside him.

"Are you sure you don't feel any the worse for your exploit yesterday?" he asked, by way of introduction to what he meant to say. "I should think you would, Morton."

"Why the deuce should I?" asked Morton, pettishly. "I'm neither a child nor a woman. Confound the exploit, Frank! can't you let it alone?"

"Oh, of course," said Mr. French, a little surprised. "I didn't know you were sensitive about it. I'm sure it made you rather a hero—at least in the eyes of the ladies. Some of them were exceedingly interested, I can tell you." Then, after a pause—"Morton, I suppose you know what you're about, but don't you think you may be going a little too far with—with one of them?"

"With one of them!" repeated Morton, giving a start. "Whom do you mean?" he asked, more quietly than his companion had expected. "I don't understand."

"I mean that Miss Tresham who lives in Tallahoma, and is a teacher, or something of the sort," answered Mr. French, who, as he had once begun, was determined to blunder through. "Of course, you know your own affairs best, and I hope you won't think me interfering; but I thought I would give you a hint. Young women's heads are so easily turned, and old women's tongues are so confoundedly long, that one is obliged to be careful."

"I am much obliged to you," said Annesley, in a tone which contradicted the words, for he was more angry than he would have liked to confess; "but I believe I can manage my own affairs—and I prefer to do so."

"I beg your pardon," said Mr. French, beginning to be a little offended in turn. "I didn't mean to be impertinent. I'm an older man than you are, and I thought I would give you a little friendly advice. It's a devilish disagreeable thing to be talked about as people *will* talk in these country places; and of course I never supposed you were in earnest about the girl.

I'm confident, I need not tell you, Morton, that such a thing would nearly kill your mother."

"You must allow me to be the best judge of that," said Morton, stiffly. And there the conversation ended.

Mr. French shrugged his shoulders, and thought to himself that he had known how it would be, but that at least he could tell Adela he had done his best; while Morton walked on, with his breast fairly in a flame. So he had made such a fool of himself as that! He had betrayed every thing so plainly that his brother-in-law felt obliged to come and force his advice upon him! Indeed, it was time that he spoke, if only for Katharine's sake, since he had committed himself, and involved her to such an extent as this. Poor Morton! In his single-minded sincerity, it never occurred to him that Mr. French had been prompted to the unusual character which he had assumed. He took it simply as the consequence of his own unguarded conduct; and it confirmed rather than shook his resolution. It would have gone hard with Adela if she could have known the result of her husband's interference.

Breakfast passed off quietly, but rather silently. Adela did not make her appearance, and, although the three others talked at intervals, there was a sense of constraint hanging over them, and they did not remain very long at table. Mr. French was the first person to leave the room, taking out his cigar-case as he did so. Then Morton rose and walked round to his mother.

"Will you come to the library?" he asked. "I have something to say to you."

She looked up at him, and, in a moment divining his purpose, her heart sank. But she had sufficient presence of mind to smile into the grave, earnest eyes regarding her.

"Certainly I will come," she answered, "but I must first see Adela, and give orders about dinner—that is, if you are not in a hurry."

"I am not at all in a hurry," he replied. "If you will come when you are at leisure, that will do. You will find me in the library," he added, as he took up a paper and left the room.

He went to the library, but he soon found that he could not read. It is one thing to hold a paper open before the eyes, and quite another to pay intelligent heed to its contents. Morton did the first diligently; but, with all his efforts, he could not achieve the second. He dreaded the interview with his mother so much that he eagerly desired it to be over; and he caught himself listening to every footstep in the hall outside the door, hoping it might be hers. At last he threw down the paper, and, rising, walked restlessly across the floor.

There was not a pleasanter room at Annesdale than this library, nor one that he liked better; but to-day it might have been an irksome cage, to judge by his impatient movements to and fro. From the fireplace to the windows, and from the windows to the fireplace, he paced, until finally he paused before the latter, and, leaning one arm on the mantel, gazed steadily at an engraving which hung above it—a "St. Cecilia" he had brought from Dresden. Something in the outline of the uplifted face reminded him of Katharine. It was not so much a resemblance as the suggestion of a resemblance. But it had struck him often before, and now it brought her face vividly to his mind. By some strange perversity of association, it also brought to his recollection that day when she sang the "Adelaide" for him, when he had chanced upon the open letter, and when her strange conduct had so chilled and repulsed him.

He was still thinking of these things, and his face looked unusually grave and troubled, when the door opened and his mother entered. She crossed the room, and, as he did not turn, she laid her hand on his arm.

"You wished to speak to me, Morton?" she said. "Here I am."

"My dear mother, thank you," he answered, turning quickly. "I did not hear you come in—how quiet you are!"

"I was afraid you would be tired of waiting for me," she said, sitting down in a deep arm-chair. "Adela is quite unwell, and I stayed with her some time. I thought that, if you wanted to see me about any thing of importance, you would have told me so."

"I wanted to see you about my own affairs," said Morton, plunging headlong into the subject he now felt tempted to avoid. "I want to ask your advice about a very important matter—to me at least," he went on, faintly smiling "Mother, I have lately thought of marrying."

The room suddenly went round and grew black before Mrs. Annesley's eyes. She extended her hand almost unconsciously, and clutched the corner of a table near by to steady herself. Her worst fears were realized; but she had sufficient self-control to look up quietly, and say—

"Well?"

"Well," he answered, knowing that the worst could not be too quickly told, "I fear that I am going to disappoint you. I fear that the woman I love, the woman I wish to marry, is not the woman whom you would have chosen for me. But in this matter, no human being, not even the nearest and dearest, can judge for us," he said, gently taking the hand which she had laid on the table. "We can only judge for ourselves, and abide by our choice through good or through ill. Mother, will you not give your sanction to my choice?"

She suffered her hand to remain in his; but her eyes looked cold, and her voice sounded hard when she asked—

"What is her name?"

"Her name," he answered, "is Katharine Tresham. My dear mother," he continued, eagerly, "don't judge her by her surroundings, don't think of the position in which Fortune has placed her. Only judge, only think of her as you will see and love her for herself, as you will—"

He was stopped by a gesture from his mother, as she drew back her hand.

"Go!" she said, bitterly. "I have heard enough. If you had the heart to come and stab me like this, you will not heed any thing I can say to you. Go! Only remember that, if you do degrade yourself in this way, you will cut yourself off from me forever. I will never receive that woman as my daughter; I will never, as long as I live, suffer her to cross the threshold of this house!"

"Mother!"

It was a cry of astonished, grieved reproach, which at any other time would have gone to her heart; but she had now so entirely lost command of herself, and of the emotion which seemed suffocating her, that it rather provoked than allayed her anger. She had feared and in a measure anticipated this for a long time; but it did not make the disappointment any less poignant when it came—it did not teach her any better how to bear it.

"Mother," said Morton, gravely, "you cannot be yourself—you cannot be in earnest when you utter such words as these."

"Go!" she repeated, once more, in a voice choked with tears.

And, as there was nothing else to be done, he walked sadly across the floor, and stood silently at one of the windows, waiting for what would come next—waiting to see whether his mother would recall him, or whether she would leave the room with only those last bitter words.

A long time passed—an hour it seemed to the young man, and it was in reality many minutes—before any sound broke the stillness of the room. Then Mrs. Annesley said:

"Morton!"

He came to her side.

"I am here," he answered, gravely but gently.

She lifted a face that was white even to the lips, and held out her hand.

"My son," she said, "forgive me. I did not mean to pain you; but the shock was so sudden, and very hard to bear."

"My mother, my dearest mother!" he said.

It was all that he did say, but he bent down and kissed the hand she gave him, and peace—or at least a semblance of it—was once more established. After a while it was Mrs. Annesley who spoke first.

"Morton," she said, "have you considered this well?"

"I have considered it well," he answered.

"Your mind is made up?"

"My mind is entirely made up."

"You are determined to inflict this distress upon me, and to ruin your own life by such a misalliance?"

"I am determined to ask Miss Tresham to be my wife," said the young man, looking pale but unshaken. "I would have asked her long ago if it had not been that I hesitated on your account. But now it is not possible for me to hesitate longer."

"Do you mean that you have committed yourself?" she asked, hastily.

"In absolute words—no. Dear mother, don't pain me by combating my resolution," he said, with his eyes full of appeal. "Only tell me that, if she consents to marry me, you will welcome and try to love her."

"Tell me one thing, Morton," said Mrs. Annesley—"what do you know of this woman whom you ask me to receive as your wife? When a man marries he should know all the previous history and all the connections of the woman he chooses. Tell me, my son, what do you know of hers?"

She touched his cause in its weakest point, and he knew it. The thoughts he had been revolving when she entered the room — the thoughts that had sealed his lips ever since the day he saw Katharine last—rushed upon him suddenly with overwhelming force, and for several minutes he could not reply. Then the truth came in one word—

"Nothing."

"Nothing!" his mother echoed, in a tone of grieved astonishment. "Nothing, Morton? And yet you ask me to welcome her as a daughter? My son, my dear son, what can you be thinking of? Where is your sense of what is due to yourself and to your name?"

"I know nothing about her," he said, "but I can trust her. She is too pure and noble ever to have done any thing that she need blush for."

"But, good Heavens! her relations, her friends—what may they not be?"

"I do not think she has any. I have never heard her speak of them."

"And you think that a good sign? Oh, Morton, Morton!"

"It is not a bad sign, mother," said Morton, beginning to look a little less patient. "Many a girl is friendless, many a girl is obliged to earn her bread as Miss Tresham is doing. It would be cruel to doubt her because Fate has dealt hardly with her. It is true that she has never mentioned her past history or her family circumstances to me; but I have never been in a position to receive such a confidence."

"And you will ask her to marry you without knowing more than this?"

"I should be a cur, not a gentleman, if I inquired into her affairs before asking her."

"Oh, my son, what madness!"

"Mother dear, be patient with me," he said, gently. "Don't you see—can't you tell how hard I am trying to do right? If I had only myself to consider," he went on, walking again from the fireplace to the window, and from the window to the fireplace, "I would sacrifice my wishes to yours. But—but I am afraid it is too late as far as she is concerned."

"You put her before me, then?"

"I put my honor before every thing."

"Your honor should lead you just the other way," she said, lapsing from self-restraint into anger again. "A gentleman's first duty is to his name. What will you be doing with yours when you marry thus?"

"I will not be degrading it," answered he, firmly. "Mother, you do not know Katharine Tresham. If you did know her—if you would know her—you could never speak of her in this manner."

"She has taken you from me, Morton. She has steeled your heart against all my entreaties; she has made you forget what is due to yourself—how can I do other than hate her? How can I stand by silently and see you marry an adventuress?"

"Mother!"

The exclamation was so stern that for a moment Mrs. Anneslev shrank. But, before she could speak, Morton gave a great gulp, and hurried on:

"Forgive me, but this had better end. There is no good in prolonging a useless discussion, and I see now that this *is* useless. I only provoke you, and am pained myself. So I will go. Don't forget that I am very sorry to have grieved you, and, if possible, still more sorry to act against your wishes for the first time in my life."

She let him go—as far as the door; but, when his hand was on the knob, her voice called him back. He returned at once, and, rising, she met him half-way.

"My son, forgive *me*," she said. "You have never in your life before grieved or disappointed me; you have often given up your will to mine; you have never once failed in respect or duty to me. It is only just, therefore, that my turn for sacrifice should come. I never thought it would be so hard; I never thought you would desire to throw away your happiness in this way. But, as you will do it—why, take my consent, and God bless you!"

The young man caught her in his arms with something that was almost a sob.

"Mother, my dear, kind mother!" he said. "You don't know how much I longed to hear those words. Thank God, they have come at last!"

He thought the tug of war was over; but, as he clasped his mother in his arms, it would have been strange if he could have known—if he could even faintly have imagined—how completely she had out-witted him, and how the worst struggle was yet to come!

CHAPTER XIII.

MISS TRESHAM ASKS ADVICE.

Two weeks went by very quietly, and brought Miss Tresham's happy scholars to the beginning of their Christmas-holidays.

"Do your lessons well to-day, children," she said, as she entered the school-room on a certain Friday morning, and found them gathering about the blazing fire. "This is the last of school until after New-Year."

They all looked up delighted.

"To-day! And Christmas not till Thursday? Oh, Miss Tresham, that's so good of you!"

"Why, we'll have two long weeks! Thank you, ma'am, so much."

"Don't thank me," said the governess, with a smile. "I should have kept you hard at work till Christmas-Eve. Your mother told me to dismiss school to-day, and that it will not be resumed till the Monday after New-Year. So, you see, you have two good weeks."

"Oh, haven't we!"

"Well, show your gratitude by giving me no trouble to-day. I will hear the geography first."

For the next fifteen minutes they were all busy locating capitals, settling boundaries, and describing countries. The children were so animated by the holiday prospect before them that they did remarkably well; and the class was about to be dismissed, when the door opened without any preparatory knock, and, instead of a servant, Mrs. Marks entered, with every sign of surprise and discomposure in her manner.

"Good Gracious, Miss Katharine, what's to be done! To think of such a thing just now of all times, and me deep in the mince-meat!"

Katharine looked up in astonishment. It was not often that Mrs. Marks used such a tone of supreme vexation, or appeared so red and worried—not often that she gave a glance so full of chagrin at her befloured dress and large domestic apron.

"What on earth is to be done?" she repeated, as Katharine's eyes met her own. "I never was so taken by surprise in all my life! To think of *her*—"

"What is the matter? Who is it?" asked the young governess. "I don't understand."

She understood the next moment, when Mrs. Marks pushed two cards across the table toward her—two cards exactly alike in appearance, and both bearing the same name:

Mrs. Annesley.

Katharine was too well bred to show exactly how much surprise she really felt. So, after one irrepressible exclamation, she hurried off at once into sympathy.

"Indeed, dear Mrs. Marks, this is very inconvenient! I hardly wonder you are vexed. Wouldn't it be possible to excuse yourself?"

"Excuse myself—to Mrs. Annesley!" Evidently that was not to be thought of.

"Well," said Katharine, with quite a practical inquiry, "why don't you go and dress? It will not take you many minutes to smooth your hair and put on your black silk. Shall I help you?"

"You! Why, I came to tell you that you must go down at once."

Was Mrs. Marks distracted? Katharine certainly thought so, as she drew back and gazed at her in sheer amazement.

"I go down to see Mrs. Annesley! Mrs. Marks, what can you be thinking of?"

"How are you going to help yourself?" demanded Mrs. Marks, impatiently. "She came to see you just as much as she did to see me—indeed a great deal more, I expect, if the truth was known. Tom said that she gave him one of those cards for Miss Tresham."

"He must have been mistaken."

"How could he be?"

"I don't know," answered Katharine; "but he must have been."

"My dear," cried Mrs. Marks, almost angrily, "what is the use of this? If you don't believe Tom, I can tell you that I listened through a crack of the pantry door, and that I heard Mrs. Annesley ask for you. Of course she came to see you; and of course you must go down as soon as you have dressed. Come—quick!"

She laid her hand on Katharine's arm and strove to lead her forward; but the girl drew back with a decided motion.

"No," she said. "If I go down at all—if you are sure she asked for me—I will go down exactly as I am."

Mrs. Marks looked aghast.

"In that old dress! Oh, my dear, consider how important it is that you should make a good impression. Mrs. Annesley is so elegant—you have no idea! What would Mr.—"

A glance from Katharine stopped her short.

"I am breaking my usual rule in leaving the school-room to go down at all," she said; and since I do it principally to give you time to change your dress, I certainly shall not make any alteration in my own.—Children, look over your sums; I will be back soon to attend to them."

Before Mrs. Marks could utter another word of expostulation, she left the room and was descending the staircase.

She would scarcely have been a woman, however, if she had not stopped a moment outside the parlor door, partly to be sure of her self-possession, and partly to glance over her dress—the same dark-blue merino which she had worn the last day Morton was there.

When she opened the door, the room looked as rigid and cold as ever—perhaps a little more so, considering that the day was gloomy—but on the stiff, black sofa sat a figure, the grace and elegance of which would have brightened even a duller scene, and which rising, with a soft rustle of silk and velvet, met Katharine in the middle of the floor.

If Mrs. Annesley had expected some timid, blushing girl whom she could awe or patronize into reverence, she must have been greatly surprised at sight of the calm, stately young lady—unmistakably a young lady—who met her with such quiet ease.

"Miss Tresham, I presume?" she said, inquiringly—for despite all that Morton had told her, she could not believe that this was Mrs. Marks's governess.

And Katharine answered with Katharine's own straightforward dignity:

"Yes, I am Miss Tresham. Pray sit down, madam. Mrs. Marks will be here in a minute. She desired me to apologize for her delay, and say that she was very much occupied when you came."

"I am sorry to have disturbed her," said Mrs. Annesley, hardly conscious of what she did say, and only noting with a sharp pang every separate charm of this girl's appearance and manner. Then they sat down, and when the lady spoke again it was with a perceptible effort.

"I have heard a great deal about you—Miss Tresham—" she did not say from whom—"and it has been a regret to me that I have not been able to pay this visit sooner; but I am a very great invalid—so much of an invalid, that my friends are kind enough to excuse a great deal of social neglect from me."

Katharine thought there were very few traces of illness apparent in the smooth, handsome face before her; but she had enough of the habitude of society to accept the apology, and answer it with a few words of conventional sympathy—wondering the while, why it had been at all necessary to offer it.

"Thanks—you are very kind," said Mrs. Annesley, in acknowledgment of her condolence. "Yes, sickness is a dreadful thing—more because it is apt to make one neglect one's duties, than for any other reason, I think. Some people don't allow it to interfere, I know; but I have never been strong-minded. If I feel badly I am sure to lie on my sofa, even with the consciousness of something that ought to be done."

"We are all of us prone to do that, I think," said Katharine; "and I, for one, really cannot admire the people who treat their bodies as cruel drivers treat their horses, and goad them into exertion whether they feel like it or not."

Mrs. Annesley smiled faintly. "You are very good to say so, when I see plainly that you have no personal knowledge—no personal experience, that is—of the malady to which I allude. Do you sing much, Miss Tresham? I see the piano open, and surely your pupils have not yet advanced as far as Mozart."

The conversation rather flagged during the "minute," which unaccountably lengthened into ten or fifteen, before Mrs. Marks entered; Katharine began to grow a little impatient, and to wonder what could possibly be the motive of this visit. Had Mrs. Annesley merely come to gratify her curiosity, or what other meaning was hidden under her cold civility, her languid commonplaces, her keen though not ill-bred scrutiny? The young governess felt that she was undergoing a sort of examination; that she was on trial, as it were, before this fine lady; and, feeling it, almost unconsciously she resented it. She who was usually so frank and cordial in her manner, was now reserved, almost haughty; while Mrs. Annesley made matters worse by a shade of patronage—half unconscious, half, it is to be feared, intended—which did not please the girl who had once told Morton that she was "unfortunately very proud." It was a relief to both of them when the door at last opened, and Mrs. Marks came bustling in, looking as if she had been hastily squeezed into her black silk, and had not yet recovered from the process.

Katharine watched the greeting between the two ladies—Mrs. Marks's hearty cordiality, a little tempered by awkwardness on the one side, and Mrs. Annesley's condescending suavity on the other—with quiet amusement. Then she kept her seat for a few minutes longer, thinking that, after they were fairly launched into conversation, she would go back to her waiting pupils; but, as it chanced, this intention was frustrated. Just as she had decided on leaving the room, Mrs. Annesley turned to her.

"I waited until Mrs. Marks was here, Miss Tresham, before I made a request which is partly the reason of my visit this morning. A few young people are coming next week to spend Christmas at Annesdale, and if you will be kind enough to waive ceremony, I should be very glad for you to make one of the party. Will you come?"

With all her self-possession—and it was even more than people gave her credit for—Katharine started. Was it possible that it was Mrs. Annesley who gave this gracious invitation?—who asked her to meet a party of young people (which was a modest way of saying the *élite* of Lagrange) at Annesdale, which was the head-quarters of gay hospitality? For a second she could not answer from absolute surprise; but she suddenly caught a glimpse of the ludicrous astonishment on Mrs. Marks's face, and it piqued her into an immediate reply.

"You are very kind," she said, looking, with her clear gray eyes, into the languid, handsome face; "I do not think much of ceremony, as a general rule, and I should be glad to accept your invitation, if it were possible. But it is not possible. I never leave home."

"You never have left home, perhaps," said the lady, smiling a little. "But, if you will pardon me, that is no reason why you should not begin to do so. Are you fond of gayety? I think Annesdale might tempt you a little in that way. Adela and Morton always manage to get up something amusing at Christmas. But I will not urge you—I will leave the matter to Mrs. Marks, and let her say whether or not you shall go."

She looked at Mrs. Marks, and Mrs. Marks, who had recovered her powers of speech by this time, was ready in a moment to take her cue.

"Indeed, I am sure Miss Katharine knows how glad I would be to see her go," she said. "It's very kind of you, Mrs. Annesley, to ask her. She has a very dull time, shut up here with Richard, and me, and the children; and I hope she won't let any of us stand in the way of her taking a little pleasure when there is such a good chance for it as this."

"I take charge of the children out of school, as well as in," said Katharine to Mrs. Annesley. "Mrs. Marks is anxious to give me pleasure, but my going would cause her a great deal of inconvenience; so I hope you will excuse me for declining your invitation."

"As for taking care of the children," said Mrs. Marks, before Mrs. Annesley could speak, "that's Letty's business, my dear, and not yours, as you know. You've spoiled her to death by looking after them yourself, and the sooner she learns to do it again, the better.—I hope you don't think we work her to death," said the good woman, turning her attention to Mrs. Annesley, with startling rapidity. "She took it all on herself, and I begged her again and again not to worry about them, though it's true they're so much improved—especially in their manners—that you'd hardly know them for the same children."

"Surely their manners would not suffer if you left them for the short space of a fortnight," said Mrs. Annesley to Katharine.

"For the matter of that," said Mrs. Marks, "I promised their Aunt Lucy that Katy and Sara should pay her a visit this Christmas; and you know, my dear, you don't have much to do with the boys."

"Mrs. Marks is evidently determined to get rid of me," said Katharine, with a smile, to Mrs. Annesley; "but I flatter myself she would miss me after I was gone. And so I think I shall abide by my resolution and remain."

"My dear," said Mrs. Marks, solemnly, "if you take my advice, you'll go."

"Take her advice by all means, Miss Tresham," said Mrs. Annesley, "or else give me one good reason for your refusal."

But one good reason, as society reckons good reasons, Katharine could not give. In our artificial condition of life, it is not considered a valid or even a courteous excuse to say that you have no desire to perform a certain action, or to go to a certain place. It is hard to imagine what could be a better reason for ordinary social refusals than the simple statement of disinclination; but, according to the rules of a certain arbitrary but very ill-defined code, it will not answer at all. If a man asks you to his house, you must not say that you don't want to come, but that you "have pressing business," or "a previous engagement," or a sick wife, or a dead uncle, or any other lie that may be convenient. If he finds you out, he will not be offended, he will take the pious fraud as it was intended. But if you had simply told the truth, and said that you felt unwilling to come, he would have had good right to be insulted. Knowing this as well as Mrs. Annesley, Katharine hesitated. She did not want to go to Annesdale, and she did not mean to go if she could help it; but still, social usages had a certain power over her, and, hemmed in by Mrs. Marks on one side, and her visitor on the other, she hardly knew what to say. Mrs. Annesley saw her embarrassment, and came to her relief.

"I am sure you think me very rude to press

you in this way, Miss Tresham; but I am really very anxious that you should make one of our Christmas party, and that anxiety must plead my excuse. I see that you are half persuaded; and I am sure that, when you think the matter over, you will find there is no reason why you should not oblige us. My son you know already, and my daughter will be very glad to meet you. If I give you until to-morrow to consider, will you promise to say 'yes' then?"

"I am sure it is quite impossible," Katharine began.

But the lady had already risen, and was holding out her hand in parting salute.

"I shall either come or send for your answer to-morrow," she said; "and I beg you most sincerely to let it be favorable.—Mrs. Marks, I leave the cause in your hands. Promise me that you will make her come!"

"I'll do my best," said Mrs. Marks, dubiously; "but Miss Katharine's very hard-headed, and I'm afraid she'll go her own way."

"So much the better, if that way lies toward Annesdale," said the mistress of Annesdale, graciously. Then she shook hands with both of them, gave Mrs. Marks an invitation to Annesdale in that vague, general way which means "good-morning," told Katharine she was sure she would not disappoint her, and finally swept out, leaving behind her a faint fragrance and a vivid impression of affable smiles and soft speeches, and shining silk and rich velvet.

"Bless my soul, how she was dressed!" said Mrs. Marks, as soon as she was safely out of ear-shot. "Did you notice the quality of that silk? I never saw any thing half as heavy in my life. It must have cost three dollars a yard, if it cost a cent; and what an elegant bonnet! Well!"—with a long breath—"I am sure I never was more surprised in my life! I thought she would have been just the other way. But there's no telling what people will do for their children; and, after all, she mayn't be as proud as people say. Nobody could have been more polite than she was this morning. I was astonished you did not agree to go," she went on, addressing Katharine, with mild expostulation. "Of course you know your own affairs best; and I don't mean to intrude my advice upon you—for advice is a thing that everybody's anxious to give, and nobody's thankful to get—but you know what she came for, my dear, and I can tell you that she has done a great deal for *her*; and, if you want my opinion, you'll be a great foo—simpleton, if you don't go to Annesdale."

"Then you will certainly consider me a great simpleton," said Katharine, coolly, "for I don't mean to go to Annesdale."

With this ultimatum, she walked off to th waiting arithmeticians, and left Mrs. Marks t return to her mince-meat with what degree of interest she could muster.

Dinner was over, and the short winter afternoon was more than half gone when Katharine opened Mrs. Marks's door, and, showing herself in her bonnet and cloak, asked if the former had any objection to her taking the children to Morton House. "They are anxious to return Felix's visit," she said (Felix had, a fortnight before, made his long-promised call), "and Mrs. Gordon was kind enough to ask me to come to see her; so, if you have no objection, we will walk out there."

"I haven't the least objection," said Mrs. Marks, looking up from her work, and wondering not a little at the grand acquaintances her governess was making. "I am glad you are going to take the children yourself, Miss Katharine, for you can see that they don't behave badly, or make themselves troublesome to Mrs. Gordon. Isn't it rather a long walk, though?"

"Not for me," said Katharine, and shut the door.

The day had been overcast from its dawn, and the afternoon was very gray and gloomy when the governess and her merry troop went out into it. Every thing looked sombre and tintless, the bare trees stood out against a dull, leaden sky, the distant hills seemed desolate and brown, the broad fields were perhaps the most cheerless element of the scene, with their dun-colored hedges, their wide expanse of sere plants, and their fragments of unpicked cotton hanging in melancholy shreds from the withered stalks. All around the horizon was a broad band of pale-yellow light, and this, together with the singular softness of the atmosphere, made Katharine sure that there would soon be a change in the weather. "It will rain to-morrow," said Jack, looking up at the sky. "Miss Tresham, don't you feel the wind? Papa says that when it blows this way, it always brings rain. There, Ponto!—there goes a rabbit, sir!"

Ponto, who was a large Newfoundland dog, had been brought along for the purpose of chasing rabbits, and was not at all averse to the amusement. In fact, he saw the poor, little furry wanderer before Jack did, and was off at a mad gallop, followed headlong by all the children. A turn in the road soon hid them from the sight of the governess, and she gave a sigh of relief. She liked them, and their bright animal spirits never jarred on her as the spirits of grown people sometimes did; but just now she was glad to have the sombre winter scene all to herself, and much obliged to Ponto and the rabbit who had secured this solitude. To her, as to a great many other people, there was a singular charm in the leaden sky, the bare woods, and brown hills, the dun neutral tints which went to make up the scene. Afar off, between some fields, there was a clump of trees, and a small house from which a column of blue smoke rose against the sky. Katharine looked at it wistfully. "I wonder if the people who live there are happy?" she thought. "I wonder if they look for any thing, expect any thing, dread any thing! Oh, me! I am sorry for them if they do!" As she went her way, between the zigzag rail fences and sear hedges, this train of not very cheerful thought colored the whole scene. She thought that she liked it because it agreed with her mood; but, in truth, if her mood had been different, every thing would have borne a different seeming to her eyes. So it is with us. If our hearts are heavy, the most beautiful landscape that ever smiled grows dark and dreary; while, if they are light, the sunshine from them overflows and colors with its own tints all the world around us. Katharine's world was made up of dull neutral hues just now, leaden grays, and cold browns, and dun, dark purples. We have no right to put the earth in mourning for our own troubles, but many of us do it nevertheless.

Morton House was farther off than she had remembered, and the afternoon was very nearly spent when she and her noisy charges walked up the avenue, and came in sight of the circular terrace and the brown old house set in the midst of it. This was Katharine's first fulfilment of the promise she had given Mrs. Gordon, and she could not help feeling a little nervous with regard to what her reception might be. Would the lady be kind and gracious, as she had been before? or would she think that, for a stranger, Miss Tresham was presuming too speedily on her invitation? "She is said to be very eccentric," Katharine thought to herself, with a slight feeling of dismay—"one of the people who can be charming one day, and freezing the next, Mrs. Marks says. Will she be charming or freezing to-day, I wonder? I almost wish I had not come." It was too late for retreat, however. At that moment, from some quarter or other, Felix espied them, and bore down with a shout of pleasure. Five minutes later, they were entering the hall.

Felix left them in the drawing-room, while he went to announce their arrival to his mother, and in a moment returned, accompanied by Harrison. "Mrs. Gordon's compliments; would the children please go with Mass Felix to the nursery; and she would be glad to see Miss Tresham in her own room." This was the substance of the message delivered by the servant; and, while Felix led off his visitors, with eager assurances that the place where he was going to take them was not a nursery at all, but a good, big room, where his playthings were kept, Miss Tresham followed Harrison across the hall, and was ushered into the pleasant sitting-room where she had been introduced before.

Mrs. Gordon was lying on a couch by the fire, and looked very ill, her visitor thought. She raised herself, however, and, extending her hand, smiled with pleasant cordiality.

"So you are really as good as your word, Miss Tresham, and have come to see me. I need not say you are heartily welcome. Sit down. Is it not very cold and gloomy out-of-doors?"

Evidently, if Mrs. Gordon was "eccentric," and had different moods for different days, this was one of her most gracious moods, and one of her brightest days. At least, so Katharine thought, as she felt that her instinct about the visit had not misled her, and as, obeying the motion of her hostess's hand, she sat down by the fire. She did not know whether to allude to the traces of suffering so plainly marked on her companion's face; but the latter relieved her uncertainty on this point at once.

"I have been quite ill," she said, "and I am sure you think that I am still, in looks at least, the worse for it. At my age, one shows so plainly things which pass unnoticed in youth. If you had come a day or two ago, I could not have seen you; but to-day I am grateful for the presence of such a bright face."

The bright face smiled and blushed a little at this, but soon recovered its usual composure.

"I am glad I came, then," said Katharine. "I was a little doubtful, thinking I might trouble you. But I always mean what I say myself, and I gave you credit for meaning what you said when you asked me to come."

"You were quite right," said Mrs. Gordon, smiling; "I meant exactly what I said, and perhaps a little more. I have lived a long time in the hottest fever of the world," she went on, "and this stagnant life is almost too much for me. In a measure, it was pure selfishness which made me press you to return. I cannot ask the people of Lagrange to come here. I have gone out of their life and their world forever. But you are different. The first moment I saw you, I knew that you were different; and I knew, or thought I knew, that you would be a person worth knowing, and a companion worth having."

"You flatter me," said Katharine, with her breath a little taken away.

"I never flatter anybody," answered Mrs. Gordon, coolly. "You know as well as I do that, although you are not particularly pretty, and, for aught I know, may not be particularly clever, you *are* particularly attractive. I don't wonder—" she paused, with a smile; then added, "Won't you take off your bonnet, and spend the evening with me?"

"I should be very glad to do so; but I have the children under my care, and I must take them home before dark."

"Can't they go home by themselves? can't Babette take them? Well"—as Katharine shook her head in reply to both propositions—"I won't press you. But leave the children at home another day, and come prepared to spend the evening. Surely, your holidays begin very soon now?"

"They have begun already. To-day was my last of school."

"I am glad to hear that. I can hope, then, to see you often in the course of the next two weeks?"

"I—don't—know," said Katharine, doubtfully. The moment afterward she caught a look of surprise on Mrs. Gordon's face, and went on, hastily: "I mean that I may not be at Mrs. Marks's during the holidays. I received a Christmas invitation to-day, and I have been doubting whether or not I should accept it. Would"—a pause—"would you think me very impertinent, Mrs. Gordon, if I asked your advice about doing so?"

"I should not think you impertinent at all, Miss Tresham; and I should be very glad to advise you to the best of my ability, leaving selfishness out of the question."

Katharine sat still and looked in the fire for a minute, puckering her brow into a slight frown as she did so. Then she turned round and smiled at her hostess.

"Don't think me very vacillating and irresolute," she said; "but the fact is, I declined the invitation this morning, and I told Mrs. Marks at dinner that I positively would not accept it; yet such is the perversity of human nature that I am half inclined to retract my own words now, and go. If one or two doubts could be solved for me, I think I should."

"And can I solve those doubts?"

"If you choose, I am sure you can. Of course, you know enough of your cousin to tell—"

She stopped short, for Mrs. Gordon raised up and looked at her with astonished eyes.

"My cousin?" she repeated. "You surely don't mean Mrs. Annesley?"

"Yes, I do," said Katharine, laughing a little. "You can't be more surprised than I was. I had never seen Mrs. Annesley before; and this morning she called on me, and absolutely asked me to spend Christmas at Annesdale—more than that, she would not accept a refusal; but, when I declined the invitation, said that she would give me until to-morrow to consider, and would send for my final answer then. Now, if I am not impertinent, pray tell me what she means by it, and what I ought to do."

Mrs. Gordon sank back on her cushions, and smiled. Instead of answering Katharine's question, she asked another:

"You say that you would like to go?"

"Yes," said the girl, frankly. "I like pleasure very much—more than is right, I am afraid—and I should like very much to go. It has been four years since I danced the last time," said she, looking at Mrs. Gordon gravely; "and I should like to go to another ball. There is always a Christmas ball at Annesdale, Mrs. Marks says. If I knew why Mrs. Annesley asked me, and if I could be sure that she really wants me, I should certainly take the goods the gods provide, and go."

"Go, then," said Mrs. Gordon. "Take the goods the gods provide, and enjoy them while you can. I am able to set your mind at rest on both those points. I think I know why Mrs. Annesley asked you; and, as she asked you, I am sure she wants you to go."

"This is your advice?"

"This is certainly my advice."

"Not given because I was foolish enough to say that I liked pleasure, but honestly and sincerely?"

"Honestly and sincerely," answered Mrs. Gordon, smiling. "You don't suppose I would think you worth much if you had not youth enough in you to like pleasure? The love of it is born in us, and is the strongest cord that draws us heavenward, as well as the heaviest fetter that binds us to the earth. Don't grudge your youth its natural impulses and pleasures. Believe me, the apathy and the distaste of later life will come on you soon enough."

"But Annesdale—" said Katharine.

"Go to Annesdale, by all means. I don't simply advise; I am bold enough to urge you to do so. Shall I tell you why? You are not a simpering, foolish young lady; so I think I may. It is evident that Mrs. Annesley, from personal reasons—don't blush, my dear, for I don't mean to be as plain-spoken as I was before—is anxious to see and know you. She has taken a better way of doing this than I should have given her credit for—a more delicate way, that is. Don't deny yourself a pleasure, and repulse her at the same time. If you have any liking, any cordial friendship, for Morton, meet his mother's advances frankly, and go to Annesdale."

"But," said Katharine, blushing deeply, despite her companion's admonition to the contrary, "that is exactly why I hesitate. Mr. Annesley has been very kind to me — if we were on the same social level, I might almost say very attentive—and I don't know what construction might be placed upon this visit."

"My dear," said Mrs. Gordon quietly, "society is a state of hollow but very useful forms. We all know that they are hollow, but still, we all observe them. Mrs. Annesley has asked you to spend Christmas at Annesdale, and you are not supposed to know any thing of the motive for this invitation. If any motive is concealed beneath it, what difference does that make? If she asks you for one reason, and you go for another, what matter of that? Have you not lived long enough in the world to know that life —this outside, social life—is merely a game of chance and skill? This visit will bind you to nothing. The day after you come away, or the day before, for that matter, you will be at perfect liberty to reject Morton if he asks you to marry him. I hope you won't do any thing half so foolish, though," she added, with a smile. "I knew his father well; and Morton is Edgar Annesley over again. No girl could ever do better than to accept him."

"I am sure of that," said Katharine, kindly and cordially. But she did not say it as if she had any personal interest in the question of accepting or rejecting the young owner of Annesdale. She spoke with her eyes fastened thoughtfully on the fire; and when she looked up, she added suddenly, "Then, once for all, you advise me to go?"

"Once for all, I do. Will you prove an exception to most advice-asking people, and take my advice?"

"Yes, I will," said the girl, rising and standing before the fire, with the ruddy light flickering over her bright face and graceful figure. "I am very much obliged to you for giving it," she went on; "and I should be very ungrateful if I did not take it after you have been so frank with me. I shall write to Mrs. Annesley to-morrow, and tell her that I accept her invitation. May I come to see you when I return, and tell you how much I have enjoyed myself?"

"Come to see me certainly, and tell me all about it. I shall be very glad to hear every thing. But must you go now?"

"Yes, it is growing late, and we have a long walk from here home. Neither the children nor myself mind it, though," she added, as the word "carriage" formed on Mrs. Gordon's lips. "I must bid you good-evening, and I hope you will be well when I come again."

With a sudden impulse which, if she had stopped a minute to consider, would certainly have been repressed, she bent down and laid her lips on Mrs. Gordon's cheek. It was a very light caress, but the latter felt it and started. Then she looked up with a smile.

"You are certainly very charming," she said. "I don't wonder that others, besides myself, have found it out."

CHAPTER XIV.

R. G.

When Mrs. Annesley reached home, she found that the whole family of Taylors, mother and daughters, had arrived at Annesdale during her absence, and were established to "spend the day," according to the irksome custom which then prevailed, and for that matter still prevails, in country districts. Their bonnets were laid aside, their work was brought out, and the drawing-room was full of the sound of their chatter and laughter, when the lady of the house entered. Poor Adela was on duty, and gave a glance compounded ludicrously of resignation and disgust to her mother. Mrs. Annesley telegraphed a reply in much the same spirit, then swept forward and greeted her guests with effusion. "Dear Mrs. Taylor, what a pleasant surprise! How kind of you to come!" etc., etc.—"Maria, how well you are looking!—Fanny, has your neuralgia quite gone?—Augusta, I need not ask how *you* are—I never saw you more blooming. Of course you have come to spend the day. I cannot think of letting you off," etc.

They all spent the day with religious exactitude. It was nightfall before the last item of news was discussed, the knitting-needles and worsted-work put away, the bonnets resumed, and the carriage ordered. Mrs. Annesley gave a heart-felt sigh as she stood at the window and watched them drive away. "What a relief!" she said. "It is dreadful to think what bores those people are!"

"The night is going to be dark, and the roads are very heavy," said Adela. "I shouldn't be surprised if they had a bad time getting home—and serve them right, too, for staying so late! Now, mamma, what news? I have been dying to hear, ever since you came; and I thought they never were going."

"Nothing very satisfactory," her mother answered, without turning round. "She declines to come, Adela."

"What!" said Adela; and, even in the soft mingling of firelight and twilight, it was evident that her face fell. "It can't be possible that she declines to come, mamma!"

"She does, though. She refused the invitation absolutely and not very courteously."

"Then what will you do?"

"What I will do is yet to be decided—what I did do was to decline to accept her refusal. I insisted on her taking a day to consider the matter, and said I would send for her answer to-morrow."

"That is more than I should have done," said Adela, flushing. "She will think she has gained every thing."

"She is welcome to think so," was the quiet response.

"It is nothing but insolence!" cried Mrs. French. "I wish I had her in my power, I'd—I'd strangle her! Mamma, I don't see how you ever submitted to it!"

"We must submit to a great deal, Adela, if we want to carry our points."

"And do you think you will carry this one?"

"I think she will come."

"But if she don't?"

"Then I shall be disappointed, but not seriously so. All I need is time; and time, I think, I can induce Morton to grant me. Since I have given a conditional consent, he has promised that he will not speak until I have seen and judged of—of this governess."

"I should make that a long process."

"No; for I hope it will not be long before I have proofs concerning her which not even Morton can disregard."

"And meanwhile?"

"And meanwhile, she cannot fail to suffer by close contrast with Irene Vernon. She is not pretty, Adela."

"N—o, mamma, not pretty, perhaps—but handsome in a certain style that men like. If you could have seen her talking to Morton at the pond that day! It was all her fault that he lost sight of that hateful child, and had such a frightful accident. Of course, Irene is a beauty—but I wouldn't trust to this girl's not being pretty, if I were you."

"Trust to it! You don't suppose I have lived to my age, without learning that there are many things besides a pretty face that make a fool of a man. It certainly is not this girl's face which has turned that poor boy's head. Let me see—what is the day of the month?"

"The nineteenth," answered Adela, wondering a little at the question.

Mrs. Annesley walked to the fire, making some calculation as she went. Mrs. French, who had meanwhile taken a seat, watched her with languid interest. She did not pretend to understand all her mother's schemes; but her reliance was, in a different way, quite as complete as Morton's. She had the most profound admiration for her mother's diplomatic abilities; and did not honestly believe that any cause was hopeless as long as she retained the management of it.

"Well, mamma," she said, at last, "what are you thinking about?"

"I am thinking," answered Mrs. Annesley, absently, "how long it takes a letter to go to London, and an answer to return."

"A letter?—to go?—" Adela sat up and stared at her mother. "A letter to go to London! Mamma, what do you mean?"

"I mean," said Mrs. Annesley, glancing round at the closed door, as if to make sure that nobody was within hearing—"I mean that I have no idea that my son shall marry an adventuress; and that I have been making inquiries about Miss Tresham for some time."

Mrs. French gave a little scream, half of excitement, half of slightly comic alarm. "Good gracious, you don't say so! Why, this is becoming quite interesting. Wouldn't Morton be vexed if he knew? Tell me all about it, mamma—how long ago did you begin, and what have you found out?"

"I can't talk about it here," said Mrs. Annesley, a little nervously. "Morton might come in any minute; and I would not let him know for the world. When I have found out what I want to know, I shall lay the matter before him; but, until then, he would not listen to any thing I could urge. His scruples on the subject are absurd."

"Most of his ideas are," said Mrs. French, coolly. "Dear me, there *is* his step in the hall! May I come to your room to-night, mamma, and hear all about it? Say yes, please."

"I suppose you may, though I am half-afraid to trust you."

"Never fear about trusting me. I'm not like some foolish women, who tell every thing to their husbands. Frank is a good fellow, and tells me all his secrets; but he doesn't hear any of mine. —Do you, Frank?"

"Do I what, Adela?" asked Frank, who entered at the moment in a very splashed and disreputable condition. "I don't mean to stop a minute," he said, hastily, as he was transfixed by his wife's glance. "I only came in to tell you what splendid luck we've had. I never saw the pond so flush of ducks before. Morton's a better shot than I am, and he bagged no less than—"

"Frank, if you don't go up-stairs this minute and take off that abominable corduroy, I will never speak to you again!" cried Mrs. French, in a high-treble key. "It smells horribly! Who cares about your miserable ducks? I don't!"

"You'll care about eating them, I expect," said the good-natured Frank, as he left the room rather crestfallen, and went to change the objectionable corduroy, which, being thoroughly wet, had, in fact, a very far from agreeable odor.

A few minutes afterward Morton entered, and, having had the discretion to change his dress, was welcomed more cordially than his fellow-sportsman had been.

In answer to his mother's inquiries, he said that they had had a very good day's sport; that the ducks were plenty, and by no means hard to approach; and that their game-bag was full.

"Frank enjoyed it extremely," he said, in a tone that was rather tired. "For my part, I am not as fond of sport as I used to be."

"I suppose it takes a fox-chase to rouse you," said Mrs. Annesley. "By-the-way, there will be some fox-hunting next week, will there not?"

"To be sure," answered Morton. "French was talking about it to-day. Langdon, and Talcott, and half a dozen more, will be here, who care for little besides fox-hunting. I wrote to Godfrey Seymour and told him to bring his hounds with him when he came."

"Isn't your own pack a good one?"

"The more the merrier, you know; and no hounds are like Seymour's. He has the best-trained pack in the country."

"I hope he will come."

"I hope so, indeed, for his own sake as well as on account of his dogs. There isn't a better fellow living than Godfrey. Is your party quite made up, mother?" he went on. "If there is anybody else to be invited, you know you ought to be attending to it. Almost everybody has made engagements for Christmas by this time."

"There is nobody else to be invited," said Mrs. Annesley. She paused a moment, then added, quietly: "I gave the last invitation in Tallahoma to-day."

"In Tallahoma!" echoed her son. "Whom did you ask in Tallahoma? John Warwick?"

"No, quite a different person. Miss Tresham."

The young man started. That name was the last he had expected to hear, and looked at his mother for a moment in surprise. Then he went round to the back of her chair, and, bending down, kissed her brow just where the hair was parted.

"My dear mother, thank you," he said, simply.

"Don't thank me," said Mrs. Annesley, in rather a hard voice. "I need not tell you that it cost me a struggle, Morton. But I promised you to see and know her, and I thought this opportunity the best for the purpose. People will wonder, no doubt; but we must submit to that."

"Let them wonder," said he, a little haughtily; but his tone softened, as he added: "You were quite right; this will be the best opportunity for seeing and knowing her. Is there nothing that I can do for *you*, mother?" he went on. "Is there nothing you could ask of me? I should like to show you in some way how much I appreciate the sacrifice you have made."

"Yes, there is one thing," said Mrs. Annesley, perceiving her advantage, and seizing it without an instant's hesitation. "You can certainly do one thing for me, Morton. I have asked this girl here for your sake. For my sake promise me that while she is here you will refrain from paying her any marked attention, that you will not give people any opportunity to couple your name and hers together."

Morton's brow contracted a little. He thought his mother had taken an unfair advantage of his offer, but he did not say so; indeed, after a moment, he saw that he had no alternative but to consent. He had rashly laid himself open to this, and he must abide by his own words.

"I promise," he said, a little coldly, "but I did not think you would have asked such a thing of me."

His mother rose and laid her hand on his shoulder.

"Why, my dear son? Why should I not ask it of you? You know where all my hopes for you are fixed. Can you wonder that I do not wish you to put an impassable barrier between yourself and their fulfilment?"

He knew what she meant—he knew she was thinking of Irene Vernon—so he did not answer. He had very sensitive ideas of his own, and he showed them in nothing more than in the reticence he always observed with regard to topics like these. Nothing would have induced him to mention Miss Vernon's name in a connection of this sort. After a while, he sighed a little, and put his arm round his mother.

"You must bear with me," he said. "Mother, dear, it is hard that at this late day I should begin to be a trouble to you; but be patient, be hopeful, and perhaps in time we may live it down."

Mrs. Annesley went to her own room early that night. She was tired, she said; her drive to town and the Taylors together had quite exhausted her, and her only chance of being moderately well the next day was to retire at an hour that Adela was fond of calling uncivilized—Adela's pet idea of civilization being to go to bed at one o'clock and rise at twelve. To-night, however, Mrs. French made no demur at the move. She yawned and said the Taylors had done for her, too; then bade her brother good-night, and followed her mother up-stairs.

"You are going to smoke?" she said to her husband, who muttered something of the sort in the hall below. "Oh, very well; take your time 'bout it; I am going to mamma's room for a while."

Her face vanished from over the balustrade, and the minute afterward the two gentlemen heard her dress rustling along the upper passage, and the opening and closing of Mrs. Annesley's door.

"They are good for a two-hours' gossip at least," said Mr. French, on hearing this. "That's their notion of 'going to bed early and getting a long rest!' Come, Morton, we'll have a smoke. Do you know where the papers are that came this morning?"

In Mrs. Annesley's chamber a large fire was blazing brightly and making the whole room radiant with that beautiful glow which a judicious mixture of pine, and oak, and hickory, can alone diffuse, when Adela entered. It rendered any other light almost unnecessary; but a lamp burned with quiet, steady lustre on the table at Mrs. Annesley's side, and, scattered around its base, were several letters and a newspaper. She looked up from the pages of one of the former when the door opened and she saw her daughter.

"I thought your curiosity would not let you remain down-stairs long," she said. "Come in, but be sure and close the door securely."

"Well, mamma, I'm all impatience," said Adela, after she had waited some time, and her mother took no further notice of her, but went on reading the letter she held.

"Look at that, then," said her mother, pushing the newspaper across the table and pointing with her finger to a particular paragraph.

Adela took it up wonderingly. The sheet was mammoth, and proved to be a copy of the London *Times*, in date five or six months old. Following the direction of the finger, her eye fell at once on the following advertisement:

"If the friends or relations of Katharine Tresham, formerly of the British West Indies, and lately of Cumberland, England, are desirous of knowing her present whereabouts and address, they can obtain this information by addressing R. G., box 1084, Mobile, Alabama."

Adela first stared, then caught her breath, and looked up at her mother.

"Is it possible you wrote this, mamma?"

"Yes, I wrote it," Mrs. Annesley answered. "I could not let matters go on as they had been doing for months past. I felt, and I still feel sure there is something wrong about the girl. Being confident of this, and seeing Morton's growing infatuation, I knew that to lift the curtain from her life was the only hope of saving him. If I have done her harm, she has only herself and her ambitious schemes to thank for it. Any parent would hold me more than justified in the means I have used."

"Oh, as for that," said Adela, "I think the means are excellent. But I wonder how you

d how did you get this

issell when he was in
He is thoroughly trust-
mention the fact nor
.s inserted in the *Times*
me this copy."
of it?"
it sooner than I had
ore the advertisement
letter was written, and

across the table, and
y. Her curiosity was
lthough she tore open
tily, she had still time
the paper, writing, and
, were unexceptionable.
y a man, and was quite

y accurate information
hereabouts and address
merly of Porto Rico, in
ly of Dornthorne Place,
will be entitled to the
d can obtain a liberal
Iessrs. Rich & Little,

last words twice over,
mother, and shrugged
think the reply gives
an the advertisement,"

nswered Mrs. Annesley,
t I had gone to work
ering to give informa-
d for it. I saw there
this friend who offers
refers me to a couple
interested as the girl
felt sure, however, that
reabouts, that he was
enlightened. In that
way, and this is what

letter across the table,
p and read:

who referred R. G. to
communicate his own
bile, Alabama, he can
desires, and be spared
'

"Well! and what was the answer to *this?*"

"The answer to this came very shortly, and puzzled me not a little. Here it is."

The second missive, in the same writing, and on the same paper as the first, was in turn handed across the table and read:

"Mr. St. John has received R. G.'s letter. If R. G. possesses any real knowledge of Miss Tresham's place of abode, and objects to communicating that knowledge through Mr. St. John's lawyers, he can address directly—

"HENRY ST. JOHN, ESQ.,
"*Poste Restante,*
"*Baden.*"

"Mr. St. John!—Mr. St. John's lawyers!" repeated Adela. "Well, Miss Tresham certainly seems to have a grand sort of person interested in her! Dear me, mamma, suppose she has run away from her friends, and is really a lady, after all?"

"She is much more likely to be an adventuress," said Mrs. Annesley, bitterly. "That high-sounding name did not deceive me for a minute. By return mail, I forwarded her address to Mr. Henry St. John, and requested some information concerning her, for personal and family reasons. No answer whatever came to that letter. After waiting some time, and finding that none was likely to come, and that evidently nothing had occurred to call Miss Tresham away from Lagrange, I wrote to the lawyer in Mobile, through whom I received these letters, and requested him to make inquiries in London about this Mr. St. John. He did so at once, and I am now waiting to hear the result. It may be some time before I obtain the facts I want, but every thing is possible to patience and money, and I shall obtain them in the end. If it takes my whole fortune," she went on, passionately, "I *will* obtain them, sooner than let my son wreck his life by marrying this woman."

"I am inclined to think that Mr. St. John is a nice person," said Adela, gravely regarding the two letters that lay open on the table before her.

"I am sure he is a sharper," her mother retorted, "and probably in league with Miss Tresham. Why he should have noticed my advertisement at all, puzzles me."

"Perhaps because he was afraid somebody else would," said Adela, too lazy to do battle for her own "nice-person" theory. "Well, mamma, when do you expect to hear something definite about him?"

"I wrote to Mr. Burns the other day, making the inquiry," her mother answered. "I was looking over his reply when you came in. There it is—you can see it if you choose."

"Of course I choose," said Adela; and suiting the action to the word, she took the indicated letter and opened it. Mr. Burns was the Mobile lawyer of whom Mrs. Annesley had spoken, and this was what he said:

"Dear Madam: Your favor of the 3d ultimo came safely to hand. In reply to your inquiries, I am able to say that I hope soon to hear from my agent in London, with regard to the information you are anxious to receive. I anticipate little difficulty in obtaining this information, if the addresses which you have furnished me are at all correct. The solicitors at Lincoln's Inn will certainly be able to satisfy you concerning the real character and standing of Mr. St. John. If we should meet with any difficulty there, it will be a little more troublesome, but quite as practicable to make these inquiries through other channels. In either case, you may be sure of receiving reliable information in a comparatively short time. I have also forwarded to my agent your copy of Mr. St. John's letter, giving the name of the place where Miss Tresham resided in Cumberland. By prosecuting his inquiries there, he may be able to learn something of this lady. I hope to receive a letter by the middle of the month, and will forward it to you immediately.

"Assuring you of my continued secrecy, and acknowledging your desire that I will not spare expense, I remain,

"Very respectfully,
"William F. Burns."

Adela philosophically folded up the letter, and returned it to her mother.

"I see now why you gave your consent," she said. "You wanted to make Morton defer matters, and so gain time."

"It was my only hope," said her mother. "I knew that if once Morton spoke to the girl, he would hold fast to his word through every thing. Now I may stave off a declaration, until I can show him who and what she is."

"If that is your hope, I should think you were very unwise to ask her to spend a week in the same house with him."

"And you don't know that by this very thing I took the surest means of binding him to his promise. He would do any thing sooner than break it now, that I have, as he thinks, made such a sacrifice for him. But that was not my only reason for asking her. I wanted her here—in my power, under my hand. When the letter from London comes, I want to give her a choice between open exposure, or leaving Lagrange. Then I do not believe that, once contrasted with Irene Vernon, she could continue to attract Morton."

Adela shook her head.

"That's your mistake, mamma," she said. "Morton has known Irene Vernon as long or longer than he has known this girl, and do you suppose he never contrasted them in his mind? I am as anxious as you can be that he should fall in love with her; but I don't think it is likely just now."

"We shall see."

"Yes, we shall see. But, for my part, I don't believe Miss Tresham will come. I am sure she has sense enough to distrust an invitation to Annesdale."

"That may be; but, nevertheless, I think she will accept it."

The event fully justified this belief. The next day was cloudy and stormy in the extreme, but Mrs. Annesley dispatched a messenger to Tallahoma, and waited anxiously for his return. In an hour or two, a damp note, woefully limp, and odorous of wet linsey, was brought to her. She opened it with two fingers, read the few lines which it contained, and looked up at her daughter with a smile.

"It is all right, Adela," she said. "She will come."

CHAPTER XV.

MERRY CHRISTMAS!

Wednesday was Christmas eve; and on Wednesday the Annesley equipage rolled majestically up to Mr. Marks's gate, and the children rushed pantingly in with the intelligence that the carriage had come for Miss Tresham, and the driver said would she please be as quick as possible, for his horses were impatient, and didn't like to stand.

Miss Tresham did not keep the impatient horses, or their more impatient driver, waiting very long. Her trunk was packed, and her bon net had been on for an hour at least; so there was nothing to do but say good-by—which, however, was very far from being a short ceremony. There was Mrs. Marks and Mr. Marks, and Mr. Warwick (it was immediately after dinner, which accounted for the presence at home of these two gentlemen) and all the children, and most of the servants, to exchange farewells and good wishes with. Mrs. Marks kissed the young governess as if she had been her own daughter, and bade her take care of herself and look her prettiest, and enjoy herself her best; Mr. Marks shook hands heartily, and hoped she would have a very merry Christmas, and they would all miss her, and keep her Christmas-gifts till she came back, and the children pressed round tumultuously, and listened distractedly, while she told Mrs. Marks that if she would look in the top drawer of her bureau the next morning, she would perhaps find that St. Nicholas had visited it; and the servants bobbed up and down in the background, and thrust forward their ebony hands with many "Christmas gift, missis! Wish you merry Christmas, ma'am!" while Mr. Warwick stood by, and looked with his quiet smile at the whole of it.

"I'll take you to the carriage, and bid you good-by there," he said, when Katharine at last turned and extended her hand to him. "You'll never get off, at this rate. Has the trunk gone out?"

"Done strapped on, sir," said Tom, appearing at the open door, and speaking over Judy's yellow turban. "Done strapped on, sir; and John says the horses—"

"Tell John to hold his tongue about the horses.—Miss Tresham, when you are ready, I am at your service."

"I am ready now, Mr. Warwick," said Katharine; and with a last bright glance around, and a last "Good-by all!" she went out of the open door, across the piazza, and down the front walk, attended by Mr. Warwick, and followed by all the children and servants. Mr. and Mrs. Marks went no farther than the piazza, but they stood there and watched the departure. "If ever I thought that such a thing would be!" said the good woman to her husband, as she saw Katharine enter the carriage, and bend forward over the closed door to shake hands with Mr. Warwick and give Nelly a last kiss. Then a touch was given the impatient horses, the carriage disappeared, like a glittering vision, round a turn of the road, and the group at the gate returned slowly to the house—all excepting Mr. Warwick, who went on to town, and, although it was Christmas Eve, and high and low, and rich and poor, were all alike rejoicing and taking a holiday, sat himself down to his grim law-books, and seemed to find the same interest in them that he found there every day.

Meanwhile, Katharine was driving at a rapid and easy pace over the country road that led past the gates of Morton House on to Annesdale. The short December afternoon was more than half gone, the shadows were long, and the yellow sunshine streamed with bright but sad pathos over the distant hills and leafless woods, as the carriage swept along; the driver and footman talked on the box, and the girl inside, leaning back on the soft cushions and watching the fields and clumps of trees fly past, asked herself if she was awake or dreaming, if she would really arrive at Annesdale after a while, or if she would rouse up in her own room in Mr. Marks's house.

On the whole, she came to the conclusion that she was awake, when the Annesdale gates flew open at the approach of the carriage, and, sweeping round the carefully-kept circle, Katharine found herself before a handsome house of soft gray color, built in the Italian style, and spreading over a great deal of space, with large wing and many piazzas. The doors of the hall were wide open, and three or four gentlemen were standing in the front portico. One of them came forward when the carriage stopped, and, putting aside the footman, began opening the door himself. He was a frank, pleasant-looking person, whom Katharine recognized as Mr. French. "I hope you have not found it cold, Miss Tresham," he said, as, after fumbling at the handle for some time, he at last wrenched open the door. "They ought to have put the windows up to protect you better. Let me bid you welcome to Annesdale. I hope you will have a merry Christmas with us. Did you ever spend Christmas in the country before?"

His voice and his smile were both very genial. Katharine felt glad that her first welcome had been from him, instead of from her formal hostess. It seemed somehow to promise better, to be a better omen of that merry Christmas which everybody just then was wishing everybody else. She answered him, as they went up the steps together, and, when they entered the door, the first thing that met her eye was the greeting—

MERRY CHRISTMAS!

in enormous letters of evergreen fronting the entrance, and running along the gallery that was part of the noble winding staircase which swept around the large octagon hall. On every side of this hall swung heavy garlands in which the deep glossy green of a dozen different perennials contrasted with the crimson berries of the holly and the glistening pearls of the mistletoe. Every picture gazed from a frame elaborately decked; and the large chandelier that swung in mid-space looked like a massive hanging basket, with its many wreaths and long drooping sprays of ivy.

"How beautiful!" said Katharine, standing still to admire. "How very beautiful!"

"Yes, it's pretty," said Mr. French, smiling. "But wait until you see the drawing-rooms. The hall was rather slighted this year, and—Ah, here's Mrs. Annesley."

He broke off thus, as a door on one side opened, and two ladies came out. One was a young and tolerably pretty girl, who ran forward and button-holed Mr. French without ceremony, while Mrs. Annesley welcomed Katharine with more cordiality than the latter had expected.

"Have you seen Spitfire? Oh, Mr. French, do tell me if you have seen Spitfire?" cried the first, in a tone of deep distress.

"My dear Miss Tresham, I am very glad to welcome you to Annesdale," said Mrs. Annesley, with pleasant courtesy.

"I am sure that some of your horrid hounds have got hold of him!" cried the anxious inquirer.

"I am afraid you were detained, and must have found it cold," said Mrs. Annesley.

Katharine was rather confused between the two; but she managed to leave the Spitfire replies to Mr. French, and assure Mrs. Annesley that she had not been detained, that she was not cold, and, that she hoped she had arrived in time for dinner—it having been understood that she should dine at Annesdale on Christmas Eve.

"In very good time," answered Mrs. Annesley. "It has not been ten minutes since the ladies went up-stairs to dress. These holiday times the servants are entirely upset," she added, "and, with all my efforts, I cannot get dinner before five o'clock. It is not so much fashion as necessity which decides my hours. Will you go to your room now?—Maggie, I suppose you will come when you find your dog?"

"I am just going with Mr. French to look for him," answered the young lady, to whom this last question had been addressed. "I don't trust a word these miserable servants say, Mrs. Annesley They all have a spite against Spitfire, and I believe they would be glad to see those hateful hounds worry him to death. I'll be up-stairs when I find him, but not before."

She walked out of the front door, followed by Mr. French, while Mrs. Annesley drew Katharine toward the staircase. "This way, my dear," she said, quietly. "That is Miss Lester," she went on, as they mounted the steps together. "She is a nice girl, but rather spoiled, and quite eccentric. We can hardly wonder, though, for she is a great heiress, and an only child, so—here—this is your room."

It was a charming apartment, large and airy, with deep, broad windows looking to the south, two canopied and curtained beds, and richly-carved rosewood furniture. A bright fire was burning on the hearth, the toilet-table was glittering with crystal essence-bottles and the like, while two maids stood before it, one engaged in holding and the other in plaiting a long braid of rich, red hair. "This is Miss Tresham, Becky," said Mrs. Annesley, addressing the former, who at once dropped a deep courtesy. "Is every thing in order?"

"Yes'm," said Becky, staring with all her might at the new-comer.

"Then, Miss Tresham, I trust you will be comfortable, and I will leave you to your toilet. I hope, by-the-way, you don't object to sharing your room. The house is so crowded, that I am obliged to quarter Miss Lester and yourself together, as you perceive. You don't mind it? I am so glad; for many persons do, and in that case a hostess is rather embarrassed. Dinner at five.—Becky, be sure you attend to Miss Tresham well."

"Won't you take a seat, ma'am?" said Becky, wheeling a chair to the fire, after her mistress had left the room. And, as Katharine took the seat, she knelt down on the hearth-rug and began unlacing her shoes.

"Never mind that," said Miss Tresham, smiling. "Don't let me take you from your work."

"Mistiss told me I was to wait on you," said Becky, looking up from the shoes. "That's my business, ma'am, as long as you stays here."

"Indeed! I hope we shall get on well together, then. And does that girl wait on Miss Lester?"

"I belongs to Miss Lester," said the girl indicated. "I'se waited on her all my life.—Becky, where'd you put the curling-tongs?"

"You'll find 'em behind the looking-glass," said Becky.—Then she glanced up at Katharine, and added, with a negro's honest admiration.

"You're the prettiest lady I've seen yet, ma am."

"Hush!" said the pretty lady, laughing. "You must not flatter me, or we shall not get on at all. If you want to begin your duties, you may take these keys and open my trunk. I must dress as soon as I get warm."

Before the process of getting warm was finished, or the process of dressing had begun, the door opened, and the young lady whom Katharine had seen below entered the room, followed by a shaggy little Scotch terrier, who incontinently rushed at Miss Tresham, with a vicious snarl.

"Spitfire, Spitfire!—behave yourself, sir!" cried his mistress, with a stamp of the foot, which Spitfire minded about as much as if she had bade him go on. "Don't be afraid of him," she said to Katharine, as Spitfire danced round and round, barking vehemently. "He is the best fellow you ever saw, and he wouldn't bite you for the world."

"I don't trust him, ma'am!" cried Becky, who had retreated into a corner and was valiantly defending herself with Katharine's shoes, while Spitfire, who had deserted Miss Tresham, devoted his energies entirely to her. "Oh, ma'am, please call him away! Oh, Lord, he's sure to bite me!—Get off, sir!—get off!"

"Hush, you silly thing!" cried Miss Lester, with another stamp of her foot, which Becky obeyed better than Spitfire had done. "Come here to me, pet—come here.—Cynthy, catch him and make him stop."

Cynthy put down the curling-tongs and made a lunge at Spitfire, who rewarded her exertions by turning his snapping and snarling against her. Katharine fully expected to see the maid badly bitten; but it seemed that Spitfire's fury was, after all, mere sound. He submitted to be captured, and, with a last futile bark at Becky, lay down on the hearth-rug and growled to himself.

"There, now!—are you not ashamed of yourself?" said his mistress, addressing him in an expostulating tone.—"Don't you ever be foolish enough to threaten him with any thing again," added she, turning severely to Becky. "If you do, he certainly *will* bite you; for nothing makes him so angry as to be threatened.—Miss Tresham, since we are to be room-mates, we might as well make friends. What do you think of Spitfire?"

"I think he is very well named," said Katharine, who had shared the panic.

"Cousin Tom named him," said the young lady. "He thought it was an appropriate name, and I kept it because it was unusual. In fact, Spitfire is a very unusual dog."

"In ill-nature, do you mean?"

"No, in sense. Look how intelligent his eyes are—I really believe he could talk if he chose. Then I like him all the better for his temper—it is such a contrast to those insipid poodles that most girls fancy. I have a bull-dog at home—a great, splendid fellow, named Bulger—but papa would not let me bring him along."

Katharine mentally applauded "papa's" wisdom as she looked at Spitfire triumphantly established on the hearth-rug, and thought that it might have been her unlucky chance to have been also domiciled with a great, splendid fellow of a bull-dog. She soon found that her new acquaintance was very pleasant and very easy to get on with—a little spoiled, perhaps, as Mrs. Annesley had said, and decidedly a little eccentric, but exceedingly unaffected and good-natured. Contrasting her with many common specimens of the genus young lady, Katharine concluded that she was fortunate in her companion; and she listened with amusement while Miss Lester's tongue ran glibly on, now to the maid, now to herself.

"Get out my purple silk, Cynthy, and the ribbons to match. Did you quill the point lace in the neck, as I told you? A pair of satin boots, while you are in the trunk.—Miss Tresham, did you ever spend Christmas at Annesdale before? No? Then I am sure you will be delighted—every thing is so charming. For my part, I am always glad to get away from home at Christmas. The servants have holiday, you know; and there is so much trouble about getting any thing done. They spend their whole time dancing in the cabins; and if you want the fire made up, even, you have to ring half a dozen times before anybody comes. I always go away from home Christmas; and, if I can, I always come to Annesdale. Adela and I went to school together. Don't you like her very much?"

She stopped after this question, and Katharine replied that she had not the pleasure of knowing Mrs. French, at which Miss Lester's face expressed the liveliest surprise.

"Why, I thought she stayed in Lagrange a great deal. I don't live in Lagrange, you see. I live in Apalatka. But you know Morton, don't you?—and oh, isn't he nice?"

"I know Mr. Annesley, and I think him very pleasant."

"He's delightful, that's what he is," said Miss Lester, a little indignantly. "Cousin Tom Langdon, and Godfrey Seymour, and Frank French, and a dozen more, are 'pleasant,' but Morton is simply delightful. I could fall in love with him," said the young lady, with startling candor.

"Then, why don't you?" asked Katharine, who began to think that her new acquaintance was more eccentric than she had at first supposed.

"Because there would be no use in it," answered the other, with a sigh of frank regret. "Everybody has settled that he's to marry Irene Vernon, and no doubt he will, after a while. She's pretty enough, as far as that goes; but, dear me, looks are not every thing—are they, Spitfire?—Cynthy, come here and take down my hair. I positively won't be dressed for dinner at this rate."

With the efficient aid of Becky, Katharine's toilet was soon completed, and, when the last touches were given, fully deserved the enthusiastic compliments of the maid. "You looks as pretty as a picture, ma'am," said Becky, smoothing down the dress of some soft, blue fabric, that was cut in a style which really made the girl resemble an old picture.

"If you only had your hair rolled up and powdered, you'd look for all the world like my great grandmother!" cried Miss Lester, turning round and much inconveniencing Cynthy, who was busy fastening the body of the purple silk. "Is that the first dinner-bell? Good gracious, Cynthy, make haste!—Here, Becky, come and help her.—Miss Tresham, would you mind looking in the tray of that trunk and handing me my jewelry-box?"

In the midst of the commotion which ensued, a knock at the door passed quite unnoticed, and, after one or two vain repetitions, they all started when it opened and Mrs. French appeared.

"Oh, Adela, you are just in time!" cried Miss Lester, lifting up her hands. "I'm only half dressed, and hurried almost to death. Do, there's a dear! come and help Miss Tresham put these ornaments in my hair."

"Indeed, I have not time, Maggie," said Adela, very coolly. "On the contrary, I have come to carry off Miss Tresham. I knew that of course you would not be ready, so I thought I would pilot her down-stairs.—I am Mrs. French. You'll let me introduce myself, won't you?" she said, turning and offering her hand to Katharine.

This was very pleasant; and in five minutes Miss Lester was left to the tender mercies of Cynthy and Becky, and Katharine was going down-stairs in amicable companionship with Mrs. French. She had time now to see the grand scale on which Annesdale was built; to admire the hall paved in black and white marble, and the staircase that swept round and round until it ended in an observatory on the roof. "It is very handsome," the governess thought to herself; but she was of the Old World, and had seen too many noble residences to be impressed by the splendors of Annesdale. "On the whole, I think I like Morton House better. It is not so new."

"Our party is not very large," Mrs. French was saying. "Not more than thirty people in all, and more gentlemen than ladies. I always like for them to be in the majority. This way, Miss Tresham—this is the drawing-room."

She opened the door, Katharine entered, and for a minute was quite dazzled. It had been a long time since she had mingled in society, and even under ordinary circumstances this large, richly-hued room, all ablaze with wax-lights and full of well-dressed people, would have made a startling contrast to the gray twilight that filled the hall. Then, no amount of social usage can make it a pleasant ordeal to face a number of absolute strangers just at the time when they have nothing to do and little to talk of, and so are at leisure for criticisms and remarks more agreeable to themselves than to the object thereof. Katharine's courage sank down to zero, but nobody would have imagined it. On the contrary, she looked so stately and self-possessed—so full of that rare, graceful ease which only the highest social culture can give—as she followed Mrs. French across the room, that everybody was immediately afflicted with an inordinate curiosity to learn who she was. All of the Lagrange people knew her by sight; but most of the present company were strangers in Lagrange; and a sort of thrill of inquiry ran round the room. "What a splendid-looking woman!" said the gentlemen. "Dear me, what an elegant girl!" cried the ladies. "Who is she?" both parties demanded in a breath.

When it was known who she was, the interest decidedly subsided. A governess who lived in the family of Mr. Marks at Tallahoma, was by no means a very important person in Lagrange estimation, and after a short time the only feeling that remained was one of curiosity to know why she should have been invited to join the

HE STOOD QUITE SILENT, WATCHING THE GRACEFUL FIGURE AND FAIR FACE.
CHAP. XV.

party. Thanks to Katharine's own prudence, there had never been much gossip about Mr. Annesley's attentions; and although some few people shrugged their shoulders significantly, and said that it would be as well to be civil, since no one could tell how soon Mr. Marks's governess might be transformed into the mistress of Annesdale, the majority passed the matter over as a whim of their hostess, and thought no more of it.

The young host was standing by the fireplace, talking to Mrs. George Raynor, when a gentleman near him said, "Who is that handsome girl who has just come in with your sister, Annesley?" And, turning quickly, he saw Katharine. She did not see him, for to her eyes the scene was one confused mingling of light, and color, and strange faces. But she had not been sitting down more than a minute when a well-known voice said:

"Won't you speak to me, Miss Tresham, and let me tell you how glad I am to see you here?"

She glanced quickly round, and the bright, handsome face she knew so well was looking down at her. With a smile, her hand went out to meet his.

"Thank you, Mr. Annesley," she said. "Of course, I know to whom I am indebted for being here. You must believe that I am very much obliged for the pleasure."

"You are mistaken," he answered. "You need not think that I have any share in the matter. I need not tell you that I am delighted, that I am happy to see you at Annesdale, but the pleasure became twice a pleasure when my mother asked you, without the slightest knowledge on my part."

Katharine opened her eyes a little; and, if it had been anybody but Annesley who spoke, would certainly have doubted the assertion. But, before she had time to reply, Mrs. French broke in—Mrs. French, whose ears were good, and who had no such implicit reliance on Morton's promise as that which her mother had expressed.

"Miss Tresham, is Morton asking you to help us in our Christmas-Eve arrangements? He said he thought perhaps you would."

"I said I was sure you would," said Morton. "Adela has arranged some *tableaux* and music for the edification of our friends; and I felt sure you would aid, if need be."

"Morton describes very badly," said Mrs. French. "Some *tableaux* and music are very indefinite. In the first place, it is no *tableaux* at all, but only a little scenic effect; and, in the second place, we have arranged the musical programme, with the exception of one part. We want a Christmas anthem—solo. Will you sing one for us?"

"What sort of an anthem?"

"Any that you can or will sing."

"Would the 'Gloria' from Mozart's Twelfth Mass answer?"

"It would be charming! Will you sing that?"

"With pleasure—but—no. I cannot. My music is not here."

"I will send for it," said Morton, before his sister could speak. "A messenger shall go instantly."

He started up, and was about to leave the room, when Katharine called him back. "I must send a message to Mrs. Marks," she said. "She would not know where to find the music else. Please tell the servant to ask her to look—"

"Had you not better come to the library and write a note? It would be much more certain."

"Don't carry Miss Tresham off, Morton," said his sister. "Dinner will be ready in a minute."

"I won't keep her a minute," he answered; and, without giving Katharine any option in the matter, he drew her hand within his arm, and led her from the room. The chandelier was lighted by this time, and the hall looked brilliant in all its guise of holly and mistletoe. To Katharine, it suggested a large mystic temple; and Miss Lester, who was just then descending the staircase, might have passed for its priestess, in her rich purple silk and pearl ornaments. She stared a little, but Morton gave her no time to speak; he led his companion hastily forward, and opened the library-door.

"You will find pen, ink, and paper, on that table," he said. "I will go to find a messenger, and be back for your note in a second."

Almost in a second he was back, and, closing the door behind him, came and stood by the table, while Katharine dashed off a few lines to Mrs. Marks.

"Tell her to send *all* your music," he said. That was the only suggestion he made.

He stood quite silent, watching the graceful figure and fair face that made such a pretty picture, seated by the table with its shaded lamp, and the dark book-lined walls behind. It looked so home-like to see her there—there under his own roof, in his own especial room—that the young man had hard work to keep his lips sealed. But in that very spot he had promised his mother not to speak without giving her warning, and he would hold fast to that promise through any temptation. When Katharine looked up, he was gazing, not at her, but at the St. Cecilia over the mantel-piece, and, when she extended her note, he took it and put it into his pocket. "I will deliver it to the messenger as soon as I have seen you to the drawing-room," he said. "I had better take you back at once, or Adela will be impatient."

Katharine felt sure of this, and rose to go; but at the door he stopped—stopped as if he must say something, however little, before letting her go.

"One word, Miss Tresham," he said, hurriedly. "You don't know how very, very happy it makes me to see you here."

CHAPTER XVI.

ST. CECILIA.

After dinner, Miss Tresham was sitting alone in a corner of the drawing-room. But let no one suppose from this statement that she was feeling snubbed or neglected, and, consequently, misanthropical or cynical, in even the least degree. She had been taken in to dinner by Mr. Langdon—the "cousin Tom" of whom Miss Lester made frequent mention—and she had found him exceedingly pleasant, while he, for his part, had been decidedly charmed. Nevertheless, after dinner he drifted away; but there were others ready to fill his place, and if, instead of being entertained, Miss Tresham was sitting alone, it was as much a voluntary withdrawal on her part, as any thing else.

In fact, the young governess soon found that she was among, but not of, these people, who laughed and talked in Mrs. Annesley's drawing-room. They were all of the best school of breeding, and, meeting her on neutral ground, they never dreamed of showing that, under other circumstances, they would not have considered her an equal. Vulgar incivility, and more vulgar patronage, were simply impossible to them; and when they accosted her there was no shade of manner to show that it was a condescension on their parts, and an honor on hers. But they had their world, and she had hers. They knew each other, and each other's friends and affairs, and had a hundred topics in common; while she might have dropped from a cloud, or been transported from the Sandwich Islands, for all she knew of these matters. One or two ladies had tried to talk to her, but somehow there was not much to be said on either side. Did she like Lagrange?—had she lived there long?—did she not think Annesdale a beautiful place?—were not the rooms prettily decorated?—Adela French had exquisite taste, and had cut out all the letters herself. Did Miss Tresham like German text?

After some disjointed efforts of this description, it amused Katharine to hear the same person turn to a group of her friends and launch into conversation of the most animated kind. She would grow eloquent on Laurie Singleton's marriage, and who his wife was, and what her grandfather's name had been, and in what degree they were related to the Churchills, and how Judge Churchill had sent the bride a diamond necklace, and how elegant were the dresses, that had been ordered direct from Paris. "After all, it is no wonder that these people find it difficult to talk to me," thought Katharine to herself. As is generally the case, she got on better with the gentlemen. Even the ordinary man inhabits a less narrow and conventional world than the ordinary woman, his very position as man giving him a wider field of knowledge and a freer scope of thought. Then, few men are not stirred into conversational effort by a fair face and a pair of bright eyes; and, where two strangers of the same sex would sit and stare at each other, two strangers of different sexes will soon find topics on which to grow sociable. "The governess is really charming," Mr. Langdon had told his friends; and few of them felt disposed to doubt the assertion. But still, they were engrossed with pretty girls, whom they knew very well, and to whom it was no effort to talk, and the charming governess, by degrees, wandered away into the corner already mentioned.

There she sat, like the historic little Jack Horner, with whom we are all acquainted; but lacking the Christmas pie with which that hero solaced his retreat. Instead, she opened a book of engravings, and tried to appear interested in its contents. A ripple of talk was sounding all round her, a pretty dark-eyed girl was singing at the piano, a glorious fire roared on the hearth, the wax-lights burned with that steady lustre which no brilliancy of gas will ever rival, the pictures gazed, the mirrors gleamed out of green-wreathed frames, people came and went continually, and the whole bright scene was, to Katharine, like a play—a picture—something scenic and unreal, but yet very attractive. She liked it better than her book, which was full of portraits of dead-and-gone beauties—as if the earth was not as rich in loveliness now as ever, or as if any one in his senses would give one face where life still brightens the eye and colors the tints, for all the cold silent beauty that ever mocked decay on canvas. "There is no one here half as pretty as Miss Vernon," thought Katharine; and, as she thought it, Miss Vernon crossed the room, and came up to her.

"A penny for your thoughts, Miss Tresham," she said, smiling. "I have been watching you for some time, and I am sure you were thinking how foolish and frivolous we all are."

"On the contrary, I was thinking how pretty you all look," answered Katharine, smiling in turn. "Why should I think you foolish or frivolous? It is only people of very superior wisdom who can afford to do that sort of thing, and, for my part, I must confess I always rather doubt their sincerity. You may be sure Diogenes would never have been able to make a success in society, or else he would not have taken up his residence in a tub, or gone about with a lantern searching for what he could easily have found by God's own day-light."

"I am glad to hear you say so, for indeed I think there is more good in the world—even in the fashionable world—than cynics give it credit for. We look too much at codes, and not enough at individuals—that is all."

"And we are too prone to judge hastily from the outside, to decide from mere appearances," said Katharine, making a personal application of her truism, and thinking how little she had expected to find this young beauty so full of the frank, sweet grace of true womanhood.

"Adela tells me that you are going to sing a Christmas anthem for us," said Miss Vernon, changing the subject. "I am so glad, for I want to hear your voice."

"I am afraid you will not hear very much."

"Will I not? Then Mr. Annesley has certainly lost all sense of truth. If you will excuse me, however, I will take the evidence of his word until I have that of my own ear. When will your music come?"

"Mr. Annesley sent for it before dinner, and it ought to be here now."

"Surely yes—since it is eight o'clock. But, no doubt, the messenger went on into town, and guns, and fire-crackers, and every description of noise, reign there to-night. No creature is so young or so old, so careless or so indifferent, as not to remember and rejoice that this is Christmas Eve."

"I know what it was last year," said Katharine, with a slight shrug. "I never saw people throw themselves with such *abandon* into rejoicing. I like to see it; yet I cannot help wondering how many have any remembrance of the cause which draws it forth."

"If you mean devout remembrance—thought of Who came to-night, and why He came—I am afraid there are but few. But still, at least they do not forget Him, and is it not better that Christmas should be celebrated thus, than passed over in cold silence?"

"Oh, a thousand times better! Don't mistake me enough to suppose that I think otherwise. But I wish the two could be united."

"Yes, so do I," said Miss Vernon, slightly sighing.

It was just at this moment that a servant entered the room with a large parcel, which he took to Mrs. French. She was talking eagerly, and opened it without thinking—whereupon a music-portfolio tumbled out.

"Oh, it is Miss Tresham's music!" cried she; and, while the gentlemen picked up the scattered sheets that strewed the carpet, she carried the half-emptied portfolio over to its owner.

"Miss Tresham, your music is come," she said, with a smile. "And you must really excuse me for opening it. I was not thinking, and Guy handed it to me without saying a word. Here is a note—I have not opened *that*, too. Do look and see if the 'Gloria' is all right."

While Katharine was looking for the "Gloria," and failing to find it, Mr. Langdon came up with several pieces of music in his hand, from one of which he was humming a few bars.

"Miss Tresham, do you sing this?" he cried. "It is a lovely thing, and I have never found any young lady who knew it. I heard Malibran sing it when I was in Europe. Won't you sing it for me now?"

"Not if you heard Malibran sing it last, Mr. Langdon.—Mrs. French, the 'Gloria' is not here. It must—"

"Here is some more music, Mrs. French," said a gentleman, coming up.

"Oh, thank you, Mr. Talcott.—Miss Tresham, here is the 'Gloria' now. Miss Tresham, Mr. Talcott. I introduce this gentleman partly because he is worth knowing, and partly because I see from his face that *he* has something he wants you to sing."

Mr. Talcott, who was young and rather diffident, bowed and blushed.

"If Miss Tresham would not mind," he said. "I see a song here—a little ballad—that my mother used to sing, and that I would like to hear."

"Your mother is not half so terrifying as Malibran," said Miss Vernon, laughing. "I am sure Miss Tresham won't refuse."

But Miss Tresham did refuse, or rather Mrs. French refused for her.

"I won't hear of such a thing," said the latter. "Miss Tresham can sing for you all to-morrow; but to-night I don't want anybody to hear her voice until he hears it at twelve o'clock. —Irene, will you come with me a minute. I want to consult you about—"

What was not audible.

The two ladies walked away talking, while the two gentlemen lingered to look over Miss Tresham's music, and show her what they wanted her to sing the next day.

Katharine had the rare art of being able to make herself agreeable to several people at once; so neither of them felt *de trop*, and both of them were so well entertained that they felt no inclination to change their quarters. In fact, they remained so long, that a lady on the other side of the room gave it as her decided opinion that Miss Tresham was a flirt.

"Look how she keeps both those men pinned to her side!" said this astute observer. "I never saw a girl who *wasn't* a flirt succeed in doing that. Of course, there's nothing in keeping one man, for the poor creature may be in such a position that he simply can't get away. But, when there are two, either one of them can go at any time, and, if they stay, it is certainly because they are well entertained."

Hour after hour the night slipped away—gay talk, laughter, and music, made it speed fast, and few of these heedless people remembered that, while they jested, the minutes rolled on to the verge of the great Feast of the Nativity. Katharine alone thought of the mystical sacrifice which all through this night circles the world, as, wherever the ancient Church has planted her standard, the midnight-mass is offered, the altar blazes with starry lights, the fragrant incense rises, the glad voices break forth, and with their triumphant strains echo those who sung, eighteen hundred years ago, to the shepherds on the plains of Judea. She alone thought of the crowded sanctuaries, and yearned to make one of th happy multitudes who, like the Magi of old, bent before their hidden Lord. But something whispered "Peace!" She stepped to one of the windows, and drew back the curtains. The night was clear starlight, and the great dome of heaven seemed fairly quivering with radiance—fairly ablaze with the splendor of myriad constellations set on a field of deepest steel-blue. In the east, one great planet glowed like a lesser moon. All the frosty night lay sparkling and still before her, but she knew that, over yonder, Tallahoma was ringing with merry uproar, and that, beyond Tallahoma, towns, and cities, and villages, echoed the same mirth.

As she turned her gaze to a hill on her left, a broad red glow met her eyes—the light from the negro-cabins, in which was seen the shifting of many forms, and from which, if the window had been lifted, she could have heard the well-loved sound of the fiddle and the banjo, and the sound of dancing feet. And it was all because of Bethlehem that for a short space the world forgot its feverish strife, and lapsed into these childlike pleasures! O Christian heart, rejoice and take hope! Better to honor ignorantly than not to honor at all, and, while you gaze forth sighing, wider and wider spreads the light of that star which once shone above the Child of Nazareth.

While she was still at the window, and Mr. Talcott still talked unheeded commonplaces, there was a stir in the room which attracted her attention. The door opened, and a servant entered carrying an enormous silver bowl filled with egg-nog, made after a receipt which was the secret of certain Southern households under the old *régime*. Another followed with a salver, bearing glittering goblets and baskets heaped with cake of every order and degree. These refreshments were the regulation "Christmas cheer," and thirty, twenty, nay, ten years ago, Christmas Eve would scarcely have seemed Christmas Eve if they had been lacking. After the bowl was deposited in state on the centre-table, the bearer turned and addressed his young master, who was standing by.

"The Kris-Kingles is out here, Mas'r Morton, and they heard as how some of the ladies said they would like to see 'em."

"*I* said so!" cried Miss Lester, starting from a sofa, where she had been *tête-à-tête* with an irresistible-looking gentleman—that is, a gentleman who thought himself irresistible—"*I* said so, Mr. Annesley. Do let them come in! I am so fond of Kris-Kingles!"

"Certainly, Miss Maggie," said Morton, laughing. Then to the servant: "Tell them they may come in, Victor."

Victor said "Yes, sir," and, apparently much gratified, retired with his grinning associate.

After a short interval, which the company in the drawing-room devoted to the egg-nog, there was a shuffling of many feet outside the door, a subdued tittering, a touch or two of the strings of a banjo, then a chorus of voices broke into the wild refrain of some negro-ditty, and, when the door was thrown open, the redoubtable Kris-Kingles—the mingled terror and fascination of every Southern child—appeared drawn up in the hall.

To Katharine alone it was a novel sight, the fantastically-dressed and masked group in the foreground, and the dusky faces, beaming with pride and delight, that made a semicircle round the wall, and peered in at the open door.

"What are they for? what do they do?" she asked of Miss Lester, who chanced to be standing by her.

"Oh, don't you know about Kris-Kingles?" cried that young lady, with surprise. "Why, on Christmas Eve some of the negroes always dress up in this way, and go round to all the cabins, and sometimes scare the others nearly to death. I can remember when I was a child I used to be awfully afraid of them. When they come in the house this way, it is for Christmas-gifts. I wish they could dance for you—you would like to see that.—Mr. Annesley, would it hurt the floor very much if they danced one dance for us? Miss Tresham never saw any Kris-Kingles before."

"It would not hurt it at all," said Morton. "Boys, give us a dance before you go."

The "Kris-Kingles" were not at all bashful, and needed no second invitation. In a minute, the measure of the music changed, and, still accompanying it with their voices, they broke into a wild, uncouth dance, impossible to imagine, and equally impossible to describe.

"I don't wonder children are afraid of them," thought Katharine, as she watched the hideous pasteboard masks bending backward and forward, the agile feet that kept such well-marked time, and the fantastic figures threading in and out of what seemed inextricable mazes. Some of the steps were most remarkable, and various double-shuffles and pigeon-wings elicited the liveliest applause from the audience. But the performance was soon over.

"Dat's 'nuff, boys," said the leader, coming to a pause. "Don't let the white folks git tired of you. Make your bes' bow now, and tell de ladies and gentlemen you wishes 'em a merry Christmas and a happy New-Year."

"Merry Christmas and happy New-Year to you all!" echoed the ladies and gentlemen aforesaid; and most of them went out into the hall to bestow that Christmas-gift which the Kris-Kingles had delicately refrained from asking. After this, the gay pageant filed out, and went its way over the hill to the quarters, the united voices swelling into fuller song as they receded, and waking all the echoes of the silent night.

"It is eleven o'clock," said Mrs. French, as she went back into the drawing-room, where Mrs. Annesley and a few elderly ladies had the fire all to themselves. "It is time to arrange our *tableaux*, as Morton calls them.—Irene, Maggie, Flora—all of you—come!"

Most of the young ladies rose at this summons, and left the room. The gentlemen fell into knots, and talked principally to each other, during the half-hour which followed. Morton snatched a few minutes with Katharine; but his mother soon managed to call him away. At the end of the half-hour, a messenger came from Mrs. French for Miss Tresham. At a quarter to twelve, a servant entered, and put out all the lights. The hush of the next fifteen minutes was very impressive. Such an idea had never entered Adela French's head; but to more than one present unconsciously solemn thoughts came, and this darkness seemed to typify the shadow which rested over the world before the blessed light of Christmas dawned. In the midst of profound silence, the clocks began to strike twelve. At the first stroke, the folding-doors which divided the two drawing-rooms, and which had been rigidly closed all evening, moved noiselessly apart; into the darkness flashed a dazzling flood of light, a scene so brilliant that it almost blinded the vision, and a chorus of silvery voices, breaking into the "glad tidings of great joy."

Not being very well used to scenic effects, the spectators held their breath in astonished admiration. The room into which they gazed was wreathed with garlands, and blazing with lights until it lost its semblance of a room, and looked rather like some enchanted palace. At the farther end, an arch of green was thrown, and above, in illuminated letters, ran the inscription, "Unto you is born this day a Saviour." Under the centre of this arch stood the Christmas-tree, glittering from the lowest limb to the highest summit with countless tapers and colored lights. Behind was a stage, arranged in careful perspective. Gazing from the darkened room, the full glory of the abounding radiance seemed to centre here, giving an effect beyond description to the figures upon it. In the foreground was an Oriental group—the Judean shepherds, as they watched their flocks—while beyond and around were slender forms clad in pure white, whose voices rose in one united chorus as they sang an anthem exultant enough to tell the world Who had entered it on that December night.

As the chorus died away, the tones of a cabinet-organ fell on the ear, and in the midst of a hush, so deep that it could almost be felt, one pure, liquid voice rose and soared aloft in the sublime "Gloria" of Mozart. In all the great world of tones, there is hardly a strain which, for triumphant majesty and noble worship, can equal this. There is scarcely more than an alloy of earth and earth's supplication in it. We forget that we are still "poor banished children of Eve," that we are yet "weeping and mourning in this valley of tears;" we catch the spirit of the angelic hosts, and our hearts are borne upward by the tones in which the master's genius and devotion live forever. "Gloria in excelsis Deo!" sang the ineffable sweetness of that silver voice, and few were so cold or so careless as not to echo the cry. In the breathless silence, every word of the grand old Latin was audible, and every word stirred those listening hearts. How full of glorious triumph rang the voice in the "Domine Deus! Agnus Dei! Filius Patris!" How it seemed smote with a sudden remembrance of humanity, a sudden yearning sense of need in the "Qui tollis peccata mundi! miserere nobis!" How grandly it rose again to the very gates of heaven in the "Quoniam tu solus Sanctus!" and, after one great burst of inspired praise, sunk at last into silence.

When the solo ended, people remembered where they were, and, turning, stared at each other. Who was it? What voice had carried them so far out of themselves, and out of the world in which they lived—the smooth, conventional, easy world, in which Christmas was only a pleasant occasion of friendly meeting and convivial sport? All these lights and wreaths, this *tableau* arrangement, and chorus of pretty girls, were a very agreeable entertainment to the eye; but here — here was something which seized them unawares, and, wrenching them out of their ordinary life, made them realize what it was they had met to celebrate, forcing upon them thoughts which to the common worldly mind are any thing but agreeable. It was the greatest proof of Katharine's triumph that her earnestness had so far communicated itself to them that they thought of her and her voice only as a secondary consideration.

"How beautiful!" they cried, when it was over; but they waited until it was over to do so There was no time to say much, for the chorus broke into the noble strains of Milton's "Hymn on the Nativity," and the last verse was still echoing when the folding-doors closed on the scene.

The company found that, while they were engrossed, servants had entered and relighted the candles; so the drawing-room looked quite like itself when they turned round—only very, very commonplace, after that glowing world of sight and sound. Mrs. Annesley was immediately overwhelmed with congratulations, and soon, to her great annoyance, beset with inquiries concerning the singer of the "Gloria." Good Heavens! what a beautiful voice! Was it really that girl who is said to be a governess in Tallahoma? Where could she possibly have learned to sing so divinely?

"For all we know, she may have been an opera-singer before she came to Lagrange," said Mrs. Annesley, striving hard to conceal her vexation, and to speak in a careless tone. "Adela was very anxious to secure her voice, which is, as you say, really beautiful; so I asked her here. But I should not like for any one to think that she is a friend of ours."

"By George! who would have thought the pretty governess could sing like that?" said Mr. Langdon to Morton Annesley

To which Morton replied, stiffly enough, that he always knew Miss Tresham had an exquisite voice, for he had often heard her sing.

"It did not astonish me at all," he said. "The pretty governess!" he repeated to himself, as he walked off. "And that is the way they talk of her! I wonder how I shall ever contrive to hold my tongue during this week which is to come?"

When the folding-doors were once more opened, and the company were bidden to admire and inspect the Christmas-tree, which was loaded with gifts, Annesley went up to Katharine and held out his hand, without in the least regarding the people standing near.

"Let me thank you for a pleasure which I shall always remember," he said. "You have given me my best Christmas-gift. I shall never again think of St. Cecilia without thinking of *you.* Don't Catholics always have a patron-saint? She ought to be yours."

It was verging close upon two o'clock when the party finally separated, and Katharine went up to her chamber. On opening the door, she found that Miss Lester had preceded her, and was sitting on the hearth-rug, engaged in petting and soothing Spitfire.

"Cynthy left him up here by himself all the evening," said the young lady, indignantly, when Miss Tresham appeared. "I can't imagine what she meant by it. Of course, she knew that she ought to have brought him down to the drawing-room to me. The poor fellow can't bear to be left alone. Miss Tresham, wasn't it all charming? There's no place like Annesdale, I think. The Christmas-tree was beautiful, and all the presents so elegant! Oh, dear!"—with a tremendous yawn—"I am terribly sleepy. I am sure I shall not get up till dinner to-morrow."

CHAPTER XVII.

THE APPLE OF DISCORD.

Miss Lester fulfilled her own prophecy, and remained in bed the better part of the next morning; but Katharine rose at a reasonable hour, and went below. As she paused at the foot of the stairs, debating in her own mind which one of the numerous doors around was likely to lead into the breakfast-room, a step sounded behind her, and a pleasant voice said:

"Good-morning, Miss Tresham. Merry Christmas to you!"

"Good-morning, Miss Vernon," answered Katharine, turning to face the speaker, who had come down the staircase in her rear, and was close at hand. "Merry Christmas to *you!* Is it not a beautiful day?"

"Delightful!" said Miss Vernon. "Let us go to the front door, and look at it."

To the front door they went, accordingly, and met the full brilliance of the sparkling winter morning—the floods of dazzling sunshine, the refraction of light from the gravel sweep, and the frost-gemmed trees and shrubs that stood out clearly in the transparent atmosphere.

"Glory to God in the highest, and on earth peace to men of good will!" sang Miss Vernon, softly, as she stood and looked out, shading her eyes with one hand, while the sunbeams turned her hair to shining gold.

"I like your translation better than ours, Miss Tresham; and, oh, I wish you would teach me to sing the Latin as you sang it last night! It seemed to me I never heard a language half so beautiful. You don't pronounce it as our university men do."

"No, indeed, I do not," said Katharine, smiling. "I call their pronunciation barbarous, and so does anybody who has ever heard the other. I'll teach you the 'Gloria' with pleasure, Miss Vernon."

"Thank you; I shall remember the promise. Do you know that, like Lord Byron, you have waked up this morning and found yourself famous—as far as it is in the power of Annesdale to bestow fame?"

"Not I."

"Well, it is true, nevertheless. Everybody is talking about your voice. Here come two of your audience now. Ask them if it is not so."

Katharine, whom the sunlight was nearly blinding, looked in the direction indicated, and perceived two gentlemen advancing along a side-path to the house. As they came near her, she saw that one of them was Morton Annesley, and the other a tall, stalwart, sunburnt person, who had been presented to her on the preceding evening as Mr. Seymour. Before she could answer her companion, they came up the steps, and, all smiling and slightly purple from the cold, were making their Christmas greetings. They had been to the stable to look at their horses; had found the morning charming, but rather cool; and were on their way back for breakfast—had the ladies been to breakfast?

"Not yet," said Miss Vernon. "We will take you in and give you some hot coffee as a reward for your exertions. What can there be so interesting in horses, I wonder, that men should go out and stand in the cold for the pleasure of looking at them? Mr. Seymour, I heard those hounds of yours making a terrible noise this morning. When are you going on a fox-hunt?"

"To-morrow morning at three o'clock, according to our present arrangement," said Mr. Seymour, smiling; and to Katharine, standing by, it was evident that this stout Nimrod was like wax in Irene Vernon's dainty hands, and before the glance of her sunny violet eyes.

"And may I go too?—Miss Tresham, did you ever go fox-hunting? It is the most delightful thing in the world.—Mr. Seymour, may I go too?"

"I am afraid it is impossible, Miss Irene."

"But why? Don't I often go, when I'm down in Apalatka?"

"Certainly you do. But it is different here. This is a rougher country, and we may have to ride eight or ten miles before we start a fox—at least, Annesley says so."

"I think there is very little doubt of it," said Annesley. "Miss Irene, I am afraid there is no hope of your going; but I am sure Seymour will bring you the brush of the first fox that dies, and you can hang it at the side of your bridle.—By-the-way," he added, turning suddenly to Miss Tresham, "won't you try Ilderim, now that you are here? I should like it very much, and, if you would like it too, there is no possible reason to be urged against it."

"Mr. Annesley, I"—here she broke down, and laughed—"I really think you ought not to tempt me so. If I would like one thing more than another, it would be to ride Ilderim."

"Then, for Heaven's sake, why do you hesitate to do it?"

"Don't be profane, and I will tell you after a while. Now, we must go in to breakfast."

They went in, and found the breakfast-room bright and cheery, and full of the sound of clattering dishes and pleasant voices. It was on the east side of the house, and the bright sunlight was pouring across it in long lines of level light. Half a dozen round tables took the place of one long, solemn board, and at five, out of the six, sociable groups were drinking their coffee and eating their steak with healthy appetites. The four who came in now took their seats at the unoccupied table, and smiled and nodded in answer to the greetings given from all sides. Miss Vernon, in particular, came in for a large share of these.

"Irene, here are some oysters!" cried one young lady. "Do you know they came from Mobile packed in ice, and Mr. French says they were brought specially for you? Take some; they are very good."

"You are very good," said Irene, looking at Mr. French. "Is it possible they are fresh?"

"Taste them, and see," said Morton, setting a dish before her. "The cold weather stood our friend.—Miss Tresham, do you like oysters?"

"Who does not like oysters, Mr. Annesley?"

"A great many people here in the backwoods, I assure you. Ask Mrs. Dargan over there what she thinks of them."

"I think they are abominable, and not fit for a Christian to look at," said Mrs. Dargan, with a shudder. "I would just as soon eat frogs."

"There is nothing better than a good fricassee of frogs," said Mr. Langdon, who prided himself on being cosmopolitan in tastes and ideas. "You are right, too, Mrs. Dargan—there *is* something in the flavor not unlike oysters."

"I said nothing about the flavor!" cried Mrs. Dargan. "Goodness, Mr. Langdon! you don't suppose I ever tasted one of the things?"

"If you went to France, my dear madam—" began Mr. Langdon.

"I should be afraid to open my mouth after I got in the country, for fear I might be made to eat some of their dreadful concoctions without knowing it," interrupted the lady.

"Then let me advise you not to go to the country, for a fasting-tour would be any thing but pleasant.—Annesley, my good fellow, what is the best way to eat an oyster?"

"Each to his taste," answered Annesley, with a smile.

"Not by any means," said Mr. Langdon. "The best way, in fact, the only civilized way, is—raw. In that case, they only need a little pepper and salt."

In this vein the conversation flowed back and forth—trivial, but very easy and unrestrained, and occasionally sparkling with a touch of humor or pleasantry. Katharine liked it, as she liked soft fabrics, and rich rooms, and delicate perfumes; for, alas! Mr. Warwick was right, and she was by nature cursed with that sensitive appreciation of refinement and the appliances of refinement which makes life in the lower grades of society nothing more nor less than a positive torture. After a while, Mrs. Annesley came over and sat down by her.

"I suppose I must not include you, Miss Tresham, in the parties made up for church this morning?" she said, by way of excuse for her advent.

"No, I shall not go," answered Katharine, who thought the question quite unnecessary.

"Fortunately—should one say fortunately about such a thing?—gentlemen are not very devout," said the lady. "If they were, I hardly know how all these good people would be conveyed to hear Mr. Norwood preach.—Irene, I believe I heard you promise Morton that he should drive you?"

"You heard me promise Mr. Seymour," said Irene, who saw Mrs. Annesley's schemes for throwing Morton and herself together, and always quietly managed to defeat them. "He asked me—or, no, I believe I asked him; but, whichever it was, I am to have the pleasure of going behind those beautiful grays of his."

"Miss Irene, you are utterly faithless," said Morton, laughing. "I shall ask Mrs. Raynor to console me for your desertion."

"She will tell you that George is afraid to trust her with your horses."

"I shall not ask George any thing about it. Yonder she is now."

He rose hastily, and went up to Mrs. Raynor, who entered the room at the moment. Mrs. Annesley watched him with a smile, then quietly took the vacant seat by Katharine. She was very gracious, and talked so pleasantly that the girl was half beguiled out of her unconscious distrust and dislike. But she noticed—even a duller woman would have noticed—how cleverly her hostess contrived that, in leaving the breakfast-room, she should be separated from Morton. It was only what Katharine herself had intended; but, notwithstanding this intention, she could not help resenting Mrs. Annesley's interference. However conscious we may be of our social drawbacks, it is not pleasant to have the perception of them thrust remorselessly upon us. More annoyed than she would have thought possible by such a trifling evidence of what she already knew very well, Katharine went up-stairs; and while she was assisting at Miss Lester's toilet, and cultivating Spitfire's acquaintance, her name, if she had only known it, was the topic of conversation with two different groups below-stairs.

Most of the young ladies were engaged in putting on their wrappings for the drive to church; but in the drawing-room a council of elderly ladies was convened around the fire, and Mrs. Annesley found herself courteously but decidedly on trial.

"My dear Mrs. Annesley, I can understand why you wished to gratify Adela in bringing her here," said one of the vigilance-committee; "but, if I had been in your place, I really would have thought twice about it. She is a dangerous girl —I can see that—and with all these young men—"

"The young men can take care of themselves, I suppose," said Mrs. Annesley, smiling, but in her heart feeling any thing but amused.

"Indeed, I think they are twice as foolish as girls," said the first speaker, hastily. "You hardly ever hear of girls acting as many of them do. There was poor Harry Anderson—*he* married a governess, and she was so extravagant that she nearly ruined him. He did not know any thing about her family, either; and I hear that she had a whole set of disreputable relations who came and lived with him."

"A drunken father," said Mrs. Dargan, solemnly. "Poor Harry at last had to order him out of the house. Do you know any thing about Miss Tresham's family, Mrs. Annesley?"

"My dear Mrs. Dargan, how should I?" asked Mrs. Annesley, becoming less and less amused. "I don't vouch for Miss Tresham in any way. I am civil to her because she is under my own roof; but she is here in—well, I may almost say in a professional capacity."

"We know that," said another lady—the mother of the Mr. Talcott who had been attentive to Katharine the evening before. "But, then, is it right to throw temptation in the way of the young? It seems to me that *that* is the light in which to look at it. The girl is certainly pretty, and, what with her looks and her singing, she might easily turn the heads of—of some of these young men. I am not thinking of my own son," said the poor woman, who was thinking of nobody else; "but there are plenty others here, and—and I can see that they find her very attractive."

"She is an atrocious flirt, that is very clear," said Mrs. Dargan, sharply. "I read her at once, like a book; and I really wonder, Mrs. Annesley, that you did not see what efforts she has made to attract your son."

"Morton paid her some attention at my request," said Mrs. Annesley, with her heart sinking lower every minute. She carried it off very bravely; but really a terrible distrust seized upon her. Had she really done mischief, after all? In the effort to bring Katharine fairly within the scope of her power, had she thrown a firebrand into her party, and made Morton's infatuation the subject of the observation which it had hitherto escaped? Almost all who deal in schemes and stratagems, must sometimes know the dread of having overreached their own end—and, having once known it, they must be aware that few dreads are more terrible. "Good Heavens! what do they find in her so attractive?" she said at last, almost impatiently. "She seems commonplace enough to me."

"Well, do you know, I think she is very pleasant," said a mild voice from the sofa, where the senior Mrs. Raynor sat—a gentle, pensive lady, all bundled up in a cashmere shawl. "She is a pretty creature, and her manners are so nice. She talked to me for some time last night, and I took quite a fancy to her. She told me a great deal about the West Indies, and I think the climate would certainly suit me. If George is able to leave home, I shall try it next winter."

The other ladies exchanged significant glances. Mrs. Raynor could afford to take a fancy to this girl, for both of Mrs. Raynor's sons were safely tied in the bonds of matrimony, and therefore not in a position to make fools of themselves. While, as for them—there was hardly one of them who had not some young man, some son, or nephew, or prospective son-in-law, for whose safety of head and heart she was at that moment quaking.

Meanwhile, the objects of all this solicitude, the young men aforesaid, were smoking their cigars in and around the front piazza, and, in their free-and-easy fashion, canvassing the governess, who, to them, simply stood on her merits as a woman. It may be as well to state that Morton was absent, for, if he had been present, the conversation would certainly have received a summary check.

"I believe I will send up and ask Miss Tresham to go to church with me," said Mr. Langdon, watching meditatively the elegant equipages which, one after another, swept up before the door. "My horses are not quite as fine as Seymour's, and my buggy isn't half as new as Annesley's; but, still, I think I'll ask her.—Here, Sam—go up to Miss Tresham's room, and give her my compliments—Mr. Langdon's compliments—and say—"

"You may spare yourself that trouble, Tom," said Talcott, who was standing near. "Miss Tresham isn't going to church."

"Did she tell you so?"

"No; I didn't ask her—but she told Mrs. Annesley so. I'd have asked her myself, if it hadn't been for that. But, then, I remembered—she is a Romanist, you know."

"How the deuce should I know?"

"You might have heard her say so—as I did. I asked her something about that song last night, and she told me she was a Catholic. I suppose that's how she came to know Latin. She must be amazingly clever."

"She is certainly amazingly pretty," said Seymour, laughing, while Langdon gravely smoked his pipe, and regarded the horses. "My test of beauty is, whether a woman will make any showing by the side of Irene Vernon. I saw them both together this morning, and Miss Tresham not only made a showing, but a very good one. Who is she? Where does she come from, anyhow?"

"You know Marks—the man who is cashier of the bank in Tallahoma?" said George Raynor. "Well, this girl is a teacher in his family. He picked her up somewhere, and they do say"—here the speaker looked significantly mysterious—"that one of our friends, not a thousand miles away, is seriously smitten."

"Who?—Talcott?" asked Langdon, looking round.

"I smitten!" cried Talcott, reddening up in a minute. "Why, good Heavens! I never thought of such a thing. She's very nice; and I got on very well with her last night—but I don't see how you could say such a thing as that, Raynor."

"There's something in a guilty conscience, Fred," said Raynor, laughing. "I was not even thinking of you. I was thinking of—well, it don't matter who. She *is* a pretty girl, there's no doubt of that," added he, candidly. "Flora tells me that Irene has taken quite a fancy to her, and that is remarkable, for Irene doesn't often take fancies—especially to women."

"She is too nice for a governess," said another smoker. "Talcott, you'd better go in for the prize. She wouldn't cost you much trouble, and that's a consideration."

"Stop that, Hal," said Seymour, gravely. "I can't bear to hear a woman talked of in such a strain. Governess or no governess, Miss Tresham is a lady, and should be treated as one. Now, I would sooner insult her to her face than behind her back."

"Who thought about insulting her!" demanded the other, flushing, and looking offended.

"You didn't, I suppose; but it is a bad habit to talk in that way, and, if I were you, I would break myself of it."

What the recipient of this frank advice would have replied, was a matter open to conjecture. He frowned, and his answer would probably not have been very amiable, if a group of brightly-dressed girls had not at that moment come down the staircase, and crossed the hall into the piazza.

Immediately all the bustle of departure began, and, before long, carriage after carriage rolled out of the open gates, and down the bright, sunlit road. Mrs. Annesley's was the last to leave, and, when her foot was on the step, she turned suddenly to one of the servants standing near.

"To-day is mail-day," she said. "Has anybody been to the post-office, Joe?"

It was at once evident from Joe's face—a good deal blank, and a little foolish—that such an idea as mail-day or post-office had never entered his Christmas-beset mind. Holding his cap between two fingers, he scratched his head with the others, as he replied: "I don't b'lieve anybody have thought about it, mistiss."

"Take a horse and go at once, then," said his mistress. "Don't forget it now—for I shall expect to find the mail when I get back."

"I sha'n't forget it, ma'am."

And, as Mrs. Annesley drove off, she had the satisfaction of seeing him take his way to the stable with laudable haste.

An hour later Katharine was crossing the hall, when a servant entered with a large and well-filled mail-bag slung across his shoulder. "Letters, ma'am?" he said, touching his cap, as if the announcement must necessarily interest the young lady. But she shook her head with a smile. "I am not expecting any thing," she said; and with that was passing on, when, through the open drawing-room door, Miss Lester's voice sounded.

"Did I hear something about letters, Miss Tresham? Oh, yes, there they are. *Would* you mind looking over them, and getting mine for me? I know mamma must have written, and I hate to move—Spitfire is so comfortable, that I can't bear to disturb him."

To prevent Spitfire's being obliged to relinquish his position on his mistress's dress, Katharine made the messenger empty the mail-bag on a table near at hand, and began looking over the different letters. There were some for almost everybody, and she soon found Miss Lester's. As she was turning away with them, she noticed that one missive had dropped to the floor, where it lay face downward. Stooping to pick it up, she saw that, although it was a large, heavy letter, the address was to Mrs. Annesley —and, seeing this, she could not help looking at it a little curiously. There could be no mistake in the character, it was "business" all over, from the seal to the very post-mark, and did "not seem like Christmas," Katharine said to herself. Such a letter should not be opened until the great festival was over, she thought; but still she laid it on top of the pile, and, leaving it with its great broad face upward, went into the drawing-room to Miss Lester.

When the party came back from church, and filled the house with the gay sound of their voices, Morton chanced to be the first person to go up to the hall table and examine the mail. The large, double letter seemed to puzzle him too. He took it up and looked at it, much as Katharine had done, then laid it on one side as if for further examination, and tossed over the others.

"Here, Seymour — Langdon — Talcott," he cried, "here are letters for all of you, and for the ladies, too. Where have they all vanished to?—Miss Irene, don't you want to hear from home? Here are two letters with the Mobile post-mark on them.—Miss Alice, here is one for you.—Yes, Miss Mary, I am sure I saw your name a minute ago."

He was soon surrounded by an eager group, for it is surprising how everybody—excepting, perhaps, a jaded business man—is excited by the prospect of letters, how fond everybody is of receiving them, and how shamefully remiss about answering them. Those who had got letters, were sitting on the chairs nearest around, reading them, and those who had not, were standing about, looking very discontented, when Mrs. Annesley entered and walked up to her son, who was opening his own.

"Any thing for me, Morton?" she asked, as carelessly as possible.

Her son looked up with a start, and held the large missive toward her.

"A letter from Burns," he said. "I wonder what he is writing to you about? He ought to know that I don't like you to be troubled with business matters."

"I wrote to *him*, and this is merely a reply," Mrs. Annesley answered. "It is about my own business, Morton—you need not be afraid that I will meddle in yours," she added, a little bitterly; and before he could reply, she had taken the letter and passed on up-stairs.

As soon as she was safely within her own room, she tore open the sheet of paper that in those days did duty for an envelope, and, without glancing at the lawyer's letter, drew forth the enclosure which it contained. She spread it on the table before her, but her excitement was so great that for a moment she could scarcely see—then a mist seemed suddenly to clear away, and, though she still trembled with eagerness, she was able to read the lines on which depended so much. The letter was addressed to Mr. Burns, by his agent in London, and ran thus:

"WM. F. BURNS, ESQ.

"DEAR SIR: In reply to your favor, I am enabled to say that I have called on Messrs. Rich & Little, and found them quite ready to afford me any information regarding Mr. Henry St. John. He is known to them as the friend and secretary of one of their clients—a wealthy Scotch gentleman; and, although they have never done business on his own account, they speak highly of him from personal acquaintance. With regard to the lady, however, they were decidedly reticent. When I pressed my inquiries on this score, I was checked very shortly, and reminded that a matter of private business could not be discussed with any but the person or persons immediately concerned, and that, if I wished information about Miss Tresham, I had better apply to Mr. St. John. I took the hint, and Mr. St. John's address, and went to Scotland to see him. When I reached the house to which I had been directed, I found it closed and deserted. The servants informed me that both the proprietor and his secretary were absent, and, it was supposed, had left the country. Being near Cumberland, I then went to Donthorne Place, and made my inquiries. Here I met with more success. The lady whom I saw answered my questions without any hesitation. Miss Tresham had been in her family for a year, and had given entire satisfaction. She had not been discharged, but had resigned the situation of her own free-will, and against the wishes of her employers. The lady knew nothing of Miss Tresham's antecedents, except that she was a West Indian, and had come to her very well recommended. She seemed much surprised when I asked her if she knew any thing of her after her departure from Cumberland, and replied at once in the negative. From none of the servants or hangers-on about the place could I obtain any more definite information. Miss Tresham seems to have been very well liked while she was in Cumberland, and to have left a good name behind her when she went away, but nobody considered her of sufficient importance to inquire about or take interest in after she passed out of their lives.

"I am very sorry that this information is so meagre, and that I have not been able to give you more satisfaction, but I have been stopped at every turn—first by the solicitors, then by Mr. St. John's absence, and finally by the complete manner in which all trace of Miss Tresham had vanished from Donthorne Place. If you wish any further inquiries prosecuted, let me hear from you without loss of time.

"Respectfully, etc.,

"T. W. Ward."

Mrs. Annesley read the letter to its end—her lips parted, and her breath coming more quickly, with every minute. When she finished she stopped a second—in blank astonishment, as it were—then let her face drop on her hands, while something like a dry sob rose in her throat. This was all! She had steadily worked herself into the belief that some terrible disclosure was to reward her exertions, some disclosure that would at once open Morton's eyes, and place Katharine in her power; and now this cruel letter came, and, after all the hope, all the expectation, left the mystery as complete as ever! Surely it was bitter! Surely it was hard! She paid no heed to the lawyer's letter lying unread before her. She knew so well what he said, that the mere thought of reading the curt, business-like sentences filled her with disgust. For a time she felt as if her whole plan, and, with her plan, the whole tissue of her life, had suddenly come to an end. If she could show him nothing worse than this, Morton would marry the girl, and then—

But she was not a woman to remain long in such a mood as this. Soon she came to herself, and the first proof which she gave of it was to take up the lawyer's letter and read it. "I will see what he has to say," she muttered. This was what Mr. Burns had to say:

"Dear Madam: Herewith you will find enclosed the letter from London of which I spoke in my last. I am sorry to say that my agent has not justified my opinion of him. The information which he sends, any child, who had been told to make the inquiries, could easily have acquired. He tells us no more than we knew before, and does not throw a single ray of light on Mr. St. John or Miss Tresham. I am very sorry, and a little ashamed to think that at my age I should have employed a man who could do no better than this.

"You ask for my opinion of the matter. I know too little yet to form or express an opinion, but if you decide to prosecute your inquiries, I would advise you to do so through certain channels of secret inquiry which are now established in all large cities, and employ agents so well trained in the work, that for a consideration—and, generally, it must be confessed, a very large consideration—it is possible to learn any thing about anybody. This mode would be expensive but secure; and if you wish to track the secret down, in the shortest possible time, I would counsel you to let Miss Tresham alone, and follow Mr. St. John and his employer. It is evident to me that there is some close connection between them, and what you desire to know. May not Mr. St. John be acting for his employer in the matter? I merely throw out the suggestion. Trusting that you will let me hear from you on the subject, I am,

"Very respectfully,
"Wm. F. Burns."

When Mrs. Annesley put down this letter, she felt that her face was burning. It was the cool proposition of the lawyer, the cool words, "certain channels of secret inquiry," which had suddenly showed her where she was standing, and what she was doing. She said "Good Heavens!" all at once, as if she had received an unexpected blow; and then she was silent, and tried to look the situation in the face.

She was a selfish woman, and a woman whose whole heart was bound up in her children and their interests—bound up, not with the tender devotion that would make some women martyrs, but with a steady force that would have sacrificed all the rest of the world to them—but she was not at all the scheming *intrigante* of romance. If she proved merciless in the case of her cousin, it was not so much from that desire for Morton House which long indulgence had fostered, as from the rankling dislike born of early envy. With regard to these inquiries about Katharine, she had begun them, and from the first looked upon them as the purest matter of duty. As she told Adela, she had made up her mind that the girl was an unprincipled adventuress, and she would have thought it wrong to hesitate at any means which would remove her from Morton's life. To-day, for the first time, a feeling of dismay came over her. What was she doing? Was this indeed a thing which no man or woman of even the merest worldly honor should be guilty of? She was coolly advised to prosecute secret inquiries into the private life of people she had never seen, and the advice struck her with a sudden sense of shame and humiliation. "It is for him—for Morton," she said, as she had often said before; but somehow the words did not bring their usual reassurance and consolation.

This, however, was not the time for considerations like these. She remembered with a feeling of impatience that it was Christmas Day, that her house was full of guests, and that her own place was down-stairs. She put the letters into her secretary, and rang sharply for her maid. But while she changed her dress, she was thinking of the great solemn dinner before her—the Christmas dinner *par excellence*, like which there was no other throughout the entire year—thinking of Katharine, thinking of the expostulating remarks she had heard that morning, thinking also of the letters she had read, thinking of the entire failure of her scheme, and wishing that she had not so uselessly thrown this apple of discord into the midst of her well-ordered party, but had left it in peace in Mr. Marks's garden.

"What on earth will come of it all?" she said to herself, as she slowly went down-stairs, and the sound of Katharine's voice rose from the back drawing-room, mingled with the rich, deep tones of the organ. Mrs. Annesley knew what sort of faces the ladies in the front drawing-room were wearing, and she actually felt cowardly about going down to meet them. It would have been strange, and consoling, too, perhaps, if she had only known that, when she laid down her weapons, Fate took them up, and from that time forth ceased not to fight for her.

CHAPTER XVIII.

ST. JOHN.

As time went on, matters, from the ladies' point of view, grew decidedly worse instead of better. Perversely enough, the gentlemen persisted in paying attention to Miss Tresham, in stoutly maintaining that she was pretty, and in finding her very entertaining. No girl of the party could gather a larger circle of admirers round her, or keep them amused for a longer space of time—not even Irene Vernon, with all her beauty. How Miss Tresham managed it, nobody was able to explain; but that she did manage it was, to say the least, amply proved. "She must necessarily suffer by a comparison with Irene Vernon," Mrs. Annesley had said, with profound confidence in her own assertion. What words, then, can describe her dismay when she found that there were others besides Morton who had sufficiently bad taste to find a charm in those gray eyes and that pretty mouth, which Irene Vernon's regular features lacked?

"There is no use denying the fact," Miss Lester said, with a little play of the eyebrows, peculiar to herself, "Miss Tresham throws us all in the shade; and for my part I should like to know how she does it."

Mrs. French, to whom this speech was made, shrugged her shoulders with considerable impatience.

"She does it simply on the strength of being

something new," she answered. "Men are such fools about a new face They talk of the fickleness of women, when the fact is, that *they* would grow tired of Venus herself."

Whether or not this was a correct solution of the matter, it was at least certain that Miss Tresham made a sensation—a sensation not to be doubted, and which took herself as much by surprise as it could possibly have taken anybody else. She enjoyed it, and entered into it with great zest. As she had told Mrs. Gordon she was fond of pleasure, and here was pleasure of the best kind, mingled with that elixir of admiration which is the sweetest draught that can be put to the lips of youth. Mrs. Marks would hardly have recognized her quiet governess in the bright, handsome girl who laughed, and talked, and sang at Annesdale, and who, all of a sudden, developed a power of attraction that quite carried the young men out of their senses. The young ladies were piqued and puzzled, but they managed to console themselves with their own sworn admirers; while the elders looked on in amazement and indignation, too deep for words. Poor Katharine! If they had only known it, they need not have grudged her this short holiday of natural, youthful enjoyment. Even while her heart was lightest and her spirits at their best, a sudden dark cloud arose, and the sunshine went out of her sky for many a long day.

Rapidly and pleasantly the time flew by. Anybody who has ever been in a country-house of this description, knows how rapidly and how pleasantly time can fly on such occasions, yet how impossible it is to give any exact description of the enjoyment that helps its flight. People, as it seems, are doing a dozen things at once, and they all go to make up an harmonious whole. There are flirting couples behind the curtains of the bay-windows, in the shady recesses of the library, in the hall, on the piazzas, walking over the grounds—in fact, flirting is the chief amusement and grand order of the day. Then, there are groups around the piano, and small card-tables, and billiard-players, and people continually driving up in carriages, and riding off on horseback; and servants coming and going, and dogs everywhere, and a perfect tide of life flowing here and there, and centring every day around the dinner-table. Usually in the morning, about three or four o'clock, there was an uproar of hounds, and horns, and horses, that roused every sleeper in the house, when all the gentlemen, with the exception of one or two who were considered hopeless sybarites, went fox-hunting—dropping in again, about mid-day, either flushed with success or dispirited by failure, but in either case quite ready to take up their respective flirtations just at the point where they had been left off.

On such a morning as this—a morning when the hunters were out and had not yet returned, and the ladies were wandering about aimlessly or yawning in each other's faces—Katharine sat by one of the drawing-room windows trifling over some needlework, when Irene Vernon came up to her.

"Are you busy?" asked the young lady, abruptly. "If you don't mind leaving that work, suppose we take a walk? It is a lovely day."

Katharine did not mind leaving the work at all; so she put it down, got her bonnet and shawl, and in a few minutes was walking by Miss Vernon's side out of the front door. They went down the piazza steps together and turned into a path to the right, that, winding down among the shrubbery, soon led them out of sight of the house. Irene gave a sigh of relief when the last glimpse of the chimneys was shut out, and they had a wall of green on one side, and a fair outlook of rolling country on the other.

"I am so glad to get away," she said, frankly. "I lose all patience with those girls; they don't seem to have an idea what to do with themselves when the gentlemen are absent. They mope about, and are *ennuyées* and stupid to the last degree, and all because they are thrown on their own resources for a few hours. It is disgusting!" said the young lady, with an expression of face that quite suited her words. "It is really enough to make one ashamed of being a woman!"

"It is natural, I suppose," said Katharine.

"Why should it be natural?" retorted Miss Vernon, indignantly. "It is not natural at all—it is the way they are taught and trained. Men are not so," she went on, with an impatience that amused her listener. "You never hear of their pining and moping because there are no women about. They like each other's society a great deal the best; and they always take it when they can get it. It is only women who are so absurdly and disgustingly dependent—who can find no zest or amusement whatever in the society of other women. Heaven only knows why! I am sure I would rather be talking to you than to any man of all the party."

"Thank you," said Katharine, smiling. Then

she added, archly, "Won't you even make an exception in favor of Mr. Seymour?"

"Why should I?" asked the young lady, carelessly. "He is a good fellow—dear, old Godfrey!—and I have known him all my life; but, excepting for that, he is no more to me than any other man. Is there anybody *you* would prefer as a companion?"

"Nobody at all," answered Katharine, still smiling. "Indeed, I should be at a loss to think of anybody, unless I chose Mr. Langdon, or Mr. Talcott, or that very singular Mr. Hallam, who makes me afraid he is going to snap my head off every time he begins to talk."

"Or Morton Annesley," said her companion.

Katharine started, and gave a keen glance at the face beside her, but failed to read any thing there. Miss Vernon was walking along tearing a geranium-leaf to pieces, and did not even raise her eyes.

"I don't know why I should make an exception of Mr. Annesley," said Miss Tresham, a little distantly.

"I thought he was a friend of yours," answered Miss Vernon. "If I had a friend, I would not speak of him in such a tone as that."

"*If* you had a friend!" repeated Katharine, a little surprised. "Have you no friend, then?"

"Of my own making, independently of family liking and hereditary connection, and all that sort of thing? Not one. All my life I have wished that I might stand on my own merits and see if I could gain a friend who would like me for myself. But I have never done so, and, indeed, it would be quite useless, for, if I cannot attract people with so many aids to win their regard, what would I do without these aids? I should be simply hated—that is all."

"You are one of the last persons in the world I could possibly have expected to hear talk in this way."

"Because I am pretty and rich? Neither of those facts make me less unamiable or less unpopular. Not that I care for the unpopularity, but I should like to have one or two friends, and I have none."

She made the statement in a quiet, decided tone, and Katharine was astonished, and puzzled, and sorry all at once.

"Miss Vernon," she said, "I am sure you do many people great injustice."

"Of course I am not talking of my own family," said Miss Vernon, "They are fond of me, as one will be fond of one's own flesh and blood, let it be ever so disagreeable. And I am very disagreeable," she added, looking the young governess straight in the face.

"I have really been considering you very charming," said the other, trying to preserve an appearance of gravity.

"Then you are the first woman who ever did so," answered her companion. "The most of them think me detestable, and, indeed, I don't wonder—my temper is so easily upset, and my tongue is so sharp. I try to keep it under control, but somehow I can't. I don't ever hear you make ill-natured remarks, Miss Tresham; and yet you are not silly either. How do you manage it?"

"I don't know that I often feel inclined to make ill-natured remarks; but, when I do, I don't give way to the inclination."

"And I always give way. Then, people think, 'How hateful she is!' and, honestly speaking, I don't blame them. As for my admirers, some of them like me for my face, and some for my fortune; but, if I were to try forever, I could not secure half as much genuine admiration as you have obtained, without trying, during the last few days."

"Miss Vernon, you do yourself as much injustice as you do other people. You are clever, and frank, and unaffected—what more could a woman wish to be?"

"I am sharp, and haughty, and ill-natured," said Miss Vernon, summing up her bad qualities with an utter disregard of this attempt at consolation. "If you knew me long enough, you would be repelled like everybody else. I really believe Godfrey Seymour is the only person who knows all my faults and likes me in spite of them; while I like him—poor, dear fellow!—as if—as if he was a great Newfoundland dog."

"No better?"

"Not a bit better."

She spoke decidedly, and Miss Tresham could not help feeling a little sorry for the gentleman who was liked in this canine fashion. "He deserves something better," she thought; but it was none of her business to say so, and they walked on silently, the bright winter day lying in still beauty all around them, birds singing over their heads, and a faint, purple mist softening the distant hills like a harbinger of spring. Again it was Miss Vernon who spoke first, and spoke abruptly:

"Miss Tresham, do you know it is a plan of our respective relations to marry Morton Annesley and myself to each other?"

"I—" Katharine was quite taken aback by

this unexpected question. "Yes, I have heard something of the kind."

"A nice idea, isn't it?" said the young lady, with a smile that was rather too bright to be natural. "I don't think I ever heard any thing more absurd. Frank French is my cousin, you know, and so Adela and Flora took it into their wise heads that Morton and I would make a good match, without any regard to the trifling fact that neither of us ever had any fancy—any special fancy, that is—for the other. Of course, he was repelled by my temper, as everybody is, while I—well, I never thought of him at all. I should have been a fool if I had, considering that he never was more than civil to me. He is a charming gentleman, though," she said, looking at Katharine, "and any woman whom he loved would do well to marry him."

They were almost the same words that Mrs. Gordon had spoken, little more than a week before, and, hearing them thus the second time, they filled Katharine with a sudden sense of surprise and amusement, which it is impossible to describe. She understood perfectly what assurance it was that Miss Vernon wished to convey to her, and the humor of the situation overpowered for the moment every other consideration. It was strange enough that his own cousin, a woman steeped to the lips in the traditions of her class and the pride of blood, should have advised her to marry Morton; but for this young beauty, this girl, who, according to the vulgar melodramatic idea, should have been her "rival," to echo such advice! A comic vision of Mrs. Annesley's horror rose before Katharine, and almost made her laugh.

"I quite agree with you," she answered, as quietly as she had answered Mrs. Gordon. "The woman whom he loved, and who loved him, would do well to marry Mr. Annesley. But how is this? We have come round to the gates."

"By a longer route than the carriage-drive, but one just as sure," said Miss Vernon, smiling. "See! there is some one coming in. Shall we turn and go back the way we came?"

Before Katharine could reply, Spitfire, who had lately taken quite a fancy to her, and had condescended to follow her out, made a wild rush at the figure just entering the gate, barking with a degree of fury almost incomprehensible, considering the size of the body from which the sound proceeded. Notwithstanding his insignificant appearance, he quite startled and overpowered the new-comer. This person—a tall, slender, well-dressed man—backed against the gate, and began kicking at his assailant with one foot, which proceeding, of course, irritated Spitfire to the extreme of canine wrath.

"Call him off! call him off!" cried Miss Vernon to Katharine. "He will bite the man, or the man will hurt him, and that would make Maggie furious, you know. Do call him off!"

Katharine called and called again; but Spitfire, who did not obey his mistress, was certainly not likely to obey her. He danced round the stranger like a dog that was possessed, and gave no sign of heeding. So Katharine went forward and addressed the other combatant, who kicked quite as furiously as Spitfire barked.

"Pray don't do that!" she cried. "He won't bite, I assure you, and—"

She stopped short. Miss Vernon, standing at a little distance, looking on, saw her suddenly put her hands to her face, and utter a low cry. The kicker dropped his foot, and, disregarding Spitfire, made a quick step forward.

"Katharine!" he said, eagerly—"my dear Katharine!"

But at the sound of his voice the girl raised her face, all white and drawn, and held out her hands, not to welcome, but to keep him back.

"You!" she said, hoarsely; "you!"

"Yes, I," he said, so much the more self-possessed of the two that it was evident this meeting was not entirely unexpected on his part. "I thought you would not be unprepared. I wrote to you not long ago. Did you not receive my letter?"

She made an effort to speak before she succeeded; then, with a sort of dry gasp, the words were articulated:

"Yes, I received it; but I thought—I hoped—that is, I was fool enough to think—to hope—that you might care for me sufficiently to leave me alone."

"To leave you alone, my dear Katharine?" His face expressed the liveliest surprise. "Am I not your natural protector, your—"

"Hush!" she said, so fiercely that he absolutely started back. "Let me hear none of that cant! What do you want with me, now that you have come?"

"I must see and speak to you," he said, a little sulkily. "Will you take me to the house?"

"To the house? to be asked who and what you are? My God, no! Wait here a moment; I will speak—"

She left him, and hastily followed Miss Vernon, who, with well-bred consideration, had walked out of ear-shot of the conversation. Hearing Katharine's step behind her, she paused and turned.

"So you found an acquaintance, Miss Tresham?" she began, with a smile, when the terrible pallor of the girl's face startled her. "Good Heavens! what is the matter?" she cried, in sudden alarm.

"Nothing — nothing," answered Katharine, striving to force a smile that only made her look more ghastly; "only I—I am obliged to ask you to return to the house without me. This gentleman is an—an acquaintance of mine, and I must stop to speak to him. You will excuse me, I am sure."

"Certainly I will excuse you," said Miss Vernon, trying hard to keep her surprise out of her voice. "But, if you will pardon me, had you not better take your friend to the house? I am sure Mrs. Annesley—"

"I cannot do that," said Katharine, nervously. "I could not think of taking such a liberty. Then, no privacy is possible in the house, and I must see this gentleman privately. My dear Miss Vernon, if you will only be kind enough not to say any thing—"

"Of course, I shall not say any thing," interrupted Miss Vernon, hastily.

Then she called Spitfire, and, without a single backward glance, disappeared down the path.

When the last flutter of her dress vanished from sight, Katharine turned and beckoned to the man, who was still standing where she had left him. He obeyed the signal with alacrity; and, as he walked quickly forward, she moved on in front of him, and did not pause until she had reached the most secluded part of the grounds — a deep, bosky dell, where a little brook ran, and where they were entirely safe from observation. There she turned and faced him—white, but by this time composed and rigidly braced, as it seemed, for any thing.

"Well," she said, with icy coldness, "what is it?"

"By Jove! my dear Katharine, your American sojourn seems to have improved the warmth of your affections," said her companion, with a smile. "Is this the only greeting you have for me — me, who have come so far to see you?"

"St. John," she cried, passionately, "let me hear no more of this! I cannot, will not, bear it! You have already worked me all the harm that it is in the power of one person to inflict upon another. You are here now, in defiance of your most solemn obligations, to injure me further; and yet—and yet you dare to talk like this! For Heaven's sake, let me hear no more of it!"

"That is just as you please," said he, with a relapse into sulkiness.

Nothing was said after this for several minutes. The two figures stood silently facing each other—the leafless trees and dark evergreens all around them, and the limpid stream flowing at their feet. Katharine's bright winter costume made a beautiful "bit" of color on the somewhat sombre landscape—her companion being, in appearance at least, less interesting. Yet he was not an ill-looking man; on the contrary, many people would have called him handsome, and been justified in doing so. He was, in age, somewhere between twenty-five and thirty—certainly not younger than the one or older than the other — he had a slender, elegant figure, and a dark, well-modelled face—a face with a good complexion, dark eyes, thin lips, and a painfully-narrow forehead. The man was not a sensualist—no man with that mouth could have been—but a physiognomist, looking at him, would have said that he was selfish and unscrupulous, and in so saying would not have gone very far wide of the truth. It was Katharine who spoke first.

"You asked me if I received your letter. Did you get my reply?"

"It was impossible for me to have done so," he answered. "I left England immediately after writing that letter. Was there any thing of importance in yours?"

"Nothing," she answered, drearily. "I asked you to let me alone—that was all, I might have known how useless that was — I might have known that you never did, nor ever will consider any one but yourself. How did you find out where I was?" she added, turning upon him suddenly. "You gave me no explanation of that, and I don't understand how it was."

"There are a great many things you don't understand, my dear Katharine," said he, in a patronizing tone. "This must remain one of them. I found out where you were just as I should find it out if you were foolish enough to go and bury yourself and all your fine talents in the South Sea Islands. I have ways and means —believe me it is useless to attempt to hide from me. I thought I should never reach this place," he went on, with a shrug of the shoulders, "and when I at last arrived, and thought all my difficulties were over, I went to the woman with whom you live, and she told me—"

"What!" cried Katharine, starting. "You have seen Mrs. Marks?"

"Certainly I have," answered he, coolly, "and a dozen or so children, besides. It was she who told me you were here. Did you think I found it out by instinct?"

"And what did you tell her to account for your inquiries?" asked Katharine, almost wringing her hands. "Oh, St. John, you surely have not told her—"

"Nothing at all," said he, roughly. "Don't make a fool of yourself! Am I the devil, or do I look like him, that you should be so afraid of claiming connection with me? I told the woman—she looks like a respectable cook, by-the-way—that I was a friend of yours, from England. She was evidently very curious, but I thought that was enough for her."

"And what am I to tell her when I go back, and she speaks of you, as she is sure to do?"

"Tell her that I am your brother."

"I will not," cried she, indignantly.

"Well, whatever lie may be convenient, then. I am ready to play any part. We might compromise on uncle, since you object to brother, for I am afraid I am rather young to attempt the *rôle* of father."

"St. John, be serious," she cried, with something like a sob in her throat. "Don't you see that I cannot bear such wretched trifling. Oh! if you had ever cared for me in the least degree, you would never embitter my life like this!"

"If you had a grain of common-sense, you would not make such a fuss over nothing," said he, impatiently. "Have I not a right to see you when and where I choose? I will go up yonder among your new associates and assert it, if you say so."

"If you dare!" said she, blazing out upon him, with sudden indignation. "Yes, if you dare! You have tracked me down, and I am willing to buy my peace of life at any price you choose to ask—short of this. St. John," she said, sitting down on a rustic seat near by, "this is too much for me. Tell me at once what you want—and—and let me go."

He walked away from her for a short distance, biting his under lip almost savagely; then he turned abruptly, and came back.

"You know what I want," he said. "It is always the same thing—the cursed need of money. Can you let me have any?"

"I can let you have the most of my two years' salary, which is in Mr. Marks's hands, if you will go away then, and leave me in peace."

"So you only care to buy my absence," he said, with a dark cloud coming over his face.

"Ask yourself how I can care for any thing else," she answered, sadly. "But such as the money is, you are welcome to it. I saved it for you, and meant to send it to you—so you are welcome to it."

He moved away, and took another turn—came back again and caught her arm.

"I would not touch a penny of it, if ruin was not staring me in the face," he said. "But, as it is, I see no other chance—not one."

"Has that man—that Fraser—thrown you off, then?"

"Curse him, yes—completely!"

"And you have only me?"

"I have only you, or you may be sure that I would not have come for any such greeting as this has been."

She rose suddenly and held out her hands to him.

"Forgive me, St. John," she cried, with a sudden pathos in her voice. "I did not understand. I thought you had come merely to disturb and make me wretched. I will do any thing in the world for you that I can—you know that. If you say so, I will go away with you, and we will try to live together, and to begin a new life, in some new place."

"And drag each other down, like a couple of millstones. That would be wise, indeed! No, I will only be cur enough to rob you of all your savings, and then I will go away and leave you in the peace you talk so much about. When can you let me have the money?"

"To-morrow—I cannot see Mr. Marks to-day. I will meet you in Tallahoma, or else you can come back here. I will show you a private way to enter the grounds, and this is a very retired place. I shall have to write a note. I suppose you are at the hotel?"

"Yes—registered as Mr. Johns. Don't forget that."

Katharine flushed. She had an instinctive horror of an alias, and this one seemed to her so unnecessary. "Who would have known the other name here?" she asked.

"Nobody, probably; but I believe in precautionary measures, always. Well, I shall look for a note to-morrow, appointing a place where I can see you again. I can tell you, by-the-way, that you are putting yourself in a very bad position by this assignation business. It would be much better, and much safer, to take me to the house yonder, and present me as a foreign friend."

"I cannot—I will not!" she cried. "It might be better, perhaps, but I would rather run more risk, and meet you where nobody has a right to question who and what you are."

"Just as you please. It is your own affair," said he, carelessly. "Are you coming to show me the private entrance you spoke of? I am sure to meet somebody about those large gates."

She went and showed it to him—quaking as she did so, lest some one should meet them; and when he was once safely beyond the boundary of the grounds, she gave a deep sigh of relief, and sped like an arrow toward the house.

CHAPTER XIX.

YOU CANNOT LET ME HELP YOU?

When Katharine entered the hall, the sounds which proceeded from the drawing-room assured her at once that the vigil of the ladies was over, and the fox-hunters had returned. On the staircase the first person she met was Annesley, who was descending as she went up. He stopped and held out his hand.

"Good-morning, Miss Tresham," he said, with a smile. "We are back again in a most dispirited and luckless condition—dogs and all fairly outwitted by a fox. Won't you come and take a game of billiards, and help me to forget it?"

"Not just now," said Katharine, hardly knowing what she was saying. "I—I am just going to my room."

He started a little, and still holding her hand, gazed earnestly into her face.

"Something is the matter," he said, quickly. "I never saw you so pale before. Katharine—Miss Tresham, has anybody done any thing to annoy you?"

"Nothing," she answered, eagerly. "Why should you think so? Everybody is very kind. There!—please let me pass. I am not well."

"Something is the matter," repeated he, still oblivious of courtesy, and keeping his place before her. "If you would only tell me—if it is any thing I could set straight—"

"It is not any thing you could set straight," interrupted Katharine, almost wild to get away. "Mr. Annesley, will you—will you please let me pass? I have told you I am not well."

He moved aside, and, disregarding the pained look on his face, she flew by, and the next moment he heard her chamber door open and shut.

The young man stood for a minute where she had left him—pain gradually giving way to surprise on his face. Then he went down, and, as he crossed the hall, his mother came out of the library and joined him.

"Are you going out, Morton?" she said. "I will walk with you a little way. I have something to say to you."

"I was not going out," he answered; "but I can go, if you wish to speak to me."

Without any further words, they passed out, and took the same path which Katharine and Miss Vernon had taken an hour or two before. After they had gone a short distance, Mrs. Annesley was the first to break the silence.

"Was that Miss Tresham you met on the staircase, Morton?"

"Yes, it was Miss Tresham," he answered, and in a moment it flashed across his mind that somebody had been guilty of slighting or annoying Katharine, and that his mother knew of it. "Something was the matter with her," he said. "I never saw her look so before. She did not seem like herself at all. Somebody must have offended her," continued the young man, with suppressed anger in his voice. "Mother, if you know who it is, if any—"

"Stop a moment, Morton," said Mrs. Annesley, with dignity. "You forget that you are speaking of your own guests—of ladies and gentlemen who are incapable of being rude to any one. Nobody inside the doors of Annesdale has done any thing to wound or annoy Miss Tresham; but what has occurred outside of them," she added, significantly, "it is quite beyond my power to say."

"What do you mean?" asked Morton, to whom this distinction was quite unintelligible.

"I mean that something has happened which I think you ought to know. I was in the observatory an hour or two ago, showing the view to Mrs. Dancey, when I happened to have my attention directed toward the entrance gates. I saw two figures which I easily identified as Miss Tresham and Irene Vernon emerge from the shrubbery just as a man was entering the gates Of course, at such a distance the action was rather confused to my sight, but I could distinguish very plainly that a recognition took place between the man and Miss Tresham, and that, after Irene Vernon had first gone on alone, he and she entered the shrubbery together. I thought it singular, but nothing more, until I went down-stairs, and, after a while, Irene came in—still alone. I asked her what had become of Miss Tresham, and she evaded the question. It was only when I told her what I had seen, that she acknowledged she had left Miss Tresham in the grounds with this stranger. She had evidently been requested to keep the matter secret, for she begged me not to mention it, and, of course, I shall not do so—excepting to yourself, who certainly have a right to know. When you met Miss Tresham, she was just coming in; and all this happened I should be afraid to say how long before."

"Did Miss Irene know the man?" said Morton, speaking very grimly.

"No, she had never seen him before. He was a stranger, she said—and young and handsome."

"And what explanation did Miss Tresham give to her?"

"She did not tell me. She was very reticent, and evidently disliked to mention the matter at all. I asked her why she had not urged Miss Tresham to bring her friend to the house. She replied she had done so; but that she—Miss Tresham—had declined."

"And there is no doubt of this?" said Morton at last, after a pause.

"There is not the least doubt of it," answered his mother. Then, after a minute: "Morton, is it not all as I told you? Can such a woman as this be trusted?"

"What has this to do with the question of her being trusted?" he asked. "Do you think I will doubt the woman who is every thing to me, because some man—some friend or relation, perhaps, of whom we know nothing—comes to see her, and she, meeting him in the open air, keeps him there, instead of taking him into a house full of people like that yonder?"

"But why should she ask Irene Vernon to keep the matter secret, if it was only some friend or some relation, as you say?"

"Did Miss Vernon say that she had asked her?"

"No; but I saw very plainly—"

"You are determined to see every thing against and nothing for her, mother," he said, a little wearily. "Can't you put the matter as if it concerned somebody else?—can't you see that if it did concern somebody else, you would not think it of any importance?"

"I see that you are wilfully blind, and wilfully determined to go your own way," she answered. "Well, I have done my duty—I have warned you. Since you will not heed the warning, you must pay the penalty of your obstinacy and folly, but my heart sinks when I consider what a penalty it will be. We had better go back to the house now—I have a great deal to do."

They went back to the house, and did not speak of the subject again; but, though Morton had so summarily silenced his mother, he could not silence the thoughts of his own mind, or the throbs of his own heart. "What did it mean?" he asked himself again and again, with the same feeling which had overpowered him when that letter, which had been the direct consequence of his mother's act, had dropped from the pages of the "Adelaide." His perplexity was not ended, nor his anxiety stilled, by the fact that Miss Tresham did not appear again that day. She was lying down—she had a headache, he was told, when he inquired about her; and, with this most unsatisfactory information, he was obliged to be content, and make, or try to make, himself agreeable to a score or more of people. It was fine social training, no doubt, but very unpleasant in the process. Any thing that teaches you to conceal your feelings, and smile in the face of the world when your heart is breaking—if hearts ever do break!—is considered a benefit; and, certainly, Morton made great strides in this branch of social art that day. He had to hear a great many remarks from other people, too; for Langdon, Talcott and Co., were quite concerned for Miss Tresham's indisposition, and kept saying how very unlucky it was, and the ball that night, too! "There is no danger but that she will be well enough for the ball," said Miss Lester, who heard some remark of this description. "What! any girl in her senses stay away from the ball—and such a ball, too! I'll believe it when I see it, and if you care to wager, Cousin Tom, I'll bet you a new collar for Spitfire, that she comes down!"

"I'll wager, certainly, Maggie," said Cousin Tom. "A new collar for Spitfire, is it?—against what?"

"Oh, any thing you choose. Shall we say a purse? I wouldn't, if I was not sure that I shall not have the trouble of making it."

"A purse, then," said he, taking out his note-book, and entering an imposing register of the wager.

Dinner was early that day, for the ball was to come off in the evening, and it was necessary that the whole force of the establishment should be employed in preparation. This was the ball of which Katharine had spoken to Mrs. Gordon, of which she had thought as the first and greatest item in her Christmas enjoyment; and now it was with a sick heart and a throbbing head that she faced the prospect of it, and the necessity of rising to dress. As she lay on her bed with the room darkened, the fire burning with a soft, crackling content, a wet handkerchief over her aching eyes, and a bottle of cologne-water in her hand, some despairing thoughts on the perversity of human circumstances occurred to her. She had come to Annesdale meaning to leave her weight of anxiety behind, and to enjoy herself for a short time with the natural enjoyment of youth; and all of a sudden every thing was dashed with bitterness! Poor Katharine! Very stern troubles were staring her in the face, but still she had time to give a sigh to her murdered pleasure. "If it had only been the day *after* the ball!" she thought to herself—and it is to be hoped that she will not be accounted utterly frivolous for doing so!

She had at last risen languidly, and was looking with critical attention in the mirror, regarding her pale cheeks, her red eyes, and her swollen nose, wondering if it would be possible to bring all these features into order, or if she had not better make a virtue of necessity, and resign the ball, when the door opened and Miss Lester entered.

"So you are up!" cried this young lady, in her liveliest tone. "I am glad of that—glad because you are better, and because I have a wager on your going to the ball. You *are* going, are you not?"

"I was just considering about it," said Katharine, doubtfully, "Come and tell me what you think. I am looking frightfully, you see."

"I don't see any thing of the kind," said Miss Lester, whose opinion was rather biassed by personal interest. "Your eyes are red and—your—nose—a little. But that is because you have been crying. If you don't cry any more, by the time you are dressed they will be all right. Then you are pale; but a little rouge—do you ever use rouge?"

"Never."

"You don't think it a sin, do you?"

"I don't think any thing about it. As a matter of personal taste, I don't like, and don't use it—that is all. I confess, however, that the sight of it affects me very much in the same way that a coarse perfume does. The two things always seem to me to go together."

"I don't use it myself," said Miss Lester, philosophically, "but a great many girls do. I have a cousin who paints dreadfully. However, paleness is becoming to you—you are generally pale—and I think you might go down. Dancing will soon give you a color. If any personal arguments are needed, Cousin Tom is half crazy to see you, and Spitfire will get a new collar if you go."

Katharine thought of the unwelcome visitor whom Spitfire had forced upon her notice that morning, and felt very little of the grateful esteem which would have made her anxious to secure a new collar for him. But still she suffered herself to be persuaded—especially as she did not need very much persuasion—and, after a short gossip in the fading twilight, the serious business of the toilet began.

The ballroom at Annesdale formed a wing of the main building, and had been built by Morton since affairs came into his hands. It was a large, and (for a ballroom), decidedly tasteful apartment—ornamented sufficiently to avoid the look of disagreeable bareness, yet not overloaded by any means, and with every facility for light and warmth. It was a beautiful apartment, Katharine thought, as she entered it for the first time that evening, and saw the lofty ceiling painted in brilliant fresco, the double line of columns down the sides, the heavy green garlands that swung in festoons from one to another, and the lights glittering in every direction, shining on the scarlet holly-berries, and reflected back from the smoothly-waxed floor. On a raised stand at the upper end of the room the band was pealing forth a march, and the guests, who had been lingering in the drawing-rooms, in the green-house, in the library, in every place that was thrown open to the public, began to pour in. A few couples were promenading in time to those strains, but with the majority there was an exciting rush to make engagements, and secure a desirable position in certain desirable ball-books.—"Are you engaged for the third set, Miss Josephine?"—"May I have the fifth on your list, Miss Annie?"—"Stand back, Tom, I have a word or two to say—Miss Mary, mayn't I have the second?"—"Bella, I wish you would remember that mamma don't like you to waltz."—"Certainly, Mr. Ford, you can have the pleasure of—the tenth set, did you say?"—"Dancey, who is your partner for the first cotillon?—Get one, man, in a hurry, and be our *vis-à-vis*—Miss Nelly's and mine."—"Stop there, George, stop—come here and help us to make up a set."—

"A polka, did you say, Mr. Anderson? I never dance the round dances."

All this was sounding at once in Katharine's ears, as she stood near a large pillar, looking very pale and pretty in her white dress, wreathed with blue convolvulus, when Annesley came up to her.

"I have been looking for you everywhere," he said, hastily, "and I have only time for a word. Will you give me the second set, and save two or three more for me?"

"I cannot give you the second set," she answered. "It is Mr. Talcott's."

"The third, then?"

"That belongs to Mr. Hallam."

"The fourth—fifth—sixth—any thing! Permit me—" he suddenly leaned forward, and, taking the little ivory toy that hung at her waist, ran his eye rapidly over the list of engagements, scribbled his initials in two or three vacant places, then, with a smile and a "Thank you," was gone. A moment later, Mr. Langdon left the side of a young lady with whom he was negotiating for a waltz, and claimed Katharine's hand for the dance about to commence. The measure of the music changed, the confused mass of figures formed into magical squares, the wall-flowers of both sexes fell back and clustered around or beyond the columns, and the amusement of the evening began in earnest. To Katharine it would have been like enchantment, at another time; but now, above the sound of the music, the tread of dancing feet, the shifting to-and-fro of brightly-clad forms, she saw one face and heard one voice that banished all gayety from her heart, and took all lightness from her step. Despite her efforts to the contrary, she seemed so unlike herself that her appearance struck a gentleman standing near the set in which she was dancing, a gentleman whose tall head towered somewhat above the throng of lookers-on—for all La Grange was in force there that night, the county people thinking nothing of a ten-miles' drive to Mrs. Annesley's Christmas-ball. His intent gaze caught Katharine's attention at last. In the course of *chasséing* back and forth, she looked up, saw him, and smiled. "Oh, Mr. Warwick!" she said, in a tone that surprised her partner.

"Mr.—*who?*" he asked, looking round.

"Mr. Warwick," answered Katharine, still smiling, and nodding to Mr. Warwick across the set. "I am so glad to see him," she went on. "It is like a home-face in the midst of strangers. I must speak to him as soon as the cotillon is over. I want to ask about Mrs. Marks, and the children, and all of them. I feel—"

She stopped suddenly, and her face changed so much that her companion absolutely stared. A sharp recollection came to her of the difference that these few days had made in her life, of the man who had seen Mrs. Marks, and the inquiries which would meet her when she returned to the familiar house in Tallahoma. Of course Mr. Langdon understood none of this, and, seeing her hesitate and turn pale, he at once conceived a suspicion of Mr. Warwick, and glanced across the room at that gentleman. Being somewhat reassured by his sedate, middle-aged appearance, he took up Katharine's sentence.

"You feel—what? Not home-sick, I trust?"

"I feel as if it had been such a long time since I left home," she answered, absently. "That is always the case, you know, when one has been among new scenes and new people.—First gentleman and lady, did they say? You are the first gentleman, Mr. Langdon."

Meanwhile, Morton was dancing with Miss Vernon, in quite another set, at the upper end of the room. He thought, and so did a great many other people, that Irene had never looked more lovely than on that night. Fashions change very much in thirty years, and to describe her costume would probably be to bring a dreadful picture before the eyes of to-day; but everybody said how charmingly she was dressed, and certainly the shining pink silk that she wore, with rich point lace falling from her shoulders, was as becoming as possible. Then her cheeks were flushed, and her eyes were bright, and her hair looked like spun gold, as it gleamed about her graceful head. Morton, who had never thought very much about her beauty, suddenly opened his eyes, and admired it with quite a fervor of enthusiasm. "I never saw you look so well," he could not help telling her more than once—though the remark strictly interpreted was any thing but a compliment.

"Perhaps you never looked at me before," she said, though she hated herself for saying it. "Nobody else seems to think that I am looking unusually well to-night."

"Shall we take a vote on the question, for I don't fancy the imputation of being a mole or a bat?"

"No, thank you. I'll take the fact of my unusual good looks or your unusual good-nature, for granted, in preference to that. *A propos* of appearance, don't you think Miss Tresham is looking very well?"

"Very pretty, but not very well. She is too pale."

"Yes, but she is one of the few people to whom pallor is becoming. And those morning-glories—are they not beautiful?"

"Yes," said Morton, catching a glimpse of the morning-glories in question, as their wearer moved forward in the dance. Then he saw his way to a sudden inquiry, and made it without loss of time.

"I met Miss Tresham on the staircase this morning, just after my return, and she seemed very much distressed and agitated. I hope nothing unpleasant occurred while you and she were in the grounds?"

"Nothing," answered Miss Vernon, with a reticence that did not escape his observation. "How did you know that I was in the grounds with her?" she added, with a keen glance at him.

"My mother told me," he answered. "Don't think that I was busying myself with matters which did not concern me," he added, with a quick flush coming over his face; "but when I met Miss Tresham, I saw at once that something had annoyed her, and I thought it might be something I could remedy, so I went to my mother"—at the moment, Morton really forgot that his mother had gone to him—"and she told me that you had been with Miss Tresham, and mentioned that she met some one—"

"I did not mention it at all," interrupted Miss Vernon, bluntly. "Miss Tresham asked me—that is, I thought it likely she would not care for me to speak of the matter, so I was sorry Mrs. Annesley had seen the—the person come in the gate. I answered her questions, that was all. I shall not answer yours, Mr. Annesley, so I beg you won't ask any."

"I am not going to ask any," said Morton, a little amused. "I would not think of such a thing as meddling with Miss Tresham's affairs. But she seemed so much agitated—"

"Things agitate at one time, that would have no effect at another," said Miss Vernon, coolly. "I should probably be agitated if I was living in Russia and you suddenly appeared before me—though there is nothing at all agitating in seeing you here, you know."

"I understand. But Miss Tresham I am sure can have no reason for concealing—"

Miss Vernon interrupted him again, remorselessly.

"Miss Tresham did not ask me to conceal any thing, Mr. Annesley; but I have learned by experience that silence is golden, and speech is silver—or base copper, rather, when it takes the form of silly tattling. I do as I would be done by. There are many reasons which might make me wish to conceal—that's a hateful word!—the visit of some embarrassing friend or relation, from people who had no right of espionage over my conduct, and so I am not quick to suspect other people for doing the same thing."

"Thank you," said Morton, before he knew what he was about. Then he added, with a blush: "You don't know how much I admire and respect such sentiments. There are not many women like you, Miss Vernon."

"There are thousands much better," said Miss Vernon, with a sharpness that quite took him by surprise.

While this conversation was going on, the cotillon ended, the last bows were made, and, as Mr. Langdon was leading Katharine away, Mr. Warwick came up to her.

"Shall we go into the drawing-room and get an ice?" the obliging Cousin Tom was saying, when he found himself summarily put aside. "Mr. Warwick!—I am so glad to see you," Katharine cried; and Mr. Warwick looked at her companion, as he said: "I have a great many messages for you, from Bessie and the children. Do you care about hearing them?"

"Of course I do," answered she, warmly; and upon this, she withdrew her hand from Mr. Langdon's arm, and took instead the one Mr. Warwick offered.

"I will see you again, when the fourth set comes round," she said, with a smile, to the former gentleman, and in this way he found himself deserted, just as he had flattered himself with the expectation of a pleasantly uninterrupted *tête-à-tête*.

"So Annesdale and all its gayety has not made you forget Tallahoma and the school-room?" said Mr. Warwick, as they walked away. "I could hardly realize that you were yourself, when I saw you dancing a little while ago."

"'If I am I, as I do think I be,'" said Katharine, with a laugh, "I have certainly not forgotten the school-room, or anybody connected with it, Mr. Warwick. How is Mrs. Marks, and how are the children?—did Sara and Katy go to see their aunt?—and has Nelly's cough given any more trouble?"

"Bessie and all the children are well, and sent you more love than I could carry—Katy and Sara did not go to their aunt's, and Nelly's cough is quite well, I believe."

"Has nothing happened since I went away? I feel as if a great deal ought to have happened."

"I think every thing has gone on exactly as usual, excepting that it may compliment you to hear that you have been very much missed by everybody. When Dick cut his hand the other day, he disgraced his manhood by crying because you were not there to bandage it up."

"Has Dick cut his hand? I am so sorry. How did he do it?"

"I was foolish enough to give him a box of tools as a Christmas-gift, and the result was three accidents in the course of as many days. Katy was very anxious to come with me to-night."

"I wish you could have brought her," said Katharine, sincerely.

They had left the ballroom by this time, and were in the drawing-room, which was thronged with people laughing, talking, eating ices, making picture-like groups everywhere.

"Is there a quiet spot to be found anywhere?" asked Mr. Warwick, looking round. "Twenty years ago, I might have liked this kind of thing; but now I find that I am very much out of my element. You know those messages I told you about. Is there a quiet place in which I could deliver them?"

"Suppose we try the library," said Katharine.

They crossed the hall to the library, and found only one or two whist-parties in possession of it. At the farther end, a sofa was fitted into a sort of alcove between two bookcases, and to this Katharine led the way. She sat down first, and looked up at her companion out of the soft gloom—her white dress and the blue flowers in her hair showing in bright relief against the dark background.

"Will not this do?" said she, smiling; and somehow the little scene came back to John Warwick long afterward, touching him again as it touched him then.

"Yes, it will do very well," he said, sitting down by her. Then he added, suddenly, "You are looking very badly. Have you been sick?"

"Not at all," answered she, growing a little paler. "I have been quite well, and enjoying myself very much. Do you know that you have terribly keen eyes?" she added, trying to laugh, and not succeeding very well.

"I hope I have serviceable eyes," he answered; "but it would not require very keen ones to see that something is the matter with you. If you have not been sick, you have been worried—and that is worse. I may be blundering in speaking of it," he went on, "and, if so, you must forgive me, but I was struck by the change in your appearance when I saw you dancing."

"I have been sick all day," said Katharine, forgetting her contrary assertion of a moment back. "That is, I have had a headache and been in bed with it. One does not look very well after a thing of that kind."

"No," said Mr. Warwick, regarding her with a pair of eyes which, for the first time, she found uncomfortably penetrating. "If you have been in bed all day," he added, "I suppose you did not see a visitor, who called at Bessie's this morning, and whom she directed here?"

Dim as the light was, he noticed—he could not avoid noticing—the crimson tide which in a moment spread over her face and neck.

"Yes, I saw him," she answered; and, as she spoke, she gave a piteous, imploring glance, that reminded him of the look sometimes seen in an animal's eyes before the knife of the butcher descends and strikes home to the heart. Its unconscious pathos touched him; but the lawyer in his composition enabled him to persevere.

"Bessie's curiosity was quite excited," he said. "You know it takes very little to excite her, and it seems that the gentleman—whom she described as young and handsome—asked many questions about you. That was enough to form the groundwork of a romance, which she has been building ever since. Her only fear is, that you may be induced to leave her, and that, she says, would break her heart."

"Mrs. Marks is very good," said Katharine, forcing a smile. "But she need not fear. I am not likely to go away. The gentleman who called to see me was"—a pause, and a great gulp of rage and self-contempt—"was a person whom I knew in England."

"So he said," remarked Mr. Warwick, rather dryly.

"I hope he did not annoy Mrs Marks in any way?" said Katharine, catching the intonation of his voice. "I—I do not think she is likely to see him again. He will leave Tallahoma in a few days—to-morrow, perhaps."

"He did not annoy her at all," Mr. Warwick answered. "I hope I have not said any thing to make you think so."

There was a pause after this. Katharine felt faint and sick, but she kept her seat—whatever he should say next, she must be ready to answer. Mr. Warwick, meanwhile, said nothing —his face looked somewhat severe, as he gazed past her; but that was its usual expression when at rest. In this lull, the voices of the whist-players sounded.

"Three by cards, and two by honors, sets us five, and four before, is nine."

"You should have returned my lead of spades, Mr. Barry, and we might have—"

"If you had led out trumps, as you ought to have done," cried an excited voice from the other table, "they could not have made a trick. I held every high diamond, sir, and every one of them trumped!"

"We threw away the game by that play of hearts, Mrs. Dargan. It gave them the lead, and then—"

This was the kind of talk which came in and bridged over Katharine's suspense. It is astonishing how oddly conscious people are of such things at such times. When the last great struggle comes, and the soul is about to go forth, shall we, even then, hear and notice the bird that sings at our window, and the child who laughs in the street below?

"Miss Tresham," said Mr. Warwick, turning round abruptly, "do you remember the day we walked out to the pond, and I told you that something was preying on your health and spirits?"

"Yes," Katharine answered, "I remember it."

"And do you also remember that I asked you if I could do any thing to relieve you?"

"Yes, Mr. Warwick, I remember that also—very gratefully."

"Well, I don't wish to force your confidence, but one glance at your face to-night told me that the anxiety which I saw then had made greater strides—had, in fact, been realized. As I told you before, if it is any thing relating to ideal troubles, I can do nothing for you; but if it is real—if it is practical—Miss Tresham, remember that I am both a man and a lawyer, and that, in either character, I am ready to serve you."

"Mr. Warwick, you are very good—you are more than good," said Katharine, almost ready to give way to the childish relief of tears. "Don't—please don't think me ungrateful. I feel your kindness in my very heart, and—and thank you for it. But I cannot do any thing else."

"You cannot let me help you?"

"No—I cannot."

That ended the matter. After a minute, Mr. Warwick rose and offered his arm. "Your partners will be looking for you," he said. "I must not monopolize you so long. Have you any message for Bessie?"

"My best love, and tell her I will see her to-morrow."

"What, are you coming back to Tallahoma?"

"Not to stay—I promised to remain here until after New-Year—but on business. There is Mr. Talcott coming for me now."

"I have been looking for you everywhere, Miss Tresham," said Mr. Talcott, quite breathless. "The dancing began some time ago, and I am afraid we shall not get a place unless we make haste."

"Don't let me detain you," said Mr. Warwick. "Good-night."

"Shall I not see you again?"

"No, I only looked in to be able to tell Bessie how you are getting on. I am going back to town now."

He was as good as his word, and Katharine had no further glimpse of him that night; but amid all the music and dancing, the gay voices and bright smiles, his voice sounded, and she heard again and again the words, "You cannot let me help you?" Her heart gave back an answer, for every now and then she caught herself murmuring, "If I only could!—ah, if I only could!"

CHAPTER XX.

MR. WARWICK'S NEW CLIENT.

About the time that Katharine threw herself down on the bed, and was foolish enough to cry until she made her head ache, Babette was tramping along the road which led from Tallahoma to Morton House. She had been sent on an errand by her mistress, and was returning with two or three large parcels under her arm, disdainfully regardless of the fact that she was the object of much attention and remark on the part of several small boys in her rear. They knew better than to come within reach of her hand, of which more than one of them had felt the weight; but, taking care to keep at a respectful distance, they followed her beyond the corporate limits. Indeed, Babette was a sufficiently remarkable figure to excite attention in a place much more used to remarkable figures than quiet Tallahoma. Besides her usual foreign costume, she had, in consideration of the muddy state of the roads, mounted a pair of sabots, and in them she went boldly clattering along, with her dress tucked up even shorter than the walking-skirt of a fashionable girl of the present day. "Good gracious, aunty, where'd you get your shoes?" more than one audacious boy inquired; but aunty's short nose only went a little higher in the air, and her keen black eyes only gave a little quicker gleam by way of reply. Her fierce appearance quite awed the good folk of the village. They had an idea that she was a sort of dragoness, whom Mrs. Gordon had imported for special guard and defence. Poor Babette, whose temper was irascible, but who was really of an excellent disposition, and whose appearance only was against her, had no idea that when she walked into a shop, with her large gold ear-rings bobbing on each side of her swarthy, stern-looking face, the clerks fairly quaked, and would have given any thing to avoid the perilous duty of serving her.

She was well served, however; and she had made her purchases and was finally on her way home—tramping along the narrow foot-path that ran by the side of the muddy road, close under the zigzag rail-fences, humming to herself in French a sort of jingling refrain, and now and then casting looks of defiance behind to see if any of her troublesome train were in sight. They had given up the pursuit, she found at last, and the gates of Morton House were almost in sight when a man's figure appeared, advancing with quick strides along the foot-path toward her. Babette hardly noticed him, her head being full of other things, for she was making a rough calculation mentally of the money she had spent, and deciding that she had been cheated beyond that point where forbearance is said to be a virtue. It was all her mistress's fault, however. She had bidden her buy the things, and never mind about the price. "Eh bien, if people will be extravagant!" Babette said to herself with a shrug. Meanwhile, the gentleman was thinking just as little of this strangely-clad figure clattering along the road to meet him. In fact, he did not notice her at all. He was thinking of other things, too, and gnawing his under lip as he had gnawed it in speaking of the money a little while before. It would be hard to tell which of them was thrilled with the strangest shock of surprise when they came suddenly face to face, and, looking up, recognized each other.

"Mon Dieu!" gasped Babette, and the parcels absolutely rolled out of her arms into the mud, as she stood helpless and aghast before him.

"What!—Babette!" cried the other, in astonishment evidently as great and uncontrollable as her own. He put out his hand and grasped her arm, as if to make sure of the fact of her bodily presence. But Babette rudely pushed him away. Evidently she had no more desire than Katharine had manifested to salute him cordially.

"Keep your hands to yourself, Monsieur St. Jean," she exclaimed, sharply. "Mon Dieu!—what are you doing here?—as if madame, poor lady, has not suffered enough for you to leave her in peace!"

"So your mistress is here!" said he, quickly. "Good Heavens! how near I was to going away without knowing it! Where—where is she, Babette?"

But the very question betrayed him. Babette saw that this encounter had been accidental, and that whatever reason had brought him here, the presence of Mrs. Gordon had no share in it. "How near I was to going away without knowing it!" he had unwittingly said, and Babette's ears were quick. So were her wits for that matter, and in a moment her reply was ready. She had no time for cunning subterfuge or evasion. The plain road to mislead him was in downright falsehood, and in downright falsehood she unhesitatingly took refuge.

"Madame is not where you are likely to find her, M'sieu St. Jean," she said, with ill-simulated triumph. "Thanks to le bon Dieu, she is far enough away, and it is not I who is going to tell you where she is. Ma foi! I would tell the devil sooner!" she added, bitterly.

"You are telling a lie," said the gentleman, coolly, "and that is not what I expected of a good Catholic like you, Babette. I wonder what the priest will say to this when you go to confession."

Babette's face fell for an instant; but she remembered what was at stake, plucked up courage, and answered boldly and volubly: "It is not for a scoffing heretic like you, M'sieu St. Jean, to tell Christian people that they are liars. I say that madame is not here, nor anywhere that you are likely to find her. And I'll thank you," she went on, raising her voice, "to stand out of the path and let me go on"

"Where have you been, and where are you going, and with whom do you live, if your mistress is not here?" asked St. John, coolly keeping his position in front of her.

"Mon Dieu! what business is it of yours?" demanded she, bursting into one of the sudden furies to which the servants of Morton House were well accustomed. "I shall tell you nothing," she continued, trembling with passion. "Madame is not here. I am staying with *une amie*—I have been to town to make purchases. If you will not let me pass, I shall go round you."

"Pass, by all means," said he, moving aside with a peculiar smile.

She carefully gathered her parcels out of the mud, and, hugging them close in her arms, marched stolidly by him—grateful for, yet half incredulous of, this welcome release. She had not gone five paces before she heard his step behind, and knew that he was following her. Instantly she faced round upon him, her black eyes gleaming, and her swarthy face all aglow.

"Comment, M'sieu St. Jean!" she cried, indignantly. "You say I may pass, and, after I pass, you follow—you dog me! Call you this conduct of a gentleman?"

"If you won't give me any information, Babette, I must simply find it out," said he, laughing at her anger. "You needn't excite yourself. I am only going with you to your friend's. There is no harm in that, I am sure."

"My friend does not wish to see you," said Babette, almost out of her senses, with indignation. "She would sprinkle holy water if you came in sight of the door."

"I have no doubt of that," said he, still smiling so provokingly that she felt inclined to throw her muddy parcels in his face; "but still, I must accompany you."

"Eh bien! then I shall not go," said she; and, to his great surprise, she wrapped her shawl around her more comfortably, and sat down deliberately on a large stone that lay in the fence corner. Once seated, she looked up at him triumphantly. "I can stay here as long as you can, M'sieu St. Jean," she said, "and perhaps a little longer."

For the first time she had the best of the situation, and, for the first time also, St. John lost his temper.

"Confound you!" he said, savagely. "Do you suppose I am such a fool as not to know that your mistress is near at hand somewhere, and that you are lying like the father of lies himself? Do you suppose I can't find out without any help from you? I have only to walk into the village yonder, and ask a few questions, to learn all that I want to know. I shall ask them, too; and you may tell your mistress, with my compliments, that I shall do myself the honor of calling on her before the day is over."

With this, he turned on his heel, and walked off toward the town. Babette eagerly watched him out of sight; she even followed him to a bend of the road, and saw his figure vanish in the distance, before she could believe that he was really gone, and that he might not return and dog her steps. Then, as fast as the sabots would allow, she hurried to the house, making no pause until she had burst in upon Mrs. Gordon with the news which she knew would be to her the most unwelcome that could be told.

"Madame!" she cried, as the startled lady looked up from her cushions in astonishment; "madame!—Ah! what a misfortune! It is terrible!—it is enough to break one's heart," said the excitable Frenchwoman, almost sobbing; "but, as I was coming back from town, madame, I met — out here — in the road — Monsieur St. Jean!"

Mrs. Gordon, who had not done more than languidly cross the room for weeks, gave one convulsive bound from the sofa, and stood erect on the floor.

"Babette!" she gasped. More than that she could not say.

"Monsieur St. Jean!" repeated Babette, lifting her arm with a tragic gesture, as if she called upon Heaven to witness the truth of the fact she asserted. "I met him in the road, madame, not farther from the gate than you could throw a stone; and ah, mon Dieu!" said she, shaking her head, "what shall I have to suffer for all the lies I told!"

"St. John!" said Mrs. Gordon; and she had hardly said it when she grew white as a sheet, and sat down suddenly. "Yonder!—that phial on the table," she panted, brokenly, as Babette hurried to her. Well used as she was to these attacks, the maid was frightened—she had never before seen her mistress look like this; she had never known her face so ghastly, or her breath so painfully short. The severity of the paroxysm did not last more than a minute; but, when it was over, Mrs. Gordon sank back on the sofa utterly exhausted. "Wait—wait a little," she said, when Babette began to speak, and the latter had discretion enough to hold her tongue. She bathed her mistress's face for some time in silence, and it was not until Mrs. Gordon opened her eyes, and said, "Well, Babette?" that she broke into a voluble history of her encounter, and of all that had been said on both sides. By the time she finished, she had worked herself into such a state of emotion, that she was fairly weeping and wringing her hands.

"Madame, let us go!" she exclaimed. "Let us not stay here. He will come.—M'sieu will come — and he will take you and make you wretched. Madame, let us go!—Mon Dieu! let us go!"

"Soyez tranquille!" said Mrs. Gordon, faintly. "We must bear what we must bear, my poor Babette. But you need not fear—he will not take us again. Go and order the carriage."

"To leave here, madame?"

"No—only to drive me into town. Don't waste time, Babette—go!"

Babette went, and, when she returned, she found her mistress dressing with trembling haste. "My bonnet, Babette," she said; and, as Babette ran to seek the bonnet, which had not been used since her mistress entered Morton House, two months before, she could not help wondering vaguely what this sudden movement meant. Whatever it was, Mrs. Gordon certainly looked more like herself than she had done in many a long day before. Her eyes were bright, her cheeks were flushed, and, as she tied the strings of her bonnet, and drew the long crape veil over her face, she felt with a strange, wild thrill, that stagnation was over, and the breath of life and combat had come to her again. It made another woman of her. It gave her strength, and will, and purpose, that no one would have dreamed of her possessing as she lay languidly on her sofa, and watched one dull day after another go by. Before she entered the carriage, she had all the windows put up, and all the curtains put down. Then she bade the coachman drive to Mr. Warwick's office in Tallahoma.

To Mr. Warwick's office in Tallahoma the lumbering old carriage accordingly proceeded, rousing a good deal of interest in the quiet streets of the little village, and startling a group of loungers who were smoking their pipes in the bright sunshine outside Mr. Warwick's door. The lawyer himself was not of the number. A man had called on business, and he had taken him into the office about ten minutes before the carriage appeared. His astonishment, therefore, was great when two or three men came tumbling into his door without any warning, and all at once. "Warwick, here's the Morton carriage!" they cried, excitedly. "What the deuce does it mean? Can Mrs.—Mrs. Gordon be coming here to see you?"

"The Morton carriage!" repeated Mr. Warwick, startled, despite himself. "I don't know, I have no idea what it means," he added. "Are you sure it is coming here?"

Before the others could reply, the carriage drew up before the curb-stone; and, the next moment, a half-grown negro boy appeared at the office door, cap in hand.

"Mr. Warruck, mistiss says she would like fur to see you on pa'tic'lar business, sir, if you is at leisure. If you ain't, she say she will come back when you is."

"Where is your mistress?" asked Mr. Warwick.

"In the carriage, sir."

"Tell her I will be there in a minute." He turned to his client, who was listening with open eyes and mouth. "Mr. Sloan, I am sure you will excuse me for deferring this business at present. Mrs. Gordon has come in from the country, and I can't put her off. Just leave the deed, and I will look over it, and you can call to-morrow."

Mr. Sloan was burning with curiosity, but the lawyer's quiet manner left him no room for appeal. He put down the deed, and made his exit, followed by the smokers. "Warwick won't want us, either," they said, and filed off without waiting for a hint to that effect. No sooner was the coast clear, than Mr. Warwick, who certainly would not have hesitated to say that he did not want them, went out to the carriage and opened the door.

"How are you, Mrs. Gordon?" he said, courteously, shaking hands with the black-draped and closely-veiled figure inside. "I am quite at leisure to attend to your commands. Will you come into my office, and let me hear what I can do for you?"

"Are they all gone?" inquired Mrs. Gordon, who had taken an observation through the carriage-window. "I wish to see you alone."

"They are all gone," he answered, extending his hand again, to assist her from the carriage.

She descended rather feebly, as he observed, and, feeling the worse for her unusual exertion, leaned heavily on his arm as they crossed the pavement. When he caught a glimpse of her face, as she put her veil partially aside on entering the office, it looked so pale, that he was afraid she might be about to faint. He placed her in a chair beside the fire, closed the door, and went hastily to a side-table, where he poured out a glass of water, and brought it to her "Will you let me suggest that you are too much muffled up about the face?" he said. "Permit me—" and he drew the masses of crape back, as she put the water to her lips for a moment. Seeing her countenance thus more distinctly, he was shocked by its appearance, and confirmed in his dread of a fainting-fit. He pulled a small table that was close by, to her elbow, and set the glass of water, which she now gave back to him, upon it. Then he crossed the room to one of several walnut bookcases that were ranged around the walls, opened a door that revealed to sight three shelves full of respectable-looking volumes bound in calf, while the fourth, and lowest, seemed to be doing duty as a sideboard. From among two or three decanters he selected one, also a wineglass, and returned to Mrs. Gordon's side.

"You look very pale, very ill, I may say," he remarked; "drink this wine. It will do you more good than water."

"Thank you," she said, taking the wineglass which he had just filled. "You are very kind. Yes, I believe I need it."

She drank part of the wine, put the glass on the table, and turned to him. "Sit down," she said, with a slight motion of her hand toward a seat opposite. "I shall not faint, and I have a great deal to say to you."

It was some time before she spoke. Whether it was the memory of the past—of the different manner in which they two had once known each other—or whether it was merely the all-absorbing thought of the threatening present, something overpowered her, and it was some time before she could collect herself sufficiently to break the silence. At last, with an effort, the first words came.

"Mr. Warwick, for a reason that I will tell you presently, I stand in need of the advice of a lawyer. I have come to apply to you for that advice. But, even more than I need a lawyer, I need a friend, and the service that only a friend can render me. I venture, therefore—you may think without any claim—to ask if you remember the old time sufficiently to care to render me this service?"

"Mrs. Gordon must surely have forgotten that she was once Pauline Morton, before she could ask me such a question," said the lawyer, flushing slightly. "There are hereditary claims of friendship between us," he went on, hastily, as he saw an answering flush rise to the pale face opposite him, "and there is, moreover, a particular claim. When I was a struggling boy, your father aided me in a manner I can never forget. What I am to-day, I owe to his generous kindness. I will gladly do any thing in my power to serve his daughter."

Mrs. Gordon understood, as not many people would have done, the delicacy which made him speak thus—which made him allude not to herself, but to her father. Understanding it, she appreciated what she had only felt before, that this man could indeed be trusted, and that he spoke truly when he said that he would do "any thing" to serve her. Instinctively she held out her hand.

"Thank you," she said. "I felt sure that I might rely on you; but I am glad to hear you *say* that you will help me. Ah, it is a terrible thing to be a woman," said she, looking at him with pathetic eyes. "If I were like you, I should not need help."

"We all need it in some form or other," answered he. "None of us are so strong as to stand quite alone."

"But it is only a woman who is entirely at the mercy of another; who may be crushed in a hundred different ways—each more cruel, more bitter than death. Mr. Warwick, tell me—what power, short of murder, does not the law give a man over his wife?"

"It gives him a great deal," said Mr. Warwick, regarding her keenly, and reading the excitement written on her face. "But what interest has this subject to you? A widow—"

He was stopped by a gesture from her. Suddenly she extended her hand, and taking up the wine, drank it off. Then she put down the glass with a ringing sound, and, leaning forward, looked steadily into his eyes.

"God forgive me!" she said—"God forgive me that I am forced to say it, but He has not been kind enough to set me free. The first thing I have to tell you is that I am no widow. My husband"—the word nearly choked her—"is living."

Mr. Warwick started, but the surprise was not nearly so much of a surprise as might perhaps be imagined. He had suspected something like this before. It is hard to tell what slight circumstances first sowed the seeds of suspicion in his mind, but he had long felt an instinct that Mrs. Gordon's seclusion and impenetrable reticence were not characteristic of a widow, but of a woman who had still something to fear, something to hide from. Then, no one knew the business of the Morton estate as he did, and he had not failed to make his own comments on the fact that, in taking possession of this estate, Mrs. Gordon had absolutely refused to go through any of the usual legal forms. There was no one to contest her claim, she said, and so she quietly assumed her right of control without any sanction from the law. Over this obstinacy, Mr. Shields shrugged his shoulders. "It's a woman's notion of doing business, Mr. Warwick," he said. But Mr. Warwick himself was of a different mind. He suspected how it was; though the suspicion scarcely took definite form in his brain. He had other and more important things than Mrs. Gordon's private affairs to consider; and notwithstanding the boyish sentiment for which his sister still gave him credit, Mrs. Gordon herself was no more to him than any old friend, liked sincerely—liked with a certain tenderness, perhaps, on account of the past—but making no part of his daily life. And so it was, that he felt very little surprise when she told him that she was not a widow—that her husband was living.

"Do not blame me more than you can help," she went on, as he did not speak. "Do you remember how proud I used to be in the old time? Well, that pride has not quite been crushed out of me. I could not bear to come back here and tell these people what bitter shipwreck had overtaken me! I could not bear to spread before them the history of—of such a life as mine!"

"Why did you come back at all?" said he, hardly knowing what else to say.

"Because it was a place of refuge—and I had no other. Because it was the one place in the world where he was least likely to come—least likely to think of searching for me. When the last awful blow fell," said she, growing fearfully white, "I looked round despairingly and wondered where I could go. Then, like a relief from Heaven came the thought of my father's house. Here I could be safe, here I would be untroubled, here I might live and die unmolested by him. But I have only been at peace a little while. To-day Babette met an agent whom he has sent in search of me."

"An agent?"

"An unscrupulous tool, whom he retains for uses of this kind, named St. John. As soon as he conveys the information of my whereabouts, that man—my husband—will come here. It is not me he wants, it is Felix—but if he takes the child, he must take me too. What I wish to ask you is this"—she rose, and stood before him, with an eager yearning in her eyes—"*can* he take him from me? Does the law give him that power—here?"

The lawyer's heart was touched with pity for her; but truth was uncompromising, and must be told. "If he can prove that he is his father, it gives him that power anywhere."

The woman—the helpless creature to whom the law gave no power—sank down again into her chair, and covered her face with her hands. When she looked up at last, that face was tense and bloodless.

"Then I must ask that service of which I spoke a short time ago," she said. "Will you take my poor boy, and put him somewhere—away from me—where he will be in safety, and—and cannot be found?"

Mr. Warwick started, and, for a moment, looked more than surprised—in fact, he looked almost aghast. Here was a proposition indeed! that a lawyer who respected the law as the most sacred of earthly obligations, should be instrumental in evading it!—that a man who was full of the dominative opinions of his sex, should lend his aid to a scheme that removed a child from the just control of its father! Pauline Morton certainly stretched the cord of ancient friendship to its utmost tension, when she made such a demand of him.

"Mrs. Gordon," he said, gravely, "I would do any thing to serve you—any thing that was right; but I am not sure this would be right. A father always has a paramount claim to his child."

Instantly all the woman in her blazed out upon him.

"A paramount claim, given by whom?" she demanded. "It is you men that make the laws that grind poor women to the earth—not God, not religion, not any thing that should be respected! It is you who tear the very hearts out of our breasts, and then talk of right and power to do so. Yes, you have a right—the right of the strong to trample the weak! You have a power—the power of the master over the slave! God knows there is no other. But I might have been sure a man would never help me against a man. Therefore, I shall do what must be done, myself—and only ask you not to betray me."

"Stop, Mrs. Gordon," he said, as she rose and moved toward the door. "Stop a moment," he added, following her. "You must not leave me like this. Remember that I have not refused to help you. I stated a general fact when I said that a father has a paramount claim to his child. It is certainly true, as a general fact: but in particular cases, that claim is sometimes forfeited. If I am to serve you, I must do so with my eyes open—I must know whether the claim has been forfeited in this instance."

"I think I can convince you of that," said she, faintly, as she sat down again. "I am not strong enough for such violent emotion," she went on, panting slightly. "Wait—wait a little, and I will tell you all."

"Take your time," he said, kindly.

"If I do that, I should never speak at all," she answered, hurriedly. "I must do it at once. You heard of my marriage some fifteen years ago, did you not?"

"We heard of it vaguely. You kept up no communication with Lagrange, you know."

"I married a Captain Fraser, an English officer," she went on, apparently unheeding his reply. "I was very much in love with him," she said, with a trembling, scornful smile; "and he—well, he seemed to be in love with me. I was beautiful then, you know, and I had been very much admired. He was highly connected, and he was very handsome—I honestly believe that those were the only reasons I had for liking him. I thought myself able to judge of character, and rank and good looks dazzled me, as they might have dazzled any village school-girl. Well, I married him, and I cannot tell you of the life I led afterward. Look at my face. Every hour of it is written there! Captain Fraser left the army, and we lived on the Continent—there is not a city of Europe that is not full of bitter memories to me. After my mother died, the life grew worse. My husband was dissipated, and recklessly extravagant. My poor brother"—her voice almost choked her—"helped me as much as he could. It was my demands that went to impoverish the estate, and—and I hear that he has all the blame of it. As time went on, and matters grew worse, I would have separated from my husband, if it had not been for Felix. He, who was my youngest child, alone lived, and I could not leave him. It would have been better, perhaps, if I had done so, for"—she stopped here, and something like a ghastly horror came over her face—"for as matters grew no better, as ill-usage increased, my brother at last lost patience. He met us at Baden, where Fraser was at his worst, and—and there was a violent quarrel. I don't know how it was—I have never heard any particulars—but he—my brother—was killed by that man whom the law calls my husband!"

Almost unconsciously, Mr. Warwick uttered an exclamation of horror, but white as was her face, parched as were her lips, she hurried on:

"The next day I was half mad, and I did not know where to turn; but on one thing I was determined—that was, never to see him again. He and this St. John had been obliged to leave Baden, but he sent me word to go to Scotland, where we had been living for some two or three years—I forgot to say that an uncle had died, and left him a large estate, with the condition that he assumed the name of Gordon. Instead of going to Scotland, I came to America. He knows how I always hated the country, and I was sure he would never look for me here—besides he had hardly more than the vaguest idea of where Morton House was situated. I relied on all this, and I thought I might live here, and—and train Felix to be a gentleman. But you see how it has ended! I might have known I could not defy the cunning of these two. It is Felix they want—not me! If they take him, it will be to make him what they are themselves. And sooner than see him that," she cried out, passionately, "I could find the strength to kill him with my own hands!"

Without a word, Warwick rose from his seat, and took two or three turns up and down the room—then suddenly came back and stood before her, looking at her worn, haggard face. "My God!" he said, "what you must have endured! And you went away from us for this?"

"Yes, for this. Don't—don't speak of the old time. I cannot bear it now," she cried out, suddenly.

"No, I will not speak of it," he answered, kindly. "I was only thinking—it seems hard that mistakes should sometimes be punished as bitterly as sins. Well, you were right. I will help you to the very utmost of my power. As long as I can prevent it, the man of whom you speak shall never obtain possession of your son."

"But the law—

"Such a man as the one you describe is not likely to have recourse to the law, in the first place—especially in a foreign land. But, if he did, the law could only assign the child to him; it could not find him for him. Get Felix ready for a journey, and I will arrange my plans, meanwhile, and will communicate with you to-morrow at latest. Do not be surprised or unprepared if I call for the child at a very early hour in the morning. That is, if there is need of haste in the matter."

"Yes, yes—there is great need of haste—immediate haste. I do not know how near my husband may be. Probably he is in America."

"This St. John cannot himself molest you?"

"Not unless he were to entice Felix away. The child was always very fond of him—he might do that," said she, suddenly rising, with terror in her eyes. "I must return at once to Morton House. He told Babette that he was coming there. Good Heavens! I don't know what may happen while I am away."

Mr. Warwick did not attempt to detain her. He saw that it would be cruel to do so. Her fears were causeless, for Babette was fully alive to the danger, and St. John could sooner have snatched Felix from the den of a lion than from Morton House, guarded by her, and garrisoned by a troop of servants; but all the same it would have been useless to reason with, and still more useless to detain, a woman whose nerves were strung to the pitch which Mrs. Gordon's now were. He saw this, and opened the office-door. "I will see you to-morrow," he said, and, as he said it, she uttered a sudden, half-stifled cry, and caught his arm—

"There!—there!" she gasped, shrinking back into the room, and pointing eagerly across the street.

His eyes followed the motion of her hand, and he saw a slender, well-dressed man sauntering along. "That is the man?" he asked, though the question was almost unnecessary.

"It is St. John!" cried his companion, with a wild burst of tears. "It is the wretch whom I have not seen since—since—"

He put her gently into a chair, and said in a quiet voice, the very tones of which were reassuring, "Trust to me, and try and compose yourself. If you allow yourself to become unnerved in this manner, you will put yourself entirely at the mercy of this man, if, by any accident, he succeeds in gaining admittance to your presence. And the child—you must think of him. For his sake, endeavor to control yourself."

Without waiting for a reply, he turned and walked to the window, and followed Mr. St. John's retreating figure with his eyes, as far as it could be seen. It was a good thing that Mr. St. John was thinking deeply; or that keen glance might have made itself felt—not comfortably. Few men like to be scrutinized in that searching fashion; and this man especially had good reason for avoiding it. When he finally turned a corner, and was out of sight, Mr. Warwick went back to his companion.

"He is gone," he said, gently. "Let me put you into the carriage now, Mrs. Gordon."

She extended her hand silently, and he conducted her out. After she was in the carriage, and the door had been closed, she leaned forward and spoke. "God bless you!" she said. That was all; but the words, and the sound of the rich, sweet voice that had spoken them, lingered with him long after he went back into his office, and sat down to Mr. Sloan's deed.

CHAPTER XXI.

MISS TRESHAM KEEPS HER WORD.

The morning after the ball at Annesdale, Katharine was one of the few people who came down-stairs at the usual hour. Most of the ladies kept their chambers, and the gentlemen dropped into the breakfast-room at irregular intervals, looking the worse for their night's amusement. Miss Tresham received many compliments on her matutinal habits—all of which she answered by a faint smile. "I don't deserve any credit for my energy," she said. "I should have liked very much to sleep longer, and probably would have done so, if I had not been obliged to go to Tallahoma this morning."

Mrs. Annesley was sitting at another table and talking to quite another set of people; but she caught the last words and turned round.

"Did I hear you say something about Tallahoma, Miss Tresham? I hope you are not intending to desert us?"

"Not unless you prohibit my return," answered Katharine, smiling. "I was only talking of going into town for a while this morning—on business," she added, as she saw a slight expression of surprise on Mrs. Annesley's face.

"Hear! hear!" cried Mr. Langdon, laughing "'On business'—that is, to buy six yards of ribbon, or a pair of gloves. How grandly you ladies talk!"

"To buy something much more important than many yards of ribbon, or many pairs of gloves," answered Miss Tresham, gravely. Then she turned to Mrs. Annesley, and asked if she could send her into town.

"Certainly. The carriage is at your service," her hostess replied. "At what hour shall I order it?"

"Immediately after breakfast, if you please," Katharine answered.

Immediately after breakfast, Miss Tresham went up-stairs, and put on her bonnet and cloak. When she came down, the carriage was standing before the door, and, while she was congratulat ing herself on her escape from companionship and questioning, lo! from the drawing-room, sallied forth Mrs. French arrayed in full out-door costume.

"You don't object to taking me along, do you, Miss Tresham?" she asked, with a smile that Katharine could not help thinking had the least possible tinge of malicious enjoyment in it. "Mamma wants me to go to the Andersons, and they live on the other side of Tallahoma. I can drop you in the village, and call for you as I return, if you say so."

Katharine said so with the best grace she could summon, and in this way found herself fairly booked to make the best or worst of Mrs. French during a five-miles' drive. For a while, the latter spared her any conversational exertion—being full of the important subject of the ball, on which her tongue ran as glibly as possible.

"Was it pleasant, Miss Tresham?—did you really enjoy yourself?" she asked. "Did other people seem to be enjoying themselves? Of course everybody told me that it was delightful; but I have said such things dozens of times, when in fact I had been nearly bored to death. After one has told stories of that kind one's self, one isn't apt to believe other people, you know. I am so glad you think every thing went off nicely. Our ball has become quite the Christmas event in Lagrange, and I always like it to be nice. It often strikes me that it is a very daring thing to bring a hundred or so people together, and leave them to amuse themselves—for that is what a ball really comes to, you know."

"Indeed I don't know," said Katharine, smiling. "On the contrary, I think it is on the hostess that the success or failure of a ball principally rests. You must not try to shirk the success of yours, Mrs. French."

"Oh, it was mamma who played hostess," said Mrs. French, with a shrug. "I took no more responsibility of that sort than any of the guests. When I come home, I tried to forget that I am married; and I generally succeed in enjoying myself quite as much as if I was a girl with a dozen or so of admirers. By-the-by, we were talking over the ball this morning, and there was quite a discussion going on as to who was the belle of it. Tell me who you think is best entitled to that distinction."

"That is hard to say," answered Katharine, trying to keep her wandering thoughts to the subject in question. "Everybody has a different opinion as to who was the belle of the ball. I think Miss Vernon was the most beautiful woman present; but whether other people thought so, or whether that constitutes bellehood, I really don't know."

"I should say that the woman who was most sought and admired was the belle," said Mrs. French, decidedly. "You were very much admired, Miss Tresham," she went on, with surprising candor. "Any number of people asked me who you were, and said you danced so gracefully. I suppose you learned to dance in Europe—in Paris, perhaps."

"Indeed, no," said Katharine, smiling and sighing both at once. "I never was in Paris. I learned to dance at home—in the West Indies—where everybody loves it so."

"But you are English."

"I am West Indian," said Katharine, flushing a little. "Please don't call me English, for I am no more English than you are. Your grandparents, or great-grandparents, probably came from England, and so did mine—that is all."

In this strain, the conversation went on until Tallahoma was in sight, and Katharine, instead of being fresh and ready for what was before her, felt already wearied and downcast.

"Where shall I tell John to stop, Miss Tresham?" asked Mrs. French, with her hand on the check-string, as they entered the town.

"At—" Katharine stopped a moment. She was about to say "Mrs. Marks," but a timely recollection of the lateness of the hour, and of the many detentions that would await her there, came over her. It was imperative that she should see Mr. Marks at once, and that the business which brought her to Tallahoma should be transacted without loss of time; so she finished her sentence by saying—"the bank."

"The bank, John," said Mrs. French, with a little arch of her eyebrows. Then she added, laughingly, "I must tell Mr. Langdon that your business in Tallahoma really was business. One doesn't go to a bank to buy ribbons and gloves."

"I am going to see Mr. Marks about my salary," said Katharine, more annoyed by this remark than was strictly reasonable, and thinking she would put an end to any and all conjectures concerning her business.

"My dear Miss Tresham," said Mrs. French, a little shocked, "I hope you don't think that I meant any thing—that I was so impertinent as to be curious about your affairs. I really beg your pardon, if I said any thing to make you think so."

"You did not say any thing," answered Katharine. "I ought to beg your pardon for mentioning them—only one certainly does not go to a bank to buy ribbons and gloves."

"This is the place now," said Mrs. French, looking out. "Shall I call for you here, Miss Tresham?"

"At Mrs. Marks's, if you please," said Katharine, as the footman opened the door, and she descended to the sidewalk. "I shall be back in about two hours," was the last thing she heard Mrs. French say, as the carriage drove off.

Watching it out of sight, the girl said: "Thank Heaven!" with fervor, then turned, and, opening a gate just before her, went up a short walk bordered with green box, to the door of a somewhat gloomy-looking brick house. She knew the place well, for, during her first year of residence with the Marks family, they had lived here; and it was only because the children were growing large, and the house, with the bank apartments deducted, was uncomfortably small, that they had removed to the outskirts of the village. Nobody was more glad of the change than Katharine; but still, her local attachments were strong, and she gave a kind smile round the yard, with every nook and corner of which she had been familiar. She even stopped a moment to examine a rose-bush, that was clambering over the porch, before she went in. The passage which she entered looked dark and cheerless, but, on a door to the right, the word "Bank" was conspicuously lettered; and, as this door was ajar, a large, well-lighted room, with a counter running across it, was visible. Here all was well-known ground; so Katharine walked in without any hesitation. Two gentlemen were standing at a fireplace behind the counter, and they both turned as she entered. One was Mr. Marks, the other Mr. Warwick. A young man was busy with accounts at the other end of the apartment.

"Why, Miss Kate, is it possible!" said the cashier, meeting her in his hearty way. He shook hands, and seemed so glad to see her, that Katharine, who was thoroughly unnerved, felt half-inclined to cry. It is astonishing how every emotion with a woman takes the form of that inclination. "Yes, it is I, Mr. Marks," she said; and, while she was making inquiries about Mrs. Marks and the children, Mr. Warwick, after speaking to her, took his departure. "I'll be back in the course of an hour," he said to Mr. Marks; and then he went out—looking, Katharine thought, a little more grave than was usual with him.

Her own business was soon transacted. If Mr. Marks felt any surprise at the demand she came to make, he had discretion enough not to show it. "The whole amount, Miss Kate?" was all that he said. "The whole amount, if you please, Mr. Marks," she answered. So, after due examination of accounts, and due adding up of interest, Katharine found no less a sum than one thousand dollars in crisp bank-notes, paid to her across the counter. Her heart gave a great leap. She had been so little accustomed to the command of money in her life, that this seemed to her a large amount—quite a moderate fortune, in fact. "Surely it will buy my freedom," she thought to herself, with a strange pang at her heart; and then, while she signed a receipt for the payment, a sudden thought occurred to her, and she startled Mr. Marks by dropping the pen, and looking up at him.

"Mr. Marks, I am sorry," she said, hastily, "but could you let me have the amount in gold?"

"In gold!" echoed Mr. Marks, so much astonished that he could not help showing it. "In gold, Miss Kate?"

"Yes—if it will not inconvenience you—if—"

"If it will not inconvenience *you*, my dear young lady," interrupted the cashier, laughing a little. "You'll find it rather troublesome, I think; but of course the bank is always ready to pay specie when demanded on its notes. Do you want all that money in gold?"

"All, if you please."

"I must go down into the vault for it, then. We don't keep specie up here," he added, smiling.

As Katharine stood waiting for him to return, she hurriedly reviewed the situation in her mind. Regarded in any light, it was a rather embarrassing one. To conceal a thousand dollars in gold about her person was simply impossible; to carry it in her hand through the streets, without exciting much observation, and incurring much fatigue, was equally impossible. Yet what was to be done? If she paid the bank-notes to St. John, he would certainly convert them immediately into specie; and, as the notes might readily be identified, this would subject her to a great deal of unpleasant conjecture and possible inquiry. The only way to avoid it was to draw the gold at once; and yet, in that case, the problem still remained—how was she to take the amount either to Mrs. Marks, or to Annesdale, being unfortunately unprovided with any convenient pocket or satchel? Necessity, however, is the best spur, not only to invention, but to fertile expedient. As Mr. Marks reëntered the apartment, a solution for her difficulty flashed through Katharine's brain. She thanked him, after he had counted the last one of the ringing yellow pieces down before her; and, while he was methodically tying them up in a canvas bag, she asked, quickly:

"Mr. Marks, would you object to my seeing a friend in the parlor yonder, across the passage?"

"Certainly not, Miss Katharine," answered Mr. Marks, speaking without the least hesitation. "By all means, see a half-dozen friends there, if you desire."

"One will do," said Katharine, acknowledging this pleasantry by a faint smile. "Now one thing more—will you give me a pen and some paper?"

Pen and paper were obligingly placed before her; and she wrote a few lines, folded, sealed, and addressed the note to Mr. Henry Johns. As she was about to leave the room in search of a messenger, Mr. Marks spoke:

"If it's a note you want taken anywhere, Miss Kate, Hugh can go for you. He'll not be sorry for a walk," he said, nodding toward the clerk.

"If Mr. Ellis won't mind," said Katharine, looking at him with a smile.

The young man put down his pen, and came forward with an air which plainly showed that he did not mind. In shy, boyish fashion, he was quite an admirer of Miss Tresham, and she knew it.

"You are always ready to oblige me," she said, giving him the note, with a smile that almost turned his head. Then she followed him into the passage. "See the gentleman yourself, please," she said; and Hugh promised that he would.

After he was gone, she went into the unfurnished parlor, and walked up and down the floor, chinking the bag of gold which she kept whispering to herself would buy her freedom—at least, for the present. After a while, however, she found it heavy, and put it down on the window-sill, for tables or chairs there were none. Then, as she stood waiting, the forlorn aspect of every thing around began to strike her. Few things are more forlorn than an empty room—a room of bare floor, naked walls, uncurtained windows—and when, together with these things, the day is cloudy, and the prospect without not a whit more enlivening than the prospect within, it would take a very strong mind indeed to withstand the effect of time and place. Some people are peculiarly susceptible to influences like these, and Katharine was one of them. Those who knew her well thought she deserved a great deal of credit for being as quiet and full of practical common-sense as she generally proved herself; for she possessed in unfortunate degree that sensitiveness to outside events, that capability of being deeply affected by outside things, which sober, phlegmatic folk are fond of calling "nonsense." Engrossed as she now was by thoughts of the coming interview, she was not so engrossed but that she noticed at the time, and remembered afterward, every separate detail that went to make up the scene around her—every grotesque figure on the sickly green wall-paper, every cobweb across the dusty, fly-specked windows, every tree and shrub in the yard outside. She was looking at her watch, and thinking how fast time was going, when the click of the gate-latch make her start, and, looking up, she saw Hugh Ellis ushering in St. John.

As they entered the passage, she opened the parlor door, and motioned the latter to enter. When he obeyed, she closed it again, and, without speaking, walked to the window where the bag of money lay. Taking it in her hand, she turned and held it out as he approached.

"Here it is, St. John," she said. "I wish it was more, but, such as it is, you are welcome to it. Don't think that I grudge you one shilling when I say—will you go now and leave me in peace?"

"You think of nothing but yourself," said he, without touching the money. "From first to last, you have thought of nothing but yourself, and of being 'left in peace.' Yet, there are people who call women unselfish."

"If I think of myself, who forced me to do so?" said she. "St. John, don't let us recriminate now. Here is the money. Take it—believe me, you are welcome to it."

"As a price to get rid of me."

"No—as a relief freely given."

"It's a devilish mean thing to take it," said he. But still he did take it—opening his eyes a little at the amount.

"You must have been hoarding, Katharine," he said. "Or else they pay like princes here."

"They pay very well," she answered, "and I

have not spent much. I have had no need to do so."

"What is the amount?"

"A thousand dollars. I took gold, because I thought you would prefer it to bank-notes."

"This is better," said he, a little absently. He weighed the bag in his hand, with an expert gesture. "Two hundred pounds sterling," said he. "Katharine, is it worth while to say that I am much obliged to you?"

"No—it is not worth while."

"Very well," said he, coolly.

He opened the bag, took out some of the coin and looked at it, put it back, and tied up the mouth again. Something slightly nervous in the action, struck Katharine; but, as he did not speak, she spoke herself.

"You will leave Tallahoma to-day, St. John?"

"No," said he, sharply. "Why should you think so?"

"I don't see what should detain you," she answered. "I—this is all I can do for you."

"I am not considering you," he said, coldly.

He turned and walked up and down the room, looking absently at the doors and windows as he passed.

"Is this rickety old place a bank?" he asked, after a while.

"Yes, it is a bank—that is, the bank is in the other room."

"Humph! They must offer a premium for feats of burglary."

"It is secure enough," Katharine answered—adding, suddenly, "St. John, don't waste time like this. Tell me what you mean by saying that you will not leave here."

"I mean that I have found work to do," he answered, coming back, and pausing before her. "I mean, Katharine, that I have found the thing I most need, and least hoped for—a claim on Fraser."

"A claim!—*here!*—St. John, are you mad?"

"If I am, it is the luckiest fit of madness that ever came to anybody," he replied, with a short laugh. "No, I am quite sane, and I tell you—"

"Hush!" said Katharine, catching his arm with a force that surprised him. "Hush!—what is that?"

They both stood quite silent, and listened—St. John full of astonishment, Katharine full of suspense. Through the closed door, there came the sound of a rustling dress and a woman's voice in the passage beyond. As soon as Miss Tresham heard this, she turned and glanced out of the window near by. To her dismay, the Annesley carriage stood before the gate.

"I must go," she said, hastily. "It is Mrs. French. St. John, don't keep me—I must go."

"Who is Mrs. French?" he asked, impatiently. "I want to see you—I want to speak to you about this business."

"I cannot stay now," she said; and, as she spoke, she moved rapidly across the room, and unclosed the door, just as there came a knock on the other side. Opening it suddenly, she faced Mrs. French, who was standing with her hand uplifted, ready to knock again.

"Oh, Miss Tresham," said she, rather taken aback. "I beg pardon—I hope I did not disturb you? The Andersons were not at home, so, thinking you might still be here, I called on my way to Mrs. Marks. Mr. Marks told me that you were in this room, and I merely wanted to let you know that I had come—I hope I did not disturb you."

"Not at all," said Katharine, perfectly conscious that, despite the obstacle of her figure, Mrs. French's eyes had fully explored the room, and fully scrutinized St. John, who was still standing near one of the windows, and immediately within her range of vision. "I am ready to go," she added. "Don't let me detain you."

"My time is quite at your service," said Mrs. French, with most obliging sweetness. "I can wait in the bank until you have finished your business."

"I have entirely finished it," answered Katharine.

In consequence of this reply, Mrs. French had no alternative but to turn from the door, and allow Miss Tresham an exit. As she walked down the passage, Katharine paused a moment, and motioned St. John to approach.

"If you are anxious to see me, you can come out to Annesdale," she said. "If what you have to say is important, you can meet me to-morrow in the place that I showed you before."

"At what hour?" he asked.

"I will try to be there by twelve," she answered, after which she closed the door, and followed Mrs. French.

"Shall I tell John to stop at Mrs. Marks's?" asked this lady, as she moved aside to let Katharine enter the carriage.

"I believe not," Miss Tresham answered. "I won't detain you. It does not matter, since I shall see Mrs. Marks in two or three days."

"Home, John," said Mrs. French, gathering her silk dress in both hands and stepping into the carriage.

Ten minutes after the equipage rolled out of sight, Mr. Warwick came down the street toward the bank. As he entered the gate, he met St. John, who was just going out. A glance only passed between the two men; but sometimes a glance can be very significant. The remembrance of the lawyer's keen eyes gave the adventurer an uncomfortable feeling as he walked along, with Katharine's thousand dollars safely stowed in his pockets, while Mr. Warwick went straight into the bank and asked Mr. Marks what "that man" had wanted there.

"That man! — whom do you mean?" inquired the cashier, in a tone of surprise.

"That St. John, or Johns, as I believe he calls himself—what did he come here for?"

"St. John!—Johns!—There has been nobody here of that name," said Mr. Marks, looking puzzled. "In fact, there has been nobody here at all since you left, excepting Mrs. French, who called for Miss Tresham."

"The gentleman Mr. Warwick means is the one Miss Tresham sent for," said Hugh Ellis, looking up. "I saw him as he went out of the gate."

"Miss Tresham sent for him?" repeated Mr. Warwick.

He said nothing more, but walked to one of the windows, and stood there for a minute gazing out. Then he turned and came back to his brother-in-law.

"Don't think I am meddling," he said, "but if it is not confidential, I should like to know what Miss Tresham's business was. Did she say any thing to you about that man?"

"She said nothing about any man," replied Mr. Marks. "She came to draw her money."

"Her money!"

"The whole of her two-years' salary," said the cashier. "A very pretty little sum it was, too," he added, approvingly. "A thousand dollars down in gold."

"Why did you pay it in gold?"

"Because she requested it—from a foreigner's distrust of our paper, I suppose. I did not think of it before," he went on, "but it looks a little as if she meant to go away. If she did, I should be very sorry, for I don't know where I could find another teacher who would suit us all as she does. As for the man, I don't know any thing about him. She wrote a note, and sent it by Hugh; but he hadn't been here more than ten minutes before Mrs. French came."

"Did Miss Tresham go away then?"

"Yes, she went away then."

Mr. Marks paused a moment, looked at his brother-in-law, and added, hastily:

"I hope there's nothing wrong about the man, Warwick? It did not occur to me to think any thing—somehow I always feel as if Miss Tresham could be trusted as we don't trust every woman of her age."

"I am sure Miss Tresham can be trusted," said Mr. Warwick, quickly. "You don't suppose I was thinking of her? Whatever the man may be, there's one thing certain—she can be trusted."

"I am glad to hear you say so," responded Mr. Marks, looking relieved.

"Surely you did not need to hear me say so? Now, about my business. Mrs. Gordon asked me to get this check cashed for her. She wants the money at once."

CHAPTER XXII.

SPITFIRE PLAYS AT HIDE-AND-SEEK.

"Mamma," said Mrs. French, entering the drawing-room where her mother was sitting with half a dozen ladies, "have you any idea where Miss Tresham is? We want to rehearse the *tableaux* for to-morrow evening, and she is not to be found."

"I saw her go to walk a little while ago," said Mrs. Annesley, looking up from her embroidery. "She went out toward the shrubbery, Adela. You had better send for her if you need her."

"Send Mr. Langdon," said Mrs. Raynor, laughing.

"I wouldn't advise you to do any thing of the kind, if you want to see either of them soon again," remarked Mrs. Dargan. "That young man is really absurd!" she added, with considerable asperity.

"Send Maggie Lester and Morton," said Mrs. Annesley. "Spitfire will soon find her for them."

"That is a good idea!" cried Mrs. French, and, by way of putting it into execution, she immediately returned to the library where the principal portion of the party were assembled. A lively examination of engravings, and discussion of costumes, was going on here, and a great deal of interest and excitement was afloat; for, thirty years ago, *tableaux* were by no means the very common and very boring amusement which they are at present. In those days they were quite novel, especially in country districts—and, in consequence of the novelty, were considered very fascinating. Not long before this, Mrs. French had assisted at an exhibition of the kind in Mobile, and she was anxious to introduce the new amusement into Lagrange. Having abundant material at hand, in the matter of pretty girls, obliging gentlemen, and an unlimited command of costume, she determined on giving a New-Year entertainment of this character. All the company received the idea with enthusiasm, and the only danger was that their zeal might outrun their discretion, inasmuch as they seemed anxious to prolong the entertainment indefinitely by representing every conceivable scene, and personating every imaginable character within the range of history or fiction. At length, however, this vaulting ambition was somewhat curbed, and the programme, after much weeding, was finally made out. Of course, the usual trouble about the distribution of parts—the trouble which is the bane of private theatricals, and all affairs of the kind—ensued. But, by judicious management, the stormy waters were allayed, and, after many compromises, peace was at length secured. But only peace in partial form. Characters being settled, dress yet remained an open question; and, when Mrs. French entered the library, a warm discussion was in progress.

"I tell you it ought to be black velvet and pearls," Miss Lester was saying, decidedly, as her friend walked up and touched her on the shoulder.

"Let the black velvet alone just now, Maggie," she said. "I want you to go out into the grounds and look for Miss Tresham. Mamma says she went to walk. I wouldn't ask you, only you are so fond of exercise; and, if you take Spitfire, he will soon show you where she is. We must have her to settle about the dress of Queen Mary. Please take Morton with you, and see if you can't find her."

"Do you hear that, Mr. Annesley?" asked Miss Lester, who was ready at once for the part assigned her. "The morning is charming, and I should like nothing better than a walk. Spitfire will like a game of hide-and-seek, too. He will find Miss Tresham for you in no time, Adela. Meanwhile"—this to the lady to whom she had been talking before—"remember that I say black velvet and pearls."

Spitfire was quite willing for a walk and a game of hide-and-seek, while Morton, for his part, was heartily tired of talk about doublets, and ruffs, and colored lights, and gauze screens.

"Oh, we can't let Mr. Annesley go—we haven't settled on the costume of the Master of Ravenswood yet!" cried one or two ladies, as he rose with alacrity to follow Miss Lester from the room.

"He won't be long," said Adela, philosophically. "What do you think Lucy Ashton ought to wear?—a bridal dress, of course; but in what shape?"

"Which way shall we go, Miss Lester?" asked Morton, as they descended the front steps together.

"We will ask Spitfire that," the young lady answered. "Here, Spitfire!—seek, sir, seek! Find Miss Tresham—Oh, I forgot," as Spitfire stood looking very confused and irresolute. "I must have something of Miss Tresham's to show him. Mr. Annesley, run into the hall and see if you can't find me something."

Mr. Annesley did as he was bid—that is, he walked into the hall, and returned after a minute or two with a long crimson scarf. "I think this is Miss Tresham's," he said. "I have seen her wear it several times."

"Here, Spitfire, here!" said his mistress, shaking the scarf at him, as if she was a matadore and Spitfire was the bull she wished to enrage. "Here, pet! and now go and seek Miss Tresham."

Thanks to the instructions of "Cousin Tom," Spitfire was tolerably well trained. He sniffed at the scarf, then trotted about a little, sniffed at the ground in much the same disdainful fashion, and finally set off toward the shrubbery.

"Come on," said Miss Lester, beginning to walk very fast; and Morton came on, as requested. Fast walking is not the most graceful thing in the world, as we who live in this day have ample opportunity for observing; but, on the 31st of December, when the sun is clouded over, and the air decidedly sharp, it is at least a comfortable thing. Miss Lester's cheeks had bright roses in them when at last she came to a halt. "Where has Spitfire gone?" she cried, laughing. "I am afraid we shall have to look for him, without the advantage, which he has, of a nose as a guide."

"This way, I think," said Morton, and he turned down a path that led into the wildest and prettiest part of the grounds. The woods, which had been enclosed here, were left almost entirely as Nature arranged them, excepting that the encumbering undergrowth of the forest had been cleared away, and now and then a rustic seat was placed in some shady nook. In spring, summer, or autumn, a lovelier spot was not to be found within the borders of Lagrange; but it looked cheerless enough on this bleak December day, with the leafless trees standing out like fine pencil tracery against a dull, gray sky, and the brown earth covered only with dry, fallen leaves.

"I don't think Spitfire came this way," said Miss Lester, a little pettishly, for she did not fancy walking down a steep hill with the assured certainty that she would have to walk up again.

"I'am sure he did," said Annesley; "but, if you are tired, we won't go on. No doubt he will bring Miss Tresham to us after a while. Here is a seat—pray sit down."

"No, we might as well go on. There!—is not that Spitfire that I hear?"

It was Spitfire, undoubtedly. From no other canine throat could such a volume of shrill sound have issued—a vehement barking, of the most indignant kind, that was borne with singular distinctness through the still air.

"He can't be attacking Miss Tresham in that way," said Morton, quickly.

"Oh, no," said Spitfire's mistress, with the coolness which characterizes the owners of bad dogs, when those dogs are annoying or terrifying other people within an inch of their lives. "He—he has met somebody else—somebody that he don't know. Let us walk faster," she went on, more eagerly, "or he may be hurt."

"The somebody may be hurt, do you mean?" asked Annesley, as he quickened his pace in accordance with her own. "Surely Spitfire will not really bite?"

"The somebody!" echoed the young lady, with an indignation that startled him. "You don't suppose I am thinking of the somebody—I mean that Spitfire himself may be hurt."

"Oh!" said the gentleman, thus enlightened—then he added, with a smile, "perhaps he may. I would not answer for what I might do under such provocation as that."

"That" was the furious sounds of rage to which Spitfire was giving utterance as they approached. Other sounds were also audible now—Katharine's voice calling him off, and a man's voice angrily bidding him be gone.

"Some one is with Miss Tresham," said Morton, stopping with an instinctive hesitation—an instinctive remembrance of that other meeting of which his mother had spoken two days before.

But he stopped too late. Urged by a fear for Spitfire's safety, Miss Lester rushed eagerly forward, and he could not decline to follow. A few more steps brought them into the little dell, of which mention has before been made, and there the combat was raging hotly—Spitfire barking fiercely, and making frantic dashes at the feet and legs of St. John, the latter defending himself with considerable bravery, and Katharine trying, by alternate persuasion and command, to draw off the assailant.

Upon this scene Miss Lester rushed, just as St. John lost patience, and, stooping, took up a stone. Before he could throw it, his arm was peremptorily caught.

"How dare you!" cried the indignant and breathless owner of Spitfire. "How dare"—a long pant—"dare you throw stones at my dog? I wonder you are not ashamed of yourself—a great big man like you to be afraid of a little dog like that!"

"Excuse me," stammered he, turning round in astonishment, and finding himself in the grasp of a young and pretty woman. "I did not mean to hurt him—but he attacked me without provocation, and"—he added, with a sudden effort to recover the self-possession that had escaped him—"'though he be but little, he is fierce.' You must confess that."

"How could you let him do it?" said Miss Lester, turning to Katharine, "and when Spitfire—poor, dear fellow—came out to look for you, too! But what is the matter?—are you not well?"

"Yes, I am well," said Katharine, trying to smile—a piteous attempt which touched Annesley—"but first Spitfire, and then you, startled me a little. I was not expecting any one."

"Adela sent us to look for you," said Miss Lester, turning her back on the gentleman, al the more determinedly because she was dying of curiosity to look at him. In her own fashion, she was a girl of very high-minded ideas, though; and she kept her eyes steadily fastened on Katharine's face. "Adela sent us for you. She wants to rehearse the *tableaux*, and you forget that you are Queen Mary and Joan of Arc."

"I did forget it entirely," said Katharine. "I will go back with you at once. Mr."—she paused a moment—"Mr. Johns, perhaps Mr. Annesley will be kind enough to show you the way out of the grounds."

"Certainly," said Mr. Annesley, with a grave

bow, "unless you will permit me to suggest the amendment that you introduce me to your friend, and that he will do me the honor to return with us to the house."

Katharine cast a quick look of mingled apprehension and entreaty at St. John before going through the form of introduction, in a voice that was not quite steady. She might have spared herself the apprehension she entertained. St. John was equal to the occasion. He bowed with easy grace, and regretted that he could not accept Mr. Annesley's courteous invitation; then bowed again to the ladies, as Katharine said to Miss Lester, "Shall we return now?"

"With all my heart," the young lady answered. "Here, Spitfire! here pet! I am afraid to leave him there," she went on, as Katharine and herself mounted the hill. "He has evidently taken a great dislike to that gentleman, and, when Spitfire takes a dislike to anybody, he never gets over it. He—your friend—was about to hurt him when I came up."

"I think not," said Katharine. Then she added, suddenly: "Don't call him my friend. I know him, and he chanced to be here and meet me—that is all."

"You know him!" repeated Miss Lester, looking at her. "Excuse me, but you say that as if you did not like him."

"I don't like him."

"Then, if I were you," said the other, with sudden frankness, "I would not meet him in this sort of way. I wouldn't do it for a man I liked, and I am sure I would see a man I didn't like shot ten times over first. Don't think me impertinent, Miss Tresham," she went on, "but I like *you*, and I thought I would tell you how people consider such things here. You are a stranger, and perhaps don't know our customs. Of course, I shall not gossip about the matter, and, as for Morton Annesley, he is true as steel; but still, if I were you, I wouldn't do it. Are you offended with me?"

"Not in the least," said Katharine, smiling faintly. "You mean kindly, and, therefore, I could not be offended. You simply don't understand."

The last words were uttered so quietly, and with so much unconscious dignity, that they had their effect upon Miss Lester. She hesitated a minute before answering.

"No, I don't understand, of course, and I don't mean to judge either. But I can see how things look, Miss Tresham, and it was of looks that I was speaking."

"Yes, I know," said Katharine, absently.

Meanwhile Morton and the companion who had been presented to him were crossing the grounds to the side-gate through which St. John had entered. A few commonplace remarks about the weather were interchanged as they proceeded; but, when they reached the gate, instead of opening it, Annesley stopped and faced the other.

"Excuse me, Mr. Johns," he said, gravely, "if I ask leave to speak a few words before we part. Of course, I do not know why you preferred to see Miss Tresham in the grounds, but permit me to remind you that the house is only a short distance from the place where I met you, and that any one of Miss Tresham's friends is cordially welcome there."

"It was by Miss Tresham's own request that I met her where I did," answered St. John, coldly. "I will bid you good-morning, with the assurance that I shall not invade your domain again."

"I hope you understand that it was on Miss Tresham's account that I spoke," said Morton, flushing a little.

The other lifted his hat with a courtesy so ceremonious that it had not a little of mockery in it.

"In Miss Tresham's name, allow me to thank you," he answered. "The only thing that puzzles me is the cause of this kind solicitude."

"Miss Tresham is one of my mother's guests," said Annesley, with a good deal of unconscious *hauteur*. He opened the gate, and raised his own hat, as St. John passed through. Nothing more was said on either side. They parted with a couple of stiff bows that would have become a pair of duellists; and, as St. John strode away in the direction of Tallahoma, Annesley went back to the house.

When he entered the hall he was at once waylaid by Mr. Langdon, and marched *nolens volens* into the back drawing-room, where a rehearsal was going on.

"No mutiny, young man," said the latter, as Morton tried to get away on a pretext of business. "I was sent in search of you, and it is as much as my life is worth to go back without you. Queen Adela is *regnant* just now, and she would think nothing of ordering my head to be taken off for disobedience of orders. In with you!"

He gave his captive no time for expostulation, but ushered him straight into the room where the stage of Christmas Eve was again erected. Strangely enough the two women whom Morton had last seen together in the grounds were the first on whom his eye fell as he entered.

They were now confronting each other in tragic attitude—Miss Lester as Queen Elizabeth, Katharine as Queen Mary, in the famous scene from Schiller's "Marie Stuart."

In these days all the world knows that scene, for all the world has seen Ristori act it. But then it was something new, and something for which the world of Lagrange was indebted to Morton Annesley. He, knowing and admiring Schiller with all the enthusiasm of a German student, had suggested the picture, and given his opinion concerning a proper selection of the characters.

"Maggie Lester would do for an immensely-flattered Queen Elizabeth," he said, laughing. "She can't deny that her hair *is* red. And, if you were to put a Marie-Stuart coif and curls on Miss Tresham, I am sure she would look like the Queen of Scots. The color of her hair and the cast of her features are not unlike the portraits of the royal beauty."

When he came in just now poor Queen Mary was thinking of any thing else but her cowering rival or her deadly wrongs. She saw him enter, and, though she could not turn her head, she shot a wistful glance out of the corners of her eyes which Mrs. French caught as well as himself.

This astute lady had made nothing of Maggie Lester's reserve and self-possession. But a look at her brother's face told her all that she wanted to know.

"He has seen him!" she thought; and the knowledge acted on her like a stimulant, enlivening her spirits as if by magic.

After that the *tableaux* went on bravely, for everybody was held well in hand by their fair ruler, and nobody ventured on any open signs of weariness or dissatisfaction.

It was not until the rehearsal ended, and most of the company had dispersed to dress for dinner, that Katharine found an opportunity of speaking to Morton. He was standing near the stage, directing the servants, who were arranging some of the decorations, when she walked up to him.

"Mr. Annesley," she said, hurriedly, "I should like to speak to you. I have something to say to you. May I say it now?"

"Certainly," he answered, turning at the first sound of her voice. "Shall we go into the library?"

"No, it is only a few words. If you will come here—"

She walked away, and he followed her. Every one, excepting the servants, had now left the room. On one side was a bay-window, and into this Katharine went.

"It is only a few words," she repeated, as Annesley followed her; "but I should not like for any one to hear them."

"There is no danger of any one's doing so here," he answered.

Then he was silent, waiting for her to speak. After a minute she began, with a nervous haste of manner that had grown habitual with her of late.

"It is not about myself, Mr. Annesley. It is about Mrs. Gordon. I know that you are much attached to her, and—and I thought I would tell you, so that perhaps you might be of service to her. She is threatened, if not with danger, at least with serious annoyance."

Now, this was the last sort of communication which Morton could possibly have expected to hear, and the surprise which he naturally felt showed itself at once in his face and manner.

"Mrs. Gordon threatened with serious annoyance!" he repeated, with a start. "Pardon me, but you must be mistaken. There is no one who would dare—"

"There is some one who has the right to dare," she interposed, hastily. "Believe me, I know what I am saying. She is certainly threatened with very serious annoyance and distress."

A sudden dark flush rose over his face, and he frowned as Katharine had never seen him frown before. She recognized then what many other people had recognized before, that to touch Mrs. Gordon was to assail him in one of his most sensitive points.

"By whom, and in what way?" he asked.

"I cannot tell you that. I would if it were my secret; but it is not mine—it is Mrs. Gordon's. It came to my knowledge accidentally, and I cannot repeat it. Go to her, and, if she wishes you to serve her, she will tell you herself. I—I am very sorry for her," said the girl, with tears coming into her eyes. "She has a hard lot. I wish I could help her. Perhaps *you* can, Mr. Annesley—you are a man."

"I will try, at least," he said. "Shall I—would you advise me to go at once?"

"At once."

He moved away a few steps, turned abruptly, and came back.

"Miss Tresham," he said, quickly, "is there nothing I can do for yourself?"

She knew what he meant. She knew that he

would not ask her confidence, or seem to request an explanation of the events of that morning. But she also knew that he gave her an opportunity—perhaps a last one—to right herself in his eyes. Some instinct told her that much hung on her reply, and she gave a slight gasp over it.

"Nothing, Mr. Annesley."

"I am sorry for that," he said.

Then, as if afraid to trust himself to speak another word, he walked away.

In the hall he met his mother.

"Where are you going, Morton?" she asked, as she saw him take his gloves and riding-whip from the stand. "Don't you know that dinner is nearly ready?"

"I shall not be back to dinner," he answered. "Make my apologies, if you please, mother, and say that important business called me away."

"Why, where are you going?"

"I will tell you when I come back. I have not time to talk now."

"But, Morton—"

She spoke in vain. Morton was gone. When she followed him to the door he was walking rapidly in the direction of the stables, and, not long afterward, she saw him, from her chamber window, canter away in the direction of Tallahoma.

It was not to Tallahoma that he was bound, however. The last sun of the Old Year had given a few golden gleams, and was sinking to rest in a bed of soft, violet cloud, when he dismounted from Ilderim before the door of Morton House. Rapidly as he had ridden, he noticed along the avenue the fresh track of carriage-wheels, and the fact puzzled him a little. Mrs. Gordon never left home, and nobody ever came to the house. At an ordinary time he might merely have thought that one of these rules had been broken; but now, with the remembrance of Katharine's vague warning in his mind, he felt an uncomfortable foreboding of ill. This foreboding was increased as he approached the terrace and saw a group of negroes loitering with sorrowful faces around the steps.

"What is the matter?" he asked, as one of them came forward and took his horse. "Has any thing happened that you all look as if you had been to a funeral?"

"Mass Felix is gone, sir," answered the boy addressed, in a tone which indicated that he thought this a sufficient reason for any length of visage.

"Felix!—gone—!" Annesley repeated. A sudden fear, common enough in that country and at that time, startled him. "Do you mean that he is lost?"

"Oh, no, sir," answered the boy, quickly. "Mr. Warwick came and took him away in a carriage. They hadn't left more'n a few minutes before you got here, sir."

"Did his mother—did your mistress go too?"

"No, sir—she's in the house."

"Very well. Keep my horse here. I shall be back directly."

He walked hastily to the house, and on the portico met Harrison, who was wearing a most lugubrious face.

"What is the meaning of this, Harrison?" Morton asked, quickly. "Where has Felix gone?—and why has he been sent away?"

"The Lord only knows, Mass Morton," said the old man, dolefully. "Miss Pauline and Mr. Warwick done it. I don't think they asked anybody's advice, sir—they just packed up Mass Felix's clothes, and took him right away. It was hard on the poor child, sir, for he didn't want to go; and if you could a-heard him a-crying, sir, it would almost a-broke your heart."

"I am glad I didn't hear him then," said Morton, who saw plainly that the whole feeling of the household was ranged on Felix's side. "But his mother must have had some good reason for sending him away. Where is she?"

"In her own room, Mass Morton," answered Harrison, following the young man into the house. "You better go into the drawing-room, sir, and I'll ask if Miss Pauline can see you. I don't mean to blame Miss Pauline," he added, with an air of severe justice. "To be sure she must a had her reasons onbeknownst to the rest of us. But it was hard on Mass Felix—and him so young."

"A great many things are hard," said Morton, "but they must be done. Send Babette to ask my cousin if she will see me."

In a few minutes, Babette entered the room, and said that Mrs. Gordon would see him. The Frenchwoman's eyes were red with weeping, and her face was sadly swollen from the same cause. Morton felt sorry for her, and said so—at which she startled him by a fresh burst of tears.

"Ah, madame—poor madame!" cried she. "M'sieur, comfort her, if you can. She is heart-broken—she will die of grief, if she is not comforted."

"I will do my best," said he; "but if Felix is gone, I fear that will not be much. Chees up, Babette! Surely he will be back before long."

"Le bon Dieu only knows," answered Babette. And, as he crossed the hall, he heard her sobbing behind him.

Poor Morton! There is no exaggeration in saying that he would sooner have faced any danger which could possibly be imagined, than the scene which fancy painted as awaiting him in Mrs. Gordon's room. The sobs, the tears—Babette's noisy grief was, of course, only a faint shadow of what the bereaved mother must feel. He set his teeth, as he laid his hand on the door-knob—then turned it, and entered.

All was quiet within. On the hearth the fire burned; outside the windows, a soft, sad requiem of the dying year was moaning through the tall trees; but no human sob or sigh was borne to Annesley's ear. A figure clad in black sat on one side of the fireplace, and held out her hand as he advanced.

"Come in," said Mrs. Gordon, quietly. "You are very welcome. Is it not cold? Draw nearer the fire. Well"—with a faint, mournful smile—"have you heard the news? I am desolate."

"I have heard it," he answered.

He could say no more; for, although he ought to have been relieved, he was, in truth, more deeply affected by her quietude than he could have been by any vehement outbreak whatever. The hopeless accent of the last words went straight to his heart, and touched it more than tears could have done. He said nothing; but he kept her hand tightly clasped in his for several minutes.

"I see you feel for me," she said—"you do not think it is foolish to mind it so."

"No words can say how much I feel for you," he answered.

"It might be foolish, perhaps," she went on, "if he was not my all. But he is, you know—literally every thing that I have on earth."

"But surely you have not sent him far—surely he will not be gone long?" said Morton, unable to contain his surprise.

"I do not know where he has gone," she answered, in the same quiet, hopeless tone; "and I do not know when I shall see him again—perhaps never."

Annesley said, "Good Heavens!"—and then he stopped. A sudden remembrance of Katharine's words and looks came to him. "It is Mrs. Gordon's secret," she had said. "If she wishes you to serve her, she will tell it to you." Here was the secret staring him in the face; and evidently it had been told not to him, but to John Warwick. For a moment, he felt wounded—more deeply wounded than it is possible to describe; but, almost immediately, cooler reason and better feeling triumphed.

"Whatever you have done, I am sure you have done well," he said, in his kind, loyal voice. "Whatever is to be borne, I am sure you will bear well. This is no time for reproaches, but I cannot help asking you why you forgot that I am your kinsman, and ready to do any service for you."

"I did not forget it," said she, holding out again the hand he had relinquished. "Morton, don't reproach me—for that *is* reproach. After Felix, there is no one so near my heart as you are—both for your own and your father's sake. If I did not ask this service of you, it was only because you were not in a position to render it. Circumstances made it necessary that Felix should be taken away—far away, where even I might not know where he is—and you had not the requisite time for this."

"I would have taken the time."

"I don't doubt that—but I could not ask it. Besides, I went to John Warwick, as a lawyer, and he advised me as a lawyer, before he served me as a friend."

"I could not have advised you, perhaps; but I would have served you against any thing—or anybody."

"There are some things one can only fight with cunning, not with force," said she—adding, after a moment, "I will tell you every thing if you will remember that I tell it only to you—not to Lagrange, or to anybody in Lagrange. Yet that is a foolish remnant of the old pride, for everybody will know it soon."

"Consult your own feelings, not mine," said he. "If it is painful to you to speak, don't do it. I will serve you ignorantly as readily as with knowledge. Don't—don't distress yourself."

"You deserve confidence from me," said she, "and you shall have it."

Then, as if it were a relief—and, indeed, after a fashion, it was a relief—she began and poured forth her pitiful story, going far more into detail than she had done in speaking to John Warwick, and eliciting far more of warm, outspoken sympathy. What the lawyer felt he had shown in deeds, not words; what Morton felt burst forth in eager language, though it would have been equally ready to prove itself by acts. The difference was less in the different natures of the two men than in their different ages.

As Mrs. Gordon went on, Morton's interest grew warmer, until suddenly there came a cold chill. It would be hard to say what the young man felt when she first spoke of St John, and an instinct—a sharp convulsion at his heart—told him that this St. John was one and the same with the "Mr. Johns" whom Katharine Tresham had that morning asked him to show out of the grounds of Annesdale. Then, the warning she had given him, the knowledge which she possessed of this carefully-guarded secret—he grew suddenly faint and sick, and turned so pale that Mrs. Gordon noticed it.

"What is the matter?" she asked. "You are thinking of something besides me."

"I am thinking of this St. John," he answered. "Don't you think that he may have come here accidentally—not in search of you, after all?"

"Babette thinks so; but I cannot believe it. However much he may pretend otherwise, I am sure he came here in search of me."

"But how did he know that you were here?"

"I cannot tell that."

Morton said no more. He would have cut out his tongue sooner than mention Katharine's name in the matter; and, although he did not know it, Mr. Warwick had been equally discreet. Mrs. Gordon had not a suspicion that St. John was connected with any one in Lagrange besides herself. Different as the two men were, they had something in common, which they proved by this reticence. Morton was right when he once told Felix that the grand test of a gentleman is the capability of being trusted; and he might have added that it is not only the capability of being loyal to a trust which has been solemnly and explicitly given, but it is also to be found in that fine sense of honor which can appreciate tacit confidence, and respect the secret for which no secrecy has been asked.

When Annesley rode away from Morton House, the last day of the Old Year had died the death common to all things mortal. The last gleam of light had faded in the west; the night hung over all things with its sombre mantle; the stars gleamed with an uncertain fitfulness through a curtain of misty cloud; and even the lights from the wayside houses looked, to the young man's fancy, more dull and red than cheery and bright. As he rode forward, his heart was strangely heavy, his mind strangely disturbed, and, in a sort of accompaniment to the thoughts that tormented him, a certain verse of a poem he had seen shortly before kept running through his brain. Almost unconsciously, as he looked at the great hosts of Night that were marching steadily forward to the death-bed of the Old Year, he caught himself repeating:

"He lieth still; he doth not move;
He will not see the dawn of day.
He hath no other life above.
He gave me a friend and a true true-love,
And the New Year will take them away."

CHAPTER XXIII

A MORNING-CALL.

GREAT was the rejoicing of the Marks children when, on the day after New-Year, the same carriage that had conveyed Miss Tresham away drove up to the gate, and Miss Tresham descended, smiling in acknowledgment of their eager welcome, but looking decidedly pale and worn, as Mrs. Marks at once perceived.

"Dissipation don't agree with you, Miss Katharine," she said, after the first bustle of greeting was over. "I never saw you look so badly. You must have danced all last night."

"I did," said Katharine, smiling. "After the *tableaux* we had a sort of fancy ball—that is, all those who had taken part in the *tableaux* were in costume—and day was breaking when I went to bed. I wish you had come to the *tableaux*, Mrs. Marks—they were so pretty!"

"I thought about it," said Mrs. Marks, regretfully. "I should have liked to have gone; but it was a long drive, and Nelly had a cough that sounded a little like croup, so I was afraid to leave her."

"But you might have sent Sara and Katy; they would have enjoyed it so much!"

"They were crazy to go, and I might have sent them if there had been anybody to take them. But Richard was tired, and John isn't here, you know."

"Indeed, I don't know," said Katharine, with a start. "Where has Mr. Warwick gone?"

"Gone to take Felix Gordon to school," answered Mrs. Marks, sending her scissors with a sharp snip through the cloth from which she was cutting a jacket for one of the boys. "You can't be more surprised than I was, Miss Katharine; for John started off without giving anybody a word of warning. It was a queer thing for Mrs. Gordon to send the child away—so fond of him as they say she is—and it was queer of John to take him; but, then, dear me! what isn't queer in this world? I told Richard last night that I shouldn't be surprised if every thing came right at last. You know what I mean; I don't like to mention names before the children."

"Yes, I know what you mean. But is it likely, do you think?"

"If this don't look as if it is likely, I wonder what would look so? Other people besides me think the same thing. I saw Mrs. Sloan yesterday, and she was telling me that Mrs. Gordon—Katy, don't stand there drinking in every word I say; go up-stairs and see if Miss Tresham's room is all ready—that Mrs. Gordon has been going to see John at his office of late, and, when a widow does that way, you know it is apt to mean something. There are a great many reports going about; but I know how people talk, and I didn't pay much attention to them till this about Felix came on me like a thunder-clap. Then I couldn't help believing. I am sure I never expected that matters would come to pass so that John could marry Pauline Morton—but this is a strange world!"

"When will Mr. Warwick be back?" asked Katharine.

"Indeed, that's more than I can tell. He said nothing about it; and, since I don't know where he went, I can't even calculate when he's likely to be back. He left a note for you, which I was about to forget. Let me see—where did I put it?"

After considerable reflection, Mrs. Marks remembered that she had put the note in her work-box, and drew it forth from among the spools and tape which filled that receptacle. Katharine, who restrained her impatience as well as she could, took it and opened it. This was what Mr. Warwick said:

"Dear Miss Tresham: I find that I am unexpectedly obliged to leave home with Felix Gordon. I shall endeavor to return within a fortnight. Will you go to see Mrs. Gordon and try to cheer her? She is suffering very much.

"Yours truly,

"John Warwick."

"Does he say any thing about when he's likely to be back?" asked Mrs. Marks, who was watching the governess's face attentively, and secretly burning with curiosity to know what her brother had written about.

"He says he may return within a fortnight," answered Katharine, with her eyes still fastened on the note. Then she held it out. "There it is," she added; "you can see for yourself what he says. It is not much. I will go and take off my things."

While Mrs. Marks eagerly read the note, Katharine left the room and went up-stairs. She found her chamber carefully arranged for her. Every thing looked fresh and bright, the fire was burning, and on the table her Christmas presents were laid out in order. It seemed like a pleasant coming home, and gave her a sense of rest and relief after the gay dissipations of Annesdale. At another time she might have thought a little regretfully of all that was going on at the latter place; of how Mr. Langdon was just then throwing a great deal of sentimental expression into his voice and eyes as he talked to some young lady who sat in the bay-window where she had herself sat yesterday; of how Miss Lester was playing billiards with Mr. Talcott; how Mrs. French was entertaining a lively group with disquisitions on private theatricals; and how the same people were loitering in the same places and saying the same things as on every day while she had been there. The habits of society are much the same on a small or on a large scale all the world over. Let a man drop out of his circle in Paris, and, even if he has been the brightest star in that circle, who misses him? So it is in every circle of every city, village, or hamlet, throughout the world. Remain, and you are liked exactly according to your deserts; go, and, whatever those deserts may have been, you are forgotten as speedily and as naturally as the events of yesterday yield in interest to the events of to-day. Until a cloud came over her brightness, Katharine had achieved quite a social success at Annesdale; but she had sufficient worldly experience to know that already she had sunk beneath the horizon, that others had taken her place, and that to-morrow people would even cease to say, "Miss Tresham did this," or "Miss Tresham did not do that." At a different moment such a reflection might have cost her a pang; but now she was too full of other subjects. Instead of thinking of the farewells of Messrs. Langdon and Talcott, she thought of Mr. Warwick and the note he had left behind. "What did he mean?" she asked herself, and, receiving no satisfactory reply, was still asking, when the door opened and Katy rushed in.

"Miss Tresham, there's a gentleman down-stairs, and mamma says will you please come down, he wants to see you."

Poor Katharine! She had expected this, but not quite so soon—not quite so unexpectedly.

"Katy," she said, with a start, "who is it? What is his name?"

"He's a strange gentleman," answered Katy, decidedly. "I don't know what his name is, and mamma didn't tell me. He came here once before, though."

"To see me?"

"Yes'm, while you was away."

"Amen," said Katharine, under her breath. She mechanically took off her bonnet and shawl, smoothed her hair, and went down-stairs.

In the passage she met Mrs. Marks, evidently much fluttered and excited.

"A gentleman in the dining-room to see you, Miss Katharine," she said. "I asked him there because there was no fire in the parlor. You needn't be uneasy on my account," she added, with a good-natured smile, "I am going into the kitchen anyhow. They are trying out lard again to-day, and I have to see about it. He's very good-looking," she said, with a significant nod, as she went out of the back-door.

Katharine did not even smile. The conclusion to which Mrs. Marks had leaped was absurd enough; but she was not in the humor for the absurdity to strike her in a humorous light. On the contrary, she felt annoyed when there was no reasonable ground for annoyance. These significant looks and smiles jarred on her.

"What fools people are!" she thought, with an impatience very unusual to her, as she went on and opened the dining-room door.

St. John was standing with his back to the fire, looking moodily down at the hearth-rug when she entered. She saw at once that something was wrong with him, and, unfortunately, was in no doubt concerning the nature of that something. He looked up when she entered, but did not move forward.

"Well," he said, "have you heard the news? Do you know that she has sent off the child, and given me the slip?"

"Yes, I know it," she answered, sitting down in the first chair she came to. "But what can I do? Why do you come and annoy me?"

"That is always the cry!—always, why do I come and annoy you! I come because I choose to do so," said he, angrily; "and because you may be able to help me in this business."

"In what business?"

"In finding out where Felix has been taken."

"What is the use of such talk as this," said she, coldly. "Do you suppose I know any thing about it?—or, if I did, do you suppose I would tell you?"

"I suppose you can find out, if you choose, for the man who took him away lives, I am told, in this very house—and, I suppose that, if you don't choose, you may repent it," answered he "I don't want to hear any nonsense, Katharine. This is a matter of life and death to me, and I will not be thwarted. You *can* find out where the child has been taken, and you shall do so."

"I might show you whether or not I would, if there were any question of finding out," she answered. "But there is not. Even his own sister does not know where Mr. Warwick has gone."

"She may say she does not—"

"She says the truth. Don't think that every body tells falsehoods, St. John."

"Everybody tells them when it suits his convenience," said St. John, coolly. "Do you suppose I don't know the world?"

"Your own world—perhaps so."

"The world is the same everywhere. If this woman does not know, her husband does."

"No—he does not."

"Then wait until the man comes back, and get the secret from him. What's the good of being a woman, and a pretty one," he added, with a sneer, "if you can't do such a thing?"

"You don't know any thing about Mr. Warwick," she cried, indignantly. "If you did, you would know that no woman in the world could make him tell a thing that he wished to keep secret. And I would do any thing sooner than ask it of him. St. John, you are cruel!"

"You are a fool!" retorted St. John, shortly. "I think there must be something between you and this lawyer," he went on, looking keenly at her. "If that is the case—"

"I won't hear another word!" cried Katharine, losing temper, and somewhat dismaying him by the angry light that came into her eyes. "You are insulting me—and I will not listen to you. If I knew where Felix Gordon was this minute, I would die sooner than tell you!" she said, passionately. "You may be sure of that."

"I think I could make you sorry for it."

"I have no doubt you could—but I would not do it!"

There was silence in the room after this. St. John had not expected such a defiance, and it quite astonished him. He drummed on his hat for some time, and knitted his brows, as he scowled at the girl, who sat before him looking pale and resolute.

"Upon my word, I had not expected this," said he, at last. "A charmingly affectionate person you are, Katharine, I must say! You'd die before you would obtain for me a certain item of information about a person who cannot concern you in the least! Will you tell me what is the meaning of this sudden interest in Felix Gordon?"

"I have no interest. But I will not play the spy at your bidding. I owe a debt of gratitude to this place, and these people; and I do not choose to repay it in such a form."

"A debt of gratitude for allowing you to come and slave among them? Humph! your ideas of a cause for gratitude are singular, to say the least. You *do* owe somebody among them a certain sort of gratitude, though," he went on, with a peculiar smile. "Pray, what do you consider the most unfortunate thing that has befallen you lately?"

"Your coming," she answered, unhesitatingly.

"I thought so," said he, coolly. "Well, you asked me, when we first met, how I discovered your place of residence. I did not answer the question then, because it was irrelevant. It is relevant now, and I shall answer it with pleasure. First, however, do you know any one in a place called Mobile?"

"No one."

"Have you ever been there?"

"Never."

"Well, your address was forwarded to me—but stop! I will tell the story in order. There is nothing like method. Read that."

He took out a pocket-book, opened it, and drew forth a slip of paper which he put into her hand. It was the *Times* advertisement that Mrs. Annesley had shown to Adela French.

"Have you any idea who inserted that?" he asked, watching her face, as she read it.

Her eyes dilated with astonishment, her face paled until the very lips were white, and he was forced to repeat his question, before she looked up and answered.

"Idea!—no. How should I have? I did not think there was any one in the world who would have done such a thing."

"Do you think it was some one here?"

"It must have been. I have never been anywhere else in America, and no one who was not of Lagrange could have known any thing about the West Indies or Cumberland."

"Those allusions prove that it is some one who knows you?"

"Yes, it is some one who knows me."

"See if these will enable you to tell who it is."

Forth from the pocket-book came two letters, and were placed in Katharine's hand. She took them, as she had taken the advertisement, and glanced over them with compressed lips. When she finished, she laid them down on the table beside her, and looked at St. John.

"I do not know who has written these," she said. "God forgive whoever it was—God grant that they may never have to endure such suffering as they have brought on me!"

"That is cant," said he. "Of course, you don't forgive them; and, of course, you can tell who the writer was. What, in a small circle like this, not be able to place your finger at once upon the person! Tell me whom you know, and I will tell you who did it."

"I do not know anybody who would have done it."

"That only proves your ignorance of the world. Do you suspect me of forging those letters?"

"No."

"Then they were certainly written by somebody who knows you, and whom you know. Common-sense might show you this. Tell me whom you least suspect, and I will tell you who did it."

"I cannot tell you. I—St. John, let me alone!" she cried, suddenly, but with an accent of almost heart-rending pathos. "I don't understand any thing! I am heart-sick and weary. Don't—don't torment me!"

"You know who wrote those letters," said St. John, watching her with unchanging scrutiny. "If you don't choose to tell me, well and good—I can find out for myself. You will be sorry for this want of confidence though, Katharine. I am your best friend."

"May God give me my worst, then!" cried the girl, who was driven beyond all power of self-control.

"I have heard some rumors about you," pursued the immovable St. John. "It is quite useless to try to deceive me—I should think you would have discovered that long before this time. Who was the gentleman that was kind enough to show me out of the grounds of the house where you were staying the other day?"

"I am going," said Katharine, rising and walking toward the door. "If you have only come to torment me as you used to do, I will not stay to afford you amusement. I am sick and weary—I am going."

"I shall remain here until you come back, then."

"St. John," cried she, facing round upon him, "what is the meaning of this? You promised me that, after I gave you some money, you would go; and you are here yet, to make life a burden to me."

"I made no promises," said St. John, "and I will make none. But I tell you that I will come here every day until you find out—as you can, if you choose—where that boy has been taken to. I have written to Gordon, and he will come, expecting to find the child here. If he is not here—if I cannot put my hand upon him—it will be worse than useless to have summoned him."

"Write and tell him so."

"No letter would reach him now."

Katharine sank back into her chair, and gazed out of the window at the desolate garden which had been so fair and smiling on that November evening when she first saw Mrs. Gordon's face. She could have cried out upon the cruelty of all this, but where was the use? All the tears of Niobe could not have moved the man before her one hair's-breadth from his purpose. The nether millstone is not half so hard as the selfish resolution of a selfish nature. While she was still sitting in hopeless silence, and St. John was still standing on the hearth-rug waiting her reply, there came a stir in the passage outside, a movement of feet, a sound of voices, Miss Tresham's name audibly pronounced, and, before Katharine could move forward, the door opened, and Mrs. Gordon stood on the threshold!

CHAPTER XXIV.

OLD FOES.

It had been a relief to Mrs. Gordon to tell her story to Annesley, and the exhaustion consequent upon long and painful emotion had made her sleep heavily during that night—the first night after Felix had been parted from her. But who can paint the waking—the next day—the long watches of the next night? As hour after hour rolled by, she endured them in much the same passive fashion as that which had so much surprised Morton. But, on the third day, this endurance began to give way to restlessness. Babette, who went in and out on various pretexts, and watched her anxiously, immediately perceived this. She had shortly before been to town on an errand, and she now bethought herself of an expedient to interest her mistress.

"Madame is not well," she said, planting herself on the hearth-rug, with an air of determination. "Madame is lonely—she should have company. As I was coming home, I met mademoiselle—the young lady who comes here with the children. Why should not madame send for her? She would cheer her up."

"Nobody can cheer me up, Babette," said Mrs. Gordon, smiling faintly. "I am used to trouble, and I can bear it; but, as for cheer—that is a different matter. Don't talk of it."

"Madame will be ill, if she is not cheered," said Babette, obstinately. "If madame would only send for the young lady—"

"Is it Miss Tresham you are talking about?" asked Mrs. Gordon, languidly. "Did you say that you met her going into town?"

"A short time ago, madame."

"Well, you may send or stay—no, I will go myself. Order the carriage."

"Madame!"

"The carriage," repeated Mrs. Gordon, impatiently. "Don't you see that I must get out of this house or go crazy? I will go into Tallahoma, and bring Miss Tresham back to stay with me. You are right. She will do me good—if anybody can."

"But Monsieur St. Jean!" cried Babette, who was aghast. "If madame goes into town, she may meet him."

"He cannot harm me," said madame, haughtily, for she could afford to be brave now that Felix was safely out of reach. "Go and order the carriage."

Babette went at once; but, owing to the fact that the horses were out on the plantation, and had to be sent for, it was some time before the carriage came round. Mrs. Gordon's fit of restlessness had by that time partly subsided, and she was half inclined to give up her intention, and merely send Babette with a note to bring Katharine. But Babette was of the opinion that it would be beneficial for madame to go herself, that a breath of the outer air would revive her, and the sight of the outer world be good for her. In

MRS. GORDON CLASPED HER HANDS OVER HER FACE.

CHAP. XXIV.

cases where the mind has too long preyed on itself, there is, indeed, no better prescription than this—simple as it seems. He must be very far gone in morbid gloom whom God's air, and God's sunshine, and the bright, rejoicing beauty of God's fair earth, cannot comfort, cannot help, cannot draw a little out of himself. Beguiled by the persuasions of her faithful attendant, Mrs. Gordon at last consented to go. The Frenchwoman put her into the carriage, and saw her drive off, with great self-congratulation. It is possible that this self-congratulation might have been slightly changed if she had only known who it was that her mistress had gone to meet.

On her way to Tallahoma, Mrs. Gordon was a little diverted from the subject of her own troubles, by thinking of the pleasure of bringing Katharine back to Morton House with her. She felt certain that Mrs. Marks would not object, for Mr. Warwick's last words had advised something like this, and she thought it probable that he might have spoken to his sister on the subject. She liked the girl—liked her bright face, her frank bearing, her sunny smile—and she felt that it would be a great relief to see her moving about Morton House, and lighting up the gloom with her graceful youth, instead of poor Babette's long face and ready tears. As she was drawing this half-unconscious picture, Katharine was going down to meet St. John, with a very pale face, and a very heavy heart, making quite a contrast to the girl whom Mrs. Gordon had seen last—the girl who even then was pictured in Mrs. Gordon's mind.

When the carriage drew up before the Marks house, two or three children were playing in the yard. They all stopped, and stared open-mouthed, as Mrs. Gordon descended. When it was evident that she intended to enter the gate, they immediately took flight, and ran full tilt to the kitchen—rushing headlong through the door, and very nearly tumbling into a pot of boiling lard.

"Mamma, here's a carriage, and a lady coming in!" cried Katy, who was first.

"Mamma, it's a lady in black—I think it's Felix's mother," panted Sara, who was second.

"Mamma—lady tummin," said Nelly, who was last.

"A lady in black!—Felix's mother! Good gracious!" cried Mrs. Mark's. "Run, Letty, and ask her in—in the parlor, mind. I'll be there in a minute. Get away, children, and let me take off this apron. Good gracious!—who was to think—"

While Mrs. Marks was hastily untying her apron, and Letty was running full speed to the house, Mrs. Gordon walked up to the front door, and was about to knock, when Jack came rushing down-stairs. He had been to the school-room to get some string for his kite, and was on his way back to the place where he had left that valuable article of property, when he was thus unexpectedly brought face to face with a strange lady. Fortunately, he was not at all troubled with diffidence; so he went forward, and, when Mrs. Gordon asked if Miss Tresham was at home, at once responded in the promptest manner imaginable:

"Yes'm, Miss Tresham's at home—she got home a little while ago. She's in the dining-room, I b'lieve."

"Can I see her?"

"Oh, yes'm—walk in. This way, please."

His hand was on the lock of the dining-room door, when, enter Letty on the scene—panting and almost breathless.

"Not that way, Mass Jack," cried she, eagerly. "Ask the lady in the parlor. This way, ma'am."

She hurried forward to the parlor-door, and Mrs. Gordon half turned to follow her, when Jack, who was always at feud with Letty, asserted his superior knowledge.

"The lady wants to see Miss Tresham," said he, in a loud voice, "and Miss Tresham ain't in the parlor, she's in here. There she is, now," he added, triumphantly, as he threw open the door, and revealed Katharine, who was sitting almost immediately in front of it.

Mrs. Gordon saw her, and at once advanced into the room. She did not see St. John, who was out of her range of vision, so she began speaking, as she crossed the floor.

"Miss Tresham, I hope you will excuse me—"

Here she stopped suddenly. Something in Katharine's face startled her, and made her look round. Then she saw her companion.

To describe the change that passed over her would be impossible. If she had expected to see him, if she had thought there was even the least reason to fear a meeting with him, she would have prepared for it—being a proud woman, and one who would suffer any thing sooner than let an enemy read her weakness. But, as it was, she had no time for preparation. When she turned and saw that so well-remembered, that so bitterly-hated face, it was as if a sudden, brutal blow had been dealt to her. She gave a sharp cry, and covered her own face with her hands.

The door was still open, and Jack and Letty

were holding an altercation in the passage, which filled up, strangely enough, the interval that followed.

"Never mind, Mass Jack—I'll tell mistis. Puttin' yourself forrard when she told me to ask the lady in the parlor!"

"You mind your own business—I'll tell mamma myself. The lady asked for Miss Tresham, and I wasn't a-going to show her in the parlor. There ain't any fire in there, either."

This was what came into the room, while Mrs. Gordon clasped her hands over her face, St. John stood undecided what to do or say, and Katharine felt a despair which bordered closely upon recklessness. She could have laughed, or she could have cried; but, instead of doing either of the two, she heard, with the odd double consciousness that came to her in moments of excitement, the recrimination in the passage, and even caught the angry whisk of Letty's dress as she departed.

Nevertheless, Katharine was the first who recovered self-possession. Seeing that St. John was about to speak, she silenced him by a glance, and walked up to Mrs. Gordon.

"Will you let me take you into the other room?" she said, gently. "I am very sorry for—for this."

The sound of her voice seemed at once to restore Mrs. Gordon to herself. She looked up with a start. Then her whole face changed—petrified, as it were—and she drew back, so that not even her dress might touch the girl—drew back as she might have drawn back from a scorpion.

"So it was you!" she said. And her voice was so cold and hard, so changed in timbre, that it made Katharine shrink.

"What was me?" she asked, as the other paused and said no more. "I do not understand. What was me?"

"It was you who gave the clew to my place of refuge," answered Mrs. Gordon, with the same repellent coldness of voice and manner. "I see it all now. I was foolish enough to like you—to welcome you into my house—to encourage my cousin in his love for you—and you gave me this return! Thank you, Miss Tresham—thank you for proving to me once more that the wisest person in the world is the person who neither gives nor hopes to receive regard."

"St. John," said Katharine, turning round, "do you hear this? Do you stand by and say not one word to exonerate me from such an accusation?"

"What can I say?" asked St. John, carelessly. "Mrs. Gordon ought to know that she is talking nonsense—that, if you had told me a dozen times over where she was, she had no claim upon you to make such an act any thing but natural.—But Miss Tresham did not tell me," he added, turning to Mrs. Gordon. "I came here in total ignorance of your having chosen this as a place of residence. After I discovered the fact, it was my duty to inform your husband; and that duty I fulfilled."

"I beg your pardon," said Mrs. Gordon, addressing Katharine with her utmost stateliness of tone and bearing. "I had no right to speak to you as I did a moment ago. I am not by nature a patient woman, and trouble has tried me severely. I hope you will let this plead my excuse. As Mr. St. John said, it is certainly true that I have no claim upon you—no right to hope that you would respect my unfortunate position sufficiently to refrain from betraying me to—to—"

She stopped, gasped slightly, as if threatened with suffocation, and her hand went up to her throat. Before Katharine could speak, however, she went on:

"I ought to apologize for this intrusion. When I entered the room, I thought you were alone. I came to see you, to ask you to return to Morton House with me, to beg you to cheer the solitude which Felix's absence has made so dreary. After this meeting, I shall not press that request. I shall only bid you good-morning."

She bowed slightly, drew her veil over her face, and turned to leave the room—a "grand lady," unmistakably, and, so far, commanding much the best of the situation.

But at this point Katharine spoke, her clear, quiet tones seizing Mrs. Gordon's attention, and, almost perforce, arresting Mrs. Gordon's steps.

"If you will allow me, madam, I have a few words to say in my defence. It seems that you disbelieve Mr. St. John's assertion. Will you disbelieve mine when I tell you that I did not bring him here, and that I knew nothing of his acquaintance with you until he himself informed me of it?"

Mrs. Gordon turned, and raised her veil again. The two women faced each other for a minute before the elder spoke—spoke with a certain quiet contempt in her voice.

"I confess that your question seems to me unnecessary, Miss Tresham. Having granted your right to inform Mr. St. John of my place of abode, I can see no reason for uselessly pro longing this discussion. Why should it matter to you whether or not I believe you to have done so?"

Katharine flushed at the tone; but she controlled herself, and held to her point with steady dignity.

"Unnecessary or not, will you be kind enough to answer my question?"

"If you force me to speak, I must answer, then, that I do believe it."

"In the face of my assertion to the contrary?"

"In the face of any assertion given by any friend of Mr. St. John's."

Hot words leaped to Katharine's lips; but she held them back. Even at this moment she had sufficient strength of will to restrain herself—to remember that he who loses temper loses many things besides, and that angry rejoinder never yet helped a cause. She had a hard fight for self-control; but she fought it bravely, and after a minute she was able to command her voice sufficiently to reply.

"I am your debtor, Mrs. Gordon, for the first direct insult that was ever offered to me in my life. I asked your attention before as a courtesy; I demand it now as a right. You have seen fit to charge me with falsehood with regard to a matter in which, according to your own admission, I should have no reason to deny the truth. I will now prove to you that you have done so without a shadow of just cause."

She walked across the floor, and took the *Times* advertisement from the table where she had laid it.

"Will you read this?" she said, coming back and offering it to Mrs. Gordon.

"I cannot imagine—" began the latter, haughtily.

"Read it," said Katharine, interrupting her with grave resolution.

So constrained, Mrs. Gordon took the slip of paper and read:

"If the friends or relations of Katharine Tresham, formerly of the British West Indies, and lately of Cumberland, England, are desirous of knowing her present whereabouts and address, they can obtain this information by addressing R. G., Box 1,084, Mobile, Alabama."

Having read it, she looked up.

"I confess that I do not understand this," she said.

"Perhaps these will enable you to do so," answered Katharine, offering the letters in turn.

The first one which Mrs. Gordon opened—the one which chanced to be the last, and in which the writer gave Miss Tresham's address, and asked information concerning her for "personal and family" reasons—startled her no little. Her eyes had scarcely fallen on the writing before she changed color. As she read on, her face assumed an expression which puzzled Katharine. It did not puzzle St. John, however. Still master of himself, and quietly biding his time, he coolly watched Mrs. Gordon, and coolly arrived at a conclusion.

"She either knows or strongly suspects who is the writer," he said to himself. "I shall remember that."

After Mrs. Gordon finished reading the letter, she stood for some time with it in her hand, apparently deep in thought. Then she roused herself, and opened the other. She merely glanced over this, folded it up, and turned to Katharine.

"Miss Tresham," she said, with formal courtesy, "I apologize. I see that you were not the person who brought Mr. St. John to Lagrange, and I retract my assertion to that effect. Are you satisfied?"

"I am satisfied, madam," answered Katharine, as coldly as herself.

"Will you allow me, then, to inquire if you have any idea who inserted this advertisement and wrote these letters?"

"I have not the least idea."

Here St. John made a step forward, and was about to speak, when Mrs. Marks appeared at the still open door, in her best company dress and with her best company smile.

"I heard that Mrs. Gordon was here," said she, advancing into the room, "and I could not help coming to—" Here the good woman stopped, awed, amazed, by the face that looked at her, overpowered by a sudden rush of feeling which swept away all thought of conventional greeting or conventional compliments. "O Miss Pauline! It can't be Miss Pauline!" she cried, with an almost pitiful astonishment in her voice. "I—I—O Mrs. Gordon! excuse me, but such a change—"

"You, at least, are not changed," said Mrs. Gordon, extending her hand. "The same Bessie Warwick that I knew once—the same Bessie Warwick, with the same honest face. Will you take me somewhere—anywhere—so that I can speak to you alone?" she went on, much to Mrs

Marks's surprise. "I am glad to see you; for I have something that I should like to say to you."

"I—certainly—if you don't object, I will take you to my own room," said Mrs. Marks, looking in bewildered surprise from Katharine to St. John, and from St. John to Mrs. Gordon. "I told Letty to make a fire in the parlor; but I don't expect it is burning yet, and I couldn't ask you to go into the cold. My room is in great confusion, for the children make such a litter; but if you wouldn't mind—"

"Anywhere," said Mrs. Gordon, faintly. Already her excitement was ebbing, her strength was failing, and the room was growing black before her eyes. "I am ready," she added.

She took Mrs. Marks's arm as a support, and turned to leave the room, but before she had made three steps, St. John stood before her—barring the only mode of egress.

"It is quite useless for you to think that you can carry off matters in this way with me, Mrs. Gordon," he said, in a tone of contemptuous amusement. "I understand, from various rumors, that you have sent Felix away, and that you intend to conceal his place of residence, as you have already concealed your own, from his father. Individually, I have no right to interfere with your plans; but I think it well to inform you that your husband"—she shrank at the word—"will be here in a short time, and that he will use every means to discover the child, and to punish, with the utmost rigor of the law, those who have aided you in concealing him."

"Oh!" cried poor Mrs. Marks, and turned a glance on Mrs. Gordon, as if to say, "Can this be true?"

But Mrs. Gordon did not heed the glance. St. John's tones and words had waked all the fire of combat within her—all the haughty spirit of resistance which years of tyranny had failed to subdue.

"Tell the man for whom you are acting," she said, with all languor gone from her face, and all weakness from her voice, "that if he is wise, he will spare himself the trouble of coming here; for no human power shall ever make me see him again. Tell him that Felix is safe from him; and that those who have the child in charge, are neither so poor nor so weak as to be frightened by threats of any penalty which it is in his power to inflict. Tell him, also," she added, with a sudden flash in her eyes that absolutely made St. John recoil a step, "that he had better think twice before he comes to seek the sister of Alfred Morton in her own home, and among her own kindred. I have only to speak, and there are men here who would ask nothing better than to take the matter of vengeance into their own hands."

"You know your husband, madam," said St. John, quietly. "You know whether such threats as that are likely to influence him."

"As for you," she went on, with passion so intense that it made her whole frame quiver, and her voice rise to that infinite height of tragic emotion which only the greatest actors have ever been able to imitate, "if I have spared you, it has been because I recognized the fact that you are simply a tool, and, consequently, that you are below any thing save contempt. But if you trouble me again, I say to you, as I said of him, that there are men who would ask nothing better than to rid me of you summarily. You will do well to remember this!"

"If your friends will be kind enough to call on me, madam," said St. John, with superb coolness, "I shall be happy to receive them. I can make *them* accountable for the words you have just addressed to me, because I have endeavored, as your husband's friend, to serve his interests."

"My dear Mrs. Gordon, let—let me take you to my room," said Mrs. Marks, breaking in here with a half-bewildered tone of expostulation. "I—had no idea of any thing like this, or I should not have come in. If this gentleman will move aside—"

The gentleman moved aside in acknowledgment of this request; but Mrs. Gordon stood still—the glow was yet on her face, and it was evident that she had yet something to say. This time she addressed herself to Mrs. Marks:

"I wished to speak to you in private," she said; "but it is not worth while. The warning which I desired to give you—which it is my duty to give you—had better be spoken in the presence of the person against whom it is directed. I find Mr. St. John apparently at home in your house. I do not know how long this has been the case, nor how long it is likely to continue; but I warn you that, if you were aware of his real character, he would not remain within your doors five minutes. I speak of this character, because I know it to my cost. He is the unprincipled instrument of another man whom it is my misfortune to call my husband. Miss Tresham has sufficiently shown that she has some close connection with him. What that connection is, it does not concern me to inquire. Whether or not it concerns you, is a matter which I leave for yourself to decide."

"Miss Katharine!" cried Mrs. Marks, with one great culminating gasp of astonishment. She turned and looked at her governess with an air of appeal. Plainly she meant to say, "Answer for yourself."

But, as it chanced, Mrs. Gordon's last words had tried Katharine's patience to its utmost limit. She had, so far, curbed herself steadily—wonderfully, in fact, considering how much she had borne before Mrs. Gordon's entrance, and how much she had been called upon to endure since then—but the last tones of scorn roused her as she had not been roused before. She answered Mrs. Marks's looks, therefore, by a few haughty words.

"Mrs. Gordon is perfectly right," she said. "My connection with Mr. St. John does not concern her in the least. I decline to explain it in her presence."

Mrs. Gordon showed her appreciation of this reply with admirable temper and dignity.

"Miss Tresham reminds me that I have not yet said good-morning," she remarked. "Will you allow me to say it at once, and to add that I shall be glad to see you at Morton House?"

She shook hands cordially with Mrs. Marks, bowed distantly to Katharine, and left the room. Mrs. Marks followed her, and, during the few minutes which ensued, St. John was able to say:

"Was there ever any thing as unlucky as that she should have found me here? If you had gone with her, you could have discovered every thing."

"You have only yourself to thank that she found you here," Katharine answered. "But, so far as I am concerned, it does not matter—I should not have gone with her."

"Why not?"

"You know why not, St. John. I should only have laid myself open to the imputation of doing what you wish me to do, of being what you wish me to be—that is, a spy."

At this point, Mrs. Marks came back through the passage—having parted with Mrs. Gordon on the front piazza. She saw the dining-room door still open, and hesitated a moment. Evidently curiosity said, "Enter;" evidently, also, discretion said, "Pass on;" and, between the two, she stood irresolute. Seeing her irresolution, St. John astonished Katharine by stepping forward.

"Will you come in, madam?" he asked. "In my own defence, and that of Miss Tresham, I should like to say a few words to you."

Mrs. Marks came in—nowise loath—but Katharine hardly saw her. It was now her turn to feel faint and sick—for the room to go round in a sort of black mist. Through this mist, she heard St. John speak as if he had been a great way off.

"Since you know Mrs. Gordon, madam, you must be aware that she is of a very excitable and impulsive disposition. This fact will account for her unprovoked attack on Miss Tresham and on myself. I came to this place in ignorance of her being here; but, as a friend of her husband, I could not conceal from him that the wife for whom he has been searching all over Europe is in America. One does not expect reason from an angry woman; but you heard how unjustly she assailed me, on account of this act of disinterested friendship. As for Miss Tresham, I will not insult her by offering to—"

"But is it really true?" asked Mrs. Marks, mercilessly interrupting this flow of language. "Is there really no doubt that Mrs. Gordon has a husband living? I—that is, we thought her a widow."

"There is no doubt, madam, that her husband is living, and that she left him in the most—"

Here Katharine rose and came forward.

"St. John, that is enough," she said. "Mrs. Gordon's domestic troubles cannot interest Mrs. Marks. Will you go now? I do not think I can stand this any longer."

She spoke quietly, but with a certain determination which, almost against his will, St. John obeyed. He started, looked at her face, and, seeing the resolution of the eyes that met his own, went to the mantel-piece for the hat he had left there.

"I will go, certainly," he said; "but I must see you again. When can that be?"

"I don't know," she answered, wearily. "I shall begin teaching on Monday, and—"

"I should like to see you before Monday."

"Come when you choose, then—that is, if Mrs. Marks does not object."

"Certainly not," said Mrs. Marks. "I am always glad for any of Miss Katharine's friends to come to see her, and if Mr."—she stopped and looked at Katharine.

"Mr. St. John," said Katharine, in reply to the look.

"If Mr. St. John will come to tea this evening, we shall be very glad to see him."

"Thank you, madam," said Mr. St. John, speaking for himself. "I am very grateful for your kind invitation, but I regret to say that I am unable to accept it. I have business-letters of importance to write to-day, and I do not think I shall be able to finish them in time to do myself the pleasure of coming."

"To-morrow evening—" began hospitable Mrs. Marks; but St. John had already turned away, and was speaking to Katharine in a tone too low for her to hear his words. As Miss Tresham replied, the coldness of her manner struck Mrs. Marks so much that she stopped short in her second invitation. She had supposed that this handsome gentleman must be a favored suitor, but now she began to change her mind. He was a lover.—Oh, dear! evidently a lover, or he would never have spoken in that voice, and with that manner—but a rejected, perhaps a hopeless lover, poor fellow! His devotion touched her, but she was too close an observer not to see at once that his cause was doomed to failure. Men are sometimes deceived by the coldness of a woman, are sometimes unable to tell whether this coldness is that which betrays dislike, or that which conceals love; but you never find another woman who is so blind. Mrs. Marks saw at once that there was no hope for Mr. St. John; and, although she felt sorry for him, although she would have liked to do something to console him, still she had sufficient discretion to feel that the invitation to tea had better not be pressed. When he took leave, she threw a good deal of respectful sympathy into her manner; and, after he was gone, she would have opened fire at once on Katharine, if Katharine had not anticipated any address on her part, by coming and putting her arms around her.

"You are very good to me," she said, simply. "I am very glad you did not let Mrs. Gordon prejudice you against me. But do not ask Mr. St. John here again, Mrs. Marks. I do not think Mr. Warwick would like it."

"I hope I'm mistress in my own house, my dear," said Mrs. Marks, a little stiffly. Then she softened, and kissed the girl. "I won't, of course, if you say not—it was only because he was a friend of yours that I asked him. I can see that he cares a great deal for you, and that he hasn't much in the way of hope to thank you for. But I don't see what John has to do with it."

"Mr. Warwick is Mrs. Gordon's friend, and, naturally, he will take her side, and look on her cause as—as she does. I don't mean to defend Mr. St. John," she went on, hurriedly. "I don't mean that they may not be right; but still, I should like to see him sometimes, as long as he stays here, if you don't object."

"My dear, I don't object in the least," said the elder woman, kindly. "Don't be afraid of my being prejudiced by Pauline Morton. I know how quick and fiery she always used to be. As for you, I would trust you with—with a mint of money, if I had it."

"You have trusted me with the children, and they are worth ten mints of money," said Katharine, smiling faintly. Then she disengaged herself, and went up-stairs.

An hour or two afterward, Mrs. Marks was in the dining-room, where Tom was busy setting the table, when she was startled by the appearance of Miss Tresham, who entered all cloaked and bonneted as if for a journey, and with a small travelling-bag on her arm.

"Mrs. Marks," she said, "will you lend me a little money?—ten dollars will do. I find I have none in my purse, and I want to catch the coach, and go over to Saxford. I cannot be back until Monday evening, and that will prevent my beginning school until Tuesday; but I hope you won't mind it."

"No—I won't mind it," said Mrs. Marks, a little taken aback. She thought Miss Tresham was growing very eccentric, for she had been to Saxford only the week before Christmas, and now to go again so soon, was quite unprecedented and singular, to say the least. She did not think of refusing her consent, however; but, on the contrary, searched diligently for her purse in the depths of a capacious pocket.

"It's late to be thinking of going, Miss Katharine," she said. "The stage is due for dinner, you know; and I'm afraid you'll hardly catch it now. Give Tom your bag, and he can put some ham and biscuit in it, for you won't be able to stay for dinner. Will two five-dollar notes do? I haven't a ten."

"Two five-dollar notes will do very well," said Katharine. "Thank you, and good-by. Kiss the children for me—I really have not time to see them. That will do, Tom—give me my bag now."

She took the bag, kissed Mrs. Marks, and was out of the door before that astonished woman had time to collect her senses. When she did, her first exclamation was:

"What will Richard say?"

CHAPTER XXV.

MORTON'S CHOICE.

The morning on which Miss Tresham left Annesdale was wearing into noon, when a note from Mrs. Gordon was brought to Mr. Annesley. It was written after her return from Tallahoma, and was brief, to the extreme of epistolary brevity.

"Morton House, Friday morning.

"Dear Morton: Come to me as soon as possible—at once, if that be possible. I have something of importance to say to you. Yours,

"Pauline Gordon."

Morton chanced to be standing near Irene Vernon when he read this, and his change of color at once struck that young lady, who was a very close observer.

"Nothing is the matter, I hope, Mr. Annesley?" she said, as he looked up and met her eye.

"N—o," answered he, a little hesitatingly. Then he glanced down at the note again, and went on: "Nothing is the matter, I hope; but I must go at once to Morton House. My cousin has sent for me."

"Oh, how provoking! What will become of our ride this afternoon?"

"I am obliged to ask you to defer it. You won't care, will you? I am very sorry, but"—

"But, if it must be done, that is an end of the matter. The weather may be as delightful to-morrow as it is to-day. At all events, don't consider me, if your cousin has sent for you."

"You are the embodiment of obliging goodness," said Morton, gratefully. Then, to the servant still standing by, "My horse."

While the horse was being brought out, the young man curbed his impatience as well as he could; and, to enable him to do so, took Miss Vernon partially into his confidence. He did not tell her all of Mrs. Gordon's story, but he told her enough to account for his abrupt departure, and to enlist her sympathy. After a while they wandered from this immediate subject to certain side issues.

"There is one thing that might console your cousin a little," said Miss Vernon, as they walked up and down the piazza, with the soft air and the bright sunshine all around them. "She has gratified the wishes and fulfilled the desires of her heart. It is not given to everybody to do that, you know. She must have tasted some sweets before the bitter came—ought not that to help her to resignation?"

"Would it help you, do you think?"

"I don't know—but it seems to me it would. Any thing is better than dull, even stagnation. A still day of leaden cloud is the dreariest thing in the world—don't you think so? Ah, how bright and beautiful it is to-day! If I knew that to-morrow would bring a blinding storm, I should still take the sunshine, and enjoy it while it lasted."

"You surprise me," said Morton, smiling. "I had no idea that you were such an epicurean. But," he added, more gravely, "you are mistaken. If you had ever known Mrs. Gordon, you would see that the lesson of her life is directly opposed to the sentiment you are advocating—a sentiment which has found its best expression in the words, 'Let us eat and drink, for to-morrow we die.' The lesson of Mrs. Gordon's life teaches with unusual force a thing which has almost grown trite in our ears—this is, that the gratification of our own wishes, and the fulfilment of our own desires, never brings happiness. Of course, we all think it would do so; and, since there are few of us who are free enough to test the matter, we go on to our lives' ends thinking so. But, in truth, when we see those who possessed the freedom which we lacked, and who marched forward to the goal of their own hopes, what is the result? Mrs. Gordon was one of those people, Miss Vernon; and, if you could see her, your own eyes would assure you that, for her, not only the end, but the very hour of fruition—if, indeed, there ever *is* an hour of fruition—was disappointment and bitterness."

"But, at all events, she has not merely existed—she has lived."

"You must give me your definition of life before I can grant you even that," he said, with a slight, grave smile. "Does life consist in a certain amount of sight-seeing, a certain number of vicissitudes to be endured, a certain depth of emotion to be sounded? I know that the idea of the day runs somewhat thus, and that discontent is rife in many places, because some people declare that life is only worthy of the name when it has known these things. But it seems to me that minds which think thus, must reason very shallowly—else they could hardly fail to perceive that, by such a standard, they exalt the worst class of the world above the best. In their sense, who has lived most thoroughly, the saint in his cloister, the philosopher in his study, the great minds and hearts that solitude has nurtured in all ages, or the reckless adventurer, the wandering sybarite, the men who sound every scale of human life, and, dying, pass from human memory like the brutes that perish? Miss Vernon, will you tell me what you meant by saying that Mrs. Gordon had lived?"

"I meant exactly what you have condemned, Mr. Annesley. I meant that her existence has not been tame and stagnant, and cast in one groove; but that it has been like a varied drama, filled with many scenes and many emotions. In short—well, I express myself badly, but I think you know what I mean."

"Yes, I think I do. You mean that, to you, her life seems like a picture, where the shades only heighten the effect; or, like a story, which would lose half its interest if it had no tragic incidents, or pathetic close. But the tragedy and the pathos are not poetical, but very bitter, when they come home to us in our own lives. If you will allow me to make a personal application of my meaning, I should judge from what you have said just now, and from many things which have gone before, that you find your life dull and tame—it may be, even weary. But does it never occur to you that this very life seems to others like one long sunny idyl of brightness and peace? Believe me, the chief secret of happiness—the only one, in fact—is content with that life, and mode of life, which has fallen to our portion. I don't mean that we can obtain this content by merely wishing for it," said the young man, with a wistful look on his face; "but we can gain it by fighting for it, and it is worth a battle. Forgive me, if I seem to be preaching to you," added he, with a smile. "I have very imperfectly expressed the thoughts your words suggested to me, but perhaps you can seize the idea through the rude garb in which I have clothed it. It has only come to me dimly and feebly, but there is a thrill about it which tells me that I am on the threshold of a great truth. Yonder is my horse, at last. Now my prosing is at an end. Good-by."

"Good-by," echoed Miss Vernon, giving her hand, unconsciously, to the one he extended. "I did not know you thought this way," she went on, abruptly. "Your creed seems to me simple, and yet—I fear I am very morbid," she said, quickly. "You have done something to make me ashamed of it."

"You are a little morbid," said Morton, smiling. "You must forgive me if I tell you so, and you must also forgive me if I suggest the remedy May I?"

"Of course you may."

"Forget yourself, then. I don't mean that you think of yourself a great deal," he went on, as he saw her flush; "but we are all prone to self-consciousness, and, in some natures, it fosters vanity; in others, a morbid habit of introspection which—pshaw! I am drifting into metaphysics, and I know you hate the stuff as much as I do. Once more, good-by. I am off for good, this time."

Miss Vernon stood on the piazza and watched him as he rode away. He looked very gallant and handsome; for, like most of his countrymen, he rode to perfection, and never appeared so well as on horseback. When he was out of sight, she smiled, to herself, with a mixture of archness and sadness. Seen just now, her face wore its very softest and sweetest expression.

"It is not hard to tell where he obtains his philosophy," she thought. "No doubt he is perfectly sincere in it, but it is amazingly easy to be resigned to success, and to be content when every desire of one's heart is gratified. The test will be when disappointment and failure come. If his philosophy helps him to bear that, it will be genuine, and worth practising. *Will* it help him to bear it, though? Who can tell?"

Regarded as an abstract question, who, indeed? Yet the time was fast approaching when the abstract question would assume practical shape, and when Miss Vernon's question would be answered in a way which Miss Vernon could not, at that moment, possibly have foreseen or imagined.

She was still standing on the piazza, still looking absently out on the bright landscape, still thinking of Morton's philosophy, and of the chances for and against his practising it, when Mrs. Annesley appeared at the open hall-door, and walked up to her.

"All alone, my dear?" she said, with a smile, in which the kindness for once was real. "I thought I saw Morton with you a few minutes ago?"

"You did see him with me a few minutes ago," Irene answered; "but he is gone now. Didn't you hear the tramp of his horse?"

"I heard the tramp of somebody's horse, but I had no idea that it was his. Where has he gone?"

"To Morton House, I believe."

"To Morton House!" The extreme of sur

prise appeared in Mrs. Annesley's face. "Why, what has taken him there? And so suddenly—without a word to me!"

"A note from Mrs. Gordon was the cause of his going," said Miss Vernon, carelessly. "He showed it to me, because he had an engagement to ride with me, which, in consequence of this, he was obliged to break."

"And what was in the note?"

"Only a few lines, begging him to come to her at once, on a matter of importance."

"Nothing more?"

"Nothing more at all."

"How very strange!" said Mrs. Annesley, with her color rising. "A matter of importance, and not one word to me—either from Pauline or Morton. My dear, excuse me, and don't think it is curiosity I feel—I am surprised, and, I confess, a little wounded, that I should be openly excluded from the confidence of my son."

"I don't think Mr. Annesley knew what Mrs. Gordon wants with him," said Miss Vernon, seeing the mischief she had unwittingly done, and being anxious to smooth the lady's ruffled plumes. "He seemed very much surprised, and, I am sure, he never thought—"

"That is just it," said Mrs. Annesley, a little bitterly. "Of course, he never thought—or perhaps he receives Pauline's confidence with the stipulation that it is to be kept from me. But we mothers must make up our minds to bear this," said she, recovering her usual manner by an effort. "As our children grow older, others supplant us in their hearts and minds, and we must endeavor to abdicate with a good grace. If we could only choose our successors, it would not be hard to do so," she added, drawing the girl's hand within her arm, with a smile.

"Dear Mrs. Annesley, you do your son great injustice," said Irene, speaking quickly. "No one will ever supplant you in his heart. I don't think you know how much he loves and admires you. It often makes me admire *him* to see it."

"You reconcile me to abdication, my dear," said the lady, smiling the same gracious smile. "Ah! if I can only choose *my* successor"—she broke off, as Irene colored and drew back a little. "Forgive me—I only meant to say that I am very happy if I am one link to draw you nearer to us. Shall we go in now? I am afraid you find it cold out here."

They went in; and no sooner was Mrs. Annesley able to make a retreat, than she retired to her own room, and rang for her maid.

"Get my wrappings, Julia," she said, "and order the carriage. Tell Sarah to have dinner an hour or two later than usual, for I am going to Morton House, and shall not be back at the ordinary time."

While his mother, at Annesdale, was preparing for her drive, Morton felt as if the ground had absolutely yielded beneath his feet, when Mrs. Gordon, who was in a state of strangely-passionate excitement, told her story at Morton House. After it was ended, she gave the reason that had made her send for him.

"I have been foolish enough to encourage you in your fancy for this girl," she said. "It was my duty, therefore, not to let you rest an hour in ignorance of her true character—not to fail to tell you at once that I consider her an adventuress of the most decided stamp. Morton, for Heaven's sake—for the sake of your name, your honor, and your friends—do not give another thought to her!"

"One moment," said Morton, who was pale, but reticent—evidently he meant to hear every thing, and say nothing that would commit him to any positive line of action—"you have not told me yet why you think this."

"Could I think it on better ground than that of her association with St. John? You don't know—you can hardly imagine—what he is!"

"But is it just to judge her by him?"

"What could be more just, when there is evidently some link of familiar connection between them? Morton, put the case as if it regarded somebody else. What would you think of a woman who was on terms of—well, we will say intimate friendship, with a man than whom the lowest sharper is not more destitute of honor—with a man whose record is one that exiles him forever from the companionship of honest people?"

"She may not know this."

"Ask her if she does not! I am willing to risk every thing on her reply, for I think that circumstances have made it impossible for her to speak falsely. Ask her if she does not know who and what St. John is."

"You are right," he said, rising. "I will ask her. That is the straightforward and honest thing to do, after all. Don't think that I doubt you," he went on, looking at his cousin "Don't think that I am ungenerous enough to blame you for what you have said. On the contrary, I thank you. I should certainly hear all that is said—if only that I may be able to answer it. You must forgive me that I cannot take any mere circumstantial evidence against her. It seems to me that I should be a very contemptible fellow, if I did."

"And you are going to her?" said Mrs. Gordon, bitterly. "Well—perhaps it may be best; but oh, Morton, don't be rash! Don't say any thing that you may hereafter regret. Give me that much credence, at least."

He bent down, and kissed her cheek—smiling with an attempt at cheerfulness which went to her heart more surely than any pathos could have done. He was mad and foolish, she thought; he was about to risk the happiness of his whole life in the blind determination to trust to the last; yet, even while she felt impatient, she could not but be touched by his simple, steadfast fidelity. It had all the elements of the highest chivalry in it, though nobody could have known this as little as Morton himself. It was Mrs. Gordon who recognized it, and who, in the midst of her anxiety and irritation, felt suddenly thrilled by admiration. Still she could not but make one last effort.

"Morton," she said, catching his hand as he bent over her, "listen to me. I am much older than yourself, and, although I am a woman, my knowledge of the world is much greater. Besides, I am your cousin—the only Morton left, the only one of the name which hereafter you will have to represent. To see you what you are—to know you brave, and true, and loyal—has given more sunshine to my life than you would readily believe. If he lives, Felix's duties will be elsewhere—some day, therefore, this house must be yours. This has been my only comfort. Morton—remember that it was through my fault my father left here; it was my fault my brother never took his place. It is a horrible thing to see, when it is too late, a direct sequence of events—to know that one's own hand has set in motion a tide which ends by sweeping away every thing that life holds dear. This has been my lot. Don't add one more disappointment to it—one more bitter memory. Don't ruin your life, and tarnish your name, by marrying this woman."

The earnestness, the passion of her appeal, touched Morton deeply. He saw plainly enough that the question of his happiness was with her entirely subordinate to the question of family pride; but he sympathized with this sentiment sufficiently to feel its supremacy no hardship. In these times, the thought that any thing is of more importance than the gratification of a sentimental fancy is quite obsolete; but, in that day, a few people (and Morton was one of these people) clung to the old-fashioned idea that there were certain claims to be considered in such a case, certain higher duties than the duty of marrying and giving in marriage, certain principles to be observed, and, if any or all of these things clashed with love, then love must give way. We of the present period know better than that. Having the grand advantage of modern enlightenment, we know that the first duty of every reasonable human being is a duty to self. And as selfishness generally culminates its strength in love—not divine love, which takes us out of ourselves into something higher, but that passion bearing its name, which is of the earth earthy—so love must needs be taught to override all the grand old watchwords of Faith, and Honor, and Duty. But, as we have said, Morton was not of this day. The jargon of the new school of moralists would have been a foreign language to his ears. The conception of sacrifice—the conception which is the key-note of every nature which deserves to be called noble—had always been familiar to him, had grown with his growth, and strengthened with his strength. As far as he was concerned, he was ready to put his own wishes down under his feet for the sake of any thing that had a right to demand the offering; and, reared as he had been, the name that he bore was one of these things. No sacrifice could be counted too costly that would help to keep it pure and untarnished.

Regarded from this point of view, his course seemed clear—but then there was another side to the question, or else all this explanation need not have been written. To Morton, life had always seemed a very simple thing, and he had never had much sympathy with those who professed to find it otherwise. "The path of duty is always clear and straight," he said, "and, if we follow it, we can't possibly go wrong. The people who are involved in moral difficulties, generally make them for themselves." Now the time had come for him to learn—as everybody who deals in such fluent generalities sooner or later must learn—that life is, after all, a very complex tissue, and that, without being addicted to the dangerous pastime of splitting hairs, we may find ourselves on the horns of a moral dilemma, and be honestly and seriously puzzled thereby. Two duties were clashing with him now, and the young man felt sorely uncertain as to which had the strongest claim to his respect. On the one side was the name to which a gentleman owes his first duty. On the other, that principle of steadfast fidelity which every tradition of his creed, and instinct of his nature, made a solemn obligation. Moved as he had been by Mrs. Gordon's passionate appeal, he was not yet ready to set this aside as naught—not yet ready to believe that the higher duty conflicted with it.

He walked away to the window, and stood there looking out. Before him lay the broad Morton fields, and the distant shadowy Morton woods. Above him was the roof which he had just heard Mrs. Gordon declare might some day be his own—at a little distance from him sat the woman rendered so sadly desolate by her own folly, the woman who had appealed to him in the name of family honor, who had bared her heart to him, and prayed him to spare her another cruel blow. Here it would have seemed as if every influence weighed heavily in one scale—as if here the side which all these things represented surely must prevail. Yet here his heart spoke to him as it had never spoken before. Here Katharine Tresham's face rose before him with a pathos and a beauty which the face itself had never owned. Suddenly the passion which he had heretofore so steadily curbed, so sternly kept obedient to his will, rose up in revolt, and swept over him in a great wave that fairly startled him. A voice seemed to speak in his ear, and to say: "If you give her up in this way, you are a dastard!" It was in obedience to this voice that he turned at last to answer Mrs. Gordon.

"Until I have seen Miss Tresham, I cannot tell what I will do," he said. "I can only say that I will try to act as seems to me right. Many things have conspired to perplex me of late; and, at this moment, I am only certain of one thing—that I will not give her up! I will trust her until she herself proves or disproves your opinion of her; and I should not deserve the name of gentleman if I did not do so."

"This is your decision?" asked Mrs. Gordon.

"This is my decision," he answered.

Something like a faint smile of pity came to the lips of the woman who had gone *her* way, and who now looked back on the results of it.

"We are all alike," she said. "Indeed, all of us must needs run our own course of folly, and wreck our lives according to our own fancy. I suppose it is useless to reason with you; and I, of all people, have no right—save the right of sad experience—to bid you stop and consider. Yet"—she paused a moment—"yet I fancied you would be different. I fancied you would rate the duty you owe to your name above your passion for a woman's face."

"And I thought you would understand me better," he answered, quickly. "I thought you would believe that I *do* rate it above every thing excepting my duty to God, and that if my love for Katharine Tresham clashed with it, I would sacrifice that love without an instant's hesitation."

"*If* it clashed with it?"

"Yes, if it clashed with it. You must pardon me that I say 'if'—but your opinion is only your opinion, you know; and, in a matter which concerns the happiness of my whole life, I cannot accept any thing but positive evidence."

"One word more," said Mrs. Gordon, as he extended his hand to bid her good-by. She did not take the hand, but rose to her feet, holding her own tightly pressed against her heart. "You will not misunderstand what I am going to say, I am sure; you will not think that I mean to influence you by any thing so foolish, and (from me) so impertinent as a threat," she went on. "But I think it right to place before you the consequences of the step you seem determined to take. Morton, that woman is allied in some way to the man who helped to ruin my life and to murder my brother. If you make her your wife, you can never be master in this house."

She spoke quietly, but in a moment she saw that she had spoken unwisely. Her warning certainly had much of the nature of a threat in it, and the man must be cold-blooded, indeed, who, in a matter of this kind, submits to be threatened.

"You might have spared me this," said Morton, with more *hauteur* than he intended. "My resolution with regard to Miss Tresham did not need a spur; and your own experience might tell you whether my sense of family obligation is likely to be increased or diminished by the knowledge of such a penalty. I see that I had better go," he added, after a short pause. "You have wounded me, and I may pain you, if I remain any longer. Forgive me if I have seemed abrupt or ungracious. I—this has been a harder struggle than you think."

She let him go in silence. But after the last echo of his step had died away, the reason of this became evident. She sat down, and a rush of tears came through the thin, white fingers which covered her face.

Half an hour later, Babette opened the door and brought in a card.

"The lady is in the drawing-room, and insists on seeing madame," she said.

"I can see nobody," answered Mrs. Gordon, languidly. Still she extended her hand, and took the bit of pasteboard. She started when she read Mrs. Annesley's name.

CHAPTER XXVI.

MR. MARKS ASSERTS HIMSELF.

Mrs. Marks's doubt of what "Richard" would have to say on the subject of Miss Tresham's flitting, proved to be well founded. When the cashier came home to dinner, and heard his wife's eager recital of the events of the morning, he looked decidedly grave. The mention of Mr. St. John recalled Mr. Warwick's opinion of that gentleman, and for Mr. Warwick's opinion nobody entertained a greater respect than his brother-in-law. Then Mrs. Gordon's warning seemed to Mr. Marks a much more important matter than it had seemed to his wife.

"Mrs. Gordon would never have spoken in that way without some cause," he said, when Mrs. Marks told her story. After this, came the news of Miss Tresham's sudden departure—at which Mr. Marks startled his wife by the astonishment of his face.

"Gone!" he said. "Gone, just at the close of the holidays, and before she had been in the house more than a few hours! What is the meaning of it?—what did she say was the meaning of it?"

"I—really, I believe she only said she was going to Saxford," answered Mrs. Marks, decidedly taken aback. "She asked me if I had any objection, and I told her no. I thought a day or two would not matter about the children, and it never occurred to me that you would mind it."

"I mind it, because I don't understand it," said Mr. Marks, with the same unusual gravity. "It don't look well for Miss Tresham to be neglecting her duties in this way; but, as you say, a day or two wouldn't matter—if a day or two's loss of time was all. What does matter, is some explanation of this strange conduct. Think, Bessie! Did she tell you nothing about *why* she was going to Saxford?"

"She did not tell me a word," said Mrs. Marks, looking and feeling a little crestfallen. "She came in here in a great hurry, just as Tom was setting the table, and asked me to lend her some money, as she had none, and wanted—Why, Richard, what on earth is the matter?"

There was reason enough for asking the question. Mr. Marks's eyes opened wide on his startled wife, and the expression of his face fully warranted her surprise. When she broke off in this way, his lips had already formed an exclamation.

"She asked you for money!" he repeated hastily. "Bessie, there must be some mistake Are you sure she asked you for money?"

"Of course I am sure! How could I be mistaken?"

"And did you lend her any?"

"Of course I did—I lent her ten dollars."

"Ten dollars!"

The cashier's astonishment seemed to have reached the utmost extreme possible to that emotion. He walked up and down the floor, then came back and stood before the fire, looking down into the glowing coals.

"This is the strangest thing I ever heard of!" he said, at last. "I confess I don't understand it."

"What is the matter?" demanded Mrs. Marks, who was, in her turn, excited by curiosity. "What is strange?—what is it you don't understand? Why shouldn't Miss Tresham ask me to lend her some money?"

Her husband turned and looked at her.

"The simple reason why Miss Tresham should not have asked you to lend her some money is, that I paid Miss Tresham no less sum than a thousand dollars no longer ago than last Tuesday."

"Richard!"

"Her receipt is at the bank to show for it" said Mr. Marks; "and now—on Friday—she comes to you to borrow ten dollars! It is very strange conduct, to say the least of it."

"A thousand dollars! Good gracious! What do you think she could have done with it?" cried Mrs. Marks, all in a flutter. "She certainly said she didn't have any money, and she certainly took two five-dollar notes from me. Richard, what on earth could she have done with it?"

"That is more than I can pretend to say," answered her husband. "But one thing is certain—I don't like the look of matters. When Miss Tresham drew that money, she was very particular about requiring gold. Then she wrote a note in the bank, and had a meeting in the parlor across the passage, with this St. John. After that she went away, and Warwick came him. The first thing he told me was that the man—St. John, I mean—was an unprincipled scoundrel; and, though he did not give me his reasons for saying so, he spoke in a manner which showed very plainly that he had reasons, and good ones, for the opinion. I confess that, at the time, I didn't pay much attention to the matter; but, looking back now, it seems to me more serious. After what has happened to-day, I feel uneasy—I feel certain that something is wrong."

"Not with Miss Tresham, Richard—I'm sure there's nothing wrong with Miss Tresham."

"What do you know about Miss Tresham, Bessie? You may forget, but I don't, that we engaged her when she was an entire stranger to us, and that, after living with us two years, she is, as far as her own affairs are concerned, as much a stranger as ever."

"But you know how nice she is!" said Mrs. Marks, indignantly. "You know all that she has done for the children, and—and all that she has done for me. You liked her yourself, Richard—you know you did!"

"I like her now," said Mr. Marks, with that stolid masculine coolness which some men possess in superlative degree, and which is, to the feminine mind, the most exasperating thing in the world. "But what has that got to do with the matter? I'm not talking about liking her. I'm talking about her drawing that money, and borrowing ten dollars from you three days later—I am talking about her acquaintance with this St. John, and what Mrs. Gordon said of it—and I'm talking of her going away without a word of explanation, just as the holidays are at an end."

Mrs. Marks sat dumb. She was a good partisan; but even the best of partisans must have something besides mere opinion with which to oppose stated facts. On any one of these grounds, she was unable to say any thing for Miss Tresham. After a minute's silence, Mr. Marks resumed:

"One of two things must happen. Either Miss Tresham has gone away for good—than which, I confess I think nothing more likely—or else she will come back at the stated time. If she does come back, there must be an explanation required from her. I must know who Mr. St. John is, and on what footing he comes here. Otherwise, I may be sorry to part with her, but my duty is plain—she must go. I cannot keep a governess who acts as Miss Tresham has been acting lately."

So spoke the head of the household in his official capacity; and much as his wife's sympathy ranged on the side of the governess, she could not deny that he spoke with reason. Miss Tresham's conduct certainly justified all that he said of it. Yet the unreasoning faith of Miss Tresham's advocate was not shaken for an instant. O wonderful instinct of woman! There is nothing like it in the world; and where it has taken one woman wrong, it has led a hundred thousand right. Yet there are people who would like to educate and "develop" it into a "reasoning faculty!" Why does not somebody come forward to paint the lilies of the field, and furnish us with patent improved sunlight, warranted to shine on every occasion?

Oblivious, for once, of his business duties in town, Mr. Marks was still standing before the fire, considering the perplexing subject which was on the domestic *tapis*, when there came a knock at the front door.

"There, now!" said Mrs. Marks, starting. "Of course it's somebody to see me—Mrs. Sloan, I expect—and what a sight I am! Go, Richard, please, and ask her into the parlor."

Mr. Marks obeyed, and, as he carelessly left the door open behind him, his wife heard him exchange a cordial greeting with the visitor; and then, without any warning, he came back, and ushered Morton Annesley into the dining-room, where the uncleared dinner-table stood in the centre of the floor—Mrs. Marks having been in such a fever of impatience to tell her story, that she had not allowed Tom to finish his duties.

"Oh, my dear!" she cried, in a tone of expostulation. But it was too late. Morton—who would have been none the wiser if there had been an elephant, instead of a dinner-table, in the middle of the floor—walked forward and shook hands with her.

"Pray don't speak of it," he said, when she began apologizing. "I hope you don't consider me a stranger. Mr. Marks, at least, was more complimentary, for he asked me in at once. I hope you are well. I have not seen you for a long time—not since before Christmas, I believe. May I wish you a happy New Year, since we did not have an opportunity to exchange Christmas greetings?—Yes, Mr. Marks—the roads are quite heavy. That rain yesterday has made them muddy. My boots show it—don't they?"

People less clear-sighted than Mr. Marks and

his wife might have perceived that the young man made these disjointed remarks very absently, that his eyes turned unconsciously toward the door, and that he started at every noise in the passage outside. They glanced at each other significantly, but were kind enough to take no further notice, and talked of indifferent things, until Morton himself came directly to the point, in his frank, somewhat boyish fashion. Mrs. Marks spoke of Miss Tresham's enjoyment at Annesdale, and Morton instantly caught at her name.

"I hope she did enjoy herself," he said. Then he added, quickly: "Is Miss Tresham disengaged just now?—I should like to see her, if she is. I am obliged to return to Annesdale very soon, and I am particularly anxious—"

He stopped short. The expression of Mrs. Marks's face warned him that something was wrong. He looked hastily from herself to her husband, and read the same expression still more strongly stamped on the masculine face.

"What is the matter?" he asked, impetuously. "Miss Tresham—"

Here Mrs. Marks interrupted:

"I am sorry to say, Mr. Annesley, that Miss Tresham is not at home. She left to-day for Saxford."

"Left!"

Morton was astounded. In a moment his mind ran over a terrible possibility—the possibility that there had been some misunderstanding between Miss Tresham and her employers, which had resulted in her leaving Tallahoma permanently.

"Left—for Saxford!" he repeated. "Mrs. Marks, what is the meaning of that?"

"Don't ask me, Mr. Annesley," said Mrs. Marks. "If my life depended on it, I could not tell you a thing more than just that—she has gone to Saxford. I am sure it didn't strike me as strange; but here's Richard has been talking about it, and—"

"It is very strange," said Richard, speaking for himself. "I don't pretend to understand it. I don't wonder you are astonished, Mr. Annesley. I was astonished myself when I came home and heard that Miss Tresham was gone."

"When will she be back?" asked Morton, catching at the first idea which presented itself to him.

"On Monday," answered Mrs. Marks, to whom the question was addressed. "She said she would be back on Monday, Mr. Annesley, and I am sure she will come. Miss Katharine never breaks her word."

"But why did she go away?" asked Morton, impatiently. "Did she not tell you why she went?"

Mrs. Marks looked at her husband, and Mr. Marks looked at his wife. This time Annesley perceived the glance, and saw plainly that there was something in reserve which he was not to hear. Determined to know if any thing had happened after Mrs. Gordon left the house, he boldly broke the ice at once.

"I have been to Morton House and seen my cousin," he said. "I am aware of the unfortunate"—he stopped a moment, as if searching for a word—"the unfortunate discussion which took place this morning. Will you allow me to inquire if that discussion, or any thing resulting from it, was the cause of Miss Tresham's leaving Tallahoma?"

On this point Mrs. Marks professed utter ignorance, and she was going on to state every thing which she had already told to her husband, when Mr. Marks broke in:

"Since you have seen Mrs. Gordon, Mr. Annesley, I need not hesitate to say to you that I am seriously perplexed and uneasy about this affair of Miss Tresham. As I was telling my wife, just before you came in, there are more reasons than the reason of Mrs. Gordon's warning for distrusting Mr. St. John, and Miss Tresham's connection with him. You know her quite well, I believe: will you tell me if she has ever mentioned the man or any thing about him to you?"

Morton flushed. He remembered the eve of New Year, and the manner in which Miss Tresham had repulsed his first and last attempt to win her confidence. Oh, if she had only been frank with him, the young man thought, if she had only trusted him, and given him a right to speak for her! But she had not done this, and there was nothing for it but to answer Mr. Marks's question by the truth.

"She has never mentioned Mr. St. John's name to me," said he. "But I have never been in a position to receive her confidence."

"Hum!" said the cashier, significantly—looking the while at his wife, and smoothing with one hand his well-shaven chin. "I cannot find," he said, after a moment, "that Miss Tresham has ever mentioned Mr. St. John's name to any one; and, even after Mrs. Gordon's visit, she gave my wife no explanation of his purpose in coming here, or of her acquaintance with him. My own impression," added he, "is, that she has left Tallahoma simply to avoid giving this explanation."

"But when she returns on Monday?"

"When she returns on Monday—or, to speak more correctly, if she returns on Monday—I shall certainly endeavor to obtain this explanation. If I cannot obtain it, Mr. Annesley, my mind is made up—Miss Tresham must leave my house."

An indignant reply rose to Annesley's lips, but he had sense enough to restrain it—sense enough to see that he would do harm, instead of good, by uttering it. What business, after all, was it of his? what right had he to interfere in Mr. Marks's domestic affairs? Angry as he was, he asked himself this question, and accepted the obvious reply. During the minute which followed Mr. Marks's speech, nothing was said. Then Annesley rose, and began drawing on his gloves.

"If you will allow me, I will call again on Monday to see Miss Tresham," he said, with unusual formality. "I am sorry—very sorry that she has left Tallahoma. But, if you will excuse me, Mr. Marks, I would advise you to suspend judgment upon the matter until she returns."

Before Mr. Marks could reply to this advice, there came an interruption. The door opened, and Letty appeared. She addressed herself to her mistress.

"There's a gentleman out here to see Miss Tresham, ma'am, and he wants to know if you can tell him when she will be back."

"Miss Tresham will be back on Monday," answered Mrs. Marks. "Tell the gentleman—or, no, stop.—My dear" (to Mr. Marks), "perhaps you had better see who it is, and speak to him yourself."

Mr. Marks went out, and Morton, after shaking hands with Mrs. Marks, followed him. At the front door they met St. John, whom Morton had seen once before, and the cashier never at all.

A glance was sufficient to show them that Mr. St. John was very decidedly out of temper. The face, which on occasions could be so bland and smiling, was now set and lowering in singularly marked degree. It did not even lighten when he saw the two men who advanced toward him.

"Mr. Marks, I presume," he said, raising his hat as Mr. Marks came down the passage. Then, glancing at Annesley, he started, and bowed without any sign of recognition. For some reason, he evidently chose to ignore their previous meeting, and addressed himself solely to the master of the house.

"I have called to see Miss Tresham," he said, "and I am surprised to hear from your servant that she has left Tallahoma. Will you allow me to inquire if this is true?"

"It is true, sir," answered Mr. Marks, with business-like brevity.

"May I ask where she has gone, and when she will return?"

"She has gone to Saxford, and will probably return on Monday—at least she told my wife to expect her on that day."

A dead pause. An expression on Mr. Marks's face, and in Mr. Marks's attitude, which said: "Your questions are answered. Take leave." An expression on St. John's face of perplexed astonishment, and half-absent thought, which Annesley, watching him closely, felt sure was not assumed. He looked silently at his boots for a second, then glanced up again at the cashier.

"Excuse me," he said, "but this news is very unexpected—and surprising. When I was here this morning, Miss Tresham gave no intimation of any such intention as this. Shall I trespass too much on your kindness if I ask you to inquire whether she left any message or note for me—that is, for Mr. St. John?"

"I can inquire, sir, but I do not think it is likely," said Mr. Marks, with the same forbidding civility.

He walked down the passage, and, without entering the dining-room, held an audible conversation with his wife.

"Bessie, did Miss Tresham leave any note or message for Mr. St. John?"

Reply of Mrs. Marks from behind the scenes: "Not a word, or a line, with me, Richard."

"You are sure of this?"

"I am perfectly sure. She never mentioned him."

"Miss Tresham has left nothing for you, sir," said Mr. Marks, returning to Mr. St. John. "I regret that I am not able to give you any further information about the reason of her departure."

"You can give me one item of further information," said St. John, manifestly proof against the plainest of hints. "Is Miss Tresham in the habit of going to Saxford?"

"She is in the habit of going there once a month or so."

"May I ask if she has any acquaintances there?"

"She goes, I believe, to see a Catholic priest," answered Mr. Marks. Then he lost patience, and showed it in a way very unusual with him. "You must excuse me, sir, if I decline to answer any more questions. Miss Tresham's private affairs *are* her private affairs; and, since she has been living in my family, I have never interfered with or inquired into them."

"Allow me to admire your discretion," said Mr. St. John, with the same bow which had once irritated Morton by its covert mockery. "I regret to have trespassed so long on your time and civility, and I have the honor to wish you good-day."

In another bow he included Annesley, and then went his way, leaving Mr. Marks with an angry sense of having had the worst of it.

"An insolent scoundrel!" said he, as soon as St. John was out of hearing. "What do you say, Mr. Annesley?" he went on, turning to Morton. "Don't you think that 'rascal' is written legibly on his face?"

"I don't especially fancy his face," said Morton; "but I should not like to say that any thing particular is written on it. One thing is certain," he went on, more slowly; "Miss Tresham's departure has taken *him* by surprise."

"That is to say, he looked as if it had," said Mr. Marks, who, what with Mr. Warwick's opinion, Mrs. Gordon's opinion, and his own discomfiture, was ready to believe the very worst of Mr. St. John. "Candidly, however, Mr. Annesley, I don't trust any thing about him."

"You think—"

"I think that I will follow your advice of a little while ago, and wait and see. Miss Tresham may come back on Monday. If she does, we can clear up matters speedily, and it is not worth while to trouble ourselves with conjectures."

"Meanwhile, however, you distrust Mr. St. John?"

"Meanwhile, I do most decidedly distrust Mr. St. John."

With this interchange of sentiment, the conversation ended. The two men walked to the gate together, and there separated—Mr. Marks going into town, and Annesley riding off in the opposite direction.

CHAPTER XXVII.

MRS. GORDON'S SUGGESTION.

When Mrs. Gordon read her cousin's name on the card, she hesitated a moment. Then she surprised Babette by lifting her face with an air of decision.

"I will see Mrs. Annesley," she said. "Ask her in here."

Babette left the room to obey the direction, and a minute or two of silence followed. To Mrs. Gordon the interval seemed much longer than it really was, and she had extended her hand to ring the bell and ask the cause of the delay, when there came the sound of foot-steps, and the rustle of silk, crossing the passage. Through the closed door she heard Mrs. Annesley's voice:

"Just left, you say?—not more than half an hour ago? It is strange I did not meet him. Do you know where he was going?"

"No, madame," said Babette, in reply.

Catching both the question and the reply, Mrs. Gordon dropped the bell-rope with a smile. "I might have known what detained her," she thought—and, as she thought it, the door opened.

The two ladies met in the centre of the floor, and greeted each other with a moderate show of warmth. They called each other "my dear Elinor," and "my dear Pauline," but, beyond this, there was not much of effusion on either side. They shook hands, kissed lightly, spoke of the weather, and sat down opposite each other, like two ordinary acquaintances. Mrs. Annesley looked at ease, but in fact she was very far from that enviable state of mind. She remembered her former discomfiture in that house; and something in her cousin's face seemed to warn her that it might possibly be repeated.

Nevertheless, she plunged boldly into conversation, and began deploring the many social duties that had kept her so long from Morton House. "I am sure you believe that I would have come if I could," said she, looking at her cousin. "Oh, my dear Pauline, how wise you were in declining to reënter society! I so often think of you, and envy you—so retired, so quiet, so surrounded by repose. As for poor me—I might as well be a galley-slave, for all the liberty I have! If it were not for the sake of my children, I really think I should give up society entirely. It tries my health so severely, and is so unsuited to my taste. A quiet day with you, now, would have been much more agreeable to me than all the gay times we have had at Annesdale."

"I should have been glad to see you, if you had come," said Mrs. Gordon; "but pray, Elinor, don't trouble yourself to make excuses for not having done so. I understood your position quite well. It is hard for any one in the full tide of social life to be able to see much of another person who is entirely apart from that life."

"My only consolation," said Mrs. Annesley, "has been that Morton sees so much of you. Riding continually about the country, he is able to come here more often than I possibly could; and I have been so glad of it. I did not feel as if I were completely neglecting you, while he was my representative."

"There was no cause for you to feel so," said Mrs. Gordon, a little coldly.

She was growing weary of these prolonged excuses, and did not see the point of them. Mrs. Annesley saw it, however, and timed her advance to it with careful exactitude.

"In fact, Morton often unconsciously shames me," she said. "He does not let any thing stand in the way of his visits to you. I don't know when I have felt as much ashamed of myself and my own neglect, as I did this morning. I saw him on the piazza with Irene Vernon—have you ever heard him speak of Irene Vernon? Ah, she is such a charming girl, and so lovely!—Well, he had been there for some time, when suddenly I missed him. I went to see what had become of him, and I found Miss Vernon alone. Morton, she said, had received a note from you, and left instantly to obey your summons—he even broke an engagement to ride with her, which he had made for this afternoon. My dear Pauline, when I heard this, I felt absolutely rebuked. Although my house is full of company, I at once ordered my carriage. I was determined not to let the hateful thing which we call society keep me any longer from coming to see you. I thought I would follow Morton, and meet the dear boy here, and that, after we had both enjoyed a visit to you, we could go home together. But your maid tells me that he has been here, and is already gone."

"Yes, he has gone," said Mrs. Gordon.

She saw the object of Mrs. Annesley's visit clearly enough now—saw it so clearly that all this careful fencing amused her not a little. She could have closed with her, and brought matters to an issue, very speedily, if she had chosen to do so; but she contented herself with this non-committal reply, and left her visitor to show her hand by force of necessity.

"It is strange I did not meet him," said Mrs. Annesley, in the same words she had already used in speaking to Babette. "He could not surely have returned to Annesdale?"

An accent of interrogation made this a direct question, and, as such, Mrs. Gordon answered it.

"He went to Tallahoma, I believe."

"Indeed!"

A pause after this. Within the bounds of civility, how could Mrs. Annesley ask the question which was next trembling on her tongue; and yet, how was it possible for her to forbear asking it? Who of us can account for certain instincts which at various times of our lives influence our actions in greater or less degree? Such an instinct had caused her to follow Morton from Annesdale, and such an instinct—now that she was on the threshold of the matter which had brought him to Mrs. Gordon—made her resolute to press forward, and in the face of civility (or of any thing else) learn what it was. After a short hesitation, she asked the question:

"Pardon me, my dear Pauline, if I appear curious, but was it on your business that he went to Tallahoma?"

"Certainly not," answered Mrs. Gordon. "I have no business in Tallahoma."

"Then you do not know why he went?"

"Yes, I chance to know why he went."

"And I am not to know, I suppose?" said Mrs. Annesley, flushing.

Her cousin looked at her gravely and silently for a minute, before she replied.

"I might answer that it is Morton's affair—not mine, Elinor," she said. "But since it is in part mine, and since I have a question concerning it to ask you, I shall not violate Morton's confidence in telling you. He has gone to see Miss Tresham."

Involuntarily, Mrs. Annesley started to her feet, and made a step toward the door.

"I knew it!" she cried, passionately, "I knew it! Something warned me that he had gone to see that—" Here she stopped suddenly, and sat down again. "I am a fool," she said, bitterly. "What could I do, if I followed him? He has gone his own way, without any regard to my wishes. How could I prevent him, if I tried, from doing so?"

Her cousin came over to her, and, strangely

enough, sat down by her, laying one hand on her arm.

"I will tell you what you can do—if you care to hear," she said.

Mrs. Annesley drew back. The instinct of distrust between these two women was so strong that circumstances could hardly be imagined in which it would not have betrayed itself.

"I do not understand," she said. "I thought you liked this—this girl!"

"You are right," said Mrs. Gordon, quietly. "I did like her. But that was when I knew very little about her. Since I have learned more, she is, so far as herself is concerned, an object of indifference to me. So far as Morton is concerned, however, she is an object of distrust, and, as such, to be dealt with—as summarily as possible. Elinor, do you wish Morton to marry her?"

"Can you ask me such a question?"

"Well, I have tested his infatuation thoroughly, this morning; and it has been proof against the strongest plea that I could urge. Yet I forced him to concede that he would give her up, if it could be proved that she was unworthy of him. If you wish to prevent his marrying her, your only hope is to prove this."

"I know it," said Mrs. Annesley, "but I have tried—" She paused suddenly here, caught her breath, and was silent.

"You have tried to prove it," said Mrs. Gordon, quietly. "Well, I know that. What I don't know, and what I would like to hear is, how you succeeded."

"I did not succeed at all," answered Mrs. Annesley, coldly. "What do you mean when you say that you know of my effort? You cannot possibly know—any thing."

"I fancy I know every thing, or almost every thing," replied the other, with the same composure as before. "Pray tell me, Elinor, did you ever hear of a Mr. Henry St. John?"

The shock of startled surprise caused by the question was unmistakable. But Mrs. Annesley never surrendered without a struggle.

"I do not understand you," she said.

"Don't you?" said Mrs. Gordon, smiling slightly. "Perhaps I can assist your memory by asking another question, then. Do you remember an anonymous letter which, by way of jest, you once wrote to Edgar Annesley?"

"I—think I do."

"I am sure you must, for the events which followed it were too marked to be readily forgotten Well, you may remember, also, that I read that letter, and admired the ease with which you wrote a hand entirely unlike your own. It is twenty-four years since I saw that writing, but the consequences arising from the letter stamped the recollection of it on my memory; and when a letter—when *two* letters—were shown to me this morning, I recognized the hand at once. *Now* will you tell me whether you ever heard of Mr. St. John?"

Mrs. Annesley saw that all attempt at further concealment was useless. However much or however little Mrs. Gordon knew, it was at least certain that she knew too much to make denial safe. In an instant she remembered the man who had met Miss Tresham in the grounds of Annesdale, and what had been before merely a suspicion resolved itself at once into a certainty.

"I have heard of him," she said—and then she added, "He is here!"

"Yes," answered Mrs. Gordon, "he is here. I have no right to blame you for the means you took to obtain information concerning Miss Tresham; but it may surprise you to hear that by those means you have brought upon me the curse of my life—the worst enemy I have ever had, or can ever expect to have!"

"Good Heavens!" cried Mrs. Annesley, in amazement. "How could I imagine—whom do you mean?"

The answer came in four bitter words:

"I mean my husband."

"Your husband!"

"I see that Morton has not told you my story."

"Not one word," cried Mrs. Annesley, eagerly, forgetting for the moment every thing else, and with the extreme of curiosity painted on her face, and quivering in her voice. "My dear Pauline," she went on, "you can surely trust me—you can surely confide in me!"

"It is a matter of necessity to tell you something of my life, Elinor," said her cousin, coldly. "Otherwise, I have learned that it is wise to 'confide' in nobody. You know that I was married. What I endured in my married life it is not worth while to tell you. I *did* endure it as long as endurance was possible. When it became impossible, I fled from my tyrant and came here, hoping to find rest and shelter under my father's roof. How long I might have remained undiscovered I do not know. Not long, I suspect. But, however that may be, it was your act which brought discovery upon me. The advertisement, which you inserted in the London *Times* before I came here, has borne bitter fruit. I have been tracked to my place of refuge, and my child has been taken from me—perhaps forever!"

"Taken from you! By whom?"

"By my own will. I have sent him away, that his father may not be able to find or claim him."

"But I do not understand," said Mrs. Annesley, in a state of perplexity which, all things considered, was very natural. "Is it this Mr. St. John who is your husband?"

"St. John! Are you mad? Have you ever seen him?"

"Never."

"He is a hanger-on of my husband's—his secretary, he was called—a sort of instrument for unprincipled purposes. Of character or position he has not even the shadow. Where he comes from, who he is, or what he is, it is impossible to say. I only know him in the position of which I have spoken. I am sure he has never had a better one."

Mrs. Annesley looked horror-stricken.

"And it was *this* man who wrote to me as the friend or relation of Miss Tresham!—it is *this* man who is here now to see her!"

"It is this man."

"And you—you let Morton go without telling him?"

"I told him much more than I have told you, and it had no effect upon him. Stop, Elinor"—as Mrs. Annesley, in uncontrollable agitation, rose to her feet—"you can say nothing to Morton that I have not already said. We have no proof of any thing beyond mere acquaintance between Miss Tresham and St. John. Think a moment. Did his reply to your letter contain nothing more?"

"I don't need to think," answered Mrs. Annesley, impatiently. "It contained not one word. Do you suppose I should have permitted matters to go on as long as they have in this way, if I had been able to produce a word of proof against her? My God! to think how helpless I am!" said she, striking her hand heavily on the end of the sofa near which she sat. "To think that this artful creature may make Morton marry her any day, and then—discovery would come too late."

"Have more faith in Morton," said her companion, gravely. "Believe, as I believe, that he will not take any extreme step, without giving you fair warning. In the mean time, you must endeavor to find out something about Miss Tresham."

"But how?"

"Do I need to tell you how? Is not St. John here, and have I not described his character? You need feel no delicacy about approaching him."

"But this is more difficult than you think," said Mrs. Annesley, hesitatingly. "Morton would never forgive me if he knew of such a thing, and how am I to see the man without his knowing it?"

"I have simply pointed out the way," said Mrs. Gordon. "The means I leave to yourself."

"But you—you know this St. John. Could not you—"

"No," answered Mrs. Gordon, with forbidding coldness. "Nothing would induce me to see or hold any communication with him."

"Not even for Morton's sake?"

"Not even for Morton's sake."

There was no appeal possible from that decided tone. Mrs. Annesley saw that, whether for success or failure, she must act for herself. After a minute's consideration, she said:

"Can you tell me where I shall find Mr. St. John?"

"It is probable that Babette can," said Mrs. Gordon, ringing the bell.

Babette appeared, and proved at once the accuracy of her mistress's judgment. She was able to gratify Mrs. Annesley with every possible particular concerning Mr. St. John; and, after that lady had heard all that could be of service to her, she dismissed her informant, and turned to Mrs. Gordon.

"I don't see my way at all clearly, Pauline," she said. "But I hope you will remember that I am acting according to your advice."

"According to my suggestion," amended Mrs. Gordon. "I never give advice, Elinor."

"If Morton discovers it, he will never forgive me."

"If you are so much afraid of Morton, you had better let him go his own way without interference."

In reply to this, Mrs. Annesley rose from her seat.

"One word, Pauline," she said, as her cousin rose also. "Have you told Morton about those letters?"

"No; why should I?"

"You will not do so?"

"I have not the least intention of doing so."

"Thank you," said Mrs. Annesley, impulsively. Then she added, with more of her usual manner: "My dear Pauline, no words can say how sorry I am that *my* act should have brought so much annoyance upon you. Can you possibly forgive me for it?"

"There is nothing to forgive," answered Mrs. Gordon. "When you wrote that advertisement—last summer, was it not?—you could not possibly have thought or known of me. Are you going?"

"I must. It is getting late, and I fear I shall not be back at Annesdale in time for dinner. I will come to see you soon again. Would you advise—that is, would you suggest, that I should offer money to this St. John?"

"I can only say there is no reason why you should hesitate to do so."

Mrs. Annesley repeated her thanks, and took leave. Once in the carriage, she looked at her watch and made a calculation of time, with reference to dinner. Having made it, she pulled the check-string and said: "Tallahoma — Mrs. Marks's."

Poor Mrs. Marks had not recovered from the combined effects of Morton's visit, and her husband's unusual assertion of himself, when this new astonishment was prepared for her. Having seen the table finally cleared off, and having rid herself of the children by dispatching them in a body to the "old field," of which mention has before been made, she sat down with a very heavy heart, to darn various small stockings full of various large holes. As she darned, she sighed; and, in fact, sighs were more frequent than stitches with her. The kind soul was lamenting her husband's resolution, and grieving much over the loss of her favorite, "Miss Katharine." She even shed a few tears, and wiped them away with the leg of Jack's sock. Impatient thoughts on the perversity of human circumstances came to her, as they had come to Katharine at Annesdale, as they come to all of us when people and events prove "contrary." Oh, why cannot things go right? Why cannot people act as they ought to? Why cannot circumstances cease to fret, or goad, or restrain us? What is the reason that every thing has its dash of bitterness, and that life seems to vibrate, like the pendulum of a clock, continually, between the painful and the disagreeable? This is the strain of thought that is going up to heaven on the wings of every minute, like the broken cry of an imprisoned spirit, panting, ah! how vainly, to be free. What is the good of it all? Ah! granted—what, indeed, is the good of it all? But then, friends, dwellers upon the earth, co-heirs of the curse laid on Adam, the question is, not what is the good of it, but how are we to help it? There is but one way known to men—the way of child-like faith—and few of us are great enough, or strong enough, to follow that.

Mrs. Marks was still darning, still heaving sighs, and still dropping a tear or two occasionally, when she was startled by the sound of a knock at the door. The dining-room was in the back part of the house, and so it chanced that she had neither seen nor heard the arrival of the Annesley carriage; so it chanced, also, that, with her work in her hand, she went out to answer the knock, and found herself face to face with no less a person than Mrs. Annesley.

Her consternation was almost as great as her surprise. The fear of something additionally disagreeable—a fear vaguely inspired by Mrs. Annesley's face—instantly seized her. Somehow or other, the greeting was accomplished, and Mrs. Annesley was ushered into the dining-room. When she had been installed in the most comfortable chair, and Mrs. Marks was sitting opposite, with her darning mechanically retained in her hand, a few remarks were exchanged, and then the visitor opened the serious business of the occasion.

"No doubt, you are surprised to see me, Mrs. Marks," she said, graciously. "In fact, I ought to apologize for such a startling visit. But, being in Tallahoma, I thought I would stop for a few minutes; and I also thought that I might find Morton here. I am anxious to see him on a matter of business before he returns to Annesdale."

"I am very sorry that you have come a little too late," said Mrs. Marks, with the utmost sincerity. "Mr. Annesley was here, but he left a short while ago; and I think he said he was going back to Annesdale."

"He *was* here, and left only a short while ago! Oh, how provoking!" said Mrs. Annesley. "What an instance of my bad luck! But pray, Mrs. Marks, what does a 'short while' mean? Do you think, for instance, that I could overtake him before he gets home?"

"Oh, no. I am sure you couldn't," said Mrs. Marks, with decision. "It's been a good hour since he left, and he must have reached Annesdale by this time—or, indeed, before this. He didn't stay long," she went on, telling of her own accord the very thing Mrs. Annesley was anxious to hear. "He called to see Miss Tresham, and,

Miss Tresham not being at home, he left very soon."

"I thought Miss Tresham was at home," said Mrs. Annesley, a little stiffly. "She left Annesdale this morning."

"She came here this morning," said Mrs. Marks, in an aggrieved tone, "but she is gone now."

"Gone!" Mrs. Annesley simply opened her eyes. It could not be possible that exposure had come so soon, and come of itself? "Gone! Excuse me, but you surprise me very much. I thought she came back to recommence teaching."

"She went to Saxford to-day," answered Mrs. Marks, unconsciously lifting the stocking, which she still held, to her eyes, from which one or two tears were drawn forth by that oft-repeated statement. She stood extremely in awe of the elegant mistress of Annesdale, but the latter was a woman, after all, and she had dropped in to pay a sociable visit, and Mrs. Marks's heart was sorely in need of a *confidante*, and so she began to open the floodgates of her feelings, and to express in words what she had heretofore only expressed in sighs.

"She went to Saxford," she repeated—very much as she might have said, "She went to be buried!"—"It is hard on me, Mrs. Annesley—it is certainly hard on me! I never meddled with Miss Tresham's affairs in my life—I never said a word, either to her or to anybody else, about them—and yet you'd hardly believe all the trouble and worry that's been in this house this day—all on account of Miss Tresham's affairs, and Miss Tresham's visitors, and because Miss Tresham has taken it into her head to go to Saxford!"

"But why has she gone?" asked Mrs. Annesley, with a very uncivil disregard of Mrs. Marks's personal grievances.

"Everybody asks me that," answered Mrs. Marks, "and Miss Tresham told me no more about why she was going than she told my little Nelly playing out in the yard. I am sure it seemed natural enough to me that she should go—she often does go to see her priest—but everybody seems surprised about it, and Mr. Marks is so provoked that he says if she don't come back on Monday, and if she won't explain every thing about Mr. St. John, she"— second application of the stocking as a pocket-handkerchief—"will have to leave us."

This good news was so unexpected, and so startling, that for a minute Mrs. Annesley scarcely realized it. Then a glow of satisfied pleasure began to steal over her, and she saw how well Fate was fighting the battle of which she had been almost ready to despair.

"Really, you astonish me!" she said. "I had no idea of any thing like this. Miss Tresham only left my house this morning, and now to have gone away so unexpectedly—and, you say, without any explanation?"

"Without even so much as a word of explanation," answered Mrs. Marks, who was now fully launched into her theme. "Perhaps I ought to have said something to *her*, Mrs. Annesley; but my head was quite upset—and then she was in such a hurry to get to the hotel before the stage left that she didn't give me time hardly to breathe. I'm sure I didn't pay any attention to what Mrs. Gordon said about her—I mean"—hastily correcting herself with a timely recollection that Mrs. Gordon was Mrs. Annesley's cousin—"that I felt confident there was some mistake—but it seems to me all the same, that Miss Katharine might have told me something before she left, so that I could have explained it to Richard. But she never said a word."

"Nothing about Mr. St. John?"

"Not a syllable."

"How extremely singular!" said Mrs. Annesley, very slowly and very gravely—so gravely that Mrs. Marks began to feel as if she had much underrated the importance of Miss Tresham's reticence, and Miss Tresham's departure. It was astonishing how infinitely more Mrs. Annesley's opinion on the subject weighed with her, than that of her husband had done!

"It *was* strange," she said, "though I didn't think of it at the time. Miss Katharine is so nice, Mrs. Annesley, and we are all so fond of her, that somehow it never struck me that—that, as you say, it was singular for her to give no explanation about Mr. St. John."

"Perhaps he may be related to her," said Mrs. Annesley, carelessly—she began to be aware that she had betrayed more interest than it was proper to show in Miss Tresham's affairs—"your governess herself is a very lady-like person; but people in her position often have very disreputable relations, you know."

"Mr. St. John is very much of a gentleman, indeed," said Mrs. Marks, greatly astonished. "I am sure nobody could say that there is any thing disreputable about him. But I don't think he is any relation of Miss Katharine's; that is"—a short pause—"I really don't know. I never heard her say that she had any relations."

Mrs. Annesley knew this before, but none the

less did she think it necessary to look as much shocked as if she heard the statement for the first time.

"No relations!" she exclaimed. "A girl of her age! Why, that is dreadful! Really, Mrs. Marks, you must excuse me if I say that I wonder very much at your courage in engaging such a person to enter your house and teach your children."

By way of reply, Mrs. Marks only stared. It had yet to dawn upon her comprehension that the misfortune of having no relations could possibly be made a social crime.

"It is hard on a young thing like Miss Katharine"—she began, when Mrs. Annesley interrupted her in her grandest way.

"It is not of Miss Tresham I am talking, Mrs. Marks, but of her position. Of course, it is only reasonable that when a girl of her age, and I suppose I may say of her refined appearance, talks of having no relations, she simply means one of two things—either that her relations do not acknowledge *her*, or else that they are themselves not fit to be acknowledged. In either case, as I remarked before, I think you must possess a great deal of courage to admit her to your family as you have done, and to be willing to trust her as you seem disposed to do. For my part, I confess that I should shudder to think of assuming such a responsibility; but then my conscience is very sensitive."

"She was so nice," said Mrs. Marks, deprecatingly, much impressed by this forcible view of the matter, and much aghast at being brought in guilty, by implication at least, of a callous conscience.

"So nice!" repeated Mrs. Annesley, in a tone of overpowering scorn. She forgot herself and her part, for a moment, and let the real earnestness which she felt come to the surface, as the thought rushed over her that all the trouble now weighing upon her, all the fear that had made her life wretched for months past, resulted from the act of this woman—this woman so far out of her life, so apart from all her associations. She had scarcely done more than bow to Mrs. Marks when they chanced to meet, once a year or so, on the village street, and yet the fateful sisters had thrown their shuttle, and across the warp and woof of her own life had woven the threads of this other homely existence. Common as such things are, when they come home to us as they came home to her, it is hard not to feel startled by them—hard to realize that they form the daily history of that which we call circumstance! Two strangers met by chance in the parlor of that Charleston hotel; the girl's face brightened into a winning smile, and the elder woman's heart was touched; a few words were said, and lo! the whole current of life was changed, not only for them, but for others then scattered in widely-different corners of the civilized world, then going each his different way, laughing, talking, smiling, weeping, perhaps, and knowing not what had been done—knowing not that, on a single breath, as it were, every aim and purpose of existence had been staked and changed—for better or worse, who could tell? Surely only He of whom it is well to think in the midst of such reflections as these—He who draws us each into our appointed path, and does not leave us to be the blind victims of a merciless Chance.

"I beg your pardon," said Mrs. Annesley, recovering herself with a faint, forced laugh. "I suppose, of course, you think Miss Tresham nice, but I was really unable to discover her attractions. What a beautiful view this room has! Do you cultivate your garden much?"

She rose and walked to the window. Well disciplined as she was, and thoroughly accustomed to self-control, she could not have sat still a moment longer and face the woman who had brought all this anxiety and possible grief upon her. An outbreak of some sort must have come, and she wisely prevented it by walking away and gazing absently into the garden, while Mrs. Marks willingly forsook the subject of Miss Tresham for that of her celery and winter lettuce.

As she talked, Mrs. Annesley's fertile brain ran over expedient after expedient for seeing St. John, and dismissed each as impracticable. How was she to do it?—*how* was she to do it?

This was the accompaniment in her brain to Mrs. Marks's conversation. Yet she was as far as ever from the solution of her difficulty, and she almost began to despair of its accomplishment, when she accidentally caught sight of a man's head above a rose-bush in the garden. In a second, she felt sure that, by some strange coincidence, her opportunity was here, ready to her hand—that St. John stood before her.

She did not stop to consider why she knew that it was he, she did not think for a moment how he came there. She only felt, by a strange, intuitive thrill, that her desire was gratified more speedily and more completely than she could possibly have hoped for it to be, and that, come what would, she must seize the fortunate opportunity.

Yet how could she escape? how get rid of Mrs. Marks? That became as great a difficulty now as the means of meeting St. John had been before. As she asked herself the question, however, she saw that there was no need of immediate haste. Plainly, St. John had entered the garden to bide his time, and plainly he meant to wait till that time came. His head had now disappeared from above the rose-bush, but Mrs. Annesley marked the place where she had seen it, and a thin, pale wreath of smoke, which now and then floated up, sufficiently indicated his present position, and sufficiently proved how he was whiling away the period of waiting.

"What is he waiting for?" Mrs. Annesley began to consider. "Is it Miss Tresham, or is it to come in and see Mrs. Marks?—Ah!"—as a sudden recollection flashed over her—"it is for *me* to leave. He sees the carriage before the gate, of course, and he has decided to remain in the garden and smoke a cigar until the coast is clear. There could not possibly be a better opportunity for seeing him, if only I could get rid of this horrid woman! But how on earth am I to do that?"

How, indeed! For, while the blue smoke floated pensively over the rose-bushes, and while Mrs. Annesley could scarcely keep her impatient hand from the latch of the door near which she stood, Mrs. Marks steadily held her ground, and steadily poured forth her flow of language with a profound unconsciousness that seemed as if it could be shaken by nothing less than a moral earthquake.

CHAPTER XXVIII.

ON GUARD.

Suddenly the ill-matched companions were startled by a terrible uproar in the back yard—the deep, angry growl of a dog was followed by the scampering rush of two animals in a short, mad chase, and then the cries of inarticulate distress, which dumb beasts can occasionally utter in their own behalf, fell painfully on the ear. Mingled with these came a Babel of sound—men shouting, women running, cries, commands, and undistinguishable confusion—in the midst of which a panting little negro rushed to the dining-room door.

"Mistiss, Rollo's caught the calf, and Uncle Jake says as how he's goin' to tar it to pieces!"

"Good Gracious!" cried Mrs. Marks, in consternation. "What did he let the dog catch it for! What will your master say! Tell him to beat him—do any thing to make him let go! I always told Mr. Marks he better not bring that bull-dog here," she added, as the child darted away. "I knew he was sure to do mischief—Goodness! what awful sounds!—Mrs. Annesley, if you'll excuse me, I'll—"

The sentence was not finished, and Mrs. Annesley had no opportunity to reply. The uproar grew worse, and Mrs. Marks followed the example of the rest of the household—she flew to the scene of action.

If the victim of Rollo's unreasoning fury had been a child instead of a calf, it is to be feared that Mrs. Annesley would equally have regarded the episode in the light of a fortunate and providential relief. The instant that the last flutter of Mrs. Marks's dress had vanished down the passage, she opened the door that led out upon the side-piazza, crossed it, and the next moment was walking rapidly down the garden-path.

She was so lightly and delicately shod that her step made very little sound on the smooth gravel, and St. John, who was comfortably smoking his cigar in a sheltered nook—waiting, as Mrs. Annesley had shrewdly suspected, for the departure of the carriage—was completely taken by surprise when, without any warning, this elegant figure stood before him.

Instinctively he took the cigar from his lips, and rose to his feet. This was not Mrs. Marks, but none the less was it somebody much more at home in the garden than he had any right to be. Therefore, the first words that formed on his lips were words of apology for his presence there.

"Excuse me," he said. "I fear I am a trespasser; but I am waiting to see Mrs. Marks."

Mrs. Annesley bowed graciously, and, instead of retreating, swept a step nearer.

"Mrs. Marks is occupied just now," she said, "and I came out to look at the garden. Don't disturb yourself, I beg. I shall not interrupt you. Mr. Marks told me something about a new perennial," added she, glancing round. "Don't let me trouble you, but pray do you chance to know where it is?"

St. John smiled, and replied in the negative.

"I am a stranger," he said, "and this is the first time I have ever ventured to invade Mrs. Marks's garden. I am sorry that I cannot tell you any thing about the perennial."

"You have no idea where it is?"

"I have not the least idea where it is."

Mrs. Annesley gave a little sigh of resignation.

"Such a pity!" she said, and, as she said it, she ran her eye with apparent carelessness, but with really keen attention, over St. John's person.

The result of her observation was discouraging. Despite all that Mrs. Gordon had told her, and despite her own distrust of the man, she could not believe that it would be expedient or even possible to approach him with any overtures of bribery. Adventurer though he was—sharper though he might be—he at least bore all the outward semblance of a gentleman; and, as he stood before her—perfectly self-possessed, notwithstanding the equivocal position which he occupied, and lightly holding his cigar between two fingers as he returned her scrutiny—she felt as much at a loss how to address him as she had before felt at a loss how to reach him. It was hardly wonderful. This man was so different—in every particular so essentially different—from the man her fancy had created, that the discrepancy in itself startled her.

As she hesitated, St. John, on his side, had time for observation and consideration. The perennial excuse had not deceived him. He had seen at a glance that this fine lady—whoever or whatever she might be—had come into the garden to meet himself. At first he had supposed that her motive might have been one of mere curiosity; but, as she still kept her place in front of him, as he felt her keen black eyes reading his face, and, as he saw the doubt unconsciously stamped upon her own face, an instinct of her real purpose came over him.

"There is something she wants to get out of me," he thought. "Well, let her try. It will be strange if in the end I don't succeed in getting considerably more out of *her* than she thinks of or bargains for!"

"Perhaps there is something else I can do for you," he said, as she remained silent for some time.

Mrs. Annesley started a little, and recovered herself.

"There is nothing, thank you," she said. "I won't disturb you any longer. Good-day."

She bowed slightly, and walked away—three steps. Then she paused, and, turning back, spoke again.

"Perhaps there is something I can do for you," she said. "Am I not right in supposing that it has been my presence which has kept you from seeing Mrs. Marks? Shall I be obliging, and take my departure?"

"I could not presume to ask such a thing," answered he, bowing gravely.

"It would not be very much of a presumption," answered Mrs. Annesley, smiling graciously. "A friend of Mrs. Marks—you *are* a friend of Mrs. Marks, I suppose?"

"I scarcely think it probable that Mrs. Marks would allow me to claim that honor."

Mrs. Annesley arched her eyebrows and looked around the garden. Plainly she meant to say, "*Not* a friend of Mrs. Marks, and yet here!"

The coolness of the glance amused St. John, and he answered it more on account of this amusement than because there was any absolute necessity for doing so.

"Under these circumstances, you are surprised to see me here?" he said. "But I think that, when I explain the reason of my presence to Mrs. Marks, she will not regard my intrusion as unpardonable."

"I am sure Mrs. Marks is always glad to receive Miss Tresham's friends," said Mrs. Annesley, using the very words which Mrs. Marks herself had used that morning—the words which had encouraged St. John to return and endeavor to learn from her something more than he had been able to glean from her husband. The coincidence struck him, and, together with the unsuspected sound of Katharine's name, made him look sharply at the speaker.

"Excuse me," he said. "I do not understand."

But, as it happened, Mrs. Annesley had grown tired of this aimless fencing; and, besides, she had not time for it. At any moment Mrs. Marks might come in search of her, and the opportunity she had been so anxious to secure would thus be hopelessly lost. Making a rapid calculation for and against success, she decided to close at once with her slippery opponent.

"Excuse *me*," she said, with a smile. "I fancied that I was speaking to Mr. St. John."

The smile told St. John infinitely more than the words. There was a shade of malicious meaning in it, which, under the circumstances, was far from wise, but which Mrs. Annesley would have found it hard to control. It was so pleasant to turn the tables on him in this style—so pleasant to show him, in three words, how well she knew every thing about him! But still, it was a blunder. It put St. John on his guard, and it made him set his teeth and think: "Confound the woman! What deviltry has she got in her head?" It galled him, too; but he had a very good armory of his own at command, and from it he immediately selected his favorite weapon of covert mockery.

"I am deeply flattered," he said, with a bow. 'I had no idea that my name had been fortunate enough to attain any degree of notoriety. I do not think that I have the pleasure of an acquaintance with yourself, madam."

"You have probably never heard of me," said Mrs. Annesley, quietly. "I am a person of no consequence whatever—out of my own family. It has merely chanced that I have heard of you," she went on. "Mrs. Marks is very much attached to Miss Tresham, and, in speaking of her, she mentioned your name to me. I also am a friend of Miss Tresham's," said the mistress of Annesdale, with a virtuous expression of face, "and as such, I am glad to meet you—glad to be able to say a few words to you, if you will allow me to do so."

"I am at your service."

"Let us sit down, then. Since you are kind enough not to consider me impertinent, I should like to be very frank with you. I am generally frank with everybody. Experience has shown me that it is so much the best way."

They sat down. Just behind the short bench from which St. John had risen, was a wall of running ivy; on each side rose tall shrubs, which, although bare, still made a seclusion of the little nook. Regarded from a short distance, the two figures, who had the nook to themselves, might easily have passed for a pair of lovers. Considered as they actually were, they much more resembled two adroit chess-players, who sat down equally matched to a game in which skill and care could alone determine the result. Mrs. Annesley made the first move—St. John contenting himself with keen watchfulness and attention.

Said the lady: "I must begin what I have to say, by explaining why I say it. I know Miss Tresham quite well, and"—a gulp—"like her very much. You can imagine my surprise, therefore, when I heard from Mrs. Marks that she has left her late home in a very sudden and mysterious manner, and that it is more than doubtful whether she will be received again when she returns."

St. John started. This was certainly news to him. Mrs. Annesley noted the start, and went on:

"I think it right to tell *you*, Mr. St. John, that the ground on which Miss Tresham will be dismissed from Mrs. Marks's house when she returns, is that of her connection with yourself. Mr. Marks has finally decided that unless a satisfactory explanation of this connection is given, he cannot retain Miss Tresham as a governess. Now, as a friend of Miss Tresham's, will you allow me to ask if it does not occur to you that it is your duty to remove the cloud from Miss Tresham's name by at once making this explanation?"

"You have set me an admirable example of candor, madam," said St. John. "Do not be offended if I follow it, and, imitating your frankness, ask if it does not occur to you that it is quite impossible for you to judge of the affairs of people who are strangers to you?"

"I thought I had explained that Miss Tresham is *not* a stranger to me."

"Evidently she is a stranger so far as regards her confidence, or else you would not need to make this appeal to me."

"You do not intend to heed the appeal, then?"

"Imitating your frankness again, I must decline to answer that question."

"Because I am not personally concerned in the matter?" asked Mrs. Annesley, resolutely resolved to keep her temper under any provocation.

"Yes—because I am unable to perceive that you have any personal interest in the matter."

"Suppose that I assume—that, if necessary, I am willing to prove to you—that I *have* an interest in the matter, that I have a personal reason for wishing to clear up the mystery around Miss Tresham, will you still refuse to give me the explanation?"

"I regret to say that I am compelled to do so."

"Do you not take Miss Tresham herself into consideration—her character? Do you not appreciate how badly this reticence looks—for her?"

St. John only smiled. Evidently, if it had been courteous to do so, he would have shrugged his shoulders, and said, "What is that to me?" As it was, his face said it for him, and Mrs. Annesley read his face. That instant she shifted her ground.

"I am anxious to obtain certain items of information about Miss Tresham," she said; "items which can harm neither her nor any one else. Do you know any one who, for a liberal reward, would show me how to obtain these?"

She looked steadily at St. John, and St. John

returned her gaze without the quiver of an eyelash.

"I do not know any one whom you could employ for such a purpose," he answered.

"No one at all?"

"No one at all."

Mrs. Annesley rose from her seat, and drew her shawl gracefully around her.

"It is growing chilly," she said, "I must go in. I regret to have disturbed you, Mr. St. John. Pray, don't let me disturb you further—pray, don't get up. I suppose it is quite useless to look for that perennial. Good-day."

A bow on both sides, and they separated. The worsted player retired with all the dignity she could summon to her aid; but, as she swept slowly down the garden-walk, she struck one gloved hand angrily against the other.

"I went to work wrong," she thought. "Some way or other, I went to work wrong! The consequence is, that this wretch has completely baffled me, and that I am not an inch nearer to my end than I was before."

As for St. John, the first thing he did, when he was alone, was to relight his cigar, and the second was to indulge in a laugh of properly-subdued tone.

"Oh, these women! these women!" he said to himself. "How is it that the devil teaches them so much cunning, and yet lets them overreach themselves so completely? Well"—with a long puff—"this has certainly been something that I did not bargain for—a little dash of intrigue that I did not expect in coming to look up my respectable friend who asks me to tea. I fancy Mrs. Gordon is not the only person *now* who has discovered the identity of R. G. After this, I can put my hand on the writer of the advertisement and the letters whenever I choose. I have two things yet to find out, however—first, her name; and, secondly, her motive."

A thought struck him. He rose from his seat, walked to the garden-gate, let himself out, and sauntered down the road to where Mrs. Annesley's carriage stood, with Mrs. Annesley's coachman and footman in attendance. Stopping to admire the horses, he easily fell into conversation with the servants, and in five minutes had learned every thing that he wished to know. No human being was ever so fond of boasting as the family-negro of the old *régime*, and Mrs. Annesley's servants were no exception to the general rule. No sooner was it evident that St. John was a stranger, than their tongues were loosed on the glories of Annesdale and of the Annesley family. Mistiss and mistiss's various splendors, Mass Morton, and Mass Morton's horses and dogs, were the favorite topics—the last especially; and St. John, who never forgot any thing, had no difficulty in identifying this much vaunted "Mass Morton" with the Mr. Annesley whom he had met in the grounds of Annesdale. Every thing was so clear to him that he could have laughed to himself as he stood on the sidewalk smoking his cigar, and listening lazily, as John and Peyton by turns descanted on the absorbing subject. It was quite a shock to Mrs. Annesley when she came out and found him there.

"Mr. St. John!" she said, haughtily, and drew back as he came forward with the manifest intention of assisting her into the carriage.

"I have been admiring your horses, Mrs. Annesley," said St. John, smiling. "They do credit to your taste. Will you allow me?"

On second thoughts, she allowed him to put her into the carriage; and, when she was seated, looked up and spoke.

"If you will take my advice, you will consider what I said to you a short time ago. It might be worth your while. I need not tell you where you will find me if you desire to communicate with me."

He bowed—making no other answer to the covert sneer in her last words—and, as he stepped from the door, the carriage drove off.

When it was out of sight, he turned, and, opening the gate, walked up to the house. Mrs. Marks had accompanied Mrs. Annesley to the front piazza, and was still standing there when he approached. In the first sound of her voice, in the first word which she spoke, he saw that a change had come over her—that she had been placed on guard against him. She answered his questions courteously; but there was none of the hearty cordiality of the morning in her manner, and she did not ask him to enter the house. After finding that her ignorance about Katharine was quite as complete as it had been represented, he had no alternative but to take his leave. Before doing so, however, he received a piece of information which startled him a little. He thought that it might be as well to verify on indisputable evidence the facts which the servants had given him, and so he said, carelessly:

"Will you allow me to inquire if the Mrs. Annesley who has just left is related to the young gentleman of the same name whom I saw here a few hours ago?"

"She is his mother," answered Mrs. Marks—

adding, involuntarily, "and the cousin of Mrs. Gordon."

"Indeed!" said St. John, starting quickly.

After this, he asked no more questions, but made his apologies, and took his leave almost immediately. As he walked down the street, the few people who met him and looked curiously at him, saw that he was deeply absorbed in thought. In fact, he was revolving what he had just heard, and considering what it meant.

"Mrs. Gordon's cousin," he repeated to himself. "What the deuce is the meaning of it all! Shall I never get to the end of all the strings and counter-strings which seem to be pulling these people to and fro?"

CHAPTER XXIX.

THE SICK LADY.

Two weeks after Miss Tresham had taken her departure from Tallahoma, a carriage, containing a solitary traveller, drove into the town of Hartsburg—a place of considerable importance, situated some thirty miles southwest of Saxford.

"The Planters' Hotel, Cyrus," said the traveller, as the carriage turned into the Main Street; "or, no—I was cheated shamefully there as we went on—the Eagle Hotel, I believe."

"Whar that be, Mass John?"

"Two squares below the other house, on the corner of the street."

Two squares below the other house the carriage proceeded, and stopped before a large, rambling frame building, two stories high, with a double piazza running the whole length of the front. An uninviting hostelry, people would think nowadays, with ideas of brick and stucco in their minds; but in that day the standard of comfort for the unfortunate travelling public was by no means a high one, and, as houses of entertainment went, the Eagle Hotel was by no means to be despised. A "tavern" look about it, unmistakably; a "tavern" odor, very certainly; but still—well, there were worse places (probably the traveller had spent the night before at one of them), and in that thought was comfort.

When the carriage stopped, a man came forward from the group of smokers and loungers congregated, according to invariable custom, on the front piazza, and reached the door just as it was opened and the traveller stepped out.

"Well, Mr. Crump, how are you?" said the latter, with a smile.

"Why, Mr. Warwick! how do you do, sir?" exclaimed Mr. Crump, extending his hand. "I had no idea it was you! You don't usually travel in this sort of conveyance. Walk in, sir—walk in. Come down to court, I suppose?"

"No; I have been below, and am on my way back to Tallahoma. Is it court-week?"

"To be sure, sir, and the house full of lawyers. I never saw a larger crowd."

"Perhaps you can't accommodate me, then?"

"Never fear about that, sir. The old woman will find you a room, if she has to turn the judge himself out.—Drive the carriage round to the stables, boy, and see the hostler about a place for your horses.—Now, Mr. Warwick—"

He turned, but Mr. Warwick was already surrounded by half a dozen men—gentlemen of the legal fraternity—who were shaking hands, and cordially welcoming him. They were all glad to see him; all seemed astonished when they heard that he had not "come to court;" and all inquired if it was possible he had no cases on the docket. While he was answering their questions, and endeavoring to make them understand that it was merely by accident he chanced to be in Hartsburg, Mr. Crump seized his portmanteau, and, carrying it into the house, called vociferously for "the old woman." This personage not being forthcoming, half a dozen servants appeared from as many different quarters, and to one of them Mr. Crump addressed himself.

"Sam, take this valise up-stairs, and ask your mistress where it's to go. Tell her it's Mr. Warwick's, from Tallahoma.—Where the dickens is she? Don't any of you know?"

"She's in the sick lady's room, sir," said a tall negro-woman, who came down-stairs as he spoke. "She says as how she'll be here in a minute."

"Deuce take the sick lady—pshaw! I don't mean that either; but it seems to me Selina's never anywhere else these days. How is she, anyhow?—the lady, I mean."

The woman shook her head with that doleful solemnity which a negro finds real and sensible pleasure in indulging.

"*Miss S'lina* thinks she's some better, sir," she said, and, with this significant mode of expressing her own opinion, vanished.

Mr. Crump gave a low whistle, expressive, apparently, of his own view on the subject, and, turning, was about to go out of the door, when he met Mr. Warwick coming in.

"Well," said the lawyer, smiling, "how is it? Can Mrs. Crump find a corner for me? I shall only trouble her for one night."

"I don't doubt that she'll find room for you, sir; but I haven't seen her yet. She's busy with a sick boarder, who's been giving us no end of trouble."

"Indeed! But Mrs. Crump don't mind trouble, I know."

Mr. Crump muttered something in reply about "court-week," and "the house being full," from which it was to be supposed that he thought it would be better for him if his wife *did* mind trouble a little more. He evidently felt injured; but, before he had time for further expression of his sentiments, a stout, pleasant-faced woman of about fifty came down-stairs and advanced toward them. She greeted the lawyer in rather a preoccupied manner, and then, instead of saying any thing about his room, turned to her husband.

"You'll have to send for the doctor again, Tom. I thought, a little while ago, that she was better; but I don't like the way her fever's rising now, and I'm afraid she's going to be light-headed again."

"But, Selina, here's Mr. Warwick wants a room, and—"

"I'll see about Mr. Warwick presently," said Selina, looking at him with a pair of kindly yet somewhat anxious eyes. "That poor child up-stairs stays on my mind; and, do what I will, I can't get her off of it. Go along, Tom, and send for the doctor, as I told you.—Mr. Warwick, you don't mind my being a little put out, I am sure. If you'll come with me, I'll try and find you a room. Somehow I had an idea you'd be here this week, and I saved you one right alongside of the judge's. I'll go and look in to see that all's right."

She led the way up-stairs, and Mr. Warwick, as in duty bound, had nothing but thanks for the room into which she showed him—it being very comfortable, according to the ideas of comfort existing at that time. While she still lingered, touching a chair here, and arranging a curtain there, he made the ordinary inquiries concerning her health and domestic affairs; and, after these were answered, she, of her own accord, led the conversation back to her sick boarder.

"A poor young thing that don't seem to have any friends, and—though I wouldn't tell Tom so —I'll venture to say, not over-much money," she said. "She come here in the stage one night, and meant to go on next morning; but, Lord bless you! she was took down with a fever, and, though that was more'n a week ago, she hasn't lifted up her head since. I've tried to get her to tell me who her friends are, so that I can write to 'em; but she won't. She says she ain't got any, which, you know, sir, would look badly, if she wasn't such a real lady."

"She is a lady—is she?" asked Mr. Warwick, carelessly. The sick woman was to him a matter of infinitely less importance than some fresh water and some hot coffee.

"A real lady, sir, as ever I saw—no half-way trash, I can tell you. That's the pity of it, and that's what makes me so anxious to find out who she is, and where she belongs. I'm as sure she's run away from home as I can be; and, if a man is not somehow or other at the bottom of it, my name isn't Selina Crump. I only wish he'd dare to come here, and set his foot inside the Eagle Hotel!"

"What would you do to him if he did?" asked Mr. Warwick, who, despite his weariness and impatience, was amused by the tone in which the landlady's last words were uttered.

"What would I do? I'd scald him—that's what I'd do! I'd put on a kettle of water specially for him, if I only knowed when he was coming; and I'd show him how he come into a honest house, after 'ticing off a pretty girl like that, and then leaving her to die, or to get well as best she could!"

"But why are you so sure that a man's at the bottom of it?"

In reply to this, Mrs. Crump became somewhat mysterious and reticent; but it finally appeared that the lady had been delirious, and, when in that state, had talked a great deal of nonsense, especially about a somebody named "John."

"She always thinks he's after her," said the landlady, solemnly, "and she's always trying to get away from him."

"Probably he is her husband," said the lawyer, basing his remark upon an extended knowledge of human nature in the marital relation.

Mrs. Crump obstinately shook her head, and obstinately held her ground—blind to the longing glance which Mr. Warwick, with the dust of a day's journey upon him, directed to the wash-stand.

"There's something about a married woman a body can almost always tell," she said. "I'm as sure as can be that this girl *ain't* married.

P'raps she's run away to do it; but that's a different matter, and all the more I'd like to send her back to her friends." A pause; then, in an insinuating tone, "I thought you might help me to find out somethin' about her, Mr. Warwick, knowing so many people as you do. I haven't said a word to anybody else, because she's such a lady that somehow I didn't like to do it. But Tom is mighty snappish about her, and, if I could only find out who she is, it might make him hold his tongue."

"I do know a good many people," said Mr. Warwick, patiently; "but it is quite impossible for me to tell whether I know the relations or friends of this sick lady among them. Pray, what is her name?"

"She wrote it down when she came, and Tom put it on the register; but my head's dreadful for remembering such things, and I couldn't tell it to you now, if my life depended on it. I saw a book lying on the table with her name written in it, though, and I'll go and get that for you."

Without waiting for an answer, she left the room, and, with another regretful glance at the wash-stand, Mr. Warwick walked to the window, to await her return. At that moment the principal thought in his mind was a wish that he had gone to the Planters' Hotel. He began to wonder if there were any "sick ladies" *there*, to be thrust remorselessly upon the attention of travellers, and defer indefinitely those ablutions of which tired nature (when just off a journey) first and foremost stands in need. "Mrs. Crump ought to know better," he said to himself, a little indignantly; and, as he said it, the door opened, and Mrs. Crump reappeared with a small, black, much-worn book in her hand.

"When she was herself, she mostly had it on the bed by her," said the good woman; "but to-day she's been light-headed, and so I put it on the table, and in that way I got it without disturbing her. Here it is, Mr. Warwick, and the name's in it."

Mr. Warwick took the volume, and, as he did so, he could not repress a start, or account for a sudden chill instinct, that seemed to rush over him. The book was a pocket-edition of Thomas à Kempis's "Following of Christ," and at once struck him as strangely similar to one that he had often seen in Katharine Tresham's hand. It was her familiar companion, and, as such, familiar to him also. Just now he could have sworn that this was the very book—he knew the very look of the worn edges, the embossed cross in the middle of the back, and the smaller crosses at each corner. "I am a fool!" he thought, and opened it at once, at the fly-leaf. There, traced in faded ink, he read, "To Katharine Tresham, from her aunt, Mary Tresham," and a date fourteen years before!

To say that Mrs. Crump was startled by the face that turned round upon her, would be to describe her sensations very inadequately—for she was in fact astounded. She fell back a little, and grasped the bedpost in a state of alarm.

"Goodness alive, Mr. Warwick!" she cried; "what's the matter?"

"Is that the name which the lady gave you?" asked Mr. Warwick, following her, and pointing to the writing on the fly-leaf—"is that the name?"

"Why, to be sure that's the name. I—I told you it was in the book." Then gaining courage—"Is any thing wrong about her, Mr. Warwick? Oh, me! what will Tom say?"

"Wrong!" repeated Mr. Warwick, in a tone that made her start back again. Then he stopped and recollected himself. "You have acted quite properly, Mrs. Crump," he said, quietly, "and your decision in this matter shows you to be a woman of good judgment, as well as of kind heart. This is a lady—" he emphasized the word—"whom I left at my sister's house, in Tallahoma, and whom I am naturally surprised to find here. I know her well, and can vouch for her in every particular. Will you sit down and tell me how she came here, and every thing that you know about her?"

Mrs. Crump willingly obeyed; but out of her verbose narrative Mr. Warwick gathered very little more than he had heard already. On Wednesday, a week before (this was Thursday), Miss Tresham had arrived in Hartsburg, and stopped at the Eagle Hotel for the night, declaring her intention of continuing her journey (destination unknown), the next morning. As the landlady learned afterward, she had a burning fever all night, and, when morning came, was not able to leave her bed. Since then, she had steadily grown worse, and lay in alternate stupor and delirium most of the time. When questioned about medical attendance, Mrs. Crump answered, hesitatingly. The doctor had not come very often—perhaps because he thought it extremely doubtful whether he would ever be paid for coming at all—and had not spoken by any means encouragingly. "I don't think he's got much idea that she'll live," said

Mrs. Crump. "He told me I'd better try my best to find out about her friends."

"Who is the doctor—Randolph?"

"No, sir; a new doctor—Joyner is his name—who, I thought, might pay more attention, because he hasn't got any practice to speak of."

"I should like to see him when he comes, and, meanwhile, I wish you would send a messenger for Dr. Randolph. I—" He stopped a moment, as there came a knock at the door. "Who is that?"

"It's me, sir," responded an unmistakably African voice. "Mass Tom sent me to see if Miss S'lina's up here."

"What does he want?" asked Mrs. Crump, going forward and opening the door.

"He say the doctor's come, ma'am, and Mom Hannah's done took him in the sick lady's room."

"You had better go at once," said Mr. Warwick, as she turned and looked at him. "Be sure and send the doctor to me before he leaves. I will wait for him here."

After she left, he sat quite still—totally forgetful of the dust now—trying to realize, and, if possible, to account for this singular freak of circumstance. But the more he thought, the more absolutely puzzled he became—the more difficult it was to believe that the woman of whom Mrs. Crump spoke, the woman who lay thus, sick and helpless at the mercy of strangers, was the Katharine Tresham whom he fancied safe in his sister's home, the Katharine Tresham whom he had seen last in her white ball-dress, with the blue flowers in her soft, brown hair! "There must be some mistake!" he said, half aloud. "It cannot be!" But, as he uttered the words, he looked at the little book still in his hand, and it seemed to answer, "It is so!" But how did she come here—so strangely friendless and alone? It was vain to ask himself that question—vain to torment himself with fruitless conjectures. Of course, he thought of St. John, of Mrs. Gordon, of his sister, of Annesley, of the money drawn at the bank, and Mr. Marks's comment upon it—but all these people and things were hopelessly confused in his mind. He could not even frame out of them a conjecture plausible enough to satisfy himself. One random thought succeeded another, until at last, to escape from them, he rose and started to leave the room. "I'll meet the doctor," he said. This intention was frustrated, however, for the doctor was at the door.

"Mr. Warwick?" said he, interrogatively.

"Yes," said Mr. Warwick. "Dr. Joyner, I presume? Walk in, sir. I wish to speak to you."

Dr. Joyner bowed and walked in. He had on his professional face and his professional manner. Having said this, it is useless to say how he looked in the matter of expression, for all doctors look alike under these circumstances. The drill of a soldier is not more exactly marked than this professional mask, which is so widely prevalent that an inquiring observer is sometimes driven to wonder if the novices of medicine are taught deportment as well as science. In the way of personal appearance, Dr. Joyner was a man who might have been twenty-five by his figure, and forty-five by his face. The anomaly of youth and age is not often seen united in the same person; but, when it is, it strikes us unpleasantly—we can scarcely tell why. It struck Mr. Warwick unpleasantly as soon as the physician entered the room, and yet he could not possibly have given his reasons for the feeling. Dr. Joyner sat down, and opened the conversation himself.

"I was referred to you by Mrs. Crump, sir. I understand that you are a friend of the lady I have just seen."

"Yes," answered Mr. Warwick, "I am a friend of hers, and, in the absence of other friends, I am anxious to hear an exact account of her case. Will you be good enough to give it me?"

This direct question seemed to embarrass the doctor a little. He had uncertain sort of eyes, that were given to shifting their gaze. They shifted it immediately, and, instead of looking at the lawyer's face, gazed out of the window

"The lady's case is a peculiar one," he said. "I am by no means sure that the illness under which she is laboring has developed itself sufficiently for me to give it a specific name."

Mr. Warwick looked astonished. "What!" he said. "She has been ill for a week, the landlady tells me, and you are not yet able to give her disease a specific name!"

"The symptoms have developed themselves slowly," answered the doctor, stiffly. "I have treated her, in a general way, for fever produced by cold and excitement; but to-day I begin to think that the brain is becoming involved. If so—" He stopped and hesitated.

Mr. Warwick turned a little pale, but took up his sentence quietly:

"If so, you think her life in danger?"

"Well, I don't go so far as that; but I think her illness may be very serious."

There was a pause. The doctor's eyes shifted from the window to the mantel-piece, and thence travelled back to his questioner's face. They rested there in keen and undisturbed scrutiny for several minutes, Mr. Warwick being deep in thought, with his brows slightly knitted, and his own gaze fastened on the floor. Without looking up, he said, slowly:

"If I only knew what to do!"

"I would advise you to write to the lady's friends, if you know them, sir," said the doctor, quietly.

The other started, and glanced up.

"I beg your pardon. I was thinking aloud. Can I see your patient?"

"You can see her, certainly."

"Will it not be dangerous? will it not excite her?"

"It cannot possibly excite her, for she knows nobody."

"She could not answer a single question, then?"

"Not when I left her, ten minutes ago."

Mr. Warwick resumed his scrutiny of the carpet, and Dr. Joyner resumed his scrutiny of Mr. Warwick. In this way another minute passed. Then the lawyer rose.

"Will you come with me to her room?" he said. "Since I am her only friend within reach, I must see her, and judge for myself of her condition."

"I am at your service," said the other, rising in turn.

They left the room, and walked down the passage together, making one or two sharp turns around sharp corners—for the house was built with a daring disregard of any plan or order whatever—and finally pausing before a door, at which the doctor tapped lightly. A negro-woman—the same who had spoken to Mr. Crump in the passage below—opened it, and, seeing the doctor, made way for them to enter.

A queer little room, with a fireplace in the corner, and dark-green walls, that contrasted strongly with clean white curtains, was what the lawyer saw. The furniture was plain and scanty, but there was not space for much; and the bed, which occupied the most prominent place, was neatly draped in spotless coverings. The best that the house afforded was plainly here, and it was evident that Katharine had suffered from no neglect at the hands of her entertainers. Without saying a word, the doctor led the way to the bed, and Mr. Warwick followed him. Standing side by side, they looked down on the sick girl.

She had fallen into a light slumber, and lay with her head thrown back over the pillows, showing the white arch of her throat, and its large arteries, beating with a rush that it was painful to watch. Her cheeks were deeply flushed; her hair fell in tangled masses all about her face; and her lips were bright scarlet. She made a lovely picture, seen in the half-darkened room, with the white draperies of the bed surrounding her; but it was a picture lovely with that awful glow of fever which hushes our breath even when we see it in a stranger. The most inexperienced person looking on could hardly have failed to perceive that, if life and death were not already wrestling here, the hour of their struggle was not far distant, and the issue more than doubtful. One hand was thrown, as if in fevered restlessness, outside the counterpane. Mr. Warwick stooped down and laid his finger lightly on the wrist. Almost immediately he lifted his face, and looked at the doctor.

"Feel her pulse," he said. "I may be inexperienced; but it seems to me that it is going at a fearful rate. I cannot count it."

Even in the dim light, it was evident to his keen eyes that the doctor changed color. He drew out his watch, and, taking the wrist, began counting the pulse, speaking after a while without lifting his eyes.

"Her fever is rising. I was afraid it would. She seemed so much lowered in strength yesterday that I ordered stimulants, and I think they have been pressed too far. She was delirious when I was here a while ago."

"She seems to be sleeping now."

"Speak to her, and see if you can rouse her."

Mr. Warwick spoke. His words roused her, for she opened her eyes at once; but there was no consciousness in their gaze. They looked at him blankly, and, when he spoke again, she answered in the aimless wanderings of delirium—few words—words without any gleam of reason—accompanied by a wild and painful glare of the eye, so foreign to its usual soft expression that it absolutely destroyed her resemblance to herself, and made Mr. Warwick almost question if this were indeed Katharine Tresham. After a minute spent in close and attentive observation, he walked to the door, and beckoned the doctor to follow him. Once outside, he stopped and turned, thus facing the other.

"I find that the case is much more serious than I could possibly have imagined," he said. "I fear that there has been some neglect."

"It was quite impossible for me to nurse the patient as well as prescribe for her," answered the doctor, coldly. "All that I could do I have done."

"Then I suppose you will not object to my calling in another physician? I have sent for Dr. Randolph."

He said this in a matter-of-course tone; but he was not unprepared for what followed. His distrust of the doctor—increasing continually ever since the doctor entered his room—made him expect very much the reply that came. The man flushed deeply, and drew back with a stiff little bow.

"In that event, I beg leave to withdraw from the case. I decline to go into consultation with Dr. Randolph."

"Be good enough, then, to make out your bill and send it to me," said Mr. Warwick. "Good-evening."

He left the man standing at the head of the stairs, and went down, smiling a little to himself. "It did not cost much trouble," he said, half aloud, as he looked round in search of Mr. Crump. That worthy was easily found, and matters were soon placed on a satisfactory footing. Mr. Warwick had very vague ideas on the subject of sick-nursing; but he knew that unremitting attention was an item of the first importance, and he provided for this by engaging the services of two women, who were to relieve each other on duty.

"Hannah's up-stairs now," said Mr. Crump, "and Elsie'll be on hand when she's wanted. Is there any thing else, Mr. Warwick?"

"I asked Mrs. Crump to send for Dr. Randolph. Do you know whether she did so?"

Before Mr. Crump could reply, a heavy step sounded in the passage outside the room in which they were standing, and a round, full voice was heard asking, "Which room?"

"There's the doctor now," said Mr. Crump.—"This way, doctor! Here's Mr. Warwick."

"This way—is it?" responded the same jovial voice; and the next instant a tall, stout man, with a frank, pleasant face, and an eye of that peculiar color which can only be called "laughing hazel," entered the apartment, lightly swinging a stick, formidable enough to have been an Irishman's shillalah.

"Well, doctor, how are you?" said Mr. Warwick, meeting him with extended hand.

"Mr. Warwick, I am delighted to see you, and to see you looking so well," said the doctor, giving the hand a cordial shake. "I was afraid, from the urgency of the message, that I should find you seriously ill. You haven't much the look of a sick man," he added, laughing. "What is the matter?—broken down from over-work? I've prophesied that, you know."

"Your prophecy is not verified yet, at any rate. But you are mistaken; I am not the patient for whom you were summoned. There is a lady here under my care" (Mr. Crump opened his eyes to their fullest extent), "who is, I fear, dangerously ill. I want you to see her."

"What is the matter with her?"

"That is what I want you to tell *me*. I am afraid, however, that she has brain-fever."

"When was she taken?"

"A week ago."

"A week ago—*here?*"

"Yes—here."

"And who has been attending her?"

"A doctor of whom I know nothing but that his name is Joyner."

At the sound of that name, Dr. Randolph dropped his eyes, which had been fastened on the speaker's face, looked in the fire, and said "Humph!" in a significant manner, that was not lost on Mr. Warwick. He at once hastened to explain.

"Don't think that *I* called him in, doctor. Miss Tresham came here a week ago, as I tell you, and was taken ill. Mrs. Crump called in Dr. Joyner. I arrived an hour ago, and I have already dismissed him. With little or no knowledge of medicine, I am still able to perceive that he has been grossly mistreating the case. What I ask of you now is to see if you can repair the mischief he has done."

"That may be harder than you think," said the doctor, gravely. "A week—however, I will reserve my opinion till I see the patient; and that I will do immediately, if you please."

Mr. Warwick led the way to Miss Tresham's room, and just at the door they met Mrs. Crump coming out.

"Oh, dear, I am glad to see you!" she said to the doctor. "She is clean gone out of her head, and the Lord knows I haven't an idea what to do with her."

The doctor did not utter a word, but passed her hastily and entered the chamber. One step took him to the bed, where, with flaming cheeks, and eyes bright with the awful glare of fever, Katharine lay tossing and raving wildly. He gave a single glance, then turned and drew back the curtain from a window near him. It chanced to be toward the west, and the rays of the setting sun streamed with a flood of golden glory into the little room, filling it with an almost dazzling radiance. The sudden rush of light almost blinded the others; but the doctor bent over the bed, felt the pulse that bounded beneath his touch, and gazed intently into the eyes that met his own.

When he raised his face, Mr. Warwick was startled by the gravity of his brow and lip. "Bring a basin here," he said to the servant. To Mrs. Crump, "Bare her arm." He drew a small case from his pocket. The next moment, there was the gleam of a lancet, a sharp stroke into the soft, white flesh, and a stream of dark-red blood pouring into the basin.

"Bandages," he said to Mrs. Crump, who was standing by. While she was gone for them, he turned to Mr. Warwick, and added, "Brain-fever of the most violent type. This is the only hope of saving her life."

"It is brain-fever, then?"

"Beyond doubt. If I had only seen her a day earlier!"

"Thank God it is not a day later!" said the lawyer, under his breath.

There was no time for any thing more. Mrs. Crump returned, and the doctor immediately devoted his whole energy to his patient. In the face of all remonstrances and entreaties to the contrary (Mrs. Crump and Mom Hannah freely treated him to both), he bled her until insensibility took the place of violent raving. Then, and then only, he stopped the flow of the blood, and bound up her arm. After this, he called for a pair of scissors and for ice. With the first, he remorselessly cut from her head the rich, brown locks that had crowned it like a glory, and, when they lay scattered over the bed, he saturated a towel with water, filled it with ice, and bound it around the burning temples.

"There!" he said, speaking for the first time, after this was done. "Remember, Hannah, this is your business — to keep a supply of towels and ice at hand, and change them whenever the chill has worn off. With the fever, that won't be long.—Mrs. Crump, I suppose you have no time to spare—"

"Indeed, doctor, I shall take the time," interrupted Mrs. Crump, hastily. "Just tell me what you want done, and I'll engage to do it, no matter what else goes undone."

"Just at present there is nothing to do, except to send for some leeches, and try and keep things as quiet as possible. Could you give those gentlemen down-stairs a hint that there is a case of brain-fever in the house, and that a little less noise would be desirable?"

"I'll give 'em something more'n a hint," answered Mrs. Crump, decidedly—and left the room, to send for the leeches, and command the peace.

"A word with you, Mr. Warwick," said the doctor, walking away to the farthest window. "I think it right to tell you," he went on, as Mr. Warwick followed him, "that this attack is a very dangerous one, and, from present appearance, the chances are that it will prove fatal in its result. If the young lady has any friends, they ought to be communicated with at once."

He paused as if for a reply; but Mr. Warwick did not speak. Situated as he was—in utter ignorance how or why Katharine had left his sister's house—it was impossible for him not to hesitate when thus summarily brought to the point of positive action. He did hesitate—he ran over in his mind the unsatisfactory condition of affairs when he left home, and the unsatisfactory conjectures that had beset him an hour ago, without arriving at any result. Finally, he looked at the doctor, and made a simple statement of facts.

"In few words, doctor, I don't like to do this without Miss Tresham's sanction," he said. "She is a foreigner, with no relations in America, and as for her friends—I can only account for her presence here by supposing that some estrangement has occurred to separate her from those who might be called her friends. Under these circumstances, I do not think that my interference could do any good—certainly not by means of letters."

"But when her life is in danger?"

"That statement would, of course, be sufficient to bring relatives to her bedside; but you know the world well enough to be able to judge whether it would be likely to have any effect on those who were simply bound to her by ties of convenience."

The doctor was silenced. He looked from the bed to the lawyer, and from the lawyer to the bed, trying to understand the matter, and failing utterly to do so. In the range of his professional experience, many sad pages of human life had come under his eye—as they come under the eye of all men of all professions, and of all physicians especially—many desolate stories had been laid bare to him, many woful tragedies had been acted before him, until out of very familiarity, he had grown callous to these varied phases of the one great drama of human suffering. But now he felt strangely touched. That this girl, so young, so fair—had she been ugly, the position would have lost half its pathos!—so evidently of tender nurture, should be thrown utterly friendless, utterly alone, upon the care and kindness of strangers, seemed to him inexpressibly pitiful. He felt for her deeply—felt as he had not felt for any one since he was young and impressionable, and new at his profession; but with regard to John Warwick, his part in the matter the doctor failed entirely to comprehend. If all that he had said were true, what interest had he in the girl, what right to make her safety his personal care? Such conduct was so unlike the quiet, reserved lawyer, always gravely courteous to women, yet always carefully avoiding them, that it seemed incredible. Reading the doctor's surprise in the doctor's face, Mr. Warwick—for Katharine's sake—addressed himself frankly to it.

"I see you think it strange that I should occupy the position I do," he said; "but if you will consider a moment, I think you will understand why and how it is. Miss Tresham has been living in my sister's house for two years, and I have learned to know her well, and to respect her highly. I do not know why she has left her position; but I am confident that it was by no fault of her own; and it would be strange if—meeting her accidentally, as I have done—I did not do every thing in my power for her. Considering that I am old enough to be her father, I am sure you will grant this."

"Leaving your age out of the question," said the doctor, with a shade of his usual jovial smile, "I grant it fully, Mr. Warwick. Your conduct is that of a true-hearted gentleman, and you have my hearty respect and support. God willing, we'll pull the poor girl through, with or without help from anybody else. Now tell me if you have any idea of the cause of her illness."

"Not the least. When I saw her last she was in perfect health."

"That was when?"

"Less than three weeks ago."

"Have you any reason to suppose that she may have been suffering from trouble or distress of mind?"

Mr. Warwick thought of St. John, and paused a moment before he replied. "I do not know," he said. "I think it probable that she has; but if so, we cannot reach the cause, and it is useless to consider it. Do you suppose that mental trouble has brought this on?"

"I cannot tell—I can only make a surmise from the condition in which I find her. Speaking in the dark, I should say that mental trouble, liberally aided and abetted by quack treatment, has brought it on."

"My instinct was right, then—that man is a quack?"

"A quack! That old woman yonder has quite as good a right to put M. D. after her name, and, I dare say, a much better amount of medical knowledge to support it. The scoundrel has hardly the barest smattering of information on the subject—as he proves by leaving a case whenever another doctor is called in. This is not the first patient he has brought to death's door—and, unfortunately, some of them go beyond it. Last week a poor fellow died under his hands—a carpenter with a large family. As clear a case of butchery as ever I saw!"

"Is there no way of stopping this?"

"There is no way as long as people, like our friend Mrs. Crump, choose to send for him. We live in a free country, you know, and when a man comes and settles among us, there is no competent authority to examine his diploma and give him a license, before he sets to work killing people."

"I think if I see him again, I shall feel very much tempted to put it out of his power to do any more mischief—for some time to come, at least."

"He is not likely to let you see him again. To give the rascal his due, he is the embodiment of discretion. As I came along the street, somebody told me that one of his other patients—his only other one, I expect—was in a critical condition. If she dies, I am inclined to think that the town will become too hot to hold him. But we must make arrangements for to-night. Somebody must sit up here—somebody who can be relied on to follow my directions exactly."

"I will do it."

"You can, if you choose—and so shall I, for that matter. But there must be somebody besides—a woman, of course. Mrs. Crump would be the person, if she was not broken down; but, from her looks, I should say that she was up last night. I'll send my wife. She will be glad to be of service."

"Doctor, how can I thank you!"

"Don't think of such a thing till we see how it turns out." He walked to the bed, and looked down at the hotly-flushed face, the parched lips, and wandering eyes, with a glance of pity. "Poor girl!" he said to himself. Then, sharply, aloud to the old woman, "More ice here—change these cloths." Then, again, to Warwick, "It all hangs on a thread. There is no telling what the end will be."

CHAPTER XXX.

AN OLD FRIEND.

WHILE Miss Tresham was lying ill at the Eagle Hotel in Hartsburg, and while Mr. Warwick was quietly journeying along the road that led to his meeting with her, matters and things in Lagrange were in a far from satisfactory condition.

To begin with the Marks family, there was growing indignation on the part of Mr. Marks, discomfiture and concern on the part of his wife, and turmoil and complaining on the part of the children, at the unaccountable absence of the governess. Two weeks had gone by, without any sign of return, or any word of explanation from her. Under these circumstances, what was left for her employers to think but that she had deliberately forsaken them? It was true that every thing she possessed, with the exception of a small bag containing a few necessary articles of clothing, had been left behind; but that might have been done merely to avoid suspicion—and then, there was that unanswerable riddle, the money! Why had she drawn it, if not to go away?—why had she been so particular about demanding gold? "It is as plain as a pikestaff," said Mr. Marks, "that she meant to leave just in this manner! It was the first suspicion that came into my mind, and it proves to be the correct one." Poor Katharine had very little idea, when she went to the bank that morning, how heavily it was to tell against her afterward, in the net that circumstances were weaving. At first, Mrs. Marks was stout in her defence, but after a while she succumbed—facts being too strong against her. "It's that hateful St. John!" she said, at last. "I'm as sure as can be that Miss Katharine has run away just to get rid of him!" It provoked her that her husband would not admit the validity of this excuse. "Miss Tresham may have run away to get rid of Mr. St. John," he said, "but it is very certain, Bessie, that she needn't have done any thing of the kind if all had been straight and clear with her. If he had no claim on her, why should she run away from him?" In the face of this masculine logic, Mrs. Marks had no reply—no relief but that of boxing Nelly's ears, when that poor little soul cried piteously for Miss Tresham to tell her a story at night.

Then there was another annoyance. Mr. St. John, who, if appearances might be trusted, seemed as completely puzzled as themselves, persisted in calling at the house, in questioning the servants, in accosting Mr. Marks, and in endeavoring by every means in his power to find out something about the missing governess. As time went on, this became a positive nuisance—and a nuisance all the more disagreeable because Mr. Marks disliked the man, and Mrs. Marks had changed her respectful sympathy into a violent aversion for him. In her eyes, he stood as the representative of the change that had given such a shock to her household, and she detested him accordingly. "Will he *never* go away?" she said to herself, pettishly, as, day after day, she saw the same slender figure, the same dark, regular profile, pass and repass the house. "If he would only go away, I am sure Miss Katharine would come back, and surely Richard couldn't refuse to let her stay." Fortunately for himself, Mr. Marks was not put to the test. St. John did not go away, and Miss Tresham did not return. Morton Annesley called vainly for news, and was always met by the same dismal shake of the head. "Not even a letter, Mrs. Marks?" he would say, with such a wistful look in his eyes that it almost betrayed Mrs. Marks into telling him a consoling falsehood. "Not even a letter, Mr. Annesley," she would answer, and heave a deep sigh as the young man went away. At such times her regret took the form of indignant reproach against Katharine. It was shameful!—Richard was right: it was shameful, she would think, as she went back to her work, and heard the children squabbling in the yard, instead of being settled quietly at their lessons.

As for Mrs. Annesley, she was simply incredulous of this great good fortune which had befallen her. That Katharine should go away of her own accord—should, without any embarrassing disclosure or trouble whatever, be removed out of Morton's life—was more than she had ever hoped in her most sanguine moments—was far, far too good to be true. She could not believe it—she absolutely declined to believe it. Some plot was at the bottom of it, she felt sure—something that would end by complicating matters more seriously than they had been complicated yet, by involving Morton as he had not been involved yet. To describe her state of mind during these two weeks would be impossible. The inaction was terrible to her, the doubt and suspense still more terrible. She went to see Mrs. Gordon, but there was no comfort to be obtained there. Mrs. Gordon knew no more than herself, but Mrs. Gordon took a view of the matter which had not occurred to Mrs. Annesley. "The girl has been sent by St. John in search of Felix!" she cried, as soon as she heard of Katharine's departure, and only her own ignorance of Felix's whereabouts prevented her from instantly setting out to guard him from this new danger. As it was, she lived in a state of restless terror which sometimes almost went beyond her control. Her only comfort, her only hope, was in John Warwick. As long as *he* was with Felix, she felt that the child was safe. Her reliance on him told her this, and did not tell her wrongly. Only sometimes she would think with dismay of his liking for Katharine, and wring her hands over it. "If he once lets her draw the secret from him!" she thought. But then, again, she would grow ashamed of this suspicion. Was it likely he would let her do it?—was it likely that, to the woman he loved best, to the man whom he trusted most, John Warwick would betray the confidence given him as a sacred charge? The woman who had once known him well, the woman whom he had once loved passionately, did him the justice to answer the question in the negative. No; John Warwick would never do this, and so John Warwick was to be trusted. But oh, Felix!—Felix! That was the burden of the mother's thought, the echo of the mother's cry. That great anxiety dwarfed every other consideration—even the consideration of Morton's folly. She still felt for him, and for the bitter distress that was hanging like a sword over his mother's head; but still Felix was at her heart, and there was no disguising the fact that she would have been glad to hear of Miss Tresham's return to Tallahoma, even although that return meant Morton's marriage with her the next day.

Under these circumstances, it may be supposed that there was not much sympathy between herself and Mrs. Annesley—yet there was more than might be imagined. They were both suffering from keen anxiety—that was one link. The anxiety of each was about the object dearest to them in the world—that was the second link. The same person, in each case, was the cause of this anxiety—that was the third link. These things were much in common, and it is doubtful whether they had ever in their lives been so nearly drawn together before. Mrs. Gordon's mode of accounting for Katharine's absence seemed to Mrs. Annesley plausible enough; but Felix was to her a person of small importance—or, to put the matter more correctly, of no importance at all—and, accepting her cousin's theory as a fact, the great consideration still remained, What would be the end of it with regard to Morton? She had heard nothing from St. John, and she had been too completely worsted to think of seeking him again herself. Besides, she had a sort of instinctive distrust of him—an instinctive feeling that she had placed herself in his power. If he saw Morton, and told him of her application, Morton would never forgive her! This was what made a coward of her, for she was very far from being a subtle diplomatist ready to walk to her end over any obstacles; but rather a woman weak with the weakness of her sex, who, having set in motion certain machinery of the power of which she had only a vague idea, stood by, shrinking from the consequences — a woman whose hands were fettered, from the use of plain means to a plain end, by a purely ideal fear—the fear of losing her son's love, and forfeiting her son's respect.

As time went on, Morton was, perhaps, the person most to be compassionated. All the others had "themselves to thank," in great measure, for their uneasiness; everybody else (even Mrs. Gordon) was suffering from the direct result of certain acts of his or her own. But Morton had done nothing to bring upon himself the keen anxiety which he was enduring. It may be perfectly true that we cry all the same whether we break our toys ourselves, or whether somebody else does the work of destruction for us, and that it is by no means a source of comfort when "one has only one's self to blame" for any of the disasters of life; but, in the matter of sympathy, this fact of personal responsibility makes a great difference and justly so. The man who has brought his trouble upon himself can, at best, advance only half the claim on our sympathy, of one who suffers through misfortune, or circumstance, or the fault of others. On this ground, therefore, it may be conceded that Morton deserved compassion more than any other of the circle whose interests were so capriciously twisted and intertwined together. Not on the ground of his love for Katharine Tresham, nor of the suffering which that love entailed upon him, but on the ground of his earnest desire to "do the thing which was right," no matter what the cost of that doing might be; of his loyal effort to reconcile the different claims that were conflicting with him, by the plain, straight rule of honor; and of his sincere renunciation of self, which deserved a better return than had yet befallen it. During these weeks he had gone about the ordinary affairs of life, and tried to meet them with his ordinary face; but, somehow, it would not do. Knocking more and more painfully at his heart, echoing more and more loudly in his ears, he heard the question, Where has she gone?—what has become of her? Had she, indeed, passed out of his life forever? Had he trifled so long with the happiness that might have been his, by a word, perhaps, that it had at last escaped him? Asking himself these questions, he took a sudden resolve. He would go in search of her, and, having once found her, he would not leave her again until all trifling and hesitation were at an end, until the fate of his life was settled as far as it was in Katharine Tresham's power to settle it. Her very absence, which told against her so strongly in the eyes of every one else, did not shake his dogged faith for an instant. He trusted her! That was his answer to all that the voice of the world could urge; and, whether it was a wise one or not, let us at least acknowledge that it was a noble one.

Having made up his mind to go, Annesley was not long in carrying the design into execution. A plausible excuse of business was soon found for leaving home, and, although Mrs. Annesley strongly suspected the real cause of his departure, she had no excuse for saying, no means of doing, any thing to prevent it. To expostulate would have been worse than useless, and there was nothing else left. "It comes of being a woman," she thought, bitterly; but, in fact, if she had been a man a hundred times over, she could have thrown no obstacle in Morton's path which Morton's impetuous resolution would not have surmounted. As a general rule, women are very much given to magnifying the disabilities of their sex, when these very disabilities often make the secret of their greatest strength. In the present instance, it was certainly so. No tangible restraint which Mrs. Annesley could possibly have placed over her son would have bound him half so firmly, would have influenced him half so much, as the intangible restraint of those wishes which appealed to him the more because she had no power to enforce them. Still, he began to consider that he had, perhaps, sacrificed a little too much to them; and, in taking his present resolution, he put them tenderly but decidedly on one side. Some instinct told him that his first duty now was to the woman he loved, and, with the simplicity of thought and intention which characterized him, he set forth to fulfil this duty.

It was on the sixteenth of January—exactly two weeks after Katharine left—that Morton drove out of the gates of Annesdale, and turned his horses' heads into the road that led to Saxford. He had not gone more than a mile when he met George Raynor. Of course, a pause and a conversation ensued.

"You look as if you were rigged out for travelling," said Mr. Raynor, after the first greetings were over. "Going down to Apalatka?"

"No—only to Saxford," Annesley answered. "I have to meet a man there on business." This was strictly true; but the speaker did not add that the man would willingly have come to Lagrange. "Why should you think of Apalatka? Is any thing going on down there?"

"Nothing that I know of; but I heard you promise Seymour to go down soon, and I thought you might be on your way to fulfil the promise. Maggie Lester went home yesterday," he added, with a laugh.

"And you think I am likely to be following Miss Maggie? Thank you; I don't care to interfere with Lawton's amusement. She didn't stay long with Mrs. Raynor, then?"

"Her mother wrote for her—company expected, or something of the sort—and she was obliged to leave. Flora was very sorry to see her go—chiefly, I think, because she took Irene along."

"Did Miss Irene go?" said Annesley, a little absently. "I am sorry to hear that, and so will a great many other people be. But she will be back soon—won't she?"

"Hardly soon, according to present arrangements. Flora is to join her in Apalatka, and they will go on to Mobile together. I fancy Lagrange won't see either of them again very shortly. I look forward with resignation to a long period of bachelor—soh, Charley!—You had better draw your horses out of the way, Pink! Here comes the stage."

Pink—the servant who was driving Annesley—drew his horses to one side of the road accordingly; while Charley, who was young and foolish, backed into a fence-corner, as the heavily-laden coach, with its six horses, its nine inside passengers, and one fortunate outsider, who had secured the seat beside the driver, rolled by with a sweeping air of grand importance on its way to Saxford. As it passed, Annesley glanced round and ran his eye over the passengers, vaguely looking for an acquaintance, as people will do, whether in stage-coaches or railroad-trains. With the exception of the driver, to whom he nodded, he saw not one familiar face—during the first instant, that is. The second after, a man, on the seat opposite from the side of the road on which Raynor and himself were, leaned forward for a look at the way-side group, and he recognized St. John.

Long after the coach had passed out of sight, after he had said good-by to Raynor, and was once more under way, with the horses trotting briskly over the smooth, well-beaten road, that face remained with Annesley to conjure up tormenting thoughts. Why was St. John leaving Tallahoma? Why was he going to Saxford? What connection did he have with Miss Tresham? These three questions formed the text of a mental discourse that occupied his attention until the roofs of Saxford came in sight, just as the sun was going down in a gorgeous bed of sunset clouds, and the whole wide panorama of Nature—its fields, and valleys, and shaded hill-sides—began to clothe themselves in the exquisite purple of the winter gloaming.

Annesley drove to the principal hotel of the place, and found that the coach had preceded him in its arrival by an hour or two. The first person he saw, on entering the house, was St. John. Involuntarily the young man frowned; the very sight of the sallow, handsome face had grown as repugnant to him as to Mr. Marks. Somehow or other this man was connected with Katharine and Katharine's disappearance—according to Mrs. Gordon, he had sent her away; according to Mr. Marks, he, at least, knew where she was, and why she had gone. In either view of the case, Annesley felt inclined to take him by the throat and demand "satisfaction" in the form of information on the spot. But the codes of civilized life discourage, if they do not absolutely condemn, such arbitrary proceedings as these; and, this consideration apart, such proceedings are sometimes attended with unpleasant consequences. Morton restrained the inclination, and passed on. After the business of obtaining a room was over, his first inquiry startled "mine host" a little. Was there a Catholic priest residing in Saxford?

"You're the second gentleman that's asked that question, Mr. Annesley," answered the proprietor, opening his eyes, but smiling all the same. "There was a gentleman came in the stage, and wanted to know the same thing. I told him, sir, what I can tell you—that there's no priest living in town, but one comes here sometimes—I really can't say how often. I referred the other gentleman to an Irish family, named Malone, for information; but, if *you* are anxious to know any thing about the priest, I'll take pleasure in sending round and finding out every thing for you."

"Thank you," said Morton, a little amused at the contrast thus strikingly marked by the landlord between Mr. Annesley of Annesdale and an ordinary traveller, who was (so far as the knowledge of that worthy extended) Mr. Nobody of Nowhere. "I will trouble you to find out, then, whether the priest is now in Saxford, and, if he is not, when he was here last, and is likely to be here again. When the messenger returns, send him up to my room, if you please."

Before long, there was a tap at Morton's door, and the expected messenger made his appearance. He was a bright-looking boy, and delivered his message very clearly. He had seen Mrs. Malone. The priest was in town—had arrived that evening to be in time for Sunday—and was staying with the Malone family. On hearing that a gentleman at the hotel wished to see him, Mrs. Malone had suggested that it would be well if the gentleman would defer his visit until the next morning—the father had come thirty miles that day, and was not very well, and a gentleman had already called on him. If the gentleman was going away, he might come that night, of course; but, if not, it would be more convenient if he would wait until the next morning.

"I'll wait," he said, absently; and, after the messenger left, he asked himself what difference it made. He had waited three weeks in Lagrange—why not wait one night in Saxford? Yet he felt impatient over the delay, as people will feel over any delay, however slight, that intervenes between the fruition of a hope or the fulfilment of an expectation.

He reasoned with himself about this folly, however, and, after a while, managed to reconcile himself to the charitable opinion that there was no real need for disturbing Father Martin's well-earned repose on that night. One thing, at least, he had gained by the application. He had learned that, instead of knowing all about Katharine, St. John, like himself, was merely on the track of discovery, and that, also like himself, the first person to whom he applied for information was the person whom Katharine would have been most likely to take into her confidence—that is, the priest.

While he was arriving at this conclusion, the person of whom he was thinking entered the hotel and passed directly into the bar-room. If Morton had seen him it is probable that he would not have felt encouraged concerning the degree of information which Father Martin was able or likely to give. Discomfiture was written as legibly on St. John's face as anger betrayed itself in his manner. On entering the door he pushed rudely against a man who chanced to be standing near, and did not trouble himself to make even the ghost of an apology. Walking forward, with an air of profound unconsciousness, he called for a glass of brandy, received it, and was about to raise it to his lips, when the man who had been so unceremoniously treated followed and touched his arm.

"I beg your pardon," he said, quietly, but with a certain tone of menace in his voice. "You are the gentleman who came within an ace of knocking me down, I believe. Did I hear you apologize for it?"

St. John turned quickly, with an insolent reply visible in his eyes before it passed his lips. He was evidently in that frame of mind when to insult somebody is nothing less than a positive relief. As it chanced, however, he had no time to speak. No sooner did he turn his face than the other recoiled a step—in sheer amazement, as it seemed.

"By ——!" he said, "St. John!"

Something in his tone, something in his manner, struck even the by-standers with surprise. They had looked with interest the minute before—anxious to see the end of what promised to be a very pretty quarrel—but the interest sensibly quickened at this unexpected recognition. Its effect on St. John was unmistakable. He looked keenly for a second in the face before him—his own growing a shade paler, meanwhile—then he put down, untouched, the glass of brandy, and extended his hand.

"*You!*" he said. "I had no idea it was *you*. I apologize, of course. Where the devil did you come from?"

The other took his offered hand and shook it with a laugh. After the first manifestation of surprise, the meeting seemed to affect him very little, either one way or another.

"Where I came from isn't half as wonderful as where you came from," he answered. "Suppose we exchange reminiscences at our leisure? Will you come to my room? You can take your brandy there, and I will order some to keep you company."

"All right," said St. John; but he said it reluctantly, and, as he allowed his companion to take his arm and lead him away, the people whom he left behind could not help thinking that this meeting was to him any thing but a pleasurable event.

They were quite right, too. He ground his teeth, and cursed his unlucky fate, as he followed the man who had claimed his acquaintance, up the steep and ill-lighted staircase of the hotel. They entered a room just at the head of the flight of steps, and, while the proprietor of the apartment fumbled about for the means of striking a light, St. John sat down on the first substantial object he came to, which chanced to be a table, and was silent.

"Deuce take the thing! Where has it gone?" grumbled the one who was stumbling about the room, kicking the chairs, and finally knocking down the pitcher and basin with a resounding clatter. "I've found the confounded candle, but where the devil has the match-box gone! Here—no. D— it, all the water's spilled, and I've stepped right into it! Pshaw! I'll get a light across the passage and not keep you in the dark this way, St. John. Excuse me for a minute."

St. John vouchsafed not a word as the speaker left the room and crossed the passage to a door just opposite, under which a stream of light was visible.

His knock was answered by a gentleman, who opened the door almost immediately, and courteously acceded to his request. He returned to a table in the room, and brought from it a candle with which to light the one presented. As he did so his face was fully exposed to view, and St. John, sitting in the darkness of the opposite room, recognized Annesley. Instinctively he drew a little farther back into the friendly shade. At that particular time, and under those particular circumstances, he had no desire to be recognized in return. There was no danger of this, however, for his position effectually shielded him; and, besides this, Morton's attention was occupied just then with the man before him. As he brought forward the candle something like recognition was plainly to be seen in his face—was evidently struggling to assert itself in his mind. As the stranger held *his* candle to the flame, and the light thus fell on his face, the recognition suddenly became clear.

"I beg your pardon," said the young man. "I did not know you at first. Dr. Joyner, is it not?"

Dr. Joyner—for it was indeed he—looked with a start into the face before him; then, according to his invariable custom, shifted his eyes back to the candle.

"You are right. Joyner is my name," he said, "but I believe you have the advantage of me, sir."

"That is natural," said Morton, smiling a little. "I never saw you but once—but my memory is good for faces. I was down in Apalatka about six months ago, and, in passing through Hartsburg, I called at your office to get a prescription for a sprained wrist. You may not remember the occurrence, but, as soon as I saw your face, it came back to me."

"Doctors see so many people that they may be pardoned for having poor memories," said the other, apologetically. "I think I remember you, though," he went on, looking again at the young man. "You were with Mr. Seymour, I believe, and he introduced you as Mr. Annesley, of Lagrange."

"The same," said Morton. "Your lotion did my wrist a great deal of good," he added, with the frankness that sat very winningly upon him. "Won't you come in? I should like to hear something of Apalatka and my friends down there."

"I regret—I am sorry—it would give me great pleasure," said the doctor, stammering, as he bowed over his candlestick, "but I left a friend in my room—in the dark, too, poor fellow!—and he is waiting for me to return. Otherwise—" Another bow completed the sentence."

"In that case I can't expect to detain you, of course," said Morton. "Good-evening."

When the doctor went back into his own oom his face wore an expression of mingled surprise and amusement, which at once attracted St. John's attention and roused his curiosity.

"You seem to be enjoying something amazingly," he said. "Considering that the brandy hasn't come yet, you might as well let me know what it is. One thing is certain"—with a look of disgust around—"I don't see much in the way of amusement here."

"I am only enjoying a new illustration of an old proverb," said the other, putting the candlestick on a rickety table that was on one side of the room, with a cracked looking-glass hanging over it. "Did you ever chance to hear that 'a prophet is never without honor save in his own country?' Well, I've just had an example of that. For want of something better to do, I have been trying my hand lately at the healing art, and the result was by no means as brilliant as I could have wished. The other doctors in the place where I settled were jealous of me, a few unpleasant accidents attended my practice, a man or two died—don't men die sometimes under the hands of regular M. D.'s?—and the consequence was that the people raised an uproar, and I had to leave—absolutely, my dear St. John, I had to leave, in preference to being mobbed. Think what a state of barbarism this horrible country is in! Well, I left the place—Hartsburg is its name—under those circumstances, and I come here, and the first person I meet compliments—actually *compliments*—me on my medical skill!"

"That young fellow across the passage?"

"Yes—did you see him? Fine-looking, isn't he? One of the first men in the country round about here, I believe. I met him, as he reminded me, in Hartsburg, with a Mr. Seymour, a wealthy planter who lives in the county of which Hartsburg is the seat. He had sprained his wrist, and I gave him a lotion for it. He says it worked excellently."

"Then why couldn't you prescribe for your other patients as well?"

Dr. Joyner indulged in a laugh—quiet, but of considerable depth and evident enjoyment.

"I sprained my own wrist once," he said, "and I got this prescription for it from a doctor. You see it's useful never to forget any thing."

"And you practised medicine on the strength of knowing one prescription? Well"—with an impatient movement—"I suppose it was as good a trade as any other that you were likely to drift into. What did you leave the old country for?"

"Humph!" said the doctor, looking at him askance. "What did *you* leave it for?"

"That's easily answered—because I felt disposed to do so."

"Oh, you did, did you? Well, then, there's a good deal of difference between us. I left because the police were so unusually pressing in their attentions, just then, that I had no alternative but to do so. I made the narrowest slip of the galleys imaginable," said he, growing pale, notwithstanding his lightness of tone. "*Ma foi!* it would be delightful to be number nine of a chain-gang just now! Practising medicine at the expense of the good people of Hartsburg is quite an improvement on that. Do you object to my leaving you for a minute? I'll step to the door and call for that brandy. In a place like this you have to assert yourself, or the rascals will neglect you."

St. John making no objection, Dr. Joyner proceeded to step to the door and assert himself. Having shouted for some time, he at last succeeded in bringing up the brandy, and half a dozen people besides, anxious to know if the house was on fire. After reassuring them on this point, he coolly relieved the servant of the brandy, shut the door in the faces of the others, and returned to St. John.

"There, now!" said he, setting the bottle and two glasses which accompanied it down on the table. "I call this comfortable—two old friends and good comrades drinking each other's health in elegant seclusion. You'll find water in that pitcher there, St. John—confound it! I forgot it was spilt. Shall I call for more?"

"Not on my account," said St. John, resignedly. "I don't care to bring up half the household again. Sit down," he went on, impatiently. "Something is on your mind—I've seen that from the first. Speak it out, and have done."

"With all my heart," said the other, sitting down and composedly draining a glass of spirits. "You haven't told me yet how you came here," he added, with a sudden furtive glance at his companion's face. "One good turn deserves another. I've been frank with you—now be frank with me. Has the pretty little game of *rouge et noir* done for you also?"

"I'm here on business," said St. John, irritably. "I thought I told you that. What is the good of, being so d—d inquisitive? I haven't been in America more than a month or two, and I shall not stay an hour longer than I can possibly help."

"Are you very closely occupied just now?"

"That depends on circumstances. Why do you ask?"

The other looked over his shoulder nervously at the door. Then drew his chair a little nearer. "Would you be willing to run a small risk for a great reward?" he asked, quickly.

"That depends," said St. John, watching him coolly; "both on the degree of risk, and the amount of the reward."

"The risk is hardly worth considering, and the amount is that of a moderate fortune. In one word, St. John, can I depend on you, or can I not? This thing has been on my mind for some time, and I have been considering day and night how I could manage it without any assistance; but when I saw you, the problem was solved for me. I said at once, 'There is the man in the very nick of time. If his head's as cool and his wits are as sharp as they used to be, I've nothing more to fear.'"

"I don't stand in any need of a dose of flattery," said St. John. "Affairs are desperate with me just now, and I am ready for any thing that won't put my neck in a noose. A person on whom I depended has just given me the slip in the most complete manner. A scheme on which I have been building is likely to come to nothing, as far as I am concerned, and so—pass the brandy, and let me hear your plan."

"It's not a thing to describe in a place like this," said the other, glancing round again. "If we talk about it at all, it must be in French. "You don't object, do you?"

"Not in the least."

"Listen then," said he, plunging at once into French, and speaking with an ease and fluency which proved his intimate acquaintance with the language. "Before I left Hartsburg, I chanced to hear that a bank of importance, which is established there, was about to send a large amount of specie for distribution among its various branch banks. I did not pay much attention one way or another to the report, until, in coming to Saxford, I travelled with a man who is well known to be the messenger intrusted with the money. This fact, and my own desperate condition, soon made me think that here was an excellent opportunity of fortune, only needing a man of courage and nerve to seize it. The courage and nerve I had, my dear St. John, but I needed a few other things—a little assistance, principally. The undertaking is too great for one person to attempt. I needed a comrade to share the risk and—the reward. As soon as I saw you, I thought 'Here is my man.' It's for you to say whether or not I was right."

"I have heard the object," said St. John, coolly. "How about the means?"

"The means are as plain as could be desired. The messenger is at present on his way to Tallahoma, where the specie will be lodged in the bank until opportunities are found for forwarding it to the other branches. Now, I have been in Tallahoma, and I have seen this bank. Write me down a fool, my dear St. John, if it would not be as easy to enter it as to walk out of this room. See here!"

He took from his pocket a morocco case of

moderate size, touched a spring, and, as it flew open, he held it out for the inspection of the other.

"What would you call that, now?" he asked.

St. John regarded it superciliously, as he answered, "I should call it a box of tooth-instruments. Have you been practising dentistry as well as physic?"

"A little. I fleshed this"—he held up to St. John's recoiling sight a formidable-looking pair of forceps—"in the—"

"Spare me a description of the operation, I beg," interrupted the other, with unconcealed disgust. "What have these things to do with the subject you were talking of?"

"Don't be impatient, and you shall hear. You would call it a box of tooth-instruments, would you? Well, you're not to blame there—and that's the beauty of it. Anybody would call it the same thing. But now—I'll show you."

So saying, he took the instruments from the box, then, with great care, removed the red-velvet cushion on which they had rested, and which turned out to be a false bottom, beneath which was a cavity containing a dozen or more of eccentric-shaped implements, the use of which it would have puzzled an ordinary observer to conjecture. It did not puzzle St. John in the least.

"You are well supplied," he remarked, with a grim smile.

"You may say so! Look at that, now, will you?"

He lifted a small saw, made of the finest watch-spring steel, and exhibited it, handling it with the same caressing touch which a painter, who has not used his brushes for some time, bestows on those beloved servitors of his more beloved art, or with which a musician passes his hand over the strings or keys of his favorite instrument.

"That walks through iron with the same ease that a good carpenter's saw passes through wood!" cried he, with enthusiasm. "And here—" He went on to expatiate upon the excellence of various of the implements, and the virtues of the box itself. "You observe," he said, "that there is room here for other matters besides these useful little gentlemen. I keep any papers of importance, that it might not be advisable to have about me, here too."

"It is a good idea," said St. John, absently. "But about this bank." He thought for a moment, then looked up with something like a flash in his eye. "The man who is responsible—the cashier, I believe they call him—is named Marks, isn't he?"

"I—yes, I believe so. I didn't pay much attention to his name. What has that got to do with it?"

"It has to do with it that he is an unmannered scoundrel, who has gone out of his way to insult me on one or two occasions," answered St. John, vindictively. "If it's *his* bank that you want to rob, I'll help you, with the greatest pleasure, on the understanding that we share the spoils fairly. But I can tell you that you will have to be very cautious in your arrangements."

"We will discuss them now," said the other, eagerly. "Help yourself to the brandy, and then we can plan the campaign."

CHAPTER XXXI.

FATHER MARTIN.

Early the next morning—as early as was at all compatible with civilized habits—Annesley set forth to pay his visit to the Catholic priest. Having been carefully directed with regard to the whereabouts of the Malone house, he had no difficulty in finding it, and, when he came to a plain two-story building, with the usual four sides, and the usual long piazzas, set back from the street in a green yard, he knew at once that it was the place of which he was in search. His knock at the front door was answered by a pleasant-looking woman, with an unmistakably Irish face, and still more unmistakably Irish accent. Hearing that he was "the gentleman to see the priest," she asked him to walk in.

"Father Martin went into the garden for a walk," she said. "I will send one of the children to tell him you are here."

"It would be a pity to bring him in," said Annesley, smiling, and winning her heart at once by his face and manner. "Can't I go to him? I have only a few words to say, and I need not disturb his walk very long to say them."

"I—yes, sir; there is no reason why you should not go," answered Mrs. Malone, after a moment's hesitation. "Straight across the yard—yonder is the garden-gate. It can't be long before you find the father; he's walking in there somewhere."

Annesley thanked her, and went his way. A path led across the yard to the gate of which she had spoken. Opening it, he found himself in a garden, which was not very much of a place in the way of size or arrangement, but which had a certain attraction, seen under that bright morning sky, with the sun shining gayly across the cabbages and rose-bushes, the birds twittering and trilling in every tree, and the fresh odor of newly-turned earth from some spaded beds. But the chief beauty of the place was in the prospect beyond—a glorious panorama of open country spreading as far as the eye could see; a sweep of level fields near at hand; then hills and valleys farther off, mingling and blending, as only Nature's perspective can blend, gleams of brightness and patches of shade, clouds drifting, delicious "bits" of harmony and contrast everywhere, and a breadth of landscape, impossible to describe, stretching to the verge of the horizon, where it was edged by a fringe of distant forest.

Annesley was charmed; but he did not have time to indulge the luxury of sight as he would have liked. He gave one minute to admiration, then looked round for the object of his search. It was not long before he discerned a black figure walking up and down under a trellis, which covered one of the walks, and was overrun by a grape-vine. Advancing to the nearest entrance, he saw a man of middle age and decidedly sacerdotal aspect—a man who wore a black cassock, and was reading from a well-worn breviary—advancing toward him. As they came within a few feet of each other, the priest looked up. Morton took off his hat, and introduced himself at once.

"My name is Annesley," he said. "I call by appointment. Mrs. Malone told me I should find Mr. Martin here."

"I am Mr. Martin," answered the ecclesiastic, courteously. He closed his book, and, coming a step nearer, offered his hand. "Your name is not unknown to me, Mr. Annesley," he said. "I am glad to meet you. Is there any thing I can do for you?"

"You can be kind enough to answer a few questions for me," Annesley replied. "May I—but are you at leisure to attend to me now?"

"Perfectly at leisure," answered the other. "I remained at home this morning because I expected your call. I was only reading my office—you don't disturb me in the least. Shall we return to the house, or will you sit down here? The air is delightful."

"If you do not object, let us remain here, by all means. Is it necessary, though, that I should interrupt your walk? I should be sorry to do so."

"Join me, then," said Father Martin, smiling. Like everybody else, he was attracted by that gift of pleasing which the young man possessed in such remarkable degree—that happy mingling of courtesy and frankness which came to him by nature, and for which he did not deserve half as much credit as he obtained. "Exercise, fortunately, does not interfere with conversation."

Annesley was ready enough to take him at his word. A great many people can testify from experience that, when one has an awkward question to ask, or a disagreeable answer to render, to ask the one, or give the other, in the course of pedestrian or any other sort of exercise, is infinitely preferable to a cold-blooded interview face to face, and eye to eye. By this time, Morton began to feel that he was in rather an awkward position. After all, what excuse could he give, what right did he have, to be making these inquiries about Miss Tresham? If Father Martin chose to "take him up" sharply, what could he say in self-defence? He had literally no excuse to offer, literally no right to show. Yet he was in for it now; and he cleared his throat, and dashed at the heart of his subject without any preliminary.

"I hope you will not be surprised by what I am about to say," he began. "I believe you know Miss Tresham quite well. Are you aware that she has left Tallahoma suddenly and very mysteriously?"

"I was told so yesterday," answered the priest, gravely. "If it is of Miss Tresham that you have come to speak, Mr. Annesley, you may rest assured that my attention is at your command."

"Your attention!" said Annesley. They had not taken more than half a dozen steps; but he stopped short, and turned round upon the other. "Your attention!" he repeated. "Excuse me; but is nothing else at my command? Is it—is it possible you do not know where she is?"

"Until yesterday evening, I was not even aware that she had left Tallahoma. Of course, therefore, it is impossible for me to know where she is."

"You have not seen her?"

"Not since before Christmas."

"You have not heard from her?"

"I have not."

Annesley looked helplessly at him. He did

not know what to do or say next. He had been so sure that Father Martin had seen Katharine, so sure that he knew where she was, that this unexpected obstacle, this barrier of complete ignorance, seemed all at once to end every thing.

"It is no temporary absence. She is gone—gone for good!" he thought, and, thus thinking, grew so pale that the priest felt sorry for him, and, extending his hand, touched his arm.

"Be frank with me, Mr. Annesley," he said, kindly. "Believe me, you can feel no interest in Miss Tresham which I do not share. The news which I heard yesterday evening," he went on, "cost me a sleepless night. I do not understand the matter, as yet. Will you try to explain?"

"There is nothing that can be explained," said Annesley, looking very downcast. "Miss Tresham has left, nobody knows why, and gone, nobody knows where. That is why I came to you, sir. Her friends in Tallahoma are very anxious about her; and I thought you must certainly have seen her, would certainly have known where she went. When she left, the impression with Mr. and Mrs. Marks was that she had come to Saxford to see you."

"When did she come?"

"This day—no, yesterday, two weeks ago—the second of January."

"I told her, when I saw her in December, that I might be here on the Sunday following that date. Unfortunately, I was prevented from coming. Well, Mr. Annesley, has she not returned to Tallahoma since?"

"No; she has not returned."

"Nor written?"

"Not a line."

"Indeed!" said Father Martin; and he walked along silently for some time, his hands, which still held the breviary, clasped behind his back, and his eyes absently fastened on the scene outspread before him. "There is one thing," he said, at last. "Can Miss Tresham's employers throw no light on her absence? Did she give *them* no explanation of why she went?"

"She did not tell them—that is, she did not tell Mrs. Marks—any thing excepting that she was going, and that she would be back on the following Monday."

Annesley spoke very quietly, for he felt intensely depressed and despondent; but he was startled by the expression that came over Father Martin's face at his last words. This time, it was he who stopped short in his walk, and looked with wonder—it might almost have seemed with alarm—at the other.

"Are you sure that she said she would be back on Monday?" he asked.

"Yes," answered Morton, with some surprise. "She certainly told Mrs. Marks that she would be back on Monday. I was in the house an hour or two after she left it; and this assurance was given to me at the time, and repeated since."

"That settles the matter, then, Mr. Annesley," said the priest, with decision. "If Miss Tresham told Mrs. Marks that she would be back on Monday, you may be sure that she intended to return on that day—you may be certain that something which she did not foresee in leaving Tallahoma has alone prevented her doing so."

"But—"

"But is it possible you can know Miss Tresham, and doubt this?" interrupted the other, looking at him keenly.

"I have trusted, I do trust Miss Tresham implicitly," said Morton, simply. "I see that you are right—I see that this assertion of hers amply proves that in leaving Tallahoma she left it with the intention of returning. Evidently, however, she changed that intention."

"Evidently she was made to change it."

"You mean—"

"Stop a moment, Mr. Annesley, before I tell you what I mean. I have answered several of your questions. I shall ask you now to answer one of mine. Suppose we sit down? After all, I believe it is more convenient to be seated when a conversation like this is going on."

He did not wait for Annesley to accede to his proposal, but, taking the liberty which social custom grants an older man, sat down on a bench placed at the end of the trellis, and motioned the other to a place beside him.

Morton instantly obeyed.

The awkwardness of the first meeting was entirely worn off by this time, and his eagerness had reached such a point that he would probably have stood on his head if Father Martin had made that a condition for gratifying this eagerness. Their position would have enraptured an artist. The trellis behind them broke the direct beams of the sun without exactly shading them, while the beautiful scene, with its purple hills and distant forests, its shifting shadows and winsome brightness, lay like a picture at their feet. Yet how little either of them heeded it! For all the thoughts they gave, it might have been as desolate as Sahara or as bleak as Siberia! And, in the face of this, we turn round churlishly and cry out upon Nature that she does not sympathize with *us* — that, in our moments of brightness, she sometimes weeps; and, in our mourning, often smiles!

"You know Miss Tresham quite well, I believe," said the priest, after a momentary pause. "Will you tell me (I do not ask the question without a reason) if you know the history of her life?"

"I know nothing of her life, excepting that she is a West-Indian by birth, and that she lived in England as a governess," Annesley answered.

"Have you ever heard her speak of Mr. St. John?"

Morton hesitated a moment before replying.

"I have never heard her speak of Mr. St. John," he said, at length, "but I met her once when—when she was with him. Circumstances made it necessary that she should introduce us. I know nothing more than that."

"You never asked any thing more?"

"If I had felt disposed to do so—which I did not—whom could I have asked?"

"Miss Tresham herself, perhaps."

The young man colored suddenly and deeply.

"You don't know me, sir," he said. "I can't be offended, therefore, that you should think I might have been guilty of such an impertinence. But you do know Miss Tresham. You know whether she is the sort of woman with whom one would be likely to take a liberty."

The priest smiled with a genial expression that lit up pleasantly his strong Irish face.

"Your *punctilio* does you no discredit, Mr. Annesley," he said, "but I assure you I made the inquiry without supposing for a moment that you had been guilty of an impertinence, or that Miss Tresham would permit a liberty. I may interpret your answer, then, to mean that you are in complete ignorance of every thing about Mr. St. John save the mere fact of his existence."

"I could scarcely be ignorant of that," said Annesley, smiling in turn, "since I have been reminded of it very recently. Do you know that he is in Saxford?"

"I had a visit from him yesterday."

"And does *he* know nothing of Miss Tresham?"

"What he knows, Mr. Annesley, I am unable to say. What he told me I violate no confidence in telling you. He came to me, as you have done, for information about Miss Tresham."

"And you told him—?"

"That I had none to give him. I did not ask Mr. St. John to walk in the garden," he added, significantly, "and our interview was quite brief—confined merely to a business-like interchange of question and answer."

There was a silence after this.

Morton hesitated what to say next, and perhaps the priest hesitated also. Frankly as they had spoken, willing as they were to meet each other's advances, there was a barrier of reserve still between them—a barrier raised by the ignorance of the one and the knowledge of the other.

It was Annesley who, with characteristic impetuosity, dashed straight at this.

"Sir," he said, "there is a great difference between us. I know nothing about Miss Tresham's life, and you probably know every thing. Under these circumstances, I should like to ask one question, and I should be glad if you would answer it."

"I am sure you will ask nothing that I ought not to answer, Mr. Annesley."

"No, I hope not. My question is simply this: Does your knowledge give you any real advantage over my ignorance? Does it enable you to form an idea why Miss Tresham did not return to Tallahoma, and where she has gone?"

Father Martin thought a moment. The young man had certainly gone straight to the only important point — the only thing that made the difference between them of any moment. After a while he answered:

"No, Mr. Annesley, I cannot say that my knowledge enables me to form any clear idea why Miss Tresham did not return to Tallahoma, and it assuredly does not tell me where she has gone. Thus far we stand on equal ground. Of course, I have certain suspicions — but so, I fancy, have you. Can you tell me whether Mr. St. John has been in Tallahoma during the whole of these two weeks?"

"He has not left the town for a day until yesterday."

"The next thing," said Father Martin, rising to his feet, "is to inquire what Miss Tresham did while she was in Saxford. Fortunately, we have the means of information near at hand. When I arrived here, Mrs. Malone told me that she had been to inquire for me. I asked no questions, and the good woman went into no details. If you will come with me, we will ask some questions now."

Annesley rose with alacrity to follow him. They left their sheltered nook and turned into a walk that led directly to the house; but, before they had gone a dozen yards, they saw a servant opening the gate and advancing with evident haste toward them.

"A messenger for me, no doubt," said the priest, resignedly. "The faithful have heard of my arrival."

"A messenger who seems to have travelled long and hard," said Annesley. "He is splashed with mud from his hat to his shoes. The roads are not so bad either."

"Toward the southwest they are. There have been heavy rains between Hartsburg and this place lately, as I found yesterday.—Well, my man, whom are you in search of?" he said, turning to the servant.

"The priest, if you please, sir," answered the boy, who had reached the two gentlemen by this time and taken off his cap. As he did so, Morton started. To his surprise he recognized a well-known Tallahoma face—no less a personage than Mr. Warwick's body-servant.

"What, Cyrus!" he exclaimed.

"Why, if it ain't Mr. Annesley!" said Cyrus, starting in turn, and staring open-mouthed at the young man.

"What are you doing here?" Annesley asked, immediately. "Where is Mr. Warwick?"

"Mass John's in Hartsburg, sir," answered Cyrus. "I've just come from there. I rode all night, sir, over awful roads. I never saw sich holes in all my life. You could almost a-put Rattler and me both in one of 'em, and—"

"What on earth were you riding all night for?"

"It was Mass John's orders, sir," said Cyrus, in an important tone. "He told me to git here as fast as I could and give this note"—he produced one from between the folds of the lining of his cap—"to the Catholic priest in Saxford. If he wasn't here—"

"He is here," interrupted Father Martin. "I am the Catholic priest. If the note is for me, give it to me at once, my good boy."

Cyrus delivered up the note immediately, and, after one hasty glance at the address, the priest broke the seal and unfolded it. Morton, watching his face as he read, saw that he paled suddenly and strangely over the very first lines. He did not raise his eyes, however, not even after the young man felt sure that he had finished the letter. In fact, he was silent so long that at last impatience got the better of civility and Annesley spoke himself.

"Pardon me, sir, but is there any news about—about the person of whom we have been talking?"

Father Martin started and looked up—with reluctance, it was evident.

"Yes, Mr. Annesley," he said, "there is news—very painful news, I am grieved to say. In a few words," he went on hastily, as he saw the young man change color, "Miss Tresham is very ill, and I am summoned to her. Here is Mr. Warwick's note."

He extended the sheet of paper, and Annesley took it without a word. This was what Mr Warwick said:

"EAGLE HOTEL, HARTSBURG,
"Six o'clock P. M., Friday, *January 16th.*

"REV. MR. MARTIN:

"DEAR SIR: Yesterday afternoon I chanced to reach this place, and, to my surprise, found Miss Tresham (lately teaching in my brother-in-law's family in Tallahoma) lying dangerously ill here. Why or how she came here I do not know, for she had lost consciousness before I saw her; but since she is in a violent brain-fever, which leaves scarcely a hope of her life, the doctor urges me to communicate with her friends, and I therefore venture to address yourself. You are the only person who, in an emergency like the present, can possibly be able to say what she would or would not wish to be done—what steps taken, who informed of her condition. May I hope that you will come to Hartsburg at once? I shall send this by a messenger who will ride all night.

"Very respectfully,
"JOHN WARWICK."

"P. S.—I have just seen the doctor, who thinks there is no hope. I ought to add, perhaps, that I should have written to you yesterday, if I had thought of it. But, in running over the list of Miss Tresham's friends, your name only suggested itself to me a few minutes ago. Once more, I hope you will lose no time in coming."

That was all. The letter—so cold, so reticent, so full of bare details, so utterly chilling to every thought of hope—fell from Morton's hand unheeded. Dying! That was the only sound he heard; the only thought left in his brain. Dying! A black mist seemed creeping over every thing round him; the very air seemed a knell that repeated the word. Dying! Youth, health, strength, all had been hers when he saw her last; and now—

It was Father Martin's hand that touched him, and Father Martin's voice that roused him from his trance of despair.

"There is nothing in that letter which need affect you like this, Mr. Annesley," he said. "Mr. Warwick is a fallible man, and so is the doctor on whose authority he speaks. Many doctors have said that there is no hope, and lived to learn that while there is life there is always hope. Will you do something to help me on my way to Hartsburg?"

"I will do any thing," said Annesley, speaking like a man who had been stunned. "What do you want?"

"I want a horse, if you will be kind enough to go up the street and engage one for me. I would not trouble you, only my own is broken down from yesterday's journey, and is quite unequal to such a ride as the one before me."

"Engage a horse!" repeated Annesley, as if the sound of the other's speech had only dimly reached him. Then he suddenly caught a gleam of his usual intelligence. "That is quite unnecessary," he said. "My own horses are at the hotel, and are quite fresh. If you will let me drive you—"

"Let *you!*"

"Do you think that I am not going?" asked the young man, passionately. "If you don't go with me, I shall go alone—so it is all the same. No power short of death could keep me from her. I have stayed too long already. This is the end of all my scruples and doubts," he added, bitterly. "She is dying!"

"She is *said* to be dying," corrected Father Martin, obstinately. "I will believe that she is dying when I see her in the article of death—not before. If you intend to accompany me—or to allow me to accompany you—will you let me suggest that you order your horses at once?"

"I will be here in ten minutes," Annesley answered. He turned to go, caught sight of Cyrus, who stood by, inwardly astonished, but outwardly stolid — and paused. "Cyrus," he said, wistfully, "did you hear anybody say what the chances were for Miss Tresham's recovery?"

Cyrus looked down at his muddy shoes. Instinct made even him pause before telling the truth.

"I heard the folks in the hotel a-talking, sir," he said. "They thought she was mighty bad off."

"Did you hear any of them say that they thought she might get well?"

Cyrus slowly shook his head. "No, sir. They all said she was bound to die. I heard Dr. Randolph a-telling Mass John so, just before I left."

"The horses, Mr. Annesley," said Father Martin, anxiously.

"I am going," answered Annesley—and this time he did go. He left the sunny garden and its bright, beautiful prospect, without even so much as a glance; yet it was long before the scene of that awful blow passed from his memory—long before he forgot one outline of the purple hills, one gleam of the golden sunshine, or one throb of the sickening pain. As he went his way to the hotel, one cry seemed to ring through his heart—the same bitter cry that had been wrung from him unconsciously so short a time before.

"This is the end of all my scruples and doubts. She is dying!"

CHAPTER XXXII.

LIFE AND DEATH.

"Is she alive?"

This was the question which Father Martin and Annesley asked simultaneously, as the exhausted horses drew up before the door of the Eagle Hotel, and Mr. Crump came forward to receive them.

"She's alive, gentlemen — that's all I can say," the landlord answered, for he knew at once to whom they alluded. "You're the Catholic priest, I suppose, sir," he went on, addressing Father Martin. "Mr. Warwick told me to be sure and ask you to walk up-stairs as soon as you come. — The other gentleman—" He stopped, and looked at Annesley. His manner said that there had been no directions about the other gentleman.

"I'll walk up-stairs also," said Annesley springing to the ground, and throwing his reins to a boy standing near. As he was turning away, he suddenly recollected that he had driven his horses very hard, and he paused to say, "Attend to these animals very carefully, if you please. Rub them down well, and let them stand half an hour before feeding them. My servant will be on in the course of an hour or two." Then, to the landlord, "Now show us the way up stairs."

Mr. Crump was quite impressed by the young man's manner. From various causes, he had lately conceived the idea that it was a disguised princess who had been lying ill at his house for more than a week, and this was only another proof of the correctness of that opinion. One illustrious person after another had seemed strangely interested in her welfare; and now this handsome young gentleman, whose horses alone showed that he was a person of importance, sprung to the ground, and, with a pale face and a manner which agitation robbed somewhat of its usual courtesy, said, quickly, "Show us the way up-stairs."

"Certainly, sir," said Mr. Crump, with alacrity. Then, to a servant standing near, "Take off those valises, and bring them in.—This way, gentlemen."

He led the way into the house and up the staircase—talking, as he went. "The doctor left only a little while ago, sir. They think the lady won't live through the night, I believe. My wife hardly leaves her at all, and Mrs. Randolph set up night before last. Last night, two ladies arrived at the house, and they've been staying here all day to help about nursing her. One of them is Miss—"

The opening and shutting of a door on the upper floor, and the rustling of a woman's skirts along the passage, stopped his flow of words. Before anybody could speak, Miss Lester appeared at the head of the stairs, and faced the advancing party.

"Has the priest come yet, Mr. Crump?" she asked, in her quick, clear tones. Then she suddenly caught sight of Morton in the rear of Mr. Crump's portly figure, and smothered a scream. "Goodness! Is it Mr. Annesley?" she cried.

"Yes, it is I, Miss Maggie," said Morton, pressing forward. "How is she? Pray tell me how she is!"

"She's as ill as she can be," answered Miss Lester, with a little catch in her voice that sounded almost like a sob. "But I don't give up hope, Mr. Annesley; and I don't mean to, either. I know how doctors talk; I have heard too many of them," said the young lady, almost fiercely. "Dr. Randolph isn't a bit better than any of the rest. No hope, indeed! What's the good of being a doctor, if he can't cure people when they've got brain-fever as well as when they've got chills. Oh, me, if *I* was a doctor! Is that the priest, Mr. Annesley?"

"This is the priest.—Mr. Martin, Miss Lester," said Morton, hurriedly.—"Where is Warwick, Miss Maggie?"

"In his own room, I think. He was in Miss Tresham's room a little while ago; but he went out with the doctor. Mr. Crump will show you the way. Mr. Warwick is very anxious to see the pr—that is, Mr. Martin."

"Walk this way, if you please, sir," said Mr. Crump; and Father Martin followed him down the passage.

Morton, however, stood his ground. Despite his inquiry, he had not come to see Warwick, but to see Katharine, and he thought that his best means of compassing the latter point was through Miss Lester.

"Why don't you go too?" asked she, in her straightforward fashion. "If you want to hear about Miss Tresham, Mr. Warwick can tell you a great deal more than I can. He knows every thing that the doctor says, while, for my part, I am at dagger's-drawing with him. I told him to his face that he wasn't worth calling a doctor if he could not save her life, and he told me that I did not know what I was talking about. So you see I am not the person to come to for Dr. Randolph's opinion."

"It is not Dr. Randolph's opinion I want," said Annesley. "I have heard quite enough of that. I want to see Miss Tresham, Miss Maggie: and I hope you will let me do it."

"You want to see Miss Tresham?" repeated Miss Lester, in amazement. "Why, Mr. Annesley, are you crazy? Don't you know she is so ill that she would not know her own mother, if her mother came? And yet you talk of seeing her! Of course, you can't see her; nobody can, except the people who are nursing her."

"But, Miss Maggie—"

"You really can't, Mr. Annesley; and that is the end of the matter."

"Not quite the end, I hope," said Annesley. "If you are determined against me, I must ask the doctor. He won't refuse, I am sure."

"He would refuse if you were her own brother," returned Miss Lester. "I—I never heard such a thing in all my life! If it wasn't you, Mr. Annesley, I really think I should be very angry. What possible right have you to see Miss Tresham?" she demanded, in a tone that provoked Annesley to a retort.

"As much right as John Warwick, I suppose," he said. "*He* has been admitted without any difficulty, I believe."

"There is a great difference between you and Mr. Warwick," said Miss Lester, severely. "It seems to me you might see it. He is an old man" (the speaker was eighteen), "quite old enough to be Miss Tresham's father; and, besides, he found her, and sent away her doctor, and got another one, and all that sort of thing. She would be dead by this time, if it had not been for Mr. Warwick. But you—Mr. Annesley, I am astonished at you! If Miss Tresham had been ill at home in a private house, you would never have dreamed of making such a request as this."

"You are wrong; you do me great injustice," said Morton, quickly. "I would have made it all the same, under any circumstances. Miss Lester, you won't refuse me—I am sure you won't—if you only stop and consider a minute."

"I might consider a hundred minutes, Mr. Annesley, and nothing would come of it. Besides, *I* am not the sick-room authority. Oh, dear, no! There is Mrs. Randolph. You would have to get her permission after you had mine."

"Please go and ask her to come here, then. Any thing is better than wasting time like this."

Even at that hour, feminine vanity was not quite extinguished in the youthful feminine breast. Miss Lester shot a keen little shaft out of her brown eyes, and made a smart little courtesy. "Thank you for such a nice compliment, Mr. Annesley," she said, and, having said it, hurried away.

In a few minutes Mrs. Randolph came out of the sick-room, and walked up to the young man. Strange to say, he found her much more disposed than Miss Lester had been to listen kindly to his petition. She read his whole story so plainly, and she had so entirely given up all hope of Katharine's life, that the grim shadow of propriety almost ceased to terrify her, almost seemed to recede into nothingness, by the side of those two phantom-shapes—Life and Death—which had met in their last awful duel. She listened, softened, and, even while she expostulated, seemed half inclined to yield.

"What good would it do?" she asked. "Miss Tresham is quite unconscious. You could not rouse her; you could not speak to her; you could only look at her."

"That would be enough," said Morton, imploringly. "Only let me look at her—that is all I ask. Dear madam, don't refuse me! Think—only think—that, if you do, I may never see her again in life!"

His tone of unconscious pathos brought tears to Mrs. Randolph's eyes. She stopped, thought a moment, hesitated, and seemed about to yield, when a step sounded on the stairs.

"There is my husband now," said she, with an expression of relief. "I am so glad! It is quite impossible for me to decide such a matter as this; and he will be able to say exactly what is right to do. I am so glad he is coming!" she repeated, as the staircase creaked loudly under the weight of her lord, and the top of his tall hat came in sight round the curve.

For his part, the doctor was quite astonished when he looked up and saw his wife in close consultation with a handsome young stranger at the head of the stairs. He had left her in chief charge of his patient; and, knowing that she was the most vigilant of nurses, he found it hard to account for this seeming forgetfulness of duty. "What the deuce—" he began asking himself, when he caught a better view of the stranger, and recognized Mr. Annesley, of Lagrange. He knew him slightly, and they were soon shaking hands. Then the petition was referred to the doctor by the doctor's wife.

"Mr. Annesley is just from Tallahoma, from Miss Tresham's friends," said this diplomatic woman. "He is very anxious to see Miss Tresham, and—and I hardly knew what to say to him. You have come just in time to take the responsibility off my hands. You can tell him all about her."

"There is only one thing I want to be told," said Annesley, a little brusquely, "that is, whether or not I can see Miss Tresham. Surely there is no harm in it," said he, addressing Mrs. Randolph. "Surely it can't injure her," he said, addressing the doctor. Then throwing all his eloquence into an appeal to both, "Only a few minutes! I am not unreasonable, and I won't ask any thing more."

"It is neither of my wife nor of myself that you should ask that much, Mr. Annesley," said the doctor, gravely. "Miss Tresham was placed under my care by Mr. Warwick. It is to Mr. Warwick, therefore, that you must apply for permission to see her. I can only say as a medical man whether or not such a visit would injure her."

"And may I ask what you do say?"

"That the visits of a hundred people could have no possible ill effect upon her now. Her disease has to-day passed from violent delirium to its second and more dangerous stage—that of stupor, which is deepening gradually into the insensibility that precedes death."

Annesley shrank. Alas! who does not shrink

when that terrible word is spoken with the cold, calm deliberation of scientific certainty in regard to some life to save which we would freely tell out our blood, drop by drop—for which we would give the very throbs of our heart, the very hours that come to us filled to the brim with the keen, fresh elixir of vitality, the very powers of health, and strength, and possible enjoyment, that mock us so bitterly at such a time!

"Doctor," said he, huskily, "is there no hope?"

Other people had asked the doctor this question, and to each of them he had given that decided answer which had so roused Miss Lester's scorn. In the name of every symptom of the case, of every teaching of experience, of every data of medical knowledge, he had replied, "No hope."

Now, for the first time, he hesitated. Now, for the first time, he felt inclined to rack his brain for something of a temporizing, it might even be of a consoling nature, felt inclined to evade the direct answer, as he often evaded it when people came to him with the extreme of love and anguish quivering in their voices to ask this same question, "Doctor, is there no hope?"

"I might answer that, while there is life, there is always hope, Mr. Annesley," he said, "but that is a mere generality which means nothing. If you want my honest opinion of this particular case, I can give it to you. Every symptom up to this point has been unfavorable. The disease has not yielded an inch to the remedies employed, but seems to be advancing steadily to a fatal termination. So far I have not seen a single sign which encourages me to hope that the patient may rally. Yet, as a medical man, I cannot say that such rallying would be impossible. In the first place, recoveries take place more frequently from meningitis occurring as an attendant upon other diseases than when the complaint is original. Miss Tresham's disorder *is* secondary meningitis. That, therefore, is our first ground for hope—slender though it be. In the second place, the disease has three stages: violent excitement, first, when it can almost always be easily arrested; stupor next, when the chances of safety are very much diminished; and, lastly, coma, or profound unconsciousness, which precedes and gradually sinks into death. Recovery from this last state is so unusual that it is hardly possible to count upon it. Nevertheless, in rare instances, it does occur—or rather the total prostration which sometimes follows the cure of violent inflammation, simulates the symptoms that mark the closing stage of the worst cases. This is our second ground for hope. Slight as it is, I shall act upon it. I shall resort to stimulants. If the symptoms are organic, they can do no harm, for death must necessarily take place; if merely functional, they may be the means of saving her life."

"And if your worst fears are realized—if the last stage is really here?"

"In that case to-night decides every thing—death must ensue before morning."

"And if she lives through the night?"

"Let us wait until the night is past, before we ask that question," said the doctor, almost solemnly. "Now I must go. If you wish to see my patient, Mr. Annesley, I can only refer you to Mr. Warwick."

He made a short little bow and went away, followed by his wife. As for Annesley, he stood still and watched them with a feeling of blank hopelessness impossible to describe. To-night! He had said that to-night would decide every thing! Involuntarily the young man looked out of a window near which he stood, and shivered. The shades of evening were falling. The sun was gone, the gray mantle of twilight was enwrapping every thing, a lovely crescent moon was cradled softly over the fringing western clouds, while faint and more faint the burning glow of sunset was fading from the sky. To-night! And night was coming—night was here! It could not be, he cried out, fiercely yet vainly—ah, how vainly! The darkness seemed like some horrible monster advancing with slow, stealthy steps to do its horrible work; to seize its passive victim from those strong arms of helpless, outstretched agony; to bear away the grace, the beauty, the glory of life, under its sombre pall, and leave only a cold white shadow of mortality to meet the gaze of the sun when he came once more in pomp and splendor from his royal couch. O fall of night! O long hours of darkness! How terrible ye are to watchers like these, to those who cry, "If she can but live through to-night!" The awful death of light—awful sometimes to the shrinking soul when there is no cause like this to dread it—seems at such times invested with a horror all its own. When morning comes—ah, morning! Will she ever see it?"

"Can you show me Mr. Warwick's room?" said Annesley to a servant passing by.

"Number thirteen—right down the passage, sir," answered the man, hastily. "You can't miss the door."

To number thirteen, right down the passage, Annesley accordingly took his way, and soon found that, indeed, it would have been impossible for him to miss the door, especially as it was standing open and Father Martin was in the act of coming out.

"It is really impossible for me to advise you, Mr. Warwick," he was saying. "You must act according to your own judgment in the matter."

"That is harder than you think," Mr. Warwick replied.

And just then Annesley appeared.

Father Martin, who was looking very pale and grave, nodded to the young man, and walked slowly away, while Mr. Warwick extended his hand cordially.

"I am glad to see you, Morton," he said. "I heard that you were in the house, and I was just coming in search of you. I suppose you have seen Randolph, and there is nothing for me to tell you."

"I saw him a moment ago," Morton answered. "He has spoken very plainly. He says that every thing depends on to-night, and that the chances are all against life."

"I suppose you have heard how I found her?"

"No, not yet."

The lawyer told him in a few brief words, adding: "It is quite useless to make wishes with regard to what is past; but, if I had reached here a day earlier, all this might have been spared. The treatment of an infamous quack brought on the disease of which she is dying; and, if Randolph had seen her twelve—nay, six—hours earlier—but this is folly. You heard the news in Saxford, the priest tells me."

"I was with him when he received your note. I had gone there to try and find out something about her. I"—he paused involuntarily. Men do not readily speak to each other with regard to matters of sentiment or feeling, do not easily conquer the strong reluctance to show the soft kernel of their natures, instead of putting forward the harder rind which characterizes them in every degree and condition of life. Even when circumstances force them to this expression, they give it with a hesitation which shows how much it goes against the grain. It certainly went against the grain with Morton now. According to his own desire, he would not have made a *confidant* of anybody; but to make a *confidant* of John Warwick—the irony of events could not go any farther, he thought. Still, he must speak plainly, if he wished to see Katharine: and plainly, therefore, he proceeded to speak.

"Perhaps I don't need to tell you, Mr. Warwick, that I have loved Miss Tresham for a long time," he said. "That love is my excuse for coming here, and for asking your permission to see her—since chance and your own kindness have placed her under your care. I can scarcely hope to interest you by speaking of my own feelings," he went on hastily—"but her death would be to me a terrible grief."

"I am sure of it," said the lawyer, with kind gravity. "You are right in conjecturing that I was aware of your love for Miss Tresham," he went on; "I have observed it, and I can understand that it brought you here, and that it makes you anxious to see her, now that you are here. But, of course, you have been told that she is insensible. It seems to me it would be more painful than gratifying to you to see her in that state."

"All I ask is to see her," said Morton. "The doctor says it could do no harm—but he referred me to you for permission."

"To me! I—stop a minute—let me think," said Mr. Warwick, in reply. He rose and walked to the window, where he stood gazing, as Annesley had done, on the gathering twilight and falling night. Objects were indistinct by this time, and his tall, dark figure was little more than an outline to Morton, who sat quite still beside the fire. After a while he came back, and, standing on the hearth, addressed the young man.

"I have been thinking of your request," he said, "and I have decided that it is you, not I, who can tell best whether or not I ought to accede to it. Your own love for Miss Tresham is no reason why you should be allowed to see her. The only thing that would give you that right would be her love for you; and, consequently, her assumed consent. Understand this, and say yourself whether or not you shall see her."

Morton was startled. "Mr. Warwick, you place me in a hard position," he said.

"The decision rests with yourself," repeated Mr. Warwick; and, having said this, he turned and went back to the window.

Annesley sat and thought. For a short time he was quite puzzled, but at length he began to understand Mr. Warwick's meaning, and to appreciate the bearing of the question which had been thus unexpectedly thrust upon him. It was a strange position, certainly. To decide, at the bidding of another man, whether the woman he loved, loved him in return; to count over her words, and looks, and intangible shades of tone, and to reckon if all these proofs went for or against his cause. At any other time, or for any other reason, nobody would have been quicker than Morton to call himself a miserable puppy for doing such a thing as this; but now it was imperative to arrive at some conclusion—it was the only hope, the only condition, of seeing her. Honestly, then, and with a strange, wistful leaning toward his own side, as far removed from vanity as one thing could possibly be removed from another, he went over the ground, faithfully summed up all the evidence, and, at last, made his decision. Then he rose and crossed the floor to Mr. Warwick, who had waited patiently at the window.

"Mr. Warwick, I think you will agree with me that this is not a time for false delicacy," he said, with quiet simplicity. "You have put me on my honor to speak the truth: forgive me if what I believe to be the truth sounds like vanity or unpardonable presumption. I have asked myself honestly if I think Miss Tresham would marry me, and, honestly also, I have answered, 'I think she would.'"

"That is enough," said Mr. Warwick, turning, and, a good deal to Morton's surprise, offering his hand. "Yes, I agree with you that this is no time for false delicacy. Your candor does you more credit than any mock modesty would. I left the question to yourself; but, since you have expressed your opinion, I will tell you that it is mine also. Miss Tresham is not a woman to wear her heart on her sleeve; but, I think if you had asked her to marry you, she would have said 'Yes.' You have my best wishes that she may say it yet," he added, smiling gravely. "Now we will go to her room."

"You will find Miss Vernon here," Mr. Warwick went on, as they walked down the passage together. "She and Miss Lester arrived at the hotel yesterday, and, finding Miss Tresham ill, they remained. They are both very kind; and Miss Vernon, in particular, has proved herself a most excellent and capable nurse. This is the room."

He stopped Annesley, who was passing on, and tapped lightly at the door before which he paused. It was opened by Mrs. Randolph, who at once admitted him. She smiled when she saw Morton, but said nothing; and, leaving them to close the door, went back softly to the bed.

Mr. Warwick passed in first, and Annesley followed. There was nothing repulsive, nothing suggestive of pain, or struggle, or death, in the scene before him. On the contrary, every thing was very quiet and peaceful. A sick-room, undoubtedly, but hardly a death-chamber, one would have thought, looking at the exquisite neatness of all the arrangements, at the white bed with its recumbent figure, at the shaded light, the soft, pretty glow of the fire, the figures sitting or standing here and there. Every thing was very subdued. If they had spoken in tones of thunder, they could not have roused that motionless sleeper, or raised those heavy lids; but, none the less, an unconscious impulse made them tread softly and speak low. Around the bed two or three were grouped. Father Martin, with his hands clasped behind his back, stood just before Annesley, as the latter approached. When a touch made him draw aside, the young man looked down on the face he had come to see.

A motionless face, out of which the burning fever flush had faded long since, a face that was almost as white as the pillows on which it rested, that was sunken in the lines a little, and bore on its serene features something of a shade of the awful change that was to come. To-night! Did they say she would die to-night? Morton could realize it, now that he had seen her. Fair, and gentle, and robbed of all terror, as that quiet sleep looked, it was not so fair and gentle but that it showed the deadly meaning underneath. It was *too* still, it was *too* full of unchanging repose. The longer he looked, the more he felt inclined to doubt whether, indeed, it was life or death on which he gazed. At last he could look no longer. With a gasp he raised his eyes, and met the gaze of another pair of eyes on the opposite side of the bed—eyes whose beauty he had known long, but whose tenderness he never appreciated until he saw them now shining like stars upon him from Irene Vernon's face.

"How is her pulse?" he heard Mr. Warwick ask the doctor, who came forward and bent over the patient.

"Feeble and thread-like — apparently failing," was the reply. "There is nothing for it but to push the stimulants. I have very little hope in them; but, at least, they can do no harm; while, as it is, she is sinking rapidly."

They went on speaking, but Annesley moved away. This was so different from any thing he had anticipated, that he was obliged to go to the other side of the room to steady himself. They had all warned him that it would be so, but, nevertheless, he had fancied something very dif ferent—something like a scene in a book, something that would sweeten all the rest of life with a taste of love's divine elixir. But this! To see her pass from him like this, lapsing from earth's sleep to the deeper sleep of death, without one gleam of consciousness, one parting glance, one farewell word—surely, this was hard! He had set aside all the obstacles, and traversed all the space that divided them; he had won his point, and was here in the same room with her; yet what were those other barriers to that which separated them now? Ah, love can do wonders! it can break through prison-bolts, it can climb mountains, it can cross oceans; but it has never yet been able to send one single tone into the ear that death has dulled, to win one single glance from the eyes that death has closed.

After a while Miss Vernon came up to him, and held out her hand. "Don't despair, Mr. Annesley! She is very, very ill; but I think the doctor has not quite given up hope," she said, gently.

"She is dying!" answered Morton. He appreciated it now, and the realization of the inevitable brought a sort of stunned quietude with it.

"I am not sure of that," said Miss Vernon, quickly. "I have seen a great deal of sickness in my life, and seen people who were desperately—so desperately—ill, sometimes recover, that I cannot despair of anybody. Besides—you may be surprised to hear this, Mr. Annesley—but Miss Tresham does not look to me like a dying person. And, what is more, Mrs. Randolph—whose experience is, of course, greater than mine—says the same thing."

"Don't try to give me hope, Miss Vernon," he said, with a faint smile. "Think how terrible it will be to-morrow."

"But you need some hope. I see that you have given up to despair."

"I was madly full of hope until I saw her. After that, I should be blind not to perceive that the doctor is right — that there is no hope."

He turned away, and, leaving her abruptly, went to a window near at hand. The solemn curtain of night met his gaze—a deep, dark shadow lay over all things, shadow hardly lighted by the faint, tender radiance of the young moon, or the steady glory of a myriad stars. It had come, it was here, that fateful time of darkness in which Life and Death would fight their last battle!

Presently Miss Lester accosted him. "Mr. Annesley, you have had nothing to eat. Come with me, and I will take you down-stairs and ask Mrs. Crump to give you some hot coffee and supper all to yourself."

"Thank you, Miss Maggie, I am not hungry," he answered. But, when she pressed the matter, he went down—careless what he did, or what became of him. He drank the coffee, and listened to Mrs. Crump's account of all that had happened, as in a dream. After some time, he found himself back up-stairs—in his own room, this time—pacing to and fro, or sitting motionless before the fire, waiting, listening, strung to the highest pitch of nervous anxiety—for they had promised to call him whenever "any change" should come.

So the long hours passed, midnight came, and it was at midnight that the doctor had said the flickering taper would be most likely to go out. In the sick-room all was quiet. The nurse nodded on one side of the fire, and Miss Lester dozed on the other: the doctor had gone into Mr. Warwick's room to lie down, leaving strict directions for the administering of the stimulants, and strict orders that he was to be called at the least sign of change. Mrs. Randolph was sleeping lightly in a deep arm-chair, while Irene Vernon, at the bed, kept vigilant guard over the sick girl. Exactly at midnight, she gave another dose of the stimulant, then remembering what the doctor had said, she laid her finger on the pulse. It crept beneath her touch like a thin, feeble thread, but still she started, and motioned Mr. Warwick, who was standing near, to bend down.

"Feel it," she said. "I may be deceived, but it seems to me it is stronger and fuller than when I felt it last."

She took away her finger, and he laid his own in its place. Her eyes were on him, and she saw that he too started.

"It is stronger and fuller," he said. "There is a change of some sort. I must go and call Randolph."

He left the room, and was passing down the passage, when a door on the right opened, and Annesley appeared.

"Well," he said, quickly, "has it come?"

"There is no change for the worse," answered Mr. Warwick. "I am only going to wake Randolph. See for yourself, if you like," he added, as Morton looked at him a little doubtfully.

In two minutes, the doctor stood in the room, and felt the pulse—his face watched by the others with breathless anxiety.

"There is a little change," he said, guardedly; "but it may be only a fluctuation of the disease—a flicker of the taper. We shall soon see. Press the stimulants, Miss Vernon—shorten the time between the doses. A few more hours will end all suspense."

The hours crept on—slowly, heavily, every minute a battle-ground with Death, who sullenly retreated step by step; not vanquished, only kept at bay. It was a night that nobody who was present ever forgot, for it is seldom, indeed, that the issue of this terrible conflict hangs on such a trembling balance, that one single error of judgment, one single fault of skill, would throw the advantage so irretrievably into the hands of an adversary who never relents. For hours it was impossible to tell whether Life or Death was winning the victory—the variations being so slight, the fluctuations so many. Nobody dared press the doctor with questions, yet everybody felt what a neck-and-neck race he was running, as he sat by the bed, and scarcely once took his finger from that slender, feeble pulse, steadily pursuing the same treatment which he had so hopelessly begun, and stimulating by every possible means the sinking system. Not once during all those hours did the set, anxious expression of his face relax, or his lips utter a word of hope. He worked with unflagging energy; but whether or not he found any signs of encouragement, no one could tell. When the first light of the cold, gray dawn began to steal into the room, the issue of the battle was still doubtful—the victory was still to be won.

Annesley, who had been in and out of the room a dozen times since he had met Mr. Warwick at midnight, was walking up and down the passage (on which a soft cloth, to deaden all sound of foot-steps, had been laid), as this chill dawn began to break. Full as he was of other thoughts, he stood still to watch it. A less enlivening occupation could hardly be imagined, especially on a winter morning, when mind and body are alike depressed by long watching at a sick-bed. In summer there is something bright and rejoicing in the birth of color, the songs of birds, the dewy freshness of awaking Nature; but a winter-day dawn is one of the most dreary things in existence. How stealthily the gray light comes! How ghost-like the white mist looks creeping along the ground, or wreathing into phantom-shapes among the bare, black boughs of trees! How barren and bereft of all beauty the earth seems! Annesley looked around him drearily, then turned and began his promenade again. Night itself was better than this, he thought. Up and down he walked with the daylight growing clearer and clearer around him, all unheeded, or, if noticed, only a discordance. The east began to glow into royal beauty, flinging out her crimson and golden banners, with a gorgeous affluence that made the glories of sunset pale into insignificance. At last, with one magnificent bound, the sun uprose, and sent his long lines of level gold flashing across the earth. One of them darted into the passage where Annesley paced, and streamed on Katharine's door, like the touch of a burning finger. At that very moment, the door opened, and Irene Vernon came out—the sunshine encircled her like a halo of luminous glory, as Annesley hurried forward to meet her.

"You want me?" he asked, breathlessly.

"Yes," she answered eagerly, with a smile —was it the smile or the sunshine that dazzled him so?—"I want you. The doctor has spoken at last, and he says— Oh, Mr. Annesley, thank God—that we may hope."

CHAPTER XXXIII.

MRS. GORDON'S SUSPICION.

A FEW days later, Katharine was sufficiently out of danger, and sufficiently in the way of recovery, for Mr. Warwick to think of returning to Tallahoma. He could not see her, or enter into any explanation with her before he went, for the doctor absolutely forbade any exciting presence or exciting topics; but he made every possible arrangement for her comfort, and finally took his departure, with the assurance that she could not be in better hands. She was still at the hotel, for the doctor peremptorily negatived removal; but it was understood that Miss Lester would claim her as soon as she was well enough to move. There had been quite a contest between this young lady and Mrs. Randolph on the subject, but the former had carried the point in her spirited, self-willed way. Mrs. Randolph was forced to resign her claim, and it was settled (as much as any thing could be settled without the consent of the person most concerned) that Miss Tresham was to be handed over to Miss Lester as soon as Dr. Randolph would give his sanction to such a step. Meanwhile, Miss Lester and Miss Vernon at last took their departure from the hotel, and, much to the relief of the down-trodden Lesters, *père* and *mère*, accomplished their return to Bellefont—the name of the Lester plantation. From this place, however, they made daily incursions on the Eagle Hotel, and sent messengers with game and fruit, and a hundred delightful things, at all hours of the day. As for Annesley, he did not trouble himself to go back to Lagrange, but quietly took up his quarters with Godfrey Seymour—who, like the Lesters, lived near Hartsburg—and he, too, left his compliments and inquiries regularly with Mrs. Crump, for Mrs. Crump's patient.

To this patient the sight and sounds of life came back very slowly, giving to life itself a dream-like unreality. It was only by gradual degrees that consciousness returned once more—that time and the things of time again asserted a claim over the spirit that had stood on the very threshold of eternity. All the weeks of pain, and the days of terrible danger, were blotted into nothingness; so that when Katharine at last opened her eyes to the things around her, she found herself in a new, unintelligible world. Her very arrival in Hartsburg was one of the memories that had gone from her forever, so her complete surprise at the strange faces and strange surroundings about her may be imagined.

"Where am I?—how did I come here?—who are you all?" she asked. But, receiving no satisfactory reply, she felt too languid and indifferent to press the matter. Day after day she lay in that profound rest which makes the luxury of convalescence, too weak to think, too weak to remember, too weak to conjecture, too weak to do any thing save smile faintly in the doctor's cheerful face, answer Mrs. Randolph's or Mrs. Crump's kind inquiries, and for the remainder of the time lie quite still, watching the sunshine on the window-sill, and Mom Elsie's black fingers as they sent the bright knitting-needles swiftly to and fro. As yet, she had seen no familiar face, heard no familiar name—not even the names of Miss Lester and Miss Vernon, not even the name of Mr. Warwick.

"I'll run no risks," said the doctor to the latter. "Take yourself off to Tallahoma—the sooner the better. Leave her in my hands, and when you come back—we will think about letting you see her then. That handsome scamp, young Annesley, had the impudence to come to me with a request of the same sort to-day," he added, smiling. "I assure you, I cut him short. He wanted a message delivered. I told him I should like to catch myself playing Mercury, or Apollo, or Cupid, or whoever is supposed to be the messenger of love-stricken youths, to a patient just out of a brain-fever."

"I need not trouble you with any thing of the kind, then, I suppose?"

"You may trouble *me* with it as much as you please; but, whether or not I'll trouble Miss Tresham—well, candidly, that is quite another matter."

Denied all access to Katharine in this decided manner, Mr. Warwick had no alternative but to take his departure, and leave her, as requested, in the doctor's hands. He did so unwillingly; but time, business engagements, and, above all, the remembrance of Mrs. Gordon's anxiety, pressed him hard. Excepting on a matter of life and death, he absolutely could not remain away from Tallahoma any longer. Feeling this, he made up his mind to go, and, having made up his mind, he was not long in carrying resolve into execution. On Wednesday morning, the twenty-first of January, he drove away from the Eagle Hotel, and, leaving Miss Tresham to be slowly won back to health by comfort and care, turned his face homeward.

Wednesday night he spent in Saxford. Thursday afternoon he was driving along the familiar roads of Lagrange, and fast nearing Tallahoma, when he met a squarely-built, middle-aged man, dressed in a suit of brown homespun, riding a horse (also squarely built) of deep-bay color, with whom he stopped to speak.

"Well, Shields, how are you?" said he.

"Pretty tol'able, I thank you, Mr. Worruck. How do you do yourself, sir?" answered Mr. Shields, with a sort of stolid surprise at the sudden encounter. "I'm glad to see you back. How did you leave the little boy?"

"Quite well, and in a fair way to be contented, I think. Has not Mrs. Gordon received my letter?"

"I don't know, sir. I haven't seen her for nigh about a week. I was at the house Tuesday; but she was onwell, they said, and, as I'd no partic'lar business, I didn't disturb her."

"Any news in Tallahoma?" asked Mr. Warwick, as he saw that the man held his ground and did not pass on as he had expected him to do.

"Well," said Mr. Shields, speaking slowly, but with evident unction—"well, yes. There's news in Tallahoma that I'm sorry to tell you, Mr. Worruck. The bank was broke into last night, and robbed of a hundred thousand dollars, they say."

"What!"

"It's a fact, sir. The excitement about it in town is tremenjous. You might a' knocked me down with a feather when I heard the news myself; and, as for Mr. Marks, he was as white as a sheet when I saw him this morning. They say the first thing he knowed of it was when he went down to the bank as usual, and found the locks all broke, and Hugh Ellis—"

"When did it happen?" demanded Mr. Warwick.

"Last night."

"Is there any suspicion as to who the thief, or thieves, were?"

"There's a suspicion of its bein' a man that went to the bank yisterday; but nobody knows who he is, nor where he is neither, for he's not about town to-day."

"Well," said Mr. Warwick, "this is bad news, and I must hurry on to town. I will stop and see Mrs. Gordon, however. Good-evening, Shields."

He nodded, and Cyrus drove on, leaving Mr. Shields somewhat crestfallen in the middle of the road. He looked regretfully after the vanishing carriage, and then pursued his way in rather a subdued frame of mind. He did not exactly think to himself that it was hard to be cut short in this summary fashion, when he would have liked to talk over all the particulars of the matter, as he had talked them over twenty times before that day; but, none the less, it *was* hard. Mr. Warwick, as he drove on, did not think of what a real and sensible pleasure he had deprived the poor man.

His road led him directly past the gates of Mortòn House. When he reached those gates, he turned in. Ten minutes later, he was shown by Harrison into Mrs. Gordon's room. She was sitting before the fire, leaning back in a deep arm-chair with a listless languor that struck Mr. Warwick at once. She did not even turn her head when the door opened, and her abstraction was so deep that he reached her side without attracting her attention.

"You see I have got back, Mrs. Gordon," he said, quietly. But, quietly as he spoke, he could not avoid startling her. She bounded in her chair at the first tone of his voice; then turned quickly, and tried to rise—did rise half-way, but, through weakness or agitation, sank back again.

"You!" she said, faintly. "I—how you startled me!"

"I see I did," he said, with some contrition. "I ought to have known better. I thought you would have heard me come in."

"No; I did not."

"I am back, you see."

"Yes, I see." She rose now, and held out her hand. "I am very glad to see you. And Felix?"

"I left Felix very well, and almost contented; no doubt, he is quite contented by this time."

Instantly her eyes filled with tears.

"Contented!" she repeated. "Away from me! Ah, that is hard—harder than you think! Yet I am glad to hear it. Sit down, pray, and tell me all—every thing—about him. I am hungry, heart-hungry, to hear."

Pressed for time, and burning with impatience, as he was, he sat down and told the story of his journey, with all those details that every woman loves to hear, and few—very few—men know how to give. She listened to him eagerly—drank in every word, indeed—while he described the kind people (old friends of his own) with whom he had placed Felix, the child's first despair, and subsequent partial content. After every thing, even to the last parting, had been told, he rose.

"I would not leave you so soon," he said, in answer to her glance of pained surprise; "but I heard some news, a few minutes ago, which startled me very much, and I feel that I ought to hasten into town. Besides, even for your sake, I had better go. I may find a letter from Mr. Lloyd. You know it was arranged that he should write to me instead of to yourself."

"Yes, I know."

As she stood up to give him her hand at parting, the light shone full on her face from a window just opposite, and he saw that it was even more pale and hollow than when he went away.

"You look badly," he said. "Have you been ill, or only fretting?"

"I have had nothing to do since you left but nurse my fancies," she answered, with a sad smile, "until I am half sick with nervous terror about Felix. I have wished a thousand times that I had not sent him from me, or that I had gone with him."

"It is not too late yet," said he, kindly. "Shall I take you to him? Only say the word, and I will do so."

"No," answered she; "don't tempt me. I might go if it were not that it would look so cowardly, so much as if I had reason to be afraid—and I have none. Let him come! He can do me no harm—now that Felix is gone."

"He could annoy you more than you think."

"Let him try!" Something like the fire and glow of combat swept into the face that, an instant before, had been so pale and listless. 'At all events, he shall find me here, if he chooses to come. Don't talk of this, however. Talk of yourself, instead. Let me thank you for having been so kind to me—and so considerate, which even the kindest people often fail to be. But I must not detain you. I see how impatient you are to be gone, and I do not wonder—I have heard of that dreadful robbery. I am so very sorry for Mr. Marks! You will come to see me again soon—will you not?"

"Can you doubt it? I would not go now but for the news of that robbery of which you speak. I must see poor Marks at once, and try to stir him up to some energetic measures for discovering the perpetrators of such an outrage. I can imagine how stunned and hopeless he is. Good-evening. If there is a letter from Lloyd, I will send it to you at once."

He shook hands with her, and was starting to leave the room, when she called him back. Like most women, she had still a "last word," and he was doomed to hear it. He could not help feeling a little impatient, as the best-natured people will feel at such detentions when they are burning to get away—yet if he had only known the importance of that word, he would hardly have grudged the time necessary to hearing it.

"Mr. Warwick," she said, when he turned back, "I am half ashamed to speak—and yet I think I ought to. It is better to give a useless hint, than to withhold one that may be of even the least service. Don't think me full of nervous fancies, when I ask if you have thought of St. John in connection with this robbery?"

Mr. Warwick started, and his face changed so much that she noticed and was surprised at it.

"No. How could I?" he replied.

"Well—I have. I don't mean to accuse him, I simply mean to say that *I thought of him* as soon as I heard of it. Was this an instinct, or merely a fancy? I don't pretend to know; but I think it right to direct your attention to him as a measure of precaution."

"What! is he so worthless a scoundrel that you should think he would commit an open robbery like this?"

"He has lived by cheating and robbing—one way or another—all his life. Why not this way as well as any other? If the chance of success was good, and the chance of detection not great, I don't believe he would have hesitated a moment."

"You say this deliberately? Stop, Mrs. Gordon—think. It is a terrible thing to make such a charge. Do you say it deliberately, weighing it well?"

"I say it deliberately, weighing it well. Whether or not he is guilty of this crime, I believe him capable of it."

"But alone—unaided!"

"How do you know that he *is* alone, unaided? God forgive me if I am judging him unjustly, but a man like him soon makes friends, and—accomplices."

Mr. Warwick did not answer. To her surprise, he turned away and looked in the fire. The peculiarity of his manner, the expression of his face, struck her. Involuntarily, she wondered what was the meaning of it—what there was in this supposition to affect him so evidently and so strongly? Before she could ask any questions, however, he turned round again—a question on his own lip, and by no means one that she had anticipated.

"Have you spoken of this before, Mrs. Gordon?" he asked. "Have you mentioned this suspicion to any one else?"

"No," she answered, wonderingly. "Even if I had felt disposed to do so, I have seen no one to whom I could have mentioned it. I heard of the robbery from the servants. I see nobody else."

"Will you do me a favor—a great personal favor?"

"Certainly," she said, wondering still more. "Can you ask me such a thing—you who have just sacrificed time, business, every thing to serve me? Tell me what the favor is, and be assured that it is granted beforehand."

"Then do not mention this suspicion to any one else. I have a particular reason for asking this," he added, as he saw the astonishment legible on her face. "For one thing, if it should be correct, it might reach Mr. St. John's ears, and put him on his guard. Promise me"—he spoke earnestly—"that you will not mention the matter again."

"Since you ask it as a personal favor, of course I will not. Otherwise—but I shall try not to be curious. You must have some very good reason for this, Mr. Warwick."

"I have."

"Reason that I am not to hear?"

"Not just now, at all events. I have not time, even if I had inclination (and, frankly, I have not inclination at present), to tell you. May I rely on your promise?"

"I hope you may—we Mortons are proud of always keeping our word."

"I do rely on it, then. Now, good-by. If I do not leave at once, it will be sunset before I reach Tallahoma."

"One word! I see you think I will never let you go; but it is only one word more. Have you seen any thing of Morton Annesley? His mother is very anxious about him."

"Why should she be anxious? Surely he is old enough to take care of himself."

"He has gone she does not know where, but she strongly suspects that it is in search of—your sister's governess, who left here very abruptly, several weeks ago."

"Tell me something about that," said he, forgetting even the bank for a moment. "Do you know why she went?"

"I do not know, but I have suspected that she was sent by St. John in search of Felix. I found—after you left—that he came here to see her, and only discovered me accidentally. There is some tie of close connection between them, evidently. I—I absolutely went to ask her to stay here as you advised, and I found *him* with her. God only knows how grateful I was for having done so. If I had brought her back with me, I might have been weak enough to tell her all that he wishes to know."

Mr. Warwick said not a word. Once again, that incomprehensible expression came over his face which Mrs. Gordon had noticed before. He looked at his boots meditatively, and, after a while, she went on:

"If Felix had not been under *your* care, I scarcely know how I could have borne the cruel suspense, the cruel doubts and fears Miss Tresham's absence has caused me. I am sure she went for this purpose—this alone—and now that I see you before me, my heart begins to fail once more. Ah, tell me, is he quite safe?—is there no possibility of her reaching him?"

"You may set your mind at rest on that point," he answered, quietly. "There is not the least danger of his being found by any agent or messenger of Mr. St. John. But I am forgetting myself. I must go. Once more, good-by."

He shook hands again hastily, and left the room before she had time for another word. A minute or two later, he was driving at a rapid pace down the avenue.

CHAPTER XXXIV.

MR. WARWICK'S INVESTIGATION.

Dusk was setting in when Mr. Warwick entered Tallahoma, and, as the Marks house was the first on that side of the village, Cyrus had already drawn up to the gate, and his master was about to descend from the carriage, when the latch was lifted and a servant came out.

"Mass John!" he exclaimed, as, notwithstanding the dim light, he recognized Mr. Warwick.

"How are you, Tom? Has your master come home yet?"

"No, sir; master ain't been home since mornin', and mistiss is just now sent me to tell him to come home to supper. The bank was robbed last night, Mass John, and—"

"Yes, I know.—Drive on, Cyrus—to the bank.—Tell your mistress, Tom, that I have come, and that I have gone on to meet your master."

Mr. Warwick was so occupied with his own thoughts that he did not notice any thing, did not even look out of the window, as he drove through the village, or he would have seen his brother-in-law, who was plodding homeward, with step most unlike his usual brisk business-walk, his head declined, and his eyes fixed vacantly on the pavement. Thus abstracted, the carriage passed him unperceived, and in a few minutes stopped at the bank.

"You need not wait," said Mr. Warwick, alighting hastily. He opened the gate, and had proceeded half-way up the walk, when, recollecting his promise to Mrs. Gordon about the letter, he went back and called to Cyrus, who was driving off. "Make haste home with the horses," he said, "and, as soon as you have given them to Jacob, go to the post-office, get my letters, and bring them here as quickly as possible."

The front-door of the bank was standing wide open, and, as he was entering the passage, he heard the sound of a key turning in its lock. The next instant, the clerk of the bank, who had just been locking the door of the cashier's room, preparatory to going out, came toward him. It was too dark to see the young man's face; but, recognizing his figure and movements, the lawyer spoke.

"Well, Hugh, I understand you have had a terrible piece of work here," he said, holding out his hand.

Poor Hugh Ellis had borne up manfully until

this moment; but his courage and power of self-control broke down now. Seizing the hand which Mr. Warwick offered, he wrung it hard, made a desperate effort to swallow a huge lump that had been stationary in his throat all day, giving him the constant sensation of choking, failed in his effort, and suddenly burst into tears.

"Come, come," said Mr. Warwick, kindly; "this won't do! There's no good in crying over a thing, you know. What we must think of is to ferret out the thieves and get the money back."

"Oh!—if y-ou *could*—do that, Mr. Warwick!" cried Hugh, sobbingly.

"It must be done. So come back into the bank with me, and let me hear all about the business. Where's Marks?"

"Just gone home to supper; but he said he would be back in half an hour," answered Hugh, with animation; for his heart was already lightened, and his spirits raised, by the confident manner of the lawyer.

Leading the way back to the cashier's room, he unlocked the door, groped his way to the fireplace—the windows being all shut close, the room was in pitch darkness—felt about on the mantel-piece until he found a box of matches, and struck a light. As he turned, with it in his hand, toward Mr. Warwick, who was advancing, the latter started in astonishment, exclaiming:

"Good Heavens! what is the matter with you?"

He might well ask the question, since the face before him was so bruised and disfigured that he could scarcely believe it to be that of Hugh Ellis. The lower part of one cheek was swollen out of all shape, and very much discolored, while the eye on the other side of the face was half closed, and surrounded with pieces of sticking-plaster, crossed diagonally by narrow strips of black court-plaster to hold them in place—the countenance altogether presenting an appearance at once ludicrous and pitiable.

"Did you have a fight with the burglars?" he demanded, his mind leaping to this conclusion before the young man had time to speak.

"Not much of a fight," answered Hugh, in a tone of mortification. "They were two to one, and too much for me, though—"

"But you saw them?" interrupted the other, eagerly.

"Yes, I saw them."

"This is better than I had hoped. Sit down, Hugh, and tell me all about it. Don't waste time, for minutes may be valuable here; but don't slur over particulars, as it is generally by some trifle that a discovery is made in cases of this sort. Go on."

He took a chair as he spoke, and Hugh, putting the candle down upon the counter, followed his example, and proceeded to comply with his request.

"I went to bed about eleven o'clock, as usual, Mr. Warwick, and soon went to sleep. How long I was asleep, I don't know—but I'm sure it couldn't have been long—when I was waked, as I thought, by a sudden, sharp noise. I jumped up and listened; but every thing was perfectly still—so still that I began to think I must have been mistaken about there having been any noise, though I couldn't imagine what else would have waked me so suddenly. Since the money was brought up from Hartsburg, I have been very wakeful—easily disturbed, and constantly starting in my sleep. Nearly every night I have got up two or three times, and struck a light to see that all was right. It was only yesterday that I mentioned to Mr. Marks that I hadn't had a good night's sleep since it came; and he laughed, and said he was glad I took such care of it, but that it wouldn't be here to trouble me much longer, for he should send off part of it to-day, and expected to get rid of the rest—all that don't belong here—the first of next week. Well, I sat up in bed, listening with all my ears, for some time—but not a sound could I hear; and then I got up and struck a light, and went round to all the doors and windows, examining them closely. Every thing was right, and I put out the candle and went back to bed. But I could not go to sleep again. Not that I felt uneasy. So far from that, I was disposed to laugh at myself for being startled at nothing. But I was so wide awake, that I felt as if I should not be able to close my eyes for the rest of the night. I lay thinking of all sorts of things for a long time, when suddenly—just as quick as thought, Mr. Warwick, and without knowing why—I jumped up in bed, all over in a cold perspiration! I had not been asleep—I'd swear to that!—for I was thinking at that very minute about Miss Katharine—who, I suppose, you don't know—"

"Yes, I know, she has left Tallahoma. Go on. You were thinking of her, and so you are sure you were awake—?"

"Yes, sir. As wide awake as I am this minute. And there hadn't been the slightest noise—and I couldn't tell, to save my life, what was the matter with me. I just jumped up as if I had been set on springs—and found myself in a cold sweat, and trembling like an aspen-leaf. It took me so by surprise that it must have been several seconds before I came to myself sufficiently to know what I was about. Then I felt sure—just as sure as I am now—that something was wrong. I put my hand under the pillow and drew out my revolver, and, without waiting this time to light the candle, I sprang out of bed, groped my way to the door, which I always leave open at night, and came into this room. I stood still to listen for an instant, but all was silent; I was just turning to go back into my own room to strike a light again, when I heard a noise in the passage outside there." He pointed to the door which gave egress from the cashier's room to the passage. "It was a slight, but suspicious kind of noise. Guided by the sound, I went close to it—to the door, I mean—and then I heard voices whispering. The door is so thick, and they spoke in such a low tone, that I could not make out a single word they said; but I could hear that it was two men talking—and that they were picking the lock. Oh, Mr. Warwick, if I had only had the presence of mind to keep perfectly quiet, so as to let them think I was asleep, and come in, I might have slipped out while they were busy picking the lock of the vault door, and obtained assistance to come and take them before they got the money. Mr. Marks always takes the vault key, and the keys of the safes, home with him at night—and the opening of them must have been a tough job. If only I had had the presence of mind! But all I thought of at the minute was to scare them off or kill them—I didn't care which. Like a fool as I was, I didn't even wait to light the candle, but called out just where I stood, 'I hear you, you thieves! I've got a revolver, and if you want me to send you to the devil, just come on!' They took me at my word quicker than I expected. I had started once more to go after the light—but before I was half-way across the room, the door was burst open, and when I turned I just caught one glimpse of two men as they rushed in, by the light of a lantern one of them carried. It was a dark lantern, and he shut it as soon as he saw that I had no light—I heard the door pushed shut, and one of them said, 'You stand against it, while I do for this bragging rascal.' I don't remember ever being afraid of anybody before in my life, Mr. Warwick; but it was an awful feeling that I had then—expecting every minute to be seized in the dark, and not knowing how I could defend myself, and, above all, how I could save the money! I knew if they killed me they'd have every thing their own way. Well, the thought flashed through my mind that if I could get into my own room and fasten the door—it locks on the inside—I might manage to escape out of the window, before they could break open the door, and, once out in the moonlight, I could give the alarm, or at least fig' them if they followed me. I was barefooted, an had the advantage of them in that—as I ma… no noise in moving. But it was pitch dark, anc I somehow got turned round in my head as to the direction of my room-door. Instead of going toward it as I intended, I went the opposite way, and suddenly came thump against the counter. The villain that was after me heard it, and I heard him coming toward me. I ought to have kept out of his way; but, instead of that, I fired at random in the direction of the noise he made in approaching, which was the very worst thing I could have done—for of course he was not hit, and the flash of the pistol as it went off showed him exactly where I stood. All was so confused after this, I can scarcely recall any thing about it. I fired twice, and the last thing that I can remember is that just as I was pulling the trigger for the third time, both the scoundrels jumped on me. I fought like mad, but I think it couldn't have been long before they overpowered me. I felt a sudden blow here"—he put his hand to the side of his forehead, which was ornamented with the yellow-and-black patches. "It seemed to me that a blaze of sparks flashed out of my eyes, and made a solid sheet of white flame before them that shut out every thing. The blow must have knocked me down and stunned me—for my mind don't go beyond seeing this white blaze for an instant, like a flash of lightning exactly. The next recollection I have is of coming to my senses gradually, and finding myself in pitch darkness and dead silence, tied neck and heels, aching all over from head to foot, and with a gag in my mouth. I tried at first to get up, but I couldn't budge an inch, I was tied so hard; and every movement I made seemed as if it would kill me with pain. As to my head, I really thought it would burst, it ached so! I think I was hardly in my right senses for some time—for, in spite of myself, I kept struggling to get loose, until I was almost strangled, besides suffering perfect agonies from the straining of my wrists and ankles, which had all the skin rubbed off of them." He held up his hands, exhibiting a pair of bandaged wrists, as he went on: "At last I lay quiet from exhaustion—and I couldn't begin to give you an idea of how much I suffered, and how long the time seemed, until Mr. Marks came in the morning. I thought morning never would come! I hope I may never, as long as I live, have such a time of it again! I knew the bank was robbed—and that it was my fault—because if I had only—"

"You are wrong," said Mr. Warwick, as the young man's voice faltered, and the tears again came into his eyes. "It was not your fault—you did your best—and that is all that can be required of any man, and you were willing to risk your life—and that is what every man would not do under similar circumstances. So, don't blame yourself unjustly. I am sure Marks doesn't blame you."

"No. He—"

"You say you saw the men?" interrupted Mr. Warwick, who was exceedingly impatient to come back to this point of Hugh's narrative, and had only constrained himself to listen to the rather verbose relation of the young man, in the hope of hearing something more about those personages. "Have you any suspicion of who they were?"

"I have a suspicion that I have seen one of them before, sir—though I couldn't be certain, as it was only just a single glimpse that I caught of them, before the lantern was shut."

"Who was it?" said Mr. Warwick, abruptly.

"I don't know his name, sir—he is a stranger hereabouts; that is, if I'm not mistaken about the person I'm thinking of. When I turned round, as the door was burst open, I saw the two men distinctly for an instant—that is, distinctly enough to take in a general idea of their appearance, and to see that they were black. But I felt sure then, and I'm still more sure, in thinking it over, that they were not negroes, but white men with their faces blacked."

"It is more likely," commenced Mr. Warwick, "that they wore—" crape masks, he was going to say—but stopped himself in time. "You are right, Hugh; they were certainly white men. This is not the sort of thing that negroes would undertake. And you think you recognized one of them?"

"I think so, sir. The one that was in front when I saw them was quite a tall man—as tall as you are yourself, or taller, and stout in proportion; the other, who had the lantern, was shorter and thick-set. Just about such a looking man as Mr. Shields." ("Not St. John—either of them!" thought Mr. Warwick, parenthetically.) "It was the first one that I thought I recognized. I never saw him but once, and that was the day before the robbery—"

"Yesterday, then."

"Yes, it was yesterday, though it seems to me a good deal longer ago. Well, this man came into the bank, while Mr. Marks was gone to dinner, with a very ragged five-dollar bill that he wanted a new note for."

"And did he get it?—did you take the bill?"

"No, sir, I couldn't. It was no bill of ours, but one of the 'Commercial Bank of A.'s' notes. I thought it was strange that the man should be so stupid as not to know that a bank has nothing to do, in this way, with any but its own issues; but I explained the matter to him; and he seemed very hard to understand. I felt a little out of patience at having to go over and over my explanation; and all the while I was talking, he stood staring round the room, and at me, in a very curious way. I noticed that he stayed a great deal longer than there was any necessity for; and seemed inclined to stay still longer, if I had not told him that, if that was all he wanted, I was sorry I could not accommodate him, and that he must excuse my going back to my writing, as I was busy. He went away then."

"And you think this was one of the burglars?"

"I think so, sir; but I wouldn't take oath to it. There was something about the tallest of the two scoundrels that at once brought this stranger to my mind; but it might have been merely his height."

"The voice—did you notice that?"

"No, sir. I was in too much of a flurry to think of noticing that. And I only heard him speak once."

"Was his dress the same as that of the stranger?"

Hugh shook his head. "Both of the burglars had on blanket overcoats. The stranger who came about the money was dressed in black."

"He was not a gentleman, I suppose?"

"Well, I can hardly say," answered Hugh, hesitatingly. "His dress was rather shabby; but still, so far as that was concerned, he might have passed for a gentleman. But there was something in his face, a hang-dog sort of look, that—but, on the whole, I suppose, yes"—rather doubtfully—"I suppose he was a gentleman. And I can't believe that he did not know better than he pretended about the bill. I think he made that an excuse to get in and take a look at the bank, and find out all he could. I saw him looking very hard at the door of the vault there. And he shut the room-door when he went out, though he found it standing open. And then, he didn't walk out at once, but stopped so long in the passage that I went and opened the door to see what on earth he was about. He walked away when he heard me coming, I suppose, for he was just going out of the front door when I stepped into the passage."

"All this does look very suspicious," said Mr. Warwick. "Did it occur to you, at the time, that he might have evil intentions?"

"No, sir. Such an idea never entered my head. All I thought was that he must be some idler who had nothing to do himself, and was loafing about, disturbing other people at their work. He had a dissipated appearance; indeed, he looked to me more like a gambler than any thing else."

"And have you made any inquiries about him, as to who and what he is, and whether he is in town yet?"

"Oh, yes, sir—we've tried to find out something about him, but nobody seems to know any thing at all. As soon as I told Mr. Marks this morning what I've just been telling you, he tried his best to trace up the fellow; and so did a good many other people. The whole town's been in a great excitement, as you may suppose, Mr. Warwick."

"Did you, or anybody, go to the hotel and inquire if the man had been there?"

"Mr. Hilliard was here himself, and Mr. Marks asked him, the first thing, whether a man like the one I described had been at his hotel. He said not; and nobody seems to have seen him except little Jimmy Powell, who thinks it must have been a man that came into his father's store yesterday, about dinner-time, and bought a pen-knife from him."

"And what has Marks—"

Mr. Warwick paused, as he heard the sound of approaching foot-steps. The next moment, Cyrus entered with some letters which he gave to his master, who, after glancing at the address of each, put all but one of them into his pocket. That one he opened at once, and read it with evident satisfaction. "Give me a sheet of paper, and pen and ink, Hugh, if you please," he said, as he refolded it. Carefully sealing it up and addressing it, he handed it to Cyrus, saying, "Take a horse and go with this at once to Morton House. Ask to see Mrs. Gordon yourself, and give it into her own hand. Now, don't lose it—for your life, Cyrus! It is of the greatest importance."

"Yes, sir."

"Have you had your supper?" said Mr. Warwick, calling him back as he was leaving the room.

"No, sir."

"Then go home and get it before you carry that letter; but don't be all night over it, for I want the letter delivered as soon as possible. And remember what I told you this afternoon—about gossipping."

"Yes, sir—I ain't forgot."

"Talking of supper, I expect I have been keeping you from yours, Hugh?" said Mr. Warwick, as Cyrus finally disappeared.

"Oh, I'm not in a hurry—I'm not at all hungry," answered the young man.

"You ought to be, then," said Mr. Marks, entering the door in time to hear the last sentence, "for you had no dinner any more than myself.—Well, Warwick," he continued, as he shook hands with his brother-in-law, who rose to meet him, "you come back to find me a ruined man."

"Not so bad as that, I hope," said Mr. Warwick, gazing hard at the face before him, which, by the dim light of the single candle, looked pale and haggard, as he had never seen it before. "It is an ugly business, I must admit," he went on; "but giving up is not the way to mend it. We must go to work and find the thieves and the money."

"That's easier said than done," replied Mr. Marks, sitting down with an air of hopeless dejection. "We've been all day trying to do something toward it, and have not succeeded in gaining the least trace to begin with. And the infernal scoundrels have got a clear start on us of sixteen or eighteen hours, at least."

"Why, surely you have sent out advertisements of the robbery to all the papers in the State, and notified the bank to stop payment of the notes stolen?" said Mr. Warwick.

"Oh, yes; I sent off special messengers not an hour after I found out the robbery. But the thieves are not likely to let the grass grow under their feet. Of course, they'll get out of the State as fast as they can.—Hugh, why don't you go to supper?"

"I'd rather stay and hear what Mr. Warwick thinks ought to be done," answered Hugh.

"I'm afraid nothing can be done to-night," said Mr. Warwick. "But, when you come back, you shall hear if we have decided on any thing."

Upon this hint, Hugh, who took his meals at a boarding-house not far off, finally went to his long-deferred supper; and Mr. Warwick inquired what was the amount of money stolen. "A hundred thousand dollars, Shields told me, but I suppose that is an exaggeration?" he said.

"Yes; the amount did not reach that figure. There was twenty-four thousand and eighty dollars in specie, a package of fifty thousand in notes still in the sheet, and thirteen hundred and twenty-seven dollars in bills that have been in circulation," answered Mr. Marks, with his usual preciseness, but by no means his usual brisk, hearty tone.

"And you sent off at once to the bank, and all its branches, giving the numbers of the notes?"

"I did every thing that could be done in that way. I sent messengers right off express to our bank and branches; and I wrote by mail to all the other banks in the State, and in the neighboring States, giving a list of the numbers of the notes, even down to the one-dollar bills. Powell, and Gibbs, and Williamson, and Horton, were here all the morning, assisting Hugh and myself with the writing—copying the lists and the advertisements—and Burgess kept the mail open to the minute the stage was starting, to put the letters in. I have offered, on my own responsibility, a reward of five thousand dollars for the recovery of the whole of the money; or a thousand for the detection of the thieves, and recovery of any considerable part of it."

"So far, very well," said Mr. Warwick. "And how about trying to detect the thieves yourself? Did you examine closely the scene of their operations?—and could nothing be found to afford a clew?"

"The whole town, pretty near, were examining—"

"You ought not to have permitted that. The thief or thieves themselves might have been among the number, for aught you know, to see if they had left any thing behind them, and to secure it if they had."

"No danger of that," answered Mr. Marks. "Hugh saw the thieves, and he says one of them was very tall—over six feet, he is sure—and the other was short and heavy built. There was nobody here that would answer to either description, and nobody that we didn't know. Just our own townsfolk. I wouldn't have let strangers come about, of course."

"And how do you know but that the robbery may have been committed by some of our own townsfolk?"

Mr. Marks shook his head. "There are some trifling men in Tallahoma, it's true; but I don't believe there's one that would be bad enough for a thing of this sort."

Mr. Warwick rose and took up the candlestick.

"Get another light, and come with me, will you? I should like to look at the vault myself," he said.

Mr. Marks did as requested. He took from the mantel-piece another candle, lighted it, produced a bunch of keys from his pocket, and proceeded across the room to a heavy-looking door set in a deep recess in the wall.

"The lock was picked, but I had another put on, though it looks very much like locking the stable after the horses are stolen," he said, as he opened the door.

Descending a narrow flight of steps that ran down against the wall, with a balustrade to protect it on the outside, they held the lights forward, and Mr. Warwick took a survey of the place. It was a small, vaulted cell rather than room, not more than eight feet by twelve, with two huge safes standing against the wall opposite the stairs. Substantial safes they were for the period, but not cast-iron, and not burglar-proof, as their present melancholy condition proved. The doors of both were wide open; but while one of them retained its contents, consisting of piles of ledgers, labelled boxes, and bundles of papers of all sizes (which had evidently been roughly handled and thrust back in utter confusion), the shelves of the other were bare.

Mr. Warwick examined the whole place with the most minute care. First, he held his candle within the empty money-safe, running his eye, and even passing his hand, over every square inch of surface on the two shelves above, and taking the drawer which was fitted between the lower shelf and the floor of the safe, for the reception of specie, clean out of its place, in order to make an effectual search.

"You'll find nothing," said Mr. Marks, who had stood by watching these proceedings with an expression of face in which apathy and impatience were rather singularly blended.

"Don't let me detain you," said Mr. Warwick, reading this expression. "I dare say you are right, but still I want to satisfy myself by a thorough examination. You were all excited this morning, of course, and may have overlooked some little matter—there is somebody coming in,

I think. Had you not better go and see, Richard? I will be up presently."

"I suppose it's Hugh," replied Mr. Marks; "but I'll go."

Left alone, Mr. Warwick next subjected the floor of the vault to as close an inspection as that which he had bestowed on the safe, until he was convinced that no object, though it had been only the size of a pin, could have escaped his observation. He then took in hand the safe containing the documents. Every separate volume, every box, and each package of papers, passed under the scrutiny of his keen eye and industrious fingers. But, as Mr. Marks had predicted, he found nothing.

It was with a sense of decided, though even to himself unacknowledged, discouragement, that he remounted the stairs to the room above. Mr. Marks was sitting in a drooping attitude, with his eyes, but not his thoughts, fixed on the clerk, who knelt upon the hearth, trying to ignite a hopeless-looking pile of wood which he had just put on the andirons. In their excitement and preoccupation of mind, both himself and his principal had forgotten the fire that afternoon—the more readily, as the day had been a very mild one. But the evening closed in cold; and poor Hugh, who was feeling almost as wretchedly in body as in mind, shivered at the cheerless aspect of the apartment, as much as at its chilly temperature, when he returned from his boarding-house. The hearth, that always gave forth such a cheerful glow and warmth, was cold and dark now—like the ill-fortune that had so unexpectedly come upon them, he could not help thinking—though he was not addicted to a poetical turn of thought usually.

Mr. Warwick walked up to his brother-in-law and laid his hand on his shoulder kindly. "Take my advice, Richard," he said. "Go home and go to bed. There's nothing more for you to do here; and you look thoroughly used up. I want to ask Hugh a few questions about his visitors of last night; but I shall not be long. Tell Bessie, if you please, to have some hot coffee ready for me—I have had no dinner."

"I can wait for you," said Mr. Marks.—"By-the-way, Hugh, hadn't you better have got somebody to stay with you to-night?"

"What for?" demanded Hugh, coloring with boyish mortification. "There's no such good luck as that those villains should take it into their heads to come back. I only wish they would. I'd know how to deal with them this time!"

"And," pursued Mr. Marks, who was a kind-hearted man, considerate of the comfort of those about him, and feeling now some self-reproach as he remembered how little attention he had paid to the pains and bruises which the clerk had incurred, though unavailingly, in the discharge of his duty—"and I don't believe Tom has been here to attend to your room to-day, has he?"

"Yes, sir, he came this morning, but it was while the house was full, and every thing in confusion; so I told him to never mind about it."

"I'll go and send him now, then.—You might as well come with me, John. It must be getting late, and I should think that, as you had no dinner, you'd be hungry."

"I am. But waiting a little longer makes no difference; and I must take a look at Hugh's room. It is only eight o'clock," he added, consulting his watch. "I will follow you in half an hour, or less time, perhaps."

Mr. Marks made no further remonstrance, but rose, said good-night, and departed.

"Now, Hugh, let me see your room," said Mr Warwick. "I am glad that it has not been meddled with. Did you look about to find if—Humph!" he exclaimed, as at this moment he stepped into the apartment in question, which adjoined the cashier's room. "Humph!"

It was a comfortless-looking dormitory at present, certainly. The bedclothing, including the mattresses, had been tumbled off one side of the French bedstead, and lay in a disordered heap upon the floor, which was strewed with strips and fragments resembling hospital-linen, for much of it was crumpled and bloody, like soiled bandages. Hugh explained that he had been tied down to the bedstead itself, which, no doubt, was bared for that purpose. The sheets had been torn up, and twisted into a rough imitation of rope, with which he was bound.

"The scoundrels seemed to understand their business," said the young man. "You see they made notches in the side of the bedstead here near the head, to keep the bands I was tied with from slipping."

Mr. Warwick bent over, and looked closely at the spot pointed out. The bedstead was of walnut-wood, and the notches appeared to have been cut into it without difficulty, as they were at least an inch deep. "The wood is soft," he remarked. "This looks as if it had been cut with a pocket-knife."

He stepped toward the foot of the bed as he spoke, and again leaned down to examine whether there were notches there too. There was one great gash—obviously the commencement of a notch—but that was all. In holding the candle so that the light would fall full upon this, Mr. Warwick's eye was attracted to a small, glittering object upon the carpet just at the side of the bed, and, stooping, he picked it up.

"What is it?" cried Hugh, as the lawyer uttered a slight exclamation.

"A fragment of the blade of a knife," answered Mr. Warwick, quietly, but his eyes sparkled. "Something may be made of this, I hope," he added, examining it eagerly.

"Oh, do you really think so, Mr. Warwick?" said Hugh, joyfully.

"I hope so. It was broken in the attempt to make that notch."

"And you think, sir, you can trace them out by it?"

"I shall try. It is a point to begin with; and in an affair of this kind, as in every thing else, the first step is almost always the most difficult. I shall sleep the better to-night for having found this little bit of metal. Here—hold the candle a minute!"

Hugh extended a hand trembling with excitement for the candle, and Mr. Warwick took out his pocket-book and carefully placed the broken blade in an inner compartment of it.

"Don't be too sanguine," he said to Hugh, as he fastened the clasp, and returned the book to his pocket. "And don't mention my having found this to any body—least of all, to Marks—for it may turn out nothing. But," he added, as he saw Hugh's face fall at these words, "I think it is a clew. Good-night. There's Tom coming, and I'll go. Oh!—don't have any sweeping done to-night. I will be here early in the morning, and we can then make a more careful search of the room, and may possibly find something else. I don't like to keep my sister waiting for me so long; and this does very well for a beginning. Mind, Hugh, that you hold your tongue!"

"I will, Mr. Warwick."

"You are not afraid of another call from your friends, the burglars?"

"Afraid? I should think not!" cried the young man, flushing, and half offended by the question.

"Well, good-night," said Mr. Warwick. "Here's Tom"

CHAPTER XXXV

TWO AND TWO MAKE FOUR.

"JOHN, John, I am so glad you have got back at last!" was Mrs. Marks's greeting to her brother, when he entered the dining-room, where a bright fire and the supper-table were waiting for him. She had been crying all day, poor woman, but the fountain of her tears was not exhausted. It gave forth a plentiful supply of briny drops, as Mr. Warwick smiled kindly, kissed her, and told her to dry her eyes, and give him some supper, for that he was tired and hungry.

"Richard has gone to bed, I hope?" said he, as Mrs. Marks began to take up from the hearth, where they were ranged in a semicircle to keep warm, various dishes, which she placed upon the table, himself hastening to assist her in doing so.

"Yes, he's gone to bed"—a profound sigh—"but there's no sleep for him *this* night, *I* know. Seventy-five thousand, four hundred and seventy dollars, John," pursued poor Mrs. Marks, with a ludicrous, unconscious imitation of her husband's manner, that made Mr. Warwick smile, despite his sincere sympathy with the distress which seemed so out of place on the round, good-natured face before him. "More than twice as much as Richard is worth, counting every sixpence he has got in the world!—and he blames himself for it all—and I'm sure he must blame me, though he don't say so"—the tears burst forth afresh—"and five little children—"

"Stop a minute," said Mr. Warwick, stemming the torrent of words that promised to flow on uninterruptedly for an indefinite time to come. "Blames himself? What does he blame himself for?"

"He says he ought never to have left the bank. That a cashier's business and duty is to protect, by his constant presence, the property committed to his charge; and that, instead of leaving poor Hugh to bear the brunt of the danger, and get beaten and bruised nearly to death, he ought to have been there himself. And you know it was *my* fault, John, that we left the bank, because it was such a nasty, cooped-up place for the children, compared to this house."

"All this sort of talk is nonsense, Bessie," said Mr. Warwick. "Marks is very much out of spirits, of course; but he will find that matters are not so bad, after all. He has been prompt in taking the steps necessary in the business, and the only uneasiness I feel now is about the specie. I have no doubt the greater part of that can be recovered—but not the whole, probably. As to the notes — you need not trouble yourself about them, I assure you. The scoundrels will find that the fifty thousand dollars might as well be blank paper so far as they are concerned. In fact, it is certain to bring detection upon them if they try to pass it."

"I don't see how that can be," said Mrs. Marks, drying her eyes once more, but looking very doubtful. "It's money. All they've got to do is to cut it apart. It's signed, every bit of it."

"And numbered too, fortunately. Never mind puzzling yourself with the matter. You can take my word for it, can't you?"

"I suppose so. But John, are you quite sure—"

"Well?" he said, as she paused, and the inexhaustible fountain began welling forth from her eyes again.

"Are you sure we shall not be ruined—and" — sob — "that Richard's character — won't—"

"Bessie," said Mr. Warwick, in such a very quiet tone, that Bessie's eyes opened wide in startled surprise, and the drops with which they were brimming stood arrested in their fall—"Bessie, have you quite forgotten that you once bore the name of Warwick?"

The poor woman was bewildered. Never very quick of apprehension, she was totally unable now to perceive the connection between this "awful" bank robbery and her own maiden name; and, after a troubled pause of consideration, she looked inquiringly into her brother's face.

"I asked the question," continued he, "because I confess that I am mortified to find that my sister"—he laid a strong emphasis on the last two words—"instead of being courageous and cheerful in this misfortune which has befallen her husband, as a brave woman and good wife ought to be, is giving way to unreasonable and extravagant lamentations that must make it twice as hard—"

"Oh, no! you don't mean that I have made it harder for Richard to bear! Surely you don't think that!"

"I know it."

She wrung her hands spasmodically. "What can I do—what can I do?"

"You can act like a sensible woman, and remember that the loss of money—even if Marks loses any, which I am not at all sure that he will—"

"He says he intends to refund every cent that the bank loses, whether it is required of him or not, and if it takes all that he owns in the world."

"He may be a few thousands out of pocket, then—but what of that? If, instead of losing a little money—or, we will say a good deal of money—he or some of the children were to die—"

"John!" gasped his sister, turning very pale.

"I think you would feel what a trifle, comparatively speaking, this whole business is," went on Mr. Warwick, without noticing her horrified ejaculation—"and be glad that trouble, which you know everybody has to endure in this world, Bessie, has come in this form, instead of a worse."

"Indeed, I am glad—and thankful to God," said she, in a subdued, rather awe-struck tone. "And thankful to you, John, for reminding me of it," she added.

He smiled encouragingly, and told her he had no doubt this wretched business might be set to rights in the end; but that, meanwhile, he expected to see her hopeful and brave. Then he went to a side-table, where a chamber candlestick was ready for him, and, as he lighted it, asked whether she thought Marks was asleep yet. "I won't disturb him, if he is; but I should like to speak to him a moment, if he is not. Will you see, Bessie, if you please?"

She went, merely opened the chamber-door, glanced in, and returned.

"He's wide awake," she said, with a sigh.

"I will go and speak to him, then. Good-night."

"Come in," responded Mr. Marks's voice, when his brother-in-law knocked at his door a minute later.

Mr. Warwick walked up to the bed, and found the afflicted cashier lying straight and motionless on his back, with his arms thrown up over the pillow, his hands folded one upon the other above his head, and the same expression of stolid endurance on his face that it had worn when he was at the bank.

"I have just been scolding Bessie, Dick," said Bessie's brother, with a smile that had humor as well as cheerful kindness in it—"and I have come to give you your share now. Why, zounds! what's the use of being a man, if you can't bear the ills of life like a man! It is natural that you should feel this severely; it is a bad business, as it stands just at present. But you must not look only on the dark side of it. The money may be recovered—will be recovered, I believe. You know whether I am in the habit of talking at random, or of boasting; and I tell you that I have not the least doubt of being able to track down the villains—in time. We must have patience, and not be discouraged because it is impossible to find them at once. I have made a little discovery since I saw you—"

"You don't say so!" cried Mr. Marks, starting up and leaning on his elbow, as he gazed eagerly up into the other's face. "What is it? —what—?"

"Never mind as to that. It is something that Hugh and myself found out after you left. Don't question Hugh in the morning. I told him not to say any thing to you about it. I should not have mentioned it myself if it had not been that I see you need stirring up a little. Between Bessie and yourself, you are making this affair twice as bad as there's any necessity for."

"It's harder to bear than you think for," said Mr. Marks, apologetically. But his face had cleared very much, and he was looking altogether ten per cent. better than he did when his brother-in-law entered the room.

"A good many things in this world are hard to bear," said Mr. Warwick; and—not at all pertinently to the subject of which they were talking—he sighed under his breath. "Well, good-night. I hope you will go to sleep now, and be yourself again in the morning. Rest assured that I am sanguine of recovering the money."

He went to his own room, and the first thing he did was to take out his pocket-book, and examine again the fragment of knife-blade which he had found. Then he sat down before the fire, stirred it, absently, put the tongs back into their place, and gazing at the leaping and curling flames, and the glowing cavern that he had made beneath them, he remained for a long time absorbed in deep thought.

He rose early the next morning, and at an hour when he was usually asleep, took his way into the village, which was just beginning to show signs of awakening life. Shopkeepers were opening their doors and windows, and drowsy-looking servants were sweeping off door-steps, and gossiping with each other, as they leaned on their brooms; exchanging items of information concerning the great bank robbery, which was *the* topic of conversation with white and black in Tallahoma just then.

Mr. Warwick paused at the entrance of a store, near the open door of which a negro boy was lazily shaking a foot-mat, wondering to himself the while, "what had brought Mr. Worruck out that time in the morning."

"Your master here yet, Bill?" said the lawyer, pointing into the store.

"No, sir—nobody's here yit but me and Mass Jimmy."

To his surprise, Mr. Warwick, instead of passing on, entered the door. Probably that gentleman had never before been conscious of the existence of "little Jimmy Powell," certainly he had never noticed the boy particularly. But he looked closely now, as he walked into the store, and encountered the gaze of a pair of remarkably quick and intelligent eyes, the owner of which was seated on the front edge of a counter, with one leg doubled under him, while the other dangled over, and kept up a swinging, kicking accompaniment to an air he was whistling. A bright face—altogether not an ordinary boy, Mr. Warwick thought—small for his age; for, though he was thirteen or fourteen at least, his size and delicate physique made him appear a year or two younger.

"How are you, Mr. Warwick? Can I do any thing for you this morning, sir?" he said, at once dexterously slipping backward across the counter, and landing on his feet on the opposite side, where he stood with the attentive and business air of a well-trained clerk.

"Yes, I wish to see some penknives," said Mr. Warwick, with a half smile at the serious clerkliness of the little man's manner.

At the word penknives, there was a flash of intelligence in the boy's face, but he said nothing. Turning quickly to one of the shelves behind him, he took from it a box, which he brought and placed on the counter, and, opening it, proceeded silently to display several kinds of knives. Mr. Warwick examined them, one after the other, and finally looked up, or, rather, looked over, at the countenance that was just on a level with his own hands. The expression of that countenance surprised him a little, there was so much shrewd interest and curiosity in it; and yet not vulgar curiosity, either, for the boy restrained it the moment he perceived that it was observed, replying with modest brevity to the questions as to the price of the knives, which his customer asked. The latter had been waiting to see whether the little clerk would volunteer some information which he wished to obtain, but, finding that there was no probability of this, he now opened the conversation himself as he paid for one of the knives.

"You have heard all about the bank robbery, of course?" he said.

"Yes, sir," was the answer; and the bright, brown eyes shot another ray of intelligence, and then looked gravely attentive.

"You know then, probably, that Hugh Ellis thinks he recognized one of the burglars in a man who was in the bank the day before the robbery was committed; and he tells me that the only information he can get about this man is, that a person answering to his description was here in your father's store that same day, and nearly about the same hour, and that you sold a penknife to him. Do you remember what sort of a knife it was?"

"It was like the one you have just bought, sir."

"Ah! You are sure?"

"Certain sure, Mr. Warwick."

"You recollect selling the knife, then?"

"Yes, sir."

"Can you describe the man's appearance to me?"

"He was as tall as you are, sir—maybe a little taller, for he stood just where you are standing now, and I had to look 'way up to see his face. He had sandy, bushy hair, and a very red face, and he was dressed in a shabby suit of black."

"Would you have taken him for a gentleman?"

The boy hesitated.

"I hardly know, sir, whether he was or not. He looked something like a gentleman, but—his linen was soiled."

"What sort of money did he pay for the knife with?"

"He offered me a very dirty five-dollar bill that was all torn. But I wouldn't take it, and then he paid in silver."

"A five-dollar bill?" said Mr. Warwick, whose interest had been quickening, and his hopes rising, with each successive reply to his questions. "Did you notice what bill it was—of what bank, I mean?"

"Yes, sir. He threw it down on the counter, and I took it up and looked at it a minute. It was a 'Commercial Bank of A—— note."

"Humph!" cried Mr. Warwick. "It must have been the same fellow who was at the bank. A 'Commercial Bank of A——' note, and very ragged, you say?"

"Very ragged indeed. I don't think it was a counterfeit," added the boy, thoughtfully; "but it was too ragged to pass anywhere; and so I told him I couldn't take it."

"Why did you think of its being counterfeit?" asked the lawyer, a little surprised at this remark.

"Because I didn't like the man's looks, sir, and I thought he mightn't be too good to pass counterfeit money. There's a good deal of it about now, you know. He never once looked me straight in the face, though I tried my best to catch his eyes. But they kept moving about, first to one place, and then to another."

"Ah!" exclaimed Mr. Warwick, with an emphasis that was almost startling.

"Yes, sir. He looked so"—and the boy glanced about him in a quick, uncertain sort of way, rolling his eyes from side to side with a restless movement that brought vividly to Mr. Warwick's recollection the eyes of the quack doctor in Hartsburg.

"Do you remember the color of his eyes?"

"They were of a light greenish blue, sir."

Mr. Warwick stood silent for a full minute, evidently in deep thought. He was trying to recall to mind the appearance of the quack doctor; but, with the exception of the restless eyes, his memory was for once totally at fault. He had a general but very vague impression that the man was tall, and that his hair was *not* "sandy and bushy." Nevertheless, the representation given of the stranger's eyes—the very pose of the boy's head while rendering the imitation—brought back so forcibly the look of Dr. Joyner, as he called himself, that Mr. Warwick felt morally sure that, in common parlance, he had "struck the trail"—and, it is needless to say, he resolved to pursue it.

"Well, Jimmy," he said, looking down with a smile, "I think you have given me some valuable information, and that you can help me still further in this matter, if you are willing to do so."

A quick flash came to the upraised face, and the boy's eyes sparkled with eagerness, as he replied: "I wish I could, sir."

"Do you think you would know the man if you saw him again?"

"Yes, sir, I'd know him anywhere."

"You are at the store here all the time, are you not?"

"Yes, sir." The little fellow sighed as he spoke.

"I ask, because I should like to see you again after breakfast. Good-morning for the present."

"Good-morning, Mr. Warwick."

"By-the-by," said the lawyer, turning back as he was about to cross the threshold, on his way out of the store; "by-the-by, my little friend, I had rather you did not mention to anybody—excepting your father, if it comes in the way—what I have been asking you, and what you have told me. I want to trace out this man that we have been speaking of, and, in a matter of the kind, talking ruins every thing."

"I know that, Mr. Warwick. I'll not say a word."

From Mr. Powell's store the lawyer went to the stage-office, as it was called, to find out, if possible, whether the man he was in search of had left Tallahoma by any of the several lines of public conveyances that ran to and from the place—Tallahoma, though in itself an inconsiderable village, being on one of the principal thoroughfares of travel in the State. He did not succeed in obtaining any information; and was feeling very much "at sea," as he walked meditatively toward the bank, when, just as he was turning a corner, he met the Chesselton hack coming in. Instantly it flashed upon him, as by an inspiration, that it was more likely a man trying to escape observation would take this, which was a less public line of travel — more merely local—than those he had been thinking of. The Chesselton hack, he remembered, ran only three times a week, and consequently, though Chesselton was but twenty-eight miles from Tallahoma, communication was much less easy and frequent than with Saxford, for instance, to which there was a double daily line—both a coach and hack line. To a man endeavoring to evade detection, it was a desirable consideration to be as much out of the way of quick communication as possible. The hack left Tallahoma on Tuesdays, Thursdays, and Saturdays, returning on the night of the same day it left; that is, making the round trip in twenty-four hours. And the rusty-looking vehicle, the appearance of which had suggested these reflections, had now just arrived from its Thursday trip for the current week. This was Friday morning, and there would be no further mail communication with Chesselton until Saturday—an excellent opportunity for a thief who had taken refuge there to make good his escape farther, undoubtedly.

These thoughts passed rapidly through Mr. Warwick's mind as he turned and followed the hack to the hotel where it stopped, in order to speak to the driver. He paused at the entrance of the stable-yard into which the carriage was driven after discharging its passengers at the hotel-door, to wait until the driver descended from his seat.

"Gillespie!" he called, as the official seemed likely to prolong interminably his directions to and gossip with the hostlers who surrounded him and his horses. "Gillespie!"—the man turned to see who had spoken to him—"just step here a minute."

"How-d'ye-do, Mr. Worruck? Was it me you was callin' to?" inquired the man, approaching him.

"Yes, I want to speak to you." He looked round, and, seeing that nobody was within ear shot, went on: "I am trying to find out some thing about that bad business which happened night before last at the bank, and I want to know what passengers you took over to Chesselton yesterday; whether a fellow who was hanging about town here the day before the robbery, and who, Hugh Ellis thinks, was one of the burglars, may not have been among them?"

The driver shook his head.

"I was keepin' a sharp lookout myself, Mr. Worruck, for I'd like monstously to have the handlin' of that five thousand dollars reward that Mr. Marks offered for the apporhension of the thieves"—he chuckled at the bare thought of handling it—"but I hain't seed nobody sence I left Tallyhomy that answered to the description of either of 'em, I'm sorry to say. There wasn't as many passengers as usual yisterday. Only one old gentleman, and a man and his wife, and—"

"But," interrupted Mr. Warwick, "did you take up no passengers by the way?"

"I tuk up two; but one was a woman, and the other didn't noways curryspond to the descriptions I heard from Mr. Ellis. He didn't have on black cloes, nor yit a great-coat, I noticed particilar. And he wore a curous kind a specktickles sich as I never seed before, that stood out like a couple of leather cups before his eyes."

"Goggles, I suppose?" said Mr. Warwick.

"Mebbe so. Anyhow, he didn't answer to the descriptions."

"He may have changed his dress, and put on the goggles to avoid detection," said the lawyer. "What sort of looking man was he, and how was he dressed?"

"He was a good-lookin' man, or would a bin, if he hadn't had on them—guggles, did you call 'em?—they give him a out-of-the-way sort of look. He was dressed well enough—drab breeches and a brown surtout. But, with them things stickin' out two inches from his face, with green glasses at the top of 'em, he had a curous look."

"What sized man was he?"

"A stout fellow. Six feet—more'n that, I reckon."

"Where did you take him up?"

"At Moonie's—the second stage-house from here, you know."

"Twenty miles from here, is it not?"

"Yes, sir, twenty miles—and good ones, too."

"How far did he go with you?"

"He stopped a little this side of Chesselton."

"And did you see any thing of him afterward?"

"Never sot eyes on him after he got out of the hack when I stopped at Spring Creek to water my horses. He said he'd git out and stretch his legs by walkin' the rest of the way, as he was goin' to a private house in the country nigh by."

"Did he have no baggage?"

"A black leather travellin'-bag, not very big, as you may know—for he tuk it into the stage with him, and sot it down betwixt his feet."

"And you don't think it likely he was the man Hugh Ellis saw?"

"I don't think it noways likely it was the same man, sir."

"Did you notice the color of his hair?"

"Well, I didn't, Mr. Worruck. But I'll tell you what I'll do. My next trip over I'll see if I can find out who the fellow was, sence it seems a matter of intrust to you."

"Thank you, Gillespie. I shall be obliged if you will do so. You go over again to-morrow, I believe?"

"Yes, sir."

After exchanging a few sentences more, Mr. Warwick bade Gillespie good-morning, and hurried on to the bank.

Hugh Ellis was expecting him impatiently.

"*I've* found something, too, Mr. Warwick," he said, quite trembling with eagerness, as he held up to view a dark crimson-and-yellow silk handkerchief that was considerably worn, and not a little soiled from use. "I got up as soon as it was light enough to see, and hunted the room over, and I found this lying behind the bed. How it was that Tom didn't find it last night when he was making up the bed I don't know."

"How do you know that it was dropped by the burglars?"

"It must have been. How else could it have got into my room? It is not mine. I never saw it, or one like it, before. They must have dropped it."

"It may have been dropped by some of the people who were here yesterday."

"No, sir; impossible. Nobody was in my room. I shut the door and locked it."

"It may be Tom's."

"I don't think so," said Hugh, decidedly; but he looked a little crestfallen. "I'll go and ask him," he continued, starting toward the door, carrying the handkerchief, which he held by one corner, fluttering along.

"Stop, stop!" said Mr. Warwick. "Look if it has a name on it."

Hugh, fingering it rather superciliously, could find no name.

"Are silk handkerchiefs ever marked?"

"Sometimes. Put it down. I am going to breakfast presently, and I will ask Tom about it. Are you certain that there is nothing else to be found in the room?"

"I am certain, sir. I searched the floor first—the whole room, indeed—and then I took every thing off the bed, and shook the counterpane, and the sheets, and the blankets, each one separately. I even took the pillow-cases and the bolster-case off! I assure you, Mr. Warwick, I have looked thoroughly."

"Very well. I need not lose any time here, then; and I am very glad of that, for I am going to start to Chesselton directly after breakfast. See here!"

He sat down to the table—they were in the cashier's room—and put down before him the knife which he had just bought from Jimmy Powell. Then he took out his pocket-book, produced the fragment of blade, and, opening the knife, he placed the fragment upon the whole blade. Hugh uttered an exclamation as he saw that the two were identical in every respect, even to the brilliant newness of the metal. Mr. Warwick explained in as few words as possible all that he had learned from Jimmy Powell, and what he had since heard from the stage-driver.

"Now," he said, when he had concluded his relation, "I am going somewhat upon a venture, which I am not in the habit of doing; but I have an instinct, amounting to a positive conviction, that the man you saw, the man who bought this knife from young Powell"—he touched the broken blade—"the man whom Gillespie describes as wearing green goggles, and a quack doctor that I met last week in Hartsburg, and who, a day or two after I saw him, had to take French leave of the place to escape being lynched, are all one and the same individual; and I shall take young Powell, who says he can identify the rascal, and see if I can't find him. I hope," he added, as he rose to go, "that—Well, Tom, what's the matter?"

Tom, who had at that moment appeared in the open door, responded to this question by another.

"Mistiss say ain't you comin' home to breakfast this mornin', Mass John?"

"Yes, I am just going now. Is this your handkerchief?"

He took up the article in question, and, holding it as Hugh Ellis had done, by one corner, exhibited it to the servant as he advanced.

"Mine? No, sir," answered Tom, with surprise. "I never saw it before, Mass John."

"Well, Hugh, I'll take it and see if I can discover the owner."

He looked round, picked up a newspaper, and, wrapping up the handkerchief, consigned it to his coat-pocket.

"I shall not see you again before I start, Hugh, so good-by. How are you feeling this morning, on the whole?"

"Dreadfully stiff, sir. I ache all over. But I don't mind that, so those infernal scoundrels are brought to taw, and we get back the money."

He said this as he walked to the door with Mr. Warwick, who paused there to shake hands and give him one parting caution.

"Not a word to anybody about the knife or about my movements. In one word, hold your tongue."

"Trust me to do that, sir."

Mr. Marks was just leaving the breakfast-table, when his brother-in-law entered the room. The little Markses, sitting demure and silent—they had been involuntary penitents during the four-and-twenty hours preceding—all started up with irrepressible and rapturous cries of "Unky! unky! Here's unky!"

Even the unnaturally-solemn visage of the cashier relaxed into a smile as the little folk bounded tumultuously forward, each eager to get "unky's" first greetings; and Mrs. Marks's face beamed for a moment. But, before the said greetings were over, Mr. Marks looked as saturnine as ever, and his devoted helpmeet was applying her handkerchief to her eyes.

"Don't go yet, Richard; I have a word to say to you presently," said Mr. Warwick, as he saw the former about to leave the room.—"Well, bairns, have you missed unky much?"

"Oh, that we have! that we have!" was the unanimous and rather stunningly vociferous reply. "We—"

"Hush, this minute, children!" cried their mother, whose temper had not improved since her brother's departure, a month before. "Do you want to deafen your uncle? Go along out now; he has other things to think about than your nonsense. Go along, all of you!—and, John, do come to breakfast!"

"In a minute," answered her brother, without moving from where he stood, just inside the door, surrounded by the children, who were, every one, clinging to him—Jack and Dick having seized each an arm, Sara and Katy having possession of his hands respectively, while poor little Nelly had nothing for it but to clasp her two little fat arms round his knee in an ecstasy of noisy delight. He looked down on them with a smile which was like sunshine to their little hearts, as he listened to their rejoicings at his return. But again Mrs. Marks began a sharp remonstrance and command to them.

"Do let them alone, Bessie!" said Mr. Warwick, a little sharp in turn.—"Here, Sara—hold your hand."

Sara's hand was extended with astonishing quickness, while all the others were breathless with expectation.

"Now, is it honor bright?" asked their uncle, appealing to them generally.

"Yes, unky, honor bright! honor bright!"

"Then, take this key, Sara, and see what you can find in my valise. Go, all of you, and stay in my room till I come. But mind—Sara is to take the things out and put them on the table, and you must all keep quiet and wait patiently."

"Honor bright!" responded they, in a breath, and were gone.

"Bessie, do you think it worth while to punish those poor children for the fault of the thieves who broke into the bank?" said Mr. Warwick, as he sat down to the breakfast-table.

"Punish them, John? I don't know what you mean! I haven't been punishing them."

"Yes, you have, and in the worst possible way—by cloudy looks and unmerited reproof. I wish you would remember what I said to you last night."

Mrs. Marks looked conscience-stricken, and Mr. Warwick turned to her husband, who stood by the fire, waiting for the word that his brother-in-law had for him.

"I have got what I believe to be a clew, Marks, and I shall start immediately after breakfast to follow it up. I don't know when I shall be back—in a day or two, perhaps; but it is not certain. All I can tell you is, that I intend to track down those scoundrels. So, keep up your spirits. You will find that this matter will all come out right at last."

"You really think so?" asked Mr. Marks, a little doubtfully

"I am sure of it. Did you ever know me to be mistaken in an opinion which I expressed deliberately?"

"Why, no; I never did."

"Rely on my opinion in this, then. If I am absent more than a day or two, I will write. Are you going to the bank now? If so, I will say good-by, as I have ordered my buggy to be ready by the time I have finished breakfast."

"I'll see you off," said Mr. Marks, drawing a chair toward the fire, and sitting down. "There's no hurry about my getting to the bank," he added, disconsolately.

"Where are you going, John?" asked Mrs. Marks.

"I am going first to Morton House to see Mrs. Gordon for a few minutes," answered Mr. Warwick, evasively. "By-the-way, Bessie—"

But Bessie, to whom the mention of Mrs. Gordon's name recalled the remembrance of the domestic trouble which had so much afflicted her —before the more important misfortune of the bank robbery occurred, and dwarfed its importance, indeed drove it entirely from her mind for the time being—interrupted him eagerly.

"O John," she cried, "every thing has been going wrong since you left home! Would you believe that Miss Tresham went away the Friday after you left, and, though she was to have come back on Monday, she's never made her appearance from that day to this? and, what's more, we haven't heard one syllable about her! What's become of her, I can't understand, for—"

"Do you recollect what I told you, Warwick, the day she drew her salary at the bank, and wanted it in gold? I remarked to you then that I suspected she was going to leave us; and, you see, I was right," said Mr. Marks, to whom it was quite a satisfaction—a little ray of light in the very dark sky that gloomed over him—to be able thus to vindicate so triumphantly, particularly to his brother-in-law, the correctness of his judgment.

"I remember your saying you were afraid she would leave you," replied Mr. Warwick. "And you have no idea why she left—have heard nothing from her?"

"Not a word—not the scrape of a pen!" cried Mrs. Marks, volubly. "All her things are here yet—two trunks, and ever so many—"

"You know she drew a thousand dollars in gold from me on Tuesday," Mr. Marks here broke in, with an animation which he had not exhibited before, since the first suspicion of the bank robbery had dawned on his horrified apprehension. "Well, on Friday, when she was going off, she borrowed *ten dollars* from Bessie! Think of that—ten dollars! Now, I say that there's something wrong about all this—one way or another—and I made up my mind that, if she didn't come back at the time she said, and couldn't give a satisfactory account of why she went—"

"She went to see the priest, Richard—she said so!" cried Mrs. Marks, who was still somewhat of a partisan of Katharine's.

"Yes, she said so," answered Mr. Marks, dryly. "But she didn't say what was the reason this St. John—you remember the man you warned me about, Warwick, when you met him as he was going out of the bank that day?"

Mr. Warwick nodded.

"Well, there is some connection—"

Here Mrs. Marks's eagerness grew quite uncontrollable, and she dashed into the conversation—taking the floor by storm from her more quiet husband—and proceeded to pour out the whole story of St. John's visit to Katharine immediately on her return from Annesdale: Mrs. Gordon's having come in while St. John was there; what Mrs. Gordon had said; Katharine's hasty departure; Morton Annesley's call; St. John's call; Mrs. Annesley's call; St. John's second call, and the manner in which the latter had persisted ever since in persecuting the whole family, in the effort to obtain information of Katharine's whereabouts; her own solemn conviction that Katharine had gone away to get rid of St. John, and that she would never come back while he remained in Tallahoma; and Mr. Marks's obstinate resolution not to receive her again into his family, if she did come back

Mr. Warwick listened in attentive silence, and had finished his breakfast before the narration was concluded. When Mrs. Marks finally stopped an instant to take breath, he turned to her husband.

"Has it never occurred to you that Miss Tresham might have been detained away accidentally?"

"Never!" answered Mr. Marks, emphatically. "It only occurs to me that there's something wrong. I'm sure of it; and, though I don't know what it is, I'll have nothing more to do with Miss Tresham. I told Bessie at the time that it was a risky business to be engaging a governess without knowing any thing about her. I have no idea that Miss Tresham will ever return here; but, if she walked into the room this minute, she should not stay very long. I'm done with her."

Mr. Warwick said nothing. He did not have time to argue the question just then, and, in fact, what could he have said? Perfectly ignorant of Katharine's motives, or the reasons which she might be able to give for her apparently singular conduct, he thought it best to be silent as to his knowledge of her present place of sojourn. He could only conjecture that Mrs. Marks's suspicion of her having left Tallahoma to avoid St. John was correct, and, as he had but a moderate opinion of Mrs. Marks's powers of reticence—or, indeed, of the capacity of people in general in that particular—he judged it most prudent to leave matters as they were—at least, until his return from the journey which he was about taking. Unwilling as he had been to entertain the suspicion suggested by Mrs. Gordon concerning St. John, he had found it impossible to put the idea from him, notwithstanding that the evidence of Hugh Ellis as to the appearance of the burglars went far to discredit its probability. The correctness of Hugh's observation in the case of one of the two—which Mr. Warwick considered fully corroborated by the testimony of the little Powell—entitled his statement to respect, and a little staggered the intuitive conviction, which had steadily been gaining ground in Mr. Warwick's mind, that Mrs. Gordon was right. Yet still, that conviction was only staggered, not done away with; and, though he thought it necessary to follow the clew which he had obtained, and which, so far as he was aware, did not point to St. John as a participant in the outrage, he was exceedingly anxious that the man should not leave Tallahoma during his own absence, and anxious, also, that he should continue ignorant of Katharine's movements. Therefore, he would not risk any thing, he thought, by premature candor. When the affair of the robbery was off his hands, he would take up this mystery about the governess, and see if he could not unravel it. So, without a word upon the subject, he rose, and, after a few more encouraging assurances that he would "bring the business" (of the robbery) "all straight," he took leave of the Markses, senior and junior, and, entering the buggy, which was at the gate, told Cyrus to drive to Mr. Powell's store.

As he was passing the hotel, his quick eye caught sight of St. John on the bench that ran along the wall from end to end of the long piazza (for the convenience of the loungers who there did congregate at all times and seasons) engaged in what, to appearance, was the business of his life—smoking. He sat apart from a group of noisy talkers, but near enough to enjoy the benefit of hearing their conversation.

No sooner did Mr. Warwick appear in sight, than one of these gentlemen of leisure, a brother lawyer, started up, and stepped to the edge of the piazza to exchange a word with him as he passed.

"Warwick! A moment, will you, Warwick!" cried he. "I did not know that you were back. When did you arrive?"

"Yesterday evening," answered Mr. Warwick, as he stopped and shook hands cordially. "But I am off again, you see."

"Ah?" said the other, with some surprise. "I thought you would have gone to work about the robbery. Don't you intend to hunt down those scoundrels?"

Mr. Warwick smiled. "You know my faith in the old saw, 'Give a thief rope enough, and he is sure to hang himself.'"

Mr. Ashe—the legal brother—smiled also, and very significantly; though, as he stood with his back to the group in the piazza, nobody but Mr. Warwick himself perceived the smile, or the glance that accompanied it. He knew Mr. Warwick's faith in the said proverb; but he knew also that Mr. Warwick invariably took the precaution, in cases of the kind, to hold the end of the rope in his own hand—and shrewdly suspected that he was not departing from his usual custom on the present occasion. A few general remarks followed after this—Mr. Ashe judiciously refraining from indiscreet questions — and then Mr. Warwick, pleading haste, went on his way. But he had taken the opportunity during the moment in which he was stationary almost directly in front of St. John—for he had not stopped the buggy until it passed a few feet beyond the group of loungers—to cast one or two rapid, apparently careless, but in reality very keen glances at that personage. Glances which were returned with interest—since, on more than one account, the lawyer was an object of no common regard to the scheming adventurer. This was the man who had spirited away Felix Gordon—this the man who, according to the unanimous belief of his townsmen, "would soon ferret out the bank thieves." St. John had no particular, or, rather, no personal knowledge of Mr. Warwick's character; but he had heard enough about it in the discussions concerning the bank robbery, which were in everybody's mouth, to excite his apprehension.

"Yet," thought he, moodily watching the smoke, as it curled away from his lips, "what can the man do?" And then he went over in his mind all the precautions against detection which his comrade had so elaborately adopted; he remembered that this comrade was accomplished in the art of deceiving London and Parisian detectives; and he smiled cynically at the idea of a village-lawyer in "this d—d backwoods country," being able to outwit such an adept in his profession. For himself, he had not the slightest uneasiness. His figure had been so effectually disguised by much clothing and a heavy blanket-overcoat, that nobody, he was certain, would ever imagine that the tall, slender, and elegant form, so familiar now to Tallahoma eyes, could have been transformed into that of Burglar No. 2, whose portrait passed from lip to lip as "short and square-built; just about such a looking man as Mr. Shields."

Meanwhile, Mr. Warwick drove on a square or two, and stopped before Mr. Powell's store.

"Is your father in, Jimmy?" he said, as the boy hurried forward to meet him.

"Yes, sir. Will you walk into the counting-room?"

He led the way to a glass door at the farther extremity of the store, opened it, ushered in the lawyer, and closed it again—looking regretfully, as he did so, at the curtain which concealed the interior of the apartment from his view. He had scarcely returned to his place near the entrance of the store, however, before the folds of this curtain were pulled aside, and he saw his father's hand beckoning to him. All elate, he bounded down the long room, and disappeared from the gaze of the wondering clerks. A few minutes afterward, the door was again opened, and Mr. Warwick, Mr. Powell, and Jimmy, all issued forth—the face of the latter beaming with pleasure.

"I am very much obliged to you, Powell," said Mr. Warwick, as they walked toward the door. "I'll take good care of Jimmy, and bring him safe back, I promise you."

"I don't doubt that, Mr. Warwick. Always glad to accommodate you in any way, sir; and particularly glad in this case—for Marks's sake as well as your own. I only hope Jimmy may be of use to you."

They shook hands, and Mr. Warwick, reëntering his buggy, pursued his way in one direction, while Jimmy, after also shaking hands with his father, and receiving a few parting injunctions from him, walked off in another.

The latter went home, and, as Mr. Warwick had advised, put his tooth-brush and a change of linen into a pocket of his overcoat, and then proceeded, by a short cut through the woods, to Morton House. So correctly had Mr. Warwick reckoned the time which his own and the boy's movements would require, that, just as he drove out of the Morton domain, Jimmy emerged from the wood on the opposite side of the road, and joined him.

"I give you credit for your punctuality," he said, with a smile. "Let me have the reins, Cyrus. I shall be back in a day or two. Good-by.—Up with you, Jimmy—this side."

He drove off, down the Saxford road, and kept it for several miles; then he took a fork to the left, and, after pursuing this for some miles farther, emerged into the Chesselton road.

CHAPTER XXXVI.

CHECKMATED.

On Saturday afternoon, St. John took his usual sunset stroll, which invariably led him past the Marks residence, into the country toward Morton House. He was in good spirits—in high spirits, in fact—for, by the Chesselton mail of the morning before, he had received a letter posted at the stage-house from which Gillespie had taken up his goggle-wearing passenger (a country post-office, as well as stage-house), advising him of the safety thus far of his associate. Added to this, he was under the impression that Mr. Warwick had "gone off on a wrong scent." Not an hour had elapsed from the time at which that gentleman halted for a moment at the hotel piazza to speak to his friend Mr. Ashe, before the group of loungers were discussing the fact of his having taken Jimmy Powell and started to Saxford. Everybody had heard Hugh Ellis's account of the man who was at the bank with the ragged note, and was aware that Jimmy Powell believed he had seen the same man, on the same day, in his father's store; it was known that Mr. Warwick had been at the stage-office, making the most minutely particular inquiries; and somebody had met Mr. Warwick with Jimmy Powell in his buggy, travelling toward Saxford. With such circumstantial evidence, the inference was clear, thought the gossiping loungers and their interested auditor — Mr. Warwick had gone to Saxford in pursuit of the burglars, and had taken the boy along to identify the one he had seen. And while Mr. Warwick's admiring townsfolk exulted in anticipation at the success which they were sure awaited him, St. John smiled to himself sarcastically, and with intense satisfaction, at the failure which *he* was as confident the lawyer would meet with.

He was thinking of this failure, congratulating his *confrère* in crime and himself on the admirable conception and execution of their daring exploit, and altogether in a better humor with Fortune than he had been for many a day before, when a curve in the road he was pursuing, brought him into an open and rather elevated space of ground, over which a crimson light from the blazing western sky was at the moment streaming. St. John was no lover of Nature. He did not turn to admire the magnificent sunset; but having just emerged from between two walls of lofty and dense forest, which had made an almost twilight gloom around him, he was surprised to find that the sun was not yet set, and he paused an instant to look at his watch. As he stood motionless, his figure was so clearly defined in the broad light, and against the background of sun-gilded forest, that Mr. Warwick, who was advancing from the opposite direction, though at east a quarter of a mile distant from the place where he stood, recognized the slender and elegant form at once. As it chanced that he was just approaching the gates of Morton House, he checked his horses.

"I have business here that I must stop to attend to," he said. "I suppose you can drive on to town alone, Jimmy?"

"Certainly, sir."

"You will find Cyrus at my office. Just hand the horses over to him." He alighted, and held out his hand with a cordial smile. "I shall not forget the service you have rendered me, my boy. Good-evening."

St. John, discovering that it was so much earlier than he had thought, walked on, with his eyes on the ground, as was his habit, and his thoughts still dwelling upon the success of his late "venture." He was considering whether it would not be safest to destroy the paper, rather than run the risk of detection at any future time in attempting to pass it. This question had already been discussed by his associate and himself; for, even before he had heard of the precautions taken by the cashier to stop the notes, he was aware of the danger attending the illicit possession of bank-paper. But it had been decided to keep it, on the chance of being able to realize at least a part of it, after the excitement about the robbery had blown over. He had intended to insist on one point—that not a dollar of it should be used, until he himself was safe out of the country. His own safety once assured, he was not uncomfortably solicitous about that of the man whom he regarded merely as a tool forced upon him by Fate.

Engrossed in meditations so interesting, Mr. St. John gave but the most careless glance at the buggy he met and passed. He had left behind him the sunny knoll which had betrayed his presence to Mr. Warwick, as the road again entered between aisles of thick forest growth, when suddenly he lifted his eyes with a sense of instinctive apprehension, and perceived at a distance of fifteen or twenty yards before him on his path, and advancing at a quick pace toward him, a man he instantly recognized as the lawyer whom he had supposed to be at that very time in Saxford. He was startled—so much startled, that, for once, presence of mind deserted him. He turned and began to retrace his way to the village, hoping thus to avoid the most transient meeting with a man for whom he had felt, from the first moment he ever saw him, a sense of unequivocal distrust — a distrust amounting to positive fear under present circumstances. After a moment or two, he felt somewhat reassured from his first panic. What pretext could the man find for addressing him? So thinking, he walked more slowly, and endeavored to collect himself to meet with a properly supercilious wonder any salutation which the lawyer might make. But notwithstanding his resolution his heart beat quickly, as near and nearer behind sounded the sharp, firm tread that was overtaking him rapidly. Just as he had left the forest shade once more, and stood in the full light of the setting sun, a voice at his side said:

"Good-evening, Mr. St. John."

He turned with an air of affected surprise, cast a single glance at the speaker, responded coldly, "Good-evening," and fell back a pace, with the obvious intention of letting the other pass on. But Mr. Warwick, instead of taking the hint, stepped a little forward, and faced so as to impede the way.

"This chance meeting has saved me the trouble of hunting you up in Tallahoma, Mr. St. John," he said, quietly. "We will sit down on this log, if you please. I have something to say to you."

The tone, the manner, above all, the expression of those piercing blue eyes, struck terror to the guilty man's soul. He quailed for an instant; but, rallying then by a great effort, answered sneeringly:

"Really, sir, you are very obliging. But, to the best of my recollection, I have not the honor of your acquaintance. You probably mistake me for some other person."

He would have moved on, but the tall form of the lawyer effectually barred the way. The only possibility of escape was by positive flight; and reckless, and morally degraded as St. John was, there still remained with him one at least of the instincts of gentlemanhood—courage. He could not fly from an adversary: on the contrary, the very sense of open antagonism gave to him an unaffected boldness of bearing and of feeling, which the consciousness of crime had almost paralyzed the moment before. He met Mr. Warwick's eye unflinchingly, as he said with supercilious *hauteur:*

"What is the meaning of this insolence, sir?"

Mr. Warwick smiled. "I am a little premature, I admit, in claiming your acquaintance," he said, in so ordinary a tone that only a very nice ear could have detected an inflection of mockery in it; "but I have a little document to present to you, which will correct the informality—a letter of introduction from your friend Mr. Gilbert Didier, *alias* Dr. Joyner, *alias* Mr. Johnson, *alias* etc., etc., etc., *ad infinitum*, I have no doubt."

He took out his pocket-book deliberately—though he kept his eye on St. John—opened it and produced a small, sealed note, which he extended.

St. John did not move to take it. His sallow face had grown actually livid, and he reeled as he stood, almost like one drunken. Mr. Warwick had the character of being a hard man; but, as he gazed at the cowering form that only a moment before had worn so brave a front, an expression very much like that of compassion passed over his face. It vanished, however, as he saw the instinct of the bravo flash into the eyes of the detected criminal. He was prepared for this; and, as St. John plunged his hand into his bosom, he himself threw forward his right hand, and St. John, before he saw the weapon, heard the click of a pistol as it was cocked.

"If you withdraw your hand, I fire," said the lawyer, in a tone not to be misunderstood. "You see that, in every sense, you are in my power—in my power absolutely. If you wish to save your life and your reputation, you will not attempt useless resistance, but will follow the example of your associate whom I yesterday evening caused to be arrested and lodged in Chesselton Jail for the late robbery of the bank at Tallahoma, and who has confessed his guilt."

He paused, and, with his pistol still covering St. John's person, waited for an answer—waited patiently enough, for he saw that a terrible struggle was going on in the mind of the miserable man, and he believed it would end in the manner he wished. So he stood, watchful but patient, as the thin and now fearfully pallid face worked with a convulsive passion frightful to behold. Suddenly the face grew calm, settling into an expression of half-sullen despair, of half-fierce defiance.

"What are your proofs against me?" he asked, with a directness which elicited Mr. Warwick's respect for his discretion in thus coming at once to an understanding of his position.

"Your promissory note in your own name to Didier, 'for one-half the specie secured in your late enterprise on the bank at Tallahoma'—I quote, you perceive, the wording of the note itself—with an acknowledgment that the whole amount of money stolen is in your possession, and that the paper shall be disposed of as hereafter agreed between Didier and yourself," was the reply, in a perfectly dispassionate and business-like tone.

St. John gnashed his teeth.

"Also," continued Mr. Warwick, in the same tone, "a letter of date of Thursday morning last, purporting to be from James Smith to Thomas Johnson, advising the latter that 'business goes on prosperously,' and so forth. The writing of this letter (though some attempt at disguising the hand was made), and the paper upon which it was written, would be recognized by a court of law as identical with those of the promissory note."

"The vile hound, so he betrayed me!" exclaimed St. John, more to himself than to Mr. Warwick.

But the latter answered:

"Joyner, or Didier, you mean, I suppose? No; I always give the devil his due. He did not betray you. I don't think he could have been induced to do so. I obtained the evidence I hold very much against his will by— Read his note. That, I presume, will explain."

Once more he held the note toward St. John, and the latter, withdrawing his hand from his bosom, this time condescended to take it, though with an air of disdain. Tearing it hastily open, he read as follows:

"Don't think that I betrayed you, St. John. I did not even make the slightest admission about myself until after this infernal lawyer—curse him! Curse his whole tribe, for they are the same all the world over, from Lincoln's Inn to this damned out-of-the-way hole that I am caged in! I was going to say that I did not make the slightest admission about myself, much less about you, until after all was up by his discovery of the false bottom in my instrument-box that I showed you. I had stowed your note and letter in there for safety. I had hoped that you would escape with the money, for there was nothing to criminate you, or even to suggest a suspicion against you, until this infernal law-ferret scented out the box, and got possession of your note, and the tools that are my letters of credit and *open-sesame* into banks and out of prisons. After that it was no good in holding out, and I made the best terms I could with him for you as well as myself. Take my advice, and follow my example. *You* will get off easy if you make no difficulty about giving up the money, which is lost to us anyhow, and it will make considerable difference for me. Don't get into one of your devil's humors and refuse to listen to reason. You see he has evidence to convict you. And you owe it to me to do all you can for me, as I would have done for you; for I'll be d—d if any thing would have induced me to betray you.

"Truly yours,

"GILBERT DIDIER."

"Have you seen this?" said St. John to the lawyer, when he had finished reading it.

"No."

"Is what he says true?"

Mr. Warwick took the note, which the other offered, with his left hand, and in turn ran his eye over its contents, without, however, suspending his vigilance as to St. John's movements.

"Yes, it is true," he answered, briefly.

"What are your terms?"

"I will spare you arrest and prosecution for the crime you have committed, and will keep your secret—not even telling it to my brother-in-law—on two conditions: first, that you at once give up the whole of the money; secondly, that you agree to leave this State and never return to it. If you refuse these conditions, I will arrest you on the spot. You look as if you thought that would not be easy to do"—he interrupted himself to say, as St. John's lip curled into a sneering smile—"but you are mistaken. As I told you a minute ago, you are in my power absolutely. The first movement that you make to possess yourself of the pistol that you have in your bosom, I will disable you. I don't intend to kill you, but I'll wing you; both sides, if necessary. I am the more powerful man of the two, and could then deal with you easily myself. But I need not be at that trouble. I have only to raise my voice and shout for assistance, to be heard by some of the Morton negroes. The quarters are just round the point of that wood, and the hands are in from work by this time. They know me, and will obey any orders I give them."

St. John's eyes sank to the ground, and he gnawed his lip sullenly, without speaking.

Mr. Warwick, after a minute's silence, resumed:

"Decide at once whether you accept my conditions. I am in a hurry."

"What terms do you offer as regards Didier?"

"I have not made public the evidence that I hold against him. He was arrested at my instance, *on suspicion* of having been connected with the burglary. I need not say that my evidence is sufficient to convict you both. He was aware of this, or he would not have made the admissions which he did to me privately—for he is a bold scoundrel. I must do him that justice. On the restoration of the money, I will withdraw my accusation against him, and he shall be released, on condition that he, too, leaves the country. I shall retain the proofs against both of you that I possess, and, if either breaks the condition I impose by coming back into the State, he will be coming to immediate arrest and prosecution."

"Your conditions won't do. I must have some of the money."

"Not a stiver!"

"You may whistle for it yourself, then. My arrest and conviction will not help you to a knowledge of where it is. Allow me five thousand dollars — the reward which that fellow Marks has offered for its recovery—two thousand five hundred apiece to Didier and myself, and I will produce it. Otherwise—do your worst! I shall at least have the gratification of baffling you, and ruining your insolent brother-in-law."

"You are not as clever as you think yourself, Mr. St. John," said Warwick, dryly. "You forget that your accomplice knows where the money is concealed. To give you a chance, he refused to treat with me himself on the subject. But I leave you to judge whether he is likely to persist in his silence when he learns that you threw away the chance thus afforded you, and as his own safety depends upon the restitution of the money. I give you terms much more favorable than you have any right to expect, because it will be less troublesome to me to receive the money immediately, and let you go, than to arrest and imprison you, and then make another journey to Chesselton to bring Didier up here. Once for all, do you take my conditions or not?"

There was a pause, a struggle—a bitter struggle in St. John's mind, before he answered, sullenly—

"Yes."

"Produce the money. I am aware that it is secreted in the woods somewhere hereabout. Deliver it to me at once."

Without a word the defeated man turned and walked toward the great iron gates that gave entrance to Morton House, his companion keeping beside him. The sun had set very shortly after the foregoing conversation commenced, and it was now deep dusk on the lonely road which they traversed; but when they entered the gates of Morton—they did enter, St. John leading the way still silently—there was something of twilight yet lingering in the more open path that they pursued; and the full moon was just rising grandly brilliant in the clear eastern heaven. St. John, after keeping the path for a short distance, plunged into the thickest of the wood, and finally stopped at a spot well chosen for the purpose to which it had been applied—a sort of miniature ravine that was shut in on all sides by a thick undergrowth, and surrounded by tall forest-trees. Halting beside the huge trunk of a fallen tree, he stirred among the dry leaves with his foot for an instant, then, stooping, took up by the handle a mattock which had been concealed there. Walking a few steps farther, to the foot of the tree, he again pushed away a quantity of dry leaves that filled a hollow caused by the violent uptearing from the earth of the roots of this forest monarch, which had been blown down by a hurricane, and proceeded to exhume with the mattock the treasure that he was forced to resign.

Mr. Warwick watched the work in silence; but when St. John, after removing the shallow layer of earth that had covered a pair of small leather saddle-bags, hauled it out with the mattock and pushed it with a heavy thump toward him, he said: "Is the money all here?"

"Yes."

"Very well. Keep your part of the agreement and I shall keep mine."

He picked up the saddle-bags, and they left the spot as silently as they had sought it; and it was not until they had regained the open path again that another word was spoken. Then Mr Warwick paused and said:

"Our paths separate here. I have been travelling and am tired—and this is rather a heavy weight to carry from here to Tallahoma. I will cross the wood to Morton House, and borrow Mrs. Gordon's carriage to take me to town. Good-evening."

St. John deigned no reply. He waited to hear the conclusion of Mr. Warwick's speech—then, without a syllable, without even a glance, he turned and walked rapidly toward the gates.

Some short time afterward, to Mrs. Gordon's surprise, Harrison ushered Mr. Warwick into her sitting-room. He carried on his arm the leather saddle-bags, and, declining the servant's proposal to relieve him of it, deposited it himself on a side-table before accepting Mrs. Gordon's invitation to join her at her tea, which she was just taking.

"You do not drink tea," she said.—"Coffee, Harrison, and something a little more substantial than this." She pointed to the table.

While Harrison went to execute this order, the lawyer told his story, and preferred his request for the carriage.

"I tell this to you only," he said, after she had congratulated him cordially on the recovery of the money. "Having received the first hint of the man's guilt from you, I do not consider it a breach of my promise to tell you that your suspicion was just."

Harrison returned, here, with a reënforcement of edibles that quite transformed the appearance of Mrs. Gordon's tea-table; and, after taking his supper with the appetite of a man who has been travelling, and is in excellent spirits, Mr. Warwick said good-evening to his friend and hostess, and once more preferring to carry his saddle-bags himself (a little to the scandal of Harrison, who was old-fashioned in his ideas of the proprieties), he entered the carriage which was in readiness, and was soon set down at the garden-gate of the Marks residence.

Passing up the walk and through the piazza, he entered the dining-room, and found Mr. and Mrs. Marks its sole occupants—the children having been sent off to bed when the tea-table was removed, an hour before. He paused on the threshold of the door, and, himself unperceived, regarded for an instant, with a smile of dry humor, the disconsolate-looking pair. Mr. Marks, solemn-visaged and pale, sat gazing with a dull stare into the fire; while his wife, her usually busy hands folded in pathetic idleness, was looking sorrowfully at him.

"Well, Marks, I have brought you back part of your money," said Mr. Warwick, advancing into the room. "Just draw that little table forward, and we will count it, and see how much is missing."

Mr. Marks sat motionless, so startled and astonished was he by this unexpected appearance and address of his brother-in-law. He looked from Mr. Warwick's face to the saddle-bags on his arm, and back again, in dumb incredulity of the possibility of such good fortune; until the latter, growing tired of the weight, deposited it upon the knees of the stupefied cashier, while he himself fetched the table he had asked for, transferred to it a candle from the mantel-piece, lifted the saddle-bags again and set them down with a sounding thud beside the candle, drew a chair to the table, and sat down. Then, as he proceeded methodically to unbuckle one of the bags, life flashed back through Mr. Marks's stagnant veins, and he drew his chair forward with feverish eagerness—impatient of the slowness, as it seemed to him, with which Mr. Warwick's long white fingers did their work. One, two, three straps; and the buckles were new and stiff, hard to open. But the flap was lifted at last, and Mr. Warwick's hand brought forth bag after bag, and ranged them before the hungry eyes that looked on. When he had emptied both bags, he began telling over their contents. Twenty-four canvas bags—the mint mark, "$1,000," bright and black on each—seals unbroken (with the exception of one, a little larger than the rest, which had been opened and was now tied at its mouth with a piece of red tape), and two packages of bank-notes. These Mr. Warwick examined first. He patiently counted the smallest package—the notes that had been in circulation. "Thirteen hundred and twenty-seven dollars," he said, as he put down the last bill. "That was the amount, was it not?"

"That was the amount," answered Mr. Marks, recovering speech.

"Now let us see whether this is right too," said the lawyer, unwrapping a newspaper that was folded loosely around the larger package.

"All right!" cried the cashier, eagerly, as he saw that here too the seals were intact. "Good God! I never thought to see any of it again, and here it is just as I saw it last! This bag" —he took up the one that was tied—"has eighty dollars over the amount in the others. It was part of what I was to keep, and I put the eighty dollars in—"

"John, how did you get it back!" exclaimed Mrs. Marks, who had been literally inarticulate with joy up to this moment. "Oh, my dear, dear John, how did you get it back?"

"Never mind about that, Bessie," he answered, smiling. "All I can tell you is that I tracked down one of the burglars and made him disgorge."

"You've got him safe, I hope, for punishment?" said Mr. Marks.

"No. I could not secure the thief and the money both—so I preferred of the two to take the money," answered he, rising and standing on the hearth-rug with his back to the fire.

"But John—"

"If you ask me any more questions, Bessie, I'll make Marks pay me the five thousand dollars reward that he offered for the recovery of the money," interrupted her brother, with his slight and rare laugh.

"Why, you don't mean, John, that you're not going to tell us any thing more than this?"

"Yes, Bessie, I mean just that. I have conjured back the money—there it is!—and that must satisfy you."

"It satisfies me!" cried Mr. Marks, speaking like himself once more. "John, I don't know how to thank you!" He started up and began shaking Mr. Warwick's hand so hard that the latter could not restrain a slight grimace of pain.

"Don't try," he said, as he managed to withdraw the suffering member from that merciless grasp. "Where are the children? Not gone to bed already, surely?"

"Yes, they are gone to bed. It's not very early," answered Mrs. Marks, apologetically. "Why, what am I thinking of!—don't you want some supper, John?"

"Thank you, no—I have had supper. Have you heard any thing from or of Miss Tresham yet?"

"Not a word. And never shall, I expect." She sighed.

"There you are mistaken. I can give you some news of her."

"You can!"

"Yes." And he proceeded to describe his having found her in Hartsburg the week before, and all that had followed. The Markses were amazed, and even a little sympathetic so far as the brain-fever was concerned; but Mr. Marks remained firm in his resolution of having nothing more to do with her. "I liked her very much," he said, "and all may be right so far as she herself is concerned; but I'm convinced there's something wrong about this Mr. St. John, and there certainly is some connection between the two; so I think it safest to have nothing more to do with Miss Tresham. I've made up my mind to it, and I hope you won't try to change my resolution, John—"

"Certainly not," interrupted Mr. Warwick, a little coldly. "If you have made up your mind, that settles the matter. All I have to say is, that you are acting very hastily and very foolishly, in my opinion. I wonder if Tom has gone to bed, as well as the children?"

"Do you want him?"

"Yes; I should like to send word to Hugh Ellis that the money is safe."

"You're right!" cried Mr. Marks, with animation. "Poor Hugh! I'll go and send at once, and relieve his mind."

The message certainly relieved Hugh's mind, but it put his curiosity on the rack; and great was his disappointment the next morning when he learned that this curiosity was not to be gratified by any more satisfactory information than that very meagre account which the Markses had already heard. Nor was he alone in his disappointment at Mr. Warwick's reticence. All Lagrange felt defrauded and indignant; and St. John, as he sat next morning for the last time in the hotel piazza (he left in the Saxford coach at noon that day), listening to the gossip of the loungers, had the satisfaction—if in his existing frame of mind any thing could be a satisfaction to him—of hearing Mr. Warwick's obstinate refusal to give any explanation of how he recovered the money, commented upon and censured in the strongest terms.

CHAPTER XXXVII.

TO WIN OR LOSE IT ALL.

February came with a burst of tender, spring-like beauty that seemed to take the world by storm. Far away on the hills and over the woods, the soft, purple mist of the spring-time—that mist to the careless eye so like, and to the observant eye so essentially unlike, the blue, melancholy haze of the Indian summer—rested like a promise of coming beauty and budding vegetation, hung like a veil of enchantment over each distant scene, rounding every outline, softening every rugged shape, clothing all things with a loveliness that charmed the senses like a draught of fairy elixir; if, indeed, we do not dishonor Nature by such comparisons, for what fairy elixir could be half as full of the delicious power to charm as her least gleam of sunshine, her palest sunset, the least flicker of her shadow upon a velvet turf? Sometimes February comes with dun skies and dropping tears, and sad robes trailing over the cold-brown earth; but then again—and this more frequently—she comes in the winsome guise of which we have spoken, crowned with flowers—who does not love them better even than the royal roses of May?—and followed by a train of joyous birds that seem to fill the air with their happy twitter and full-throated song. "Singing, perhaps, does not so much make them happy, as it saves their little hearts from bursting because they are so full of happiness," says one of the sweetest and most tender of writers; and sometimes we think this must be so. Sometimes we feel as if they utter *our* happiness, as well as their own, *our* thanks to God for the bounteous gift of all this His fair and glorious creation.

It seemed so at least to Katharine, as she felt the world waking to new life all around her—felt it as she felt the health that was coming like new wine into her veins, and flushing her cheek. She was by this time domesticated at Bellefont, and every thing was very pleasant around her

Luxurious appointments, plentiful attendance, kind faces, cordial tones, smiles that seem only the faint reflections of warm hearts—who has not been cheered by such a haven once or twice in life, at least? Who has not gone forth warmed, invigorated, grateful for what has been, and courageous to meet what may be? Just now it was the time of rest with Katharine. The first period of convalescence was past, and she was well enough to make one of the family circle into which she had entered; yet the habits of illness still clung to her, and the task of getting well was as yet far from complete. Repose was still a necessity; and this repose the Lesters took especial care to secure for her. Though the house was thronged with company half the time, Katharine found that every thing had been arranged so that she could see as much or as little of it as she chose; and when she chose to see exceedingly little, nobody found fault or was offended. Mrs. Lester, a quiet, motherly old lady who wore black-silk aprons, and carried a huge basket of keys, sympathized with the young stranger, and spent much time in concocting delicate, dainty dishes with which to tempt her appetite; Colonel Lester made her welcome in very pleasant and hearty fashion, and promised her exercise on a "splendid" riding-horse that would bring back her roses as soon as she was able to sit in the saddle; Miss Lester was charmingly kind, and kept her dozen or so of boisterous cousins to herself as much as possible; Miss Vernon Katharine liked better every day; Spitfire condescended to remember that he had formerly made her acquaintance, and to greet her with tolerable amiability; and the redoubtable Bulger (whose teeth in themselves were enough to terrify a nervous person into hysterics), suavely permitted her to pat his head, when he was triumphantly marched in for inspection by his doting mistress. Even the maid who was detailed for her special service had a bright, pleasant face; and any one who has ever suffered from a sour, sullen, or unwilling servant, will need no assurance that this was a very far from inconsiderable item in the general sunshine.

On the whole, Katharine felt as if she was in a sort of dream. Tallahoma!—Mrs. Marks!—the school-room!—St. John!—Mrs. Gordon! What had become of them all? Which was real, that life or this one? What had befallen all those people since she parted from them so long ago? What chance had led these kind Samaritans to the way-side where they had found her? It all seemed strange—nearly as strange as when she first waked from unconsciousness and asked those bewildered questions which nobody would answer—which nobody had answered to her satisfaction yet.

One evening, a few days after her arrival at Bellefont, she was down-stairs, in the cosy sitting-room where the family assembled when there was no company, where Mrs. Lester placidly knitted in one corner, where Colonel Lester read the papers, and occasionally nodded over them, where he played whist, and never nodded over that, where Miss Lester had her particular seat by the fire (the same seat on which she had nursed her doll a few years before), from which she chattered nonsense unceasingly, where Spitfire basked luxuriously on the hearth-rug, and where a little darkey with an unnaturally solemn face and an unnaturally-clean check apron, sat in a corner by the fireplace on a low stool, ready to hold Mrs. Lester's yarn, to bring chips, and run errands generally, for anybody who wanted any thing. It was a pleasant, home-like scene, Katharine thought, as she sat back in a corner (it is astonishing how many corners a room of this description can manage to have), and watched and listened, herself quiet and silent. There was a piano in still another corner—somewhat in the shade—and at this Miss Vernon was singing that softest and sweetest of Scotch ballads, "The Land o' the Leal." The clear voice—which had no power in it for bravura execution—sounded very sweetly in the touching cadences of the tender melody. They were all silent, and all listening — even Colonel Lester, who cared no more for music in general than for the beating of a tin pan—when there came a step in the hall. "Some of the ubiquitous cousins," thought Katharine, with a sigh of regret; but a familiar voice was heard saying, "Yes, I know the way," and Godfrey Seymour entered the room. The music did not cease. Miss Vernon only nodded to him with a smile, and went on singing, while he made the tour of the fire, shaking hands with every member of the circle, and only recognizing Katharine when he came to her last of all. "Miss Tresham!" he exclaimed. "What a pleasant surprise!" Then he greeted her warmly, and sat down by her side. Katharine did not feel much like conversation, but it never required any effort to talk to Seymour. He was so frank, so simple, so free from all effort himself, that, unconsciously, he forced others to be natural also. Miss Tresham was startled when at last she glanced at the clock and saw how long she had been talking to him.

"I must go," she said, smiling. "I am an invalid still, and keep invalid hours. You will excuse me, won't you?"

"Of course, I excuse you," he answered, "especially since I hope to see you very soon again."

He went with her to the door, shook hands when he said good-night, and then, in turning back, cast a quick glance round the room, that took in the occupation of every one of its inmates. One of the ubiquitous cousins *had* arrived, and was entertaining Miss Lester, Colonel Lester was nodding over a newspaper, Mrs. Lester was winding some yarn which Flibbertigibbet, (a name of his young mistress's bestowal), held solemnly on his two little black paws. Miss Vernon was still at the piano, singing softly to herself. To the piano, therefore, Mr. Seymour took his way.

"I don't know what you will say to me," he began, as he settled himself in a seat by the keyboard. "I have broken faith with everybody, and told Miss Tresham that Morton is staying with me."

"Indeed!" said Miss Vernon, stopping in the midst of her song. "And what did she say?"

"Nothing in particular," he answered, "though I assure you I was frightened enough when I found I had let out the secret. I had been warned so solemnly against any indiscretion of the kind, that I fully expected her to faint; but, instead of that, she had not even the grace to turn pale."

"How foolish you are!" said the young lady, smiling. "Of course, nobody ever expected her to faint, or even to turn pale. In fact, there is no reason why she should not be told about him. You know it was by the doctor's orders that every thing has been kept from her up to this time; but I think she is well enough now to bear something a little more exciting than dear Mrs. Lester's nice soups and omelets."

"I bring a message from Annesley, anyway. The poor fellow wants to know when he can come over. I was charged to make intercession for him, and I can do so most sincerely. It is amazingly dull for him over at our place."

"That is a slander on your place which I won't sanction. Because Mr. Annesley happens to be lovesick, and unable to find any pleasure in any thing that is not brightened by Miss Tresham's eyes"—(then with some contrition)—"there goes my sharp tongue again! I wonder if I never shall cure myself of saying ill-natured things? Honestly, I am very sorry for him, and it was only to-day that I told Maggie that she ought to write a note and tell him he might come. I am very glad you paved the way by speaking of him to Miss Tresham. By-the-by, this reminds me that Mrs. Lester has received a letter from Mr. Warwick, begging her to keep all accounts of the Tallahoma bank robbery from Miss Tresham, and adding that he will be down here soon to take her back to Lagrange."

"He seems to take a great deal of interest in Miss Tresham. I hope it does not bode ill for Annesley."

"Nonsense! I should as soon think of a volume of Blackstone falling in love as Mr. Warwick. Miss Tresham was his sister's governess, and he has been very kind to her—that's all. Men are twice as fanciful as women are about such things as this."

"Perhaps because we know each other better. Miss Tresham is amazingly pretty," he added, candidly, "and very attractive, very sympathetic. I should not mind falling in love with her myself."

"Do it, then, by all means. Your chance would be quite as good as Mr. Annesley's, I should think."

"I might, perhaps, if—no man can serve two masters, you know, much less two mistresses. Now, I found mine long ago. Fortunately, or probably unfortunately, for me, I could not change my allegiance, if I would."

"It is a misfortune to be too constant," said Miss Vernon; but she said it very gently, and then changed the subject abruptly. "And Mr. Annesley wants to make an appearance on the scene, does he?"

"He sent me over specially to intercede for him. Not that I needed much persuasion to induce me to come," he added, with a slight grimace. "I am always ready enough to singe my wings. Tell me what message I shall take back to the poor fellow."

"We must go and ask Mrs. Lester that. I can't venture to bid him come merely on my own responsibility."

Mrs. Lester being propitious, it was finally decided that Mr. Annesley might venture to make his appearance at Bellefont the next morning; and, with this comforting news for his friend, Mr. Seymour took leave.

The next morning was unspeakably lovely. The sky had not a cloud, the air was soft and warm, yet full of buoyancy—so full of buoyancy that it almost seemed as if it were possible to feel the buds expanding, the flowers opening, and the grass springing all around. As Miss Vernon sauntered back and forth on the front terrace, her bright beauty looked akin to the bright day. She almost dazzled Seymour and Annesley when they came riding up, and, dismounting from their horses, looked up and saw her standing at the top of the steps, with the sunshine pouring over her slender figure, her fresh morning-dress sweeping the gravel-walk, and a knot of violets fastened at her throat.

"I am very glad to see you," she said, greeting them both with a smile. "Is not the day charming? I could not stay in the house, though there are half a dozen people there who have come with the deliberate intention of spending the day—the Roystons, and ever so many more. Mr. Seymour, you need not look so much alarmed. You can stay out here with me, if you choose, and that will give me a good excuse for not going back. I can say you kept me."

"And put all the blame on my shoulders," said Godfrey, laughing. "Well, they are broad enough to bear it, and I accept the responsibility with pleasure. We will certainly stay. It is a sin to go in-doors such a day as this."

"But how about me?" asked Annesley. "Am I to be left to the tender mercies of Royston & Co., or am I to be allowed to remain and enjoy the beauties of Nature also?"

"You are to come with me and be shown what you are to do," answered Miss Vernon.—"Stay here, Mr. Seymour, if you please, I will be back in a minute.—This way, Mr. Annesley."

Somewhat amused, and a little puzzled, Morton obeyed, and followed the young autocrat around the terrace. She led him to an angle of the house, and quite out of sight of the drawing-room, before she paused. Then she stopped, and pointed to three French windows that opened on the terrace, just where the terrace overlooked the garden, which lay to the south.

"Do you know where those windows lead, Mr. Annesley," she asked, gravely.

"I think I do, Miss Irene," answered Morton, with equal gravity. "They lead into the sitting-room."

"Well, if you choose to go through one of them, you will find Miss Tresham in the sitting-room. I left her there half an hour ago."

"But is there no fear of startling her?"

"None at all, I assure you. She knows you are expected, and I don't think she troubles herself to be the least bit excited about it. She said she should be glad to see you—she wanted to hear from Lagrange. Go in, by all means, and give her the news from Lagrange; only remember" (and her voice changed from bantering to earnest) "that you must not mention the bank robbery. For some cause, Mr. Warwick has prohibited it."

"You may depend on my discretion," he said, and was turning away, when she extended her hand and touched him.

"One moment, Mr. Annesley," she said, smiling and blushing. Many a long day afterward the scene came back to Morton; he remembered the sweet spring sunshine, the slender white hand on his coat-sleeve, the beautiful face bending toward him, the frank, tender eyes, and the delicious fragrance of the violets fastened at her throat. "One word, Mr. Annesley," she said, hastily. "Don't think me impertinent, but we are old friends, and—may I wish you success?"

For one moment Annesley was surprised; the next, he felt deeply touched. The few words had been so sweetly and so gracefully said that the veriest churl must have acknowledged their charm. It was fortunate that they were out of sight of the drawing-room windows, for, following his first impulse, he bent and kissed the hand.

"Thank you, Miss Irene," he said, simply.

Then, before she could answer, he was walking away toward the French windows.

As it chanced, Katharine was sitting immediately in front of one of these windows, leaning back with supreme comfort in a deep arm-chair, enjoying idly all the fresh beauty of the scene before her, and so wrapped in the dreamy reverie which such weather inspires, and which does not deserve to be called thought, that a book she had been attempting to read had dropped from her hand to her lap, and lay there unheeded. She hardly started when a crisp, ringing step—step that she knew well—sounded on the gravel walk, when Morton drew aside the curtains and looked in at the window, thus finding himself face to face with the woman he had come to seek.

"Miss Tresham! How happy I am to see you!" he exclaimed, making one long step through the window to her side. "How happy I am to see you! and to see you looking so entirely yourself!"

"How happy I am to be well enough to be seen again!" she answered, letting him take both her hands in his warm, eager clasp. "You are very good to—to look so glad," she added, with a little laugh. "Everybody is so good to me! You have heard how these kind people insisted on bringing me here to get well?"

"I have heard considerably more than you have, I believe," said he, laughing in turn. Then he released her hands, and, stepping back a little, looked at her.

Her illness had not left any very terrible traces. That was his first thought. The worst was certainly the loss of her hair; yet, even that did not disfigure her as much as might be imagined. The head had only been shaven on the top of the scalp, and that was covered by a light and infinitely becoming cap of muslin and lace; elsewhere the brown hair, which was not more than an inch or two long, had an inclination to curl, that saved it from the horribly-ungraceful aspect of short straight hair. Round the forehead it lay in soft, pretty rings, that seemed to suit the delicate complexion, which had an exquisite transparence, that is often seen after severe illness, but rarely ever at any other time. Even the eyes he knew so well had caught, Morton thought, new beauty; they were so full of dewy lustre, as they looked up, dazzled and drooping a little from the sunshine! Perhaps this dewy lustre sprung from tears. At least, there was something like a suggestion of tears in her voice when she spoke.

"Everybody is so good to me!" she repeated, with much feeling.

"How could anybody help being good to you?" he asked, in a tone that carried with it an unmistakable accent of sincerity. After he said it, something rose in his throat and choked him a little. With that face before him, and the golden day all around, a sudden remembrance came of the night when this bright life had seemed passing away from earth, and the things of earth, into that realm of darkness and shadow which to him, as to many people, the night served to typify. Was it real? Was it she, sitting before him there with the sweet, flickering smile—smile half akin to tears—on her lip? Or was that other only a dream—that memory of past danger, darkness, and distress? He found it impossible to realize them both. Yet, he looked at her, and said:

"You don't know how grateful I am that you are gaining health and strength once more."

"Can you imagine how grateful I am?" she asked. "It is so pleasant—no words can say how pleasant—to feel life coming back with every breath one draws! The most common and trivial things of existence seem to have new sweetness and value, when one has so nearly lost them. This day—no doubt, it is charming enough to you, but to me it seems like paradise! So it is with every thing. I cannot describe the sensations that beset me; or, perhaps, I can sum them up in one—I am so glad to get well!"

"And glad to be here, are you not?"

"Very glad, indeed, though everybody was most kind in Hartsburg. I don't understand matters quite yet," said she, looking puzzled; "but I suppose I shall after a while. I was surprised to hear that you were expected to-day How do you chance to be down here?"

"Oh, I—I am staying with Godfrey Seymour," said he, smiling a little. "What are you reading?"

She held out the book. It was a volume of the "Faerie Queene."

"I wanted something that would not excite me," she said; "and this is an old and dear favorite, that has gone with me many a ramble. Perhaps it is from this association that it seems to me as if it should always be read with bright sunshine and beautiful scenes all around. I am so glad to see you!" she went on, with an abrupt change of subject, as Annesley took the volume and began turning over the leaves. "I want to ask you about Lagrange. I feel as if the world might have come to an end while I was lying sick in Hartsburg; so I really have not dared to write to anybody. Tell me something, please, Mr. Annesley."

"What shall I tell you?" asked Mr. Annesley, becoming much interested in the "Faerie Queene."

"Any thing," answered she, impatiently. "Don't look that way, or I shall think there is something you don't want me to know. Mr. Annesley"—growing pale—"tell me, please, *is* there any thing?"

"On my honor, not a thing," answered Morton, hastily, quite startled by her sudden change of color. "What should there be? and, if there were any thing, why should I not tell you? I—I'll go and bring Mrs. Lester to you, if you don't get your color back," he added, becoming more alarmed.

"No, don't!" said she, holding out her hand as he half turned to go. "Stop; the color will come back in a minute. I fancy your fright is only an excuse to escape from my questions," she went on, smiling faintly. "I have not asked them yet, you know. Did you see Mrs. Marks before you left Lagrange?"

"Yes, I saw her, and she was quite well.

Please let me go and get you something—some water or wine."

"I need nothing at all; thank you. Did Mrs. Marks say any thing to you with regard to me or my absence?"

Poor Morton cast about in his mind for an evasive answer, found none, and plunged headlong at a reckless truth.

"She mentioned you, of course, and expressed great concern at your absence. You—she—it seems you did not tell her how long you meant to be away?"

"How could I, when I had no idea of any thing like this? It is like a dream," she said. "You don't know how strangely vague every thing seems. Almost immediately after I arrived in Saxford, things waver and grow dim in my recollection. I stayed there two or three days—longer, perhaps—waiting for Father Martin. I think, in fact I am sure, that the fever was on me then. My remembrance of those days is of continued, dull, heavy pain, and burning thirst. If I had been myself, of course, I should have gone back to Tallahoma; but I was full of cowardice and terror—terror of a person whom I did not like—and I had no control over my nerves. Day by day this grew worse, until it became a wild desire for flight. My last tangible recollection is of making up my mind to leave Saxford and going to sell my watch, for I had brought very little money with me. After that, every thing is a blank till I waked up in Hartsburg, and they told me I had been at death's door. I don't know what they think of me in Tallahoma. It has been six weeks, you know, since I left there—but I have felt a quietness about it that amazes myself. I am glad to come back to life; but it seems as if many things that troubled me before have dwindled in importance, have less, far less power to disturb me than they formerly had."

"Then that is one good result, at least, arising from your illness."

She looked a little startled.

"Why, is there any thing that I must hear?"

"How quick you are to suspect what has no existence! There is nothing at all that I know of I am simply glad that you have reached an enviable state of indifference to things sublunary, which are more often disagreeable than pleasant."

"I did not say I was indifferent. I hope I never shall be. I think indifferent people have hardly a right to live in a world that is full of things to take interest in. Never mind about that, however. Tell me how many days it has been since you left Lagrange."

"Days!" He first stared, then hesitated. "It has been a month since I left home."

"Indeed!" The extreme of astonishment was in her face and in her voice. "A month!" she repeated. "Then you must have been elsewhere? You cannot have been here all that time?"

"If by here you mean Apalatka, I am obliged to confess that I have been here all the time."

"But, Mr. Annesley—"

"Well, Miss Tresham?"

"I beg your pardon," said she, coloring. "I was so much surprised that I was on the point of being very uncivil. I was about to ask what you had been doing here."

She spoke with perfect unconsciousness; but her words seemed charged with meaning to Morton. He had gone in search of her with one fixed purpose in his mind: he had waited to see her, steadily resolved to accomplish that purpose as soon as practicable; and now, here was the opportunity to do it. Morton did not fear his fate very much, as his frank assertion to Mr. Warwick on the night that Katharine lay, as they thought, dying, plainly showed. Poor fellow! He had been so spoiled and humored, so praised and taught to consider himself irresistible all his life, that the wonder was, not that he had a little vanity, but that he had half so much honest humility. There was nothing of offensive puppyism—in fact, there was nothing of puppyism at all—in his belief that Miss Tresham would accept him. He wondered at it himself, and, despite his apparent grounds for confidence, could not help doubting it a little. He even flushed suddenly at her last words, more like a boy than like a man of the world; then looked straight at her with his clear eyes.

"I will tell you what I have been doing here," he said. "I have been waiting to see *you*."

"To see me!" repeated Katharine. She was stupid just then, and it did not occur to her what he meant. On the contrary, her head was so full of Tallahoma, and St. John, and Mrs. Gordon, that she turned pale again, and gave a low, trembling cry. "I know it," she said. "You have something to tell me. O Mr. Annesley, pray be kind and tell it at once."

"I think I am the most bungling fellow that ever lived!" cried Annesley, out of patience with himself. "This is the third time I have startled you without any earthly reason for it. Please believe, once for all, that there is nothing I could tell you if I wanted to—of a disagreeable nature, I mean. There is something I wish to tell you, and mean to tell you," he went on, hurriedly; "but it certainly cannot have the merit of novelty, and I hope it will not be disagreeable to you. Miss Tresham, do I need to tell it? Don't you know—you, without any help from me—why I came here, and why I have remained?"

In a second she knew what he meant. A flush came over the pale face, then died away, leaving it paler than ever. Looking at her, Annesley was startled; he did not know whether to hope or to fear. Only one thing was certain—a good sign, it is usually considered—she did not speak. Still there was something about her, now as ever, which kept him at a distance, which made him speak with humility when there was every reasonable ground for speaking with hope.

"Miss Tresham," he said, "don't be angry with me. I only mean this: that I love you so well I cannot keep silent longer. I—what is the use of talking!" said the young man, with a sudden, passionate burst of excitement. "You are every thing in the world to me; words are too poor to tell you what you are. I never knew what love was till your face kindled it in my heart. I should have spoken long ago if—if you had given me one sign of encouragement. But you are so cold, so self-contained. Even now—"

He stopped suddenly—stopped without any apparent cause—and, turning, walked away.

He was right. Words were too poor to tell her what he felt, to utter the great love, the faithful, honest devotion which lay at her feet ready for her to take up and make her own. But then, again, no words were needed to tell him that he had spoken in vain, that there was no answer to his passionate pleading in that averted face, that the hand lying so lightly on the arm of her chair would never be extended to him, never—ah, never! The knowledge came on him with a rush—a force that was equivalent to a physical blow. He stopped, turned pale, and walked to the other end of the room. Then there was a silence. A bird just outside of the window was twittering and trilling as if in the very exuberance of happy content, a ripple of gay voices and laughter sounded across the hall from the drawing-room, and a gardener just below the terrace sung to himself a negro melody as he spaded.

Katharine was the first to speak, her voice telling nothing of the struggle it had been to command it, as she uttered his name. He came back instantly, a light of wistful hope in his eyes that touched her heart, and gave her tones a sort of quiver when she went on:

"Mr. Annesley, forgive me that I did not speak. You surprised me so much, and I—I am not very strong yet. What can I say?" she added, after a moment's pause. "It seems useless to tell you that I am grateful for the honor you have done me. I admire you so much, I esteem you so highly, that I shall be prouder all my life, and yet sadder, too, to think that you should have loved me. But you know—ah, why have you been so foolish?—you know it cannot be!"

"I only know that it depends on you," said Annesley. "On nothing—on nobody else. Understand this, you hold my life in your hands. Keep it, or throw it away, just as you please; all the same, it is yours."

"Hush!" said Katharine, gently. "Pray, don't talk like that. Your life—ah, Mr. Annesley, how much you have forgotten when you speak so to me. Your life can be nothing to me, my life less than nothing to you. Not a single interest or possibility of one crosses, or can cross, the other. Why have you forgotten this?"

"Rather ask why I should remember—why I should believe it."

"You know it is impossible," said she, speaking with an earnestness that startled him. "You have acted on a sudden impulse—a generous impulse, I am sure—but you must see and feel that it is impossible; that I am nothing, that I never can be any thing to you."

"You are every thing to me," he answered, standing before her, pale and resolute, determined evidently to obtain a definite answer before he left her presence.

"I—oh, how foolish I am!" said Katharine, as a sudden rush of tears ended her sentence almost before it was begun. She *was* foolish—very foolish—but this was a great temptation; and that fact may, perhaps, excuse her. How forlorn she felt, just now, especially, among strangers, and without a single friend on whom it was possible to rely; and, in the very midst of this loneliness, a hand was extended, a voice spoke, and she knew that care, kindness, home, wealth, position, best of all, earnest love, was offered to her. Was it strange that, realizing this, her resolve almost failed, her heart gave a great pang when she tried to speak the words that would put them forever from her?

"Don't distress yourself," said Annesley, to whom the last, worst evil of earth was the evil of seeing a woman's tears; "pray, don't distress yourself; I shall never forgive myself if you do! I think I had better go," he said, desperately; "I shall make you ill if I stay any longer. All this agitation must do you harm. I will come again to-morrow. Please think of what I have said, and—and try to make up your mind to come to me. I think I could make you happy, if you would," he added, wistfully, "and I am sure you could make me more than happy."

With these words he left the room, Katharine making not an effort to detain him. In truth, she was literally incapable of doing so. Weakness and agitation together had proved too much for her. She was so completely exhausted that, after he was gone, she could hardly remember where she was, or what had happened.

When Morton went back round the terrace (for his exit, like his entrance, was by way of the window), he found that Miss Vernon had disappeared, and that Seymour was standing by the horses, smoking a cigar, and looking rather gloomy.

"Have you spoken to the good people in the house?" asked Annesley, coming up. "I wonder if it is necessary to do so before we go?"

"No, I have not," answered Godfrey, with a start. "And I don't think it is necessary. They are not ceremonious people, or people likely to be offended. If you have finished your visit, we might as well be off. As certainly as we go in, we shall have to stay to dinner."

"Let us be off, by all means, then," said Annesley, springing into his saddle with ungrateful haste.

The other followed his example, and, riding briskly, they were soon out of the Lester domain. The Seymour place was several miles distant. They had ridden a mile or two before Annesley roused sufficiently from his own abstraction to notice his companion.

"What is the matter, Godfrey?" he asked. "You don't seem like yourself—you don't even look like yourself."

Godfrey rolled a cloud of blue smoke from between his lips before he answered. Then he laughed shortly.

"A man is apt to look gloomy after he has made a fool of himself," he said. "I have made an egregious fool of myself; so, as a logical conclusion, I have a right to look gloomy. It is only the old story," he went on, meeting Annesley's eye. "Every six months, regularly, for the last three years, I have asked Irene Vernon to marry me. She has told me, regularly, in the gentlest and kindest manner, that she cannot think of such a thing. Each time I say to myself that it shall be the last time; yet I go back and commit the same absurdity over again. With the best possible intentions to the contrary, I committed it again this morning."

"And the result?"

"The result was that I made her cry, and that I should like to give myself a sound drubbing, if that would do any good."

"Cry!" repeated Annesley, somewhat aghast. "Good Heavens! I wonder if women always cry on occasions of the kind?"

"Not if we may believe the testimony of some lucky fellows," said Seymour, dryly. "However, I don't think a man is worth much until he has been rejected once or twice," he added, resignedly. "It is like getting well thrashed at school—part of that sound, but unpleasant process called 'finding one's level.' One or two straightforward noes would not do you any harm, my good fellow."

"Thanks. I suppose you mean that I am a puppy?"

"No; I only mean that you are a little conceited, as, perhaps, you have some right to be. If you won't consider me impertinent, have you ever been rejected?"

"Never!" said Morton, who had reasons of his own for being reticent on this point.

"Then you have some of the needful discipline of life yet to undergo. Let that be your consolation when the time of your discomfiture comes."

"I hope it may never come!" said Annesley, with perfect sincerity.

But, in his heart, he could not help thinking that there was a very good chance of its coming on the morrow.

CHAPTER XXXVIII.

MEA CULPA.

After Annesley left, Katharine went to her own room, partly because she was obliged to lie down, and partly because she wanted to be alone and think over all that had occurred.

From this process resulted great self-contempt, and greater self-reproach. Why had she been so foolish?—why had she been so undecided?—why had she let herself be swayed from what she knew was right?—why had she let him go away under a false impression that she might perhaps say yes?—and, oh! above all, why had she been so silly as to cry? She asked herself all these questions, and did not find a single satisfactory answer for one of them. The more she thought of the matter—of that unsatisfactory, pointless proposal—the more vexed with herself she became. She could not walk distractedly up and down the floor, because she was much too weak for such an exercise; and she could not tear her hair, because there was hardly any left to tear; but she did every thing else that people under stress of strong emotion are usually expected to do—she set her teeth, she wrung her hands tightly together, and every now and then impatient exclamations (far from complimentary to herself) burst from her lips. Nothing is more true than that "some people seem by intuition to see only truth and right; others must needs work out their faith by failing and sorrow. They realize truth by the pain of what is false, honor through dishonor, right by wrong repented of with bitter pangs." Katharine was one of the latter class. Looking back over the events of the last few months, regarding them as having culminated in the events of the last few hours, no words can express the self-contempt and self-reproach that rushed over her. "St. John was right, I have thought of myself—of nobody but myself!" she said. "And this is the end. Ah, me! Are people always punished so much for considering themselves? If so, I wonder that anybody ever does it."

The more she thought of Morton, the more the temptation of his offer gained strength, and yet the more firmly she determined to put it from her. "I should make a base return for his generous kindness if I accepted him," she thought; yet what an attraction there was in himself and in all that he offered her! There is neither sense nor truth in saying that a woman only feels this attraction when she is in love. Plenty of women feel it about plenty of men; yet instinct tells them that it is not the right feeling—not the feeling that will endure, and, enduring, sweeten all that even the happiest married lives must know—so they resist it; and so, likewise, it often takes as hard a struggle to say No, as it is sometimes reported to take for saying Yes. The probabilities are that, if Katharine had loved Annesley as much as Juliet could possibly have loved Romeo, she would still have held firm to her refusal; for with all her weaknesses—and her story shows that she had a sufficient number of them — she possessed no inconsiderable amount of that rare strength which enables a human soul to come victorious from the most fierce and terrible combat known to earth — the combat where self takes part against self, and the flesh rises against the spirit. But Fate had been kind enough to spare her this last, worst trial. She was *not* "in love" with him, as far as that common phrase can be taken to mean the eager, impetuous passion that no obstacle of rank, time, distance, or age, can overawe. Very probably she would have fallen in love after the most approved mode, if she had been of an equal social position with himself, if she had not known that insuperable obstacles lay between them, or if she had not been occupied with other and graver considerations. As it was, however—at the risk of making her a little less interesting, the truth must be told—her struggle had not the romantic savor which a desperate passion hopelessly combated can alone give; the attraction that drew her toward Annesley was, in great degree, an attraction apart from himself.

Yet not the attraction of those merely worldly advantages which went with him. They had their weight, of course; it is only in Arcadia that people are entirely independent of such considerations; but their weight was infinitely less than that of the faithful love, the warm devotion, the shielding protection, that would be hers, if she held out her hand to him. Think of her for a moment—think how lonely and friendless and desolate she stood! Then, if possible, wonder that the temptation was almost beyond her strength. Let it not be supposed, however, that any grandiloquent ideas of not loving him sufficiently made her hold back. She loved nobody else; and she did not doubt that a *grande passion* for this young paladin would come soon enough with time and opportunity to help it. That was not the consideration. Yet she—him—oh, what was the consideration? Her head felt singularly dull and heavy. Before she was aware of it, tired Nature asserted itself, and she fell asleep.

How long she slept, she had no means of telling; but the sun, which was streaming over the crystal essence-bottles of the toilet-table when slumber overtook her, had entirely veered round, and was dancing like a will-o'-the-wisp about the white ewer and basin on the wash-stand, when she woke—woke with a start, and found a bright face surrounded by crisp, red curls bending over her.

"Well," cried Miss Lester, "it is not possi

ble that you have really concluded to open your eyes at last! I began to think that you were going to sleep straight on into to-morrow. Dinner has been over ever so long, and mamma has been up two or three times to see about you. She came to me at last, and wanted to know if I thought you could have taken morphine or any thing of the sort. What is the matter? Does your head ache?"

"No, not now," answered Katharine, putting her hand to the member in question, and trying to remember what made her feel so vaguely uncomfortable. Suddenly, it all came back to her with a rush. Mr. Annesley! Oh—yes—that was it! How painfully bright the sunshine was! Why could she not have been left to sleep in peace?

"It *does* ache, I am sure," said Miss Lester, who was watching her. "Is it the sun that dazzles you? I'll close the blinds, if you say so."

"No, thank you," said Katharine, rising languidly. "I believe I will get up. I am sorry to have troubled Mrs. Lester so much. I really did not mean to sleep so long."

"People can't be expected to wake themselves," said Miss Lester, composedly. "If you are going to get up, I will ring for your dinner. You must feel the need of something to eat."

The dinner was rung for, and the dinner came up—a sight to tempt the worst valetudinarian appetite. Even in the midst of difficulties, people can sometimes be tempted by dainty dishes served on fine old china, with damask of dazzling whiteness, as Katharine satisfactorily proved. She ate her dinner with considerable appetite; and, after it was finished, Miss Lester cleared her throat, and made a plunge into conversation.

"I would not tell you before you had taken your dinner," she said, "for a little thing often takes away one's appetite; but there is somebody down-stairs to see you—somebody who came after you went to sleep."

Poor Katharine! This was dismaying intelligence indeed, for she thought of nobody but St. John; and, thinking of him, she gave such a gasp, and grew so pale, that Miss Lester was quite frightened. "Good gracious!" cried she, making a wild dart at a cologne-bottle on the toilet-table. "Surely you are not going to faint. I had not an idea—dear, dear! why, it is only Mr. Warwick, Miss Tresham! What on earth is the use of looking like this about him?"

"Mr. Warwick!" repeated Katharine, and she gave another gasp, and tried to laugh. "Oh, how much you startled me! I was thinking of another and—and quite a different person. I am glad Mr. Warwick is here. But surely he has not come to see *me?*"

"To see you, and nobody else," answered Miss Lester, keeping the cologne-bottle still in her hand, and looking suspiciously ready for all possible emergencies. "He drove over from Hartsburg, and arrived just before dinner. You were asleep then, and mamma would not let you be waked; besides, Mr. Warwick said he was in no hurry. Take your time, therefore, about seeing him. If you don't feel like it just now—"

"Of course, I feel like it," said Katharine, rising and walking to the mirror. "I like Mr. Warwick extremely, and it is very kind of him to come and see about me," she went on. "I wonder how he found out? Oh, my poor hair! How much he will be astonished to see me such a fright!"

"Who—Mr. Warwick? Why, he saw you when you looked a hundred times worse!" cried Miss Lester, heedlessly. Then she stopped, and stammered, as Katharine turned round in amazement: "I mean, of course—I forgot you did not know—oh, pshaw! Miss Tresham, it is all nonsense, and I am sure you ought to know that, if it had not been for Mr. Warwick, you would not be alive now. He found you there in Hartsburg, when you were lying ill, at the mercy of that abominable quack who, I hope, is hanged by this time."

"He found me? Mr. Warwick found me?" said Katharine, in the depths of astonished bewilderment.

After this, there was no help for it. Whether Miss Lester would or not, she was forced to tell the whole history, as far as she was acquainted with it; and Mr. Warwick had to listen resignedly to Mrs. Lester's gentle commonplaces below, while Katharine, above, listened breathlessly to the account of his good deeds. When, at last, she went down-stairs, the remembrance of what she had just heard was flushing her cheeks and lighting her eyes, until John Warwick, who had naturally expected to see a pale, languid invalid, was quite startled by the eager, impetuous girl who opened the sitting-room door and walked up to him.

"Mr. Warwick," she said, "I have just heard—I did not know before—how very, very kind you have been to me. Forgive me—oh, pray, forgive me—for having given you so much trouble! I am very grateful to you! They tell me

I should have died, if you had not found me. I should not like to die, and—and I am so grateful to you!"

She spoke hurriedly, clasping her hands eagerly together; then stopped suddenly at the last words, and extended them toward him, with an impulsive warmth that he had never seen her display before.

"My dear Miss Tresham, they have been imposing upon your credulity, I fear," he said, laughing, as he took the hands and shook them cordially. "I am delighted to see you looking so well!—You have done wonders with her, Mrs. Lester." Mrs. Lester, who was sitting by, smiled a bland acknowledgment.—"I had not expected to find you so entirely recovered in such a short time; but Mrs. Crump told me that your convalescence was very rapid. I saw Mrs. Crump as I came through Hartsburg; I spent last night at the Eagle Hotel. She sent her best wishes to you."

"And Mrs. Crump—deceitful woman!—kept me in ignorance about you. And Dr. Randolph—Mr. Warwick, why did you forbid them to tell me? You might have known that I would find it out sooner or later."

"On my honor, I did not forbid them. I never thought of such a thing. You must pour out the vials of your indignation on Randolph's head, not mine. By-the-by, this is the first opportunity that I have had to return an article of your property which, strangely enough, chances to be in my possession."

He put his hand in his pocket, and drew forth the little, worn volume of Thomas à Kempis, on which Katharine darted at once, with a cry of recognition and delight.

"My 'Imitation of Christ!'" she exclaimed. "Oh, thank you, Mr. Warwick! I am so glad to see it again! I thought I had surely lost it during all that dreadful time of which I remember nothing. It is such a pleasure to recover it!"

"If I was fortunate enough to be instrumental in saving your life," he said, "you may thank that book for my having done so. If the landlady had not brought it to me, I should have gone away totally unconscious that I had passed the night under the same roof with you."

Katharine opened the book, and pointed to the faded writing.

"It seems like a blessing accorded to *her* prayers," she said, softly. "I can hardly think that I deserved it. But you have not told me—I don't understand—how did you chance to be in Hartsburg?"

"Your memory is bad," he said, smiling. "Have you forgotten a note that I wrote you when I left Tallahoma, nearly two months ago?"

"A note?"

"Yes, a note. Stop and try to think what it was about. That will tell you how I chanced to be in Hartsburg."

She stopped and thought for a minute, before she succeeded in grasping the missing idea. Then, like a flash, her face cleared, and she looked up at him.

"I remember! You said you were going to take Felix Gordon to school. Were you on your way back to Tallahoma when you stopped in Hartsburg?"

"Yes, on my way back."

"And you found me accidentally?"

He pointed to the book.

"If we may call that accident."

Her glance followed his.

"No," she said, reverently; "it was not accident. I hope I am sufficiently grateful—to God first, and to you afterward. You have done so much—so very much—for me, and I, alas! can do nothing for you."

"Yes," answered Mr. Warwick, smiling slightly, "you can do something for me, and you must not be surprised when I tell you what it is."

"I shall not be surprised, no matter what it is. I am only too glad to hear that there *is* something," she said, earnestly.

Mrs. Lester, with commendable discretion, had left the room by this time, and they were alone. Miss Tresham was sitting on a low chair at one side of the fireplace, while Mr. Warwick still stood before her, in his favorite attitude, with one hand on the mantel. After her last words, he sat down, and looked at her kindly with his clear blue eyes.

"I did not expect you to make such a rash promise," he said. "But, since you have done so, I will take advantage of it. What I ask of you, then, is—confidence."

She started, colored, and looked at him a little apprehensively.

"Pray be quiet," he said. "I won't distress you, if it is possible to avoid it. Can't you trust me—a little?"

"I trust you a great deal," she answered, simply.

"Very well, then. Trust me thus far—tell

me candidly, as you would tell your own brother, the reasons why you left Tallahoma."

There was a minute's silence. Katharine checked a question which rose to her lips, struggled with herself a minute—the varying color made that evident—then lifted her eyes, and spoke as quietly as he had advised.

"I will not ask why you think it necessary to make this inquiry, Mr. Warwick. I am sure you must have some good reason, or you would not do it. You don't know how strangely your question strikes me after—after some thoughts I had this morning. It seemed to me then that, looking back on the last few months, I could trace all that I have suffered to one thing—my own cowardice. I ought to have spoken plainly from the first—spoken as I will endeavor to speak now, if you have patience enough to listen to me. Don't be astonished if I go very far back, though; I must do it to make you understand."

"I can spare you a little, perhaps," he interposed here. "Do you know that the Catholic priest—what is his name?—Mr. Martin, from Saxford, was summoned when you were so ill? I sent for him principally that I might inquire if you had any friends or relations. I thought he was more likely to know than any one else. Well"—as she colored deeply—"I see that you anticipate what I am about to say. You must not blame him. I pressed him hard, and he thought you were certainly dying. Under these circumstances, he finally told me that you had a brother—the Mr. St. John I had seen in Tallahoma."

"And you thought—"

"I thought nothing, believe me, that I need hesitate to tell you. If I ask your confidence now, it is because, knowing thus much, I find it necessary to know more; why, I will tell you presently."

"You don't despise me for having been so—so cowardly about acknowledging him?"

A dark cloud came over the lawyer's face, a cloud which absolutely frightened Katharine, and yet which had no possible relation to her.

"I do not even blame you," he answered. "More than that I can not say, until I know more. I am sorry to impose such a hard task upon you, but—"

"It is not a hard task," she interrupted, eagerly. "It is almost a relief to tell it to you. I" (she looked at him wistfully), "I begin to wish that I had told you every thing when you asked me some time ago, if you remember."

"It would have been much better if you had."

"Yes, I see that now. But then it seemed so useless, it seemed like a confidence without a purpose. You could not help me, I thought, and so why should I trouble you? Afterward, after he came, of course, it was harder to do. You can't tell what he has been to me all my life," she said, covering her face with her hands.

"I can imagine."

"My first remembrance is one of terror and dislike of him. We lived in Jamaica with an aunt—our parents were both dead—and even yet it makes me burn with indignation to think how her life was robbed of all peace and sunshine by St. John. Mr. Warwick, I can't go into particulars. They would not interest you, and they would make me uncover some bitter ashes which I tried—tried hard to bury in her grave. Only believe that he repaid her kindness by ingratitude and bad conduct of every possible description. I ought to explain, perhaps, that she had adopted us from our earliest childhood, from my earliest recollection. We never bore any other name than hers."

"Yet your brother—" he began.

"Is named St. John," she interrupted. "Yes, I know. But St. John is merely one of his baptismals, the one by which we always called him, and it was only when he finally separated from us that he dropped Tresham and adopted his second Christian name as a surname. Well, at last it became impossible that my aunt could endure him any longer. She wrote to his guardian in England, a man whom he had never seen, and represented matters so forcibly that St. John was removed from her nominal control. The guardian desired that he should be sent to England, which was done. After that, as a means of escaping from him in case he came back, she left Jamaica and went to live in Porto Rico. It was in vain, however, as far as her object was concerned. After a while he followed us; he was in need, and wanted money. Slender as my aunt's means were, she was forced to comply with his demands, as a condition of getting rid of him. This left her too poor to move away again if she had felt disposed to attempt it. That was but the beginning. St. John did not come very often, but he continually wrote for money; and you can imagine what it was to have this continual cloud hanging over one's life and home, and the face one loved best in the world. What his life was in Europe, meanwhile, I cannot even pretend to say; I cannot bear to think. There was a man named Fraser, who seemed his special comrade; or, rather, I should say, his leader in the life on which he entered. That man—well, you have heard of him. St. John told me that he is Mrs. Gordon's husband."

"Yes; I have heard of him."

"Perhaps, then, you know better than I do how St. John lived during the intervals of months, sometimes years, in which we never heard of him. As I have said, he only came or wrote when he was in need. He had not been heard from for a long time, when my aunt died and left me desolate. Almost her last words implored me to leave the West Indies and go to some place where he would not be able to trace me. 'He will ruin your life if you do not escape from him,' she said. 'He will destroy every prospect of happiness that you could possibly have if he knows where you are, and if you acknowledge him and give him a claim upon you.' She was dying, Mr. Warwick; you may believe that I was ready enough to promise to avoid him if I possibly could. Well, I left the West Indies, and went to England to an old friend of hers, who obtained a very good situation for me at Dornthorne Place. I had lived there a year—contented, at least, if not happy—when one day St. John appeared. By some means he had tracked me down; from the mere desire to torment me, I honestly believe, for he knew I was in no position to aid him. This man of whom I have spoken, Fraser, I mean, had inherited a large Scottish property, and St. John was living with him as his secretary. The knowledge that he was living near me, the knowledge that he knew where I was, filled me with the old terror. I remembered my dear aunt's dying admonition, and, coupled with my own inclination, it made me resolve to leave England and come to America. I felt that I should be more safe from him here. You know how I came, how kindly your sister took me, how quietly and happily I lived. But it all ended on that November evening when you brought me his letter; the same evening that Mrs. Gordon arrived. Do you remember it?"

Mr. Warwick's memory was very good. He said, with perfect truthfulness, that he remembered it.

"After I received that letter, the terror of his coming grew upon me to an almost morbid degree. At one time I had nearly made up my mind to leave Tallahoma, but then that was very hard to do; I had grown so much attached to the children, and Father Martin (to whom alone I told my story) counselled me against it. 'Wait,' he said; and I waited, alas! too long. I was very miserable during that time, though you were the only person who perceived it. I remember one day I was reading St. John's letter over again, in the parlor, when somebody came in, and I hastily put it out of sight in a sheet of music and forgot it. Not long afterward Mr. Annesley was turning over my music and found it. This seems a trifling thing, no doubt, but you don't know what a shock it was to me. I seemed to *realize* who and what he was so clearly when it came to the point of speaking of him to somebody else. Of course, the feeling grew because it was indulged. I did not combat it as I should have done; and, at last, it reached such a point, that I felt as if I would sooner die than acknowledge him. I see now how wrong it all was, how nothing but selfish regard for the opinion of the world, and wretched human pride, was at the bottom of it; but then I gave way, and tried to make myself believe that it was right to give way to it."

"I can't say that I think it was wrong," observed the lawyer, gravely.

"Yes," she said, "it was wrong. I see things more clearly now; somehow it seems as if I almost see them as clearly as I might have seen them on that death-bed which I so narrowly escaped. We are not put into this world to think of ourselves. Now, I thought of nobody but myself. I shirked the plain duty, I tried to throw off the plain burden which God put before me, and all out of mere worldly opinion and fear lest my name should be linked with—with—O Mr. Warwick, nothing can ever do away with this! It was cowardice, it was wretched cowardice, and all that has followed is my fault."

"Pardon me if I remind you that you are wandering from the point," said Mr. Warwick. "It is a bad thing to be discursive. Suppose you go back to causes, and let effects alone."

She saw what he meant. "I won't excite myself," she said. "There is no use in that, you know. But, all the same, it is my fault. Well, St. John came; and, of course, after he came, matters with me grew worse. After I took the first false step—I see now that it *was* a false step—in the way of concealing his relationship, and attempting to conceal his visits, I went deeper and deeper into difficulties. At first it seemed very simple. He assured me that he would leave as soon as he received the money I was able to give him, and I counted certainly on his keeping his word. But then came his recognition of Mrs. Gordon, and his writing to her husband, and all the rest. Have you seen Mrs. Gordon, Mr. Warwick? have you heard how she came in and found St. John with me, and how she charged me with having brought him there?"

"Yes," he said, kindly. "I have heard both from herself and from Bessie. Don't trouble yourself to go over that."

"Well, after she left, a sudden impulse seemed to take possession of me; I felt desperate, felt as if I *must* get away, let what would be the consequences. I chanced to remember that Father Martin would be in Saxford on the Sunday following New Year. I thought I would go and ask him what to do. If you had been in Tallahoma, I am inclined to think that I should have asked your advice; but you know you had gone. That was Friday. I had barely time to catch the coach and go to Saxford. Acting on impulse, I went." She then told him substantially the same that she had told Annesley with regard to the days she spent in Saxford, the nervous, feverish desire of flight which had beset her, and the manner in which she went to Hartsburg. After this, she added: "There is only one thing I have neglected to mention. On that last morning, just before Mrs. Gordon came in, St. John told me for the first time how he had discovered where I was. Mr. Warwick, don't refuse to credit me when I tell you that it is somebody in Lagrange, somebody whom I could never possibly have imagined, who was cruel enough to advertise in the London *Times* for information concerning me."

"I have heard that, too," said Mr. Warwick. "I see you think that I have heard every thing," he added, smiling; "but you forget how natural it was that Mrs. Gordon should mention this advertisement to me."

"I remember that she saw it, that I showed it to her."

"Since you have mentioned the matter, perhaps you will not be surprised if I ask you a question concerning it: have you any idea who was the author of that advertisement?"

"Idea! How could I have? I knew so few people out of Mr. Marks's family; I flattered myself that I had not an enemy, or any thing approaching to an enemy, in Lagrange."

"Stop and think a moment. Is there nobody in Lagrange whom it was in your power to disappoint, and—after a certain fashion—injure? Miss Tresham, brain-fever certainly has not improved the keenness of your perceptions."

"Mr. Warwick, you do not mean—"

"Well?" (as she paused).

"You cannot mean Mrs.—Mrs. Annesley?"

"I do mean Mrs. Annesley."

"But this is only a conjecture on your part; you are not sure?"

"Pardon me—I am perfectly sure."

"Mr. Warwick!"

"Well?" (smiling again).

"Oh, don't smile!" cried she, passionately, covering her face with her hands. "It—it is so horrible! That she could—that she would—Oh, what had I ever done to injure her! How had she the heart!"

"Be reasonable," said he, gently. "I was indignant too—as indignant as you could possibly be—when I first heard of it; but, after thinking it over coolly, I saw that a woman—a merely worldly woman like Mrs. Annesley—was not so much to blame for taking this step. Miss Tresham, she did not even know you personally when she wrote that advertisement."

"But she knew—anybody must have known—that it was a cruelly dishonorable thing to do! How could she tell what she might bring upon me?"

"She probably thought much more of herself than of you; and more, perhaps, of her son, than of either. Have you yet to learn how easily people reason themselves into a belief that a thing which they wish to do, is a thing that it is right to do? I have no doubt that this advertisement, and every thing connected with it," he went on, "seemed to Mrs. Annesley a solemn duty."

"Does that excuse her?"

"Well—no. Morally speaking, I suppose it does not. Philosophically speaking, however, it may. Try to be a philosopher, Miss Tresham," he continued, with an effort to divert her that might have amused Katharine if she had been in a humor to be amused. "I should not have told you had I supposed that you would take it so seriously; in fact, I should not have told you at all, if I had not been sure that, in thinking the matter over, your own suspicions would point to the right mark."

"They might have done so," she said, a little wearily. "I cannot tell."

Her head sank on her hand with a dejection that touched the lawyer. "She loves Morton, and this is hard on her," he thought. "Poor girl!" He rose, walked to the window, stood there a moment looking out, then turned and came back.

"Miss Tresham," he said, seriously, "shall

I tell you something else that made me speak of this? I thought you might perhaps respect my opinion—a man of my age is apt to be vain on that point, you know—and I thought that, if you were inclined to take an extreme view of Mrs. Annesley's conduct, I might throw all the weight of this opinion into the other scale. You have no friend in the world," he went on, with energy, "who feels your interest more than I do, or who would be quicker to resent your injuries. But, on my honor, I do not think that Mrs. Annesley can be very much blamed. Remember that we must not judge people by our own standard of honor and dishonor, of right and wrong. We must, as much as possible, judge them by their own. Mrs. Annesley's code is of the world, worldly: judge her by that, Miss Tresham, and see if you cannot excuse her."

"No," said the girl, with a hard, set look about the mouth. "Judged by the merest code of worldly honor, this was a dishonorable act. Don't try to make me think otherwise, Mr. Warwick; I cannot. Besides, what does it matter?—Mrs. Annesley is nothing to me."

"I am not sure of that," he said. "She may be a good deal to you some day; that is, if you are wise. You must excuse me if I speak of something that does not seem exactly my concern. Miss Tresham, you would not let such a thing as this weigh against Morton's honest, unselfish love?—Morton," he proceeded, earnestly, "whom I have known ever since he was a child, and who is certainly one of the very best fellows in the world?"

"No," said Katharine, quietly, "I am glad to say that it has not weighed with me. In utter ignorance of his mother's act, I told Mr. Annesley this morning that I could not marry him."

"Miss Tresham!"

"Well," said she, a little surprised at the astonishment on his face, "what is there so amazing in that? Surely, Mr. Warwick, you did not think that I would marry him?"

"I thought so—yes," said Mr. Warwick, beginning to recover himself a little. "Why should I not think so? If you were my own sister, I could not wish a better fate for you than to be his wife. A woman could scarcely ask more than Morton Annesley is able to give."

"And you advise me to accept him?"

"I do, most emphatically."

"I had not expected this of you," she said, impulsively. "Think what a position you would place me in! Mr. Annesley himself is every thing that is kind, and generous, and disinterested; but his mother—his friends—what just ground they would have for complaint if I were selfish enough to accept him! It looks, perhaps, as if it would be doing a good thing for myself," she went on; "but in truth (unless I was willing to find happiness in fine dresses and jewels, and the like), I should be doing the worst possible thing. Such a marriage would be too ill-assorted for any hope of happiness. As Mr. Annesley grew older—he is little more than a bright, warm-hearted boy now—he would feel it himself. Can you not think what it would be to him—he so proud, so sensitive to the least shadow of dishonor—to know that his wife's brother was—was— O Mr. Warwick, don't you see how blind and foolish I should be, even to my own best interests, if I did such a thing?"

"I see this," said Mr. Warwick, whose ear was quick enough to catch the pathetic ring in her voice, "that you are on the eve of doing what many high-strung natures have done before you; that is, of throwing away substantial happiness for an unsubstantial scruple. I am a practical man, Miss Tresham, and, you may take my word for it, that all these things of which you have spoken are not worth considering when placed in comparison with a heart like Morton's. If you love him—"

"If I loved him," interrupted she, "I might not be able to reason as I have done. But I don't love him!"

"You don't?"

"No—I don't. I am sure I don't know why," she said, with half puzzled frankness. "Nobody knows better than I do how charming he is, nobody could admire or respect him more; but I do not love him. Perhaps because I have had other things to think of, or because I knew how many insurmountable barriers were between us, or, again, because I have learned to put little faith in the admiration and attention that any moderately-attractive woman is sure to receive."

"But are you certain of this; are you certain that you are not deceiving yourself?"

"I am certain. He was here this morning, and I have had all day to think about it; that is, until I went to sleep. I assure you that saying No to him did not cost me a pang, unless (I will be quite frank with you) it was the pang of feeling my own loneliness."

"You feel your loneliness, then?"

Her eyes softly filled with tears—tears that had no bitterness in them. She looked at the little, worn volume closely clasped in her hand; then round the pleasant, home-like room.

"They are all very kind to me," she said. "But how could I feel other than lonely here?"

Something in the simple words, something in the pathetic glance, went to the lawyer's heart like a shaft. He knew more—much more—than she did the loneliness of her position; much more than she did of the difficulties that surrounded her. Looking at her as she sat in the deep, old-fashioned arm-chair, she seemed so fair, so delicate, so little fitted to cope single-handed with that world over which only the sternest triumph, that an impulse which he could not resist—an impulse which he afterward bitterly regretted—made him speak words that Katharine little expected to hear.

"Yes, I can see that you are lonely," he said, with something—a gentleness that she did not quite understand—in his voice. "Miss Tresham, do you think it would be a hard fate to exchange this loneliness for care, and protection, and love, even though there were little besides these things to win your heart? I am old enough to be your father, but if you can resolve to trust yourself with me, I do not believe you will ever repent it; at least" (with an unconscious inflection of pathos), "I promise you that no effort shall be wanting on my part to prevent your ever repenting it."

For one bewildered moment the room seemed going round with Katharine. Was she awake?—was she asleep?—was it Mr. Warwick who had spoken these words? Was it he sitting there, or—or— How foolish she was! He had not meant *that*—she was sure she had misunderstood. He, of all men, had not meant to ask her—

"Mr. Warwick," she said, turning pale, "it cannot be—it is not possible—you do not mean—"

Mr. Warwick cut the confused sentence very abruptly short.

"I mean," he said, quietly, "that I have asked you to marry me. Will you do it?"

CHAPTER XXXIX.

MISS TRESHAM'S REPLY.

This time, at least, Katharine could not mistake the meaning of what she heard. Deliberately—with his eyes open, and every outward appearance of a sane man—Mr. Warwick asked her if she would marry him! It is not too much to say that amazement literally superseded every other feeling with her. It is seldom, indeed, that an offer comes with quite such a force of unexpected surprise. Usually, if there is no positive preparation, there is a suspicion at least, a word, a glance, or, it may be, only a tone, to show what is coming. But here there was absolute want of preparation, absolute astonishment, and, for a time at least, absolute incapacity to reply. Then the realities of the occasion began to assert themselves; and Katharine tried to meet the emergency.

"It seems impossible that you can be in earnest, Mr. Warwick," she said; "but if—if you are, I scarcely know what to say to you."

"Would you like time to consider?" he asked. "If so, take it."

"No, I do not require time to consider," she replied. "No amount of consideration could teach me any fitting words in which to thank you—in which to say to you how deeply I feel the kindness which has made you speak to me thus. I see, I feel, why you have done so; but"—clasping her hands, and speaking passionately—"you certainly cannot think so poorly of me as to believe that I would repay all that you have done, all that you would do for me, by marrying you because I am poor and lonely; because I need a home and a friend?"

"My dear Miss Tresham," said he, smiling gravely, "I am not a romantic or passionate lover like the man whom you have already rejected. I was not very much addicted to passion or sentiment in my youth; but now—well, now I am equally beyond the age and the inclination for either. Still I think I may say that I love you well enough to be willing to be accepted even on those terms. Don't look so much astonished"—as her eyes opened on him large and startled. "I have spoken on the strength of an unaccountable impulse. When I entered this room, I had not the least intention of such a thing. I was sure you would marry Annesley. It was only when I discovered my mistake that I thought I might give you the option of accepting or rejecting—a man old enough to have left love-making behind him! Only"—here he took a short turn up and down the room—"the heart will not grow old with years. We may think that it does, we may flatter ourselves that it has, until suddenly there comes an hour when passion, strong as any passion of youth, seizes it, and we know that age has left one citadel unconquered. I tell you this," he went on, pausing again in front of her, "because I do not wish you to think that I have asked you to marry me simply on account of your lonely position. I have *loved* you longer than you can imagine—longer than I knew myself—but it never occurred to me to think of telling you so. My age alone put such a declaration out of the question. Now, however—"

"Now you think of me!" cried Katharine, with a rush of tears—a softer shower than that which had driven poor Morton from the field—"O Mr. Warwick, I am so sorry, if I had known this earlier, I might perhaps have learned to love you, I might have been able to marry you; but, as it is, I—oh, pray forgive me—I cannot."

"You cannot promise to marry me, and trust that the love will come with time?"

She shook her head mournfully. Through their brimming tears, her eyes said again "Forgive me," as she answered, "I dare not."

"Think a moment," he said, in evident agitation. "Believe me, I do not press you from mere selfishness. Do you not think you like me even well enough to marry me for the sake of that home and that friend of which you spoke a moment ago?"

"I like you too well, much too well for that," she cried, passionately. "Don't you see—ah, don't you see how it is! If I liked you a little less, I might marry you for such a motive; while if I liked you a little more, I should marry you for your own sake. But, standing between the two, I only feel your generous effort to make me happy. I am only sure that I should repay you very ill, if I accepted you for any reason but the right one."

There was silence for some time after this. Through her tears, Katharine glanced up into Mr. Warwick's face, and was surprised to see how grave and thoughtful it looked, as he stood with his eyes absently fastened on the fire. He did not know that she was looking at him; so he allowed an expression of troubled perplexity to betray itself, which he would otherwise have kept concealed. Something in this expression struck the girl with a vague foreboding of ill. The fear that had found such frequent expression when Annesley was with her, suddenly sprang to her mind and to her lips again. Before she was conscious of what she was doing, she leaned forward and touched his arm.

"Mr. Warwick," she said, as he turned quickly toward her, "I am sure something is the matter—something in which I am concerned. Tell me what it is."

The quickness with which she leaped to a conclusion would have taken anybody but a lawyer by surprise—would have thrown anybody but a lawyer off his guard. It required all Mr. Warwick's professional command of countenance not to show how closely her shaft had struck home. As it was, he had only just presence of mind enough to smile.

"Why should you think that?" he asked. "Can't you imagine that I was thinking of myself, and my own great disappointment?"

"No, you were not thinking of yourself," she answered. "You were thinking of me—I am sure of it. Mr. Warwick, if it is any thing about St. John—it *is* something about St. John!" cried she, suddenly springing to her feet, as she caught an expression on his face that it was beyond his power to control. "I knew it! I felt sure of it! Oh!"—with a ring of imploring agony in her voice—"tell we what it is."

"Sit down, Miss Tresham," said Mr. Warwick, almost peremptorily. "There is no knowing what harm you may do yourself by this excitement. There has been a little trouble in Tallahoma, and Mr. St. John was mixed up in it," he added, quietly; "but I assure you every thing is right and straight now. Still, if you insist upon hearing about it—"

"Oh, indeed I do!"

"I can give you an outline of the matter. I am sorry, however, that you force me to it, for I think you have had agitation enough for one day. Why, you are quivering like an aspen-leaf!"

"Never mind. I cannot help it, it is purely nervous. Go on, please; tell me what he has done."

As gently as possible Mr. Warwick told her, softening the blow by every means in his power. But no gentleness, no softness, could break its awful force, could shut out from her sight the hideous truth. "O my God!" she exclaimed, when she first clearly understood *what* it was that he had done. But after that, no sound came from her lips. She sat with her face buried in her hands, and only now and then a long, shuddering sigh seemed to shake her whole frame from head to foot. Even after Mr. Warwick ceased speaking—after he had made his last attempt at pitying comfort—she still sat bent down, crushed, as it were, by the double blow of anguish and disgrace.

"Miss Tresham, this will never do," said he, at last. "This is not like you—is it worthy of you? Can you find no comfort in the fact that no one is aware of Mr. St. John's complicity in the matter? Have you not sufficient reliance in me to feel that the secret is as safe with me as with yourself?"

"I should be the most ungrateful human being in the world if I *did not* feel it," said she, lifting her face—so pale and drawn, that it absolutely startled him—"but not even your kindness can alter the fact itself—the terrible, awful, overwhelming fact! Mr. Warwick, I never, never thought I could sink so low as *this!*"

"Which do you consider worst," said Mr. Warwick, coolly, "this conduct, or that of which you have spoken with regard to yourself?"

"Oh, this, this!"

"There I don't agree with you. The man who robs a defenceless woman, as this man has robbed you, does not, it is true, make himself amenable to the law, as when he breaks into a bank; but he does transgress the higher law—the moral law—as much, or, perhaps, more; and the man who violates the one, will not hesitate to violate the other, whenever he thinks that he can do so with impunity. Miss Tresham, believe me, you need not regret Mr. St. John's moral degradation—I mean that you need not think he has taken any deeper step. When he entered the bank to rob it, he was committing an act which made him liable to the penalties of the law, if the law could detect him; but he was not, even in degree, taking a deeper step in abstract dishonesty, than when he entered it to rob you!"

"But the disgrace—the terrible disgrace!"

"So far as that goes, so far as the opinion of the world goes, a thing cannot be disgraceful which is not known. If you trust me at all, trust me this far, nobody ever shall know of this."

"O Mr. Warwick—" Once more the tears came, and ended all further speech. He made no effort to stop them, but walked away to the window, and left her to herself; sure that those tears would do more to relieve her heart and clear her brain than any words of his could. As he stood there, feeling sad and sore enough at heart, he watched the last red glow of sunset fade from the top of some distant trees, and the lovely veil of spring twilight begin to steal over the earth. Something in the scene and in the hour carried his thoughts back to that evening when the doctor said that the life so near him now, the life at that moment throbbing with the emotions and sorrows of earth, would pass before morning into eternity, when he had gazed at the steady advance of night, and waited for Morton Annesley to decide whether or not the heart of that dying girl was his. "Poor fellow!" said the lawyer, half aloud, forgetting his own cause for wounded feeling in pitying the young man who had been so full of honest, impulsive grief. Strangely enough, he was standing at that moment exactly in the place where Morton had stood a few hours before waiting to hear his sentence. Katharine noticed it when she turned to speak, and saw that he had left her side.

"And, knowing this, you counselled me to marry Mr. Annesley!" she cried, her voice, with a sudden flash of indignation in it, making him start, as it rang through the silent room. "Oh, how could you do it? how could you think so meanly of me? how could you think that I would carry such a stain as this to a man who loved me?"

"You do not seriously think that your brother's conduct leaves any stain on you?" said he, coming back, with something of his usual slight, grave smile on his lip. "Miss Tresham, I am astonished at you! Such talk sounds like melodramatic nonsense in a novel or a play! If Annesley were here, he would tell you what I tell you for him, that Mr. St. John is not of the least importance when considered in connection with yourself. As for this affair in Tallahoma, I see but one result springing from it, and that is a good one. It has taken the scoun—the man out of your path. Trust me that, as long as you remain in Tallahoma, you have nothing to fear from him. He will never return there, for he knows that I hold evidence against him which would convict him in any court of law."

"And yet you let him go?"

"Yes, I let him go."

"On my account?"

"Do I need to tell you that? do you suppose any other motive could have induced me to spare him?"

"And you have done all this for me, while I—" she stopped, and covered her face with her hands, held them so a moment, and then looked up. "Mr. Warwick," she said, with exquisite gentleness, "I begin to appreciate your offer of a moment ago; I begin to see more clearly why you made it. I begin to understand that, when you offered me a home, you did so because no other home is open to me. You have not spoken of Mr. Marks. I feel sure that he does not wish me to return to them."

For the second time during the course of this interview Mr. Warwick's face betrayed him. The climax to her speech came so suddenly, that he was not prepared for it; and, feeling her eyes steadily fastened on him, he knew that evasion or concealment was useless. The truth had already shown itself, and the truth must be told.

"You are right, Miss Tresham," he said; "my sister's husband has fallen many degrees in my estimation, by his refusal to receive you again. But you mistake very much when you think that I asked you to marry me merely to offer you a home. It is true that your loneliness encouraged me to tell you of my love, but that love existed long before this loneliness came upon you."

"But still it is true—Mr. Marks does not wish me to return?"

"It is true," he answered. He could say no more, for he was too indignant with his brother-in-law to attempt to make excuses for his conduct (which really, if he had looked at it dispassionately, did not merit indignation), and he could not but be wounded by Katharine's indifference to those last words of his—words which had been so full of earnest feeling.

"Oh," said the girl, wearily, "how desolate I am, how very desolate! I cannot stay much longer with these kind people, and yet where to go, what to do? Mr. Warwick, am I asking too much of your kindness and forbearance when I beg you to advise me what to do?"

Mr. Warwick might have replied that he had already advised, and that his advice, in two different cases, had been unhesitatingly rejected. But he was one of the rare men—rarer, by far, than heroes, or geniuses, or exceptional wonders of any other description—who, on emergencies, can put themselves aside, and speak or act for others without any bias of egotism. He considered for a moment, and then he said:

"I think that Tallahoma would be the best place for you just now, because Tallahoma is safe from Mr. St. John. You are not well enough to be molested by him, and you are only safe from that molestation when you are where he will not dare to venture. Will you allow me to ask if you gave him all the money which Marks paid to you?"

"All. I borrowed ten dollars from Mrs. Marks to go to Saxford—by-the-way, I must return it to you for her—and in Saxford I sold my watch, when I hardly knew what I was doing, to enable me to go farther. They were very honest at the hotel in Hartsburg. I found all that money safe in my bag when I got well. I have it still, for Mrs. Crump would not receive any before I left. She laughed, and told me I could settle the bill when I came back. Dr. Randolph said the same thing. After those bills are paid, however, I scarcely think there will be any left."

"Never mind those bills. I have already settled them. Surely"—as he saw a deep flush come over her face—"you do not mind being indebted to me for such a trifling amount, and, I hope, for such a short time. Remember, Miss Tresham"—smiling a little sadly—"I am old enough to be your father. I assure you that I have the bills, and you may pay me the full amount as soon as you are able to do so. Wait, however, and don't attempt to pay me until you are able. Give me the pleasure of helping you a little. Now"—hurrying on—"the question is, have you money enough to come and board in Tallahoma while I endeavor to obtain another situation for you? I am sure I can do this in a short time."

"I believe I have a hundred and fifty dollars. The watch had been my aunt's, and was richly jewelled. It should have sold for much more; but I—I was not in a condition to do any thing but take the first sum that was offered me. Nevertheless, this amount is enough to support me for a time, is it not?"

"For a short—" Mr. Warwick began, when the door behind him opened and shut quickly, a silk dress rustled across the floor, and through the dusky gloom Irene Vernon came forward, her eyes shining, her cheeks glowing, and herself looking like some radiant picture that had stepped from its canvas to walk the earth in guise of flesh and blood.

"Mr. Warwick," she began, abruptly, "and you, Miss Tresham, pray pardon me when I tell you that I have overheard a little of your conversation. I was passing along the terrace a moment ago, and, as I stopped by the window, I caught the sound of your voices, and heard a few words—enough to send me in upon you, and make me venture to ask you" (addressing Katharine) "a question. Am I right in gathering from those few words, that you do not intend to return to Mrs. Marks?"

"Yes, Miss Vernon, you are quite right," said Katharine, quietly. "I do not intend to return to Mrs. Marks, for the simple reason that Mrs. Marks does not wish my services any longer."

"And you are talking of going to Tallahoma to—to board?"

"Mr. Warwick has advised something of the sort."

"Well, I will give you better advice than Mr. Warwick's, then," said the young beauty, with her most royal tone and look. "You can go back to Tallahoma—in fact, I think it is a good thing to do—but you must go back with me. No—not a word! I positively won't hear a word until I have finished what I have to say. It is very uncivil to interrupt people, is it not, Mr. Warwick?—Well, Miss Tresham, I was about to tell you that I heard to-day from my sister, for whom I have been waiting here, and she cannot join me. My troublesome brother-in-law has managed to break his leg—Flora says she thinks he did it on purpose to keep her at home—and she begs me, instead of going on to Mobile, to come back to Lagrange and wait for her. Now, I will go back on one condition—that you go with me. Flora took a great fancy to you, and so did George, and they will both make you heartily welcome, not to speak of the pleasure of my society. You can get well there at your leisure, and—and—indeed it is just the thing for you.—Mr. Warwick, tell her that she ought to go!"

"Miss Vernon, you are too kind, much too kind," began Katharine, in that tone which inevitably presages a refusal; when Miss Vernon broke in upon her with an utter disregard of her own theory about interruptions:

"You are mistaken, Miss Tresham, I am not at all too kind—nobody ever was too kind in this world. If there were such a thing as being too kind, it might not, perhaps, be quite as hard a world to live in as it is. That is social cant; and you know how I hate social cant. I see plainly," she went on, "that you are going to say something about 'deeply grieved,' and 'impossible to accept,' and all that sort of thing. I will take it for granted that you have already said it; and I will ask you to give me one reason—a single reason—why it is impossible for you to accept the kindness (saying that it is a kindness) which I have offered you?"

"I have no claim upon such kindness," Katharine said.

"You have the claim of my liking you; what better could there be?"

"I have not even that claim upon your sister."

"Upon my sister! Why she likes you exceedingly; and, even if she did not, she would be glad to see you all the same.—Mr. Warwick, did you ever hear any thing quite as absurd as the idea of her making a bugbear out of Flora, of all the people in the world?" (Persuasive), "Tell her, please, that she ought to come!" (Imperative), "Tell her that she must come!"

Said Mr. Warwick, looking a little amused: "Miss Tresham, don't you think it would be well to consider Miss Vernon's proposal? It seems to me that it is a very clear way, and a very pleasant way out of all your difficulties—present ones, at least."

"But I really cannot," said Katharine. "Miss Vernon is mistaken if she thinks it is social cant when I say that she is too kind—that her kindness blinds her to the objections against her plan."

"Name them," said Miss Vernon, with business-like brevity.

"I am under very many obligations already," said Katharine. "I cannot consent to increase their number."

"That is nothing more nor less than pride," said Miss Vernon, concisely; "and pride, no doubt you are aware, is the besetting sin of human nature, and the one we are most called upon to struggle against. I was reading in your —what do you call it?—your manual, the other day, and I saw that you were specially told to mortify your will. Now, here is a good opportunity for you to mortify your will by going with me to Lagrange."

Katharine laughed. It was impossible to do otherwise—the girl's manner, half-serious, half-whimsical, made such a strange and complete contrast to the highly-wrought frame of mind which she had dispelled by her entrance. She had brought a fragrance of violets into the room with her, and as she stood in the soft gloaming, with the firelight gleaming on her silk dress and a gold locket that hung round her throat, she seemed to have brought an atmosphere of other things besides violets—of sweet thoughts and noble impulses, and generous, kindly deeds.

Katharine was won by her now, as, indeed, she had been from the first; and, when two soft, white hands took hers, and a gentle voice said, "See! I ask it of you as a favor to me. Won't you come?" she remembered how tenderly those hands had nursed her through her desperate illness, and she felt that refusal was no longer possible.

"Yes," she said, "I will come."

And so it was settled. Thus, swayed as it seemed by the merest chance, yet led, who can doubt, by the kindest care, she took the road back to Lagrange—that road that was leading slowly but surely to the end.

It was determined that they would leave the next morning. Miss Vernon, on her own (that is, her sister's) account, was anxious to do so; but she good-naturedly proposed to wait several days if Miss Tresham desired. To her surprise, Katharine begged that the journey might not be deferred on her account.

"I am quite well enough to travel," she said; "and, if I could only go away from here to-morrow morning early, I should be so glad—so very glad!"

"But Mr. Annes—," began Miss Vernon, in amazement. Then she paused, her bright-blue eyes turned keenly on her companion's face, and in a moment the truth flashed over her.—"Miss Tresham," she cried, sharply, almost angrily (they were alone in Katharine's room a little while before supper), "you don't mean to say that you have rejected Morton Annesley?"

"Miss Vernon," answered Katharine, with a touch of the besetting sin of human nature, "did you think it likely that I would accept him?"

"Did I think? Of course, I thought you would accept him," returned Miss Vernon. "Why should I not think so? You seemed to like him, and he is certainly every thing that a woman could wish to like. Miss Tresham, you can't have done such a thing!"

"Yes, I have," said Katharine, who was tired of the subject, and could not bear the idea of running another gantlet of remonstrances. "Yes, I have; and, if you only knew my reasons for having done so, I am sure you would not blame me."

"I *would* blame you!" cried Miss Vernon, indignantly. "I don't believe that, if I knew any or every reason that could possibly have influenced you, I should blame you a single degree less than I do now."

"Don't make rash assertions," said Katharine, smiling faintly, "I cannot go into a detail of all the motives that influenced me; but, putting most of them aside, one is, or ought to be, enough to exonerate me from blame. Miss Vernon, I grant all Mr. Annesley's good qualities so cordially that I think the woman who marries him ought to love him devotedly. Now, I don't love him at all. Would you advise me to return all the generous devotion that is willing to give so much by a cold sort of liking that is not able to give any thing?"

"But is it possible that you really do not love him?"

"It is certainly possible; and—ah, me! I must write to-night and tell him so. The letter can be delivered after we leave, in time to prevent his coming here to-morrow morning."

"You are determined to go, then?"

"The decision rests with you; but I should like to go."

"Of course, then, the matter is settled; we will go.—Heigho!" sighed the young lady to herself, as she left the room. "Poor Morton!—poor, dear fellow! How strangely contrary to what we expect, things turn out sometimes!"

That night Katharine sat down to write her letter to Annesley. Taken at any time, or under any circumstances, it was a hard letter to write; but, with an aching head, and, worse yet, an aching heart, the difficulties of composition were many times increased.

Everybody does the same thing in a case like this. Everybody spoils one sheet of paper after another; makes beginnings with the desperate intention, "This *shall* do!" becomes disgusted at the third line, throws it aside disdainfully, or wrathfully crumples it up, and dashes at another fair page, with the same result. One stilted address follows another; the gamut of endearing, or respectful, or uncivil terms is run from end to end, until at last—if common-sense can manage to get a hearing—the grand conclusion of so many experiments is simple, and generally brief.

Thus it was with Katharine. After getting well on in half a dozen lengthy epistles, she at last thought how foolish and vain all words besides the few strictly necessary ones were, and the result of this thought was the following note:

"Dear Mr. Annesley: Miss Vernon has kindly asked me to accompany her back to Lagrange and spend a few weeks at her sister's house until I am strong enough to find another situation. I shall leave with her to-morrow morning. This arrangement, made since I saw you, renders it necessary that I should write and tell you how deeply I feel your kindness, and how impossible it is for me to accept all you have offered me. I will not pain you—as I know I should do—by speaking of the great disparity in our social positions, and of other greater obstacles, which under any circumstances would stand between us. It is enough for me to say that the woman whom you honor with your heart should love you as you deserve to be loved—as some woman far more worthy of you than I am will yet love you—and that this love it is not in my power to give you. Forgive me, Mr. Annesley, if this sounds ungracious—sounds as if I had forgotten all the many kindnesses which are, in truth, written on my heart. I must speak frankly, and make myself clearly understood, for your sake, as well as for my own. Every feeling, except the one feeling which alone you would be willing to accept, I have for you. Each one of them makes me your warm and life-long friend; but all of them put together are not strong enough to make me your wife. God bless you, Mr. Annesley! God make you happy! God reward you for all your generous kindness! It is hard to close this letter here, and yet there is nothing more to say, unless I ask you again to forgive me.

"Faithfully, your friend,

"KATHARINE TRESHAM.

"BELLEFONT, *Thursday night.*"

It was done. For the second time that day Katharine deliberately put aside the love and the protection which two different men, each well worthy of trust, had offered her, and with the blind, heedless, yet sometimes divine impulse of youth, turned from the golden gifts of life, those gifts for which some wretched women are willing to sell themselves into legal bondage, and went her way alone. It had been a struggle, a hard struggle, in both cases; it was a struggle, even after this letter was written, to seal it and lay it aside, saying: "Lie there, happy days, full to the brim of love and content, and soft belongings, and tender care, and glittering pleasure! Lie there, sweet dreams of what might be, of affection ripening into love, and trust growing in sweetness and strength with every passing year! Lie there, words, and looks, and tones, that will never see the light; days possible, yet forever unborn; emotions never to be felt, and the whole current of a life never to be lived!" It was hard to hold out the arms, saying: "Come, weary days filled with toil, uncheered by any smile from kindred lips, or glance from loving eyes! Come, days that lead among the rough by-ways of the world, and toss the living, yearning human heart from one strange household to another, that teach in every hour of your flight how some paths are strewed with roses only that others may be filled with thorns! Come, days within whose very bitter lurks a sweet that only those who meet you willingly can ever taste—a sweet like that grand victory which noble deeds wring from defeat, which come when the spirit has dropped its arms after long conflict, and the divine secret of content begins to steal upon the soul, the first knowledge of good and evil, the first startled, humbled thanks to God that He guided the blind eyes and the faltering hand, and gave at last the leaden casket with the precious jewel shrined within!"

CHAPTER XL.

GOOD SAMARITANS.

GREAT was the astonishment, and greater the consternation, of the Bellefont household when they heard of the intended departure of Miss Vernon and Miss Tresham. With Miss Lester in especial, these feelings verged strongly on indignation.

"Your sister is absurd. If Mr. Raynor chose to break his leg, surely she is able to nurse him without any assistance from you!" cried this young lady to Miss Vernon. "I thought you might be content to stay with me for a little while; you are not nearly strong enough to travel yet," she said, reproachfully, to Miss Tresham.

Miss Vernon laughed, and Katharine apologized, but they both remained firm in their intention. Bellefont charmed wisely, but charmed in vain.

"We must go," said Miss Vernon, decidedly, and Katharine echoed, "We must really go!"

They did go, notwithstanding all the persuasive eloquence employed by their kind hosts. And, when these last saw that the resolution was firm, they made a virtue of necessity and yielded gracefully, remembering that the law of hospitality is double, and that it is as incumbent to speed the parting as to welcome the coming guest.

"You won't forget us, I am sure," said Mrs. Lester, wistfully, when she kissed the young stranger who had taken such a hold on her heart.

And she was right. In all the years of her life Katharine never forgot the pleasant home which had opened its doors to her in the hour of her need, nor the cordial faces and warm hearts that had surrounded her with kindness and care.

When the last thanks had been uttered, the last farewells—many times repeated—were over, and the last glimpse of pretty Bellefont, crowning its stately terraces, had vanished from sight, Katharine could scarcely restrain her tears. She felt as if she were bidding adieu to peace, as if she were leaving quiet behind her, and turning her face toward turmoil. She had seemed to escape out of that uneasy current of life in Lagrange, to be able to spread her wings for wider flight and freer air, yet, of her own accord, she was now going back—she was now drifting again among the scenes and the people that haunted her like uneasy dreams of delirium, and inspired her with a strange shrinking impossible to analyze and hard to resist.

"I have an instinct approaching to a certainty that I ought to have turned my face in the other direction," she said, to Miss Vernon, as the horses trotted gayly along the smooth road, and she felt that every moment was taking her nearer to Lagrange.

"And I have an instinct approaching to a certainty that you are doing the right thing in taking this direction," answered Irene, smiling. "Now, the question is, which instinct is entitled to the most respect?"

"Mine, I think, since I have a reason for it."

"A good one?"

"A very good one."

"Suppose you let me judge of that."

"It would involve a long story," said Katharine, "and that, I fear, would tire you."

"What, with a day's journey before us, and not even a novel to read! My dear Miss Tresham, what are you thinking of? If you have a story, and if you would not object to telling it, there is nothing I should like better than listening to it, especially if there were any good end to be gained by doing so."

"There is no good end to be gained," said Katharine, "but, since I accept your hospitality, I certainly owe it to you to be quite frank about myself. I don't know what may or may not be said about me in Lagrange, Miss Vernon; but, having so generously extended your hand to me, it is only right that you should be able to judge intelligently of the truth or falsehood of any reports which may be afloat."

"Miss Tresham, if those are your reasons for telling your story, let me assure you that you need not do so. I rarely hear gossip, and I never believe it."

"Nevertheless, it exists; it is heard by everybody, and believed by the vast majority. Mrs. Raynor may like some explanation of—"

"I can answer for Flora, that she will not dream of such a thing."

"At all events, you must allow me to speak," said Katharine, smiling faintly. "For once in my life I have been betrayed by cowardly folly into that tangled web which deception in any form is sure to weave. The sooner I can clear myself of it, the sooner I may be able to forgive myself for having fallen into it. Shall I begin at the beginning, and tell you a tolerably long story?"

"If you insist, I can only be frank, and say that I should like nothing better."

So, as the carriage rolled along the pleasant country-road, with a changing panorama of sunny landscape all around, drifting clouds throwing sudden shadows over distant hill-sides, green valleys on either side, orchards in the full glory of tinted bloom, and dogs rushing out to bark from every way-side house, Katharine told the story of her life, in all its details, to a very sympathizing listener.

These two advanced nearer toward friendship during this day than in all the days of their former acquaintance. For it is with friendship as with love—to be perfect, it has two requisites, congeniality and confidence. Without the former, it is a merely fictitious sentiment; and, without the latter, it is a sentiment dwarfed at best, and restrained. Confidence is a golden key to almost every heart, and certainly a golden link to every affection, let its form or degree be what it will.

Says Miss Thackeray, very sweetly and truly: "If love is the faith, then friendship is the charity of life."

And so these two women were to find it. Neither of them was an ordinary woman; both of them had much of the rare sweetness that is born of strength, and in which a frivolous or petty nature is invariably lacking; and both of them had felt at different times, and in a different manner, the need of a friend.

There had been a certain attraction between them from the first; but they were not quick to come together. Both of them had seen too much of the world for this. When at last the league of friendship—a league which was to last all the rest of their lives—was struck, they made no protestations to that effect. It was understood somehow, and none the less felt and respected because it was tacit.

"Now," said Katharine, when she had finished, "you will do me a great favor if you will tell as much or as little of this to your sister as she requires to know or as you think fit. Remember that I leave the matter entirely to your discretion."

"My discretion, then, will be likely to leave Flora very much in the dark," answered Irene, smiling. "It is better to err on the side of tell ing too little than of telling too much, you know —at least there is a remedy for the first, but no remedy has ever been devised for the second. I shall tell her just as little as she will be satisfied to hear, Miss Tresham."

Judging from her experience of human nature in general, and the feminine nature in particular, Katharine was inclined to think that this would not be very little; but she thanked Miss Vernon for her discreet intentions, and it was decided that Mrs. Raynor's curiosity was, if possible, to be left ungratified.

On the afternoon of the second day, many familiar signs began to show that they were approaching the bourn of their journey—familiar Lagrange scenery around, familiar Lagrange faces on the road.

Miss Vernon saw that Katharine was growing nervous, and tried to reassure her.

"It is very absurd that you should persist in making bugbears of two of the most inoffensive people in the world," she said. "Miss Tresham, do you think I would have asked you to come with me, if I had not been able to promise you a cordial welcome?"

Katharine acknowledged the truth of this, and much more like it; but still she was uncomfortable—as, in fact, it was not remarkable that she should have been.

It was almost a relief when at last the dreaded moment of final arrival came, when the carriage turned from the main-road, entered a wide gate, and, after half a mile of trotting along an avenue so full of sylvan beauty that it looked as if it might have led into the heart of a forest, came to a bridge crossing a pretty creek, a smooth lawn sloping on all sides like green velvet, and the usual country-house, with many piazzas, and wide, cool hall, where Mrs. Raynor was standing in the door waiting to receive them.

"O Irene, I am delighted you have come!" she cried. "I hardly expected you so soon—in fact, I did not know whether or not to expect you at all.—Miss Tresham, I am charmed to see you"—she looked a little surprised, nevertheless —"I am glad that you are well enough to travel. Irene wrote me an account of your illness; it must have been dreadful!"

"I have brought Miss Tresham to stay with us for some time," said Irene, before Katharine could answer. "She looks badly, does she not? We must try to bring back her roses before we let her go.—How is George?"

"Dreadfully cross," answered George's wife, with the most literal promptness. "The doctor says he is getting on very well, however; and, indeed, I suppose crossness is one sign of it.—Miss Tresham, I am very glad to hear that you are going to stay with us. I am only afraid you will be dreadfully bored. I confess I am bored myself nearly to death. Bella and Louisa have been over continually, Irene. They are dear girls, you know; but by no means the liveliest of companions."

"Where is George?" asked Irene.

"In his own room. Will you go in and see him? He will like to hear all the Apalatka news. I will take Miss Tresham up-stairs.—This way, Miss Tresham. Dear me, how pale you are! You must lie down immediately, and take some refreshment. Do you prefer wine or cordial?"

Katharine's mind was soon set at rest on the score of her welcome. Mrs. Raynor was unaffectedly glad to see her—glad of any thing or anybody to break the monotony of sick-room nursing, for which Nature had rendered her singularly unfit.

"George is so disagreeably cross that I am glad to get away from him for a little while," she said, as she sat down in the room into which she showed Katharine, and plainly manifested her intention of remaining some time. "I have a horror of sick men," she went on; "they are so impatient, and ten times harder to manage than sick women, or sick children either. I am so glad Irene has come to relieve me a little. I am very glad, too, that she has brought you, Miss Tresham. I hope you will not let Mrs. Marks deprive us of you soon."

"I shall not return to Mrs. Marks at all," said Katharine, meaning to give an explanation of her position at once. But Mrs. Raynor merely opened her pretty blue eyes a minute, and then rambled on with her own grievances; she had a habit of paying very little attention to what was said to her, especially if she chanced to be interested by something else at the time.

Miss Vernon soon discovered that her sister's curiosity was not at all troublesome on the subject of Katharine. Not to give her too much credit, however, it must be premised that this would scarcely have been the case if she had entertained even a suspicion of any thing unusual in the matter. True, Lagrange was full of gossip about Miss Tresham and Mr. Annesley; but Mrs. Raynor had been full of her own concerns, and had heard very little of this gossip. Besides, Katharine was certainly very "nice." She herself had thought so, and Irene had taken quite a fancy to her. As Mr. Raynor had once remarked, Irene did not often take fancies, especially to women, and when, by some chance, she did take them, it was an understood thing that they were to be humored. Then, in her present desperate and doleful condition, Mrs. Raynor was so glad to see her sister that there was no doubt but that she would have welcomed the most disagreeable person in the world whom Irene might have chosen to bring back with her.

"I believe there is a good deal of talk about Miss Tresham," she said, indolently; "but, of course, we have no reason for minding that. These stagnant Lagrange people would talk about a straw. By-the-by" (with some animation), "Irene, have you any idea where Morton Annesley is?"

"Certainly I have," answered Irene. "He is down in Apalatka, staying with Mr. Seymour. Why do you ask? Have his good-natured friends been talking about him, too?"

"Indeed, they have; and, what is more, I fancy that Mrs. Annesley and Adela have been very uneasy."

"Uneasy!" repeated Irene, with a curl of her scarlet lip. "Pray what mischief did they think he was likely to get into? Surely he is old enough to manage his own affairs without being kept in leading-strings by his mother and sister."

"They have every disposition to keep him in leading-strings; but I don't think they succeed very well," answered Mrs. Raynor. "He has a will of his own, notwithstanding that he looks so gentle. Adela French was here not long ago—just before George broke his leg, that is—and, although she said nothing on the subject, I could see that she was very uneasy."

"About what?"

"About the danger of his marrying Miss Tresham, I presume. For my part, I never believed that there was any probability of it. I always felt sure that he has entirely too much sense for such a thing."

"It would be the best thing in the world for him," said Miss Vernon; "and, I am sure, it will not be his fault if he does not succeed in doing it. Is Adela French in Lagrange yet?"

"I don't know, but I think not. George has kept me so closely at home" (in an aggrieved tone), "that I hardly know any thing. I will ask Bella when she comes to-day. She may know, and she can tell you all that people are saying about Miss Tresham."

"Thank you; but I have not the least curiosity on that score. I give them credit for any amount of ill-nature, just as much as if I had heard all they say."

When Miss Raynor came, she proved fully capable of retailing all the gossip of which her sister-in-law had spoken. Miss Vernon listened with a disdainful curl of the lip; but still, she did listen; she felt that it was necessary to know exactly what was said of Katharine, in order to use to the best advantage those discretionary powers which the latter had given her. After all, however, the talk proved to be harmless and indefinite enough with all its ill-nature. Lagrange had known nothing; and, therefore, Lagrange had found it difficult to say very much. The chief hubbub seemed to have been raised about poor Morton Annesley. The kind friends, who always know all the particulars on these occasions, had declared, unhesitatingly, that he had "given his mother the slip," and eloped with Mrs. Marks's missing governess. Why he should have thought it necessary to give his mother the slip, or why—if he wished to marry Mrs. Marks's governess—an elopement on either side was requisite, nobody was able to say; but circumstantial evidence being strong against the two, they were formally condemned after the most approved form of popular justice. It was useless to hint (as one or two skeptical people did) that Mr. Annesley had not left Lagrange until two weeks after Miss Tresham's departure. *That* the wise ladies and gentlemen concerned were ready to reply, was by special arrangement. It was meant to lull suspicion, and throw people off their guard. No doubt Miss Tresham had gone on before to some appointed rendezvous, where Mr. Annesley had followed in due time, and a marriage had taken place. This point being settled to the satisfaction of everybody but the most stoutly incredulous, people became undecided whether Mr. Annesley would take his bride away somewhere (to Europe, probably), or whether he would return, and, with a high hand, "have it out" with his outraged family. Being, as usual, very stagnant for subjects of interest, Lagrange hoped much for the latter event. Parties ran high on the question. Would or would not Mrs. Annesley continue to live at Annesdale? "Mrs. Annesley is a Christian woman; she will bear this severe trial as a Christian woman should, and remain with her son," said one party. "Mrs. Annesley is a woman of spirit and self-respect; she will certainly leave Annesdale, and go to Mobile with Adela French," said another party. Chorus of both parties, "What a sad pity for Mrs. Annesley! Such a charming person! Mrs. Marks's governess for a daughter-in-law! Only what she might have expected, however; the idea of inviting such a person to Annesdale! Might have known what would follow," etc., etc., etc.

It was not to be doubted that Miss Vernon felt a considerable degree of malicious enjoyment when, after a month of uninterrupted gossip (to which the only drawback had been a decided and uncomfortable dearth of material), the news fell like a thunder-bolt on the county, that she had returned to her sisters, bringing Miss Tresham—who was still Miss Tresham—with her. At first Lagrange was incredulous, then Lagrange was indignant, and finally Lagrange stood on its dignity, and said things more scornful and slighting than agreeable and complimentary, about the governess who was no longer a governess. Why had she left Mrs. Marks? Lagrange was not curious, by any means; but still, it wanted to know that. Where had she been all this time, and what was the reason that Mr. Annesley had not yet made his appearance? Lagrange did not absolutely request people to tell their story to the marines, who were foolish enough to make statements about brain-fever, and Colonel Lester's, and no connection with Mr. Annesley; but, in its secret heart, it did not believe a word of the whole story, and waited grimly for what it was pleased to call the "upshot of the matter."

This did not come for some time, however. Miss Tresham remained quietly enough at the Raynors', and Mr. Annesley still lingered in Apalatka. Poor Morton! That letter of Katharine's, written the night before her departure, had dealt him such a cruel and such a terribly unexpected blow, that he felt cowardly about going back to Lagrange, about taking up again the familiar life from which so much sunshine had gone, he thought, forever. He felt more inclined to remain with Seymour, to spend his days strolling about the woods, with a gun on his shoulder, and a dog at his heels; his nights in talking or not talking to Godfrey, as he felt inclined, while they both smoked countless cigars. It was a dull, quiescent sort of life, but it suited his mood. It was doubtful when or how he would end it; and, all this time, Lagrange talked unceasingly, and Mrs. Annesley's anxiety nearly drove her into a fever.

All this time, too, Katharine was winning back health, and strength, and bloom, and making herself very attractive and very necessary in the Raynor household. The power to charm, the gift of diffusing brightness, was hers now as much as ever, and these new friends began to look a little injured when she talked of intended departure. "Why can't you stay?" Miss Vernon would ask; "why need you be in such a hurry to procure a situation? Flora and George are both absolutely in love with you, and both thank me on an average once a day for having brought you here. I am almost sorry to see Mr. Warwick come; I fear, every time, that he may have found a place for you."

"He is trying to do so," said Katharine. Then she added, gratefully: "Mr. Warwick is very kind to me. He is the best friend, by far, I ever had."

"One of the best," corrected Irene. "I am sure he has no better disposition to serve you than—than Mr. Annesley, for instance. He has better opportunity, that is all."

"Don't you think one is apt to be more grateful for realities than for possibilities?" asked Katharine, smiling. "Not but that I am very much obliged to Mr. Annesley," she added. "He, too, has been a very kind friend to me."

"Nevertheless, I see plainly that you prefer Mr. Warwick."

"Do you mean that I am more grateful to him?"

"Well, yes; and that you *prefer* him. That includes liking as well as gratitude, doesn't it? you are twice as cordial to him as I ever saw you to Mr. Annesley."

"He is different," said Katharine, blushing in a manner which Miss Vernon thought quite unaccountable. "I have known him so much longer and so much better. And—and there is no danger of misconstruction with him. Now, with Mr. Annesley, I felt as if it was necessary to be on my guard all the time."

"Against his vanity, do you mean?"

"Oh, no; how could you think I meant such a thing? Against gossiping tongues, and ill-natured comments, and all that sort of thing It must be a very foolish woman who does not learn a little discretion from being tossed about the world as I have been."

"I hope you will never be tossed about again," said Miss Vernon. "I wish you would be reasonable, and let it be over at once."

The two ladies were sitting in a pretty morning-room, which opened on the lawn, while they talked in this manner. A soft, spring shower was falling outside, but every thing looked very bright and pretty within, when the door opened, and Mr. Warwick was shown into the room. They greeted him cordially; and, after the first salutations were over, he turned to Katharine.

"I see you are getting quite well," he said. "Are you almost ready for work?"

"I am quite ready," she answered, eagerly. "Have you found any thing for me?"

"I cannot say positively," he answered, "but I have a strong hope of doing so before very long. Have you any objection to going to R—— County?"

"I have not the least idea where R—— County is; but I have no objection to going anywhere."

"How very obliging you are!" said Mr. Warwick, smiling. But Miss Vernon gave a cry.

"R—— County!" she said. "Why, Mr. Warwick, that is so far away, that we need never hope to see her again if she once goes down there. Is it possible you could not find a situation for her nearer Lagrange?"

"It does not at all matter that it is so far away," said Katharine, hastily, for she understood Mr. Warwick's reasons for choosing R—— County better than Miss Vernon did. "I—I am not at all diffident about going among strangers," she went on. "Mr. Warwick, do you really think that there is any certain hope of a situation?"

"Read that," said Mr. Warwick, taking a letter from his pocket, and giving it to her.

She opened it eagerly; and, while she read, Miss Vernon was summoned from the room. A little negro boy, whom Mrs. Raynor called her page, came in with a message from "Mass George" of a very imperative nature, necessitating her immediate attendance on that gentleman. She went at once, though it was with some reluctance. "George is spoiled to death!" she said, to Mr. Warwick. "I have no doubt he will send a message for you when he knows you are here. He seems to think that people exist merely for the purpose of ministering to his amusement."

"It is not worth his while to send for me," said Mr. Warwick. "I shall not be here ten minutes longer. Tell him that, if he has any such intentions, if you please, Miss Vernon."

"I will," she said, with some malice, and the door had hardly closed on her when Katharine looked up.

"I like the tone of this letter," she said. "You have answered the questions, I presume?"

"Yes," he replied. "I answered them yesterday. I know Major Wright well," he went on, "and I am sure you will find a situation in his family pleasant. I should not have entertained his proposal otherwise."

"I am sure of that," she said, gratefully. "You think of me a great deal—much more than I deserve."

"Let me be the judge of that," said he. "When Wright's next letter comes—no doubt empowering me to offer certain terms for your acceptance—you will be ready to close with them, then?"

"Oh, yes; most gladly."

"You won't feel inclined to regret that R—— County is so far from Lagrange?"

"How could I? The last few months have given me very painful associations with Lagrange." Then, remembering how ungracious this sounded, she hesitated and blushed. "*You* will come down to R—— sometimes, will you not?" she said. "There is no one else I shall care to see."

"I don't know," he answered. "It has been two or three years since I was down there last, hunting up evidence in a troublesome case. It may be two or three more before I have such another matter on hand. Do you think you will remain with the Wrights that long?"

"I cannot tell," she answered, a little wounded by his tone. "'A rolling-stone gathers no moss,' you know; so I shall endeavor to be a stationary one. Very likely, therefore, you will find me in the Wright household two or three years hence. If so, I hope you will come to see me."

"There is not much doubt of my doing that," said he. "But I shall hope to see you in a home of your own, no longer a waif and stray of Fortune, as you are now."

She looked at him reproachfully. It was astonishing how they were playing at cross-purposes, these two. He meant to show her that she had no troublesome persistence to fear from him; while she felt aggrieved by the manner in which he seemed to ignore much that she thought he might have remembered.

"You have forgotten," she said, in a low voice. "You must have forgotten a great deal before you could say such things to me. I shall never marry, Mr. Warwick."

Mr. Warwick shrugged his shoulders a little over this positive declaration.

"Why not?" he asked.

"You know why not," she answered. "My burden is heavy enough on myself; I will not take it to any one else."

"Not even if he were willing to bear it?"

"No, a hundred times, no!"

"That is foolish, Miss Tresham. You must

forgive me for saying so, but it is very foolish. Your brother has nothing whatever to do with yourself. A man who loved you—a man whom you loved—would never hesitate for such a consideration as that."

"You should not judge all men by yourself," she said, smiling faintly, yet very sweetly. "There are very few who are able to sacrifice themselves as you have proved willing to do. I—I never knew anybody before who was."

"Don't think that I mean to reopen a subject which was closed finally," he said, "when I beg to correct you in the use of that word. 'Sacrifice' means something which we do unwillingly for the sake of another. Now, when I asked you to marry me—don't start! I have not the least intention of repeating that act of folly!—I was making no sacrifice at all; I was simply following the instinct of human nature, and endeavoring to win for myself the happiness I most desired. Take my word for it, that this will be the case with somebody else before long—somebody," he added, kindly, "to whom you may be able to give a different answer."

She shook her head, but something—a most unaccountable something—rose in her throat, and she could not speak.

He saw her agitation, and walked away, to give her time to recover herself.

"Poor girl! no doubt she is afraid of another sentimental scene with a man old enough to be her father," he thought, with a strange mixture of bitterness, and amusement, and sadness, as he stood looking across the lawn, watching the rain as it fell, and the sun as it tried to struggle through the clouds. After a while he turned round and took up the thread of conversation again, with a tolerably successful attempt at cheerfulness.

"You have no idea how anxious poor Bessie is to see you," he said. "It would really be a deed of charity to give her that pleasure when you chance to be in Tallahoma some day. I am sure you don't bear malice, or I would not ask such a thing."

"Bear malice!" repeated Katharine. "What an expression! Why, I am quite as much attached to Mrs. Marks and the children as ever; and I really have not been to Tallahoma because I could not bear to think of not calling to see them. Miss Vernon asked me to go with her yesterday, but I declined."

"You must understand that Bessie has all the time been very anxious for you to return," he said. "It was Marks who made a fool of himself. I can see very plainly that he is sorry for it now. Perhaps the fact of Mrs. Raynor's august protection may have something to do with his change of sentiment," he added, with a smile.

"It has been for the best," said Katharine, a little sadly. "I cannot blame Mr. Marks at all; and I am sure it is better that I should leave Lagrange. I have done little besides mischief since I have been here."

"Will you be good enough to tell me what kind of mischief?" asked Mr. Warwick, with the humorous accent she knew very well.

"Don't laugh at me," she said. "I assure you I am serious. Looking back, I can trace every thing to myself. If I had not come here, there would have been none of this trouble about St. John and Mrs. Gordon, or about Mr. Annesley, or—or about yourself."

"And if you had not been born, you would not be living," said he. "If I laugh at you, it is because you deserve to be laughed at for such absurdity! A quickness at perceiving the connection between cause and effect is a very good thing in its way, Miss Tresham, but it is possible to carry it too far—it is possible to torment one's self uselessly with past and irretrievable issues. No man is wise enough to foresee the to-morrow, or how the events of to-day may influence it. If we act with an honest intention for the best in the present, it is all that God will require of us. Nobody in the world stands alone; life is a very complex tissue, and every human soul influences others directly or indirectly. The conduct of some one else affected the course of your life; your conduct, in turn, affects the lives of others, and so on, *ad infinitum*. If you want to be logical, you must go far beyond yourself."

"You give me comfort as well as teach me logic," she said. "Must you go?" (as he rose). "Well, give my love to Mrs. Marks, and tell her I will certainly come to see her soon. Are the children all well?"

"Quite well, and eager for a sight of you. I may hear from Wright next week. If so, I will come and let you know."

"Thank you." She held out her hand. "You are very good to me," she added, softly.

The tone of her voice, the look in her eyes, haunted him after he left the room, after he rode away, and even after the ordinary distractions of life began to assert themselves once more. It was with difficulty that he finally banished the intrusive recollections.

"I have been a fool once," he thought,

"Nothing shall induce me to make a fool of myself a second time. I am old enough to have left such absurdities behind me."

CHAPTER XLI.

THE LAST DEFIANCE.

"The slow, sad hours that bring us all things ill" went by, slowly and sadly enough; brought little enough besides ill to Mrs. Gordon, as the days lengthened, the heavens smiled, and earth budded, and Nature, wakening from her brief winter sleep, prepared for her long summer carnival. Spring came, with its soft airs, its sportive breezes, its glittering sunshine, and bright flowers; but no change of season or of weather lightened her gloom; no lapse of time softened her sorrow, or taught her resignation. Round the old house that had been silent so long, and at last had come to shrine this one lonely life, all was rejoicing beauty; but within its doors there was a hush that seemed to speak of desolation—a subtile and penetrating sadness that human grief sometimes seems to impress even upon inanimate surroundings. People—the few people who ever came—felt it as soon as they entered the door, and left it behind them, like a weight, when they emerged again into the fresh air and bright sunshine. Day after day of stagnant, weary calm, rolled by; and the pale woman, lying on her sofa, grew daily more pale and more hollow-eyed. Who can wonder? Trouble, suspense, and bereavement, are grim phantoms which prove hard enough to fight when the daily cares of life—cares merciful at such a time—are pressing on the heart, and giving at least the relief of partial distraction to the mind. But trouble, when there is nothing to do but brood over it; suspense, when it is only possible to sit and wait for the dreaded day, or the dreaded object; bereavement, when not one human source of consolation has been left; oh, where is the tongue or the pen that can speak of these? As people who sit by warm hearths, and for whom luxurious tables are spread, shrug their shoulders, and say, "Poor thing!" when their sympathy and their attention are claimed by some gaunt, thinly-clad form out beyond in the night and storm, so we utter a few set words of pity and condolence when a face, white with the awful footprints of despair, looks in on our life. But have we—we, warmly clothed, and fed, and lodged, and hedged about with love—even the least conception of how bitterly the cold cuts, how heavily the rain falls, how dark and full of terror is the night to that poor, houseless wanderer? If we had, ah, vain words! even if we had, what could we do? The needs of the body can be supplied, the wants of the body can be filled, but who has yet been able to comfort the soul sick with lonely grief, or feed the heart starving for absent love?

So the days went by—one after another, with dreary sameness—and so the woman, whose life of fevered emotion had sunk at last into apathetic lethargy, watched them, from sunrise to sunset, all alone. Sometimes she shivered, as a keen realization of her position came over her; as, in a mirror, she saw herself sitting in the desolate solitude of her father's house, waiting for the man whom she had once loved, and now hated; the man who had wrecked her life, and made her what she was; the man whom she dreaded, abhorred, yet longed to see again—longed to pour out upon him the bitter tide of reproach, defiance, scorn, and hate. Sometimes she would shrink and shiver at a footstep, thinking, dreading that it might be his; then, again, she would pace the floor, and clasp her hands together, longing that he would come, that the worst might be over, that the utmost which could be said might have been said. But the weeks wore on, and he did not appear. John Warwick came often—as often as possible, and as he had news from Felix—and did his honest best to cheer and lighten the gloom which he found; but even he, when he went away, felt depressed; even he felt how hopeless were any efforts to bring sunshine where sunshine was not.

"If you only had a companion!" he said, to Mrs. Gordon, one day. "Such a life as this is enough to kill you! your own thoughts are the worst possible company; anybody or any thing would be better."

"And where would you find me a companion?" she asked, languidly. "Not that I would desire such a thing, but, if I did, where would you find one? A companion! think of all that a companion means. Not somebody to sit there and distract me with set looks, and composed manners, and talk about the weather and Lagrange gossip; but somebody who would have quickness enough to read my moods, and change with them; who would cheer at one time, and soothe at another; who would not be too gay, nor yet too dull; toward whom I need feel no reserve, yet who would not pry into my heart; somebody who— Ah, what is the good of talk ing? All this means a friend, and where have I a friend?"

"I know where I could find such a person for you," he said. "If—if you would only consent to it."

She looked at him a little suspiciously. "Whom do you mean?" she asked.

"I mean Miss Tresham," he answered. "If you would only believe—"

She interrupted him, passionately. "I will believe nothing that would bring her into this house! I don't trust her, Mr. Warwick; say what you will, I don't trust her! St. John's sister cannot be other than false, and you will live to find it out!"

"I am rather of the opinion," said he, "that you and some other people will live to find out that it is neither just nor reasonable to condemn one person for the faults and crimes of another, no matter how nearly related that other may be."

"And you trust her? Trust anybody with that blood?"

"Stop a moment, Mrs. Gordon; consider how little you know of the blood, or are able to judge of it from one representative. It is impossible for you to tell how many brave and noble ancestors this very St. John may have had, ancestors whose blood has made his sister what she is."

"She *is* his sister!"

"That settles the matter, I see," said he, slightly shrugging his shoulders. "Well, perhaps you may be glad to hear that this dangerous person will soon be removed from the neighborhood of Morton House. I received a letter to-day from an old friend of mine in one of the lower counties, offering Miss Tresham the position of governess in his family. She has requested me to accept it for her, and to say that she will leave Lagrange in a few days. I am going home to write that letter now."

"Does your friend live near Felix?"

"No; very far from Felix. Surely, after all that I have told you, you do not cling to that idea yet?"

"It has been an instinct with me from the first One cannot disregard instincts."

"Yes, one can, especially when they are contrary to reason and common-sense. You see I talk plainly to you. On my honor, I think you need it. Have you seen Annesley since he returned?"

"He was here yesterday. He tells me that this girl has finally rejected him."

"And will not even that fact alter your judgment of her a little?"

She made an impatient gesture. "Why should it? No doubt she would have married him if she had dared to do so; that is, if she had not known that his family would never recognize her."

"Morton is tolerably independent of his family," said Mr. Warwick, dryly. "If Miss Tresham had married him, no doubt they would have found it tiresome to stay away from Annesdale because his wife was mistress there; and that is all that their not recognizing her would have come to, you know. Well, the afternoon is wearing on, and I must leave you. Don't you ever go out to get a little fresh air?"

"Scarcely ever," she answered, languidly, giving him her hand as he rose to take leave.

After he went out, he carried a dreary picture back to town with him—the room, which looked dark and confined, as any room will look on a day when Nature is taking one of her royal holidays; the sofa, with its cushions, and the pale, thin face pillowed thereon; the relaxed form; the sad eyes; the books, tossed aside in utter weariness! He seemed to see it all as he rode along, with the lovely day around him; and he could not help saying over and over again, "Poor woman!"

The poor woman, who well deserved his compassion, lay, meanwhile, where he had left her, watching dreamily the shadows lengthening on the stretch of emerald sward beyond her window, the fruit-trees looking like pink-and-white clouds in an orchard far away, and the golden afternoon, with all its spring-time wealth of sight and sound, drawing toward sunset. Sunset, however, had not yet come when she fell into a light sleep, her face still turned to the window, and the soft breeze playing gently over it. Something of peace, something even of beauty, came to her as she slept, as we see it often come to world-worn faces when the stillness of this mimic death steals over them, winning back a little of the lost grace of youth to the heavy, deep-set lines of age or care

She had not slept more than half an hour when the stillness around her was broken, slightly broken by a step on the sward that sloped so gently from the window before which her sofa was placed. The sound was so slight that it did not rouse her, and she still remained unconscious—still slept with a faint, sweet smile on her lip—when a shadow fell across the floor, a figure drew near the window, and a man, pushing back the gently-swaying curtains, stepped into the room.

Not Mr. Warwick, not Annesley, not even St. John, but a stranger, who steps into this history, as he stepped into that room, for the first time—a tall, handsome man, with an air at once unmistakable and indescribable, which only much intercourse with the world confers, with a bearing of marked distinction, and with a look of youth—despite certain significant lines that told of the wear and tear of reckless years and more reckless passions—in singular contrast to that pale, faded woman on the sofa. Evidently, he had walked round the house, and entered the first window which he found open. Evidently, also, he had not caught a glimpse of the sleeping figure before he made his unceremonious appearance. He started when he saw it, drew back a step, then smiled a little, and came forward.

At the same moment, Mrs. Gordon woke—woke suddenly, with a wild start. In recalling the scene afterward, she remembered that, in the midst of a happy dream about Felix, her heart seemed, without any warning, to give a great bound, and with a terror which she did not understand she sprung to a sitting posture, and, half sleeping, half waking—was it dream or reality?—saw before her the face that had haunted her last waking thoughts.

She gave a low, inarticulate cry, then clasped both hands to her heart, and kept them there, striving vainly to still the passionate throbs that made speech impossible. She had expected him, looked for him; sometimes, in a strange, wild way, longed for him; yet, now that he was before her, the realization of it turned her faint. She could say nothing; her lips seemed parched; her tongue refused to speak; it almost seemed as if she was still asleep; and yet she knew that she was awake, and that her husband was before her.

"I have come, Pauline," he said, coolly. "I suppose, of course, you expected me. You have acted like—well, like a foolish woman; but I presume you knew that I would come."

All the past rushed back over her in the first tone of that cold, careless voice—all the memories, how bitter, how stinging, none but she could tell! Rage, scorn, defiance, hate—where were they all? Only an overwhelming horror came to her, as in these words he asserted his claim over her—this man who was her husband, and the murderer of her brother, yet who stood there under her father's roof!

"How did you come here?" she demanded, haughtily. "This is my father's house, a house only fit for honorable men. My servants long ago received orders not to admit you."

"I gave you credit for that measure of precaution," he answered, in the same coldly-careless manner, a manner on which it was evident that St. John had modelled his own, and which, therefore, possessed all the advantage that an original possesses over a copy. "I did not trouble your servants to admit me," he went on. "The front of the house was entirely deserted. I walked around until I came to this window. Seeing it open, I entered."

"It is still open," she said. "If you do not leave the room instantly, I shall do so myself. I am determined never to see or speak to you again. If there is any thing that you wish to say to me, any arrangement that you wish to make with me, I refer you to my lawyer."

He only answered by walking across the room, and closing the door. Then, coming back, he placed a chair so as to intercept any possible retreat on her part, and quietly sat down.

"All this is folly," he said, with unmoved composure. "I thought you knew me well enough to be aware how worse than useless such a tone as this is. You seem to forget—or I suppose you really do not know—that I am the injured person in this freak of yours. Your conduct, from first to last, has not a single excuse, not a single palliation. I directed you to go to Scotland, and you deliberately came to America, thereby robbing me of Felix, and endeavoring to conceal yourself from me. It was a woman's idea," he said, with contemptuous amusement, "and has had the success that might naturally have been expected."

"You mean that you have found me?"

"Yes, I mean that I have found you, and that I am lenient enough to give you your choice whether you will return to Scotland with me, or whether I shall leave you in the seclusion you have chosen, and simply take Felix."

The tone of subdued but unmistakable malice with which he spoke the last words roused Mrs. Gordon like the blast of a trumpet. Suddenly, the remembrance came to her that she was not, as heretofore, helplessly in his power. It was evident that he thought to bend her to his will through her fears for Felix; yet Felix was safe, was far away, was where this man could not possibly seek or find him. The sweetness of that one moment repaid her for all the months of desolate sorrow she had endured. Watching her face, her husband was startled by the change that came over it—the sudden glow that seemed to light up the sunken eyes and the pallid features into something of their old beauty.

"I decline to make any choice," she said. "I have already told you that I refer you to my lawyer for any thing you wish to say to me. However long you may choose to detain me, you will obtain nothing further from me."

With something like a mocking smile, he leaned forward, and laid his hand on a bell-rope that hung against the wall, just at the head of her sofa.

"I will ring for Felix, then," he said. "It will save time and trouble if I take him away with me at once."

"You can ring if you choose," answered Mrs. Gordon; "but you will not find Felix. Do you suppose I should have sat here quietly if there had been any danger of your finding him?" she asked, scornfully. "I should have defied you to keep me! But, thank God, Felix is safe! Three months ago, I knew that you would be here, for your miserable instrument appeared before you, and I sent the child away. It was like tearing the very heart out of my breast; but I did it, and now I am repaid."

"You—you dared to do it?"

"Yes, I dared to do it."

It was well that she came of that brave Morton blood which had never been known to quail at danger in any shape, for there was that in the baffled face looking at her which might have startled the firmest nerves. All his cold smoothness of manner gave way, as she had before seen it give way on a few memorable occasions, and the savage of the man's nature stood out clear, and dark, and unutterably repulsive. He was silent for a moment. In that moment the veins rose like cords on his forehead, and his eyes glittered as eyes only glitter in passion that, for violence, is next to insanity. When he spoke—well, it is scarcely worth while to transcribe such scenes as these. Who cares to write, who cares to read, who cares to dwell upon them? Fortunately for Mrs. Gordon, she had served her apprenticeship of endurance; and the knowledge of years is not readily forgotten in a few months. Besides, she was fired with new spirit. One of those moods in which she had longed for him to come, that she might pour out her hate and scorn, rushed over her. She gathered all her old haughty strength and pride, and faced him—once, at least—on equal ground.

"I defy you!" she said, after he had sworn a bitter oath to make her repent. "You have done your worst and your last. You have wrecked my life, you have murdered my brother, you have insulted and injured me in every possible way. There is only one more channel through which you can strike me—that is, Felix: and Felix you will never see again, even if the price I must pay for it is the price of never seeing him myself! Once more I repeat that I am safe—that I defy you."

It seemed as if she could not repeat the last words too often. Their very sound in her ears was as the echo of music, and, when she uttered them, she looked like another woman—like a vision of the regal beauty who, long years before, had gone forth from this very house, and who now faced the direct result of her own wilful folly. Gordon could scarcely believe that it was his wife who spoke to him. Not on account of her fiery spirit—he knew that well enough of old—but at sight of the transforming power which excitement had over her, and which seemed to kindle the dead light in her eyes, and bring back the dead roses to her cheeks. He had hardly ever been wrought to such a pitch of fury against her, yet, again, he had hardly ever been forced to such a degree of reluctant admiration. He made a quick step forward, and caught her arm.

"The devil is surely tempting you to your own ruin," he said, bitterly. "Have all the years we lived together taught you no better than this? Have you not learned yet that there are no possible circumstances which could make it safe for you to defy me? You had better stop a moment and think—you don't know what you are doing!"

"I know perfectly well what I am doing," she answered. "I am trying to save Felix—and, with God's help, I will save him—from you, and what you would make of him."

"And do you really think that you have concealed Felix so effectually that I, with unlimited means at command, cannot find him?"

"I am sure of it."

He read her face keenly, and, being well skilled in physiognomy, saw that she spoke from no mere bravado—no mere attempt to simulate confidence in order to deceive him. From some cause, of which he knew nothing, she was sure, she was perfectly secure, that the child was placed beyond his reach.

"No doubt you were confident of being safe when you came here," he said, with the mocking smile which she knew so well. "Can't the failure of one attempt teach you wisdom with regard to another? But that is a foolish question, women never learn wisdom, especially women like you. I see one thing, however, that you have not arranged and carried out this precious scheme alone. You have had assistance. Ah!"—as she changed color a little—"I knew it! Well, that makes matters a trifle easier than they would have been otherwise. I can find your instrument, and, having found him, you know me well enough to be aware—"

"I know him well enough to be aware that your threats are useless," she interrupted. "You will gain nothing from him. He is not a man whom you can either bribe or intimidate. I sent you a warning once," she went on, excitedly. "I don't know whether you ever received it; but if so, you would do well to heed it—you would do well to remember that I am here in the midst of my friends, and that to attempt to harm me further is only a certain means of harming yourself. I am no longer in a foreign country, and helplessly at your mercy. I am at home, and you—if you only knew it—are at my mercy!"

"I suppose you mean that some of your highly-civilized kinsmen and friends would be ready to shoot or stab me at your bidding," he said, carelessly. "For that I have only one answer—by all means let them try. How much you must have forgotten, before you thought it worth your while to take a tone like this."

"I have said all that I shall think of saying," she answered, coldly. "It is for you to heed or not, as you think fit. Once more, will you go? I have defied—I do defy you—to do your worst. There is nothing to add to that."

"Yes, there is something," he said. "Not on your side, perhaps, but on mine. I will inflict my presence upon you long enough to add it."

He had loosed his grasp of her arm by this time, and he now sat down again in the chair from which he had risen. His change of manner warned her that something worse than what had gone before, was yet to come. She tried to conjecture what it could be; but a dizziness seized her, and she could think of nothing. Felix! Felix! That was the only thought which rang through her brain. He could not touch him. She was sure of that. What did any thing else matter? With a great parting flash of glory, the sun went down; the whole sky was glowing with the lovely reflection of the incarnadine west, melting into softest rose-colors, and violets, and blues, when he began to speak.

"I gave you your choice when I first came in, to return to Scotland with me, or to resign the child to whom the law gives you no claim. Considering the defiance of my authority, which has been your only reply, I might reasonably retract that offer. But, as it is, I give it to you once more, and for the last time. Stop!"—lifting his hand when he saw that she was about to speak—"you must understand fully, as you do not understand now, the alternative that is placed before you. In the first place, I am sure that it is in my power to find Felix—if you considered a moment, you would be sure of this too. But to do so will cost both time and trouble, neither of which I desire to expend. I *shall* expend them, if necessary," he said, with energy; "but I am willing to make a compromise to effect his recovery without them. I shall not speak to you of your duty, nor of the false and groundless charges that you make against me in the matter of your brother's unfortunate death—"

"If you are wise, you will leave that name unspoken," she said, in a tone that came with something like a hiss through her teeth—teeth set to keep back the fierce tide of emotion that struggled for expression. "If you utter it again—here, under this roof—I think I could almost find strength to murder you, as you murdered him! Say what you have to say while I am able to control myself sufficiently to listen to you. It is the last time that I shall ever see you, or hear your voice."

"You forget that you are my wife, and entirely in my power."

"I am your wife—God help me!—but I am not in your power, nor ever will be again."

"We shall see about that," he said, smiling again. "I was on the point of saying, when you interrupted me, that I shall not speak to you of your duty, but of your interest. If you consent to produce Felix, I will allow you to accompany him back to Scotland. If you refuse, I will find him myself, and in that case I shall take him alone. Do you understand?"

"I understand."

"And refuse?"

"And refuse."

"Very well. That point is settled—irrevocably. We will not return to it again. Now I give you another alternative—either you will produce Felix, or you will alienate from him, by your own act, the inheritance which would naturally be his. I swear to you solemnly—and you know whether or not I am likely to keep my oath—that unless he is resigned to my guardianship, he shall never inherit a fragment or a pittance of the Gordon estate."

"You are counting too much on my ignorance, when you make such threats," she said, haughtily. "I chance to know that you are unable to fulfil them—I chance to know that your uncle's estate is entailed upon your son, and that you are powerless to alienate it from him."

"You are right," he said, with a flash of triumph in his eye. "It is entailed upon my son, but upon my *eldest son*."

"Well?"

Something like a dim foreboding of the truth began to dawn upon her. The excitement died out of her face, she turned white to her very lips, and leaned back against the cushions of the sofa.

"Well," he replied, coolly, "Felix is *not* my eldest son. For reasons that will be apparent to you hereafter, I have preferred and do prefer him as an heir. But he is not the legal inheritor of the estate. It depends upon you whether or not he will ever own an acre or touch a penny of it."

"Upon me!" A gathering mist seemed closing round her; but she fought it bravely—she struggled desperately against the rising faintness that threatened to sweep away all powers of combat. One thought only gave her strength—Felix's rights! They were assailed—falsely, unscrupulously, assailed, she was sure—and she was their only defender.

"I do not believe you!" she cried out, passionately. "Why should I? You have never failed to deceive me when you could do so with any advantage to yourself. Why should I believe any thing so stamped with falsehood as this?"

"Believe it or not, as you please," he answered. "It is a matter, fortunately, which admits of proof."

"You can prove that Felix is not your eldest son?"

"I can prove a former marriage when I was quite a boy, and the existence of a legal heir to the Gordon estate in the person of my son by that marriage."

"He is living?"

"Yes, he is living. I can put my hand on him whenever I choose. You need not look so incredulous," he said, as he saw her eyes grow larger and larger, her face whiter and whiter. "As I have said, it is a case in which assertion can have no weight; it is capable of proof that can, if necessary, be taken into a court of law. Perhaps you may be convinced if I give you a short statement of the matter?"

She made a gesture, signifying assent; and yet it was hardly necessary. Something in his manner — something in his tone — above all, something in his face (and she knew that face well)—told her that he was speaking truth, and not merely a cunning falsehood devised to annoy and intimidate her. Every thing had seemed so plain to her a minute before, and now all was confusion. Felix! Felix's rights! What were they? where were they? what ought she to do? This was the accompaniment to her husband's words when he began to speak.

"I need not trouble you with particulars," he said. "It is enough to give you a bare outline of facts. When I was a very young man—in fact, little more than a boy—my regiment was stationed in the West Indies. I had not been there very long when I accompanied one of my friends on a visit to Martinique. This man—I have forgotten his name, and it does not matter—had a letter of introduction to an Irishman named O'Grady living on the island. He took me with him; and, since our welcome was very warm, I soon became intimate in the family. The man himself—O'Grady, I mean—was a widower, and his family consisted of two daughters. One of them was a widow, a Mrs. ——. Confound my memory! I have forgotten that name, too. The other was a young girl, pretty enough, I dare say; but I have little recollection of her now, excepting that she turned my head completely at the time. A love-affair followed, of course, notwithstanding that I was in a much better position to cut my throat than to think of marrying. My father had paid my debts twice, and I was in deep disgrace with him. The beggarly allowance which he still continued, and my pay together, barely sufficed, or rather did *not* suffice, for my own wants, since I was a third time deeply in debt. To marry under these circumstances was simple insanity. This I knew perfectly well. Still, I was young, and ready for any act of folly. The consequence was that I compromised with an elopement and private marriage. The girl was easily worked upon; and, for the rest, matters were quite easy. There is hardly the least communication between the different islands of the West Indies, and there was nobody to follow or make disagreeable inquiries. Her father, who was infirm, died almost immediately after her departure, and there were no troublesome brothers or cousins in the matter. I took her to the island where I was stationed; but nobody in the regiment had any suspicion of the marriage. I was particularly cautious on this point, because any rumor reaching my father's ears would have ruined me. Well, before long, I appreciated my folly as it deserved, and grew heartily tired of the whole affair. I fancy it did not answer well on either side. Kate—that was the name of the girl—was sufficiently full of complaints, if complaints are any signs of unhappiness. At last, to my great relief, the regiment was ordered home. I left her as well provided for as possible, but hardly had I sailed from the island when (as I afterward learned) she wrote for her sister—a thing I had expressly forbidden. Her excuse was that she felt sure of dying at the approaching birth of a second child. If that was the case, her foreboding was verified, for, as it chanced, she did die. The sister wrote to me then with regard to the children—one, the boy of whom I have already spoken, the other an infant, and I believe a girl. To be burdened with such dead-weights as these would have been equivalent to suicide, in so far as my prospects in life were concerned. A lawyer answered her, by my directions, offering a yearly sum for their support, provided I was never troubled with any thing concerning them, and provided also that they did not bear my name. Since the entire proof of the marriage rested with me, to produce or to suppress as I thought fit, she had no alternative but to consent. She gave them her own name, and kept them with her until the boy grew toward manhood and became unmanageable. Then she addressed the agent through whom the yearly stipend was paid, and requested that some arrangement might be made, removing him from her control, also requesting that, if necessary for this, the whole of the allowance might be taken, as she was able to support the sister herself. This was accordingly done; and the boy was placed at school in England. Before long he was expelled for some disgraceful scrape. Then I took him, to see of what material he really was, and soon found—"

He stopped, for Mrs. Gordon had risen again to a sitting posture, and faced him in the gathering twilight with a look of horror that words can only fail to describe. It awed even him, seen through the falling gloom; yet he recovered himself with a slight movement, as if to shake off some unconscious influence.

"Well," he said, lightly, "what is the matter?"

"What is his name?" she asked, in a tone that fell sharply on the still air. Then, in a lower voice, "My God! It cannot be! It is too horrible even for you! What is his name?" she cried, again, more sharply than before.

"You might know his name by this time," he answered, in a tone of mingled disgust and triumph that did not escape her highly-strung ear. "The man to whom you will give the Gordon estate, if you still refuse to surrender Felix, is the man you have so long scorned and hated, the man whom you have held as less than the dust beneath your feet—is, in short, St. John!"

For a full minute after that name was spoken, not a word further broke the silence of the room. Face to face they sat in the dusky gloaming, the tempter and the tempted, and the only audible sound was that of Mrs. Gordon's breathing, which came in short, painful gasps, as she sat with her hand once more pressed to her side, trying to still the wild throbs of her heart, trying to command her voice sufficiently to speak. She was silent so long that at last Gordon himself broke the stillness.

"The choice is before you," he said. "Surrender Felix, and I make him my heir; refuse, and I shall prove my first marriage, which will give the estate to St. John. I need not tell you what is my choice in the matter. It will be no pleasant task to acknowledge a son in one of the most profligate adventurers and swindlers in Europe."

"And who made him either an adventurer or a swindler?" she cried, with a sudden vehemence that startled her listener. "Who made him a tool for all the base uses that your own hand disdained? Who taught him to scorn every law of God and man? If he *is* your son—if you have spoken truly—you have prepared for yourself an heir who is worthy of you! If I surrendered Felix, it would be for the same result. You would make him what you have made this poor instrument of your vices! Do you hear me—do you believe me—when I tell you that I would rather see him dead before me?"

"Do you think that Felix will appreciate these heroics?" he asked, with a bitter sneer. "Do you think that, if he lives, he will thank you for having stood between him and his inheritance—for having made him virtually a beggar?"

"If he has a drop of Morton blood in his veins, he will thank me for having spared him the example of such a father, and the shame of having purchased worldly prosperity—the enjoyment of property that rightly belongs to another —at the price of moral degradation."

"Then your decision is finally made?"

"Yes, it is made. Nothing that you can say, nothing that you can do, will change it!"

He rose to his feet and half turned away, then stopped a moment, and came back to her.

"I suppose you know that you have no right whatever to this property which you are enjoying," he said, "that the law gives all control of it to your husband. If I choose, I can sell this house, and every acre of land you call your own, to-morrow."

"I am not sure that the law gives you such power," she answered. "But, granting that it does, I have only one reply to make—try, if you dare, to enforce it."

"Do you think that the law will stand your friend, because you chance to be a Morton, and to be at home?"

"I think—I know that the law is sometimes powerless to act in the face of public opinion. And, if it comes to an issue of high-handed outrage like this, a Morton will never lack friends or defenders in Lagrange."

"You may find yourself mistaken."

"We shall see. But, if you had the right, and if you were able to enforce it, there would be no difference. If I were obliged to live on charity, or to beg my bread by the way-side, I should still defy you. Let that be the last word between us—the last I shall ever speak to you—I defy you!"

"Very well," he said, grinding his teeth together in irrepressible rage.

Recalling the scene afterward, Mrs. Gordon wondered at her own fearlessness. She was entirely alone, she was utterly helpless, and she had good reason to know of old how brutal and how reckless he could be. Yet she rose to her feet in the excitement of passion, and uttered those last quivering words, like a haughty challenge.

He made a step forward, almost as if he would have struck her; but she did not quail. She stood before him, like a pale wraith of a woman, in the ghostly twilight, daring him to do his worst. After a short interval of silence, that worst came in the form of words.

"You have taken your choice," he said, "and, indeed, you shall abide by it. I swear to you that I will find Felix, and that I will make you repent this defiance in sackcloth and ashes. When I find him, and when your hour of repentance comes, then I will see you again, and not before!"

His tone, often as she had heard it in moments like these, involuntarily made her shudder; it was so full of concentrated bitterness, hatred, and revenge, that the wonder was, not that he had for a moment threatened her with personal violence, but that he was able to restrain himself from executing that threat. If she had felt inclined to reply, he gave her no time to do so, but left the room immediately through the window by which he had entered.

As his shadow passed away, the woman—his wife—sat down, sick and shuddering. It was over. *Was* it over, or had she only waked from a hideous dream? Had he really been there, and had the last bitter defiance been exchanged between them? Had she really told him that Felix was safe from him, and that, for herself, she was ready to face the worst that malice, aided by the strong arm of legal power, could devise against her? Her head seemed giddy; she could not tell. A darkness, that was not the darkness of approaching night, closed round her. She made a vain effort to cry aloud; but it ended in a low, gurgling moan. Then she sank down on the pillows.

Gordon, meanwhile, was walking quickly and fiercely—as men always walk under the influence of strong passion—round the house. It was not by any means so late as it appeared in the room he had quitted; but, still, dusk had fallen, and objects near at hand were becoming indistinct, while those farther off were entirely wrapped in obscurity. This fact, together with great preoccupation of mind, prevented his observing a man who was nearing the terrace, as he emerged from the shadow of the house, and descended the stone steps that led down to the avenue.

He had scarcely taken half a dozen steps on the latter, when his path was barred; a voice, quiet but somewhat menacing, said, "A word with you, if you please," and, looking up, he found himself face to face with St. John!

CHAPTER XLII.

ON THE THRESHOLD OF MORTON HOUSE.

It was time that Morton Annesley had at last returned to Annesdale, and that Lagrange had at last been rewarded for long and impatient waiting, by the appearance of the hero of the melodrama it had arranged with so much artistic skill, and such dramatic situations—arranged, alas! for nothing. It was a very tame conclusion indeed, the crestfallen gossips thought, when Annesley quietly came home, two or three weeks after Miss Tresham's return, and looked and seemed, in every respect, very much as usual.

It was a very blessed conclusion, his mother thought, however; and her joy was so great that she even refrained from any reproaches or any complaints of the long and bitter anxiety she had endured—anxiety concealed as much as possible under a suave manner and a smiling face, but suffered like the gnawing of a vulture, while Lagrange talked itself hoarse, and her own heart was sick to the extreme of heart-sickness. It might have been that his pale face and listless manner pleaded for him more powerfully than any words. He had suffered—he was suffering! After all, there is no excuse like that, especially to a woman. Of her own accord, and quite silently, Mrs. Annesley buried out of sight the tomahawk which had been kept in bright, sharp readiness for combat, during all this period of absence. He was back again, he was safe—what did all the rest matter? It is true it mattered sufficiently to fill her with an inexpressible mixture of relief and indignation when she heard that the girl against whom she had expended so much effort, the girl whom she had unhesitatingly denounced as a scheming *intrigante*, had absolutely refused the grand chance of becoming mistress of Annesdale, when the owner of Annesdale had been insane enough to offer it to her. There is no exaggeration in saying that contending emotions nearly choked her when she heard this; and that the relief and the indignation, already mentioned, were at least equal in her breast. "Oh, what a blessing to be free at last from that haunting dread, and yet—oh, how dare she, the miserable creature!" That was the way thanksgiving and reproach were mingled to her. Is it not always so? Few things are more singular than to consider how seldom in our lives we have ever known a pure, unmixed emotion of any sort. Whether it be joy or sorrow, it is always dashed by and blended with something else; it is almost always complex in its nature. God is good to us in this, as in all things else. Strong revulsions of feeling would be too powerful, if they came with unmixed force—if joy were joy, and sorrow were sorrow, pure and simple, not as now, the hues of each blended with exquisite care into the other. Yet people complain of this, and call it "unsatisfactory." If they called themselves ungrateful, they would be considerably nearer the truth.

The day after Morton's return home, he went to see Mrs. Gordon. The one following this—his third in Lagrange—he spent in Tallahoma, attending to various arrears of business. It was sunset when he left the town, and turned Ilderim's head in the direction of Annesdale. His road led him past the Marks house, and something in the hour and in the sight of the children, who were playing in the garden, brought to his mind with singularly vivid remembrance that November evening when he had stood at the gate talking to Katharine, and Mrs. Gordon went by—when her face entered for the first time the current of their existence. It is only as we pass on in life — only when we have reached some height of time, and can thus overlook the road winding through the valley—that the mist clears a little, and we begin to understand the true significance of events that seemed purposeless or puzzling at the time of their occurrence. To Annesley, looking back, it seemed as if every change of the last few months dated from that evening—as if all the perplexities and annoyances which had encompassed him took their rise then—as if the quieter life, and the hopes that had brightened it, went down into darkness with that long-vanished day. He sighed a little to himself—a short, quick, half-impatient sigh—then pulled his hat over his eyes, and touched Ilderim with the spur. Ilderim, who always resented any liberty of this kind, immediately indulged in a few rearing and plunging exercises, which had the effect of diverting his master's attention from useless and by no means enlivening retrospection. When he was brought to terms, and had at last settled into a sharp, steady canter, a proverb familiar enough to a certain class of thinkers was on Annesley's lips. "*Che sarà, sarà!*" he muttered to himself. "After all, who can tell? Every thing is for the best, no doubt. The only difficulty—Soh, Ilderim! What the deuce is the matter with you, sir?"

He broke off with this impatient question, as Ilderim suddenly gave a bolt from one side of the road to the other. It was just where a footpath led across some fields, and a stile crossed the hedge that bordered the main road. As Annesley turned quickly to see what had caused the fright, he caught a glimpse of the top of a hat sinking below the hedge, and thinking that some little imp had startled the horse for amusement, and was now hiding from the probable consequences, he gave Ilderim's bridle a peremptory jerk, and, in a good deal of a fume, rode up to the stile. "Come out, you miserable little rascal," he said, "and let me tell you that if you ever try such a trick as that again—"

He stopped short, full of amazement. Instead of a child, a man rose up from behind the hedge, at his bidding, and, with the full glow of sunset falling on him, he recognized St. John. They faced each other silently for an instant—Annesley overcome by astonishment, St. John full of mortified rage, and neither knowing what to do or to say, until the adventurer, who, having been most prepared for the encounter, broke the awkward silence first.

"I beg your pardon," he said, with a sort of insolent defiance. "Did you speak to me?"

"I beg your pardon," answered Annesley, recovering a little. "No, I did not speak to you. That is, when I spoke, I thought some mischievous boy had frightened my horse, and was hiding behind the hedge. I had no idea it was you—that is—I mean—"

"You had no idea that *I* was hiding behind the hedge," said St. John, grimly. "Thank you, Mr. Annesley, for that much courtesy. You are right, too—I was not hiding. I have been in the country to see a friend, and, returning to Tallahoma by this short cut, I stopped here a moment to rest. I regret to have startled your horse. I know by experience that nothing is more provoking. Good-evening."

Annesley returned the salutation, and rode on; but as he rode, he thought of the encounter, and the longer he thought, the more singular it appeared to him. "That fellow is a slippery scoundrel," he thought, "and I am as certain as I can possibly be of a thing I don't know, that he was hiding when I startled him. 'A friend in the country,' 'resting on the stile'—as if he imagined I would credit such a story! What the deuce is he up to, I wonder? He can't be meaning to turn highwayman; and yet this looks amazingly like it. Ah!"

He pulled up Ilderim with a jerk that almost threw that astonished horse on his haunches, and stopped a minute in the road to think. Like a flash, the recollection of Mrs. Gordon came to him, and he remembered that this stile was almost exactly opposite the gates of Morton House. Was St. John on his way there?—did his appearance mean any thing like annoyance to her? Such a thought was enough to fire Annesley at once. He did not stop to consider whether or not it was probable—that it was possible, was quite sufficient to put his blood in a glow. He wheeled Ilderim about, and in a second was galloping back along the road he had come.

At the gates of Morton House, however, he paused. He did not want to startle his cousin unnecessarily, or make himself ridiculous, yet he could not banish an uncomfortable impression that St. John's appearance in that particular place meant mischief. While he was still debating what he should do, the thought of John Warwick came to him as a sort of inspiration. "He will know," he thought. "He has been on the scene, and knows much more of matters than I do. He may be able to tell what the fellow is after; and, at all events, I need not startle my cousin without first learning whether or not she is likely to be annoyed." Under such circumstances, and with such a person, resolve and execution are very nearly synonymous terms. In the course of another minute, he was galloping rapidly toward Tallahoma.

Dusk had fallen, as he rode down the village street—his evident haste making more than one person gaze curiously after him—and drew up before Mr. Warwick's office just as that gentleman, with his letter to Katharine's would-be employer in his pocket, stepped into the street.

"Why, Annesley!" he exclaimed, as the eager horseman reined up at the curb-stone. "I am glad to see you back," he continued, coming forward with extended hand. "How are you?"

"Tolerably well, thank you," said Annesley, shaking hands absently, and in a great hurry. "You won't be surprised, or think me very foolish, if I ask you a rather abrupt question, will you?" he added, quickly. "I have a special reason for it."

"A lawyer has no business ever to be surprised," replied Mr. Warwick, noticing the eager concern on the face before him. "Ask away—a hundred if you like."

"Anybody in your office?"

"Not a soul."

The young man leaned out of his saddle, and spoke low and quickly. "You know more about Mrs. Gordon's affairs than I do," he said. "Is it possible that that fellow St. John could annoy her in any way?"

The lawyer started a little.

"It is possible, certainly," he answered, coolly; "but it is not at all probable. Why do you ask?"

"Because I met him half an hour ago, at the gates of Morton House."

"What!" exclaimed Mr. Warwick, absolutely recoiling a step in his amazement. "You must be mistaken, Morton," he went on hastily. "It can't be—it is not possible—that you met St. John!"

"I saw him as plainly as I see you, and spoke to him, besides," answered Morton, somewhat surprised. "Why should it not be St. John? He—"

"Never mind about that," interrupted the other hastily. "If you are sure it was the man himself—"

"I am—perfectly sure."

"Well, then, are you also sure that he was going to Morton House?"

"Not at all—as you may judge for yourself." He then proceeded to detail the incident as it occurred. "You see," he went on, when he had finished, "it is all pure supposition on my part—and for that reason, I would not run the risk of disturbing my cousin until I had spoken to you about it. If he can annoy her in any way—"

"He can annoy her," interrupted Mr. Warwick, "and his venturing to reappear here looks very much as if he had that intention. You are mounted, Annesley. You had better ride on to Morton House at once—I will follow you as soon as I possibly can."

"Then you really think—"

"Hallo, George! Stop a minute!" cried Mr. Warwick, suddenly interrupting him. And when Morton turned, he saw that the person addressed was a young man who came riding down the street in their rear. "Good-evening, Clayton," he said, recognizing one of the young "men about town" of Tallahoma; and, as Clayton drew up and returned the salutation, Mr. Warwick went on: "George, you are going home, are you not? I thought so. Lend me your horse, then, for an hour or so. I want to go to the country in haste, and haven't time to wait for my own."

"Certainly, Mr. Warwick," said the young man, dismounting instantly. "He's quite at your service," he continued, with evidently cordial sincerity. "You need not be in a hurry about returning him; and, if you want to go any distance, he's quite fresh—I've only been out to the plantation and back."

"Thank you," said Mr. Warwick, hastily, and mounting the horse without loss of time. "I am in a great hurry—it is most fortunate that you happened to be passing, George. Good-evening.—Now, Annesley!"

Annesley needed no second bidding, and side by side the two men whom Fate had of late seemed capriciously determined to throw together, rode out of town on their way to Morton House. Considering that both horses were put on their mettle, it was not surprising that in a few minutes they reached the large iron gates of the Morton domain, and, in still another minute, were cantering up the avenue—looking almost like spectral horsemen as they rode rapidly under the bare trees in the dusky gloaming.

Their anxiety and uncertainty had in some intangible manner been communicated without any agency of speech; for certainly each knew what the other was feeling, and yet certainly also, not a word had been spoken on either side after they left Clayton, standing full of surprise and curiosity on the curb-stone in Tallahoma. They were half-way between the gate and the house when the first sound broke the stillness. Suddenly, on the soft evening air, the report of a pistol rang sharply out. Both horses sprang—reared—plunged—and before a word could be exchanged—in the midst of the struggle for the mastery, which ensued on the part of both riders—two other reports followed in quick succession.

"What on earth can it be!" said Annesley, as soon as Ilderim, quivering in every limb, was again under his control.

Mr. Warwick did not answer. He galloped hastily forward, and the other followed. In another minute, they reached the terrace-steps, and came upon a scene that neither of them ever forgot.

The reports which they heard had evidently startled the entire household. Notwithstanding the obscurity of the twilight, they were able to see that figures were running eagerly round the terrace and descending the steps, at the bottom of which a confused movement was taking place. A group of servants were bending over some object, or objects on the ground; but they all drew back instinctively as the two gentlemen galloped up.

"What is it, Harrison?" asked Mr. Warwick, almost before he drew rein.

"The Lord only knows, sir," answered Harrison—evidently in a state of the wildest excitement. "Two men shot theyselves sir — right here—and the first we knowed of it was when we heard the reports. I was in the kitchen sir, and I jumped up and come a-running, and—"

"Stand back, all of you!" said Mr. Warwick, impatiently. He and Annesley pressed forward. It was true. Two figures were lying on the ground where there was every trace of a fierce struggle—one slightly breathing with a pistol still in his hand; the other fallen across the lower step of the terrace—on the very threshold of Morton House—stone dead!

For a moment, the unexpected horror of the situation held both men powerless. They looked at each other through the gathering shades of evening, with white faces; but neither of them said a word, until the thought of Mrs. Gordon came to both. What had preceded this tragedy, they could not even guess; but it would have been strange if their first care had not been for her.

"You will see what can be done here," said Annesley, after a moment. "I must go to my cousin."

"Yes—go at once," answered Mr. Warwick, quickly. "She must have heard the reports, and she may come— Stop that, by any means."

Morton did not think this likely; but he gave one or two agile bounds up the terrace-steps, and strode hastily toward the house. He had not gone a dozen paces before he met Babette, running in the direction of the scene of action, wringing her hands, and crying aloud. She did not recognize him, and he was forced to claim her attention peremptorily before she would even notice him. When she found who it was, however, she seized his arm with both hands, and poured forth a pitiless lamentation.

"M'sieur, what is the matter?" cried she. "I went in madame's room, a minute ago, and I found her—poor lady—lying in a dead faint on the sofa. I knew—ah, mon Dieu! I felt sure that M'sieur Gordon had been there. Then I heard the guns, and I saw all the servants running; but I could not leave madame, and she—"

"Has she come to herself?" asked Morton, who could not help thinking that a dead faint was the best possible condition for Mrs. Gordon just then.

"I can do nothing with her!" cried Babette, hysterically. "I have tried to bring her to, but I could do nothing with her; and I came to see about the guns—O m'sieur, what is it?—has M'sieur Gordon—"

"You are just the person!" said Annesley, interrupting her; and, much to her surprise, taking her, in turn, by the arm. He led her forward, without giving her time for a word, and stopped at the head of the steps.

"Here's Babette, Mr. Warwick," he said. "She will be able to tell more than anybody else. My cousin, she says, is in a swoon. Why don't you send for lights?"

"I have done so," answered Mr. Warwick's voice out of the dusk. "There they come now."

They came as he spoke—three or four excited negroes running as hard as possible, some with candles, which they shaded with their hands, and some with pine-torches caught from the kitchen fire—the red flames streaming out wildly on the night air, and lighting up the whole scene with the peculiar glare that only pine produces. It was a singularly picturesque group, if anybody concerned had been able to think even for a moment of its possible effect. Afterward Annesley remembered how he stood at the top of the steps holding the trembling, sobbing Frenchwoman by the arm; how Mr. Warwick directed every thing below; how he glanced back at the grim old house behind them, thinking of the insensible woman within it; how, at that moment, a shrill, piercing scream from Babette made him look round again; how the red glow of the torches fell just then full on the face of the dead man, and how he shivered from head to foot as his companion cried wildly:

"Ah, mon Dieu!—M'sieur Gordon!"

An hour later, Mr. Warwick came out to Annesley, who had left the house and was walking up and down the terrace before the front entrance. Mrs. Gordon insisted upon being left alone with the dead body of her husband, and the doctors were in consultation over St. John, so there had been nothing for Morton to do; and he had come out to see if he could not shake off the numbing horror that seemed to oppress him, in the fresh air, and under the great, silent canopy of heaven. He had not made more than half a dozen turns, however, and the cigar he had mechanically taken out was still unlighted in his hand, when the lawyer walked up to him.

"The doctors have decided that there is no possible hope for that poor fellow," he said. "The ball has entered his lung in a place which renders extraction impossible; and death must take place in a few hours—probably sooner. He has recovered consciousness, and I think his sister ought to be summoned Morton you must go for her."

"For his sister!" repeated Morton, in bewilderment. As much as he had time to think, he was certainly inclined to believe that Mr. Warwick had taken leave of his senses.

"I forgot that you did not know," said the other. "Miss Tresham is his sister; and she is at Raynor's—George Raynor's. Will you go for her?"

"I—of course, instantly," said Annesley, swallowing this new cause for astonishment with a great gulp. "But—if you will excuse me—are you sure—is there no mistake—"

"I am quite sure," answered Mr. Warwick, cutting him short. "There is no mistake whatever about her being his sister; but it is a long story, and I cannot begin to tell it now. Take every thing for granted, my good fellow, and go at once—remember, it is a case of life and death."

"I am not likely to forget that," the other replied.

Nothing more was said by either. Men, when they know they can rely on each other, are not much given to speech. With his unlighted cigar still between his fingers, Annesley walked away to the stables where some officious servant had taken Ilderim, while Mr. Warwick went back into the house. His foot fell softly as in crossing the hall he passed a closed door, under which shone a stream of light. As he sprang into the saddle, he chanced to turn one look at the house, and caught the same light—shining steadily over the terrace from a flower-wreathed window. He drew his breath quickly at sight of it, for he knew what it meant —he knew that in the room where little more than an hour before the last bitter defiance had passed between them, the widow now watched by her husband's corpse.

He had no time for reflection, however. "Remember, it is a case of life and death," Mr. Warwick had said; and the young man, as he had answered, was not likely to forget it. He gave Ilderim a sharp taste of the obnoxious spurs, and, after one wild plunge, was away—cutting straight across the park, and taking a plantation by-way that led through the fields to the Raynor estate. He did not trouble himself much about gates or bars; but when he came to a fence—and fences, it seemed to him, had never before been so numerous—gave Ilderim his head, and went straight at it.

At this rate, it was not long before he came in sight of the Raynor house—or rather, of the Raynor out-buildings; for his approach was made from the rear. Fortunately, he knew the place well, and was at no loss where or how to proceed. Opening one of the usual large plantation gates, he let himself into the stable-yard, and riding forward soon came upon a group of servants lazily talking and smoking together.

"Here, one of you boys," he said, startling them very much by his unexpected appearance, "take my horse, while I go to the house. Is your master at home?"

"Yes, sir—Mass George's at home," answered several of the astonished boys. Then two or three of them advanced. "It's Mass Henry Dargan, ain't it?" asked the first; for the starlight made personal appearance very much a matter of conjecture.

"No—it's Mass Morton Annesley," said another, before Morton himself could reply. "I knows his horse.—Shall I put him up for you, Mr. Annesley?"

"No"—answered Annesley. He stopped and thought a moment. "Is Charley in the stable?" he asked.

"Yes, sir—been up all day."

"Change my saddle to him, then, and put a side-saddle on Ilderim. Make haste about it, and when they are ready, bring them both to the house. Do you understand?"

"A *side-saddle*, sir?"

"Yes—a side-saddle. Don't waste time over it. Change my saddle as quickly as you can, and bring the horses on."

He walked away, leaving the astonished grooms to bewilder themselves with conjectures about this strange order, and took a familiar path to the house. Following it directly, he soon found himself on a side piazza, and, looking through a glass door, saw that the family were at supper. Involuntarily, he stopped a minute—he began to realize now that it was hard to take the next step.

Standing thus, he saw Katharine for the first time since that well-remembered day at Bellefont. She was looking pale, but very pretty, he thought, as he watched her sitting exactly opposite the door through which he made his observation. The family party was not large, and supper—if the light meal merited such a heavy name—was set very informally on a small round table. George Raynor, with his crutches beside him, was comfortably established on one side of this, while his wife poured out coffee on the other. Irene Vernon, with a book in her hand, stood by the hearth, where a servant was toasting bread. Being the person most discengaged, she first caught a glimpse of Annesley's face through the glass door, and made a slight exclamation. After that, he had no alternative but to push it open, and enter.

CHAPTER XLIII.

THE VALLEY OF THE SHADOW OF DEATH.

Something in Annesley's face and manner told his story for him as soon as he came in upon the astonished group. Raynor was the first person who looked up as the door opened, and he made the first echo of Miss Vernon's exclamation.

"Why, Annesley!" he cried, making an effort to rise, and sinking back again, when he remembered his leg. "Good Heavens, Morton! What is the matter?"

Morton came forward, and tried to smile, as he held out his hand.

"You must excuse my being so unceremonious," he said. "I came through the stable-yard, and followed the side-path to the house. I hope you are all well. It was a shame to startle you so! — Indeed, Mrs. Raynor, you need not be alarmed. Nothing is the matter, I assure you—at least nothing that concerns you."

"Something that concerns somebody else, then," said Raynor, impatiently. "The deuce, man!—don't try to tell us that nothing is the matter when you look like this! What is it?"

"I have come for Miss Tresham," said Annesley, looking at Katharine, and thinking—poor fellow!—that he had better make a desperate plunge into the matter at once. Impulsively, he went over and took her hands—there was something very pitying in his face and eyes. "I am very sorry for you," he said, "I must beg you to come with me at once. You are wanted —at Morton House."

"Wanted!—by whom?" she asked, for Morton House was the last place she could possibly have expected him to name.

"Wanted by"—he hesitated a moment—"by Mr. St. John. He has been in a difficulty, and, I am sorry to say, is badly wounded."

"Ah!" she gave a low cry, and grew suddenly pale. "But—but he cannot be there!"

"Yes, he is there. I cannot tell you any more now," he went on, hastily, as he saw the amazement in her dilated eyes. "You had better change your dress at once. I have ordered a horse for you—it will be the quickest way of reaching Morton House. The sooner we start the better."

"Is—" She stopped, and drawing her hand out of his clasp, clutched nervously at the back of the chair from which she had risen, while her words came with a slight gasp—"is he dying?"

Annesley did not answer, but, being inexperienced in dissimulation, his face answered for him. Everybody who was looking on read the reply written there as plainly as Katharine did. She gave a shuddering sigh, put her hands to her face for an instant, then let them fall, and turned to leave the room.

"I will be ready in a minute," she said, in a repressed sort of voice.

"I will help you," said Miss Vernon, breaking the trance of surprise that held them all. She came forward quickly, and drew the girl's hand into her arm. There was something very gentle in the action, and in her face, as she looked back at Annesley.—"She shall be ready in a minute," she said. "Don't fear any delay."

They passed out of the room, and then Morton was beset by questions—to which he gave very unsatisfactory answers indeed. "I don't know much more about the matter than you do," he said, at last. "And of what I do know, I am bound to say nothing, because it is no affair of mine. You may hear all about it soon—God knows; I don't. Who is shot? That poor fellow St. John, for one, I can tell you.—George, I had a side-saddle put on Ilderim for Miss Tresham, and ordered out Charley for myself. You don't object, do you?"

"Object! Of course not," said George. "Charley has been standing up in the stable eating his head off, ever since I broke my leg. But, Morton, you can at least tell us what this—St John is his name?—has to do with Miss Tresham?"

"No, I can't," answered Morton. "Miss Tresham will very likely tell you herself," he continued; "until then, my dear fellow, you must restrain your curiosity as best you can.—Mrs. Raynor, will you give me a cup of coffee? I have had no supper this evening."

He made the right diversion. With all a woman's ready sympathy, Mrs. Raynor was at once intent upon administering to his bodily wants, even in preference to the gratification of her own curiosity. Notwithstanding his protest, she insisted upon making him eat as well as drink, and she was so full of this important matter, that she did not find time to ask another question, before Miss Vernon and Katharine came back, the latter equipped and ready to start.

"Mr. Annesley, are you not afraid to put her on that wild horse?" Miss Vernon asked, as they stood on the piazza and Morton led Ilderim up. "Minnie is in the stable. Surely she would do."

"She would do excellently well for a pleasure-ride," answered Annesley; "but not for such a purpose as this. Charley is by no means safe," he added, "so Ilderim is our only resource.—Miss Tresham are you afraid of him?"

"Not in the least," Katharine answered. "I should not be afraid of any thing, Mr. Annesley, that would take me there at once."

"Ilderim will take you there like lightning," he said, lifting her to the saddle. And, as he said it, a sharp recollection came to both of them of the evening when she had given the name which had come to bear such a significance. "Ilderim—it signifies 'the Lightning,'" she had said; and now it rested with Ilderim whether or not she should reach her brother's death-bed in time to hear or to speak one last word of love, or pardon, or hope. "Oh!" she said, under her breath, "do you remember?" just as Annesley for his part said, "Do you remember?" then added quickly, "You are riding him at last."

"Take care of her, Mr. Annesley," came from the piazza, in Miss Vernon's voice. It was the last sound that followed them as they rode away.

"Where are we going?" Katharine asked, as they passed out of the stable-gate together. "This is not the road to Morton House."

"Yes, it is—the shortest road," he answered. "A cut across the plantations which will take off two or three miles of the distance. Are you afraid?"

"Afraid—with you? Oh, no."

She said the words very simply, but, out of their very simplicity, they touched him deeply, making that strange, lonely ride—that gallop at full speed across the great silent fields, and now and then through a dark stretch of woods full of the weird, inarticulate voices of the Night—an era in his life to be ever remembered. What man is wise enough to be able to tell when passion is born, when it reaches its full height, or when it dies? Does the turn of the tide always come when the waves have reached their highest point? As they rode along, with the hoof-strokes of their horses the only audible sound, themselves uttering scarcely a word, Nature in silent grandeur all around them, man so far distant, and the great hosts of heaven marching steadily overhead, it seemed to Annesley as if much that had before been unintelligible was now made plain to him. He could not possibly have given expression to the different emotions that swayed him, to the different thoughts that came to him, or to the strange flux and reflux of feeling that possessed him. But all the same, these things left their mark upon his life—all the same, he looked back afterward to this night as to one of those periods of transition which every human soul must undergo. The forces may be long in marshalling, the causes may be long in preparing their effects, but we may know the thrill of final issue when it comes, even though we may not know till long afterward the final result.

Annesley had no means of judging what length of time they had been on the road, when at last they reined up before the door of the great stables of Morton House, and, springing to the ground himself, he received the slight, swaying form of his companion in his arms.

"Courage, Miss Tresham! Here we are at last!" he said, kindly. "Don't give way now, after holding out so well. Shall I send for some wine for you, or shall we go to the house at once?"

"Let us go," she answered, panting slightly. "We must not wait a minute. He—O Mr. Annesley, do you think he is alive?"

"Let us trust so. But you ought to have something to strengthen you before—"

"No," she interrupted, with feverish eagerness. "Take me in. I—I am quite well."

"Just as you please," he said, with that consideration which comes from the heart, and knows, therefore, when it is vain to press even that which is best on an unwilling recipient. He drew her hand into his arm, and she remembered afterward how gently and carefully he led her to the house, speaking now and then kind words of cheer and comfort. During the last half-hour of their ride, he had told her all he knew of what had occurred, and who had been St. John's adversary in the quarrel that had ended so fatally. Shocked she was, undoubtedly; but almost less so than he had expected. "It is horrible—horrible for Mrs. Gordon—that he should have been killed there," she said, with a shudder; "but, oh, you cannot tell how his influence has led St. John astray, and how much this seems to me like retribution!" That was all she said of the man who had so suddenly and so fearfully gone to his account. All her thoughts seemed filled by her brother. Annesley was astonished to hear with how much tenderness she spoke of him; he could not tell how the news of his danger and extremity carried her heart back to the days when they had been children together, and loved each other as only children can love. All the intermediate time of terror and repulsion, of shame and disgrace, was swept out of her memory. He was her brother, that was enough.

As they neared the house, Annesley pointed to the light which streamed from the windows of Mrs. Gordon's room—the room where Katharine had spent the first evening of their acquaintance.

"My cousin's husband was here this afternoon," he said. "He must have seen her in that room, and, as well as we can judge, had just left her, when—when this took place. His body is there now."

"And she?"

"Is with it."

The girl looked at the light and shivered, Vaguely and dimly she wondered at the possible depths of emotion existing so near her. Out of her own anxiety, she had time for a throb of pity toward the woman who, under the roof that had sheltered her girlhood, received the dead body of the man she had once loved, and, through love, learned to hate.

"Does she know how—how it occurred?" she asked.

"She knows all that we do," Annesley answered; "but that is not much. This is the door, Miss Tresham."

He led her into the house, and the first person whom they met was Mr. Warwick.

"Thank Heaven, you have come at last!" he said. "I thought you would be too late. He is sinking rapidly.—Miss Tresham are you able to see him at once?"

"Oh, yes, yes—at once," she said.

"Then bring her on, Annesley—this way."

He led the way, and Annesley with Katharine followed. St. John had been insensible when he was brought into the house, so they had carried him up-stairs, to one of the chambers. It chanced to be the one that had been occupied by Felix, and the first thing that met Katharine's eye, as she entered the door, was a number of boyish playthings arranged carefully at the end of the room. The hobby-horse, drum, and gayly-painted bow and arrows, made a strange contrast to a table near by, which was covered with surgical instruments and an open medicine-case, such as doctors practising in the country always carry; and to the bed, with its muslin curtains thrown completely over the old-fashioned canopy, while the bandaged form of the wounded man rested on top of the coverings. Two doctors were in the room—the only two of any skill that Lagrange could boast. One of them was sitting by the bed, the other stood by the table, measuring out some medicine, when Katharine entered. Mr. Warwick walked up to the latter.

"Here is Miss Tresham, doctor," he said. "I suppose there is no danger of her exciting the patient too much?"

"I suppose not," answered the doctor, a little ungraciously. He looked keenly and somewhat suspiciously at Miss Tresham. He did not understand matters at all, and he did not care to conceal his resentment of this fact. Who was Mr. St. John?—how had he been shot?—what was this about a dead man in the house?—what the deuce did this girl, whom he knew as the subject of a great deal of Lagrange gossip, have to do with it all? Doctors are subject to the infirmities of human curiosity as well as other men, and do not like to be kept in the dark a whit better. Perhaps this doctor liked it a shade less, as his tone showed, when he said, stiffly: "I suppose not—the patient is considerably past being harmed by any thing."

"Oh, doctor, is there no hope?" asked a voice, against the pathetic sweetness of which even the doctor was not proof. He glanced quickly at the gray eyes lifted to his face—then looked away again.

"I thought you would have told her that the man must die," he said, addressing Mr. Warwick.

"He did tell me—that is, I have heard it," said Katharine, before the lawyer could speak. "Only I thought I would like to hear your opinion myself. He is my brother," she added, after a momentary pause. "You will forgive me for asking how long he can live?"

"That is a question which it is hard for me to answer," said the doctor, more gently than might have been expected; then he shot a glance half questioning, half indignant, at Mr. Warwick. "Mr. St. John's wound is mortal," he went on; "but in these cases it is hard to determine exactly when death will ensue, so much depends on the vital power of the system. He may live two or three hours—possibly even through the night—or he may die within ten minutes. I cannot tell."

"Which do you think most probable?"

"As far as I can judge, he is sinking rapidly. He has already lived longer than I anticipated."

Annesley, on whose arm she still leaned, felt her shudder from head to foot; but she said nothing. Her face grew a shade whiter, perhaps, and her lips set themselves with painful rigidity, but that was all. The doctor thought to himself that she had no feeling. "She calls the poor man her brother, and takes the news of his certain death like this!" he thought, as she drew her hand from Morton's arm, and crossed the floor alone, to the side of the bed.

St. John lay in what was apparently a deep stupor, or what was, perhaps, the prostration which precedes dissolution, and verges on insensibility. The hæmorrhage from his wound had been so excessive that his face was bleached to a deathly pallor; but otherwise it showed no signs of the approaching death which the doctor prophesied. Looking at him, Katharine could scarcely believe that it was indeed so near, until suddenly a sharp convulsion of agony passed over the face, and roused it from its repose. The lips sprang apart, then closed tightly over a groan, while the eyes opened full on her face. In an instant she saw that he was perfectly conscious. As soon as the paroxysm abated—it did not last more than a minute—he strove to speak, but, failing in this, lifted his hand, and motioned her to come nearer. The doctor silently resigned his seat, and, sinking into it, she bent her face down almost on a level with his own, while her hands clasped eagerly over the one he had extended.

"Don't try to talk, dear," she said, gently. "Here I am—I shall not leave you."

"You won't be needed long," he answered. His voice was very weak, and had a slight catch between the words; but otherwise there was no change, and the old mocking cadence still rang in its notes.

"Oh, St. John—" Her own voice broke down in the quiver of sobs that were hastily choked back. This was neither time nor place for them—especially since the doctor's hand was laid heavily on her shoulder, and the doctor's voice said in her ear, "The least excitement will kill him in a minute." She fought hard for self-control, and after a time gained it. At last she was able to say, quietly, "I will not leave you—but pray keep quiet. The doctor says the least excitement is very dangerous."

"Confound the doctor!" answered St. John, peevishly, apparently quite unconscious that this personage stood just by his side. "What is the use of keeping quiet?" he went on. "Why," with a singular inflection of contempt, "I know, as well as he does, that I'm done for! Only there's one or two things I must say to you, if—if I can."

"Don't try—oh, pray don't try!"

"I must, I tell you!" This quite impatiently—then, more faintly, "Water—my throat is dry—I—can hardly talk."

Katharine turned, but the doctor was already at hand, with a glass of water in which a stimulant was infused. "He is sinking fast," he said, as he leaned over her. "If he has any thing on his mind, let him say it. He may go off any moment."

But, after drinking the water, St. John seemed to sink back into stupor. Holding his hand, Katharine chanced to rest her fingers on the pulse, and she was startled to feel how weak and slow it was. Life was ebbing fast—even her inexperience began to appreciate this, especially when she noted that awful grayness which is the first shadow of approaching dissolution, and which no one, who has seen it once, can ever forget or mistake, stealing over the face. He looked very handsome as he lay with closed eyes, and slightly-heaving chest. All that was repulsive about the face seemed to have been fined away as by a sharp chisel. The features stood out with the pure clearness of sculptured marble, and the dark lashes and brows made the only contrast to the deadly-white pallor of the complexion. Mr. Warwick and Annesley exchanged a glance—was it only imagination, or did they notice a strange, subtile likeness coming out on this face, to that other face lying even more still and white, below? Just now, they thought it *was* imagination, but afterward—when the full horror of the truth was known to them—they knew that fancy had not played them false, but that the hand of death had brought out with a force not to be mistaken the trace and the proof of common blood.

Several minutes passed, then Mr. Warwick came up to Katharine, and, standing in the shade behind her chair, bent down and spoke.

"If he rouses again, you must ask him how this occurred," he said. "The other man is dead, and it is important that we should know."

"Very well," she answered, under her breath—and just at that moment, with a slight start, St. John opened his eyes.

"Katharine—are you there?" he asked, his voice having become much weaker since he spoke last.

"Yes, I am here," she answered, bending forward so that he could see her. "Is there any thing I can do for you?"

He muttered something, but so low that she did not catch his words. Then, while she was still straining her ears, he turned his head, and said abruptly, "Is Gordon dead?"

Katharine had been so entirely unprepared for such a question, that she did not know what to reply; she did not know what the effect might be of the unsoftened truth. She looked at the doctor; but the doctor's face was non-expressive—at Annesley, but there was nothing to direct her there. It was not until Mr. Warwick said, in a low voice, "Tell him," that she found courage to answer.

"Yes, St. John; he is dead."

"You are sure?"

"I am quite sure."

There was silence after this. St. John drew a deep breath—to every one of the bystanders it sounded almost like a sigh of relief—and lay quiet for some time. Katharine was on the point of speaking again, when he anticipated her, uttering his words faintly, and with evident effort.

"So that is settled," he said. "Well, I didn't mean to kill him; but I should be a canting hypocrite if I said it was not a good riddance to everybody! He tried me too far," he went on, gathering a little more strength. "It was all his fault—not mine. He was in one of the devil's own rages, and I was desperate. They have told you all about it, I suppose, Katharine."

"How could they?" she answered sadly. "Nobody knows any thing about it."

"Don't they?" said he, with the old mocking sneer on his white lip. "It would be a pity if their curiosity should never be gratified. Of course, *you* know how it was, though. When a man is hungry, and footsore, and penniless, he is next to a wild beast, and I was all those things, a few hours ago. I knew Gordon would be here about this time; and I had been wandering about the country for days, keeping a sharp lookout for him. At last I met a boy—to-day, was it?—who had driven him to Tallahoma. Then I came on as quickly as possible, and I thought Morton House would be the best place to find him—the safest place for me, that is. Just as I got to the terrace, he came down the steps. It seemed he had found out that the child was gone, and that his wife was out of his power. If you knew any thing about him, you'd know what sort of a scene we had then. He was out of his head with fury, especially against me, who had brought him here for nothing, while I was just as ready as not to have out all the old scores! There was plenty of them, for I had been his cat's-paw for many a day, with most of the labor, and all the risk, and hardly a taste of the profit. I told him he should not stir till he had promised to give me something—any thing—to live on, and, in that case, I engaged never to come near him again. He had not sense enough to close with the offer—considering all that had gone before, an amazingly liberal one, I can tell you—but he dared to say that he would give half his fortune to take me to the gallows, but not a penny to keep me from it. At that, I lost *my* temper. I—oh, this cursed throat! Give me some water."

It was given to him, and, after drinking, he went on of his own accord:

"You need not think I fired without provocation at an unarmed man. I did not mean to use the pistol—in fact, it was in my pocket, and I had forgotten all about it. I would not have touched it, if I had not been at a terrible disadvantage. But he fought like a tiger, and he soon got the better of me. In the scuffle the d—d thing went off, and gave me this wound. Then I knew I was done for, and the devil entered me, and I was determined to kill him. I managed to draw it, and fired twice. I—I don't believe he stirred afterward."

"He is exciting himself too much," said doctor No. 2, in the midst of the pause which followed the last words—words over which the dying man's voice had sunk into inarticulate weakness. "He will kill himself in ten minutes, at this rate! Miss Tresham, you must not let him talk."

"But I will talk," interrupted St. John. "If I choose to kill myself in ten minutes, whose business is it? Not yours, at any rate!—Katharine, I—I have something to say to you."

"Had you not better be quiet, dear?"

"I can't think what it was"—a strange gasping and catching was now audible in the weak voice, the gray shade stole more plainly over the face, and an awe settled on those around him. "I—yes, I wanted to tell you that I am sorry I have been such a drag and terror on your life. I don't know, but—but it seems now as if I might—perhaps—do a little better, if it were to live over again. It is too late now for any thing of that sort; but—I am sorry."

"Oh, St. John!" The tears came now in a hot, burning shower, as she sank on her knees by the bed. "Oh, my brother—my dear, dear brother! don't you know—can't you tell—how little it all seems? It was my fault too—don't think it was all yours. If it were—oh, if it *were* to live over, I should be more patient, more loving, more kind—then all might be different. But, dear love, try to think of your soul, and of God. Oh, remember how near death is! St. John, have you quite forgotten and disowned the dear Lord who died for you? Oh, try, try to make one good act of contrition—it is all you can do, but He is strong enough to do the rest."

"I—cannot."

How strangely his faltering tones contrasted with her passionate accents! All was silent around. The figures about the bed might have been of graven stone, for all the sign of life they gave by word or movement. It seemed as if the forces of Good and Evil had met to fight their last awful combat over this erring soul.

"Oh, try!" she cried, "for God's sake, try! Think—think that you may have to face Him in another minute! You *are* sorry for all this life of sin and violence, are you not?"

He murmured something in reply. The others could not hear it, but she did. Whatever it was, it must have been affirmative, for she lifted a crucifix, which was attached to a rosary at her girdle, and held it before his eyes. "Try to follow me," she said, and then she poured forth a fervent Act of Contrition. It was only the ordinary form, but her voice uttered it with a passion and pathos that touched the heart more than any pomp of language could have done. It was the very cry of an anguished, shipwrecked soul, mounting in its last dire extremity to Him who once ended His bitter passion on Calvary. St. John tried to follow; but strength was failing fast. When she held the crucifix to his lips, he kissed the sacred figure fastened thereon; but he could not articulate any longer. The awful moment of final agony had come. God and the pitying angels only knew what strong and powerful wrestling in passionate supplication the girl beside him did, during that short time. One familiar prayer after another rose from her lips; and at last, by a sudden impulse, she began the "Memorare." In a second, something like the light of conscious life flashed into the failing eyes. The lids lifted, the lips faintly smiled—the sound of the long-forgotten but still familiar words had apparently taken the thoughts of the dying man far back into his childhood.

"Katy—little Katy," he murmured. And just at the words: "Oh, let it not be said that I have perished where no one ever found but grace and salvation," there came one strong shiver and all was over.

CHAPTER XLIV.

IN THE DAWN.

The first gray chill of daylight was stealing over the terrace and gardens of the house, when Mrs. Gordon's door at last opened, and coming out she asked a servant, who was loitering and shivering in the hall, where Mr. Warwick was.

"He's in the dining-room, ma'am," answered the boy. "Mus' I tell him you want him?"

"No—I will go myself."

She walked a few steps, then stopped and turned round.

"Is he quite alone?" she asked. "Is there nobody with him?"

"Nobody at all, ma'am; the doctor is gone, and Mass Morton, he went up-stairs a minute ago."

Thus reassured, she walked forward, and opened the dining-room door. A fire was burning on the hearth, and throwing its flickering light over the walls panelled in old-fashioned style, and the portraits hung round them. It also threw a fantastic glow over the face of Mr. Warwick, who had leaned back in a deep arm-chair, and quietly fallen asleep. This sleep was only a light doze, however, for the opening of the door roused him at once, and he started when he saw the figure that came across the floor toward him.

"Mrs. Gordon!" he exclaimed, not quite sure in the dim light whether or not his sight played him false.

"Don't let me disturb you," said Mrs. Gordon, as he rose. "If I had known that you were sleeping, I should not have come in. You must be very tired."

"No—not tired at all," he said, moving a chair toward her. "Pray sit down—you look very weak. Can I get any thing for you—any thing in the way of stimulant or refreshment?"

Her pale lips answered, but no sound was audible. She shook her head, and, sinking into the chair he had placed for her, motioned him to resume his own seat. As he turned to do so, he perceived the pale, gray daylight which began to struggle through the blinds of a window at the end of the room, and, walking to it, threw them open. He felt as if it might be possible to throw off something of the ghastly horror of the night with these first tokens of God's day.

When he came back to the fire, he was startled to see the change which the last few hours had made in Mrs. Gordon's appearance. She looked inconceivably old and haggard, as she sat there in the pale morning light—inconceivably worse than he could have imagined that even the long watches of this fearful night would have made her look. Before he could speak, she anticipated him.

"Sit down," she said. "I have something to say to you, and I can say it better now than hereafter." She paused a moment, then added, gently, "Is that poor man up-stairs dead?"

"Yes," he answered, a little surprised, not at the question itself, but at the tone of it. "Yes, he is dead—he has been dead for several hours."

She gave a deep sigh, and, leaning back, closed her eyes. There are few stranger things in this strange world than the similarity and association of sound. This sigh immediately recalled to Mr. Warwick's mind the sigh which St. John had uttered on hearing of Gordon's death. In both there was a cadence of unmistakable relief which his ear was able to detect, though it had been mingled with a singular chord of other emotions. Some instinct warned him that he was not yet at the end of this night's eventful history—that there was something yet to hear, something yet to do, before the sun should rise. Thinking of this, he did not observe that Mrs. Gordon unclosed her eyes, and when she spoke, her voice startled him.

"Where is Miss Tresham?" she asked. "Was she sent for? Is she here?"

"Miss Tresham is here," he answered—then added, after a second, "she is lying down, I believe. The agitation which she underwent at her brother's death was too much for her. He had scarcely ceased to breathe, when she fainted."

"But she has recovered—has she not?"

"So the servants tell me. I have not seen her since I carried her out of the room."

"Babette is an excellent nurse," said Mrs. Gordon, with more interest than he had expected. "Has she seen her?"

"She is with her now, I think."

"Ah!" with a faint sigh, "then she is in good hands. There is no fear of her dying," she went on, a little bitterly. "Neither grief nor trouble is merciful enough to kill. I will speak of her again, after a while. Now, I should like to ask you something else. Did he—did St John—give any account before he died of how all this occurred?"

"Yes; just before he died, he told his sister." He then related all that the dying man had said, adding, when it was over: "Every thing goes to corroborate this statement. The time at which Morton met him—the time we occupied in coming from Tallahoma—the shots we heard, and the condition in which we found the two men. The doctors also say that the position of the wound proves it was given accidentally and in the manner described."

"Then there is no doubt that he killed my—my husband?"

"There is no doubt of that. I can only ask you to think for a moment of his provocation, and you will scarcely be able to condemn him, as we condemn a cold-blooded murderer."

"Condemn him!" Her tone and manner surprised the lawyer so much that he could only gaze at her in astonishment. Excitement sprang into the eyes, passion quivered in the voice—some overpowering emotion seemed to seize and shake her form from head to foot. "Condemn him! My God! I can only pity him, till pity grows into pain. I can only look with horror—as I have looked all this night—on the terrible retribution which even in this world crime sometimes works for itself!"

Was she mad? Had the shock proved too much for her mind? Mr. Warwick almost feared that it had, as he met those burning eyes. The daylight began to broaden by this time, and he saw more plainly the ravages of fierce emotion, already suffered, on that white, haggard face.

"Try to be quiet, Mrs. Gordon," he said. "I am afraid I ought not to have told you all this. You have undergone too much excitement. You are not yourself. Let me beg you to rest—to talk no more."

"I must," she answered. "It is a work of justice, and it must be done. Don't fear about me. I shall have strength enough to do it, and, after that, nothing matters. It does not even matter if I never see Felix again, for he is safe now. Does that sound horrible? Should not I think of it now, while *he* lies dead?"

"It is natural that you could not avoid thinking of it," he said. "But let me entreat you—"

He spoke in vain. She did not even hear him, but went on with what she was going to say:

"Was it yesterday afternoon that you were here? Every thing appears so long ago that happened before he came. Well, I fell asleep after you left, and, when I woke, he was entering the room. I told him that Felix was gone, and that I—I defied him! It seems to me that was all I said; at least"—passing her hand wearily across her brow—"I cannot remember any thing else. By various arguments he tried to induce me to surrender the child; but, when he found that every thing else was useless, he threatened me with the entire loss of his inheritance. I knew that he could not possibly alienate this, and I told him so. Then"—she shuddered visibly—"then he said I was mistaken—that he *could* alienate it, that Felix was not his eldest son, that there was another—another who—"

She stopped—so ghastly pale, that he was about to rise and go to her assistance, when she lifted her hand with a gesture which signified "Keep still," and went on:

"He said he had another—a son whom he had never acknowledged—the child of an early, private marriage. He told me the history of that marriage, and it was so much in character with the record of his whole life that I could not doubt it. But conceive what I felt when he said that this son was the man whom I have known as his partner and instrument in dishonor and crime!"

Mr. Warwick started to his feet. The horror of the revelation was too much even for his self-control.

"Good God, Mrs. Gordon!" he cried. "You don't mean that it was—"

She looked up and finished the sentence as he paused. "I mean that it was St. John!" she said.

"It is impossible!" he exclaimed.

"It is true," she answered.

"But have you thought—have you considered?"

"The horror of it? Yes, I have thought of it all. I scarcely think this tragedy has shown it to me more plainly than I saw it when he spoke—when he told me who St. John was."

Mr. Warwick sat down again. A chill seemed creeping over him which he tried vainly to shake off. It *was* horrible! He began to appreciate it a little—but only by degrees. It was not a thing to take in all at once. He could not feel, all at once, how that woman had felt as she faced the terrible secret through the long watches of the night—he could not all at once realize the real tie which united those two men, both of whom were lying dead under the roof of Morton House.

"There is one thing to be grateful for," he said, at last. "That wretched man, St. John, died in ignorance of this."

"And therefore I asked you if he was dead," she answered. "I felt that it was impossible to utter the truth—even to you—while he lived. If all ended with him, I should let the horrible secret die and be buried in the grave of the man who from the beginning to the end of his life worked little beside ill. But—there is some one else to be considered."

"Miss Tresham?"

"Yes, Miss Tresham. She must be told."

"Why?" he asked, eagerly. "Why should you distress her by such a terrible story? Why not be merciful, and never suffer her to suspect it?"

"I have thought of that. But, granting that it would be a merciful concealment, it is one which I have no right to make. It is *her* right to know this story; and I am sure you would not be willing to accept the responsibility of keeping it from her. Besides, I have wronged her very much, and I can only make reparation by means of this explanation."

"But what good end will be gained? I do not see."

"Do you not see that I cannot suffer her to remain in her present position—she who is my husband's daughter, and Felix's half-sister? And do you think that she would be likely to accept any thing from me unless she was made aware of her own claim upon me?—unless she knows that she is a Gordon?"

"But you are not certain of this," he persisted. "You have only your husband's assertion, and—and the story may have been devised merely to terrify you."

"I have told you already that I am absolutely certain of its truth. If you wish to be convinced, however, go and bring Miss Tresham here. Her answers to two or three questions will be sufficient."

"Bring Miss Tresham here!" he repeated, looking absolutely aghast. "I must really remonstrate against this, Mrs. Gordon," he went on. "Neither Miss Tresham nor yourself are in a condition to bear further excitement. Such a story would be a fearful shock to her. I must beg you to defer it."

To his surprise, she answered by rising to her feet. "Come with me," she said, walking toward the door.

Half mechanically he followed. She crossed the hall, and led the way into the apartment where she had spent the night. It was the sitting-room which he knew well. On the couch where he had left her the afternoon previous—the couch where she had been sleeping when her husband entered — the body of the dead man lay, with a shawl thrown over the figure, while the face remained uncovered. Before leaving the room, Mrs. Gordon had extinguished several candles on a table near by, and opened the blinds of the window through which he had entered. It looked toward the east, and as much of daylight as there was, streamed freely into the apartment—streamed over the couch and the white face pillowed on its cushions.

She moved so as to command a view of this face, and motioned him to approach. He did so, and thus, for the first time, saw clearly in death the man whom he had never seen in life. Handsome as that face had always been, it was something far more than handsome now—it was almost beautiful, under the refining touch of death, and with the peculiar serenity of expression which sometimes comes to the clay when the spirit has left it. But that which struck Mr. Warwick at once, and startled him most strangely, was the likeness to St. John—as St. John's face had reminded him of this, though he had only seen the latter hastily and indistinctly. There had been no likeness between them in life—even now, the whole cast of feature was so entirely dissimilar that it was difficult to determine where the resemblance was, and in what it consisted. But no one could possibly have failed to perceive that there *was* a resemblance—that, in some subtile manner, the blood which they owned in common asserted itself, and stamped each face with a token which even the most superficial gazer must have observed. Mr. Warwick certainly observed it, and it banished from his mind the last doubt of the story Mrs. Gordon had told him. She was standing by him, when he said, half unconsciously:

"It is true. It is *there*."

"So you see it, too?" she said. "I brought you for this purpose," she added, after a moment. "We will go now. I—I cannot talk here."

She led the way again to the door, and again he followed her. They were in the dining-room, when she spoke next.

"That was why I took you in—to show you the likeness which death has brought out so strongly," she said. "The perception of this resemblance first made me think of telling Miss Tresham the terrible truth at once. Remember, I have not the least proof of the story, save my own word, and—and that. But I am sure it would be impossible for her to look at that face and refuse to believe me."

"I agree with you that far, but why be in such haste?—why not rest, yourself, and let her rest? A few hours hence—"

"Can you answer for the change which an hour may make in that face? And will the force of the blow be less great to-morrow than to-day?"

He saw that she was resolved; so he did what it would have been wisest to have done at first—he submitted.

"What do you want?" he asked.

"I want you to go for her, and, if possible, bring her here. But first, one moment—give me a pencil and a piece of paper."

Somewhat puzzled, he produced a pencil and that inevitable last resource for writing emergencies with a man—the back of a letter.

"Will that do?" he asked.

"That will do," she answered. She wrote a few words, then tore off the strip of paper, folded it, and, greatly to his surprise, handed it to him. "Keep it," she said, "and when I ask Miss Tresham one or two questions which I must ask her, see if her answers correspond with what is written there. Now, go and bring her. Remember—bring her, if she can possibly come."

With those words—words the earnestness of which it was impossible to disregard—sounding in his ears, he went up-stairs. As he was looking round for a servant to send with a message to Katharine, he saw Annesley standing with his back to him at a large window which ended the upper passage, and overlooked the front entrance. He went to him immediately, and touched his shoulder.

"Do you know how Miss Tresham is?" he asked, as the young man turned quickly round.

"Miss Tresham!" repeated Morton. "Did you ask *how* she is, or *where* she is?"

"How she is, of course. I thought you might have heard."

"She is much better—so much better, that she is in that room"—he nodded in the direction of the chamber where St. John had died—"I was staying there, but she came in, and begged me to leave her alone with—with the body."

"And is she there now?"

"Yes, she is there now."

To Annesley's surprise, Mr. Warwick turned and walked into the room thus indicated.

Every thing had been put in order, and the chamber, seen in the light of early dawn, looked singularly calm and peaceful when he entered. The white bed, with the motionless figure upon it, occupied the centre of the floor, and candles still burned at the head and foot. By the side, Katharine knelt with the little crucifix in her hands, on which the dead man's last glance had been fixed. It was a touching picture, the lawyer thought, as he paused a moment, with unconscious reverence, on the threshold. Twelve hours before, and how great had been his scorn, how profound his contempt for that man!—now the great sanctification of death had come, and he lowered his voice, and softened his tread, even in presence of that poor forsaken dust. Truly we live in the midst of mystery — who shall explain even this?

Katharine had heard his step, light as it was, and, rising to her feet, she looked round. When she saw who it was, she smiled a faint, pitiful sort of smile, and motioned him to draw nearer.

"Come and see," she said, pointing to the still face. "Does that look as if it had ever known violence or sin?"

Certainly it did not. Even more marked than on the face below—because here the end had been less sudden—was the peculiarly serene expression which always follows death from gun-shot-wounds. The placid lips seemed almost about to smile, and on the brow, and around the closed eyes, there was a seal of ineffable calm—calm almost like that "pathetic peace of God" which, on the faces of those who in the beautiful language of Holy Writ have "fallen on sleep," sometimes hushes into awe the very sobs and tears of mourning. But here—even as below—was the likeness—intensified, if possible, since he had noticed it first. It startled him at once into a remembrance of the errand on which he had come.

"Miss Tresham," he said, "Mrs. Gordon is very anxious to see you. Will you come to her?"

Much to his surprise, for he had expected to meet with some difficulty, Katharine assented at once.

"I can do nothing here," she said, mournfully —"nothing, save pray. I am only too glad if I can be of the least comfort to Mrs. Gordon. Is she very much prostrated, Mr. Warwick?"

"She is supported by excitement now," he answered. "I am afraid she will be terribly prostrated when it is over."

That was all that was exchanged. Annesley looked surprised, when they passed him on their way down-stairs; but he said nothing, and the silence lasted until they reached the dining-room. Then—before opening the door—Mr. Warwick thought it well to give a slight warning to his companion.

"Don't be astonished," he said, "if Mrs. Gordon asks you some questions that do not seem to you exactly relevant. She has a good reason for doing so, and I am sure you will confer a favor on her by answering them frankly."

"I—of course I will, if I can," said Katharine, already much astonished.

After this, he opened the door, and they walked in. Mrs. Gordon was sitting by the fire, where he had left her; but she looked up when they entered. Then rising, she advanced a few steps, and held out her hands to Katharine, with a grace which, even at that moment, was somewhat stately.

"Miss Tresham," she said, in the rich, sweet voice which had charmed Katharine when she heard it first, "I cannot claim your sympathy, nor offer my own in the grief that has fallen upon us, until I have asked you to forgive me."

Notwithstanding the grace and the stateliness, there was much of hesitation both in her voice and manner—for she remembered the day at Mrs. Marks's when she had last seen Katharine, and she did not know how her advances were likely to be received. She need have felt no doubt on this score. Almost before she finished speaking, those outstretched hands were taken eagerly and warmly.

"Dear Mrs. Gordon," said the girl, gently, "there is no need to utter such a word. I have nothing to forgive. I can only love and pity you—if you will let me."

It was so sweetly, so simply, so earnestly said, that, by a sudden impulse, the elder woman opened her arms. In a second, the first tears which either of them had shed, flowed together.

Mr. Warwick walked away to the other end of the room. It was a very long apartment, and he might almost have been out of it, for all that he heard of the words spoken, or the tears and sobs mingled by the fire. There was not very much of the latter: neither of these women was of a demonstrative nature; and, with both, the grief which oppressed them was not of that tender kind which can be "cried away." A few hot, bitter drops; a few dry, choking sobs, and that was all. Before very long, Mrs. Gordon's voice recalled him.

"Mr. Warwick," she said—and Mr. Warwick turned instantly and came back to the fireplace. A small round table, on which some supper had been arranged for Morton and himself, was still near the hearth-rug where it had been placed. Mrs. Gordon and Katharine were standing on one side of it as he advanced from the other. In this manner they faced each other. There was something almost judicial about the scene, he could not help thinking.

"Mr. Warwick," said Mrs. Gordon, a little formally, "will you look at the paper which I gave you a few minutes ago, and see if Miss Tresham's answers correspond to the answers written there?" Then she turned to Katharine.—"Don't think that I intrude upon your reserve," she said, gently, "when I ask you to tell me how you are related to—to Mr. St. John?"

"I have no reason for reserve upon that point," Katharine answered. "I have not had for some time. I am his sister."

"His own sister?"

"Yes—his own sister. There were"—her voice faltered—"there were only two of us."

"And will you let me ask what was your mother's maiden name?"

Katharine looked a little surprised. She did not understand—she did not see the point or meaning—of these questions. But she felt somewhat apathetic and indifferent about them. It was strange that Mrs. Gordon should ask such things at such a time; but there was no reason why she should not answer them; and so—after a second—she replied:

"My mother's maiden name was Katharine O'Grady."

Mrs. Gordon looked at Mr. Warwick. He glanced up from the paper, with a slightly-significant expression. Nothing was said—only that glance was exchanged—and then the lady turned again to address Katharine.

"Forgive me for pressing you, but I should like to ask one or two further questions. Was your grandfather an Irishman by birth, and did he live in Martinique?"

"So I have heard my aunt say," Katharine answered. "I never saw him—he died before I was born. My mother and my aunt were both native West-Indians," she went on. "They were born in Martinique."

"And do you remember your mother?"

"I? Oh, no. She died when I was a few weeks old. My aunt was my mother," she said, softly.

"And did she never tell you any thing about your father?—who, or what he was?"

"Never. My impression always was that he was dead—though I cannot remember that my aunt ever absolutely said so." She paused a moment, then added: "Since her own death, I—I have sometimes thought this might not be."

Mrs. Gordon extended her hand across the table, and took from Mr. Warwick the slip of paper, which he at once surrendered. She gave it to Katharine, saying:

"I wrote those answers to the questions I have asked you before you came down—read them."

Wondering more and more the girl obeyed. This was what she read—written hastily in pencil on the torn fragment of a letter.

"Maiden name of mother—Katharine O'Grady.

"Time of her death—soon after the birth of her second child.

"Grandfather an Irishman by birth, who lived in Martinique."

Katharine looked up with profound astonishment visible in her face.

"I gave the paper to Mr. Warwick, when he went for you," Mrs. Gordon answered.

"But how—how was it possible? How did you—know?"

"Child," answered the other, so gently and sadly that her voice seemed, as it were, to still instead of excite emotion, "I know, because I heard the whole story from your father's lips."

Mr. Warwick, who was looking on apprehensively, notwithstanding this apprehension, was alarmed by the change that at those words came over Katharine's face. She turned deadly pale, and quivered from head to foot. Did something like an instinct of the truth dawn upon her? It almost seemed so. It almost seemed as if fear, doubt, terror, and amazement, were all struggling in her eyes and in her voice when she spoke.

"Mrs. Gordon"—it was fairly a wail—"what do you mean?"

But having gone thus far—having made retreat absolutely hopeless—Mrs. Gordon's courage failed. Woman-like, she looked at the man standing by with a glance that asked, "What must I say?"

Mr. Warwick answered the glance quietly, almost sternly.

"It is too late to hesitate now," he said. "Tell her."

"Yes, tell me!" cried Katharine, clutching

the table with one hand, and looking up with eyes full of passionate appeal. "I—I must hear it now. Tell me—tell me at once!"

"Have you never thought—have you never suspected—who your father might be?" asked Mrs. Gordon.

"I—how could I?"

"Have you never thought that the man who ruined your brother's life—that the man who ruined my life—and the man who ruined your mother's life, might be one and the same?"

"My God!—no!"

Mrs. Gordon pointed to the paper in her hand. My husband," she said, "came to me yesterday evening. He demanded Felix, and, when I refused, he threatened me with the loss of the child's inheritance. When I was incredulous of his power to fulfil the threat, he told me that he had an elder son living—the child of an early marriage—and that the name of this son was—"

But here Katharine interrupted—her voice ringing, with a tone of horror in it through the quiet room:

"It cannot be!" she cried, almost wildly. "O Mrs. Gordon, stop—stop and think! Don't utter any thing which *is* so horrible, which *must* be so untrue! It—" she made a motion with her hands, as if thrusting it from her—"it cannot be true!"

"I see that you know what I mean," said Mrs. Gordon, calmly—and again her quietude seemed to still Katharine's passionate excitement. "Come with me," she added, in a lower voice. "What I have to say to you can best be said in *his* presence."

She drew the girl's hand within her arm, and —before Mr. Warwick could interfere—led her from the room. They crossed the hall, and entered the apartment where the dead man lay. Outside the windows was all the dewy freshness of Nature's happy morning wakening—birds twittering, leaves softly rustling, life everywhere —inside was the terrible quietude, the settled stillness which pervades the air of a death-chamber, and makes our very pulses seem to ourselves out of unison with its deep repose.

When they both stood by the couch, looking down on that marble face, Mrs. Gordon spoke.

"This man," she said, "wronged me more deeply than he could ever have wronged any one else—save, perhaps, that poor victim of his vice and crime who lies dead above us. I have struggled all this long night for the power to say that I forgive him. Thinking of all that he has done —of all that he had the will to do—I have not yet been able to say this. But, standing here with you now, I feel that your debt against him is even heavier than mine. Your mother and your brother—he ruined and killed them both. He made your life the hard and bitter thing which it must have been. He—your father—left you without a thought or a care to struggle alone, in your woman's helplessness, against the world. Count up all these things, as I have done—add up every sigh, and tear, and drop of blood. Then see if you are Christian enough to stand here—here by his side—and say that you forgive him!"

Her words rang through her listener's heart with a strange power, her voice was full of the modulations of a passion for which language has no name. As she spoke, her very soul—her quivering, stricken, human soul—seemed laid bare before the girl who listened. The horror of it was too much for Katharine. The still, white face swam before her eyes—a deadly faintness came over her. She fought hard against the rising tide of unconsciousness; but fought vainly. Things tangible faded away from her for a time—how long, or how short, she could not tell—but when she came to herself, she was sitting before the window with the fresh air playing over her face, and Mrs. Gordon's hand resting on her brow.

"I shall never forgive myself," she was saying. "I ought to have thought—I ought to have known—"

"Never mind," said Katharine, rallying a little. "I have not fainted yet. I—I don't think I shall." Then she roused herself, and caught the hand which was on her brow. "Is it true?" she asked, passionately. "I cannot think—I cannot reason and consider all the links of evidence. I shall believe you, if you tell me it is true."

Mrs. Gordon bent down and kissed her tenderly. "It is true," she said.

Nothing more was uttered for some time. Katharine sank back again, and closed her eyes. Mrs. Gordon stood, like a statue, by her side. Into fuller and yet fuller radiance glowed the east—royal tints of every imaginable color melting and changing, and softening into each other, and waxing more glorious with every succeeding moment, on the wide panorama of sky. Who can look on such a scene with the mere eye of sense, or the mere thought of earth? "Heaven and earth are full of the majesty of Thy glory!" rises instinctively to the mind and to the lips. I sunset comes to us like a sweet, solemn vesper, after the weary, busy cares of day, surely sunrise is like a grand, triumphal symphony, bursting and thrilling from a million notes into one noble harmony of exultant praise! It seemed so to Katharine when she opened her eyes and saw the dazzling glory spread before her. With an impulse that startled her companion, she rose to her feet, and half turned toward the dead man, on whose changeless face the glowing splendors fell.

"Oh, who are we, to talk of forgiveness!" she said—and her voice, with a deep, pathetic thrill in it, fell strangely on the hushed calm—"is there any wrong so great that it is not easy to forgive it if we only think of the dear Lord who will one day need to forgive us so much? Can we harden our hearts over any thing, if we only remember that our free, generous, willing pardon of all wrongs may touch His heart, and make Him more merciful to the soul that has gone forth to meet His justice? O Mrs. Gordon, we do not know—we cannot tell how, in what degree, our forgiveness may benefit this life which has passed forever from our life, which, in all the ages of eternity, can never, never harm us again! Let us—oh, let us—here—now—say that we forgive him—that we forgive him for ourselves, and for those he has injured far more than us!"

Her earnest pathos startled and awed Mrs. Gordon; bent her, as it were, without any resistance, to the higher passion, the stronger will. They advanced to the couch, and side by side said the words together.

As they uttered them, the sun rose, and, with the first flood of golden light, a myriad of birds burst forth into rejoicing. The night was past, the day was come. As the glory of the sunlight streamed over their bending figures, it seemed like the promise of a brighter, happier future—like the earnest of a day of tranquil peace, after the night of troubled terror.

CHAPTER XLV.

A TURN OF FORTUNE'S WHEEL.

A WEEK after the double tragedy at Morton House, and while all Lagrange was still ringing with the noise of it, Miss Vernon walked across the lawn of her brother-in-law's residence with Morton Annesley.

The young man was on his way to bring Felix Gordon home, and had only stopped a few minutes to deliver a note and a message from Miss Tresham to her late kind entertainers. But, when he rose to make his adieux, he suddenly recollected something else that he wished to say, and, much to Mrs. Raynor's regret, asked Miss Vernon to walk "down to the bridge" with him. Irene consented, and they were soon on their way to that spot—a very favorite spot with every *habitué* of the place. The lawn was exceedingly pretty now that every thing began to wear the light, silvery-green livery of early spring; but the special charm of it, the special thing which made it different from other lawns, was the creek which flashed along under a fringe of willows and laurel, and the graceful bridge which was thrown across it. When they reached this spot, they paused—the bright water flowed beneath their feet, the soft shadows flickered overhead, and a lovely perspective of lawn and shrubbery opened behind them. On the other side of the stream—set, as it were, in an archway of green—a travelling-carriage with servants in attendance, and a trunk strapped on, was standing in the shade—the horses switching their tails leisurely, and the servants amicably gossiping. The whole sweet, spring wealth of tender beauty and indescribable charm was all around and all about them, until indeed one might have wondered

> "——how it was
> That any one, in such a world might grieve,
> At least for long, at what might come to pass;
> The soft south-wind, the flowers amid the grass,
> The fragrant earth, the sweet sounds everywhere
> Seemed gifts too great almost for man to bear."

The day was rapidly advancing toward its meridian, but Annesley seemed in no haste to begin his journey. Irene wondered a little at his delay, as, instead of saying good-by, he stood before her, and looked and listened while she talked of Katharine.

"I suppose there is no hope that Miss Tresham will return to us," she said, twisting the note which he had brought around her fingers. "I am very sorry—we are all very sorry. We have missed her so much since she went away. She is one of the most attractive and sympathetic persons I ever knew. George said only last night that he would be willing to go to school himself for the pleasure of securing her as a permanent inmate."

"Mrs. Gordon needs her more than you do," said Annesley, smiling a little. "Will not that console you? Ah! you don't know all that she has passed through!"

"She! Do you mean Mrs. Gordon, or Miss Tresham?"

"Both—but I mean Mrs. Gordon." He stopped a moment, then added: "Of course you have heard the whole terrible story!"

"No, I have not," she answered. "I believe there is a great deal of gossip afloat, but I rarely heed gossip."

"Still, you have heard—"

"Something, undoubtedly."

"How those wretched men were killed, for instance?"

"Yes," she said, in a low voice. "How horrible it was!"

"How much like retribution it was!" returned the young man, with a dark cloud coming over his face. "I confess that my pity all went with that poor fellow St. John," he said. "He was hardly used in every way. Miss Irene, did you ever trace out a sequence of cause and effect?"

"Never," she answered—then added, smiling, "I am like the lilies of the field, not worth much either for toiling or reflecting."

"You are like them in another respect also," said he, pointing the compliment by the admiration in his eyes as they lingered on her face, which was indeed like a lily in its stainless beauty. "But I am sure you have sometimes noticed the strange connection between events, the strange manner in which circumstances seem to act and react on each other."

"I assure you I never have. I eat my daily bread, and am thankful for it, without troubling myself to think that somebody must have sowed and reaped and garnered it yesterday. I remember, however, that you once suggested something of this kind—about Mrs. Gordon."

"It is a very fascinating occupation, when you once get fairly into the spirit of it," said he, leaning against the railing of the bridge.

He could have stayed there all day, he thought, with the pretty music of the stream in his ears, and those wonderful blue eyes gazing at him. In the midst of his reflections, he forgot to think what a strange comment on this strange self-absorbed life of ours his very mood and the very tone of conversation made. The awful tragedy which had carried two souls into eternity, and wrung two living hearts with the bitterness of death, had become a topic to be discussed with philosophical curiosity in the midst of a scene like this.

"Tell me the facts as they really occurred," said Miss Vernon, "that is, if I am not asking you to violate confidence."

"No," he answered, gravely, "facts can harm nobody now. Indeed, there is so much exaggeration of them, that it is well the truth should be known."

Then he began, and told her all that had occurred—soon drifting by insensible degrees into more than the bare outline of events. Something in the sympathetic face and honest eyes made him sure she could be trusted; and so, while the servants and horses waited as patiently or as impatiently as they could, while the water rippled, and the shadows flickered, he gave a sketch of the different causes that had led to this result. Her interest and astonishment were almost beyond power of expression. St. John the son of Gordon! Katharine the step-daughter of Pauline Morton! Little as he felt inclined for such a thing, Annesley could almost have laughed at the overwhelming surprise on her face.

"It is true," he said. "My cousin tells me that the last assurance her husband gave her was of his first marriage, that St. John was his eldest son, and the heir of the Gordon estate."

"And—and does Mrs. Gordon mean to make this public?"

"No—making it public would involve too many painful disclosures. The horror of the tragedy would be doubly augmented, if people knew that a son (however ignorantly) had killed his own father. Besides, it is unnecessary. My cousin is going to Scotland soon, and the affairs of her life matter nothing to the people she leaves behind—this time forever."

"But Miss Tresham?"

"Miss Tresham will accompany her."

"Indeed!" Miss Vernon started a little. "I am surprised to hear that," she said, simply, almost involuntarily.

"Why should you be surprised?" he asked. "Don't you think it is the natural thing and the right thing—on both sides?"

"Yes—oh, yes, I"—she stopped, hesitated, blushed somewhat—"I was not thinking of that. I was thinking, if you will pardon my candor, Mr. Annesley, of *you*."

"Of me!" said he, blushing himself, in the boyish fashion which he had never quite outgrown, yet smiling at her embarrassment. "And may I ask what you were thinking about me?"

"I am sure you don't need to ask," answered she, with a direct frankness which some carping people called *brusquerie*. "Perhaps I have no right to speak on such a subject, but"—a winning smile, half-bright, half-soft—"my excuse as, that I should be very glad to see you both happy."

"I hope we may both be happy," said he, earnestly. "But, dear Miss Irene, I think it will be apart—not together. Miss Tresham has rejected me."

"I never thought you lacked perseverance."

"I don't think I do—when there is any thing to be gained by it. But you would not advise me to waste time and effort in a hopeless suit? Did you read the letter which Miss Tresham wrote to me the night before she left Bellefont?"

"I! How could I?" she asked, flushing. "What a strange opinion you must have of Miss Tresham if you think she would show such a letter; or of me, if you think I would read it!"

"Don't be indignant!" said he, smiling. "You forget that Miss Tresham and yourself were in the same house, and good friends besides. There would have been nothing reprehensible in her showing you the letter—nothing, certainly, that I should have been inclined to resent. It was a very charming letter," said he, with a slight grimace. "The only misfortune was, that I was not exactly in a frame of mind to appreciate this, when I received it. I read it over last night, and appreciated it better, I think. It is exceedingly kind, but very decided. If I had it here, I would show it to you, and ask you if you thought it worth while to persevere in the face of such a 'No' as that."

"You certainly take your disappointment very philosophically," said Miss Vernon, with a slight tinge of sarcasm in her voice.

He changed color a little.

"I hope you don't think that I take it lightly," he said. "I assure you it has been a very serious matter with me. I was as wretched down there in Apalatka, as—well, as anybody could possibly wish to be. But no man with any sense or self-respect will spend life pining and moaning because a woman has rejected him. I fought hard for resignation, and I think I may say that I have gained it."

"You are resigned?"

"I am quite resigned."

Miss Vernon looked at him with an expression on her face which he did not understand—a mixture of half-puzzled surprise and struggling remembrance, which puzzled him in turn. She could not tell of what his tone and manner reminded her, until, like a flash, she recalled the day when they had walked up and down the piazza at Annesdale, and he had spoken of Mrs. Gordon, and of the content with life and the things of life which could be gained—so he said—by fighting for it. She remembered how she had questioned whether this philosophy of his—a buoyant, healthful philosophy, which, even in theory, had commanded her respect—would bear the test of disappointment or failure. Was her question being answered now? Was this, indeed, the content which is the victorious fruit of struggle, or was it only that mask of indifference which often betrays, instead of hiding, the deepest wound?

"You astonish me," she said. "I had an idea—I really don't know why—that you were very constant, very tenacious, in your affections. This makes me think that I was mistaken in that opinion."

He colored again, and looked at her with an expression which she, in turn, did not quite understand.

"Won't you distinguish between constancy and obstinacy?" he asked. "I think there is a distinction. One may be constant to an affection as long as there is hope of return; but, surely, it is the height of folly to hold obstinately to a sentiment which causes, and can cause, only pain. Don't you think it is desirable to control one passion as well as another—the passion of love, as well as the passion of anger or revenge? I won't pretend to tell you how much it has cost me to be able to say that I am resigned; but if you did know—if you could know—you would not, I am sure, accuse me of being inconstant or light."

"I—I did not," said Miss Vernon, a little contritely. "The fact is, I am unreasonable," she went on, half-laughing. "It would be difficult to please me, I am afraid. Nobody would have been more sorry than I, if you had taken Miss Tresham's rejection to heart after the approved romantic mode; and yet, you see, I find fault with you for showing yourself a sensible young man of the nineteenth century. Desperate love has quite gone out of fashion," she said, with a shrug of her shoulders. "Nowadays you are all so reasonable, that it is quite edifying. I have been wasting a good deal of sympathy on you; I see, now, that I must change it to respect."

"And I see that you are determined to give me a liberal taste of mockery," he said. "I thought you would be more kind—more just."

"Indeed, you are mistaken," she answered. "Indeed, I am glad, heartily glad, that I am able to change sympathy to respect. You must not think otherwise. I should be very sorry if you were—were suffering."

"Since I am, not suffering, however, you think I am able to bear a little sarcasm on my unfortunate exemption."

"You are provoking!" she said. "You know better, and I shall not reason with you any longer. Let me inquire if you have any intention of reaching Saxford to-day?"

"There will not be the least difficulty in doing so; the roads are excellent, and my horses perfectly fresh. It is growing late, though," he said, with a regretful look at the shadows round him. "I suppose I ought to go—I suppose I must go. Before doing so, however, I should like to convince you—"

"Never mind," she interrupted, hastily; "I am quite convinced. Besides, it is not a matter of any importance. My opinion—"

"Is of great importance to me," he said, eagerly. "I want to show you—I want to prove to you—that I am neither inconstant nor light."

"That expression — which, by-the-way, I don't at all remember having used—seems to rankle with you!" she said, trying to laugh, yet feeling vaguely conscious that the scene was growing too earnest for her taste. "I don't mean to be inhospitable," she went on, "but I really think you ought to go; those poor servants look so tired, and I fancy they are gazing reproachfully at me, thinking that I keep you."

"They make a great mistake, then," he said, smiling; "for it is I who am keeping you—unwillingly enough on your part, as I perceive. It is amazingly hard to go. This is certainly the pleasantest and prettiest spot in Lagrange. I wish I was an artist; I would paint you as you stand there now. The whole scene is lovely, and you—pardon me, if I say so—never looked more beautiful."

"You are not an artist, though, and I am not standing for my portrait," answered Miss Vernon, turning away. "I see I must make the first move," she went on. "I hope you will have a pleasant journey. Good-by."

He followed her, and held out his hand. "If I am obliged to go, at least you must tell me good-by after a more cordial fashion," he said. "I shall be back soon. Shall I find you still here?"

She gave him her hand and smiled. "Very probably you will," she said—"unless George becomes more amiable than he is at present, about letting Flora go. Give my love to the Lesters if you see them in Apalatka," she added. "Once more, good-by."

This time he echoed her farewell, and took his departure. But long after he had left the pretty lawn, and silvery creek behind, her fair face, her tender eyes, her bright smile bore him company. Try as he would, he could think of—he could see nothing else. "How beautiful she is!" he caught himself saying again and again. Yet something told him that her beauty was the least part of her, that the regular features, the lily-white complexion, the golden hair, and violet eyes, would have been worth little indeed without the brave, noble soul, the strong, sweet nature, which shone through these outer coverings, and glorified them, "like the lamp of naphtha in the alabaster vase." He had only lately learned to know this. Until within the last few months, Irene Vernon had been to him a woman merely like other women—a girl like the majority of girls, only a little less attractive, perhaps, on account of her haughty beauty. Now an instinct began to dawn upon him that henceforth in his life she was to be set apart from all other women. The memory of his fevered passion for Katharine seemed to fade away. That graceful figure, that exquisite face, still stood there on the bridge, with the bright water flowing beneath, the tender green of earth's renewed life all around, and heart, and hope, and fancy, seemed to bow down before her and say, "Lo! we are thine!"

Two weeks after this, Mrs. Gordon's preparations for leaving America were so nearly completed that the day of her departure was fixed, and not far distant. Felix was once more at home, and all that now detained her in Lagrange was the final disposition of the Morton property, and its transfer to Annesley. The house which his mother had so long coveted for him was at last to be his, through the kindness of the very woman whose arrival had caused Mrs. Annesley so much of bitter heartache, so many fruitless schemes and plans. Where were they all now?—what end had they gained? Morton, with his loyal honesty, had seen the straight path and followed it; while she had wandered off into dark and devious byways. And, after all, it was Morton, not she, who won at last the prize on which her heart had been set. Did the perception of this teach her wisdom? Doubtful, indeed Few things are more rare, than that the eye once accustomed to darkness should learn to love the light; than that the nature which finds pleasure in hidden paths, should learn that plain roads lead best to plain ends, and that open weapons are more effective, as well as more honorable, than concealed and stealthy ones. Still, Mrs. Annesley was heartily glad of this auspicious end, and, in her own way, felt a little ashamed of herself. "I should have tried to do more for Pauline, if I had only known," she said—and that was the whole secret of it. If she had only known—if she had only been aware that something was to be gained by cousinly kindness and championship, she would have buckled on her armor and entered the lists as fearlessly as Morton himself; but, as it was, why should she have been expected to do such a thing? "I had my children to think of," she would say, "and we were never fond of each other at the best of times." Every thing had turned out very well, and she was glad of it; but she could really see no cause for blaming herself in any thing she had done, or failed to do, although—well—yes—she might, perhaps, have been a little more cordial to Pauline.

As to Lagrange, it was thunderstruck by the news of Mrs. Gordon's impending departure, and by the rumor — tenfold exaggerated — of her wealth and rank. And this was the woman who had lived in their midst for six months, whom they had persistently ignored, and about whom they had circulated any number of ill-natured reports. A Morton, too! The last direct representative of the oldest blood in the country! What could they have been thinking of!—Lagrange waked up, as it were, from a sort of trance, and felt, in a measure, half-dazed, and totally unable to account for its own conduct. One thing was certain, however: Mrs. Gordon must see her old friends—and, what was considerably more important, her old friends must see Mrs. Gordon!—once more, at least, before she bade a final farewell to the home of her youth. The door of Morton House was suddenly besieged with visitors, and Harrrison grew weary of receiving cards, and saying, over and over again, that Mrs. Gordon begged to be excused from seeing company—she was preparing for her departure, and was, besides, not very well. Only the few friends who had come forward to welcome her, were admitted to say farewell before the wanderer once more turned her face —this time forever—from her father's house. These few were struck by a singular change in her appearance. They had expected to see her looking much older, much more broken by the late terrible scenes through which she had passed; yet fragile, and pale, and worn as she was, underneath all this there was something which had not been there before—a glimpse of the Pauline Morton of old coming out under the ghastly change wrought by years and trouble, a possibility of reviving power which no eye could have been keen enough to see before The worst part of the change which had so shocked her friends was gone from her. She was even yet a woman on whom the signet of fiery trials had been branded too deeply ever to fade; but she was no longer a woman resting helplessly under the torturing, haunting dread of a terror that might come to her any day or hour. Peace at least was hers at last, and the seal of peace—the promise of the calmer life upon which she was entering—was plainly to be read upon her face.

"In time, perhaps, you may even teach me to be happy," she would say, wistfully, to Katharine.

And, indeed, the thing which seemed to give her most pleasure was the thought of this bright and gentle companion whom she had won, this girl who all her life long had managed to find some pearls of happiness under the stormiest water.

Katharine, for her part, made her preparations to leave Lagrange with a reluctance that surprised herself. She did not understand the intangible sadness and regret which oppressed her—she often asked herself what it meant—she often wondered why a dimness should come over her sight, and a choking rise in her throat when she looked out over the fair hills and woods clothed in their lovely April green, and thought how soon she would leave them, never to return.

"Why should I care so much?" she would ask herself, half indignantly. "It is no native home of mine—it is not as if I had been born and reared here! Then, indeed, it might be hard to go; but now, I do not understand it. Why should I care so much?" A little while later it was all so clear to her that she could have laughed at the remembrance of her own perplexity; but that *was* a little while later. At the time of which we speak, no one would have suspected her hidden sadness, her unaccountable reluctance; but, all the same, it existed—all the same, she would move about the rooms, and galleries, and gardens, of Morton House, brightening and cheering every spot to which she came, but deplorably conscious, meanwhile, of a very heavy heart, and asking herself, in puzzled honesty, what it possibly meant.

At last the day of departure drew near at hand. They were to leave on Tuesday morning. On Monday afternoon a heavy shower of rain was falling; but Katharine wrapped herself up in a large cloak, and, armed with an umbrella, set forth to pay a farewell visit to Mrs. Marks. Mrs. Gordon was somewhat shocked, remonstrated, and insisted upon ordering the carriage; but the girl obstinately declined.

"I much prefer to walk," she said. "I don't mind a rain like this, and it looks as if it might clear. I can stay as long as I please if I walk, you know; and then"—a slight quiver of the voice here—"it is for the last time."

So Mrs. Marks, who felt sufficiently doleful, and had entirely given up all hope of the promised visit, was equally astonished and delighted when there came a shout from the children on the front piazza, and the next minute a drenched apparition of Katharine, with glowing cheeks and rain-gemmed hair, walked in upon her.

"So you have come!" she cried, joyfully. "Oh, I am so glad! I didn't look for you at all after it began to rain."

"And you thought an April shower like this would keep me away from you, when it is for the last time?" said Katharine, dropping her wet wrappings in the middle of the floor. "You must have given me credit for wanting to see you very badly—mustn't she, children?—Katy, my shoes are quite damp. Can you take them into the kitchen to dry, and get me a pair of your mother's slippers to wear?"

While Katy eagerly darted away on this errand, the other children crowded around the young ex-governess, and drew her into a chair. What an afternoon it was that followed! There was so much to say, so much to tell of the past, so much to promise of the future, that the wonder was how it all was said, even in the three or four hours which were consumed.

Katharine made several fruitless attempts to leave before she rose at last and said that she must go.

"I am afraid it will be dusk before I can reach the house," she said, "and Mrs. Gordon will be uneasy.—No, no, children, don't do that"—as several audible sobs were heard—"this is not good-by. You must not think so. Mrs. Gordon, and Felix, and I, are all going to stop to see you to-morrow morning."

It may not have been "good-by," but still it was a very lugubrious leave-taking. Mrs. Marks broke down as well as the children, and Katharine herself was on the brink of tears when she left the sobbing group behind, and hurried along the front walk. These tears were blinding her to such an extent that she did not recognize—she did not even see—a man who had reached the gate as she came out of the house, and stood there waiting for her.

"Good-evening, Miss Tresham," he said, as she fumbled for the latch, and his voice, which was very unexpected, made her start violently. "Are you going to Morton House?"

"Good-evening, Mr. Warwick," she answered, as the gate at last yielded, not to her touch, but to Mr. Warwick's, and she came out into the road. "Yes, I am going to Morton House. I have been spending the afternoon with Mrs. Marks," she added, looking up at him with her brimming eyes.

"I think you came very near spending the evening also," he said, smiling. She caught the smile, and it made her feel aggrieved. She did not, of course, expect him to be in tears like Mrs. Marks, and the children, and herself, but still he might have felt the solemnity of the occasion a little, and he need not have smiled in that way, just as if nothing more than usual had happened or was about to happen. "You are late for such a lonely walk," he said. "Give me your umbrella. I will see you safely to the house."

"Indeed, you need not take that trouble," she said, with a shade of coolness in her tone. "It is not very late," she went on. "The road may be lonely, but it is entirely safe, and I had much rather you did not."

Her speech was cut short very summarily. Mr. Warwick took the umbrella out of her hand, and held it over her head, as he walked along the foot-path by her side.

"I am sorry if you would 'much rather' I did not accompany you," he said; "but I cannot reconcile it to my conscience to let you go alone into the country at such an hour as this. Besides, if you must know the truth, I was on my way to Morton House when I saw you; so the only difference is, whether I shall go alone or with a companion."

"In that case, I am very glad that you chanced to see me," said Katharine, conquering her momentary grievance. "I need a companion," she went on, a little sadly. "My frame of mind is any thing but cheerful. Oh, how hard it is to say good-by to people that one loves!"

"Yes," said he, with something of unconscious dreariness in his voice, "it is hard."

Nothing more was spoken for some time

They walked along, side by side, and both so much abstracted that they scarcely noticed how the rain had ceased, and the sun, which was not yet down, seemed about to break through the western clouds. They were by this time fairly beyond the last outskirts of the town, and the sweet, wild odors of forest and field—the peculiar spicy woodland fragrance which loads the very air after a spring rain—were borne to them by every breeze that, in passing, shook myriads of glittering rain-drops from the boughs under which they walked. Katharine laughed a little as one of these quick showers sprinkled her face.

"The very trees are weeping," she said. "I wonder if I may flatter myself that they, too, are sorry to see me go? How fresh and fragrant every thing is! Surely there is no month like April; and yet it seems to me that, after this, April will always be sad to me."

"You are like a child who thinks to-day's clouds will not be gone to-morrow," said Mr. Warwick, smiling again; but this time in a manner with which she was not inclined to find fault. "Is it possible that you do not know that before another April comes round Lagrange will seem to you like a dull and painful memory? By that time you will wonder how you ever endured such a life as this, from which you are now sorry to part."

"You think so because you don't know me," she said, a little resentfully. "Whatever else I may be, I am not fickle nor ungrateful. I love Lagrange now, and I shall love it always. If I live to see a hundred Aprils come, I shall always think of this one, and—and be sorry."

"Sorry to have left poverty and toil behind you, and gone to ease, and luxury, and happiness?"

"No, sorry to have left so much kindness and so many dear friends behind me—kindness shown to me in the days of my need; friends who proved their friendship when I was desolate. O Mr. Warwick! you do not really believe that I can ever forget these things?"

"No," said Mr. Warwick, touched by her earnestness. "I do not believe any thing unworthy of you. I am sure that, go where you will, you will retain a kindly remembrance of us, and that, perhaps, is as much as we could ask."

"I shall always think of *you* as the best friend I have ever known," she said. "I—I cannot say good-by without thanking you once more for all your kindnesses to me—they have been so many, so great."

"Don't call them kindnesses," he said, hastily. "They were not that—they were pleasures to me, and I was only glad that they were also services to you. I—"

He stopped. What he was on the point of saying, he scarcely knew; but an instinct warned him that it was something which had better be left unsaid. He was a self-contained man, well accustomed to controlling himself on all possible occasions; so he had very little difficulty in restraining words which he told himself could serve no good end. Why distress and pain her uselessly?—why give her a last disagreeable memory of him to take away? What folly it was, after all! She had unhesitatingly rejected him when she was poor and desolate, without a home on earth; and was it likely—was it even possible—that she would reconsider that decision now, that she would turn from the brilliant future which opened before her, to share his homely, commonplace life? He gave a sort of mental laugh—a laugh singularly devoid of merriment—at the very thought.

"Is not this the view of which you are so fond?" he asked, pausing abruptly on a knoll which they had reached, a gentle eminence that commanded a prospect of the surrounding country—of all the fields and meadows clad in brightest green; of the hedges in full blossom; of groups of trees near by, with feathery, tender foliage; of shadowy woodlands far away; of hills melting and stretching in graceful undulations to the east. Toward the west there was an expanse of open country, and the sun (which had now come forth) was gilding all things with the red glory of sunset, turning all the rain-drops into diamonds, and all the little rain-pools into miniature fiery lakes.

"Yes, this is the view," said Katharine. "Is it not lovely?"

She stood quite still, and looked with lingering, pathetic gaze on the fair scene. The light of the glowing western sky was on her face and in her eyes—soft, sweet eyes, that were none the less lovely for the tears that filled them.

"It is hard to leave," she said at last, simply, and almost as if she were thinking aloud.

Those words, and the tone in which they were uttered, were too much for the man beside her. After all, what did it matter? He could only hear again what he had heard before—he could only receive the answer which was, of course, the sole possible answer for a question such as his. Still he would ask it. He could do no harm, at least; and a strange, wild hope—which he sternly tried to repress—rushed over him unaccountably, and without a moment's warning. The struggle with himself occupied a minute. During that minute, the sun quietly sank out of sight, and Katharine, with a wistful sigh, turned her face around.

"Perhaps we had better go," she said. "Mrs. Gordon will be uneasy."

"We will go in a second," he answered, quietly—so quietly that she had not the faintest suspicion of what was coming. "You say it is hard to leave," he went on. "Has it ever occurred to you that there is a very easy way of remaining? I suppose it is worse than folly for me to ask such a question, but do you like Lagrange well enough to give up all this bright future which is opening before you, and make it your home for life—with me?"

The strong passion which, under these circumstances, he did not feel inclined to betray—which, under any circumstances, he was not a man likely to betray—rang in his voice despite himself, and startled her. Something dazzled her—something seemed to rush over her with a thrill beyond expression. Was it joy, or surprise, or relief, or only a great unutterable sense of rest, which came suddenly, like a blessing, and, in its coming, showed how sore and deep had been the conflict to which she was only able to give a name now, that it was forever ended? She stood for a moment quite silent—striving to realize, striving to understand all that was revealed to her so simply and so strangely. Mr. Warwick grew pale, despite his self-control, and set his lips in a way peculiar to him. He was bracing himself for the reply, telling himself that, of course, he had known all the time what it would be, and that, at least, he was prepared for it.

If this was the case, he certainly was not prepared for what came. After a short pause—it *was* short, though it seemed to both of them very long—a white hand was extended, and a voice with a quiver—half of archness, half of tears—said:

"I am afraid that I do not like Lagrange sufficiently to give up for its sake all this of which you speak, but—but I do like *you*."

It was not very clearly expressed, perhaps; but John Warwick had no difficulty in comprehending what she meant. He knew then, as well as he knew long years afterward, that the happiness of his life had come to him at last; and as he saw the sweet face—with the sunset glow still on it—turned toward him, wearing the look that no man was ever blind enough to mistake, his first words were those which, for the smallest as for the greatest blessing, should be ever on our lips:

"Thank God!"

THE END

CHRISTIAN REID'S NOVELS.

VALERIE AYLMER. 8vo. Paper, 75 cents; cloth, $1.25.

MORTON HOUSE. 8vo. Paper, 75 cents; cloth, $1.25.

MABEL LEE. 8vo. Paper, 75 cents; cloth, $1.25.

EBB TIDE. 8vo. Paper, 75 cents; cloth, $1.25.

NINA'S ATONEMENT, and Other Stories. 8vo. Paper, 75 cents; cloth $1.25.

A DAUGHTER OF BOHEMIA. 8vo. Paper, 75 cents; cloth, $1.25.

BONNY KATE. 8vo. Paper, 75 cents; cloth, $1.25.

AFTER MANY DAYS. 8vo. Paper, 75 cents; cloth, $1.25.

THE LAND OF THE SKY. 8vo. Paper, 75 cents; cloth, $1.25.

HEARTS AND HANDS. 8vo. Paper, 50 cents.

A GENTLE BELLE. 8vo. Paper, 50 cents.

A QUESTION OF HONOR. 12mo. Cloth, $1.25.

HEART OF STEEL. 12mo. Cloth, $1.25.

ROSLYN'S FORTUNE. 12mo. Paper, 50 cents; cloth, $1.25.

A SUMMER IDYL. 18mo. Paper, 30 cents; cloth, 60 cents.

MISS CHURCHILL. 12mo. Paper, 50 cents; cloth, $1.00.

A COMEDY OF ELOPEMENT. 12mo. Paper, 50 cents; cloth, $1.00.

THE LAND OF THE SUN. (*In preparation.*)

JULIAN HAWTHORNE'S NOVELS.

BRESSANT. 8vo. Paper, 50 cents.

GARTH. 8vo. Paper, 50 cents; cloth, $1.25.

SEBASTIAN STROME. 8vo. Paper, 75 cents

NOBLE BLOOD. 16mo. Paper, 50 cents.

MRS. GAINSBOROUGH'S DIAMONDS. 16mo. Paper, 25 cents.

DAVID POINDEXTER'S DISAPPEARANCE. 12mo. Paper, 50 cents; half cloth, 75 cents.

CONSTANCE AND CALBOT'S RIVAL. 12mo. Paper, 50 cents; cloth, 75 cents.

F. ANSTEY'S NOVELS.

TOURMALIN'S TIME CHEQUES. 16mo. Half cloth, 50 cents.

VICE VERSA. 16mo. Paper, 50 cents; cloth, $1.00.

THE GIANT'S ROBE. Illustrated. 16mo. Paper, 50 cents; cloth, $1.00.

THE TINTED VENUS. 12mo. Paper, 25 cents.

THE BLACK POODLE, and Other Stories. Illustrated. 12mo. Paper, 50 cents.

New York: D. APPLETON & CO., 72 Fifth Avenue.

THE PYGMIES. By A. DE QUATREFAGES, late Professor of Anthropology at the Museum of Natural History, Paris. With numerous Illustrations. 12mo. Cloth, $1.75.

In this interesting volume the author has gathered the results of careful studies of the small black races of Africa, and he shows what the pygmies of antiquity really were. The peculiar intellectual, moral, and religious characteristics of these races are also described.

WOMAN'S SHARE IN PRIMITIVE CULTURE. By OTIS TUFTON MASON, A. M., Curator of the Department of Ethnology in the United States National Museum. With numerous Illustrations. 12mo. Cloth, $1.75.

"A most interesting *résumé* of the revelations which science has made concerning the habits of human beings in primitive times, and especially as to the place, the duties, and the customs of women."—*Philadelphia Inquirer.*

"Mr. Mason's volume secures for woman her glory as a civilizer in the past, and by no means denies her a glorious future."—*New York Tribune.*

SCHOOLS AND MASTERS OF SCULPTURE. By A. G. RADCLIFFE, author of "Schools and Masters of Painting." With 35 full-page Illustrations. 12mo. Cloth, $3.00.

"The art lover will find in Miss Radcliffe's work a book of fascinating interest, and a thoroughly painstaking and valuable addition to the stock of knowledge which he may possess on the history of the noble art of sculpture."—*Philadelphia Item.*

"It would be difficult to name another work that would be so valuable to the general reader on the same subject as this book."—*San Francisco Bulletin.*

"The work is free of all needless technicalities, and will be of intense interest to every intelligent reader, while of inestimable value to the student of art."—*Boston Home Journal.*

"Invaluable as a history of sculpture that can be understood by the general reader."—*Philadelphia Press.*

"The book is immensely useful as a reference guide, while the main object of the author—that of stimulating interest in the mind of the pupil—seems to have been very well attained."—*Boston Beacon.*

BY THE SAME AUTHOR.

SCHOOLS AND MASTERS OF PAINTING. With numerous Illustrations and an Appendix on the Principal Galleries of Europe. New edition, fully revised, and in part rewritten. 12mo. Cloth, $3.00; half calf, $5.00.

"The volume is one of great practical utility, and may be used to advantage as an artistic guide-book by persons visiting the collections of Italy, France, and Germany for the first time."—*New York Tribune.*

www.ingramcontent.com/pod-product-compliance
Lightning Source LLC
Chambersburg PA
CBHW031333070726
47496CB00018B/1840

* 9 7 8 3 3 3 7 0 2 6 3 3 2 *